CW01662495

Myrtlewood Mysteries

BOOKS 1-3

IRIS BEAGLEHOLE

Iris Beaglehole

ISBN: 978-1-99-117354-6

Te Rā Aroha Press, Wellington, New Zealand

Accidental Magic

MYRTLEWOOD MYSTERIES BOOK 1

Prologue

Thunder roared and lightning crashed through the sky, illuminating the clouds above Thorn Manor. The sky darkened again and all that could be seen was the light from the manor's tower, shining above the dark forests of Myrtlewood and the restless sea along the Cornish coast.

"Ah... that's it," Galderall Thorn muttered.

The storm raged outside, shaking the very foundations of Thorn Manor. Lightning flashed again followed by a loud boom of thunder, as if the gods themselves were at war. Inside the tower room, Galderall stood upright and proud, her white hair tied back in a red scarf as she gazed out into the night with shrewd eyes. She may be an old witch, but she had a deep connection to the magic that flowed through the earth, and pooled, concentrated, around the village of Myrtlewood. She had lived here her entire life, and had dedicated herself to protecting it from the darkness that threatened to consume it.

But on this night, the darkness was closing in. Galderall could sense the malevolent forces approaching, drawn by her power and the ancient magic that flowed through her veins. She knew that she had to act quickly, before it was too late. She gathered her ingredients and began to mix them together in her cauldron, stirring them with a powerful hand. Fresh herbs and protective crystals, mandrake root, obsidian and colloidal silver – mixed with the power of the moon and the strength of the crone goddess, Cerridwen.

She would fight off her enemies if she could, but she was no fool. She knew she was old, and her magic was beginning to wane.

She searched through her shelves of occult implements until she found it, its dark surface gleaming against the light: her black mirror. She used it often, to check on her wonderful bubbly granddaughter, Rosemary, and her great-granddaughter, Athena with the acerbic wit. She hadn't seen them in person for years, for their own protection. Tonight she was relieved to see that they were safe, in their shabby flat in Burkenswood. She watched them, sitting around their battered kitchen table eating a simple meal of beans on toast and commiserating about their days. If only they knew what was coming.

They were safe, for now, but Galderall could sense that something was wrong. Lightning struck again and the scent of danger hung heavy in the air.

Like many witches, Galderall Thorn knew that nature had its cycles and patterns; the full moon always rose at sunset; the high tide would be an hour later every day and, observing the seasons, garlic should always be planted on the shortest and longest days and harvested accordingly. She knew when her time was coming to an end. However, like many people who look up and suddenly realize it's a full moon, Galderall had been busy, distracted by life. She hadn't noticed the sand running out in her own hourglass until a short time before it happened.

The clouds cleared above and Galderall looked at the moon. She realised that her time was coming to a close, just like other natural cycles. She knew that she could not hold off her enemies forever. She had to prepare one final spell and a message for Rosemary and Athena that would guide them on their journey. She had to trust that they would take on the Thorn legacy, and save the town of Myrtlewood from the darkness that threatened to consume it.

With a fierce determination, Galderall began to chant. She used all of her remaining strength and magic, pouring it into the words and the incantation. The spell was a powerful and ancient incantation that had been passed down through her family for generations. The words flowed from her lips like a river of power, filling the room with a sense of ancient magic. She could feel the energy gathering around her, swirling and pulsing with a life of its own.

I call upon the powers of the earth
To protect the Thorn family, and give us strength

I call upon the powers of the wind
To keep us safe from harm outside and within

I call upon the powers of fire
To burn away the darkness, and never tire
I call upon the powers of water
To cleanse and purify, and make us stronger

By the power of the ancient ones
As I do will it shall be done
By all the powers of land and sea
As I do will, so mote it be!

With a final flourish, she cast the spell, a shield of pure magic that enveloped the manor and all within its walls. She breathed a sigh of relief, knowing that she had done what she could to protect her family and her home. But she knew that it was not enough. She could sense her enemies approaching, stronger than ever.

A blinding light filled the room. The magic flowed through her, filling her with a sense of peace and calm. She knew that this was her final act, and she was ready to face her fate.

She could feel the magic gathering around her. She spared one last glance towards the black mirror, and her dearest kin.

"Everything is about to change, my darlings," she muttered.

A crashing sound alerted her that it was time. But Galderall Thorn, despite her respect for natural cycles, wasn't going to go without a fight, and her enemies had no idea what was coming to them – not now, and certainly not in the future. Rosemary would have to make sure of that.

The light of her spell might be fading fast, but Galderall Thorn was at peace. She knew that her time had come, and she was ready for the next stage of her journey into the realm of the ancestors. Her granddaughter, Rosemary, would have to take on the legacy that her own children had never accepted.

"You might not be ready, my dear, and you might want a nice quiet life, but fate has other plans for us."

One

Rain bucketed down outside the rusty old car. Rosemary groaned.

"It's just water," Athena said from the passenger seat, picking at her chipped purple nail polish.

Rosemary sighed and looked at her teenage daughter. Athena's red hair hung over her face, the same fiery tone as Rosemary's but straighter and easier to tame.

"Just water...sure," said Rosemary. "Easy for you to say. You're not the one who has to get out of the car." She smoothed down her curly locks in anticipation of the rain that was sure to make them even more wild and frizzy than usual.

"What are you, a cat?" Athena teased with a smile.

"Just because you've always loved the rain, it doesn't mean the rest of us have to."

Athena patted her mother's shoulder. "You used to love it too. Back before..." She didn't finish the sentence and she didn't have to.

There was a moment of silence before Athena added gently, "You do need to go in."

Rosemary felt a chill that had nothing to do with the weather.

"Can't you come with me?" she asked.

"You know that wasn't the instruction," Athena said. She put on a posh voice and recited, "Rosemary Thorn, granddaughter of Galderall Thorn, must come alone to meet with the lawyer administering the estate."

"You should go into comedy," Rosemary said, laughing at her daughter. She looked up at the old building with its stone gargoyles. "I don't get it. Why would she do this?"

"She was *your* grandmother," Athena replied. "How should I know? I hardly knew her."

"But there are other family members who should probably be here too, not that Granny had a lot of money to leave behind or anything, but I don't know why she asked for me, in particular."

"Maybe she had something sensitive to tell you..." Athena said.

Rosemary grimaced. "Maybe I'm not ready to find out there's a deep dark family secret."

"Stop being silly, Mum."

"Or is it that I was really adopted and not part of the family at all – you know it's something I used to wonder since I never fit in."

"Mum..."

"You know, even our hair colour is different."

"What about Granny? You said she used to have red hair like us."

"Well, yes. But if it wasn't for that I'd be absolutely sure we weren't related to those other nasty Thorns, and perhaps we aren't. Maybe this is my formal disowning."

"Stop being paranoid."

Rosemary mock-pouted. "How dare you say that to your mother on the day of her formal disowning."

"Mother!"

"Alright, alright." Rosemary opened the door and a gust of wind whipped the rain into her face. "Yuck!" She tried to pull the door closed, but Athena was too fast and gave her an encouraging push, jolting Rosemary out into the weather where she made a dash towards the lawyers' office.

Rosemary ran through the rain, using her arms to ineffectively shield her head.

Despite the dark moods that had plagued her lately, there was a ray of hope that she had been hiding from Athena. It was just possible that her late grandmother might have bequeathed her something, anything...and even a small sum of money might be enough to give them some respite from the hole they were in.

That ray of hope shrivelled up like a deflated balloon as she saw the huge plumes of smoke pouring out of the building. An alarm rang out, deafeningly loud. Rosemary covered her ears as she watched the people scurrying out of the lawyer's offices, ducking their heads against the rain.

She stood there for a moment, stunned.

"What the..." Athena came to join her.

"Just when you thought things couldn't get worse," Rosemary yelled, through the rain and the screeching alarm and the sirens as the fire brigade arrived.

"Hey – at least you aren't in there, somewhere," Athena said.

"Too true, kid," Rosemary said, wrapping her sopping wet arm around her daughter. "Let's get out of here. It's not like we can do anything to help and the lawyers certainly aren't going to be in any mood to meet with us now."

The drive back to the flat was a quiet one. Athena seemed either dejected or lost in thought and Rosemary was too caught up in her own worries to find out which particular teenage mood her daughter was in.

Athena let out a long sigh as they pulled into the driveway of the dingey flat, which, despite its unpleasantness, they could barely afford. "I don't suppose there was any inheritance waiting for us in that building anyway."

Rosemary let her shoulders slump. "I didn't want to even bring that up as a possibility," she admitted. "I didn't want to–"

"Get my hopes up?"

"Something like that. I mean, I can't have you running wild with fantasies of inheriting a dynasty or anything."

Athena sighed. "I don't need a dynasty, Mum. I don't think you even know what that means. But it would be nice to go back to something like our old life in Stratham."

They went inside and took turns to shower under the pathetic trickle of water from the old broken fixture in the mouldy dilapidated bathroom before getting into dry clothes and watching broadcast TV on the couch, sipping the cups of hot cocoa that was Rosemary's specialty comfort drink.

"You know, you should really sell these," Athena said holding up her drink.

"Wow, things must be bad," Rosemary replied.

"Why do you say that?"

"The situation must be pretty dire if my sixteen-year-old daughter is trying to cheer me up."

"You make me sound like a monster." Athena squinted at her mother and then laughed. "I'm serious though. You make the best hot chocolates, and it wouldn't kill you to dream a little – maybe about creating a chocolate dynasty."

"Now that's a deluded fantasy I can get behind," Rosemary said. "My speciality would be Turkish delight flavoured hot chocolate – you know, the one I make with the rosewater."

"Tastes like soap," Athena complained, wrinkling her nose. "Actually..." Her voice became more serious. "Wasn't there a strange soapy smell in the air, outside that building?"

"Was there?" Rosemary asked. "I can't recall."

"Yes, something a bit like lily of the valley."

"That can't be right," Rosemary said. "I would have noticed that. It would have reminded me of my cousins. You know, the Bracewell-Thorns."

"Yes, I know. You always said they smelled like that flower. How do you think I recognised it? Remember, when I was a child you told me and I insisted you take me to the perfumery to see what it was like – you even got me a little bottle of the scent."

"Nasty stuff."

Athena crossed her arms and pouted. "That's what you said whenever I wore it."

"Well, you reminded me of my nasty cousins. They always smell like that icky poisonous plant."

"That's not a polite thing to say...hey, you don't think there's a chance that they were there today?"

Rosemary thought for a while. "Well, they weren't supposed to be there, unless they had a separate appointment right before ours with Granny's lawyer."

"Do you think that..."

"You're not implying my wealthy cousins could be arsonists?" Rosemary said, raising her eyebrows. "It seems like a stretch, even for them."

But the thought wedged its way into Rosemary's brain and refused to dissipate. Something strange was definitely afoot.

Two

Rosemary lay awake that night, in her uncomfortable bed. She let the full force of the disappointment wash over her.

She didn't want Athena to see her cry, but that meant holding back so much. Granny had always been so sweet and kind and patient. Even though Rosemary hadn't visited her in Myrtlewood Village for years – which she regretted dreadfully – she'd always appreciated the endless empathy Granny provided.

Rosemary felt the ache of the fragmentation inside her. She couldn't remember where it started, but she knew it intuitively. There were two disconnected parts of Rosemary Thorn. This, at least, was how she explained to herself the wide berth between her actions and her inner world. Things could make sense inside her mind, but as soon as she tried to enact them or speak them, they'd scramble and warp and scatter into erratic nonsense. It wasn't easy to hold down a solid job or parent a teenager under such conditions. It was hard enough just to look after herself.

It must have been after Dain had left the first time, that Rosemary had stopped visiting Granny as often. It was the shame of it all – not the separation itself, but all the debt that he had dug them into that just kept getting worse.

Rosemary hadn't been able to bear the look in Granny's eyes – was it pity? Rosemary didn't want to take money from an elderly relative, no matter how much Granny had insisted. She couldn't bear the thought of being indebted to anyone, especially not the only living relative she really connected with.

Granny's generosity was the reason that Rosemary felt some hope about the meeting with the lawyer. But all her hope had gone up in smoke along with the lawyer's office.

*There's no will now...*Rosemary thought. *It probably burned along with everything else. I don't have a hope in Hades of getting out of this debt, and it's not going to disappear all on its own.*

It wasn't a good night of sleep that Rosemary woke from – and it wasn't a gentle waking either.

"What the heck?"

She opened her bleary eyes and tried to shake the feeling of shame and dread from her body. There was a sound. A terrible, horrible sound. It was some kind of yodelling.

It was her phone ringing.

"Athena!" she yelled down the hall. "I told you not to change my bloody ring tone!"

Rosemary grabbed her cell off her bedside table and mashed the icon to end the call, only she missed and hit the little green phone instead.

"Drat!" she yelled and then remembered there was someone on the other end of the phone, listening. *Oh well, too late to turn back now.*

She held the phone up to her ear. "Uhh, yes? I mean...Hello."

Not for the first time, Rosemary wished that she was a morning person, but who on Earth was calling at this hour on a Saturday?

"Miss Thorn."

"Ugh...Speaking."

"Apologies for...disturbing you," the silky and rather old-fashioned male voice on the other end of the line said. Rosemary pictured an elderly man in a velvet smoking jacket. "It seems we missed our appointment yesterday. Unforeseen circumstances."

"We did?" Rosemary said, wondering who this strange caller was.

"Allow me to introduce myself," the caller purred. "I'm Perseus Burk, of Clifford and Burk Associates."

"Clifford and...oh blast, you're from the law firm."

"Indeed."

"I had nothing to do with that fire," Rosemary said, a little too quickly. "I mean, my daughter and I had just arrived and – I mean...umm. I'm glad you're okay. Are you okay? Of course, you are okay enough to call, but I saw those big flames and...and I'm...I'm rambling. Sorry." She ended rather meekly.

"Thank you for your well-wishes. I assure you we are fine. We have rather sophisticated fire-proofing, believe it or not. And I can assure you I'm not calling to in any way accuse you of arson. I'm merely aware that we had an appointment yesterday, which I intend to reschedule at your earliest convenience."

"You're calling me on a Saturday to reschedule an appointment when your whole office just went up in flames?"

"Something like that, yes."

"Why?"

"I'm a lawyer, Miss Thorn. When I make an appointment, I intend to keep it. And as things did not go according to plan yesterday..." he said, with a tone of disapproval.

Rosemary was unsure if he was disapproving of the fire itself or of her missing an appointment in order to avoid being torched alive by an inferno. Judging by his tone, either was possible.

"I decided to call to reassure you that we can meet as soon as you are able," he continued. "I assume you still want to attend this meeting?"

"Oh...oh yes," Rosemary said. "But...uhh, your office is kind of charred right now."

"Indeed it is. Our main offices in Burkenswood will be out of commission for at least a few weeks, however we have a smaller office in Myrtlewood."

"Myrtlewood?" It took Rosemary by surprise to hear the name of her grandmother's village spoken aloud by someone in a fancy accent. It was a small town, a place that hardly anyone knew of. "I guess it makes sense you'd have an office there if Granny was your client, because she was always saying everyone should shop local and support the businesses. She even insisted on buying locally made loo paper made by old Marjie Reeves out of recycled newspaper, even though it was like wiping your arse on sand– oh...I'm doing it again, aren't I?"

"Indeed, you are," Perseus said. "And while I'm sure the rest of that sentence would have been endlessly fascinating, let us return to the matter at hand, shall we?"

"At hand?"

"Yes, our meeting. Your grandmother, Madam Galderall Thorn, insisted that you have a private meeting for the reading of her will, as you may recall."

"Yes," Rosemary said, feeling too embarrassed to say much else lest she begin rambling uncontrollably again.

"And when would you like this meeting to take place?" Perseus Burk prompted.

"Oh, uhh...as soon as possible?" Rosemary suggested, suppressing a tiny squeak of excitement.

"Very well, let me check my diary. How about this afternoon?" Perseus said. "Three o'clock."

"Oh...okay," Rosemary said. "I didn't know lawyers worked on Saturdays."

"I find Saturday much like any other day, Miss Thorn."

"I guess it is," Rosemary said, and then literally held her tongue with her hand to stop it from misbehaving.

"I'll see you at three o'clock this afternoon," he said with a hint of amusement in his voice, as if he could tell exactly what Rosemary was doing to keep herself from blathering on. Rosemary ended the call, the full ramifications of the lawyer's words hitting her as she wandered out of her room.

"Oh, crud!"

"What is it, Mum?"

"I told him we'd be there at three," Rosemary said, still bleary-eyed as she entered the small dishevelled kitchen where Athena was pouring muesli into a chipped bowl.

"Told who?"

"The guy."

"You're not being very specific," Athena said.

"You know – the legal guy."

"Granny's lawyer?"

"That's the one," Rosemary said and sighed, sitting down at the table.

"What's wrong with that?" Athena asked.

"Oh...nothing, just that I told him we'd meet him in Myrtlewood, and I don't think the old car will make it that far without overheating. The last time it happened the mechanic said it would need more serious repairs, only we couldn't afford that, and unless you have a carriage of fine stallions or maybe a pair of racing llamas we can ride..."

"Okay, okay, I get it," Athena said. "So, reschedule."

"But I'm dying to know what's so important that he called me on a Saturday."

"So, we'll take the train," said Athena.

"The train?" Rosemary asked. "Since when do you take trains?"

"You always said you took the train to Myrtleweed when you were a kid."

"It's Myrtlewood."

"Whatever."

"Fine," Rosemary said. "We're taking the train."

"Why do I have to come?"

"Moral support. Plus, it's a really cute town. I know we haven't been there since you were very small, and you probably don't remember but..."

"Yeah, I know. You go on and on about it."

"It's settled then."

"Fine." Athena shrugged. "It was my idea, anyway. Besides, I'm dying to get out of this awful hole."

Just as she spoke those words, a kitchen cabinet door swung loose and fell right off its hinges, clattering loudly to the floor.

"Point taken," said Rosemary.

It turned out there was only one train on Saturday afternoon, so Rosemary convinced Athena that they'd have to stay the night in an affordable inn before catching the Sunday train back. Athena had consented, provided Rosemary could guarantee there would be no bed bugs. They'd had a rather unpleasant and traumatising experience at a boarding house once. Rosemary made bed bug promises that she wasn't entirely sure she could keep, but what choice did she have? She didn't want to leave her teenage daughter all alone in a dodgy neighbourhood, and they hardly had any close friends they could call on at short notice.

They packed their bags and boarded at the Burkenswood train station. Rosemary felt a nostalgic thrill – the excitement of being twelve again and going to visit Granny Thorn in the countryside. Young Rosemary had felt so grown up, leaving her parents behind and travelling on the train all by herself.

Athena was quiet as she took her seat. Rosemary followed her daughter's lead, stowing away the luggage before sitting silently by the window. She savoured the sound of the horn blowing and the rhythmic sound of the train as it began to make its way along the track. There was something so peaceful about a train-ride, a gentle inevitability that the train was going to take her exactly where she needed to go. All she had to do was relax.

Rosemary liked that it was an old-fashioned train – not one of those new fandangled super-fast beasts. This one was more fitting for Myrtlewood.

She listened to the soft whistling of the wind through window and watched the countryside fly past, enjoying the sight of orchards and little villages here and there. As the ride progressed, she even caught glimpses of ocean.

At some point, Rosemary dozed off and dreamed of Granny Thorn serving her tea. She awoke to the scent of lily of the valley, though she couldn't tell if it was from her dream, or whether it was actually in the carriage. She looked across to check if Athena could smell it to find that her teen was fast asleep, slumped over on the padded bench.

The smell had disappeared. Rosemary poked her head into the passageway, just to check. Walking away, quite far down the aisle, was a thin woman with light-coloured hair that looked slightly familiar.

It was possible that Elamina was there on the train, but Rosemary considered it highly unlikely that her snobbish cousin would deign to travel via public transport. She would have brushed it off entirely as just her imagination playing tricks on her, but then she recalled Athena smelling the floral perfume during the fire.

It doesn't mean anything, Rosemary told herself. *Even if Elamina is hanging around, it's probably more to do with the lawyers and the inheritance than it is to do with me.* She hadn't spoken to her cousins in years, and had no desire to after the way they'd always treated her.

The train continued to roll along, and Rosemary enjoyed the view out the window, despite now feeling oddly unsettled. Occasionally, she glanced at her daughter. There was a strong family resemblance between them; the same green eyes and high cheekbones. Athena's features were more delicate and her skin a darker shade from her father's side. Dain never said anything about his heritage other than that he was "Eastern". He'd grown up in foster homes and Rosemary knew not to ask too much. Besides, she reasoned, he probably didn't know much about his birth parents, anyway. Rosemary certainly didn't have that problem. The Thorn family tree was long and lengthy, including a number of quirky characters.

Athena slumbered, blissfully unaware of all their problems. She wore a purple dress that contrasted with her hair, along with stockings covered in holes that Rosemary thought were tacky. Of course, Athena thought that Rosemary's trusty jeans and t-shirt combo was drab and unoriginal.

Athena knew they were poor, but she didn't know how far below the black line they were. Rosemary wasn't treading water financially; she was drowning, and the debt just kept mounting up, the interest accruing faster than her measly pay-check from the grocery shop could keep up.

Athena's life was already busy and complicated enough with schoolwork, and dealing with the mean kids, and trying to fit in and find proper friends even when no one seemed to quite understand her.

All that was enough for a teenager to worry about, and so Rosemary was determined to protect her from the truth as much as possible.

The carriage darkened. Rosemary looked back out the window to find they were trundling through a dense forest. She vaguely remembered this part of the journey.

We're getting close to Myrtlewood.

It was a thrilling realisation, a feeling of home-coming that Rosemary hadn't anticipated. There was a hint of something resembling connection, as if the town might hold a balm capable of healing her life. She'd been blocking out her memories of the village and of Granny Thorn in order to protect herself from regret and grief, but she hadn't realised she was also shutting herself off from feelings of joy. Now that she was getting nearer to Myrtlewood, a part of her didn't ever want to leave. It was the very same sensation she'd had as a child every time she had to return from her holidays with the wild and wonderful Granny Thorn, who always had a pantry full of contraband treats that Rosemary's parents would consider sinful and indulgent.

Granny would take young Rosemary to the beach or foraging in the forest or into the Myrtlewood village for dances and fairs. There was always an adventure to be had, and Granny never judged Rosemary for anything she did or for anything she wanted. It was the only time she'd ever felt truly free.

As soon as the forest opened up into bright sunshine and prairie again, the train began to slow.

Athena stirred and stretched, opening her eyes. "Are we there yet?"

"Yes," Rosemary said. "Almost."

"It's...like a fairy tale," Athena said, looking out the window at the row of silver birch trees lining the railway tracks on both sides, tied with ribbons and arrangements of spring flowers in white and pale pink and yellow.

"What is this place?"

"Oh yes. I should have told you. Myrtlewood village is a pretty special place."

"You did tell me that – only about a million times!"

"Well, for the million-and-oneth time, it's special. It's hard to explain exactly how, but this is one of the things they do – they celebrate the seasons. This must be for the early spring festival."

"It still feels like winter to me," Athena said, crossing her arms and shivering.

"Spring often does," Rosemary pointed out.

"So, you're saying they celebrate the spring by cutting down spring blossoms and tying them to other trees?"

"Yes," said Rosemary, matter-of-factly. "They do other things as well."

"Like dancing naked in a circle?"

"Possibly. We'll have to stick around to find out."

"Ugh. No, thank you."

"Look, here's the station," Rosemary said as the train pulled to a stop in front of an old-fashioned brick railway building.

"It is very cute," Athena admitted. "In a kind of old-timey way."

They exited the train and made their way from the station to the town square.

"Where's the lawyers' office?" Athena asked.

"I don't recall, or maybe he didn't say."

"You've got to be joking," said Athena.

"Well, Myrtlewood is a small place. I'm sure we'll find it. Anyway, it's only quarter-past-two. We should have a spot of late lunch and a cup of tea before I go to the meeting."

"Fine," Athena said, in that sullen teenage tone that Rosemary had become accustomed to.

"Look, we can ask this man for directions." A short but somehow lanky chap with close cropped hair approached. He looked to be in his thirties and had an unusual gait, as if he was deliberately trying to keep his back impeccably straight. He wore wire-rimmed spectacles and a chocolate brown cap with a matching brown jumper tied around his neck.

Athena's eyes widened in concern, as if interacting with this slightly odd man might affect her social status for the worst, despite being many miles from school.

"Excuse me," Rosemary said, waving him down as he walked with purpose along the footpath.

"You're excused," the man said.

"Uh, uhm, thanks," Rosemary stuttered. "But can you tell me how to get to...what was it, Thistle and Burk? Borgen and Balks? You know, the lawyers."

"Clifford and Burk?" the man asked in a slightly nasal voice.

"That's it! That's the one."

"Oh," the man said, frowning.

"Don't tell me it's on fire," Rosemary said.

The man looked surprised. "No. Why would it be?"

"Long story," said Athena. "Can you just tell us where it is?"

Rosemary smiled at her daughter, half pleased that she was eager to step in to stop her mother making a fool of herself with terrible rambling, and half embarrassed that this was so often required.

"I could," said the man and kept walking.

Rosemary and Athena followed behind him.

"Why are you following me?" he asked.

"You said you'd tell us where the lawyers' office is," Rosemary reminded him, trying to keep her tone calm and patient, even though she was feeling frustrated and confused.

"I said I *could*," the man corrected. "I didn't say I would."

"Well...will you?" Athena asked, flashing him a smile.

"Oh...fine. If you really must know!" he blustered. He turned back around and led them back in the direction in which they were originally walking.

He waved his hand, as if flicking water off it, towards a corner of the town square. "Over there!" he yelled. "And that horrible man is probably there, too. Whatever you do, don't trust him. I doubt he's even human."

"Uh, thank you, Mister..." Rosemary said.

"Ferg is the name," the man responded, quickly recovering his composure and reaching out a hand towards Rosemary. She cautiously shook it.

"Thank you, Ferg. I'm Rosemary."

"Rosemary," he said. "Of course you are." And with that, he walked off.

"What an odd man," Rosemary said to Athena.

"You can say that again."

"What an odd–"

"It's an expression, Mum!"

"I know, but I'm still processing, and I thought it might be helpful to say it twice."

Athena sighed. "It's still only two thirty. What are we doing now?"

"Look – over here. It's a teashop," Rosemary said. "I'm sure they'll have something to eat. You can settle in there and read while I go to the meeting, and then we can check in at the inn."

"I hope you at least made reservations for us to stay," Athena said.

Rosemary shot her a look that revealed she hadn't.

"Mum!"

"What? It's out of the way – a small town. I thought they might give us a special deal if we just showed up."

"You're always looking for special deals," Athena protested.

"Yes, well..." Rosemary's words trailed off. She didn't want to explain why. It would have been cheaper for her to come on this trip alone, and she might well have just slept at the station overnight, but Rosemary was determined to do whatever she could to keep her daughter company, despite all the sighing and eye-rolling associated with the teenage years. It had been hard for Athena with her deadbeat dad and always being the odd one out at school, and never having money for new clothes. Even though Athena was sometimes grumpy and surly, Rosemary knew deep down her daughter was hurting and she wanted, more than anything, to take that pain away.

As they approached the teashop, Rosemary noticed that there was something familiar about it. A bell rang as they entered, and a large woman with bright red hair and walnut-toned skin appeared behind the counter. She wore a floral dress and a white and red checked apron and looked flushed. She smiled at them, dimpling her rosy cheeks.

"Oh, my!" the woman said and her eyes lit up. "Little Rosemary Thorn! Look how you've grown!" She bustled out from behind the counter and wrapped her arms around Rosemary, who was baffled for a moment before deducing who this overly friendly shop lady must be.

"Marjie?"

"Oh, but of course!" Marjie crowed. "I'm surprised you remember me, what with you been gone away so long."

Marjie had been close friends with Granny, who'd often taken young Rosemary to visit the little cottage where Marjie lived with her husband, Herbert. Marjie was always cooking up new business ideas –

such as the locally made loo paper that Granny insisted on using, and she'd had a few different shops over the years. Rosemary had never seen the teashop before, but the overtly floral décor and furnishings were much the same as Margie's previous entrepreneurial ventures, such as the make-your-own lemonade stand, or the pot-plant emporium.

"This is new," Rosemary said, gesturing around.

"Oh no," Marjie said. "I always say it's my new shop, but it's been here for over ten years – so that's a long time of you not visiting us! And who is this? Not your wee babe?"

Marjie unwrapped herself from Rosemary and flung her arms around Athena instead. "My, how you've grown, you little lass. Practically a woman now. And last time I saw you, you were barely walking!"

"Oh...err. Hi," Athena said, mildly baffled by the very warm greeting from a woman she didn't remember knowing.

Rosemary smiled. Usually, Athena had a quick quip for every situation, but this time, her daughter could barely string a sentence together.

"Now what will you have?"

"Uhm, tea?" Rosemary suggested.

"Of course you will!" Marjie cried, and bustled back to the kitchen. "Tea and cake! What takes your fancy?"

Rosemary and Athena surveyed the cabinet full of mouth-watering cakes, lamingtons, shortbread and slices.

"That one," Athena said decisively, pointing to a large chocolate cake with strawberries on top.

"I should have known you'd want that," Marjie said, poking her head out of the kitchen. "And for you, Rosemary?"

"What do you recommend?" It was a copout. Rosemary hated making decisions and generally got other people to make them for her whenever possible.

"You'll be having the lemon sponge cake with cream," Marjie said knowingly. "Now just take a seat, and I'll be over in a jiffy."

Rosemary and Athena shot each other an amused look and took a seat at the table by the window with a petunia-print tablecloth.

"Now. This pot is for you," Marjie said, bustling out with a tea tray. She placed a deep purple teapot in front of Rosemary, with a matching cup and saucer. "It's Lady Grey, just how you like it." She winked. "With a little something extra for the nerves."

Rosemary couldn't help smiling at Marjie's strong intuition. How did she know about her taste in tea blends, let alone her nerves?

"And here, love. This one is your favourite." She placed a pale blue teapot in front of Athena, speckled with daisies. "Strawberries and cream, am I right?"

Athena gave her a blank look, but as soon as she caught a whiff of the tea in front of her, she couldn't help but smile. "It smells amazing!" she exclaimed.

"She's a bit magic, I think," Rosemary said to her daughter as Marjie bustled away to retrieve the cakes.

"There's no such thing," Athena said. Though, just moments later, she took a sip of tea and a look of pure joy crossed her face. "Actually, you might be right."

"What did you mean about the nerves?" Rosemary asked cautiously when Marjie returned. "Did you...spike my drink?"

"Oh...well," Marjie put down the tray and fumbled nervously. "I knew you must be here because Galdie's gone. We all know about that, of course. Nasty business."

"Galdie?" Athena asked.

"Your great grandma, dear," said Marjie. "Galdie Thorn, and what a woman she was. I miss her so."

"Nasty business?" Rosemary said. "I thought...I thought it was a heart attack."

"That's the official word," said Marjie. "But the local constable says it was suspicious. That's all I know...and to think, someone could have deliberately hurt poor old Galdie!" She clutched at her heart.

Rosemary felt a rushing in her ears. It had only been a few weeks since she'd heard the news about Granny Thorn passing and though it had been years since she'd last seen her, Rosemary had cried for days when she found out. She was still awash with intermittent waves of grief that she hadn't yet processed. Hearing that foul play may have been involved made things that much worse.

"I didn't know," Rosemary said, taking a sip of her 'special' tea. It was a lovely fragrant Lady Grey blend, which she could smell and taste, but she couldn't quite enjoy it, as if the pleasure part of her brain had checked out. It sent a warm feeling radiating through her, despite not tasting at all like alcohol.

"I'm sorry, dear. We're all such gossips here. Everyone knows everyone else's business. Anyway, you just sip your tea and take a bite of cake, and you'll be right as rain."

Marjie went back to the kitchen, humming to herself as she clattered plates around.

"Are you alright?" Athena asked.

"I...I think so," Rosemary said. The warm feeling had only intensified with each sip of tea, and she was starting to feel quite light, almost giddy. She took a bite of her lemon sponge and just about melted into the table as the intense, delicious flavour radiated through her. "Oh, my goodness. This is amazing."

Athena raised her eyebrows and took a bite of her own cake. "Wow! This is heavenly. Try some!"

Rosemary took a bite of the velvety, creamy chocolate cake. "Oh...no!"

"What?"

She glanced down at her watch.

"I'm late!"

Three

Rosemary rushed toward the Myrtlewood office of Clifford and Burk, juggling the conflicted anguish from the knowledge that her grandmother might have been deliberately killed with a bubbling warmth from Marjie's "special" tea, which was now making her feel rather jolly. It was all very confusing, and though the tea seemed to be having a soothing effect, the jovial feeling probably wasn't a good thing when she was about to be in a very-serious-meeting with a very-serious-lawyer.

As she passed the town square, she noticed people milling around, carrying more boughs of the spring blossoms they'd seen tied to the trees earlier, preparing for whatever the festival was called. They all seemed so calm and tranquil compared to the intensity inside Rosemary's mind.

She crashed through the front door of the building to find the beige-on-beige reception empty.

It's Saturday, Rosemary reminded herself. *The lawyers are probably all out playing golf, or whatever they do. I wonder if Percy-whatsit has given up on waiting for me and has gone to join them for 18 holes.*

Just then, the sound of a throat clearing startled Rosemary. She turned to find a tall, dark-haired man in a black suit. He seemed too young to be the lawyer Rosemary was looking for.

"Uhm, hello," she said. "I'm looking for Percy Burk."

The man cleared his throat again, looking put out. "I'm Perseus Burk," he said.

"Oh, yes...Perseus, right. Like the ancient warrior or something?" Rosemary mumbled. "You sounded older on the phone, and more...well, kind of old-fashioned, but you must be younger than me, and you know what they say about young people these days – Gen Z or whatever letter we're up to—"

"I take it you're Rosemary Thorn," Perseus said, thankfully cutting Rosemary off from her rambling.

"That's me."

"You're late," he replied. "And I assure you, I'm certainly not younger than you."

He smirked a little as he said that, and Rosemary wondered if he was recalling some kind of inside joke she wasn't privy to. She also wondered what his skincare regime was like.

"Right this way, Miss Thorn," he said.

"Okay, but please don't call me Miss," Rosemary said, taken aback by his cool and distant demeanour. He was quite good looking, in a movie-star-from-a-spy-film kind of way, but he was clearly full of himself and that detracted from his appeal.

"Ms then?" he said, drawing out the "Mizz"-sound as if it were slightly offensive to him.

"Just Rosemary, please."

"Very well," he said, though he didn't really sound as if he meant it. "Please take a seat." He ushered her into an office with a large wooden desk and leather armchairs. She sat down in one of the chairs, which made a creaking sound beneath her almost like a fart, making Rosemary blush. "It wasn't me," she said.

"I'm aware of that, Miss Tho– I mean, Rosemary. I beg your pardon."

"So, what's this all about, then? The letter said that Granny's will instructed you to meet with me alone."

"Indeed, it did."

"And...?"

"Miss– Rosemary," Perseus said.

She smiled, both at the fact that he was clearly struggling to break out of his usual way of doing things, which amused her, and also because he was trying, which was satisfying.

He cleared his throat. "You may be aware that the circumstances around your grandmother's death were...unusual."

"Unusual how?" Rosemary said, the sinking sensation returning to her along with the roaring in her ears.

"I'm not permitted to discuss any details that may still be under investigation by the authorities," Perseus said.

"But there is an investigation?" Rosemary asked. "Someone hurt Granny."

A sense of panic erupted inside her that she tried to dismiss as illogical. After all, she had already been told this, more or less, just a few minutes ago. Then an even more reasonable voice in her head assured her it was a normal part of grieving to experience these waves. Meanwhile, she realised she was speaking all this aloud while crying inside the lawyer's office – the very same lawyer who was looking mortified at her apparent display of insanity and emotion and handing her a box of tissues.

"Thank you," Rosemary said, dabbing her eyes. "It was a risk to have me come here without my chaperone. She usually stops the worst of it."

"Your chaperone?" Perseus asked, looking even more mortified.

"My daughter, Athena. She knows when to shut me up."

"Oh," he said, recovering and letting out a little chuckle, as if finally realising Rosemary was joking.

"But why was it you wanted me to come all the way here today? Is this to do with the 'suspicious circumstances'?"

"My apologies, Rosemary. I should have explained better from the beginning." He pulled out a stack of old papers. "Your grandmother's will states that you, and your daughter, are the sole heirs to her entire estate, which she intends for you to look after with great care and pass on to your descendants."

Rosemary's jaw dropped open.

"Are you quite alright?"

"Excuse me?" Rosemary said. "I didn't quite catch that last part. It sounded like you said Granny left everything to me. But that can't be right. I hadn't even seen her in years!"

"It is, in fact, right," said the lawyer, his tone dry. "It seems the late Madame Thorn had a very old will."

"Oh – well, I guess that makes sense," Rosemary said. "We used to be close. That's the sort of thing other relatives might contest, isn't it? I mean, if there's actually any money involved, which I'm sure there isn't much. Granny's house was quite old and the upkeep must have been far too much for her to manage alone. It might well be in a shambles by now. I'm sure there are hefty land taxes, so there's probably more debt than there is value. That's what they always say with pensioners – a penny saved is a penny in the coffin or something. Maybe I just made that up."

Rosemary was aware that she was talking herself down from a ledge of potential disappointment, only she was doing it out-loud and the lawyer seemed perturbed by her continued rambling.

"I'm sorry," she added. "You can blame Marjie – she spiked my drink, though actually this is how I normally behave, so it's probably no excuse."

"If you'll allow me to finish," Perseus said. "Her will *was* very old, however she changed it just two months ago..."

"Oh," Rosemary said. "So I don't inherit–"

Perseus cleared his throat again.

"Sorry," Rosemary said. "I'll shut up now."

"That might be wise if you want to hear the rest," he said curtly. "To continue. The older version of Madame Thorn's will dated back to the year before you were born and prescribed an equal division of all her wealth between her decedents, aside from the manor, which was to go to one particular descendant: the oldest granddaughter."

"But that's me," Rosemary said.

"Yes," he said patiently. "However, as I said, just two months ago Madame Thorn came to us – her lawyers – and asked for a new will, one that bequeathed her entire fortune to you."

"Fortune?"

"It is a sizeable inheritance. Some might call it a small fortune or even a medium-sized fortune. It all depends on context. And that is referring to only the cash assets. There are also significant artifacts of value. And the house, too, will be worth a tidy sum. However, as you mentioned, it is old and falling apart, and as you're not local, I assume you probably want to sell it, despite what it says in the will."

Rosemary felt numb.

A fortune! Whether small or medium-sized, a fortune must surely be enough to get her out of debt and more.

"Can I have a look at that?" Rosemary asked, gesturing to the will Perseus Burk was holding. He handed it over, and Rosemary read it several times, not quite believing her eyes. It didn't contain any details about the size of the fortune. However, it did clearly state exactly what the lawyer had just told her.

"Now, it isn't for me to judge," Perseus said. "And please understand that from our legal perspective, Madame Thorn was of sound mind at the time she composed this will. However, just between you and me, the police may find it suspicious."

"Suspicious?"

"Suspicious that she changed her will significantly only weeks before her death – which they also consider *suspicious.*"

"Oh, I suppose it is," Rosemary said, folding her arms and frowning.

"If you know of any *reason* that she may have done so, I'd be happy to discuss the legal ramifications with you, free of charge – off the record, of course."

"Reasons?! Are you implying tha–"

"I'm not implying anything," Perseus said silkily, interlacing his fingers and leaning back in his chair. "I'm merely offering you support – just as I intend to offer you support to sell the house."

Rosemary was taken aback. *Sell the house.* Thorn Manor was indeed a rambling old building that needed a lot of work, but Granny was quite specific in her wills – both of them – that the house was to go to Rosemary, the eldest granddaughter, and that she was supposed to take good care of it. And that was exactly what she intended to do – or at least as much care of it as she could afford.

"I don't think that will be necessary," Rosemary said. "I can't very well honour Granny's memory if I'm selling her house the moment I inherit it."

"Take you time; think it over," said Perseus. "In fact – here are the keys."

He handed her a large keyring, full of rusty old keys.

"Why not spend the night there and think about it," he said. "You might find that it's more work than you're willing to take on. And I must inform you that the inheritance is all pending the police investigation. It will be a while before the funds from your grandmother's accounts can be released to you."

"You mean, they have to clear me of any wrongdoing?"

"Something like that. I'm afraid I can't tell you much more. The house isn't officially yours yet, however as you are family of the late owner no one is going to stop you from staying there – though consider yourself warned, it is in quite a state."

Rosemary reached out to take the keys, and her finger brushed against Perseus Burk's hand, which was frightfully cold. She shivered. "Are you alright?" she said.

"Why do you ask?"

"Your hand – it's freezing."

"It's just a condition I have," Perseus said, turning away. "It affects my... blood-pressure. I'm prone to cold extremities."

"If you say so," Rosemary said. "Uhm. Thank you, I guess."

"It has been a pleasure, Miss Thorn," he said, and he didn't even try to correct himself that time.

Rosemary left the lawyers office feeling worse than ever that Granny had died before she'd gotten the chance to visit her again, but it was wonderful to feel so acknowledged by her grandmother – to be left everything, while the rest of her miserable conniving family got nothing.

Serves them right, after the way they treated me.

She didn't like to dwell on the past. It was too uncomfortable and heart-breaking, and anyway, she had just inherited a medium-sized fortune.

Rosemary was practically jumping for joy as she skipped along the street to meet Athena, who was sitting contentedly at the teashop, exactly where Rosemary had left her. Marjie was in full flight, gesturing wildly as she regaled Athena with a story.

"We was just sitting down for tea when young Rosemary came screaming into the living room, waving her hands in the air, certain there was a bear after her...only it was just my Herbert in the shed with his circular saw!"

Athena bent over the table, laughing. Her cheeks were rosy, and Rosemary was happy to see it.

"I see you're having a jolly old time at my expense," she said, coming to join them.

"You look like you've perked right up," Marjie said. "I told you my special tea was just the ticket."

"It was certainly *something*," Rosemary said. "What did you put in it, anyway?"

"Now that's a family secret I'm not willing to share," Marjie said. "But trust me, it'll do you some good."

Rosemary sat back down at the table and examined her watch to find that only half-an-hour had passed, and her cake was still good.

She took another mouthful, letting the delicious tart lemon curd revive her senses while Marjie went off to make her a fresh pot of tea.

"So?" Athena prompted.

"Where do I start?"

"What do we inherit?"

"Umm, everything!" Rosemary said. "And I didn't even realise there was anything much."

"Money?" Athena asked. "Really?! Will it be enough to make us not-poor?"

"It sounds like it might be," Rosemary replied. "Though the lawyer was a bit vague on the details – something about the investigation still pending."

"Yippee!" Athena crowed. "We can go back to Stratham, and I can go back to my old school, and we can live in a nice normal house, and everything will be wonderful! I'll have friends again!"

"Well...here's the thing."

"Oh no – don't use that voice."

"What voice?"

"That how-can-I-let-you-down-easy voice. You always talk like that when you're about to disappoint me."

Rosemary sighed. "Really?"

"Really."

"But I try so hard to protect you from the harsh realities of the world."

"That's exactly your problem, Mum. Trying to protect me only disappoints me more. I'm not a baby – just tell me the truth."

"So, the thing is, Granny left us her big old house."

"That's okay," Athena said. "You can sell it."

"You sound exactly like him."

"Like who?"

"That ridiculous man with his silky voice and his nice Italian suits."

"The lawyer? He was good looking, wasn't he?" Athena narrowed her eyes.

"How can you tell?"

"That's the voice you use for good-looking men."

"Oh – shut up! The thing is, it's a special house. It was special to Granny Thorn, and it was special to me as a child."

"But you haven't even visited for years."

"You know I regret that. Don't rub it in."

Tears sprang up involuntarily in Rosemary's eyes, and she did her best to suppress them.

"I'm sorry," Athena said, more gently. "It's just that...you're hardly a handy-woman. How are you going to take care of a big old house that probably needs loads of work?"

"I don't know," Rosemary admitted. "But Granny left it to me in her will with specific instructions to look after it."

Athena crossed her arms. "You're kidding?"

"No. Not kidding."

"You want us to move *here*?"

"Well, I don't know yet. It's all a bit sudden. Let's just go and check out the house. I have the keys from the lawyer. We can even stay there tonight and save money on the inn."

"I thought the inheritance would mean that we don't have to scrimp and save anymore."

"Well, we still will for a while. I don't know when the investigation will be through and anyway, being frugal is a good thing, isn't it?"

Athena rolled her eyes. "Fine. We'll stay in the big old house that belonged to your dead grandma tonight. It better not be haunted."

A strange sensation passed over Rosemary, an almost-yearning feeling as if she hoped Granny was still around, haunting the place. At least that would give her a chance to properly say goodbye.

And with that yearning came a hint of destiny.

Four

Thorn Manor was only a short walk from the town centre, but what might have normally taken ten minutes took a lot longer with Rosemary and Athena both lugging their bags. Athena grumbled and complained, but Rosemary was too busy enjoying the sights of the village as it gave way to countryside again. It was lovely to be back, reassuring somehow, as if the world didn't have to be as tough as it had been for the past few years.

"Here it is," Rosemary said, as they drew up to an overgrown driveway.

"Here *what* is? All I can see are trees and vines."

"That's exactly how it should be," Rosemary said. "That's what Granny used to say. Plants want to grow and there's no use in trying to get them to follow human rules."

"She sounds a lot like you," Athena said.

"Thank you."

"It wasn't a compliment."

"I know, but I choose to take it as one."

Rosemary took in the familiar scene, the rambling bushes and wild weeds giving way to the forest that surrounded Thorn Manor. Though she couldn't see the house yet, she could almost sense its presence, and something else, a feeling of being watched. Rosemary shivered and glanced around, though no one else was in sight.

"So, what am I looking at?" Athena asked.

"This is just the entrance to the driveway," Rosemary said.

As they stepped closer, they could make out the shape of the old house, through the trees, on the hill.

"It's like something from a movie, isn't it?" Athena said, and Rosemary thought she detected a faint tone of awe in her daughter's voice.

"It's pretty special," Rosemary said. "Let's go."

As they stepped onto the driveway a flock of tiny gold butterflies took flight and the wind whistled past, ruffling the bushes as if the land itself was breathing a sigh of relief to be inhabited by its rightful guardian again.

The gravel driveway was steep as it wound up the hill into a forested area overlooking the sea. Athena had stopped complaining, giving Rosemary an uncommon sense of peace. She watched a little robin flit from branch to branch on the path ahead of them, welcoming them home.

Home... It certainly felt that way. Rosemary hadn't felt at home for so many years, having to move from flat to flat, each seeming more squalid than the last. Her life had felt so caged in, so cramped and desperate. Here, things were so open and calm, wild and wonderfully free.

They neared the house. Rosemary could tell it was much more dilapidated than the last time she'd seen it. The shutters hung at odd angles from their hinges, and vines were taking over the east wing. The lower roof appeared to be caving in, and the tower had seen better days.

"This is definitely the part of the fairy tale where we meet the witch," Athena said.

Just then, a crashing sound startled them.

"Is someone in there?" Athena asked as Rosemary raced towards the house. "Mum! You're supposed to run *away* from the scary noise. Honestly, this is just like a horror film."

"Don't be silly," Rosemary called out as she reached the building. "It was probably just a cat. But if someone is in there burgling our inheritance, they've got another thing coming."

Rosemary peered in through the front windows at what used to be the parlour. It was bad. The house was practically a ruin. Inside, it looked dingy and dusty.

"It looks as if no one has lived here for years," Athena said, joining her.

"I can't believe I left Granny here to rot."

"Can't we just go back to the village?" Athena asked. "I don't want to go in there. It doesn't look safe. What if the roof caves in, or the floor gives way?"

"Just let me..." Rosemary said, fumbling with the keys, "take a look."

"Fine," said Athena, crossing her arms again. "But I'm waiting out here in case I need to call the emergency services to get you out."

Rosemary found the green key, which she assumed was the right one for the green front door, and tried it. It fitted perfectly, and as the lock turned, a small sparkle appeared.

Rosemary stepped back and squinted at it, not sure whether to believe her eyes.

"Is it electric or something?" she muttered to herself.

"Not bloody likely," Athena said, standing a few metres away at what she must have considered a safe distance from the crumbling old house.

"No," Rosemary said. "Look!"

"I am not coming any closer," Athena insisted.

The sparkle began shimmering out in a radius around the door knob, leaving it a deeper, darker green. It continued out, appearing to clear the dust and years from the wooden door frame leaving it looking fresh and polished.

"I must be hallucinating," Rosemary said.

"Well, at least you're finally admitting it," Athena quipped.

"What on Earth?" The shimmer continued to radiate out until the entire front of the house looked fresh and well-maintained. Rosemary took a step back to see that even the roof pushed itself up and back into rows of orderly tiles. "Are you seeing this?"

"Seeing what?" Athena asked.

"Oh, crud. That special tea must have had some kind of psychedelic component."

"Uh, Mum, are you alright?"

"Of course I'm alright," Rosemary said. "I'm just not used to seeing houses fix themselves."

"What are you talking about?"

"Look?" Rosemary gestured back at the house, only to find that it had returned to its dilapidated state. "Oh...well. Never mind," she muttered, pushing open the door. "I might need a lie down and a cup of non-special tea."

Inside, the house was dark, but not quite as bad as Rosemary had feared. The floor was still solid and so were the walls. There were a few noticeable vines growing inside, but at least it seemed safe to enter. Her vision had mercifully returned to normal. There were no more shimmery sparkles to deceive her. It felt reasonably dry and almost inhabitable, but it still upset Rosemary to think that Granny had lived like this, with the roof caving in and the vines growing indoors.

She stifled a sob and suppressed a well of guilt at not coming to help.

Granny's much-loved ornaments and china were strewn across the filthy floor. Mildew covered the wallpaper, and paintings of landscapes and still-life bouquets hung askew on the walls, where they remained up at all.

As she passed the open door to the room which used to be her grandmother's library, Rosemary had a sense of foreboding, as if something was lurking there in the dark. She stepped quickly past and came to the staircase. It, at least, looked solid. The banister was gleaming under a layer of dust. Rosemary took the steps two at a time, the way she used to as a child. She reached the top story to find everything largely in-tact and quite a lot tidier than it had been downstairs.

This must have been where Granny was spending all her time, she thought as she walked along the hallway. The realisation gave her a sense of relief. *It's much more inhabitable up here. At least she wasn't living in total squalor.*

Rosemary checked the other rooms, which all looked fine, even her old bedroom from when she was a child with its floral patchwork quilt. The room wasn't dusty, as if Granny had kept it there waiting for her. The thought brought a tear to her eye.

Rosemary didn't want to go into her grandmother's bedroom. She wasn't quite ready to face it yet, but as she returned down the hallway, prepared to update Athena on the state of affairs in the house, Granny's door creaked open, and Rosemary couldn't help but take a peek.

The bed was perfectly made with Granny's lavender quilt. Even the windows were clean, letting bright sunlight shine in. The wood-panelled walls glowed warmly, as if recently oiled.

Rosemary noticed a piece of folded cream paper sitting propped up on the bed, as if waiting for her.

She entered the room, and the door closed softly behind her, giving her an eerie feeling.

"Is that you, Granny?" she whispered. "Are you still here in some form?"

There was no response, but Rosemary comforted herself with the knowledge that if anyone could stick around beyond the grave, it would certainly be Granny Thorn with her sharp wit and strong character.

Rosemary picked up the letter, written in her grandmother's long sloping cursive.

My dearest Rosemary,

My time on this earthly plane is almost up. I can feel it drawing nearer, and it is also time that you knew the truth. You know I've never been one to dither about, and so I'll put it bluntly.

You, my dear, are a witch – yes, really, a witch – just like we all are in the family, like it or not.

The reason I couldn't tell you before is due to something that happened many years ago. I had to make a tough call to bind your powers – all the powers in the family, including most of my own magic. It was decades ago, and you won't remember because I had to bind your memory as well. I'm afraid it might have had a detrimental effect on your mind, but let's just say you have plenty of character development yet to do!

I'm so sorry for all this secrecy, and I'm sorry for the distance as well. It was a side-effect of the spell that, as it took hold, you became more and more removed from this place so that it was even hard for you to visit. It was the only way to protect you and young Athena – to keep you away from this place and removed from the source of your powers. I know you felt awful about abandoning me, but you see, dear, it really wasn't your fault.

Now the danger is truly upon us. I've done my best to keep it at bay for this long, and now I know I cannot hold this fortress of energy any more. I only wish I could have told you about it, properly – that I could have taught you – but I was naïve – yes, even old biddies like me can be naïve. I thought I could hold it back for much longer – just to give you a little more time and a shot at normal life.

I'm sorry that I was wrong, and now I can only hope that you are able to free your powers. You will need them if you are to have any chance of fighting the enemy. I cannot say much here, lest someone finds this note before you, however, I will tell you this:

They come by tooth, claw, and fang.

That is all I can say.

I love you infinitely, and I wish you all the blessings I can muster.

Eternally yours,

Granny.

. . .

Rosemary read the note through twice and then sighed, feeling even more guilty than before.

Granny was mad and senile, and I didn't even think to find out...I did nothing to help her.

She took the note back downstairs, through the grimy entrance way and walked out towards where Athena was waiting for her.

"Took you long enough," Athena grumbled, then she stopped when she saw the look on Rosemary's face. "What's wrong?" she asked. "You look like you've seen a ghost."

"It feels a bit like that," Rosemary said. "Look at this."

Athena took the thick cream paper and read it. "So...we're all witches and we're in danger from some kind of beast with claws?" she summarised.

"That's certainly what Granny seemed to think before she carked it. I can't believe I abandoned her here – senile and living in squalor."

"So, it's just as bad inside?" Athena asked.

"Downstairs is pretty dire, but upstairs is actually quite nice."

"Are you still going to be a tight-arse and make us stay here instead of paying for the inn?"

"What, stay here and risk you running off to find refuge at Marjie's cottage without me?" Rosemary said.

"You've got me there. I was just wondering if the old bird had a spare room I could kip in."

Rosemary sighed. "I guess not. I have to admit, it's a lot worse than I thought – well, outside and downstairs is, anyway. Upstairs is almost exactly as I remember it. It doesn't really make sense."

"Are you sure you didn't just hallucinate it being nicer upstairs?" Athena joked. "You and your magic tea!"

"Hey, that wasn't really my choice. Marjie just handed me the tea, and it seemed rude not to drink it. But yes. I'm sure. This time, there was no magical shimmering. It was just normal. Anyway, we can head back to town and stay the night there before leaving on the train in the morning."

Rosemary looked out at the darkening sky. They'd be lucky to make it to town before proper nightfall. Movement caught her eye. She glanced towards the forest to see the glint of eyes staring back at her from the darkness. Her heart raced, but she reassured herself it was probably just some wild animal, a squirrel or ferret perhaps, even a fox. The woods around here were full of such creatures. Nothing to alarm Athena over.

The sound of an engine distracted Rosemary, and she turned to see what looked like an old-fashioned police car rumbling up the driveway. She glanced back, but the creature, whatever it was, was gone.

An officer got out of the car, dressed in a uniform that also looked like it was from another time. He seemed to be in his fifties and slightly rotund, with greying hair that curled around his ears, and steel-grey eyes.

"Good day, Ma'am...Miss," he said, nodding to both of them in turn.

"Uh, hi," Rosemary said, confused. "If you're looking for a hen's party you've come to the wrong place."

"Excuse me?" he said. "Hen's party?"

"Well, you're hardly an ordinary copper in that uniform or with that car, so I figured you must be a stri–"

"Mum!"

"What?"

"Just let the man speak before embarrassing us both!"

"Oh, sorry."

"I see, I see," the officer said, with an unduly serious expression. "I'll have you know I am a real copper. We just do things differently in Myrtlewood, see. We're off the beaten track here, and no one ever checks up on us to see if we've got the latest doodaddys, so we do as we see fit."

Rosemary giggled, but the police officer retained a serious face.

"Now look here, I'm Constable Perkins," he said, raising his hand in a small wave. "And you must be Galdie Thorn's relatives – you certainly look like her."

"I'm Rosemary Thorn and this is my daughter, Athena."

"The goddess and the plant," Constable Perkins said.

"Excuse me?"

"Oh, you know – Athena, the goddess, and rosemary is a plant – I have some in my back garden, come to think of it."

"How can we help you, officer?" Athena prompted, clearly used to getting conversations back on track.

"Oh right, well. I'm gonna have to ask you a few questions."

There was a pause while Rosemary and Athena waited for the questions. When none came, Athena prompted again. "Such as?"

"Such as what?"

"What questions do you have for us?"

"Oh...such as, where were you on December the twenty-second?"

"We were in Burkenswood, getting ready for Christmas," Athena replied.

It was true, though the memory saddened Rosemary, as it had been such a pitiful Christmas due to lack of funds.

"And I don't suppose you have an alibi?"

"Each other?" Rosemary suggested.

"How convenient," Constable Perkins said. "Anyone else?"

"Our neighbours, I guess," Athena said.

"And I suppose if I was to check with those neighbours, they would corroborate your story."

"I suppose they would," Rosemary said, though she wasn't sure that old Marcy Podge would remember seeing them, given she was blind drunk at any opportunity, whereas their neighbour on the other side, Mr Finch, was just plain blind.

"Very well, very well," Constable Perkins said, pulling at his suspenders. "When was the last time you saw Galdie Thorn?"

Rosemary's shoulders slumped and Constable Perkins got a gleam in his eye.

"Well, well. Is this the body-language of guilt I see here?"

"It is," Rosemary said. "But not for the conclusion you might be jumping to. It's just that I hadn't seen Granny Thorn in years. Not since Athena was a toddler. I've been such a terrible granddaughter."

"And yet she left this whole place and all her money to you, I hear," Constable Perkins said, suspicious. "Not to that other lot who visit every month."

"What other lot?" Rosemary asked.

"*You* should know. They're *your* relatives."

"I...I don't know," Rosemary admitted. "I don't know why she left it to me, other than, maybe it was something about me being the oldest granddaughter – isn't that what she put in her original will?"

"How do you know that?" Perkins asked. He furrowed his brows, glaring at Rosemary.

"The lawyer told me."

"Did he, now? What else did that Mr Burk tell you?"

"Not much," Rosemary admitted. "I wish I knew more. Really, I do. Was it my cousins who were here visiting Granny so regularly? Elamina and Derse?"

"Could be," Perkins said, leaning back on his heels. "I'm not at liberty to say."

"Either that or he can't remember," Rosemary said quietly, under her breath so that only Athena could hear. Athena nudged her to shut up.

"What was that, Ma'am?"

"Nothing," Rosemary said. "I just...I don't know my cousins very well. That's all."

"Interesting," Perkins said, taking a small notebook out of his pocket and jotting something down. "I'll be back to continue this investigation," he said. "Consider yourself warned. Don't leave town."

"What?" Athena looked aghast.

"But..." Rosemary said. "We just came to visit for a night."

"And you can stay visiting until all this is over," he said, sounding very satisfied with himself.

Rosemary and Athena watched as Constable Perkins walked slowly back to his car, pausing every few steps to look back and shoot them suspicious looks. It was almost comical. They would surely have been trying not to laugh if they hadn't been feeling so stressed.

"What the heck was he on?" Athena said, as the police car rambled back down the driveway. "Stay here – in this cooky little town until he finishes his 'investigation', which sounds more like a wild goose chase than anything. How dare he suspect us when we have nothing to do with it. It's just not fair!"

"Easy on," Rosemary said. "I'm the one who's supposed to ramble like that. You're supposed to have the quick quips, remember."

"But..."

"I know."

"This trip just keeps getting weirder!"

"Yes, it does, but hey – we're set to probably inherit a smallish fortune," Rosemary said. She had downplayed the already-vague sum of money so as not to get Athena's hopes up, and also because she still didn't want to reveal the exact state of the current hole in their accounts.

"If we don't get thrown in jail for murder first. And given his uniform, I bet their local jail still has dungeons and torture implements."

"At least today can't get any worse," Rosemary offered.

As if in response to her statement, the sky above them darkened and thunder rumbled overhead, followed quickly by a deluge of icy-cold rain.

"You shouldn't have said that," Athena said.

"Quick, let's get inside!"

Rosemary grabbed her bag and took her daughter's hand, then ran with her towards the house.

"I'm staying in the entranceway," Athena said, as Rosemary pushed open the door. "I don't want to go in there. It's creepy."

"Oh, it is not," Rosemary said, peering into the dark house. "And besides, the rain is coming in sideways, so you'd better get indoors or you'll catch a cold."

"Fine," Athena said, although she didn't sound fine at all.

The shadowy interior of the house looked to be in better shape than when Rosemary had come inside only a handful of minutes before.

"It's not that bad," Athena admitted. "It looks worse on the outside. It just needs a good dusting in here."

"See, I told you," said Rosemary, though she was concerned that somehow she'd imagined all the additional cobwebs and disarray she'd seen before.

Maybe that special tea is still affecting my senses.

"The lights don't work," Athena said, flicking a switch too many times.

"No. I suspect the power has been cut off. It's been a while since Granny was around to pay the bills."

"So, what do we do?"

"Look." Rosemary pointed to a candlestick on the mantlepiece. "We can do this the old-fashioned way." She found a box of matches and lit the three white tapers, sending candlelight cascading around the room.

"It's actually kind of nice in here, in a creepy-old-house kind of way," Athena said.

"Nice and creepy?"

"Pretty much. So, what do we do now?"

"I'm going to try to make some tea," Rosemary said, walking to the kitchen.

"But the power has been shut off."

Rosemary held up the matches and rattled them.

"Please don't build a bonfire to make tea," Athena said.

"I'm not," Rosemary assured her. "Granny has– I mean *had* an old wood-fired stove as well as a more modern one. I guess it's ours now, along with the rest of this stuff."

"Is any of this valuable?" Athena asked, following Rosemary towards the stove.

"Don't even think about hocking your great grandmother's possessions."

"I was just asking," Athena said defensively. "And surely we don't need all this old stuff."

"The lawyer did mention that there were...uhm...what did he call them? Artefacts? Something like that. Maybe just antiques. He seemed to be interested in them – actually he tried to buy the whole house from me." Rosemary said all this before she could stop herself.

"Perfect! So sell it to him!" Athena said. "We don't need this old junk and you know you can't take care of an old house like this. You can barely change a lightbulb."

"Granny managed it alright," said Rosemary. "And it was just her here with her old patchwork cat, Molly."

"What happened to the cat?" Athena asked.

"Molly? She probably died years ago," said Rosemary sadly, as the realisation hit her. "She was old even when I was a child."

"Alright, sorry about that," said Athena. "But you have to sell the house. It's our chance to have a normal-ish life, and you're not exactly handy. An old house like that would just crumble around us."

"Athena."

"What? It's true."

"Can we please stop talking about selling my grandmother's house when she's only just willed it to us?"

"But—"

"Please? At least for the night. I'm just...there's only so much I can handle."

"Fine, but we're talking about it tomorrow."

"We can talk about it, sure," Rosemary conceded, and she rummaged around in the cupboards. "Just please understand that the house has a lot of sentimental value for me. It's special."

"I'm going to have to call the psychiatrists and tell them my mother is in love with a house, aren't I? They're going to have to come and drag you out of here before you end up living with a hundred cats and the whole place falling down all around you."

Rosemary shrugged. "You have always wanted a cat."

"That's true," said Athena. "Can I have a cat? Especially if you're going to end up with hundreds. It would be unfair if you get all the cats in your new ramshackle cat lady lifestyle."

"I won't rule it out," Rosemary quipped as she found some kindling and began lighting the old wood stove. "It wouldn't be my worst life choice."

"No – that would be Dad."

Rosemary frowned. She knew Dain had messed up their lives over and over, though for some mysterious reason she could never remember the details. Despite this, Athena wasn't wrong. "Don't rub it in."

The fire crackled to life and Rosemary stood back to admire her handiwork. "See, your mother is not completely useless."

"I'm actually kind of impressed," Athena admitted. "But just because you can set fire to stuff effectively, that doesn't mean you can look after an old broken-down house like this."

Rosemary sighed. "You're probably right," she said, picking up the old kettle and filling it with water from the tap. "But this place is important to me – it was important to Granny, and I can't just sell it. I already feel guilty enough.

Athena put her arm around her mother. "You really like it here, huh?"

"You really don't, huh?"

"It's creepy, and even if there's money to pay for the restoration, a house like this will require constant upkeep. The money won't last, and it will be about as fruitful as pouring water into a bucket full of holes."

"Since when did you get so wise?" Rosemary asked her daughter.

"Since forever."

"And even if we could afford it, you wouldn't consider moving to Myrtlewood?"

"Mum, we've already moved so many times because of...money problems."

The words stung, barely masking an accusation and Rosemary took a step back as if slapped.

Athena blamed her, and sure, it was her choice to get together with Dain in the first place, though it had always felt out of her control. That man had a power over her she couldn't explain.

Rosemary didn't like to think of herself as a weak woman who'd throw her life away for a man, and yet in Dain's presence, she melted like goo.

"You're thinking about him, aren't you?" Athena said. "You're thinking about Dad."

"How did you know?"

"You always have that dazed look on your face when you think of that man...and you're right. Our problems are mostly his fault, as I keep reminding you – but you are the one always letting him get away with it."

Rosemary could feel the sharp edge of the rift in their mother-daughter relationship, the one caused by Dain. As a young child, Athena had idolised her father, but once she hit teenage years, she saw through him.

"You just forget everything bad he does," Athena continued, her hands on her hips. It was something she'd pointed out several times before. "You have this weird memory blind spot when it comes to him. When he does something sneaky or flaky, you'll get mad for a few minutes, sometimes even to the point of plotting revenge, and then it all disappears."

"Surely, I'd remember something like that," said Rosemary. "And besides, if I forget things, it's not my fault. My memory had been addled, remember?"

"It's still your responsibility."

Rosemary let her shoulders slump. "Is it one of the laws of nature that teens must blame their parents for everything?"

"I believe so," Athena said. "Though being a teen doesn't come with a handbook. Sometimes I wish it did. I just want a normal life, you know, like when we lived in Stratham and I actually had friends?"

The kettle whistled, interrupting their slightly stilted conversation. Rosemary made the tea, thankful for finding a carton of long-life milk in the pantry, so that it didn't have to be served black because the tannins gave her a headache.

The rain bucketed down outside and the sky darkened even further as Rosemary and Athena sipped their tea on the window-seats in the alcove near the front door.

"It doesn't look like this is going to let up anytime soon," Rosemary said. "We'd better just kip here. Like I told you, the rooms upstairs are much nicer and cleaner than downstairs."

"Can't we just call a ride-share or something?" Athena asked hopefully.

"You think they have Uber all the way out here?" Rosemary laughed.

"Well, it was worth a shot."

"Come on," said Rosemary. "I'll show you."

She led a hesitant Athena up the staircase.

"You're right. It's not even dusty up here," Athena said. "It looks almost like a normal house."

"Enough with the 'normal' already."

Rosemary wondered, for the millionth time, what was so good about 'normal' anyway. Her parents had desperately wanted a normal life, moving her away from Myrtlewood and away from the eccentric Granny Thorn and devoting themselves to their Christian church. They were humble people who cared more about God than anything else, unlike Granny, who said God better watch out because she had designs on the job. Being such devout Christians made her parents abnormal in Rosemary's eyes. It also meant they tithed all their additional earnings to the church and were never in a position to help their daughter out, not that they would have, anyway. They'd disowned Rosemary in her early twenties, the moment they realised she was having a child out of wedlock, pushing her further into the arms of the man who was to be her ruin. This was the kind of thing Rosemary tried to spare Athena the details on, saying as little as possible about her parents' rejection.

"This is my old room," Rosemary said, showing Athena in. "You can sleep here if you like. It's very cosy. I'll take the guest room."

"Why don't you sleep here since it's your room, and I'll take the guest room?"

"Okay. Sure," Rosemary said putting on a cheerful voice, though it meant taking the single bed instead of the double. "If that's what you want."

She showed Athena next door to the room Granny kept made up for guests. She had often enjoyed the company of unusual guests in Rosemary's youth. Sometimes they wore cloaks and capes, other times, top hats or old-fashioned embroidered dresses. When Rosemary had asked her grandmother about the strange clothes her friends wore, Granny had just mumbled something vague about "medieval fairs and other such things."

The guest room was done up in matching forget-me-not blue. It was perfectly clean and tidy like the other rooms upstairs.

"It's nice," Athena said. "You're really going to take the single bed and let me stay in here?"

"Sure, why not?" said Rosemary.

"Or there's that other room – I guess that was hers."

"Granny's room. Yes. No. I'm not going to stay in there."

"Too soon?"

"It feels like it will always be too soon," Rosemary said.

Athena patted her gently on the shoulder.

"Are you hungry?" Rosemary asked.

"Starved."

“I saw some tins of beans downstairs, and I bet there’s other stuff we can have for supper.”

“At this point, I’d eat anything.”

Supper was indeed cans of beans on toast, a favourite food of Athena’s growing up. Rosemary had very frugally brought half a loaf of bread from home to save it going stale and to provide at least one meal on their trip. She toasted two slices each, using the toasting fork over the fire while the can of beans simmered in a pot on the stove.

“This is good,” Athena said as they ate their make-shift meal at the kitchen table after Rosemary had cleared it of a thick layer of dust. “Do you think it tastes better because we had to toil over it?”

“Toil?” Rosemary laughed. “What kind of fairy tale are you living in? I did all the cooking, you just stood there telling me that it wasn’t going to work.”

“I’ll have you know that took a great deal of concentration,” Athena quipped.

“Alright then, you poor toiling teen – time for bed.”

They made their way upstairs, feeling exhausted, and said goodnight on the landing.

Rosemary slipped into her childhood bed and fell quickly asleep.

Five

A loud bang startled Rosemary awake, followed by a shriek from the next room.

Athena!

Rosemary's mind raced with awful possibilities of dangerous intruders and natural disasters. She leapt out of bed and flung open the door to find her daughter standing there in the dull moonlight, pale and trembling.

"What? What is it?"

"Didn't you hear that noise?" Athena asked.

"Of course I heard it. Why else would I be standing here?"

A loud crash sounded from downstairs.

"Oh...crud," Rosemary said. "We really are being burgled, aren't we?"

"Shh!"

"Oh sorry," Rosemary said in a whisper. "You're right. We don't want them to know we're here."

"Obviously!" Athena hissed. "Where's your phone? Call the police."

"It's downstairs, I think," Rosemary said. She didn't mention that it was probably out of battery as she'd forgotten to charge it because that was exactly the kind of irresponsible thing Athena always grilled her about.

"Crud," Athena whispered. "So is mine."

"Is this a bad time to wish you were always glued to your phone like normal teenagers?" Rosemary muttered. "I'm sure they don't leave their phones in downstairs."

"Shush, Mum," Athena hissed. "What's the point in me being glued to my phone when I have no friends?"

There was another crash, and another, interrupting their pointless and frustrating conversation.

"Do you think we should try to sneak up on them?" Rosemary asked quietly. "You know – startle them with the element of surprise. Hit them with a bat?"

"Do you *have* a bat?" Athena asked.

"No, but I do have..." Rosemary looked around before picking up a heavy-looking lamp from the sideboard. "This."

"Great, we'll startle them with a lamp."

"Have you got a better idea?"

Athena shrugged. "Wait 'til they go away?"

"That's great, but what if they don't?" said Rosemary, trying hard not to show how terrified she felt and failing miserably. She'd never seen Athena so scared, her teeth chattering and eyes wide.

"Listen," Rosemary whispered.

"To what?"

"Exactly. There's silence now. Maybe they've gone away – or maybe it was just an animal or something, a broken shutter blowing in the wind."

Athena looked doubtful, but it was true. The rain had stopped outside, and the house was completely silent. "Uhm...Mum."

"What?"

"If it was just a shutter in the wind, then how do you explain that sound?"

"What sound?"

"It's like...music of some sort."

Rosemary strained her ears to listen, and sure enough, there was a sound a bit like chimes.

"This is way too creepy," Athena said, reaching for Rosemary's arm as if she were still a small child needing to hang onto her mother.

"It's probably wind chimes or something."

"I didn't hear any wind chimes earlier, did you?"

Rosemary shook her head. "Look, let's just check it out, okay?"

"Okay, but you're going first and take that stupid lamp with you."

They crept down the staircase, treading softly to try to avoid any creaking steps. It was so dark, looking down into the ground floor of the house, that Rosemary almost turned back, but Athena urged her on.

"It might be dangerous," Rosemary hissed. "There could be a serial killer with an axe down there just waiting for us."

"Don't you think a serial killer would have just wandered on up here and chopped us into tiny little pieces by now?" Athena whispered back. "Let's just go and figure out what's causing that sound. I have to know now. There's no way I'm going to sleep without finding out."

"Fine," Rosemary said. "But I notice you're not curious enough to go first."

"You're my mother. It's literally your job to protect me."

Rosemary took a deep breath and breathed out slowly, just like the online anxiety videos told her to do, though those had not specifically envisioned a situation where one was holding an old lamp in preparation for confrontation with the musically inclined axe-wielding serial killer that her imagination was busy fabricating.

The house remained silent, apart from the chiming sound that continued to ring out softly, as if beckoning them closer.

Rosemary and Athena followed the sound down the staircase and along the passageway to a closed door.

"Not in here," Rosemary said and shuddered.

"Why not? What's in there?"

"I just got a feeling, earlier – like there's something big and powerful there."

"Was that when you were trippin' on magic tea?" Athena jibed.

"Probably," Rosemary said. "But that doesn't mean I was wrong."

"What is that room, anyway?"

"Granny's library. She never let me go in there when I was a kid."

"Look. It's probably just an old music box or something," Athena said, pushing open the door.

The room was just as dark, except for a rectangular shape in the centre that looked to be glowing. Light shone out from it revealing an intricate pattern, which looked lacy, illuminating the glossy surface of Granny's big wooden desk.

"It *is* a box...of some sort," Athena said, taking a step forward. Rosemary reached out and tried to hold her back.

"It might be dangerous."

"It's a freaking box, Mum."

"Maybe it's an explosive or something."

"Mum!"

"What?"

"Stop being ridiculous – it's just an old music box. It probably got disturbed during the storm or something."

"You know that doesn't make sense, right?" Rosemary said.

"Well, what do you think it is?" Athena asked.

The box continued to chime, and after a moment, Athena pushed her mother forward.

"Hey! Watch it."

"Go on," Athena said.

"What do you want me to do?"

"Open it, of course. Let's see what's making the sound."

"Fine then," Rosemary said, noticing that her own voice sounded as petulant and teenage as Athena's was when she was in a sulk.

She took a step forward and reached out towards the box. As her fingers brushed against it, the lid flew open, blasting the whole room in blinding white light.

"What the...?" Athena said.

Rosemary ducked, pulling Athena down beside her, terrified that this was some kind of explosion after all, but as the light faded to a golden glow, she saw the sparkling that she'd assumed she had hallucinated earlier.

It was moving faster this time, radiating out, clearing the dust from the big desk and then moving further into the room.

"Do you see that?" Rosemary asked, rubbing her eyes.

"Of course I see it!" said Athena, no longer bothering to keep her voice down.

"Get back," Rosemary said. "It might be some kind of bacteria."

"Bacteria?" Athena said, doubtfully. "Really?! You think this is dust-eating bacteria?"

"Well, what do you think it is?"

"Some kind of hallucination we're both having. Did you slip me some of that special tea?"

"No. Of course not."

"Well, if this 'bacteria' eats dirt and grime, we'd better both get out of the way. We're not exactly sparkling clean," Athena said.

They both stepped back as the shimmering golden light put the room to rights – not just dusting, but also plumping the cushion on the chair and straightening the books that clung to the shelves encasing the room.

"This is really weird," Athena said as they promptly exited the room, walking backwards. "I can't stop watching; it's too cool – like Mary Poppins or something. I should have had some of that tea *earlier.*"

"I told you I didn't dose you," Rosemary said.

"Well, someone did. This can't possibly be real."

"Even if we are both hallucinating, how likely is it that we're seeing the exact same thing?"

"I don't know," Athena said. "I'm hardly an expert on psychedelics."

Just then, the shimmering glow reached the boundaries of the library. It slowed and then burst out – illuminating the house around them, cleaning, clearing, tidying and fixing everything in sight.

"This is impossible!" Athena said as they ran outside to get away from the flying household objects – including a broom, a chair, several books, and the cups and plates they had carelessly left by the window seats. "What kind of house tidies itself?"

"The perfect house?" Rosemary suggested.

They stood outside and watched as the exterior of the house received a rapid makeover, turning from weather-worn and crumbling into what appeared to be gleaming paint and freshly scrubbed stonework. The lower roof pushed itself up, and every tile slipped satisfyingly into place, and the tower re-built itself.

"Super weird," Athena said.

"Yep," Rosemary agreed. "It's just like before – and that only lasted for about thirty seconds. Let's see how long this lasts."

"You mean this hallucination?"

"Or whatever it is."

"What else could it possibly be?"

"Who knows, kiddo," Rosemary said, draping her arm around Athena's shoulders. She couldn't help but recall her grandmother's note from earlier – *you're a witch. We all are in the family*. The words echoed in her mind as the house continued to bloom like a rose, restoring itself back into a pristine state, the shutters pulling themselves up by the hinges, and the ivy creeping back to a slightly less chaotic level.

"No freaking way," Athena said. "This is some potent drug we're on, huh?"

"I don't think it's a drug, love," Rosemary said. "But I also can't quite believe it's real. Do you think we could be dreaming?" She pinched herself but found she didn't wake up.

"Must be," Athena said. "Ouch."

"You pinched yourself too, huh?"

"Theoretically, it's possible to pinch yourself in a dream and feel pain, right? It would just be dreamed pain," Athena said as the house finally stopped righting itself and stood, calm and still and grand before them set against the blooming light of the early dawn.

"I guess," Rosemary said.

"You must be in *my* dream," Athena said.

"No, you're definitely in mine," Rosemary argued.

"That's just what dream-Mum would say."

"Very well, oh wise and powerful master of this dream, do you think it's safe to go back inside the house? I think it's starting to rain again, and my feet are cold and squidgy."

Indeed, a light pattering of rain had begun to fall all around them.

"I guess," Athena said. "Or maybe it's super dangerous and the danger will wake us up."

They trod back into the house. Every surface was spotless and gleaming in the low light. Their eyes were wide as they made their way upstairs. Rosemary insisted on them wiping their muddy feet with towels from the linen closet, despite Athena's insistence that it wasn't going to matter when they woke up, anyway.

"Can you sleep in the same room as me?" Athena asked. "This has all been way too freaky, and I don't want to be alone in case something even freakier happens."

"Freakier than a house fixing and tidying itself?" Rosemary asked.

"...maybe?" Athena said.

"Sure. We can both fit in the big spare bed, but you have to promise not to kick me."

"I make no such promises," Athena said.

They got into bed and immediately felt drowsy.

"It's strange," Athena said with a yawn. "I don't think I've ever gone to bed before in order to wake myself up."

And with that, they both fell fast asleep.

"The birds are too loud," Rosemary moaned into her pillow. "And the light is too...light."

"What time is it?" Athena asked, sitting up in bed.

"I don't know. My phone is downstairs, remember."

"Well, according to the clock that's still ticking on the chest of drawers over there, it's nine o'clock."

"It's a Sunday," Rosemary grumbled. "They should start the day later."

"That's not how it works, Mum," Athena said, getting out of bed. "Hey, I had the weirdest dream last night."

"You mean – that there were loud noises and then music and a bright exploding light box, and then the house fixed and cleaned itself?" Rosemary asked.

"You dreamed it, too?!"

"Uhm, Athena," Rosemary muttered, still half asleep and dazed.

"What?"

"If that wasn't a dream, then why do you think we're sleeping in the same room?"

"No...way!" Athena shouted. "It's not possible."

She jumped out of bed and ran out of the room. Rosemary heard her footsteps down the stairs, but despite her daughter's excitement, she still wished the daylight would just go away and let her sleep for an extra hour. The thumping of footsteps sounded again, and Athena burst into the room.

"No way! No way!" she said, jumping up and down.

"Hey, settle down," Rosemary said. "I'm trying to sleep here."

"Mum. Get up, now!"

"But..."

"Now!"

Athena grabbed her mother's arm and started pulling.

"Hey! Leave me alone."

"Mum!"

"Fine," Rosemary said, and pushed herself out of bed.

As she made her way down the staircase, it slowly dawned on her that Athena was right to be excited. The house, including the ground floor, really was clean and as lovely as Rosemary remembered it being on her earlier visits when Granny was still alive.

The wallpaper was spotless and fresh-looking. The paintings all hung exactly as they should, and even the vases, crystals, and crockery on display on the hall cabinet up ahead looked to be in order, as if Granny had just dusted that very morning. Rosemary bit back the hope that Granny's death had all been a terrible misunderstanding and that she'd emerge at any moment to tell them to take their grubby shoes off and put the kettle on immediately. Grief had a funny way of defying all logic, and though Rosemary knew in her mind that her grandmother was gone, her heart had other ideas.

"How do you explain this, then?" Athena asked. She was standing at the top of the staircase with her arms crossed, looking at her mother as if Rosemary was a naughty child and Athena was the parent who'd just caught her with her hand in the biscuit tin.

"How do *I* explain it?" Rosemary said. "How do *you* explain it?"

"Either we are still hallucinating now, or we were when we first arrived," Athena suggested weakly.

"Or the house magically restored itself after I touched that...thing."

They both turned in the direction of Granny's library. On closer inspection, the box still sat on the desk, innocently. It had somehow closed itself and looked like an ordinary carved wooden item.

They both took a step closer and then looked at each other cautiously.

Just then, a rumble sounded outside. They turned back to the front of the house. Through the now-clean window, they could see a pale pink car making its way up the driveway towards the Thorn Manor.

"Not another visitor," Rosemary said.

"At least it's not that cop again," said Athena. "He was hard work."

Rosemary sighed. "You'd think being out in the middle of nowhere in a dead-lady's house would be enough reason for people not to visit."

"Come on, Mum. Let's just go and find out what they want."

"But it's raining again."

Rosemary and Athena watched from the window as the car door opened and a navy blue sensible-heeled shoe popped out below it, followed by another. Then an umbrella appeared, and the door closed, revealing a rather short, dark-haired woman with a perfectly straight fringe. She wore a navy-blue pencil skirt and a pale pink cardigan, which matched both her car and her handbag.

"It's like something out of a cartoon," Rosemary said, as the woman paused and eyed the house before resuming her approach.

"Shush, Mum. Just because it's not your style, it doesn't mean you have to judge."

"Well, then why are you always judging my sense of dress?"

"Look at what you're wearing."

Rosemary looked down at her worn blue jeans and dark red long-sleeve t-shirt. It was a perfectly normal outfit, but Athena often judged such an ensemble as drab.

"So rude!" Rosemary said, poking Athena in the shoulder. "How did I raise you to be so insolent? Anyway, what's wrong with jeans and a red t-shirt?"

"It's not even a style. You just throw on whatever clothes you find first. Take a good long look at yourself," Athena joked.

There were three sharp knocks at the door, and Rosemary went to answer it.

"Hello?" she said.

"Why, good morning, Madam," the woman said in a high, slightly raspy voice. "Allow me to introduce myself. My name is Despina Crepe, and I'm from the local estate agency in town."

"I didn't know Myrtlewood had an estate agency," Rosemary said. "Next thing you'll tell me, they have their own zoo and prison, too. Everything you need – right here— ow!"

Athena had jabbed her in the ribs. Rosemary scowled.

"Are you quite alright there?" Despina asked.

"I'm fine, thanks," Rosemary said. She wasn't exactly fine. In fact, Rosemary had a mild phobia of estate agents, brought on through some bad experiences when she was younger, and the particular anxiety she got around them sometimes made her break out in hives. This had led her to believe she was allergic. At that very moment, she noticed a slight itch near her wrists, cementing her urge to cut the interaction as short as possible.

"Very well," said Despina. "May I come in?"

"Uh...well, actually, we were kind of in the middle of something, so if you don't mind," Rosemary tried to shut the door, but it bounced back. Despina had already wedged her shoe inside.

"Well, I shan't be a minute," Despina said. "And your name is?"

"Rosemary Thorn, and I really must be going," Rosemary said, trying to will the itch away.

"Rosemary – of course! Now, I heard you inherited Galdie's old place. I must say, I came to have a look the other day, and I'm sure it was in much worse repair. You must have worked your magic on it," she winked.

What does this woman know? Rosemary wondered. *And why does she give me the creeps – as well as hives?!*

Despina smiled a sickly sweet smile. "Well, I can't imagine city people like you two would want to live in an old place like this. I won't keep you any longer, but know that I'm here anytime you want to talk about selling. Here's my card."

She held out a pale pink business card. As she did, Rosemary noticed a flash of something silver. It was a brooch in Despina's lapel, bearing a circular coat of arms with a crow, snake, and wolf, as well as a symbol that looked like some kind of Celtic knot. It was unusual enough for Rosemary to do a double-take despite her itching desire to get the woman out of her vicinity.

"That's an interesting brooch," she said.

"This old thing?" Despina said sweetly, clutching it. "Just a family heirloom. You get a lot of that kind of thing around here. This whole village is just full of old stuff. I bet there's plenty of junk you want to get rid of in that big old house." Her eyes gleamed as she tried to look past them into the house.

"Not really, no," Rosemary said.

"Mum!" Athena nudged her mother.

"Got to go now," Rosemary said.

Despina removed her foot from the doorframe and Rosemary quickly closed it before the estate agent decided to try anything else.

"What?" Rosemary asked as Athena glared at her.

"That could have been your chance."

"My chance to what?"

"To make some cash, so we can get out of here and go back to a normal life."

"Oh." Rosemary's shoulders slumped. "You're still fixated on that idea, huh?"

"Of course. Why wouldn't I be?"

"I just thought that after last night..."

"You mean the hallucinations?"

"Or magic?"

"Are you serious?" Athena asked. "You're supposed to be the adult here."

"I was just thinking that...wait a minute."

"What?"

"We haven't eaten."

"So?"

"So – remember how our brains stop working properly when the blood sugar runs low?"

"Speak for yourself," Athena said. "*My* brain is perfectly fine."

"No. I'm getting the woozy feeling."

"Okay. Let's have some food, and then you can call that woman and tell her you're interested in selling."

The problem was, Rosemary wasn't interested in selling at all. In fact, calling the estate agent was pretty close to being the last thing she wanted to do, but her blood-sugar was too low for her to properly articulate any of that.

In the sparkling clean kitchen, they found not just the old wood burner stove but a new-looking oven, and to their astonishment it turned on – as did the eclectic kettle.

"I thought the power was off," Athena said.

"It was!" Rosemary insisted. "Maybe it was a power cut because of the storm? I'm sure most of this stuff wasn't here last night."

"It was quite dark," Athena said, but her tone was uncertain.

Rosemary laughed.

"What?" Athena asked.

"Don't you think it's funny that we're freaking out over a kettle after what we saw last night?"

"I don't think any of this is funny."

"Oh, love, you're always so serious when you need to eat. Let's see..."

Rosemary opened up the previously bare pantry, looking for the rest of the bread she'd stored there the night before, only to find it now contained an assortment of canned food. She checked the refrigerator and found various edible items in there too. Upon examination, nothing was past its expiry date.

She decided to keep all this from Athena, at least until after they'd eaten. She cooked up some bacon and eggs and served them on toast with cups of tea. Athena was so hungry she didn't even think to ask about the ingredients until after she'd wolfed down her breakfast at the polished wooden kitchen table.

"Where did all that come from, then?"

"It was in the kitchen – though, I don't remember seeing it..."

"Must have just been another thing we missed last night." Athena said, settling on the most plausible explanation. "Alright, so now that you've gotten us both fed, it's time to call that Despina woman."

"No."

"Why not?"

"You know I'm allergic to estate agents," said Rosemary.

"Oh, come off it. You are not!"

"They give me a rash."

"That's preposterous and you know it."

"So, I'm preposterous, then."

"Mum!"

"That's not the only reason," Rosemary admitted. "I don't want to sell the house. In fact, I love this place."

"More than you love me?"

"Athena!"

"What?"

"Don't be ridiculous."

"Don't you want me to be happy, Mother?"

"Of course I do, and I'm not going to make you move here, but I'm not going to sell it either. It's all I have left of Granny." Tears welled up in Rosemary's eyes, and her voice took on a high note as she braced herself so as not to completely break down.

Athena sighed and put her arm around her mum.

"Hey, I get it. It's okay," Athena said. "You don't *have* to sell the house."

"Thanks for your permission," Rosemary said, wiping her eyes.

"Well, I didn't want you to have a full melt-down."

"I'm serious, though. Thank you."

"For what?"

"For understanding that this is important to me."

"What are daughters for?"

"Clearly they are for making their mothers another cup of tea."

"Oh, fine," Athena said, taking their cups and plates to the kitchen.

Rosemary smiled to herself and got up from the table. She shook out her arms and legs and then wandered around the ground floor, looking at Granny's things while Athena put the kettle on.

At the wall facing the bottom of the staircase, Rosemary came eye-to-eye with the familiar portrait of a slightly younger Galderall Thorn than she'd ever met. It was deftly painted in oils in that classic romantic style, though it also held something so lifelike about the visage. Out of the corner of her eye, Rosemary could have sworn she saw her grandmother wink at her.

"Weird."

"What?" Athena said, coming to join Rosemary bearing a laden tea tray.

"The painting. It's just so lifelike."

"I'm not sure how your eyes work, but this image does not represent what I see of life," Athena said. "It's too misty and swirly."

"She must have been, what? Forty-something when this was painted? That's only a little bit older than me."

"So, this is the famous Granny Thorn, is it?" Athena said. "She looks... different to how I imagined."

"You met her, you know."

"Oh sure, when I was what? Two?"

"Probably."

"Two-year-olds aren't known for their attention to detail, Mother."

"I wish you had got to spend more time with her," Rosemary said. "She was...she was amazing."

Rosemary thought the painting in front of her might have just smiled slightly, but decided that they'd had enough excitement for one day already and did not try to bring up the possibility with Athena. Instead, she followed her daughter back towards the kitchen and then sat with her on the window seats, drinking tea.

"So, what now?" Athena asked. "Can we pack up and go back?"

"I guess we have to. You have school tomorrow."

"Oh, don't remind me. School is awful at the moment."

"That bad, huh?" Rosemary asked.

Athena didn't usually tell Rosemary much about her school life these days. She was at the age where she preferred to withhold a lot of information about her life from her mother.

"It's not just the teachers or the classes," Athena said. "I mean, they're alright. It's more..."

"The social stuff?" Rosemary suggested.

"Yeah, it sucks being an outcast."

"Tell me about it, kid."

"Wait a minute," Athena said. "Didn't that police guy say we had to stay here until he'd finished his investigation?"

Rosemary scratched her head, trying to remember a detail as far back as yesterday. "I think he did. But surely, he can't stop you from going to school – I mean, what power does he have to get us to stay in the village? The country, sure, the region, maybe, but the village?"

"It does seem strange," Athena admitted. "But everything about this place is."

"So, what do we do?" Rosemary asked.

"Uhm, you're the adult, remember?"

"Oh yeah...crud. I don't know."

"We can go and check in with him, see if he actually meant it," Athena suggested. "Maybe ask to speak to his supervisor. That guy must surely be a rogue cop."

"So sensible," Rosemary said.

"Why am I trying to get myself *into* going back to school, when by all rights, I should be trying to find a way out of it?" Athena asked.

"I thought you hated this freaky place and wanted to get as far away as possible."

"That might be true," Athena said. "But then you brought up school, and that's a whole different kind of freaky that I'd rather avoid."

"Tough luck, kid," Rosemary said. "Let's get dressed and pack up and we can figure out how to continue your gainful education."

"You know, when you put it like that, staying in Myrtlewood isn't such a bad idea."

"I know you are only saying that because you hate Burkenswood," Rosemary said. "So, don't get my hopes up that you would move here when you really want to be in Stratham."

"Things were just better in Stratham," Athena said.

"You always say that, but you forget that it wasn't all roses there either. Your friends kept falling out with each other, and it upset you a lot."

"At least I had some friends."

"You'll make more. I promise."

"What if I just stayed here and hid away from the world?"

"Not going to happen. If we do decide to move here, you'll have school here to look forward to. Let's go back into town and see if we can shed some light on what we're actually allowed to do while 'under investigation.' If we don't get back to Burkenswood soon, I'm going to lose my job!"

"Maybe you won't need to work behind a counter after you inherit that small fortune."

"Gosh, I hope that's the case. If I never have to deal with another coupon again, it'll be too soon."

They put on their coats and shoes and locked up the house, then made their way into town, enjoying the views of the countryside. The weather had fined up and the birds all seemed to be out, singing to one another as if gossiping about the rainstorm the night before.

"Can we go back to get more cake?" Athena asked wistfully.

"After that woman spiked my tea? I don't think that's wise," said Rosemary, but as they entered the village, Marjie popped her head out of her shop door and greeted them warmly.

"Come in for some lunch," she said.

"Uh, no," Rosemary replied. "We really have to be going. We have some errands to run."

"Nonsense," Marjie said. "You have plenty of time to run errands once you've been fed and watered."

"The thing is..." Rosemary said, struggling to find the words to raise her grievance, especially since Marjie was so warm and kind. "Yesterday you slipped something into my drink."

"Oh that," Marjie said, with a dismissive wave. "Just a special blend of lemon balm and cardamom. It wasn't alcoholic, if that's what you were thinking."

"I did think that, originally," Rosemary said. "Really, it was just ordinary herbs and spices?"

"And a little charm of my own," Marjie said. "It should have given you a nice bright warm feeling, that's all."

Rosemary looked at Athena, who shrugged.

"Any chance it could have caused me to...err...see things?"

"See things, dear?"

"Yes – you know...like hallucinations? I mean...Athena and I both saw some strange things last night."

"Certainly not," Marjie said, ushering them into the tea shop and setting them up at the table. "That's not something I would do, and anyway, it was just you I gave the charm to, not your girl."

Rosemary and Athena looked at each other, perplexed as Marjie brought them both menus.

"What kind of strange things did you see, dear?" Marjie asked.

"Oh, it's hard to explain." Rosemary said, perusing the menu and settling on the mushroom pie. Athena ordered the bangers and mash, and Marjie went off to the kitchen to tell her husband, Herb, to get cooking. She was back a moment later with a tray of tea, which she assured them was perfectly normal this time.

"It was the house, wasn't it?" Marjie said knowingly.

"Excuse me?" Rosemary asked.

"The house – Thorn Manor – it was playing tricks on you, wasn't it?"

"Playing tricks, how?" Rosemary asked.

Athena looked alarmed at the possibility of a sentient house. It wasn't something Rosemary would have considered possible either, though the experiences of the previous night had set a whole new bar for what "possible" meant.

"Is it...alive?" Rosemary asked, and Athena kicked her gently under the table.

"Not in the way you or I are," Marjie said. "But it has a certain presence...a power, a will of its own, one might say. What exactly happened, dear?"

Rosemary wasn't sure whether she ought to reveal the details of the very strange occurrences to anyone else yet, not even a close friend of her grandmother's like Marjie. The last thing she needed was rumours flying around that she was bonkers when she was apparently involved in a murder investigation.

It did strike her, though, that Marjie might hold the key to interpreting Granny's note, which was seeming more and more reasonable as her world became less and less so.

Is "witch" a code for something else, or is it really what Granny was talking about?

Rosemary wanted to ask, but held back, unsure. She resolved to make a note of all her questions and then bring them up at a later date, preferably when Athena wasn't there to kick her.

Six

Rosemary and Athena stopped talking as they enjoyed the delicious food that Herb had brought out with a curt nod.

"He's a man of few words," Marjie explained. "You'll get used to him." Then she spun around on her heels and squealed. "Oh, it's just so good to have you home!"

After that, Rosemary had to forgive Marjie completely for the magic tea incident. It was impossible to hold a grudge against someone so genuine and warm and welcoming, and yes, Myrtlewood did feel a lot like a home, at least to Rosemary.

They finished up their meals and made their way over to the police station, which Marjie had told them was across the town square. The building looked just as old-fashioned as Constable Perkins' uniform.

As they crossed the square, two rows of young children wearing pastels were walking in a circle, holding wicker baskets. Rosemary also noticed a tall, thin woman in a bright red cape, who wore her black hair pulled back in a tight bun.

"Such a strange place," Athena said as they pushed open the doors to the police station. The foyer was empty, and the whole building was still and silent.

Rosemary walked up to the front desk and rang the silver domed bell that sat in its centre. She jumped back at the sudden movement as a dark shape emerged from behind the other side of the counter.

"What the...!" Rosemary and Athena both shrieked.

"Hello there. How can I be of service?" Constable Perkins said, straightening his cap.

"You!" Rosemary said.

"Oh, it's you," said Constable Perkins.

"What were you doing under there?" Athena asked.

"I'll be the one asking the questions, young lady," Constable Perkins replied, taking his small notebook out of his breast pocket and clicking his pen.

"But we were the ones who came to see you," Athena argued.

"Oh, right," he said. "So, what can I do for you?"

"Okay, so here's the thing," Rosemary said. "Yesterday you came to the house and told us not to leave town until you're finished with the investigation, but we live in Burkenswood. Athena needs to get back to school and I need to go to work."

"That may be the case, Ma'am, but we can't have you running off while the investigation is ongoing. How am I to know if you might just skip the country or not?"

"Really?" Rosemary said.

"Really. You must stay in Myrtlewood until you've been cleared of any wrongdoing."

"But that doesn't make sense for us – I have to work for a living, and if I don't turn up, I don't get paid," Rosemary said, feeling desperate. She didn't know when the inheritance money would come through, or how much of it there actually was.

"That's not my problem," said Constable Perkins. "I'm just here to be a professional and...professionally do my job of upholding the law...professionally."

"I'll be speaking to my lawyer about this. I don't even think it's legal to hold people in a particular town."

"Be my guest, Miss Thorn," said Constable Perkins. "But I think you'll find we do things differently in Myrtlewood, regardless of what any fancy-schmancy lawyers say."

Rosemary looked at him, aghast that a uniformed police officer would use a term like fancy-schmancy.

"I want to speak to your superior," Rosemary said.

"I think you'll find that no one is superior to me," Constable Perkins said, flicking his moustache.

"I mean, your manager."

"I manage myself just fine, thank you," he replied.

"Are you saying there isn't a police chief or anyone above you I can ask?"

"Oh, there was, but he retired and moved to Bath."

Rosemary and Athena left the police station feeling bewildered.

"On the bright side, I don't have to go to school," Athena said. "But then again, I'm trapped in this insane little town in the middle of nowhere that's a kind of parody of itself, where things behave in ways that defy the laws of science."

"So, you're finally coming around to the fact that the house did, indeed, fix itself?" Rosemary asked.

"I don't know what to believe anymore."

Rosemary wrapped her arm around Athena. "The problem is, we have no idea how long this investigation is going to take. If it's going to be months, then you will need to enroll at the local school so you don't get too far behind before exams."

"Oh, no. Please don't say that!" Athena said. "I've changed schools too many times already, and I bet the school here is hopeless."

"Come on then, let's go to the lawyer's office and see if they can give us better advice on what our rights are."

"But it's Sunday," said Athena.

"Well, he was the one who insisted I come here on Saturday, so maybe the office is open on Sunday as well."

They walked down the road towards the Myrtlewood branch of Clifford and Burk, which was indeed open. A pale, thin woman who looked far too young to have silvery hair sat behind the reception desk with a frown on her face. She seemed to be solving complex mathematical equations on the notepad in front of her.

"Hi," Rosemary said.

"How can I help you?" the woman asked, though she looked disgruntled about being interrupted from her equations.

"I'm wondering if Perseus—I mean, Mr Burk, is available."

"Do you have an appointment?"

"No."

The woman frowned again and rifled through an old-fashioned leather-bound appointment book. "He's not due in the office today," she said. "He's in Burkenswood and is...err...golfing this afternoon."

"Of course he is," Rosemary said, before she could stop herself.

"Pardon me?"

"I just mean, isn't that the stereotypical thing that lawyers are supposed to do on Sundays? Come to think of it, why are you even open?"

The woman's frown deepened, and she muttered, "We're always open. That's part of the problem with this place."

"Okay. We'll just be going."

"Message?" the receptionist asked.

"What?"

"What message shall I leave for Perseus?"

"Oh...uh." She looked at Athena, who nodded encouragingly. "You can just tell him that Rosemary Thorn wanted to ask him about some things."

"Very well," the woman said and went back to her equations without writing the message down.

Seven

Athena followed her mother out of the lawyer's office. The sky above was overcast, and the air was slightly muggy, giving her the sense that the clouds were cloaking the land in a snuggly blanket. It was the kind of observation she seldom shared with her mother, partly because she didn't want Rosemary to get carried away with even more unusual thoughts than usual, but mostly because she wanted to maintain the air of seriousness about her that commanded respect.

Rosemary was the silly one. Athena was the logical one.

This was part of the game Athena played in her head that allowed her to feel slightly more in control of a life that was often uncontrollable. Athena knew it was only partly her mother's fault. Rosemary, at least, tried. Her father, on the other hand, was a total loose cannon, and Athena had vowed to stay away from him and anyone like him.

This went some way to explaining why she'd never had much of an interest in boys. But as they'd left the lawyer's office and headed towards the town square, Athena couldn't help but notice him. His dark hair flopped across his face as he sat under a stark leafless tree, reading a rather large hardback book.

There was something insatiably romantic about the image of him sitting there. He was so lost in his book that Athena felt he might never notice her, and the thought caused a slight jolt of pain through her chest that she wasn't expecting.

As if in response to her emotion, he looked up, his pale blue-grey eyes meeting hers.

It was definitely a moment of...*something*.

Athena had no words for what to call it, but the boy was looking at her as if seeing her...all of her. She almost felt he could reach right through her mind, into her memories, seeing everything laid bare...*but of course, that's impossible,* she told herself.

She realised she was staring and blushed. Then she quickly wrenched her eyes away from him and hurried to catch up with Rosemary.

Something in her mind whispered: *I see you...*

As Athena walked away, she glanced back in the direction of the boy, only to find he had disappeared.

Eight

Athena trailed behind as Rosemary made her way across to the town square so preoccupied with worries that she walked right into someone.

"Sorry," Rosemary said, taking a step back.

"Sorry for what?" the man asked. Rosemary recognised him as Ferg, the odd chap who had given them directions the day before. Only, he was wearing a blue cap with a matching blue sweater draped over his shoulders, rather than yesterday's brown ensemble.

"Sorry for bumping into you, I guess," Rosemary said.

"We meet again, Rose Thorn."

"Rosemary," she corrected.

"If you insist," he said. "Next time you should look where you're going, you know." He said the comment not as an admonishment but offhandedly, as if it were an idle fact.

"I intend to," Rosemary assured him

"Very well. While you're here, you Thorn women can assist me with something."

"Uh...we can?" Rosemary asked, looking at her daughter, who had been oddly quiet since their visit to the police station. Athena merely shrugged.

"Yes. With the festival preparations for Imbolc," Ferg said in his somewhat wooden tone.

"Imbolc?"

"Yes. Imbolc is the festival of first light. It marks the ending of winter, the first signs of spring. That's why we have the flowers. We must honour the goddess, Brigid."

"You say first signs of spring," said Athena, "But it looks like the season's already in full flight with all these blossoms and daffodils everywhere."

"When we honour the gods and goddesses, they show us favour in turn," Ferg said.

Rosemary and Athena gave each other a puzzled look, as if trying to work out if Ferg was serious or speaking in metaphor.

"What is it exactly that you want us to do?" Rosemary asked.

Ferg raised his arm, revealing he'd been holding on to dozens of pastel-coloured ribbons. "Tie these to the trees around the town circle."

"You mean the town square."

"No, the circle – the circle of trees and the big round lawn within the square."

Rosemary looked across the square to see that a large circle of trees was dotted around inside it.

"Oh...well." She looked at Athena.

"We'd love to help," Athena said.

Rosemary stared at her, shocked. That was not the reaction she was expecting from her teen.

"Great!" Ferg said. "Here you go." He handed them the ribbons he was holding, plus another bag of them. "Just tie them in bows. It shouldn't take very long."

"All of them?" Rosemary asked, eyeing the bag full of ribbons. "There must be at least a hundred in there."

"Yes, all of them. You can tie them with your hands or with your magic if you're in a hurry, but I don't want to see a rushed job."

"My magic?"

"That's what I said."

"Ohh...kay."

Ferg gave her a strange look. "The whole town knows, you know."

It was a slightly creepy thing to say, and Rosemary had the urge to get as far away from this strange man as possible, but he seemed to mean whatever it was in quite a matter-of-fact way.

"I don't know what you're talking about," Rosemary said. Only perhaps, she did. It was all starting to fall into place in her mind: the letter from Granny insisting the family were all witches but saying that she'd had to bind their power years ago, the house fixing itself, the box on Granny's desk that lit up like fireworks. *Could it all really be magic?*

Ferg nodded slightly, as if he'd understood Rosemary's thought-process. She gave him a funny look, hoping that he wasn't actually a mind-reader or she'd have to remember to keep as far away from him as possible.

"So, what is this Imbolc festival like?" Athena asked, changing the conversation as she took some of the ribbons from Rosemary. "Will the whole town be there?"

"Of course," Ferg said. "But as for the details, you'll have to wait and see. We have to have some surprises."

"As long as there are no human sacrifices or naked dancing," Athena said, and this time, it was Rosemary who gently kicked *her*.

"That would be hugely inappropriate," said Ferg. "It's hardly the season for them. Too cold. And anyway, that's not the modern way of doing things." He shook his head sadly, as if lamenting the loss of tradition. "If we burn anything in rituals these days, it's just herbs and the occasional wooden figure that goes on the autumn bonfires for Samhain."

"Err...very good then," Athena said, though she looked as if she wasn't so keen on helping anymore.

"Just start in the east and move around the circle sunwise," Ferg said, not seeming to notice that he'd said anything strange or off-putting.

He walked away, leaving them standing there with the ribbons.

"How did we get landed with this?" Athena asked. "This place is even weirder than I thought."

"You were the one who enthusiastically volunteered to help."

"Yes, but that was before I heard Ferg's nostalgia for the good-old-days of human sacrifice."

"That *was* decidedly uncomfortable," Rosemary agreed. "Let's get started, though. Otherwise, he'll come back to find us, and we'll have to talk to him again."

They got to work, tying ribbons on trees. It was more enjoyable than Rosemary had expected. In fact, in performing the simple act, she felt she might also be tying parts of herself back together, even if it was rather clumsily and haphazardly. It wasn't a permanent fix, more like an old muscle being stretched for the first time in ages. It had been a while since she had done something quiet and relatively solitary. She and Athena divided the ribbons and took different trees, then moved between them, trying the silky strips of satin into pastel bows. Just as she was tying a lemon-yellow ribbon to a silver birch tree, her phone rang.

Rosemary was astonished at the sound. She was absolutely sure her phone battery would be well flat by then, having only charged it for a few minutes that morning.

"Hello?" she answered, her tone cautious.

"Mis– Rosemary," a familiar voice said.

"Mister Burk?" Rosemary asked.

"Please, call me Perseus. If you want me to refer to you on a first-name basis, then it's only fitting."

"Alright then, Perseus. How can I help you?"

"I was actually wondering how I could help you," he said. "You called into my office, remember."

"Oh yes," Rosemary recalled. She'd somehow forgotten, even though it must have only been fifteen or so minutes before. "I figured you were busy with your golf and wouldn't call me back on a Sunday. What is it with lawyers and golf, anyway? Is it some kind of status thing or is it possible you actually enjoy it? It seems a bit dull – no offence. Are all lawyers born liking golf or is it a learned thing?" she wondered out loud, then clamped her hand over her mouth to stop herself from rambling any further.

"I beg your pardon, Rosemary. I called to see how I could help, not to be casually insulted."

She could hear the smile in his voice, and it made her laugh.

"I'm sorry, Perseus," she said. "Next time I'll be sure to insult you more formally."

"I appreciate it," he said. "Now. What it is you need?"

"They won't let us leave town," Rosemary said, recalling what pre-empted the visit to the lawyers.

"Who won't?"

"The police...Constable Perkins said we couldn't leave Myrtlewood until we were cleared from the investigation. The thing is, we have lives in Burkenswood. Athena has school. I have what passes for work, though it pays terribly. I still need that terrible pay to, you know, pay the rent and not be homeless."

"Rosemary, you just inherited a rather large home and a medium-sized fortune."

"Kind of," she said. "Like you said, it isn't coming through yet, and we don't have any money until...well, who knows when. You don't seem to know. Anyway, it's disruptive for Athena to miss school, and she doesn't want to live here."

"She doesn't?"

"No, not really. She doesn't much like Burkenswood either, but she likes Stratham more and wants to move back there if possible."

"And what do you want?"

"It hardly matters what I want at the moment, does it? We have no choice, apparently. We can't leave here and...well...can we leave? Is this even legal?"

"I'll look into it for you," Perseus Burk said. "Though I'm afraid that while this investigation continues, you are likely best placed to stay in town and help...err...resolve the issues."

"What on earth do you mean by that?"

"Things appear to be quite complicated, and you may have vital information that will find the person – or people – who harmed your grandmother," he said, and then hesitated. "Not only that, but I've just received word of another unexpected development."

"What kind of development?" Rosemary said through rising dread.

"Your cousin Elamina has issued a legal challenge on the will of Galderall Thorn."

"You're joking!" Rosemary said. "What would Elamina want with an old house? It's certainly not cash. She's loaded."

"She has not stated a particular objective, just that she believes the new will made by Madame Thorn is compromised, somehow."

Rosemary's mind was racing...*compromised? Is she implying that I tried to twist Granny's arm into giving me her entire fortune?*

The thought of the implied accusation made Rosemary furious. "Well, she can go suck on a toadstool," she said. "I didn't even speak to Granny in all that time, let alone try to manipulate her. Elamina was the one who was visiting her regularly according to that cop. Maybe it was just her personality that turned Granny off."

"That could well be the case," Perseus Burk said. "Though it does create certain...complications for you."

"How do you mean?"

"Well, given the suspicious nature of Madame Thorn's death..."

"Oh no – no, that's just great! Maybe that's what all this is about. Elamina is trying to frame me!"

"I suggest refraining from jumping to conclusions," Burk said. Rosemary had tried but could not really think of him by his first name. He was far too formal. "I do not seek to alarm you," he continued. "Just to make you aware of the risks. The police, after all, will be looking for a motive. A legal challenge to the will such as this will rouse their suspicions."

"So, tell me then, who would stand to gain if I was thrown in jail for murder? Who would inherit then?"

"I expect the will and estate would have to be re-litigated before a judge," he said. "Depending on how good your cousin's lawyer is, as the second-oldest granddaughter, Elamina might well stand to inherit the property. Or it could be sold and the money would likely be divided up equally among eligible family members."

"So, there's Elamina's motive!" Rosemary crowed. "That's what I'll tell that ridiculous constable."

"I understand you're upset, Rosemary," Burk said.

"Upset? No. I'm livid. Can you even imagine being thrown into this situation?"

"As a matter of fact, I can," Burk said calmly. "I was in a similar situation some years ago with my own family, and based on that experience, I advise you not to throw stones. Avoid making any strong accusations until you have concrete evidence, and if you want to raise your concerns with the authorities, do it subtly."

"You've got to be kidding," Rosemary said. "There's nothing subtle about being framed for murdering the only family member – aside from my daughter – that I actually love!"

"Rosemary. The police like to think they are clever. They like to be the ones to work things out. That is the only reason I'm advising you of this as your legal counsel. It's practical advice. If you subtly lead the authorities to work it out 'on their own', they are much more likely to see things your way than if you accost them with furious and spurious accusations."

Rosemary sighed. "I suppose you're right."

"Very well. Is there anything else I can help you with?"

"No," she said, then added a slightly sullen, "Thank you."

"I'm happy to help, as I said. Anytime you need legal advice, please do call me. Golfing advice, however, is not included."

Rosemary laughed and hung up the phone.

"What was all that?" Athena asked from behind her.

Rosemary turned to find her daughter smirking.

"All what?" she asked. "I was simply seeking legal advice."

"You were flirting!"

"Oh, nonsense. You know I don't know how to flirt!"

"Well...you *were* doing it badly."

"Athena, this is hardly the time to be accusing me of more things. We are in the middle of a murder investigation."

"Oh, that old chestnut."

"Yes. That old rotten, slippery, slimy chestnut that keeps getting worse."

"What *are* you talking about?"

"Elamina is contesting Granny's will, which makes it look like we are guilty of something."

"Great...but by 'we', you mean 'you', right? I didn't murder anyone."

"Thanks for the support, kid," Rosemary hissed. "But I'd like to remind you that neither did I! And furthermore – keep your voice down when you say suspicious things like that. You never know when that oddball policeman is going to pop up with his notepad and use our silly jokes against us."

"Sorry," Athena said, raising her palms in surrender.

They both looked around, but Constable Perkins was blessedly nowhere in sight.

"So, I take it we can't just leave town?" Athena asked.

"Apparently 'it is in our best interests' to stay," Rosemary said. "Whatever that means."

"I expect it means exactly what it sounds like."

Rosemary shrugged.

"So, what do we do then?" Athena asked. "We can't just stay here in limbo and do nothing."

"That's it!" Rosemary said, excitedly.

"What?"

"We are going to solve this damned investigation ourselves!"

"Mum, you can't 'solve' an investigation. You *carry out* investigations, you maybe *conduct* them. You solve problems."

"You know what I mean. We will figure it all out."

"You're sure about that?" Athena asked sceptically.

"Yes," said Rosemary, feeling more and more determined. "We just need to gather all the evidence together and figure out the patterns and the motives and stuff. Surely, it can't be that hard."

"Uh, Mum, you've been watching too many murder mysteries on the telly. In real life, this stuff is really hard. That's why people train to do it – professionally!"

"Are you saying you don't think we could make a better go of it than old Perkins over there?" Rosemary said, gesturing towards the police station.

"You might have a point," Athena said. "So, what do we do?"

"We talk to people, ask questions, not like an interrogation, but just as if we are friendly people."

"I'm not friendly, and I'm not a good actor," Athena said.

"Oh, yes, you are – on both counts – when you want to be. We'll get information together and when we work it out, we'll drop subtle hints to Constable Perkins just like Perseus suggested."

"Perseus?" Athena said, raising her eyebrows. "You're on a first-name-basis with the lawyer?"

"Long story," Rosemary said. "Though I still want to just call him Burk. He's kind of stuffy. And stop giving me that look. It's not going to happen."

"So, what exactly did *Perseus* say? Why are we dropping subtle hints instead of being more to-the-point?"

"Because cops have big egos," Rosemary improvised. "And they want to figure everything out themselves. If you tell them something directly, they will assume you're wrong because they think they're smarter than you. So, you have to kind of approach things sideways and lead them without their knowledge, so that they think they are the clever ones working everything out."

"That's an overly complicated way of putting it," said Athena. "But I think *Perseus* might just be onto something."

Nine

They finished up tying the ribbons and made a quick stop at the grocery store as Athena had convinced Rosemary that they were sorely in need of snacks.

"We've got food back at the house," said Rosemary. "It would be better if we didn't waste money."

"Ninety-nine pence on Jaffa Cakes is hardly going to break the bank," said Athena. She was selecting a second packet, much to Rosemary's disapproval, when a voice startled them.

"Rosey?"

She turned to look straight into the blue-green eyes she remembered from long ago.

"Liam?"

"Of course," he said, brushing his light sandy hair out of his eyes. Rosemary recalled that he always did seem to have a problem with getting haircuts on time, but the look also suited him. Liam had been a gangly youth, but he'd bulked up to the point where he was almost embarrassingly attractive in a slightly rough way, as if he belonged in a Men's magazine photo shoot about living in a log cabin. Rosemary took in the stubble frosting his chin and the definition of his muscles evidenced even through his shirt.

She was awash in old memories – that first mid-winter carnival in Myrtlewood, where she and Liam had snuck away from the crowd to kiss, sweetly and innocently, under the mistletoe when they were only fourteen.

The summer they had spent together, after getting to know each other through a year's worth of letters. It had been bliss – walking down by the river, holding hands in jubilant teenage infatuation. The autumn where Rosemary had realised it was never going to work – her heart ached from the long-distance and their letters had become few and far between. Furthermore, another young man had caught her eye. She'd called Liam to tell him it was over, hearing his voice shatter into tears on the other end of the phone.

The other young man had turned out to be very, very bad for her, and it always made her wonder what would have happened if she'd stuck with sweet and earthy Liam.

"You're still in Myrtlewood," Rosemary said, blushing slightly.

"Of course. As far as I'm concerned, it's the best place I could possibly live, and you?"

"Oh..." Rosemary said. "Well..."

"We're here for the moment," Athena added, trying to help her mother find the right words without launching into the whole murder investigation thing.

"You must be...?" he said, looking at Athena.

"This is my daughter, Athena."

"Oh gosh," Liam said. "I heard you had a daughter, Rosey, but I didn't realise time had..."

"It does pass quickly, doesn't it? Especially when you're not a parent."

"Mum!"

"Anyway, as Athena said, we're here for the moment."

"Of course," said Liam. "Your grandmother. I was so sorry to hear about that."

He looked down at the floor, as if unable to proceed.

"Yes," Rosemary said, trying to hold back from launching into the entire story, then she realised that, as a local, Liam might have helpful information. "Actually, I'd like to know what you've heard about the situation. We've had a few...mixed messages."

"From Madame Thorn?"

"No. How would Granny be sending us messages?" Rosemary said, and then recalled the box and the note and the strangely smiling painting. "Never mind. I was thinking more about what people are saying 'round town. Who do they think might have had a role in her...well, you know."

"I'm not one for gossip, but this is a small town and people do talk,"

Liam said. "All I know is she was found up at the house. I heard there were animal footprints of a few different kinds – could have been birds and dogs."

"Oh," Rosemary said, feeling herself growing pale. "I wasn't expecting that."

"Sorry, Rosey," Liam said. "I didn't mean to..."

"No, it's fine," she said, though she didn't feel particularly fine. "Anyway, we best be getting on."

"Look – here's my card," Liam said, handing her a small yellow square of card with 'Haversham Books' on the front.

"Your...card?"

"Yes – I run the bookshop just across the way. Pop in anytime you want to chat or...you know, call me if you need anything."

"Thanks, Liam."

Rosemary watched as he walked away, then turned back to Athena.

"What was all that?" Athena asked.

"What?"

"All that gushing, *Rosey*! All the doe eyes!"

"Don't be silly. He was a childhood crush. That's all."

"Are you going to *call* him?"

"Not like that, Athena. You know I don't date. Anyway, he's probably married or otherwise occupied."

"You always make excuses like that."

"Athena!"

"What?"

"Can we please just stick to the matters at hand? Such as, oh, I don't know – solving a murder so we don't get blamed for it?"

"Oh fine, spoilsport," Athena said, plucking two bags of crisps from the shelf to add to the basket. "Let's get back to the house, then. We can't keep talking about murder all around town, or we'll look even more suspicious."

They left the grocery shop and made their way back to Thorn Manor.

The house still looked grand and well-maintained. Rosemary was grateful that it had not regressed back to a run-down shambles, though how the house had seemingly fixed itself in the first place remained a mystery.

"I suppose we have to let my boss and your school know that we won't be in tomorrow," Rosemary said.

"I guess," Athena replied. "It still seems so weird. I don't particularly want to go to school, but it feels like we're trapped here, and I don't like it."

"I know, love," Rosemary said. "It's an unusual situation, but I believe we are up to the task. Let's solve this mystery and get our freedom back."

"How do you suggest we start?"

"A cup of tea?" Rosemary suggested. "Yes, that's always the best way to start: a cup of tea and we can chat about the things we've learned so far."

They went inside and Rosemary put the kettle on and readied the teapot. When the tea was brewed, they sat in the window seats and thought through some possible suspects.

"Who would stand to gain from the situation?" Athena asked. "Apart from us, I mean."

"Well, there's obviously Elamina," Rosemary said. "She's certainly up to something – who does she think she is, contesting the will? I bet it's all her fault. Her and her brother Derse and their hoity-toity parents, aunt Cecilia and uncle Cyril. The constable said that some family had been visiting Granny regularly. I bet it was her, trying to wear Granny down."

"I thought you said she didn't need money. That side of the family is loaded."

"Maybe they made some bad investments, got into money troubles, or maybe there's something else they want. They were always so competitive. I bet they just can't bear to lose anything. Including the old family manor."

"We'll put them down as *potential* suspects, okay?" Athena said, writing in her notebook. "But don't get too obsessed with thinking it's them. That's how they always miss the real killer on telly. You know, it's a red-herring or something. Puts you off the scent."

Rosemary shrugged. "Fine, who else is there?"

"What about the people who want the house? There was that really odd estate woman."

"Ugh, don't remind me," Rosemary shuddered. "I feel the tingle of an itch on my hands just at her mention."

"Don't be such a hypochondriac," Athena said. "There is no way you can actually be allergic to estate agents."

"You don't believe your own mother!"

"Would you, if grandma said something like that?"

"Probably not," Rosemary conceded. "Okay, write her down. Look—" She picked up the pink card off the coffee table. "Here she is: Despina Crepe."

"Of course, it could be her or someone else who she's an agent for," Athena suggested.

"Oooh...like a double agent," Rosemary said.

"No, Mum. A single agent. That is literally her job."

"I guess you're right. Maybe we can ask her more questions to see what we can ascertain about the prospective buyers she has in mind, pretend we might be interested in selling so that she gives us more information."

"Good idea," Athena said. "And we can find out more about your cousins too. We could even ask them questions directly."

"Oh, yes. That's going to go well," said Rosemary. "Hey Elamina, how are you? It's been so long. Did you change your hair? It looks nice. Oh, and by the way, did you happen to kill Granny?"

"No, Mother. Not like that. Just a normal conversation where we can figure out if they are tense or nervous about anything."

"We don't have normal conversations," Rosemary said. "A normal conversation in our family is us talking about each other separately, in our separate homes. I'm sure they are having their normal conversation about how hopeless I am right now."

Athena sighed.

"Okay, okay," Rosemary conceded. "It's a possibility."

"Who else is there?" Athena asked. "Has anyone else shown an interest in the house?"

"Well, Marjie's interested in everything," Rosemary said.

"Come on, Mum. She can't possibly be a killer."

"It's always who they least suspect," said Rosemary.

"That's on television, not in reality," said Athena. "Although she did dose you with that 'charm' or whatever it was. What if she dosed Granny too?"

"Why? Why would her best friend do that?"

"You're right. That's too creepy," said Athena. "Besides, Marjie is not the murdering type."

"How would you know that?"

"I'm a good judge of character, remember. Anyway, who else was interested in the house?"

"There was Burk," said Rosemary.

"You mean your lawyer friend, *Perseus?* He wants the house, too, does he? *Interesting.*" Athena said it in *that voice* and Rosemary gave her an evil glare.

"When we first met, he was very keen on me selling it, that's all. It seemed strange since I hadn't even come out here to see it at that point."

"I'll write him down, but now you can't date him."

"Since when do I date anyone?" Rosemary asked. "And why not?"

"It would be a conflict of interest," Athena insisted. "Oh, actually...you should date him!"

"So consistent."

"No, seriously. That would give you a reason to get to know him and ask questions."

"Like, please pass the salt, and by the way, have you committed any casual murders lately?"

"In a non-suspicious way," Athena said. "You know, ask about how long he's been around here and why he's interested in the house."

"It certainly is an interesting house," Rosemary said, looking around at all the gleaming wood. "Yesterday, I have to admit, I was terrified of it, but now it just feels so..."

"Cosy?" Athena suggested, looking around the room at all the doilies and ornaments.

"Yes, and welcoming. As if it's here to look after us."

"Well, I hope that's the case, since there's a murderer on the loose. What other suspects do we have?" Athena asked.

"I can't think of any just yet, but maybe after we chat with other people around town, we can add more. Hey! Why don't we find a big piece of paper so we can write down all the names and all the connections, like one of those police whiteboards on telly."

Rosemary got up and looked around for something to use. Of course, Granny's library was the obvious place to look for paper, but she'd been avoiding that room since the light-box-house-fixing incident.

She peeked around the door, but the scene seemed quite ordinary. Even the box sitting on the desk appeared to be innocent and wooden. She pushed the door open wider, cautiously stepping into the room and giving the box a wide berth as she walked past.

The library was well-stocked with stationery. It didn't take Rosemary long to find a large piece of paper on one of the shelves behind the desk. She turned back, intending to take it straight out to Athena, but the box caught her eye again. Rosemary was curious to know what was inside and what could have happened the night before to spark such a reaction.

How dangerous could it possibly be? Her curiosity got the better of her. She set the paper down on the desk and reached for the box. As she touched it, the sound of a chime rang out.

Rosemary stared at the box. She could detect a slight glow inside that hadn't been there a moment earlier.

Part of her wanted to run away as quickly as possible, but the other part wondered if this was some kind of message from Granny.

She thought back to the note telling her about the family's supposed magic powers, and the painting that seemed to smile at her, and the light from the box that somehow repaired and cleaned the old house.

If this really is magic and it somehow cleans a house, how could that possibly be a bad thing?

She thought about calling out to Athena, but then again, she didn't want to scare her.

"Granny?" she whispered. "Is that you?"

The interior of the box seemed to glow brighter.

"Granny?"

Rosemary reached back out towards the box. As her hand touched it, the glow started to spread from the tips of her fingers and up her arm.

She wanted to pull back in surprise, but the light was warm and pleasant and soothing, reminding Rosemary of the way Granny would sing her to sleep as a young child. Instead of pulling away, Rosemary leaned in further. The light flooded through her entire body. This time, there was something else in the box. Her index finger brushed against its cool, hard surface.

Rosemary grasped the object, lifting it up away from the bright light to see she was holding a quartz crystal.

It glowed brightly in her hand, and the room around her faded to black.

She was standing in a void.

"Athena?" she called out. Her voice echoed into the empty space around her. Rosemary's heart raced. *What just happened? Where am I?*

She walked tentatively into the dark. The crystal glowed like a lantern in her hand, radiating light that fell into the darkness without illuminating anything around her.

It all just seemed like nothing, a vast black emptiness. The ground beneath, at least, was solid but just as pitch black as everything else.

"Hello?" she called out, and then fear caught her heart. If anything dangerous was out there, she was alerting it to her presence. As if the light was not enough.

She cupped the crystal in her palms, trying to mute its glow. It stubbornly continued to shine from between her clenched fingers.

Another source of light flickered close by. There was a flurry of movement, and Rosemary froze, but so too did whatever she was looking at. As her eyes adjusted to the new light source, she realised that it was some sort of mirror – a reflection of her. It breathed when she did and turned its head in time with her, but this woman was wild and confident, clad in intricate dusky lace with beautiful tattoos of botanical plants up her arms.

Rosemary stared at the woman in the mirror, who was both her and not her. The woman stared back, so strong and confident. Rosemary felt a deep tug, as if the woman she was staring at was the long-lost part of her she'd been searching for, imprisoned in the glass, or perhaps a future self, waiting to unfurl like a wild blossom. Another light flickered up ahead, and the reflection dispersed like smoke. Rosemary stepped towards the brighter light. It seemed welcoming and safe, drawing her in.

Up ahead, another woman stood on a platform of stone, stooped and slender, wearing light grey robes. She had long white hair, half-plaited and trailing down her back. She held a large bowl made of stone. Her smile was genuine, warm, and somehow familiar.

"Who are you?" Rosemary asked. "Do I know you?"

"Of course, dear," the woman said. "You are of my line and likeness. My blood flows through you, as it has through generations before you."

"You're...my ancestor?"

"I am your elder," the woman said, nodding. "And it's time for you to reconnect with your life blood."

"What do you mean?" Rosemary asked.

"Here," the woman said. "Drink of this to regain your link with the family line."

The woman took a silver goblet and scooped it into the stone bowl she was holding. Shimmery liquid, like mercury, dripped from the sides and Rosemary wondered if this was a trick, an enemy, trying to poison her...but the woman's smile was so kind and, really, what choice did Rosemary have? She had no idea where she was or how to get back.

Rosemary reached out for the goblet, taking it into both palms. She eyed the liquid, which seemed to move as if it had a life of its own. She lifted it to her lips and took a great gulp then closed her eyes to savour the complex flavour.

It tasted like rust and honey, and cool summer nights, and fresh cut grass and elderberry wine. It tasted like Granny's mince pies and Sunday morning lie-ins, and late nights at the beach, and lolling out on a blanket underneath the stars in the throes of youthful infatuation. It tasted like secrets and velvet, and coming out of the cold rain to drink hot toddies. It was bitter and tart and sweet and a little bit salty. It was delicious and also slightly painful to drink, and yet Rosemary wanted more.

Rosemary opened her eyes to find the woman had vanished. She was in the dark again. She called out, but nothing responded. She felt a distinct discomfort...a creeping fear, and then—

"Mum!"

Athena was shaking her awake, and Rosemary opened her eyes to the blinding daylight of the library.

"I wasn't ready," Rosemary said.

"What?" Athena asked. "You fell asleep."

"No. I was...I was somewhere else, and I drank a potion and then it was dark and uncomfortable but...I get the feeling something else was supposed to happen."

"What are you talking about?"

"Oh, never mind," Rosemary said, picking herself up off the floor. "I'll explain later."

"Did you at least find the paper?"

"Oh...oh yes, paper," Rosemary said, reaching out towards the desk. Just as she did so, the paper twitched and then flew straight into her hand.

"Did you just see that?" Rosemary asked. She turned to see Athena's jaw dropping. "That was weird. Let's get out of here."

"No," Athena said. "Try it again."

"Why?" Rosemary asked. "It was weird enough the first time."

"Just try it," Athena said. "I want to see if you can actually move paper with your mind or if it was just the wind of something."

"Right. It's blowing a gale in here," Rosemary said into the perfectly still room.

"Or static electricity. I don't know. Just try it."

Rosemary held out her hand towards the stack of paper on the bottom shelf, willing it to come to her. Everything remained still and ordinary.

"What did you say last time?" Athena asked.

"Uhm, paper?"

Still, nothing moved from the shelf.

"Try it again, but more commanding," Athena said.

"Paper!" Rosemary cried. The stack of paper remained perfectly still, and Rosemary, despite her initial hesitation, was oddly disappointed. "Maybe it only works sometimes," she said.

"What works sometimes?" Athena asked.

"My magic," said Rosemary. "The elder restored it. At least I think that's what happened. She gave me some kind of silver potion to drink from a goblet which tasted like...well, like everything good with just a tinge of sadness."

"Did you hit your head, or something?"

"No, I'm serious," Rosemary said. "You saw it with your own eyes. That paper moved. It came to me."

"I saw something, but I'm not convinced it's magic."

"And the house!" said Rosemary. "You saw the house fix itself."

Athena shook her head, as if trying to shake off cobwebs. "Come on," she said. "I think we need another cup of tea."

"Seriously," Rosemary said, following her daughter out to the kitchen. She reached into her pocket and pulled out the note from Granny. "Remember this?"

"You thought she was mad and senile, remember?"

"Sure, I did, at first...but with everything that's happened."

"You really think it's magic?" Athena asked. "That you're magical?"

"Our family is. That's what Granny said in this letter, only somehow, we lost it. There was some grave danger and Granny bound the family's powers. That's why we never knew, and that's also why I stopped spending so much time in Myrtlewood. Granny says here that it was all part of the spell."

"Convenient that she basically excuses you for neglecting her," Athena said.

"Ouch. That's harsh."

"Well, you were going on about how guilty you felt, and then all of a sudden, you have a reason for your actions."

"I'm not trying to use it as an excuse," Rosemary said.

Athena had filled the electric kettle with water by this point. She tried to put it on, but the switch didn't light up. "It's not working. Maybe it's another power-cut. Drat. We'll have to use the wood-burner again." She started filling the old-fashioned kettle instead.

"Or we could use the gas stove," Rosemary suggested, gesturing to the gleaming stainless-steel oven with gas hobs on top. "We'll just need to use matches to light it. It will be a lot quicker than lighting the wood-burner."

"Then why didn't we do that when we first arrived?"

"I don't think the gas stove was here," Rosemary said.

"Oh, nonsense. Here." Athena passed the filled stove-top kettle to Rosemary.

"You really don't believe me, do you?" Rosemary said, still holding the kettle. "I mean...I can understand why. It's not easy to believe this stuff...but when you've seen it with your own eyes."

"It's ridiculous, Mum,"

"I know it's ridiculous!" Rosemary said. She could feel a slight tingling in her fingers, which were unusually warm, but she ignored it in favour of continuing the impassioned conversation. "Don't you think I realise that? I'm a grown woman. Why would I make this stuff up?"

"I never said you made it up," Athena said, using her calming voice. "I just think you're getting carried away."

"Carried away?!"

The kettle started to whistle in her hands around the same time that Rosemary realised it was unbearably hot.

"Ouch," she dropped it down on the unlit stove. "What...?!"

Steam billowed out of the kettle, which continued to whistle and then died down, as if the stove had been turned off beneath it.

"No way!" Athena cried. "No freaking way. Did you just boil the kettle with your *hands*?"

"I...I think so," Rosemary said.

"Is the water safe to drink?" Athena asked.

"I don't see why not," said Rosemary.

"You might have magicked it to be all weird."

Athena picked up the kettle and poured a little of the hot water into the sink, just to check it, but it was quite ordinary looking. She made the tea and carried the tea tray over to the window seats, while Rosemary wrung her hands and paced around, muttering undiscernibly to herself.

"The tea tastes fine," Athena said. "I hope it doesn't make us hallucinate again."

"I think we've established that it wasn't a hallucination," Rosemary said.

"Do you think you can do it again? Boil the water, I mean."

"Oh, I don't know," Rosemary replied. "I couldn't make the paper move when I tried to do it deliberately. Maybe this is the kind of magic that only works by accident."

"That's a *kind*?" Athena asked. "Oh, hello, Rosemary, what type of magic do you practice? Just the accidental kind."

"Oh, stop it," Rosemary said. "You know about as much as I do."

"Give me that letter then," Athena said.

Rosemary begrudgingly handed it over, though she was at least satisfied that Athena finally seemed to believe her.

"It says it's family magic," Athena said. "So where are *my* powers?"

"I don't know," Rosemary said. "It's all to do with that box in the library, I think, but the elder also said that magic would be restored to the family line. Maybe you have the magic, too, and you just haven't accidentally used it yet."

"We could ask Marjie about all this," Athena suggested. "She seems to know about charms and the like."

"We could, but we haven't completely ruled her out as a suspect yet," Rosemary reminded her. "I really hope she isn't the one who hurt Granny, because that would be awful. Her own best friend."

"It won't be her," Athena said.

"How do you know?"

"I told you, I have an instinct for these things."

"You mean you've watched too many crime dramas?"

"No. In a crime drama she would be a likely suspect, but in real life she can't be."

"And why is that, madame investigator?" Rosemary asked.

"She's too...good," Athena said. "You can just tell with her. She's good and kind and warm through and through. There's no way she's the one who killed your grandmother."

"Well, I'm not quite so hasty," Rosemary said, retrieving the large piece of paper. "Let's get started on this. We have to be methodical. Who were the people in Granny Thorn's life that might have hurt her? Who had it in for her? Who had something to gain from her passing? There's that estate lady. Despina. Who else?" She began scrawling on the paper.

"What about that lawyer man you like so much?" Athena said, teasing.

"Perseus Burk. Yes, I suppose we can't rule him out. He did seem strangely eager to help with all this, and he was keen on me selling the house. Okay. That's two. Then, of course, there are our dear relatives, the Bracewell-Thorns. I'll write down Elamina and Derse for now, though their parents are just as bad, but more distant. I have a feeling that if it was them, they'd all be in on it together. Oh...and that constable. He was a weird one. I wonder if he has something to hide."

"Surely, there are a bunch more people that we just haven't heard of yet," Athena said.

"You're right. We need to start asking questions, and what better excuse than to go into to town for dinner and strike up innocent conversations to find out more details."

"You've got to be kidding me," Athena said. "*You* having an *innocent* conversation? You're bound to put your foot in it. Besides, you keep saying how broke we are, but you keep suggesting we go out for food."

"I'm too tired to cook," said Rosemary. "I suppose our financial situation stretch to a pub meal."

"Says the woman who didn't want to spend less than a pound on biscuits."

"Biscuits are hardly food. But you're right. I *am* bound to say something stupid. I'll try to be careful."

"Oh, fine," Athena said. "Let's go. I'm starved."

Ten

Athena and Rosemary put on their coats against the chilly wind and made their way towards the Myrtlewood village.

It was late afternoon, fading into early evening, and the sky was just beginning to darken. Athena delighted in seeing a snowy owl, who watched them from a hollow in a nearby tree. They paused to admire it.

"Maybe it's not so bad here," Athena said.

"Oh, okay, so you don't take my word for it, but trust in this owl."

"Of course. Owls are innately trustworthy," Athena said, but just as the words escaped her mouth, they heard a loud scratching sound from the stand of trees nearby, followed by an unearthly squawking.

"Let's get out of here!" Athena whispered, and Rosemary agreed. They hurried on, and both breathed a sigh of relief when they reached the village. Marjie's tea shop was closed, as were most of the other shops, giving the whole place an eerie dusky feeling, but the lights were on, and jolly sounds were booming from the building called the 'Witches Wort', the only pub in town. They made their way, gratefully, into the warmth.

All the other patrons turned their heads to watch as they entered. There was a hush and all Rosemary could hear was the sea shanty playing quietly over the speakers.

The woman behind the bar smiled at them. "Welcome," she said. "And who do we have here?"

The woman was not much older than Rosemary, with a round face and long strawberry blond hair, which she wore in a plait.

Rosemary wasn't used to such a personal greeting from someone she didn't know, but she decided to go along with it. After all, this was a small town.

"Uhm, I'm Rosemary," she said. "And this is my daughter Athena."

"Why, I never...Rosemary Thorn!" the bartender said. "You don't remember me?"

"Uh, no," Rosemary admitted.

"I'm Sherry Hume. I used to help your grandmother out around the house when I was a kid. I'd give you piggy-backs around the garden."

Rosemary smiled, a flicker of memory helping her to nod in agreement, though it was so vague she never would have recognised this woman without prompting.

"Sit down, sit down! I'll bring you two some menus."

Rosemary and Athena took their seats in an empty booth.

"Well, that's gone and put a dampener on our investigations, hasn't it?" Athena said.

"What do you mean?"

"The whole town knows who we are now, and who we're related to. They're hardly going to spill the beans and tell us they killed granny."

"Well, the murderer isn't," Rosemary whispered, trying to encourage Athena to keep her voice down. "But they probably weren't going to waltz up and tell perfect strangers about their terrible crime, either. The thing is, there are probably tons of people here who know a thing or two and would want to tell us because they want the crime to be solved – for Granny's sake."

"I didn't think of it like that," Athena admitted.

Sherry brought them the menus as promised, along with two small brown pottery mugs that were steaming and smelled delicious – sweet and spicy.

"What's this?" Rosemary asked. "We didn't order drinks."

"On the house," Sherry said. "This is some of our famous mulled mead!"

Rosemary looked at Athena, whose eyes were wide as she stared at the unusual beverage.

"—and don't worry," Sherry continued. "It's not too alcoholic, more like a ginger beer, I promise."

"Uh. Okay," Rosemary said. "It's not spiked with...anything else, is it?"

Sherry cackled. "Oh, you've been spending too much time with Marjie, haven't you?"

"Some," Rosemary admitted.

"Look, I'll level with you," Sherry said. "Our mulled mead is made with an old and very secret recipe, and it does involve a little bit of magic – nothing serious. It's just something to give you a bit of a pick-me-up and protect you from the cold, that's all."

"Magic," Rosemary said. "Of course."

Sherry smiled again and left them to consider the menus.

Rosemary took a sip of the mulled mead. It really was delicious and warming. Athena did the same and smiled. She looked in Sherry's direction at the bar.

"So, it really is just something they talk about casually here," Rosemary said, looking around the pub. "Magic – as if it was needlework or tennis or Szechuan pepper."

"So it seems," said Athena. "Unless it's a metaphor."

"You're too sensible for your own good," said Rosemary.

"These prices are good," Athena said, ignoring her mother and scouring the menu.

"It's just as well," Rosemary replied. "We are short on cash for the foreseeable future. Payday isn't until Thursday, and it won't be much if I can't get back to do more shifts."

"All the more reason to figure out what happened to Granny Thorn," Athena said. "If we can solve that mystery, then maybe we can get our freedom back and—"

"'scuse me," an old woman said, stumbling into the booth. She had wild hair and an eye patch. "Allow me to introduce myself. My name is Agatha Twigg and I couldn't help overhearing what you young ladies were saying about old Galdie."

"Oh, yes?" Rosemary said, blanching. She didn't realise they'd been talking loud enough for anyone else to hear. "You knew my grandmother, then?"

"O'course I did," Agatha said, shaking her head sadly. "And what a shame it was to lose her in her prime like that."

"In her prime? She was in her eighties."

"Exactly," said the old woman. "I bet she had a good few decades left. She was a strong 'un."

Athena raised her eyebrows at Rosemary in a way that suggested they'd be better off not believing anything the old woman said, but Rosemary was less incredulous. After all...magic was probably real. Who knew how long a magically enhanced life-span might be? And Granny Thorn had always been fit as a fiddle.

"Do you know anything about what happened to her?" Rosemary asked. "We want to know, you see. As family, it's so hard to think of her passing without even knowing what happened."

"It wasn't me, if you're asking," Agatha said. "I mean, Galdie had her enemies, but I wasn't one of them. I'd know better than to cross someone so powerful."

"Enemies?" Athena asked, seemingly forgetting her own distrust for a moment. "Who were her enemies, then?"

"Well, she didn't like all that many people, see. She never got along with the police force around here, or the postman, for that matter. She loathed courier companies. She didn't like that bloke at the bookshop – kept muttering about how he didn't know real magical books from the fake ones. She was definitely offside with the Bloodstone Society..."

"The what?"

"Oh, you know. No one is supposed to know they exist, but naturally, everyone does. They're just one of those secret societies. Think they're better than anyone else. Old Galdie hated them with a passion. Told them to stay away from her house."

"It seems like lots of people were after her house," Rosemary said. "I mean, I've already had a few people trying to buy it, and it's not even mine."

She'd meant to say "yet," but something told her to hold her tongue. After all, she didn't know if she could really trust this unusual stranger.

"O'course, lots of people want that house. Legend says that's where the power is hidden."

"What power?" Athena asked.

"The old Thorn magic. Y'see, you'd both be too young to remember it, but once that power was so obvious. You could feel it miles away. Then, probably only a few decades ago, it vanished from the radar. The house was still there, and Galdie was still there, but though she still seemed to have a bit of power for odds and ends, there wasn't the great loads of it there was before. The Thorns were one of the old magical families, see, and the power just grew and grew over generations. Now, don't get me wrong, Myrtlewood is a special place, and just about everyone here has a trace of some kind of power or other, but it's nothing compared to that old magic...nothing," she muttered.

"Are you ready to order?" Sherry said, and Rosemary realised she must have been standing within earshot for some time. "Sorry if Agatha is bothering you. She's a great story-teller, this one."

"Yes, I'm starved." Athena said. "I'll have the fish 'n chips, please."

"Great, and for you, Rosemary?"

"I'll have the same, thanks."

"Anything else?"

"No thank you," Rosemary and Athena chorused at the same time.

"That young lass is too big for her britches," Agatha grumbled. "Thinks she owns the place. Well...she does. But that's only because old Merle died and left it to her. No one knows why he didn't leave it to his own kids. It was right suspicious if you ask me, but try telling that to the local law enforcement. What a joke."

Agatha Twigg took a big swig of her pint and then toddled away, muttering to herself.

"Well, I supposed we should take all that with a grain of salt," Rosemary said.

"Or a bucket load," said Athena. "Perhaps a whole salt-lake full of saline."

"I'm pretty sure half of what she said made absolute sense," Rosemary said. "I'm just not sure exactly which half."

"Oh, don't mind old Aggie," Sherry said. She was back again holding two plates full of delicious looking golden deep-fried food.

"That was quick!" Rosemary and Athena both exclaimed as both plates were placed down on the table in front of them.

"Well, I have my ways," Sherry said, tapping her nose. "She, on the other hand." She gestured back to where Agatha was now standing, near the bar, accosting a young couple who sat there. "Well, she's a troublemaker. Pay no mind to anything she tells you."

"She talked about Granny Thorn," Athena said. "You wouldn't happen to know anything, would you? About what happened to her?"

"I've heard some whispers that her own magic might have backfired," Sherry said. "Other people in here say that wasn't it, but I can't bear to think that someone would hurt that lovely old woman intentionally."

"Agatha said she had enemies," Athena added, clearly fishing for more information.

"Oh, don't we all?" Sherry said. "No one can please everyone, and Agatha least of all. She and Galdie never saw eye to eye."

Rosemary cleared her throat. "Agatha said she wasn't counted among Granny's many enemies."

"Of course she'd say that," said Sherry. "No one wants to be seen as the enemy of the dead, especially not when that death was suspicious."

"So, you do think it was suspicious?" Rosemary asked. "Not just her own...accidental doing?"

She couldn't quite bring herself to say "magic", despite the way everyone else around Myrtlewood seemed to talk about it, as if it was as plain as daylight.

"It's not up to me now, is it?" Sherry said. "I'm no expert, but one thing is for sure. It was magic that killed your Gran."

"How can you tell?" Athena asked.

Rosemary wasn't sure if she was bluffing or starting to get her head around the magic thing.

"I went up there the next day," Sherry said. "I was supposed to drop off some pickles for Galdie. When I arrived, the police was blocking the entrance. I didn't see nothing, but I could feel it in the air. That was definitely some strong magic. So, either Galdie was messing with something more powerful than she should have reckoned with, or someone was using some strong forces against her. Anyway, enough of me. I'll let you eat."

As Sherry walked away, Rosemary and Athena gave each other a significant look.

"It couldn't possibly be us," Rosemary said.

"Uh, Mum, we knew that already, remember?"

"*We* knew it already, but the authorities? All we have to do is convince that constable that we don't know the first thing about magic, and that therefore it couldn't have been us who hurt Granny."

"Sure, but how are we going to explain that to the coppers? Hey, so we didn't even believe in magic until five minutes ago, therefore we couldn't possibly have killed an old lady with it."

"That's exactly what I want to say," Rosemary said. "But in different words."

"You're really going to go to the police and talk about magic?" Athena asked. "They'll lock you up for being mad."

"Not just any police," said Rosemary. "The Myrtlewood authorities.

You know they're already at least half-mad, so my insanity shouldn't bother them too much."

Athena shrugged. "You have a point. Shall we eat now?"

They tucked in to their meal to find it as crispy and satisfying as it looked, and still piping hot despite all their distracting conversation.

"We'd better be getting back," Rosemary said, after they'd finished up their dinners. "It's still slightly light outside, but it will be completely dark soon, and I'm not sure there are street lights."

"Couldn't we stay just a little bit longer?" Athena asked. "Surely, there must be some kind of taxi service here."

"What's got into you?" Rosemary asked her. She followed her daughter's gaze across the room to where a pale, dark-haired boy sat. He looked only slightly older than Athena, and he was definitely looking back at her.

"Oh...I see," said Rosemary, smiling. "Your sudden affection for the Myrtlewood pub has nothing to do with the fine dining experience, or even the warm small-town atmosphere, and almost certainly something to do with a certain—"

"Mum!" Athena said in an urgent whisper. "It's none of your business who I fancy."

"I knew it! You fancy him!"

"Keep it down, will you? I want to leave here with some shreds of dignity intact."

"Oh, fine," Rosemary said, folding her arms in a sulk. "But we really do have to be getting out of here soon, and I'm pretty sure there are no taxis in Myrtlewood."

"Did someone say taxi?" Ferg appeared at the side of the table.

"Uh..." said Rosemary, taken aback.

"Yes!" said Athena. "We'd like to catch a taxi a bit later, but we don't know if there are any in Myrtlewood."

"I happen to run the only preeminent taxi service in town," Ferg said.

"Is it preeminent if it's the only one?" Rosemary muttered.

Athena kicked her, and not as gently as usual.

"Ouch."

"So, you can take us home then, in about half an hour?" Athena asked.

"I can, indeed. I basically spend my evenings here waiting to see if anyone needs a lift home. Can't condone drunk driving, after all," said Ferg.

"Uh, how much will it cost?" Rosemary asked. "It's only a five or ten-minute walk to Thorn Manor, so it will hardly take a minute to drive."

"The first trip is free," Ferg assured them. "After that it's 20p per minute."

"That's very reasonable," Rosemary said.

"Thank you," said Ferg. "People don't often call me that." He saluted like a sailor. "I'll be back in twenty minutes."

"That was quite strange," Rosemary said. "Are you sure you want to ride in a car with that man?"

"Oh, he's harmless," Athena said. "*I'm* a good judge of character, remember?" She gave Rosemary a significant look.

"Hey, how long are you going to blame me for your father?"

"I don't know. How about forever? I have to live with his genes, after all."

"Huh, fair enough," Rosemary said. "But you turned out alright." She reached out to pat Athena's shoulder but was quickly brushed away as Athena gave her a significant look and then turned her attention back towards The Boy.

Rosemary sighed and got up from the table. She figured she might as well pay the bill before Athena decided she wanted dessert and cost them extra money they didn't have. She took a final swig of the mulled mead, emptying the cup and enjoying the spicy warming sensation, then she mumbled something to Athena about getting ready to leave soon, but was deliberately ignored.

As Rosemary approached the empty bar, Sherry re-emerged from the back room.

"Just settling up," said Rosemary.

"Oh no," Sherry insisted. "This was your first meal here for a donkey's age. You can't expect me to charge you for that."

"Can't I?" Rosemary asked, perplexed.

"Certainly not. We have our customs in Myrtlewood, and the first meal is always free for people who move here."

"But..." Rosemary said. "We may not be moving here. We're just here because of Granny..."

"Oh, nonsense," said Sherry, matter-of-factly. "You belong here. It's obvious. And your daughter will see that soon enough. See, she's already getting friendly with the locals."

Rosemary looked back and was slightly alarmed to see the boy from across the room had approached Athena and was standing by their booth, chatting to her. He wasn't smiling though, as Rosemary thought he ought to be. Instead, he had a sullen, brooding look. *Teenagers!*

"You know what?" Rosemary said, turning her attention back to Sherry. "I really hope you're right. I do love it here. It's so different from the rest of the world – or at least the other places I've lived. Myrtlewood is special. It's like a cosy blanket and a hot cup of tea on a cold rainy night."

"That it is," Sherry said.

Rosemary glanced back across the bar to see Athena was still chatting away to the glum young man. She would have given her pinkie toe to know what they were talking about, but she knew better than to try to eavesdrop. Athena would have none of that. She tried not to stare, but something else caught her eye. In the corner booth sat an ominous, hooded figure. Whoever it was had the hood of their cloak – yes, cloak – pulled forward so far that it obscured their face.

She turned back to Sherry to ask after the strange character only to find her busy pulling a pint for another patron.

"You look like you've seen a ghost," Sherry said, bustling back moments later.

"Oh, it's just..."

Rosemary turned to gesture towards the corner booth only to find it empty. The hooded figure had disappeared. "Oh, you get a few strange characters in here, don't you?" she asked Sherry.

"We're all strange characters here, love," Sherry said warmly.

"Touché," Rosemary replied. "It's just—"

"Look, Rosemary, I've been meaning to tell you something since you first walked in," Sherry said. "Only, it's probably not going to make a lot of sense."

"What is it?" Rosemary asked. "I mean, I'm used to not making any sense, if it's any consolation. I don't know if that increases or decreases my chances of misunderstanding whatever it is you're going to tell me."

"So, the thing is, old Galdie knew something. Something she shouldn't have known at the time. In fact, most people still don't know it. I only know because she confided it in me one day when I was delivering some dinner to her. She liked to order the mutton stew, and I never minded running it up to her. One day, about a month or more ago, I go to deliver the stew, see, and she's in a right state. She wasn't too clear about what it was, but she'd been down at the council buildings to pay her rates earlier that day and walked in on...Oh, I don't know what it is, but it was something to do with the town mayor. I'm dead certain he was up to no good."

"No good as in embezzlement, or an affair or..." Rosemary still couldn't bring herself to suggest magic, even though it seemed more and more likely over the past twenty-four hours.

"I don't know the details. That's why it doesn't make any sense, really. I just thought you should know, in case it helps. It sounds like you've been poking around, trying to figure out who had it in for her."

Rosemary blanched again. *So much for our secret investigation...*

"So, you think she witnessed something bad at the council office, and the mayor then went to great lengths to shut her up?"

"You didn't hear me say anything of the sort, mind," said Sherry. "I won't go on record with anything like that, in case it comes back to bite me in the bum."

"I see," said Rosemary.

"The thing is, it might not have even been intentional. The mayor, Mr June, is just not very good at spells. He's all pomp and ceremony, sure, and no one else wants the job of listening to the complaints of every Tom, Dick, and Harry, so he's had no competition. He just keeps getting re-elected, but if he did go up there, trying to erase your Granny's memory, it might have backfired on him."

"Interesting theory," Rosemary said. "And yes, we are trying to figure out what happened to Granny Thorn. It's awful not knowing."

It was also awful being a potential suspect, too, but Rosemary didn't exactly want to broadcast that to the entire pub.

"I suppose we'd better get going," Rosemary said. "Apparently, Ferg is our taxi driver for the evening. Is he trustworthy?"

"Who? Fergus?" Sherry said. "Oh, aye, he's a good lad. A bit odd, but who am I to judge?"

"I'll take your word for it," Rosemary said.

"Very well, but where's your young girl?" Sherry asked.

Rosemary looked back towards their table to see it empty. Athena was nowhere in sight.

Eleven

Athena sighed as her mother prattled on about her largely unwarranted suspicions. She took another bite of her crispy battered fish. It was good food – magical or not. The whole magic thing was starting to sink in, though Athena's logical mind wanted to dismiss it completely.

Things had been getting weirder and weirder inside her head, and she didn't want to tell Rosemary about it. The pub was fairly crowded, and that only made things worse.

There were strange sounds, as if her mind was a radio station being tuned in and out – and being around people made it worse.

It would have been easier if the sounds were comprehensible, but they were mostly gibberish, half-formed sentences and single words out of context. She sometimes felt as if she was hearing bits and pieces of people's thoughts, but nothing clear enough to be interesting, just incoherent noise. Athena worried she might be losing her marbles.

It had all started when she'd seen that boy.

I see you...

That was the first time she'd heard a voice in her head and been sure that it wasn't her internal monologue. But he'd disappeared oh so quickly, and Athena was left with only questions and incomprehensible sounds.

She'd begun to wonder if the boy had ever existed at all, or had he merely been her mind playing tricks on her? *Have I become so lonely that I'm making up imaginary friends?* She stifled a laugh. *Even my hallucinations don't want to talk to me.*

Rosemary gave her a strange look, but Athena simply looked back blankly, and they continued to eat in silence.

There you are...

The voice said again. Athena froze. She looked across the table at her mother, who seemed focused on her chips and clearly hadn't noticed anything unusual. Athena made the most of the small moment of privacy where Rosemary was so engrossed in fried food that she didn't notice her daughter scanning the bar, looking for someone in particular.

*He has to be real...*she thought to herself. *And if he is, Mum will see him, too.*

There he was. Sitting at the edge of a booth across the room was the boy from earlier. Athena recognised his dark hair. He turned towards her, flashing those grey-blue eyes in her direction.

*It's you...*Athena thought.

Yes, it is, came a surprising reply in her head.

Athena shook herself, relieved that Rosemary was still preoccupied with scoffing dinner. Only a moment had passed, but it felt like an age.

She turned back to the boy.

You can hear me? Athena asked.

The boy nodded from across the room.

Athena blushed, wondering how she could possibly drown out her thoughts so as to retain some privacy around someone who was clearly a mind-reader and...*a mind speaker? Is that even a thing?*

She refocused her attention on finishing her dinner. All the while, her heart was racing, as was her mind.

Am I totally nuts? Is it possible that I just had a telepathic conversation with a stranger? I need to stop thinking...He can probably hear all of this!

She took a gulp of the beverage Sherry had brought them and felt it soothing her.

Don't worry, the boy's voice said in her mind. *I can't see everything in your head. I can just hear the thoughts you broadcast clearly. Think of it like a conversation.*

*Oh...okay...*Athena thought back.

I can help you learn to master it, if you like, the boy offered.

Just then, Rosemary said, "We'd better be getting back. It's still slightly light outside, but it will be completely dark soon, and I'm not sure there are street lights."

No... Athena thought. *I was just starting to figure out the mystery.*

She wasn't ready to tell her mother about what had been going on in her head. Firstly, because she wanted to maintain as much privacy as possible. Living in small flats and boarding houses over the years meant Athena had to fight for every ounce of privacy she could muster. Secondly, she didn't want to worry Rosemary – not after everything else that had happened recently. She glanced across at her mother who was looking rather too thin. She hadn't been eating enough, perhaps due to stress or trying to save money. There was already far too much to worry about!

Athena looked back across the room towards the mysterious stranger who could somehow communicate with her. "Couldn't we stay just a little bit longer? Surely, there must be some kind of taxi service here."

"What's got into you?" Rosemary asked.

Athena couldn't help it. Her eyes darted back in the direction of the boy.

Rosemary followed her gaze across the room to where he sat.

"Oh...I see," said Rosemary, smiling. "Your sudden affection for the Myrtlewood pub has nothing to do with the fine dining experience, or even the warm small-town atmosphere, and almost certainly something to do with a certain..."

"Shush!"

Athena tried to stop herself from blushing. She was relieved that, at least, her mother could see the boy. He wasn't a figment of her imagination, after all. However, she did not appreciate Rosemary's tone.

Athena already had too much on her mind and being heckled for fancying a boy wasn't helping. It wasn't even that Athena fancied him. She didn't know anything about him at all except for his unusual ability, but she wasn't about to tell her mother any of that.

Nevertheless, she needed to resolve the mystery and was relieved when that unusual man, Ferg, offered to taxi them home. It was even better moments later, when Rosemary went over to the bar to pay and became distracted by a conversation with Sherry. Athena finally had time alone to think, or at least that was what she thought.

Finally, alone, his voice said in her head.

Yes, what of it?

Good. Can I come over and talk to you?

I guess so, Athena replied, though she felt a nervous jolt at the proposition. Her nervousness only worsened as she watched him get up and walk towards her. Though she was sitting down, she could tell he was around a foot taller than her, and his hair hung over his eyes in a cool way. She gulped, not knowing what to say.

"What's your name?" he asked.

"Athena," she replied, looking down at the wood grain on the table to stop herself from staring into those stormy eyes.

"Athena, goddess of wisdom," he said.

"Something like that," Athena replied. "What about you? What's your name?"

"Finnigan," he said.

There was a moment of silence, in which a thousand deafening thoughts rushed through Athena's mind, creating a roaring effect.

"So..." she said, finally. "Why did you come over here if..."

"If I can already talk to you in here?" he said, pointing to his temple. "I wanted to meet you properly." He twirled his hand in an elaborate gesture and bowed.

Athena laughed, surprised.

"I can't see you smile inside your head," he said.

Athena gulped. *Is he...flirting with me?*

"So, what is this, anyway?" she asked. "Telepathy?"

"Shh," Finnigan said, raising his finger to his lips. "You really don't know anything about it?" he asked.

Athena shook her head, unsure what was okay to say aloud.

"Come with me," said Finnigan.

"Where?"

"Just out of here."

"But..." Athena said.

"We won't be a minute."

Athena hesitated. She knew next to nothing about this boy, and yet she absolutely needed to figure out what was going on inside her head, and he seemed to have the answers. She glanced up to the bar to see her mother still focused on talking to Sherry.

"Okay," she said, though she wasn't sure if Finnigan could hear her since he'd already walked away. She got up quickly, and followed him.

Twelve

"Athena? Athena!"

Rosemary called out across the bar. Many heads turned her way, but none bore the face she wanted to see. Her heart raced.

How long does it take to abduct a teenager? Probably not very long, especially if the teen has gone willingly! How could Athena do this? She is supposed to be the sensible one – at least in her mind she is. She's always telling me off for being careless and brash. Now look at her, disappearing in the night off to goddess-knows-where!

Rosemary strode furiously around the pub, checking in all the corners and booths, but Athena was nowhere to be found. She looked outside the front door, but there was no one in sight. The empty street chilled her blood.

At least I hope she went willingly, Rosemary thought, her anger quickly transmuting into terror. *What if someone – The Boy – threatened her? What if he had a weapon, or used some kind of bewitching charm!*

Her fury was now firmly aimed at The Boy, and she intended to make him regret he ever looked at her daughter. She turned back to the pub, hoping that Athena would blossom out of the woodwork or emerge from the bathroom and tell her to stop being so silly, but the stalls were empty. She strode back out into the main room again and checked the table to see if her daughter had left a note. Nothing.

"Athena!" Rosemary called out again. She turned back towards the door, only to walk straight into something solid. It was a large, tall man, with a scarred face and greying scraggly hair. He gently gripped Rosemary by both arms and said in a quiet voice, "Calm down, lass. She's just out here."

"Oh, thank goodness!"

Rosemary gratefully followed the man towards a side door.

"Here." He gestured through the window.

Athena was sitting on the stoop next to The Boy, his hand lay on the stone beside them and her hand rested on top.

She's holding hands WITH A BOY!

Rosemary took a deep breath and reminded herself that this was quite ordinary teenage behaviour. So normal, in fact, that she should have been more surprised that Athena hadn't taken much of an interest in boys previously – as far as she'd told her mother, anyway. But this was a boy she'd just met!

"Thank you," she said to the older man, not taking her eyes off her daughter this time.

"A pleasure to do a good deed," he said. "The name's Covvey."

"Covvey," Rosemary muttered. The name sounded familiar, but Rosemary couldn't think why.

"You ever need anything, I'm happy to help." Covvey said. "Galdie did me many a favour, and I owe her more than my life."

"Thank you," Rosemary said, risking a glance at his wrinkled and scarred face before turning back towards her daughter again.

"I'm Rosemary."

"I know you are," Covvey said.

Rosemary turned back towards him, wondering if she'd known him years ago, but all she could see was his back as he limped back towards the bar.

Rosemary took a deep breath and pushed open the door.

"Excuse me, young lady. Exactly what do you think you're doing?"

Athena jolted away from The Boy. "Such a cliché, Mum! Give me some privacy."

"I'll give you privacy when you show me enough respect to let me know where you're going before I tear the whole pub apart looking for you in a right panic!"

"Woah, take a deep breath!" said Athena, embarrassment blooming on her cheeks in a bright blush.

"I already did."

"Ready for your transportation?" a reedy voice said from behind Rosemary's left shoulder.

"See? Time to go!" Rosemary said, reaching for Athena's arm. "No time for privacy – or anything else." She glared at The Boy, who gave her a disinterested stare in return.

Teenagers!

Athena brushed off her mother's hand but got up just the same.

"Fine, I'll go, but let me at least say goodbye to Finnigan."

"Finnigan," Rosemary repeated, under her breath, trying to remember the name so she knew who to track down if Athena made any other unexpected disappearances. "Fine. Say goodbye. You have two minutes, and I'll wait right inside, by the door."

"Mum!"

"Don't push it."

"Ugh!" Athena huffed, crossing her arms.

Rosemary stepped back inside the blessedly warm pub to find Ferg standing there, holding her jacket for her.

"Oh...uh, thank you," she said.

"You left it at your table, Ma'am."

"I didn't realise this taxi came with the full valet service."

"Pardon?"

"You know, valet – like in fancy hotels where they drive your car for you."

"I think you'll find I do not know about the val-aye," Ferg said. "And no one drives my car but me. Sorry to disappoint."

"Uh, never mind," Rosemary said. "I'm not disappointed, don't worry."

Athena re-emerged from the side door, glaring daggers at Rosemary, and followed her glumly out front to where a bright orange VW bug was waiting. Ferg opened the door.

"Just like a valet," Athena joked, clearly recovering from her bad mood.

"No, you may not drive my automobile, young madam," Ferg said.

Athena shot a confused glance at her mother.

"Don't ask," Rosemary replied. She was still feeling quite scratchy and mad at Athena.

"Why are you reacting like this?" Athena asked her.

"You gave me a right scare back there. I'm starting to wonder whether it was a good idea trying to move to Myrtlewood in the first place."

"You are the one who loves it here," Athena said.

"You're right. This place seems like a dream come true, but it could so easily turn into a nightmare. Maybe I've been too hasty in wanting to move."

"Oh, don't start this now," Athena said. "I was just starting to like the place, and also..." She gestured to Ferg, who had a serious expression, as if he was concentrating hard on the road. "Keep your voice down," Athena whispered.

"So now you like it here?" Rosemary said, not caring if Ferg heard her. "And what am I supposed to do if you go off the rails?"

"Don't be silly, Mum. You're totally overreacting. We went outside to look at the stars for five minutes! Finnigan was showing me the constellations."

"Well, that's just lovely. Stargazing while I was running around frantically through the pub, calling your name. Feeling like an awful mother, scared you'd been abducted, for Pete's sake."

"It's not my fault you overreacted," Athena said.

"Overreacted? Really? And what if you had been abducted, in a strange town in the middle of nowhere?"

"But I hadn't been."

Rosemary sighed. "You've never done anything so careless before, and yet, within a day or two of being here you're throwing caution to the wind and stepping outside with a boy you don't even know without telling me!"

"Oh, come on," Athena said. "I didn't want to have to go up to you and explain...Can't you give me a bit of privacy?"

"I hate to break it to you, love, but in a small town like this, there's no privacy."

"She's right, you know," Ferg said from the front seat.

Athena looked at Rosemary, mortified.

"See, I told you."

"Do you want some advice?" Ferg asked.

"No!" Rosemary and Athena said at once.

"Suit yourselves," said Ferg, as he turned the car down the driveway to Thorn Manor.

"That took longer than I was expecting," Rosemary said, trying to keep a neutral tone as it wasn't really Ferg she was annoyed with.

"I took the scenic route, since you're new in town."

"At night?"

"It *is* night," said Ferg.

"Oh...well, thank you," Rosemary said, as they pulled up at the house.

Something looked different. Rosemary could tell, even from the car. Thorn Manor seemed more imposing than usual – ominous and dark, against the blue-black sky.

"I do hope you'll be in attendance at the spring festival next Saturn day," said Ferg.

"Saturday?" Athena suggested.

"I prefer not to use the shorthand for the day of Saturn. I revere the gods."

"Oh, okay, fair enough," said Athena, shrugging.

"Here's my card, in case you require any more transportation." Ferg held out the card for Rosemary to take. She slipped it into her pocket and thanked him. Then both she and Athena got out into the chilly night air and made their way towards the house.

"Is it just me, or does the house look different?" Athena asked.

"It's not just you," Rosemary said. "And don't think you're off the hook for what happened earlier."

"Oh, come on, Mum!" Athena said, shivering in the cold. "What is up with you? It's really not such a big deal. I shouldn't have slipped out without telling you, and I'm sorry for that. But *you* should have trusted that I can look after myself for five minutes. I didn't go far. I was being responsible."

"Oh sure," said Rosemary. "You were fine – you were being responsible – but what about him? What about The Boy?!"

"Finnigan was fine, too."

"I don't know anything about him, and neither did you. He could have been a total creep."

"I'm a good judge of character," Athena muttered under her breath. "And as much as I should have told you where I was going, you shouldn't have freaked out like that. It's daft. I'm sixteen, not six!"

Rosemary huffed, too ruffled for a response as she fumbled with her cold fingers on the house keys. The front door swung open to reveal...nothing.

A swirling black void was the only thing visible inside the house. The darkness had engulfed everything. At its edges, silvery waves shimmered as they circled in a chaotic vortex. It seemed to pulse with its own kind of life force, which gave Rosemary an ominous feeling. She definitely did not want to mess with it.

"What the...?"

Rosemary pulled the door closed immediately.

"What just happened?" Athena asked as they both took several steps back from the house for good measure.

"You really expect me to know?" Rosemary asked, her voice acerbic.

"Well, no, I guess I can't expect you to know, or to be reasonable. I can't expect much from you at all."

"Oh, Athena."

"Stop being so mad at me," Athena grumbled.

Rosemary folded her arms against the freezing night air and gave Athena a stern look, certain her daughter was hiding something from her.

"Oh, I give up," Athena said, throwing her arms in the air. "Don't you think we have bigger problems right now, like the fact that our newly-inherited house is a gaping void of doom?"

They stood in silence for a moment, their breath fogging up in front of them, looking up at the house which seemed to loom above them.

"You might have a point," Rosemary admitted. "It might well have been a normal teenage thing, and I might well have issues, which are being triggered."

"I'm glad that's settled then," Athena said, crossing her arms. "Now, back to the other pressing matter at hand. What do we do about the house?"

Rosemary took a few deep breaths to calm herself, and thought about their situation. "We could call someone to help us," she suggested.

"That Ferg man? He gave you his card."

"I'd rather not," said Rosemary. "And why is it that every second person in this town has a business card? What are we in a corporate 80s movie or something?"

"I hope not," Athena said. "My hair is far too flat."

"Well, mine is all frizz today, so I'll fit right in."

"If not Ferg, then who?" Athena asked. "We don't have anyone's number here."

"Haven't you ever heard of a telephone directory service?"

"Actually, no. What's that?" said Athena.

Rosemary was taken aback. "It's like a phone book, but you look it up online or you call a person and they just put you through."

"Really? That sounds like a massive violation of privacy."

"Well, I think it only works on landlines," Rosemary said.

"People still have landlines?" Athena asked. "You're lucky I know what *they* are. We haven't had one since we lived in that big old shared house in St Austell, and that was *years* ago."

"Well, these outdated technologies turn out to be quite helpful at times like these," said Rosemary. "Oh drat!"

"What is it?"

"No reception."

Athena checked her phone too. "Me neither."

"Great," Rosemary said. "So, we're stuck out here, in the middle of nowhere, cold and exhausted...and the house is a swirling doom vortex, and it's too dark to walk anywhere else."

"That about sums it up," Athena said. "Strange, I'm sure I had reception earlier."

"You think *that's* strange?" Rosemary laughed. "Wait 'till I show you to the kitchen."

"Do you want to try again?" Athena asked.

"The door, you mean?"

"Sure, why not. What do we have to lose?"

"I'd say the stakes are quite high, really," Rosemary said, finding this all suddenly absurdly amusing. "We could lose our entire selves into a great spiralling abyss."

"True," Athena admitted. "How about you try the door, and we'll hold onto the veranda posts just in case the house tries to suck us inside. They look reasonably solid."

"Do you really think that's such a good idea?" Rosemary asked.

"Mum, it's freezing out here, and if we don't get out of the cold soon, we might just die of hypothermia."

"I suppose you're right. Okay. Here goes."

Rosemary approached the door, cautiously, and took hold of the veranda railing with one hand while she fitted her key into the lock with the other. "Ready?" she called to Athena, who was standing a much more comfortable distance back.

"As I'll ever be," Athena replied.

"Right. Hold on tight!"

The two Thorns braced themselves against the unknown potential powers of the house's new vortex. For a split second, Rosemary was awash with fears of giant beastly creatures escaping the void to eat them, but she pushed through her terror and turned the key. The door swung open, with an innocent creak to reveal a perfectly ordinary entrance way.

Rosemary sighed with relief.

"Now that's the kind of anti-climax I can get behind," Athena said, stepping closer.

"Wait," Rosemary said. "What if it's just an illusion?"

"You think it's more likely to be an illusion now that we're seeing the normal house that we've been in before than the glimpse of absurd mayhem we saw, briefly?"

"Probably not *more* likely," Rosemary admitted. "But I'm not sure I trust it."

"Fair enough," Athena said. "Let's just go in, slowly and carefully for now, and we'll dash back out if another vortex appears, alright?"

"Alright."

They stepped tentatively into the house, grateful to find the floor was solid beneath them. It was also blessedly warm and toasty – much warmer than it probably should have been, but Rosemary wasn't about to begrudge it that oddness when they needed to warm up. She found the light switch and flicked it to reveal that everything seemed to be as it was when they'd left earlier.

"Tea?" she asked, walking to the kitchen to put the kettle on.

"Yes please," Athena said. "I need to warm my insides. It's freezing out there. I'm glad the house is warm. Is there central heating or something? I'd have figured a place as old as this might just rely on fire places."

"Given the experience we just had, I really hope it's just central heating. I've had enough of all this magic stuff to last a lifetime. I'm seriously hoping to get back to normal life as soon as possible."

"I'm just starting to enjoy it," Athena said.

"Really?"

"Yes. I mean, it's not every day you discover your mother has magic powers. Hey...you don't think that..."

"What?" Rosemary asked.

"Maybe it was you who made it weird in here."

"I certainly did not."

"But you were all flustered, Mum."

"Flustered? You should have seen me back at the pub. If I could create a void of doom in here, then why didn't I turn the entire establishment into magical chaos?"

"Good point," Athena said. "Maybe your magic is connected to the house."

"How so?"

"Well, it only seemed to work – accidentally – when we were here earlier. Nothing odd happened when we were in town. Maybe it's kind of – *bound* – here."

"It's a good theory, though I can't be made responsible for whatever that thing was. I mean, firstly, we don't know I definitely caused it – there could have been any other number of factors – and secondly, even on the off chance that I did, I had no idea!"

"I'm not blaming you, Mum," Athena said. "But please try to keep a calm temper, just in case."

"Alright. Fair enough," Rosemary said, yawning as the full exhaustion from the day caught up with her. "But don't go off gallivanting with surly young men without my knowledge or permission."

"I wasn't gallivanting. The real question is, why is it so triggering for you?"

"Oh fine," said Rosemary. "It's just that you reminded me of your father."

"Harsh."

"No..." said Rosemary. "It was something he was known for doing. He could walk into a bar and have women pawing at him in five minutes flat."

"You're joking!" said Athena.

"I wish I was. It was like...like he had some kind of power over them. And maybe he really did, now that we know magic is real."

"That's ridiculous."

"That may be so, but it's also the truth. You blame me for going back to him, over and over...or rather, for taking him in every time he turned back up in our lives, but the thing is, I never felt I had much power over the situation. Dain just had this charm that dissolved all my defences."

"That's gross, Mum."

Rosemary sighed. "Not like that."

"I'm not Dad," Athena said firmly. "I'm not like Dad at all."

"In many ways, that's true," said Rosemary. "But you have to admit, tonight was...well it was unusual. You were gazing over at that boy you'd never seen before in your life."

"That's not true. I saw him earlier."

"What? When?"

"When we were leaving the lawyers' office. I saw him sitting under a tree, with a book, and he looked so...well, anyway. I saw him. He saw me." Athena shrugged.

"There was a moment?" Rosemary suggested.

"Yuck. Please don't say sappy things like that. But yeah, I guess. Then I saw him in the pub, and it seemed like...oh, I don't know. It was a nice co-incidence, I suppose."

"So, you looked at each other," said Rosemary. "That part is normal, but what happened next is just a little bit strange. He came over to your table, and then you went *stargazing*!"

"It was totally normal, Mum," Athena said, though Rosemary noticed her voice was rather defensive. "He came over and introduced himself and said he didn't recognise me, was I from out of town?"

"Shy and brooding teenagers just do that, do they?"

"Sometimes."

"Just don't do it again, please?"

"Fine."

They drank their cups of tea in silence, overcome by tiredness, which was compounded by the lack of sleep from the night before.

Rosemary yawned. "Bed time."

"What's that?" Athena asked, sounding scared.

"What?"

"Out there. I'm sure I just saw eyes watching us from the woods."

"It's probably just a fox or a rabbit or something," said Rosemary, looking out into the darkness. "I saw something like that before when we first arrived."

"And you didn't tell me?"

"The woods are wild around here," Rosemary said. "There will be loads of creatures out there. But don't worry."

"Sure, Mum. Way to make me not worry."

"They're harmless," Rosemary insisted as she got up from the couch and made her way cautiously upstairs, but everything on the upper level seemed to be in order, too.

"Do you want me to kip in your room again?" Rosemary asked.

"No, I'm safer alone," Athena said. "Given how out-of-control your newfound magic powers are."

"Fair enough."

"It's not really fair though, is it?" Athena said, crossing her arms.

"What are you referring to?"

"You get to have powers, and I don't."

"You can have mine," Rosemary said. "I don't want them."

"Are you serious?" Athena asked. "You really don't want to be magic?"

"It's more trouble than it's worth, trust me."

"That's even more unfair. You don't even want your powers, and I want them, but what do I get?"

"Oh, just go to bed, will you?" Rosemary said, smiling warmly at her child. "Let's hope this all makes more sense in the morning."

"I appreciate your wild optimism," said Athena. "And I am sorry about before. I promise to let you know where I am next time we're in a strange small town and I meet a boy."

"I appreciate that," Rosemary replied, lifting her arms for a hug. "I'm sorry for going off at you – and you are really not much at all like your father."

"Thanks, Mum," Athena said, returning the hug.

They parted ways. Rosemary went back to her childhood bedroom and remembered to plug in her phone, which had miraculously regained its reception.

"Figures," she muttered to herself, as she got changed and climbed into bed. "It's never there when you need it."

She closed her eyes and drifted off to sleep, praying to any magical deity who might be listening for things to settle down and become safe.

Thirteen

A howl tore through the night air, waking Rosemary just in time to be jolted by a loud crash.

"Oh, no...not again!"

She jumped out of bed, pushed back the curtains, and peered out into the night.

"Something's attacking the house!" Athena cried, rushing into Rosemary's room.

"Shhh. I'm trying to see what it is."

"Isn't it downstairs again?" Athena asked. "Like last night."

"Could be. I heard something out here. Look!"

A bright orange flame burned in the darkness, quickly building in size as it moved closer.

"It's heading for the house!" Athena shrieked. "Duck!"

They both ducked as another crash sounded. The house trembled and Rosemary peeked up to check the damage, expecting to see flames.

All was dark and still again outside.

"Weird," she said. "It's like nothing happened."

"You spoke too soon," Athena said. "Look, there's another one."

Another bright fiery ball had appeared and was heading directly towards them. They watched this time, bracing themselves for impact, but too curious to duck down completely. Just as the great ball of fire reached the perimeter of the front lawn it seemed to flatten, as if it had collided with something invisible in the air.

"Holy cow!" Athena exclaimed. "It's a forcefield!"

"No way!" said Rosemary. "Did I do that?"

She looked at her hands as if examining them for magic powers.

"Not bloody likely," Athena said. "Remember we're in a house that can fix itself. Well, chances are it can also protect itself from stupid thugs."

"Thugs?" Rosemary asked. "Is that what you think is going on?"

"How else did the fireballs appear, Mum?"

"I don't know. I'm unfamiliar with fireball lore and etiquette." She squinted down into the forest where the fire had originated from. "I think I can see something moving around down there."

"Look. There they are!" Athena pointed to the far side of the lawn.

Rosemary could see what looked like people, clad in black, moving like shadows in the night. "They've gotten through the forcefield!" she cried.

"Maybe it only deflects magical attacks, not just people wandering in," Athena suggested.

"How did you get to be such an expert?"

"It's just a bit of calm rationality, but I don't expect *you* to understand that," Athena said.

A rattling sound came from below, followed by the tinkle of breaking glass.

"Oh, drat. This hardly seems like the time to be calm," said Rosemary, keeping her voice low so as not to attract the attention of the intruders.

"Someone is definitely breaking into the house this time!" Athena said in an urgent whisper. "Do you think it's the same people who made that racket last night?"

"Sounds plausible," said Rosemary. "I wonder if all that scared them off, or if the house has more defences than just a forcefield."

"Should we leave them to it?" Athena asked. "I don't much feel like confronting burglars, if that's what they are – especially ones with big fireballs at their disposal."

"Not a chance," said Rosemary, adrenaline pumping through her body along with righteous rage, making her feel at least fifty percent braver than usual. "Offence is the best defence, remember, and I'm not going to take the chance that they might come up here. Where's my trusty lamp?"

She found said trusty lamp on the dresser and began inching her way downstairs. “Stay back,” Rosemary said. “I’m only doing this to keep you safe.”

“I don’t know if you’re brave or just foolish,” Athena muttered, following at a safe distance.

Rosemary made it to the foot of the stairwell to find absolute silence. It was too quiet, in fact. She took a tentative step out, towards the west side of the house, where she suspected the breaking glass had been.

“Ahh!”

Rosemary ducked as a winged creature flew at her, clawing at her face and arms. She lifted the lamp up and tried to fend it off.

“What are you doing?” Athena whispered from the stairwell.

“Ahh – this beast! It’s attacking me,” she shrieked.

“It’s just a crow, Mum,” Athena said, trying to suppress a giggle.

“It’s evil!” Rosemary cried, trying to whack the crow with her lamp. It managed to find purchase, and at the same time, golden sparks flew out of her fingertips, paralysing the bird mid-flight. It fell to the ground, dazed, and Rosemary breathed a sigh of relief. She raised her hands up to her face to feel only minor scratches left by the bird.

“What a show,” a man’s voice said. Rosemary turned to find a dark silhouette standing in the doorway to the kitchen. She couldn’t see his face in the shadows, though something about his voice was familiar. She could tell he was leaning casually against the doorframe – far too relaxed for what this situation warranted in her view.

“Excuse me?” Rosemary said. “What are you doing in my house? Get out!”

“This isn’t your house yet,” the man said. “And I suspect, with those killer instincts it never will be. You’d be better off hopping on the next train out of town – if you want to live, that is.”

“How sweet of you to have my best interests at heart,” Rosemary sneered. “Now get out or you’ll meet the same fate as that crow. You saw what I did to it.”

The man laughed. “You have no mastery over your magic. You hardly have any access to it at all. Your powers are more of a danger to you than they are to anyone else. I, on the other hand...”

“Oh, no...” Rosemary said, as the man held his palms about a foot apart and began chanting. Fire flared in the centre, and she was NOT prepared to deal with fireballs in the house.

The flames flickered and then puttered out.

"What?" the man asked, clearly gobsmacked.

Rosemary smiled.

"It seems you've underestimated the Thorn family magic, after all," she said, patting the wall near her in appreciation for the house.

"No matter," the man said. "I have other advantages."

He lunged towards her, all muscle and strength, which clearly meant he had the upper-hand over Rosemary's fairly un-muscly frame, but she centred herself just like her self-defence teacher had told her, planting her feet. She lifted her lamp high in the air and sent it crashing down onto the intruder's head.

The lamp cracked into pieces, and Rosemary's powers crackled through it, glinting in the dark. She smiled, triumphantly, hoping that would be enough to stun the man, but though it seemed to addle him somewhat, it only enraged him more. He lashed out, kicking Rosemary to the floor. She instinctively rolled away and then crouched down, ensuring her balance was stable. When the man turned back and lunged at her again, she was able to grab hold of his arm, swinging him around and sending him crashing into a side-table.

Gran's knickknacks scattered across the floor, and Rosemary hoped there wasn't anything too special on display that had been permanently damaged. She was surprised at her own strength, and fighting instinct for that matter. She didn't know if it was the adrenaline pumping through her veins or the magic somehow giving her the advantage over her clearly more muscular opponent.

The man righted himself and growled. Fangs popped out at the corners of his mouth.

"No sodding way," Rosemary said. "You've got to be kidding me. This is not some paranormal teen drama. How can it possibly be real?"

"You'll find real-life in Myrtlewood is far more dangerous than you expected."

"I'm starting to get that impression," she replied as the man – *or vampire* – lunged towards her again.

This time, she simply ducked and stepped to the side, allowing him to crash directly into a wall, splintering the timber panelling.

That's it...I'm definitely being helped by magic in this fight.

Rosemary decided to embrace her newfound power. The man pulled himself up to attack again and was met by several kicks to the legs and chest, followed by a sharp punch in the face.

"Ouch!" he cried, hopping back.

"Bet you didn't expect that now, did ya?" Rosemary said, hopping up and down and pumping her fists in the air like a boxer.

She jumped forward, sending another swift kick towards the area Granny would have referred to as his nether-regions. The intruder doubled up in pain, and Rosemary shot a satisfied glance up towards the stairwell where Athena was cowering on the landing.

Big Mistake.

She turned back to the vampire and saw a predatory gleam in his eyes as he caught sight of the teenage girl.

"Oh. No. You. Don't!"

Rosemary grabbed at him, intending to haul him in another direction, but it was too late. He had escaped her grasp and bounded towards the stairwell.

Wood. Granny's voice rang out in Rosemary's mind.

Of course, she realised. *Wood kills vampires.*

Rosemary snapped out her hand and grabbed the closest piece of wood: a splinter of panelling that happened to be just the right size to wrap her fist around. *Thank you, house.*

She jumped higher than she thought possible and lunged towards the man as he clambered up the stairs, mounting his back like a bull-fighter. She raised the wooden makeshift stake up high and stabbed it down, driving it into the man's back.

He let out a groan of pain and turned his head toward her, terror in his eyes. Up close, in the low light of the stairwell, Rosemary could see a clear resemblance in his face to Perseus Burk, just before the intruder burst into a cloud of dust, sending her thudding down onto the steps.

"So...vampire?" Athena asked, coughing.

"I guess so," Rosemary replied, feeling slightly mortified.

"That was awesome!" Athena said. "You're a freaking superhero."

"Oh, nonsense," said Rosemary. "And keep your voice down. We don't know if it was just one intruder – and his crow – or whether there are more fights to be had. I sincerely hope there aren't."

"But Mum," Athena said, more quietly this time. "You're the chosen one."

"Cut that out."

"Seriously, Mum, even the scratches on your face have healed up. You do have superpowers."

Rosemary reached up to trace her fingers across her cheek where the scratches had been, only to find smooth skin. "What the..."

Athena giggled softly. "In every generation, a slayer is born." Then she held her ribs, doubling over on the stairs, trying to muffle her own hysterical laughter.

"Will you stop with the Buffy references?" Rosemary hissed. "This is a serious situation. We're sitting in a dark house with no idea if any other intruders are about to attack or what kind of...special abilities...they might have."

As if in answer to her words, all the lights in the house suddenly flickered on.

Rosemary and Athena looked at each other in surprise.

"The house?" Athena asked.

Rosemary shrugged.

They waited in silence for a few moments, but there were no unusual sounds, so they got up and began to investigate.

As Rosemary stepped away from the downstairs landing, she tripped over something.

"Oh, blast," she said, regaining her balance. Then she realised what it was. "Blast. Blast. Blast!"

"What is it?" Athena asked.

"It's...a body?" Rosemary said.

Indeed, a man's form lay on the floor, clad entirely in black.

"I thought he turned to dust," Athena said. "Did he actually just teleport or something?"

"Just teleport?" Rosemary said. "As if it's the more ordinary of the two options?"

"Oh, you know what I mean."

"It's a different man," Rosemary said, examining his face, which did not at all look like Burk. This man had dark cropped hair with smaller eyes and thick dark eyebrows with a scar on his cheek. She pressed her fingers to his neck. "And he's not dead, either, which I guess is a good thing?"

"How do you figure that?" Athena asked.

"Well, we are in the midst of a murder investigation." Rosemary reminded her. "I suspect the less murder we *actually* commit, the better."

"Fair call," Athena said. "Hey! He's surrounded by feathers. You don't suppose this is the crow?"

"Is that another Hollywood reference?" Rosemary asked.

"Well, sort of," Athena said. "I mean, if vampires are real, then maybe shapeshifters are too. I think this guy might have been the crow that attacked you before."

"It seems a bit far-fetched," Rosemary said dismissively. "Anyway, wouldn't he be naked if he was a crow a minute ago?"

"Mum, surely if magic can transform him into a crow, it could make him clothed too, and all of this is far-fetched. Get with it!"

"Oh, fine," Rosemary said as she began to wander around the house, checking rooms. "I'll consider it a possibility. At least it doesn't look like there are any other intruders to worry about. Maybe if there were more, they've already run away when they saw how strong I am."

Athena laughed. "That part is the most far-fetched of the lot."

"Hey! I took self-defence classes," Rosemary said. "My instructor said I showed great promise."

"Was that before or after you broke his nose with your handbag?"

"That was a prime example of self-defence!" Rosemary insisted.

"Well, it might have been if you weren't supposed to be in hand-to-hand combat with someone entirely different."

"Oh, shush. Don't remind me. Anyway, let's go and have some tea."

"And just leave old crowy here?" Athena asked.

"He's out cold. We'll figure out what to do with him. I'm in strong need of a cup of tea to help my brain work," said Rosemary.

"Let's at least tie him up first," Athena said. "Before we wander off, leaving ourselves open to another attack."

"Good point," said Rosemary. "I was going to think of that."

"Sure, you were," Athena said. She'd already rummaged in a drawer and found some thick twine. "This will do for now."

"I suppose we should call the police."

"Actually, we should have done that about an hour ago when we first saw the fireballs," Athena pointed out.

"You're probably right. For some reason, Constable Perkins didn't cross my mind when faced with imminent danger."

"Fair enough," said Athena, following her mother to the kitchen to make tea.

Rosemary put the kettle on and then sat down at the kitchen table and rested her face in her hands, pressing gently against her closed eyes in the vain hope that she might wake up from this very strange dream.

"It's all a bit much, isn't it?" Athena said gently.

Rosemary nodded.

"I'm sure things will settle down soon, Mum. I mean, surely those attackers were the ones who killed Granny Thorn. It's too much of a co-incidence otherwise. Call Constable Perkins and tell him what happened."

"Do you think he'll even believe us?" Rosemary asked.

"He'll have to, once he sees the damage, plus there's old crowy over there."

"Alright," Rosemary said. "I'll call him. But I still don't like our chances staying here. What if there are more of them, whoever *they* are? What if they come back to finish the job? What if they hurt you?"

"I'll be fine, Mum."

"It's too dangerous," Rosemary said. "We have to get out of here."

"Typical."

"What?"

"When I hate the place, you want to stay, but as soon as I start liking it, you want to get out of here as fast as you possibly can."

"For good reason," Rosemary grumbled. The kettle whistled, and she got up to make tea. While it brewed, she looked up the number of the local police station and gave them a call. Even though it was just before dawn, Constable Perkins answered, sounding as if he'd just woken up. Rosemary wondered if the police station phoneline re-directed straight to his bedroom! She gave him the short version of what happened. He told her wearily and warily that he would be right over after he saw to some urgent business, which she assumed was his morning routine.

Rosemary poured the tea into cups at the table, but was too restless to sit still. She got up and paced around, sipping her tea and darting anxiously from thought to thought, then decided to assess the damage by the stairs.

"Oh...drat!"

There was an ominous space on the floor, surrounded by several black feathers and twine, where the intruder should have been lying.

"What is it?" Athena called out as she approached Rosemary.

"He's gone."

"No!" Athena shrieked. "But we didn't hear a thing!"

Rosemary felt her spine prick in cold fear at the possibility that the man was still in the house – in humanoid form or any other. She looked around, but there was no sign of him. She checked through most of the house, but could not shake the eerie feeling. Even when she was satisfied he had gone, there was the possibility that he might return at any moment, and this time they might not be so lucky.

"This is all too much," she said. "Athena, pack your bags!"

"What? Where are we going?"

"Away from the vampires and were-crows, for Goddess' sake! This is no place for a young woman to live!"

"But I like it here!"

"Athena!"

"Come on, Mum. That was way more exciting than Burkenswood has ever been, and you were awesome. You totally kicked arse."

Rosemary couldn't help but glow at the rare praise.

"I did, didn't I?"

Athena nodded. "Very impressive."

"Still, as your mother it is my prerogative to keep you out of danger. We have to get as far away from this place as possible."

"And what do you suggest we do at four thirty in the morning?" Athena asked. "I'm not lugging my bag all that way again. It nearly put my back out last time."

"Fine," Rosemary said. "I suggest we get dressed and pack. Then, to save your delicate back, we call Ferg to take us to the train station. We'll catch the next thing that will get us out of here – train, bus, broom – I don't care what it is."

"What about Constable Perkins?"

"We'll tell him what happened and then explain that we have to get out of town as soon as possible for our own safety, unless he's prepared to hire armoured guards for the house 24/7, which I can guarantee is out of budget for a small town like this. We are leaving whether he likes it or not, and I don't care if I have to go to court to overrule him."

"But..."

"No. This is non-negotiable. We both could have died just minutes ago."

"Oh, you're no fun."

"That's just tough, isn't it? We're going."

Rosemary cajoled Athena into following her upstairs. They packed their bags in silence.

"You're going to regret this, you know," Athena grumbled as she hoisted her bag back downstairs.

"Oh, yeah?" said Rosemary. "I'm going to regret protecting my daughter's life by getting her away from danger, am I? And why is that?"

"Because this town is special – like you kept saying. I actually think it's the only place you've ever fit in...that you've ever felt at home."

"You're just saying that because you want to see the dashing and broody Finnigan again," Rosemary teased, though a part of her knew that Athena was right. Myrtlewood had always felt like home, so much so that Rosemary had yearned for it sometimes when she was away, never quite understanding why it was she couldn't stay in the quaint, quirky village for long.

I suppose I have Granny's spell to thank for that, she thought to herself as she lugged her own bag, following Athena. *And now that the spell is broken, I still can't stay here. Typical.*

It had been a common pattern in Rosemary's life that the things she wanted moved out of her grasp just as she thought she could reach them.

She sighed and looked out the window at the lightening sky. *Surely, it's late enough to call Ferg now. If it goes straight to voicemail, he could come as soon as he gets the message, and the sooner we get out of Myrtlewood, the better.*

Ferg picked up on the second ring. "Ferg's Useful Services, how can I help?" said the unusual voice that had already become rather familiar.

"Good morning, Ferg."

"Is it?"

"Well, perhaps not. Anyway, it's Rosemary Thorn here. Athena and I need to get to the train station and could use your taxi services."

"Right away, Ma'am," Ferg said and hung up the phone before Rosemary could try to exchange anymore unsuccessful pleasantries with him.

"He's coming now," she said to Athena. "Let's wait on the porch."

"Please reconsider," Athena begged.

"Not a chance. We are not staying here a moment longer – and we are not coming back until we know for sure that it's safe."

She approached the front door and tried to unlatch it while still carrying her bag, but was unsuccessful.

"Oh, bother," she put her bag down and tried again, but the latch didn't move. "What is wrong with this door!?"

"Is it stuck?" Athena asked.

"It's more than stuck. It's not doing anything at all! I bet those intruders did something to it. They wanted to trap us in here so they could come back and finish the job."

"Or maybe it's the house."

"Of course it's the house, Athena. The door is part of the house."

"No – I mean, maybe the house is trying to stop us from leaving. It wants us to stay."

"That's even worse!" said Rosemary. "We will not be trapped here because of a stubborn sentient building! If the house is really acting in our best interests, it would let us make choices for ourselves. I can't believe I just said that. See what this place is turning me into? I'm over it. I'm over all of it. I want to get as far away from Myrtlewood as possible."

She looked frantically at Athena.

"I'm sorry to hear that, dear," Granny Thorn's voice said, coming from the direction of the door.

Rosemary snapped her head back in shock to see her grandmother's likeness imprinted on the gleaming mahogany surface in front of her.

"Granny?"

"Of course it is. Who else would it be?"

"Are you...a ghost?"

"I don't seem to have a corporeal form, so yes, I suppose so."

"Uhhh..." Rosemary shot Athena an even more frantic look. "Are you seeing this, too?"

Athena smiled nervously and nodded.

"It's good to see you," Rosemary said. "Even if you are...disembodied. I've missed you."

"I've missed you too, love, but there isn't much time. I'm using up a lot of my energy just to speak to you now, and I need you to understand that you must stay in Myrtlewood."

"Oh." Rosemary deflated. "Not you too! Can't you see it's dangerous?"

"I'm afraid I do see that...a little too clearly, actually."

"Oh...sorry, of course you do," said Rosemary. "So, then why do you want us to stay?"

"It was with great regret that I had to lead you into this danger," Granny Thorn said. "However, it was only in order to protect you and many others from an even greater risk."

"Well, that's just spiffing then," Rosemary said sarcastically. "Isn't there anyone else who can deal with this while we nip out of town?"

"No, Rosemary. You are the only ones who can wield the Thorn magic. I do not trust your cousins and neither should you. There is no escaping what has been set in motion. If you were to leave town now, the danger would follow you. However, you wouldn't be as well-protected as you are here, in my house."

"Drat," Rosemary said.

"Stay in Myrtlewood, Rosemary," said Granny's ghost. "It is your rightful home, and I'm sorry that I created such distance, that I kept you away for so long. It was out of fear for your safety and Athena's, but now that you are both powerful women, you are ready."

"I'm not ready," Rosemary insisted. "And Athena is absolutely not ready. She's only sixteen."

"A powerful age."

"Too powerful, if you ask me," Rosemary grumbled.

"Let me look at you, dear," Granny said, beckoning Athena closer.

The girl stepped tentatively forward.

"Oh, yes. You are indeed powerful."

"I don't think so, Granny Thorn...I mean, Mum is the one with the superpowers."

"You don't know it yet, but it's right beneath the surface, and not just from our side of the family, either," Granny said, winking. "You're a special one."

"Granny," Rosemary said. "As much as I love and respect you, I really can't subject Athena to this. It's not right. You should have seen the men who invaded this place – your home – last night. They had fireballs and fangs and...uhm, birds."

"Our enemies are trying to drive you out. Don't you see?" Granny replied. "They think you're weak. They're trying to scare you off."

"But why? Why would they go to so much trouble? I don't understand," said Rosemary.

"Don't tell anyone else you saw me. I can't have every Tom, Dick and Harry calling me up to ask for help with magical odds and ends."

Granny's image in the door was fading fast. "No! Don't go!" Rosemary cried. "We need you!"

"I'm sorry, dear. My energy is running out. Much love and blessings to you!"

With that, she vanished into the polished mahogany.

"Drat!" Rosemary said. "Drat, drat, drat! We didn't ask her who her killer was!"

"Mum!" Athena said. "That should have been so obvious! Not to mention, it would have saved us a whole lot of trouble. What were you thinking?"

"I didn't hear you ask her, either," Rosemary said, glumly.

"You're supposed to be the adult here."

"Well, according to Granny, we are both strong women, and you're special. What on earth was she talking about, saying it wasn't all from our side of the family? I mean, your father is...he's *special* in his own way, but it isn't generally a *good* way."

"I have no idea," Athena said. "I like to think I didn't inherit any traits from him at all."

"He's not magic, though, is he?" Rosemary asked. "I mean, he's got enough charm to woo all the ladies, but he's never had sparks fly out of his hands or fought a vampire and won, as far as I know."

"It's not a competition, Mum," Athena said. "Anyway, how do you know we can trust her?"

"Granny? Of course, we can trust her. She's the most trustworthy person I know."

"Except for the fact that she hid the family magic from us and cast a spell to drive us away from this place?"

"Well, she had good reason to do that," said Rosemary, but a bitterness lingered on her tongue as she realised Athena had a point. Granny was at least partially responsible for all this, and she hadn't bothered to let them know anything while she was alive. Rosemary felt an uneasy crumbling of one of the few things in her life she'd felt was certain – her relationship with her beloved grandmother. All the while, Athena nattered on, oblivious to her mother's inner turmoil.

"Even if that's the case and Granny Thorn did have good reasons, how do we know that...that apparition on the door...was really her?"

"It was definitely her," Rosemary muttered. "There's no one quite like Granny Thorn, and it's not something you could fake."

"Not even with magic?"

"I don't think so," Rosemary said, though she wasn't entirely sure, herself. "We have to get her to come back!"

"What?" Athena asked.

"Yes – that's it," said Rosemary. "We can get her to come back and ask her who killed her straightaway and then we can think of a test that only she would know to make sure it's her and not some kind of trick."

"How do you suppose we do that?"

"Granny!" Rosemary said to the door. "Granny! If you can hear me... uhm...knock three times?"

Just then, there was a knock at the door.

Rosemary looked triumphantly at Athena.

"Uh, Mum," Athena said, glancing around through the side windows.

"What? It worked!"

"No, it didn't," Athena assured her, in a furious whisper. "Not unless you were really trying to summon Constable Perkins!"

"What!?"

Rosemary glanced through the window to see that the strange police officer was indeed standing on the doorstep.

"Oh bollocks!" Rosemary cursed under her breath. "What's he doing here?"

"You called him, remember?" Athena whispered.

"That seems like years go."

Constable Perkins knocked again.

"More like an hour. What do we do?" Athena said, keeping her voice low.

"I suppose we have to let him in," Rosemary said. "I mean...we can show him the mess that the intruders made and everything...That's why I called him, after all."

"Of course, you have to let him in!" Athena said. "What else would you do?"

"Pretend we've already gone?" Rosemary suggested.

"Oh yeah, and when he comes in to investigate, what then?"

"I didn't think of that."

"Just let him in," Athena said. "And try not to say anything too ridiculous, or we'll end up in even more trouble."

"What about the door?" Rosemary said. "It wasn't working before."

"Just try it."

"Fine," Rosemary said, turning the handle and latch to find they clicked open effortlessly.

"Took you long enough," Constable Perkins grumbled. "Now what's all this about?"

"It's..." Rosemary began and then lost her train of thought.

"There were intruders, Sir," Athena chimed in, perhaps sensing the immediate danger of her mother spouting off more incriminating nonsense.

Constable Perkins shifted his disapproving gaze on Rosemary into a more mollified glare at her daughter. Evidently, he liked being called "sir."

"Go on," he said.

"We were sleeping in the bedrooms upstairs, and we heard noises," Athena said, attempting to walk him through the chain of events.

"Loud crashing, howling noises!" Rosemary added enthusiastically.

Athena nudged her subtly with her foot.

"They woke us up, Sir. We went to the window to have a look, and we saw some people out there, all wearing black."

"More than one?" Constable Perkins asked.

"At least two," Athena said.

"But it was dark. How can you be so sure?" he asked.

"We know there were at least two because they came inside the house, and we saw them," Athena said. "Mum fought them off. It was actually quite impressive."

Rosemary gave a satisfied smile until she remembered the fate of the vampire she dusted. She wished that Athena hadn't mentioned how many there were, just in case. Still, the story was vague enough that there was a chance that particular dusting wouldn't be traced back to her.

"Where did all this happen?" Constable Perkins asked.

"Over there, by the landing," Athena said gesturing down the hallway, towards the staircase. "I'll show you."

"Wait a minute!" Constable Perkins said in such an abrasive and accusatory tone that Rosemary wondered if he'd somehow already figured out the vampire homicide.

"What's with the bags?" Constable Perkins asked, pointing to the bags that still lay on the floor nearby. "You weren't thinking of skipping town, were you? After I specifically told you not to?"

"We certainly weren't going to stay in a house plagued by intruders," Rosemary snapped. "We were going to stay...oh I don't know, somewhere else in town, maybe? I suppose we could ask Marjie. Anyway, we're not the ones you should be suspicious of. I'm pretty sure whoever broke in last night were the exact same culprits that killed Granny, or were strongly connected to them."

"Hang on, hang on. I'm the one who does the accusing around here," Constable Perkins said. "What if you made all this up, so you'd have an excuse to leave the country and never return?"

"Constable Perkins," Rosemary said in her mum voice. "As much as you might inexplicably despise me, please believe me when I say I have no intention of becoming an international fugitive."

Athena gave Rosemary an alarmed look that told her to shut up now.

"You Thorn women are so cantankerous, the lot of ya," the police officer grumbled. "Now show me the damage, then."

"Damage?" Rosemary asked.

"From the fighting you supposedly did in the middle of the night."

"Uh, of course. Right this way," Rosemary said, leading him towards the stairways. "Oh, blast!"

"What is it, Mum?" Athena asked, following behind the constable.

"This was a right mess before!" Rosemary exclaimed. "Honestly! I never thought it would be such trouble to have a self-fixing house."

The whole area below the stairs looked perfect and polished without even a crow's feather to mess up the floor.

"What are you on about?" Constable Perkins asked.

"It's..." Rosemary tried to find a good excuse but quickly gave up. "Oh, sod it. It's just – this house kind of fixes and tidies itself. I know that sounds mad—"

"No," Constable Perkins said. "Not mad, just magic. And I do believe this is the most honest you've been with me since we first met."

"You...do?" Rosemary asked.

"I can always tell when people are hiding things from me, and you have secrecy written all over you," he grumbled. "That's another problem with you Thorn women, you always seem to hide the truth. Even if you think it's in other people's best interests. It's not."

"So, you believe me?" Rosemary asked.

"About the house fixing and cleaning itself, sure. That sounds plausible."

"*That* sounds plausible?"

"It would be just like old Galdie not to want to do her own housework and maintenance," he said. "Though it's a mystery to me how she keeps her spells going after she's already gone to the other side."

"Good," Rosemary said. "So that clears things up, then."

"It most certainly does not," he replied. "You're still hiding things from me. I can't believe what you say about the intruders because there's too much secrecy getting in the way. The one thing I do believe is the house is self-fixing, but everything else is just a story as far as I'm concerned."

"But it's true...and...and..." Rosemary was grasping at straws, trying to remember the other thing she had been meaning to tell the police officer. "We can't possibly have killed Granny!" she said triumphantly.

"Oh yeah, and how's that then?" Constable Perkins asked, suspiciously.

"Well...well...someone told us her death was definitely caused by magic. Powerful magic. You see, so it couldn't be us. We didn't know about any of this stuff before we arrived back in Myrtlewood."

"Any of what stuff?"

"Magic," Athena said, trying to help fill in the blanks in Rosemary's haphazard explanation. "We didn't live here before, you see, Sir. We lived in ordinary towns where people don't believe in spells and charms or anything like that, so it wasn't until we came to Myrtlewood and stayed here, in this house, that things started happening that we couldn't possibly explain except through magic. Everyone talks about it around here as if it's the most normal thing in the world – like sunshine or electricity."

"I never did trust electricity," Constable Perkins grumbled.

"Uh...anyway," Rosemary said. "Athena and I are telling the truth now. You must be able to tell with your...ability. We honestly didn't know about magic before we came here on Saturday."

"Fair enough, fair enough," Constable Perkins said, tugging at his suspenders as he shifted from side to side. "I've seen enough, here."

"You have?" Rosemary said, hopefully. "Does that mean we're cleared?"

"Certainly not," he said. "I'm yet to carry out the full investigation. Just because you tell the truth about a few specific things, it doesn't mean much on the whole. You're still hiding some things." He looked at them suspiciously. "I need to get the full picture, you see."

"Oh...okay," Rosemary said, following the police officer out of the house to find Ferg standing on the veranda, this time wearing a yellow cap and sweater.

"Hello there," he said. "Taxi to the train station, ready and waiting."

"To the train station, eh?" Constable Perkins said, his voice dripping with suspicion. "I thought you said you were going to stay with old Marjie."

Rosemary sighed. She was backed into a corner, and she knew there was nothing for it but the truth. "Actually, to be perfectly honest, I was in a right tizz this morning, and I wanted to get as far away from Myrtlewood as possible."

"Oh, you did, did you?"

"I was going to tell you," she said. "I mean – otherwise why would I have called you?"

Rosemary's voice sounded a tad more doubtful than she intended it to.

Constable Perkins raised an eyebrow. "Why indeed?"

"It was just...terrifying. I was scared for my life, but most of all, I was trying to protect Athena. One of the attackers...he lunged at her."

"Oh, yes," Constable Perkins said, scratching his chin as if he'd just remembered a small detail he'd forgotten to ask about. "These attackers, what did they look like?"

Rosemary's gut seemed to form into a stone at the question. "Uh...well, like Athena said, they were wearing black...and it was dark, so I didn't see much. They were men, though...erm...with short hair."

"You seem nervous," the police officer said.

"I was terrified," said Rosemary, wondering whether it was considered a heinous crime to dust a vampire or more of a community service. She wasn't about to take the chance of finding out for herself. "And I still am. What if they come back? I mean...it seems likely, especially if they're the ones who killed Granny. Maybe they're after us or looking to steal something she hid in the house...I really don't know."

"You know more than you're letting on, that's for sure," Constable Perkins said. He nodded at Rosemary and Athena. "Make sure you *do* stay in town."

He tipped his hat at Ferg, who saluted in response and said, "Good day, Sir."

As Constable Perkins's car puttered away down the driveway, Ferg looked from Rosemary to Athena. "I take it we are not going to the train station now?" he said.

Rosemary had the sensation of the entire world spinning around her. The last few hours had been such a rollercoaster of terror and anger at the intruders, of stubbornly wanting to escape Myrtlewood, of seeing her Granny again. Even if it was in two-dimensional ghost form, which gave her a pang of loss and happiness and confusion all at the same time. Granny had told her to stay, and that was more powerful than anything the constable might have said.

"I guess we're staying," said Rosemary, looking at her daughter, who shrugged but looked rather pleased all the same.

"Very well," said Ferg, walking backwards towards his orange car.

"Actually, I could do with some breakfast," Rosemary said. "How about you, Athena?"

"Yes! I'm starved," Athena said.

"Ferg, instead of the station," said Rosemary, "how about you take us down to Marjie's, so we don't have to walk? It has already been a full morning, and I don't know if we have the energy to get there ourselves."

"Very well," Ferg replied. He walked over to his car and opened the back door for them.

"Yellow is a good colour on you, by the way," Rosemary commented as she followed Athena into the car.

Ferg shrugged. "It's Monday."

Rosemary waited for him to explain the relevance of Monday to his choice of clothing, but Ferg got into the car without elaborating.

"Is Monday something to do with yellow?" Rosemary prodded, trying to make small talk despite her creeping sense of exhaustion.

"Of course," Ferg said. "Monday is the bright day where the week starts. I wear a different colour every day. Saturn Day is brown, Sunday is blue, Moon Day is yellow, Tuesday is orange, Wednesday is purple, Thursday is green, Friday is red."

Rosemary and Athena looked at each other in astonishment.

"Great," Rosemary said. "So, I can tell which day of the week it is based on what colour you're wearing."

"If it suits you," Ferg said.

"It's like a rainbow," said Athena

"No."

"But—" Athena started, but Ferg interrupted.

"No, it's deliberately not in that order – and it includes brown. Rainbows don't have brown," Ferg insisted.

"Okay then," said Athena.

"I'm an individual."

"That, you are," said Rosemary with a slightly amused grin. She was no longer amused. However, an hour later when she checked her phone to find a message from her boss, telling her she had been fired for not turning up for her early shift that morning.

Rosemary pressed her palms to her face. She didn't want to tell Athena, not just yet. It was mostly her fault. She'd meant to call and tell him they were staying away for longer, but either she'd put it off or forgotten, probably both. Of course, it was possible that she would have been fired for missing the shift either way, even with good reason, but now it was too late. Fate had made up its mind for her.

Fourteen

They pulled up outside the tea shop just as Marjie was putting out the "open" sign.

"Hi Marjie, ready for your first customers?" Rosemary asked, as she and Athena got out of the car.

"Absolutely!" Marjie said. "Get yourselves inside and out of the cold, and I'll bring you both some tea. It looks like you need my special blend today."

Rosemary shrugged. "Actually, you might be right. It has been one shocker of a morning."

"Say no more, say no more," Marjie said, ushering them inside.

As Marjie bustled about in the kitchen, making tea, Athena nudged Rosemary's arm.

"What?" Rosemary asked.

"Do you think we should tell her?" Athena asked, keeping her voice quiet so that Marjie wouldn't hear.

"Tell her what?"

"Everything," Athena said.

"Why on earth would we do that?" Rosemary asked.

"We need an ally," Athena explained. "We need someone we can trust who lives here, someone who understands this place inside-out who can help us to get our head around all this."

"What if we can't trust her?" Rosemary asked.

"Oh, come on, Mum. Does it look like Marjie was outside our house sporting a black ninja outfit last night? What do *you* think?"

"No, that's not what I was implying," Rosemary said. "It's just...what if her loyalties don't lie with Granny? What if she's some kind of mastermind...behind the whole thing?"

"Does that seem like a criminal mastermind to you?" Athena said, gesturing in the direction of the kitchen where Marjie was busy donning a floral apron.

"No, but..."

"I think at this point, the benefits of having an ally outweigh the risks of Marjie being a dark wizard," Athena said.

"Oh, fine. We'll tell Marjie."

"Tell me what, dear?" Marjie said, as she approached with a tea tray laden not only with tea but with toast and soft-boiled eggs in little floral egg cups.

"You brought us breakfast!" Athena said, with much more enthusiasm than Rosemary was used to from her teen.

"Of course I did," Marjie said. "The two of you need fattening up. Now, what was it you wanted to tell me? I'm all ears."

Rosemary took a sip of Marjie's special blend and instantly felt warmed and reassured. She began the long story about the house: the noises and the magic box and the self-fixing and the attacks and the intruders, omitting only the part about the vampire staking, which she wasn't sure was a safe topic to broach at that point.

Marjie smiled and nodded and ummed and ahhed, her expression growing gradually more concerned as they explained about the attacks to the house. She looked quite impressed with that last detail.

"You really fought him off, did ya?" Marjie asked, with more than a hint of pride in her voice.

"So, it seems. I guess it was something to do with the magic. I still don't understand it very well," Rosemary said.

"Oh, magic isn't for understanding up here." She tapped her head. "All that logic will do you no good. You have to understand it here." She held her palm to her heart. "That's where magic really lives."

"I see," Rosemary said, though she wasn't quite sure she got it.

"I'm surprised you don't want to skip right out of town after all that, though," said Marjie.

"I did want to, actually," Rosemary admitted. She wasn't sure if she should tell Marjie about Granny appearing and decided to err on the side of caution. "Constable Perkins has forbidden us from leaving town."

"I'm glad you haven't left us," said Marjie. "You'll be a lot safer here. But rest assured, I'll be giving that Constable Perkins a piece of my mind for troubling you."

"Who's troubling whom, now?" a rich booming voice sounded from the door.

"Now, now, Mr June. You're early this morning!" Marjie exclaimed.

Rosemary turned to look at the customer who had just entered. He wore a black embroidered jacket with a royal-purple collar, and though he might have been about her age, he carried a black stylised walking stick with a silver top. His hair was slicked back. The look was so old-fashioned that Rosemary assumed he was actually older, or that he was going for a particular goth look. She couldn't tell which.

Marjie left to fuss over Mr June instead, bringing him his usual English breakfast tea and a slice of carrot cake.

"The doctor says I have to eat my vegetables," he boomed, taking a large bite of the cake.

Rosemary and Athena gave each other a questioning look.

"Perfect, as always, Marjoram," Mr June said, smacking his chops. "And who are your lovely lady guests? I don't recognise them. You'd think, as mayor, that I'd have a good handle on all the goings-on in town, but it's quite frankly not the case."

Mayor...alarm bells rang in Rosemary's mind. She couldn't quite remember what it was she'd heard about the mayor of Myrtlewood, or who had told her. She racked her brains, wanting to ask Athena if she recalled anything, but not wanting to appear suspicious by whispering. Athena did not look suspicious, just perturbed by the unusual character.

"Why, this is Rosemary Thorn and her daughter Athena, of course! Can't you see the family resemblance?"

For the first time, Rosemary wished that Marjie wasn't quite so friendly, especially after everything they'd just told her about the past few days. She wished she'd had a mind to let Marjie know the entire conversation was in the strictest confidence, and now it would be hard to say anything. She tried to shoot Marjie a warning look.

"Of course! The Thorny descendants," Mr June said. "See what I did there."

"Yes, uh, very clever," Rosemary said.

Athena rolled her eyes, and Rosemary was grateful that the mayor didn't notice. It was her turn to kick her daughter softly under the table, an action that earned her an angry glare.

"Here to check out the old house, I imagine," Mr June continued. "I expect you'll want to put it up on the market as soon as possible. An old manor like that is a lot of work to maintain."

"Actually," Rosemary said. "We have decided to stay in Myrtlewood."

Athena looked at Rosemary, startled by the certainty in her mother's voice.

"Oh, ugh," Mr June spluttered, choking on his tea.

Rosemary wasn't actually quite as sure as she had tried to sound. She was really just trying to gauge the mayor's reaction to see how likely he was to be their prime suspect, but it was starting to seem likely they'd stay in Myrtlewood. After all, she'd just lost her job and there wasn't much to go back for, plus she trusted Granny's instincts.

"Really?" he asked. "Because I know a few people who'd be willing buyers – people who love old heritage houses like that."

"Really. We're staying," Rosemary said.

Mr June looked perturbed for a moment, and then he clapped his hands together enthusiastically. "Two new members of Myrtlewood! Two new constituents! Welcome!"

He strode over to their table and shook hands with both of them.

"Thank you, Mr June," said Rosemary.

"Oh please, call me Don," the mayor said.

"Don June?" Rosemary asked, trying to suppress a giggle.

"That's my name. What of it?" he asked.

"Nothing," said Rosemary. "It's just...an unusual name, is all."

"I pride myself on being extraordinary," he said, tugging at his purple collar.

"I can see you're successful at it," Rosemary said, trying to sound complimentary rather than mocking. After all, he could well be a murderer whose bad side she didn't want to get on, and even if he wasn't, it would pay to have an official on their side if things got worse with Constable Perkins.

"Now, if you'll excuse me," Mr June said. "I'll be over there, reading my paper. It's the best way to start the day – a cup of tea and the morning paper, don't you agree?"

Rosemary and Athena both nodded enthusiastically, hoping he'd clear off and leave them in peace. They ate the rest of their breakfast in silence, while more customers arrived and the noise around them built up.

After a while, the mayor folded up his newspaper with a flourish and announced to Marjie that "duty calls" before striding out of the tea shop.

Rosemary turned to Athena. "What do you think?" she asked. "Suspect?" She gestured to the table where Mr June had been sitting moments before.

"I don't know," Athena said. "Why do you say that?"

"Someone told me something dodgy about him, only I can't, for the life of me, remember what it was. Do you know?"

"Mum, your memory is shocking, but honestly, how would I know?"

"Well, chances are you were there with me when they said it."

"Not ringing any bells. What was it?"

"I told you, I can't remember. If I could recall who said it, I could go back and ask them. Hang on, that's it!"

"What's it?"

"It was right before you went missing. That bar woman told me something, and it must have been so interesting I took my eyes off you for a minute too long – big mistake."

"Hey! I thought we were over all that."

"We're over some of it," Rosemary corrected. "I'm still processing. Anyway, what was her name?"

"Sherry," Athena said. "And I only remember that because I thought it was funny that she worked in a bar with a name like that. That's this place all over though, isn't it? I can't believe you are now so sure we're moving here. This morning you couldn't get away fast enough."

"Well...I'm not a hundred percent sure, but Granny told us to stay, so we're here for now. I was just trying to test him."

"Test who?"

"The mayor, of course. I wanted to see the look on his face. If he was trying to scare us off, then he wouldn't be happy about us sticking around, now, would he?"

"He seemed pretty happy about it to me," Athena said.

"Actually, at first, he looked shocked and choked on his tea, remember? Only after he recovered from that did he come over and roll out the welcome wagon."

"So, what did your test tell you?"

"I'm not sure yet."

Rosemary took another sip of tea and watched as a smile spread across Athena's face.

"We're really staying, then?!"

"So, it seems."

"Don't you have a job to get back to?"

"Uh, about that..."

"What?"

"Apparently I don't have a job. Not anymore."

"What? Oh no...you didn't!" Athena said. "You forgot to call Mr Lindon, didn't you?"

Rosemary sighed. "Don't give me a hard time, okay. It's been a rough few days and...I'm sure he was likely to fire me even if I did call up and tell him I couldn't make it in for days – or weeks – without a good non-incriminating explanation or an idea of when we'd be able to leave. And, well, *you* wanted to stay here, anyway. You should be pleased."

"I am pleased," Athena said. "But it's the principle of the matter."

"And that principle is?"

"You're always wrong," Athena teased.

"Harsh!" said Rosemary, giving her a playful push.

"But true," Athena insisted. "What are we going to do about money now that you're gainfully unemployed?"

"We'll figure it out," Rosemary said. "We always do."

Fifteen

They thanked Marjie for breakfast and Rosemary tried to pay, to no avail.

"Your Granny wouldn't approve of me charging you," Marjie insisted. "You Thorns are like family to us. There will be no charging going on what-so-ever."

Rosemary felt terribly guilty, though her dwindling bank account would have expressed gratitude if it could.

"Well, at least let me return the favour and treat you sometime," said Rosemary.

"Oh, if you must," Marjie said.

"Thanks again, Marjie. You're brilliant." Rosemary said, giving the older woman a peck on the cheek.

"Oh, it's nothing really," Marjie insisted.

"Come over for dinner, sometime," Rosemary said as she turned to go, then remembered the other thing she needed to tell Marjie. She turned back. "Uh, and please don't tell anyone what's been happening to us up at the Manor. It's strictly confidential, all right? It's not that we have anything to hide. We just don't want the attackers to find out through the grapevine that they've ruffled us."

"O'course not," Marjie said. "Mum's the word."

Rosemary and Athena left the shop, slightly reassured by Marjie's promise of a secret kept, though they really knew so little about her it was hard to tell how loose her tongue was.

"She could be the town gossip, you know," Rosemary pointed out on their walk back to the manor.

"Your Granny trusted her. That should be good enough," Athena reminded her mother. "Besides, what were you thinking, inviting her over for dinner like that? What if we're attacked again?"

"Actually, that's a brilliant idea!"

"What!? Being attacked is not something you aspire to," Athena scolded.

"Not being attacked, per se, but dinner."

"Dinner is always a good idea," Athena agreed. "What's your point?"

Rosemary lowered her voice and looked around as they neared the edge of the village. "We'll have a dinner party and invite all the suspects and watch them to see what they do and who is acting suspicious."

"So, you want to get all the potential murderers in the same room as us, and feed them?" Athena asked.

"Yes."

"Ridiculous! What if they slip you poison or attack you?"

"I'm hoping the house will help us a little," Rosemary said sheepishly.

"A great lot of good it did Granny Thorn," Athena muttered.

"We can invite that police officer, too," Rosemary said. "And everyone who is being friendly to us, so that there are more pairs of eyes watching for anything untoward."

"You really want to do this?" Athena asked.

"Yes. Just think about it. It will be our hello-to-Myrtlewood party. We can invite all the suspicious people like the mayor and that lawyer, Burk..."

"I thought you liked him," Athena said with just a hint of teasing in her voice.

"I thought he was okay," Rosemary admitted, looking around the picturesque countryside as they walked, to make sure no one was listening to what she said next. "But did I tell you how much that vampire guy I dusted looked like him?"

"No, you did not," Athena said. "Do you mean to inform me that you managed to dust a lawyer?"

"No, love. It wasn't him, but there was a definitive resemblance."

"Well, that's incredibly suspicious."

"Yes, and I bet he knows more than he's letting on."

"So, you really think this dinner is a good idea?" Athena asked.

“Of course it is. We’ll hold it in the formal dining room.”

They had reached the long rambling driveway to Thorn manor, and Rosemary once again had a creeping feeling of being watched.

“What will we serve them? Jaffa Cakes and crisps?” Athena asked, clearly not noticing Rosemary’s discomfort, which was probably for the best. She didn’t want to worry her daughter.

“No. I’ll cook.”

“Really, Mum? It’s been ages since you’ve cooked properly. You know I miss your cooking...well, especially the desserts.”

“You never much liked my fancy dinners when you were younger, you fuss-pot. I got out of the habit of making proper meals when all you wanted was baked beans on toast.”

“It’s normal for little kids to be fussy. I’m not so bad now. I even eat a variety of vegetables,” said Athena as they reached Thorn Manor.

“Sure,” Rosemary said. “A somewhat limited variety...”

“Anyway, how are you supposed to cook a fancy meal and host the party at the same time? That’s more than one person can do – let alone spotting nefarious villains.”

“It will be fine, Athena. I’ll just make most of the food ahead of time.”

Athena sighed and followed Rosemary into the house, and they went directly to the kitchen to put the kettle on, as usual.

“We better at least get that big piece of paper and make sure we’ve got all the suspects. I guess it needs updating now.” She retrieved the list and set it down on the kitchen table while Rosemary made tea.

“So, we need to add Mr Don June the mayor, and...who else? Burk is already on here because he asked about you selling the house. Why does everyone seem to want you to sell it?”

Rosemary shrugged. “It’s a pretty special house.”

“Yes, but do they all know about how it fixes and cleans itself, or was that one of Granny Thorn’s many secrets?” Athena asked.

Rosemary shrugged.

“And why does it do that?” Athena continued. “Where is the magic coming from? Maybe if we understand that, we’ll know why everyone’s so interested in buying the house.”

“Your guess is as good as mine,” said Rosemary. “In Granny’s letter it seemed like she thought it was to do with the family magic, remember? She bound the family magic years ago because people were after it, and those people eventually came after her.”

"Are you sure they're people?"

"Hey, vampires are people too," Rosemary said. "Even if they're not humans."

"You're the expert...Buffy."

"Oh, shut it!"

"Hey. Do you think you've released the magic, like Granny Thorn's letter told you to do? I mean, there was that thing with the box and then you said you went to another world and met an addler."

"An elder!"

"Whatever. Did that release the family magic, or just part of it? You've definitely got some magic, at least when you're in the house."

"I see what you're getting at," Rosemary said. "The power must still be bound up in here, and people who are after that power want to buy the house so they can get at it."

"*Finally*, Mum," Athena said, bemused. "You know you're not the sharpest tool in the shed."

"Did you just call me a tool?" Rosemary said. "How rude."

"Ha, ha. Very funny," said Athena.

"Seriously, though. We need to figure out how this magic works. We need to know more than our enemies."

"Up until a couple of days ago, our only enemy was Dad," said Athena.

"He's not an enemy, just a...problem."

"A big problem, Mum. And if he ever tries to come back, I'm casting a spell on you to stop you falling for his codswallop again."

"That sounds like a wise course of action," Rosemary admitted. "Though I seem to be the only one with magic at this point."

"Don't rub it in," Athena said. "It's *so* not fair that you get super strength to fight off vampires with sparks flying out of your hands and the power to move things and boil a kettle—"

Just then, the kettle whistled.

"It wasn't me that time," Rosemary said, going to make tea.

"Still not fair," said Athena.

"None of that was my choice," Rosemary said, carrying the freshly made pot of tea to the table to sit next to her daughter. She glanced at their makeshift investigation map. "Is there anyone else we're missing?"

"I don't know, you were the one catching up on all the pub gossip. What else did Sherry say?"

"If only I could remember," Rosemary said. "Everything she said was overshadowed by your sudden disappearance."

"Stop bringing that up, already."

"I will not," Rosemary said. "As your parent, I have rights...and that includes the right to hassle you about your behaviour."

"I suppose it's only fair, seeing as I hassle you about yours."

"It should be a right that only *I* have," Rosemary grumbled.

They sipped their tea and then spent the next few hours going over the details of what they knew.

"There was some kind of group someone told me about that Granny didn't like," Rosemary recalled. "The Blueblood Clan? The Bluetooth Group? Something like that."

"They sound like a tech firm," Athena scoffed.

"Yes, I'm sure a tech firm is trying to embezzle our magic for their own nefarious digital purposes."

"Stop saying nefarious all the time," Athena complained. "It's a stupid word."

"But it seems so *fitting*," Rosemary protested.

She poured their tea, and then the two of them sat in silence for a while, sipping and pondering.

"We have to go back to the pub, don't we?" Athena said.

"I suppose so, but only if you don't run off without telling me where you're going."

"I won't!" Athena insisted.

"Promise."

"I promise not to run off without telling you, not even if I'm only five metres away."

"Very good. Thank you," said Rosemary, patting her daughter on the arm.

Athena grimaced and pulled away.

Teenagers! Rosemary thought. *Grossed out at any show of affection... unless it happens to come from a mysterious boy!*

"Let's hope Sherry is working again tonight," Rosemary said. "We could even bring this piece of paper to write down what she says."

"What an idea, Mum. Bring a huge piece of paper so that everyone can see that we're conducting our own investigation and probably get in the way. You know this town is full of weirdos and busybodies just waiting to give us their opinion on everything and lead us off-track, accidentally or on purpose."

"You just reminded me of something," Rosemary said. "Remember that woman? The strange old bat who came over to our table last night? What was it she said?"

"Granny Thorn had enemies, some other nonsense."

"It could have been useful nonsense," Rosemary lamented. "I just wish I could remember it!"

"Your memory is like a sieve at the best of times," Athena said. "Don't worry about it. That woman was clearly batty. Didn't Sherry say as much?"

"Sure, but how do you know we can trust Sherry?" Rosemary asked.

"This isn't Cluedo, Mum. Be reasonable."

"I am being reasonable. It really could be anyone – even Marjie – and now we've gone and told her almost everything."

"Well, whoever is responsible would already know half of what we told her, since they were the ones who planned the attack," Athena said. "Come on. Get your coat."

"Where are we going?" Rosemary asked.

"To the pub, for lunch," Athena replied.

"Good call," Rosemary said. "We can ask Sherry whatever it was she said last night."

"Plus, I'm starved," Athena added.

"Already? We only just had breakfast."

Athena shrugged. "Blame it on a growth-spurt, if you must."

Rosemary took a snap of the large piece of paper with her phone just in case they wanted to refer to it inconspicuously at the pub. They put on their walking shoes and headed out the door and back into town.

It was lunch time when they reached the pub, and it was bustling with customers, but to their disappointment, Sherry wasn't behind the bar. A man was there, instead, standing with his back to them, polishing the glasses. Rosemary noticed his muscular frame and his casual sandy hair before he turned towards them, flashing familiar blue-green eyes her way.

"Liam?" she said. "You...work here?"

Liam looked startled. He put down the glass he was holding and straightened his apron a little. "Rosey. Hi. Uh...not usually. I just help Sherry out sometimes on the days that the bookshop is closed."

"Where is she?" Athena prompted.

"Oh, yes," Rosemary said. "Where is Sherry today? We were hoping to have a wee chat with her."

"She's come down with something," Liam said. "Excuse me."

He turned to a customer at the bar and began pouring pints.

"I wonder if she's okay," Athena said.

"It's probably just a cold," Rosemary replied. "I'm sure she's fine."

"Knowing this town, it's some kind of magical malady," Athena said. "Or worse – what if the people who came after us have gone after her too?"

"Don't be so paranoid," said Rosemary.

"Paranoid about what?" Liam asked.

Rosemary turned back to find him leaning on the bar, smiling. "Sorry – didn't mean to eavesdrop," Liam said. "It's a bad habit, I know. I'll just go over there and sort the cutlery."

"Hang on a minute," said Rosemary. "Don't go just yet. While you have a minute, is Sherry alright? What's she come down with?"

"I tried to find that out myself," Liam said, blushing slightly. "But she fobbed me off, didn't she? Typical Sherry. She told me she'd be right as rain in no time."

Rosemary felt somewhat reassured by that explanation. At least Sherry was well enough to talk and be stroppy. Even Athena looked somewhat satisfied.

"So, what brings you two to this fine establishment?" Liam asked. "Lunch?"

"Oh, yes," Rosemary said. "Yes, please."

"Take a seat." Liam handed them a couple of menus. "I'll be over in just a jiffy."

"Shall we go back to where we sat last time, or are there too many bad memories for you?" Athena asked Rosemary.

"We'd better take the same seat," Rosemary replied. "Seeing as it's the only booth that's empty, and I'll just have to push through the bad memories and make good ones – you know – get back on the bicycle."

"Gross, Mum!"

"It's not gross. I do not think you know what that phrase means."

"It sounds sordid."

"Well, it's not, it just means, you know...when you fall off, you should get back on, so that you keep riding and don't develop a phobia. At least I think that's what it means."

"Still sounds gross," Athena said, noticeably scanning the bar before sitting down.

"I give up," Rosemary said. "What do you want to eat?"

They both scanned the menu, Rosemary occasionally glancing at her daughter to see if she was looking out for anything else the pub had to offer, namely The Boy, though he was nowhere in sight.

"Maybe the pie," Athena said. "It's steak and mushroom today."

A man's voice interrupted them. "The steak and mushroom pie is excellent."

Rosemary looked up to see Burk standing next to their table.

"Oh...hello," she said cautiously.

"I'm glad you decided to stick around town," Burk said. He glanced at Athena.

"Uh, Athena, this is the lawyer I told you about, Perseus Burk," said Rosemary. "This is my daughter, Athena."

"It's a pleasure to meet you," he said, holding out his hand to Athena, who reluctantly shook it, a puzzled expression on her face.

"I take it you've had quite an eventful time," Burk said.

"How do you figure that?" Rosemary asked, suspicious. She wasn't about to let a handsome lawyer throw her off track.

"Constable Perkins informed me. As your lawyer, I have a duty to know what's going on."

"But you're not..." Rosemary said. "I mean. It's very generous for you to offer to help, but you're not officially my lawyer. You were Granny's lawyer, but I never signed anything to say you were mine."

Burk looked taken aback. "I thought you were taking up the offer of my legal assistance," he said. "You called me, after all."

Yes...but that was before your evil twin attacked me! Rosemary thought, though she managed to hold herself back from saying it.

"I did," Rosemary said coolly. "And thank you for your offer, but I feel uncomfortable about you talking to the police behind my back."

Athena shot her mother a look of warning that said: *keep your mouth shut. Don't start rambling. This is serious.*

"It wasn't...it wasn't like that," Burk said, noticeably ruffled for the first time since Rosemary met him, which admittedly hadn't been that long. "The constable actually came to me this morning, concerned for your welfare. I told him I would check in to see if you were okay. I was about to give you a call after lunch, but then I saw you were already here."

"How thoughtful of you," Rosemary said, smiling politely, but not warmly. "What exactly did Constable Perkins tell you?"

"He said that there had been a disturbance at the house – that you'd told him you were attacked by intruders. I'm suspecting they had something to do with your grandmother's passing."

"We suspect so, too," Athena said. "But how do we know we can trust you?"

Rosemary kicked Athena under the table.

"I suppose you don't know that," Burk said.

"Perhaps you could refrain from speaking to the authorities about us for the time being?" Athena suggested.

"But...I'm sorry...Rosemary...?" Burk stuttered.

"Is this man bothering you?" Liam asked, approaching the table.

Rosemary watched as a look of challenge passed between the two men.

"We were just chatting," Burk said.

Liam looked from Rosemary to Athena.

"It's fine, Liam," Rosemary said. "Perseus was just leaving."

Perseus Burk gave her a slightly pleading look and then raised his palms in surrender and walked away.

"That man is a right prick," Liam said. "He struts around here as if he owns the place.... Just because he's some fancy-pants lawyer...Sorry he was bothering you."

"It's fine, really," Rosemary said. "Can we order some lunch?"

"Of course," Liam said, seemingly remembering why he was standing there. "What will you have?"

"Steak and mushroom pie?" Rosemary asked Athena.

Athena shook her head. "Actually, I think I'll just have the pumpkin soup, thanks."

"Well, I'll have the pie," said Rosemary. "And a ginger ale."

"Make that two ginger ales," Athena said.

"Perfect," said Liam. "It won't be long. The cook here is magic."

Rosemary smiled, assuming Liam meant that literally.

"I think I'm starting to get used to Myrtlewood, with all this paranormal-normalness," she said to Athena.

"It's a wonder, with how open they are about it, that you didn't pick up on it earlier," Athena said. "You spent summers here as a kid; did it all just sail over your head?"

"I presume it was part of Granny's spell that I didn't remember," Rosemary said, frowning. "Maybe she's responsible for my sieve-like memory. Hey!" Her expression brightened. "Maybe when we've unbound the magic, it will fix my memory."

"It's magic, not miracles," Athena said sceptically. She glanced around the pub again.

"He's not here, you know," Rosemary said.

"Who?" Athena asked, feigning innocence.

"Your Finnigan chap."

"I wasn't looking for him," Athena insisted. "I'm just...you know... looking for suspicious behaviour."

"Sure, sure," Rosemary said. "Speaking of suspicious behaviour. What do you think all that was about before, with Burk and Liam?"

"So he's Burk now? Moment's ago, he was Perseus. 'Oh Perseus, do you think I should order the steak and mushroom pie?'" said Athena, batting her eyelids and putting on a cartoony accent.

"Oh, shut it," said Rosemary. "I did not say – or sound – anything like that. From the tense interaction before, I was sure that both men knew something. I bet one, or both is involved with the plot to steal our magic."

"Seriously, Mum?"

"What?"

"Are you that blind?"

"What are you talking about?" Rosemary asked.

"They're both keen on you, and they're getting all weird and blokey and territorial over it."

"Don't be silly," Rosemary said. "Burk is just Granny's lawyer, and Liam...well he's an old adolescent flame, sure, but I'd be surprised if he's not seeing Sherry. Did you see the protective way he responded before when we asked about her?"

"Still..."

"No," Rosemary said. "Neither of them are my type, and besides, I don't date, remember."

"Do you even have a type – except for drop-kick?"

"Athena, it's rude to talk about your father that way."

"Rude, but true."

"Come on. Dain's not that bad. He just has issues – lots of them."

"Dad's not the only one with issues," said Athena, giving her mother a meaningful look.

"Here you go," said Liam, appearing back at the table with a laden tray and placing their meals and drinks in front of them.

"That was quick," Rosemary said. "No wonder you have this whole place under control with just you behind the bar."

Liam beamed. "Sherry has this whole place under control, even when she's bedridden," he said with a look of pride in his eyes.

Rosemary shot Athena an I-told-you-so glance.

"About Sherry," Athena said. "We'd love to see her when she's well. Could you pass on the message?"

"Of course," Liam replied. "I'm sure she'd love to pop 'round to the old house. She's always adored that place."

Rosemary's expression changed to one of suspicion, but Athena subtly shook her head.

"Thanks, Liam," Rosemary said. "Tell her to give us a call and pop around when she's well, or we'll catch up with her here."

"No worries," Liam said and made his way back to the bar.

Rosemary and Athena had just started tucking into their meals when another interruption arrived.

"Rosemary Thorn!"

Rosemary looked up at the sound of the woman's voice to find her heart sinking, and her hands starting to itch.

"Oh, hi...Despina?"

"That's the one!" the estate agent said. She was entirely clad in cornflower blue this time, with a matching bow on her head. "And this is my... niece, Geneviève."

A young girl stepped forward who couldn't have been more than about twelve, though she was wearing much more mature clothing than her aunt – a mauve suit, more appropriate for a professional office than a country pub, and certainly not commonly worn by tweens. Her curly chestnut-coloured hair was pulled back into a tight bun, and Rosemary empathised. It was so hard to tame curly hair. She herself had entirely given up and let her hair do its own wild thing, but when she was younger, she'd slaved for hours to try to control her locks, to no avail.

"Hi Geneviève," Rosemary said with a smile.

Athena frowned from across the table.

"We were just popping in for lunch," Despina said.

"Yes. Can we join you?" Geneviève asked.

"Oh...uhm." She glanced at Athena, who stared bloody murder back. "Well..."

"Oh, come now, Gen. I'm sure Athena and Rosemary are enjoying quality time. They wouldn't want to be interrupted by people they hardly know."

Geneviève looked downcast, pulling at Rosemary's heartstrings.

"Maybe not today," Rosemary said. "But we are planning a dinner for later this week, a sort of welcome-to-the-town kind of thing. We'd love for you to join us."

Rosemary felt a sharp kick to her shins. She grimaced to stifle a yell and then managed to turn her expression into a smile.

Geneviève's face lit up. "Really?"

"Yes, *really*," Rosemary said, giving Athena a meaningful look.

"How wonderful," said Despina. "We look forward to further details. Enjoy your lunch." She gave a little wave and then ushered the young girl away.

"What was *that*?" Athena said. "You looked like you were about to adopt that brat!"

"Oh, don't be jealous," Rosemary said, dismissively.

"I am not!"

"You always hated it when I held other babies when you were little. I don't see how this is any different."

"You were just instantly all gooey over little miss twelve-going-on-thirty-two. It was weird and inappropriate. I can't believe you invited them to our party!"

"She's charming," Rosemary said. "I wish I could say the same for her aunt." She shuddered and scratched at her hands. "And besides, Despina is on our invite list already, remember. She's a suspect, as someone who's expressed an interest in us selling the house."

"That's because she's a freaking estate agent!" Athena hissed. "It is *literally* her job to sell houses. She's almost the least-suspicious person we've encountered, apart from Marjie."

"So why are you getting so riled up, then?" Rosemary asked. "If she's not guilty, she'll just be another guest. It's going to be my problem, really. I don't know how I'm going to tolerate a whole evening with itchy hands. The rash might even spread to my—"

"I do not want to hear about your imaginary rashes, or where they might spread," Athena snapped. "Nor do I want to spend an evening with that child, who clearly thinks she's an adult. How tiresome!"

"Oh, you've always hated younger kids," Rosemary said.

"And you've always loved them."

"It's probably because you're an only child, you know."

"And thank goodness for that," said Athena. "Imagine if I got a younger sibling who dressed like Margaret Thatcher."

"Thatcher always wore blue, you know."

"Not the point, Mum."

"So, what if I liked the kid? She's a much snappier dresser than her aunt."

"And that's what's important to you, is it?" Athena teased. "If only I knew...I could have been gaining parental approval points just from power-dressing."

"Since when have you ever cared about *my* approval?" Rosemary asked. "You know, I love you very much, but you were practically born with a judgemental glare."

"Harsh, Mum."

"It's not a bad quality to have," Rosemary assured her. "You're naturally shrewd, and it has only increased with your teenage brain-changes. It probably kept you out of danger fairly well, aside from the other night."

"You mean, last night? In which I was perfectly safe? And five meters away?"

"Without telling your mother, yes," said Rosemary. "Anyway. Your judgement can be an asset. Like you say, you are a pretty good judge of character. You just have to learn to keep it in check."

"If I'm such a good judge of character, then why don't you trust my judgement on little miss-high-flyer?" Athena asked.

"Because you're being petty," Rosemary said. "And it shows."

Athena sighed and focused on quietly slurping her soup.

Rosemary properly dug into the steak and mushroom pie. Up until that point she had only picked at the chips and salad, which were rather nice, but the pie itself was exceptional. Burk had been right about that, at least.

Sixteen

While Rosemary ate, savouring every mouthful of the delicious meat pie, she gazed over to the far corner of the bar. She wasn't paying attention at first, but by-and-by, she noticed a couple of people had walked out through the shadowed door with its red-velvet curtains, into darkness. Though they had not returned, however, different people had walked in.

It was perplexing, as it wasn't marked with an exit sign like the other doors. It also had a whiff of secrecy about it. She wondered if it was a secret gambling room, or perhaps something more magical. She thought about asking Liam, but he was nowhere in sight.

Rosemary was startled when Despina and Geneviève both walked out that way, clearly not staying for lunch, after all. For a moment she worried about the young girl being taken through a door like that into some dark, sinister location, perhaps frequented by multiple estate agents. Rosemary shuddered.

"What?" Athena asked her.

"What do you think that is?" she asked Athena, pointing to the unusual door.

"Erm...a doorway?"

"Don't you think there's something...shady about it?"

"Not really, Mum," Athena said, clearly not in the mood to chat.

Rosemary decided to investigate. She took her last mouthful of pie and excused herself. She went to the loos first, hoping not to look too suspicious, then she skirted the room so that she ended up near the mysterious door.

There was a slight cavern to one side of it, like a badly lit cloak room. She stepped into the shadows and listened.

Nothing.

Rosemary tentatively pushed open the door, only to find her wrist seized as, from out of nowhere, she was shoved firmly but politely back into the far corner of the shadowy alcove.

"What the...!" Rosemary said, blinking in the darkness in an attempt to see the gentle assailant who was still gripping her arm, holding her up against the wall.

"Do *not* open that door," a familiar silky voice said. "Whatever you do."

"Mr Burk?"

"Perseus," he corrected.

"What do you mean by this?" Rosemary asked.

"I can't explain," Burk said, stepping back. "Just trust me, please."

Again, there was a vulnerability in his voice that bordered on pleading, but that Rosemary instinctively responded to, intuiting that he was trying to protect her.

"I don't understand," she said. "I just saw Despina and her little niece go through there."

"They have their reasons," Burk assured her.

"And I'm not allowed to know them?" Rosemary asked, feeling stroppy. She pushed herself away from Burk, though a part of her had enjoyed the intimacy of having someone so close. As she did, she noticed how cold his hand was on her wrist. *Poor circulation*...that's what he'd said back at his office, but now Rosemary wasn't so sure.

"Something strange is going on here, isn't it?" she said.

Burk laughed. "In Myrtlewood? Of course."

"But everyone is so open about magic here. Why won't you tell me what's going on behind the door?"

"I have my reasons," Burk said. "And they are chiefly concerned with your safety." He bowed his head slightly.

"Fine," Rosemary said. "But I do intend to find out, one way or another."

She stepped back towards the light, but Burk's hand shot out, lightning quick, and barred her way.

"Wait, Rosemary."

"Call me Ms Thorn," Rosemary said, feeling it was only appropriate to rescind the invitation to use her first name given the distance she intended on putting between herself and Mr Burk.

"Ms Thorn..." Burk said.

Rosemary had to brace herself against the discomfort of the polite title. It was almost as unpleasant as being in the presence of estate agents.

"What?" Rosemary said, and there was a harshness to her tone that even she didn't expect.

"Is there a reason for your being so distant, all of a sudden?"

"There might be," Rosemary said. "But I don't have to explain myself to you."

"That's fine," Burk said. "I do have one other question, though. And then I promise I'll stop bothering you."

"What is it?" Rosemary asked.

"Constable Perkins told me about the attack, but he couldn't describe the intruders to me."

Rosemary's gut tightened, recalling the face of the vampire just as he burst into dust, the face uncomfortably similar to the one directly in front of her.

"It's confidential to the investigation," Rosemary said.

Burk visibly deflated. His expression was so sad that Rosemary was caught off guard, and her wayward tongue got away from her. "One of them had dark hair and a goatee, I think. Oh, and a scar on his cheek. The other one..." She paused, managing to restrain herself. "Uh...I didn't see the other one."

"Verikus," Burk said, under his breath.

"Excuse me?"

"Verikus Wyrt," he explained. "He's been a right pain in my neck ever since he learned to walk and talk. I don't suppose my wayward brother was with him?"

Rosemary felt as if her insides had frozen solid.

His brother! I killed Perseus Burk's brother!

She managed to utter a strained, "I told you, I didn't see."

"That would be just like them," Burk said. "If you ever have the misfortune of meeting my brother, run the other way. He's rotten to the core."

*And he's a vampire...*Rosemary thought before remembering the swiftness of Perseus Burk's movements and the chill of his skin.

Does vampirism run in families? I have so much to learn.

"My brother makes his money as a hired goon," Burk admitted, bowing his head further, as if in shame. "He'll do anything for a chunk of cash or gold...or even stolen goods. He once took a job against me – *his own brother* – in exchange for a box of smokes and bag of jewellery, probably nicked from some wealthy old woman."

"I'm...sorry," Rosemary said. After an awkward pause she added, "I have to get back to my daughter."

"Of course," Burk said, dropping his hand.

Rosemary stepped past him and back into the light and bustle of the pub.

"If you ever need anything, the offer still stands," she heard Burk say as she walked away.

"There you are!" Athena practically shouted as Rosemary returned to their table. "You've been gone for ages! I was about ready to send out a search party!"

"Oh, really?"

"No – but if I had disappeared for that long, you'd have had the army out looking for me."

"That's because you're a teenager and I'm your mother."

"It sometimes feels like the other way around," Athena said, crossing her arms. "Where were you, anyway?"

"I'll tell you later," Rosemary said, looking around the pub, which had emptied out, somewhat.

"What? Why? What happened?" Athena looked worried.

"Nothing much," Rosemary said, keeping her voice low. "I just discovered something that I don't want to share in a place where it might be overheard."

"Okay – let's go."

Rosemary took some cash out of her wallet and left it on the table.

"Don't we pay at the bar?" Athena asked, looking around for Liam, who was nowhere in sight.

"Sure," said Rosemary. "I just don't want to get into another argument about why we should or shouldn't pay for meals."

"Despite the fact that you soon won't be able to afford to go out for them? You lost your job, remember?" Athena said.

"Yes, despite that. I still have some shreds of pride left, and I'll just have to find a new job more locally. Until then, we can go back to your favourite childhood meal of beans on toast."

"Great," said Athena, "just when I was starting to like vegetables. I suppose I'll have to regress again."

"That reminds me," Rosemary said. "We need to enrol you in the local school! I can't believe I hadn't thought of that."

"I had," Athena admitted. "I was actually thinking about it a lot, hoping you'd never remember that I'm still school-aged."

Rosemary sighed. "How could I forget something so obvious? I mean, not your age, clearly, but school?"

"Give yourself a break, Mum. It's Monday. It has only been one school day, and you just decided this morning that we're staying here for the time being. Let's take a few days to figure things out."

"I see what you're trying to do there," Rosemary said, putting on her coat as they made their way through the pub and out the front door. "And it's not going to work. I'll call up the local school as soon as we get home. And don't be hoping I won't remember!"

Athena laughed. "Oh well, it was worth a try. The school here is probably bonkers, but it can't be any worse than the one in Burkenswood. Have you forgot we have a flat back there, filled with all our measly possessions?"

"No, I have not forgotten," said Rosemary as they walked back to Thorn Manor. "I've been thinking about that a lot since Constable Perkins insisted we stay in town. I just haven't figured out what to do about it. I mean, our stuff is bound to fit in the car – we don't own very much, and I'm not keeping that terrible excuse for a bed!"

"So, we get rid of the crappy furniture or just leave it in the flat for the next unfortunate tenants?" Athena suggested.

"Unfortunate to inherit the furniture, or the flat?"

"Both," said Athena. "You have to admit, Thorn Manor is a huge leap above anywhere else we've lived."

"That's true," Rosemary said. "And we haven't even explored the house. We've only been in the central part. There are two whole other wings – plus the tower."

"I bags the tower!" said Athena.

"For what?"

"It's going to be my bedroom."

"It'll be freezing in winter," Rosemary said. "With windows all around. Plus, it's tiny. You'd barely get a bed in there."

"I don't care. It's mine," Athena said. "I am determined to have every moody teenager's dream bedroom."

Rosemary sighed. “Impractical and romantic.”

“Exactly!” said Athena. “But not in a gross touchy-feely way. Romantic in a classic gothic historical sense.”

“If you insist,” said Rosemary. “How about, as soon as we get back, I’ll ring up about the school and then we can explore Thorn Manor and see what else it’s hiding? Granny only used the central part of the house. I do remember wandering around the other wings as a child, but as you know, I don’t remember all that much. I’m pretty sure there’s an old-fashioned glass conservatory out the back too.”

“Cool!” Athena exclaimed. “It’s just like something out of an old novel.”

“Since when do you read the classics?” Rosemary asked.

“Since now, I guess,” Athena said. “I have to get into the spirit of my new home, after all.”

Rosemary laughed. “You’re full of surprises, you are.”

“Wait a minute, you’re just trying to distract me, aren’t you?” Athena said in an accusatory tone.

“What are you talking about?”

“You’re trying to distract me from your mysterious disappearance earlier with talk of the tower and conservatory.”

“No,” said Rosemary. “I was intending to tell you about that. I...I just haven’t figured out the right words.”

“Were you accosted in the loos by an assassin woman with a weapon for a handbag?”

“Well...not exactly.”

“Then what?” Athena demanded.

“I found out who our attackers were,” Rosemary said, keeping her voice quiet in case there were eavesdroppers hidden behind the trees nearby, or perhaps eavesdroppers that *were* in fact trees, given that in a place like this anything could be possible.

“What!?” Athena exclaimed. “How? Who are they?”

“I ran into Burk again.”

“Oh, really?” Athena said, raising her eyebrows. “I thought we were staying away from him.”

“It wasn’t intentional,” Rosemary argued. “Anyway, it turns out the crow man is someone called Vikivis or Ver...Verikus? Yes, I think that’s it Verikus Wyrt.”

“Interesting name. And what about Burk’s vampy doppelganger?” Athena asked.

"Well, it turns out they're related. The vamp I dusted was Burk's hooligan brother."

"No way!" Athena cried.

"Shh, keep your voice down."

"Does that make him a vampire, too?"

"I'm pretty sure it doesn't work like that...but...maybe? There are a few weird things about Burk – he's super-fast and his hands are so cold!"

"Super-fast at what, exactly?" Athena asked.

"Nothing like that!" said Rosemary.

"Well, if he is a vamp, then how was he out during the day?"

Rosemary sighed. "It's possible that Buffy lied to us."

"Blasphemy!" said Athena. "Anyway, she was right about the bursting into dust thing."

"That's true – but just because we now believe in paranormal beings and other such things, it doesn't mean they follow the exact same rules as on TV and movies – I mean – even they don't follow the same rules as each other, and I'm willing to bet that vampires do not sparkle!"

"So, do we or do we not think your good friend Burk is a vampire?" Athena asked.

"I don't know! He might not be one, but there is definitely something unusual about him – something supernatural."

"I guess it does kind of kill off your budding romance."

"There *is* no romance, I assure you," said Rosemary, thinking back to the brief brush of intimacy in the dark earlier. It wasn't exactly her idea of romance, though there was a closeness about it she hadn't experienced in a long time...that she was definitely *not* going to inform Athena about. "But yes – 'I murdered your brother' would kind of put a dampener on things."

"You didn't *tell* him?!" Athena cried.

"Of course not. I don't want to incur family vengeance or wind up in prison, if that's even a possible consequence of murdering someone who's technically already dead."

By this time, they had reached the house and Rosemary had definitely *not* forgotten about calling the local school to ask about enrolments. Or rather, she had forgotten several times and then quickly remembered again.

As soon as they got through the door and taken their shoes and coats off, she made the call.

"Well, that's strangely convenient," Rosemary said, hanging up the phone a moment later.

"What is?"

"I called up the local school only to listen to a message informing me that the rest of the week is a holiday due to the Imbolc Festival." She shrugged. "I suppose you can start after that."

"Is that even legal?" Athena asked. "I mean, I'm not complaining, but don't they have to have the same holidays as everywhere else?"

"I suppose, if it's a special character school..." Rosemary said. "Oh, I don't know. Things are different in Myrtlewood. Just take their local police department as an example of that. Besides, I bet you're secretly delighted about going to school here, hoping to see Finnigan again."

"No," Athena said, crossing her arms.

"No?"

"He said he didn't go to school around here."

"I suppose he busses to some fancy private school," Rosemary said. "He seems like the type."

"Now who's judgemental?"

"What? He does! Anyway, I'm relieved about that."

"Why? Because you want me to stay away from him and that will be hard if we're at the same school?"

"Because if he's in boarding school, he'll be locked up safely, far away from you – at least on weeknights, and that alleviates approximately forty percent of my worries."

"What are the other sixty?"

"Weekends and holidays."

Athena sighed. "Fine, you've made your paranoia abundantly clear. Can we at least explore the house now?"

"Of course we can," said Rosemary. "It'll do us some good to take our minds off the investigation into Granny's death."

"Thanks. Now that you've put it that way, I'm going to have a lot of trouble taking my mind off it."

But despite Athena's protestations, it didn't take long before she was sufficiently distracted. The magic of the house that kept it clean and well-maintained seemed to weaken the further they moved away from the central rooms. The east wing was covered in a thick layer of dust, which made them both sneeze. And try as they might, they could not find the entrance to the tower. Rosemary couldn't ever remember going up there as a child, and even though it looked like it might stem from the east of the manor, it remained a mystery.

Feeling grimy, with snivelling sinuses, they gave up on the exploration but vowed to return in the near future, armed with cleaning implements – if only they would find the laundry room. They had planned to explore the west wing next. However, assuming it was in a similar state, they searched for the laundry instead.

They found it, just by walking out of the kitchen's back door. It was an old room, but sported new laundry appliances and quite a few different mops and buckets and brooms.

"No witchy brooms, though," Athena said.

"I'm sure *that's* a myth," said Rosemary. "I am not co-ordinated enough to ride one of those things and fly around in the air, even if I do happen to be a witch."

"I'm glad we found this place, though," said Athena. "I'm onto my last pair of clean underwear, and all my clothes need a wash. We were only supposed to stay for a night, remember?"

"Yes," said Rosemary. "And it's only been *two* nights. Can you believe that? It feels a lot longer."

"We are definitely going to need to go back and get the rest of our clothes soon," Athena said. "It's not like we can afford whole new wardrobes."

"Hey – look!" Rosemary said, picking up a set of keys off a hook by the laundry room's back door.

"We already have keys to the house."

"Yes, but these are car keys...I wonder if..."

She pushed open the back door to reveal a poorly lit garage.

"You didn't tell me Granny had a car," Athena said, squinting into the low light. "It looks like there's something vaguely car-shaped in there."

"No...well, she used to, quite a nice old classic Rolls Royce. But I figured she must have sold it. She was far too old to be driving."

Athena switched on the light to reveal a vehicle covered in a large grey sheet. They both stepped forward and pulled the sheet off to reveal a perfectly waxed burgundy and gold Rolls Royce.

"It looks good," Rosemary said.

"Good? It looks bloody brilliant! Is it...is it ours?"

"I guess so, once the will has gone through properly."

"Does it go?"

Rosemary took the keys and opened the car door with them, then she tried the ignition. The engine purred to life. "Sounds like it!"

"Great, so we can drive this back to Burkenswood to pick up our things," Athena said.

"Not now!"

"Okay, first thing tomorrow morning," Athena insisted.

Rosemary sighed. "I guess you're right. We do need to clean up our old life eventually, but for now, try to relax. How about I put the washing on and you can go upstairs for a nice hot bath."

"That sounds like the best idea you've had all day," Athena said.

Seventeen

Rosemary perched on the window seat, sipping a cup of tea. She looked out at the wild tangle of garden that lay just beyond the front lawn, wondering how hard the upkeep was going to be on the grounds of Thorn Manor.

In that moment, she was convinced that the magic of Myrtlewood wasn't just the stuff of fantasy. It was also something simple she felt deep in her bones, as if being here had begun to knit the disconnected parts of her back together like a quilt, or perhaps like a vine, wildly entangling the order with the chaos, creating something that made its own kind of beautiful sense in her inner world, something that might help her become a coherent person, or at least someone who wasn't objectively a failure in the eyes of the world.

She could hear the subtle hum of the washing machine, and, occasionally, the sound of Athena singing to herself in the bath upstairs. When she stopped worrying about how she was going to mow the lawns, it was all rather relaxing. That was until a car pulled up the driveway – a newer Rolls Royce in gleaming dark charcoal that could only mean one thing.

Rosemary sculled her hot tea and tried to tame the static from her hair. She wanted to present the impression of being on top of things.

The knock came, half a minute later, and Rosemary was already at the door, ready to slam it at any moment.

The overpoweringly soapy scent of lily of the valley wafted into the house, making Rosemary cough. A petite woman with ice-blond hair and an ice-cold gaze stood behind the door, along with a taller man, his dark hair gelled back and a permanent sneer on his face.

"Elamina, Derse..." Rosemary said. "What a surprise."

She couldn't quite manage "nice" before surprise, but lying was never really Rosemary's forte, anyway.

"Rosemary," Elamina said. "It has been too long, cousin."

"Really?" Rosemary asked. "I would have thought ever seeing each other again wouldn't have been too long – for either side. You never gave the impression that you ever wanted to spend any time with me, in particular."

"Still," Elamina said, peering around, behind Rosemary, into the house. "Family is family. Aren't you going to invite us in?" She put on the biggest fake-smile Rosemary had ever seen – which was startling and a little frightening. Rosemary couldn't recall seeing her cousin ever smiling before, outside of a malicious gleam in her eyes when something went her way.

"I don't believe I am," Rosemary said. She wasn't about to let her cousins walk all over her like they had in the past. "I was in the middle of something, so this is not the best time."

Derse coughed and cleared his throat. Rosemary looked towards him, but he didn't say anything.

"But surely, this is a family house," Elamina said. "We belong here as much as you do."

"I don't think so," Rosemary said. "According to both of Granny's wills, the house belongs to me, and in the more recent one so does everything else."

Elamina wrinkled her perfectly smooth and pale face into a grimace. "I think you'll find we are contesting the will," she said. "Our lawyers advise that our side of the family should get more."

Rosemary laughed. Her grown cousin was about to have a tantrum on her front doorstep, and given the way Elamina had always treated Rosemary, it was a satisfying sight.

"Well, Granny's lawyers don't seem to think so. She was sound of mind when she made both wills, and you get nothing," Rosemary said.

"Rubbish," Elamina replied. "We deserve half the house – at least! Probably more. After all, I was the one who organised the funeral that you didn't bother to attend."

Rosemary winced. She hadn't attended precisely because Elamina had organised an elaborate function near her swanky mansion, not something that Granny would have wanted at all.

"And I visited Granny regularly in her last few months." Elamina pouted and batted her eyelashes. "Where were you?"

"Trying to survive and feed my daughter. Thanks for asking," said Rosemary. She had a right mind to slam the door in their faces and leave it at that, but she couldn't help herself. "Granny knew me, and she knew you. She knew you were just greasing up to her to try to get the house. Lord knows why you need it when you're already filthy rich."

"Oh, poor, sweet Rosemary," Elamina said. "You think this is about money. How crude. If you only knew..."

"I do happen to know about the magic," Rosemary said, testing her cousin.

Elamina's eyes widened.

"How...how do you know?" she stuttered. "Did you find something?"

"More than you can imagine," said Rosemary.

"But the family magic is still bound, otherwise we would..."

"You'd what? Sprout wings and fly around?"

"You think this is all some big joke, don't you?" Elamina said. "I'll tell you this. When Daddy first married Mummy, he knew she was from an old magical family, and it showed! She could do all sorts of things – we all could! But when we were just kids, it all stopped. You must remember that? It was like the well ran dry, and so did my parents' marriage."

"I thought they were still together."

"They are, on paper," Elamina said. "But Daddy is obsessed. He was always hounding Granny to find out what happened to the magic – of course we still have some – from his side of the family, but the Thorn magic virtually disappeared. Only Granny seemed to possess any at all, and even that...well, she was a shadow of her former self."

"Something did happen," Rosemary admitted. "I don't know what it was and I don't know any of the details, so don't ask. Granny was trying to protect herself – and us. That's all I can say."

"From whom?" Derse asked, continuing with his perpetual sneer.

"I had actually wondered if it was from you," said Rosemary. "I'm still not convinced otherwise."

"You think *we* had something to do with Granny's death?!" Elamina cried. "Oh, you must be joking! I know we've never gotten along, Rosemary, but *this*?"

"You have a motive," Rosemary pointed out. "Your side of the family wanted the magic."

"And you didn't?"

"We didn't even know about it. It's hard to explain, but it's all part of what Granny had to do to protect the family magic. She bound it and altered my memory and did something that kept me away from this place. I didn't know about any of this until we came back to Myrtlewood."

"Did she tell you all that?" Elamina asked.

"She wrote me a letter, if you must know." Rosemary wasn't about to tell her cousin about the ghostly apparition as well.

"Can I see it?"

"No, it's private."

"So, I'm just supposed to take your word for it?"

"I'm not going to tell you what you're supposed to do," Rosemary said. "I'm not the hoity-toity one in the family. Go and tell yourself what to do... and do it elsewhere!"

"Rosemary, please?"

"Oh, very well. You can come back on Friday night, if you must."

"Friday night?"

"We're having a dinner party, here, and I thought you might like to come, you know...to meet some of Granny's friends?"

It sounded like a weak excuse, but the cousins were on the big piece of paper, and Rosemary's hairbrained dinner party was only going to work if all the key suspects were there. If the killer was not among them it, it would just be a party of oddballs – entertaining, but useless for their cause.

"You're inviting us to dinner?" Elamina said the words as though they left a foul taste in her mouth, and Derse's sneer deepened.

"That's what I said." Rosemary held her ground, waiting in silence until they caved in.

"Oh, very well," Elamina said. "What's the dress code?"

"I don't know, Elamina," said Rosemary. "How about 'dress as your true self?'"

"What's that supposed to mean?"

"Think about it," Rosemary said. "You'll figure it out." Though, by the time the words had escaped her lips she had already become confused about what she'd meant.

“Fine. We’ll see you Friday. What time?” said Elamina.

“Seven p.m.,” Rosemary replied.

“Seven it is.” Elamina lifted her palm and gave a little wave. She turned and sauntered down the front steps, through the car door that was being held open by the chauffer, and into the back-seat. She didn’t look back at Rosemary as the car backed to turn around and drove away.

Eighteen

The rest of Monday evening flew past, blissfully uneventful.

Rosemary prepared the customary Thorn delicacy of beans on toast, and while they ate, she filled Athena in on the visit from her unpleasant relatives, with much ensuing laughter.

"You should have called out to me," Athena said. "I would've loved to see that."

"Well, you'll have your chance to get reacquainted with the Bracewell-Thorns," said Rosemary. "I've invited them to our dinner party."

"Really?"

"Yes – they're on our big piece of paper."

"And they accepted?"

"They did indeed."

"I would have thought snobs like them wouldn't stoop to dine with us," said Athena.

"Under normal circumstances, I think you're right – but they want the magic, so they'll be here."

Rosemary and Athena went to bed early and slept peacefully that night, with no loud disruptions for a change. They got up early the next morning in preparation for the trip back to Burkenswood to retrieve the rest of their belongings – aside from the terrible furniture.

"Shall we go?" Rosemary asked first thing in the morning.

"What about breakfast?"

"I thought we could stop in at Marjie's on the way. We should tell her what we're up to – so someone knows to come looking for us if we don't return."

Athena shuddered.

"I meant that as a joke," Rosemary said.

"That may be so, but it's too close for comfort. Anyway, aren't we going to get in trouble with that coppa for leaving town?"

"We'll be back before he even realises we've gone," Rosemary said.

The engine of Granny's old, but well-maintained Rolls Royce purred to life, and they cruised into Myrtlewood village, to Marjie's tea shop.

They were the first customers to arrive again.

"Making a habit of this!" Marjie said, kissing them both on the cheek. "You'll be my best customers!"

"Only if you let us pay," Rosemary said.

"Oh, nonsense," said Marjie. "Your presence is payment enough. Now what'll you have?"

"Anything, really," Rosemary said. "Just whatever is convenient for you. We want to be quick. We're driving back to Burkenswood to pick up the rest of our things from the flat – since we're going to be staying in Myrtlewood for a good while."

"Very good, very good," Marjie said. She brought them a big pot of Earl Grey tea and disappeared into the kitchen again.

"So, we'll go straight to the flat and clear out everything we want and then I'll call the landlord to say I won't be renewing the lease," said Rosemary.

Athena nodded. "And we'll be back before nightfall, won't we?"

"I should think so. Why is that?"

"I don't like the idea of travelling at night," said Athena. "Given the danger we're in."

"Fair enough, though logically, we'll be at more risk at the house. That's where all the attacks have been so far."

"Yes, but it's also where my mother has superpowers to protect me with," Athena said.

"Inconsistent powers that I can't seem to control," Rosemary reminded her. "I'm just a normal person most of the time, remember."

"Normal is a stretch." Athena's eyes glittered with myrth. "Anyway, what's your plan when we get back to Myrtlewood? It's now Tuesday, and you told the Bracewell-Thorns our dinner is going to be on Friday...so we have a couple more days to prepare for all these people – some of whom you actively dislike – to descend on the house. How is that going to work again?"

Rosemary sighed. "Well, first I have to invite them all."

Athena sighed. "Yes, that is something you should have already done by now. It's only a few days away. And what if our true villain doesn't come?"

"They will," said Rosemary. "They won't be able to resist a peek inside the house and a chance to steal the magic."

"Very well," said Athena. "Exactly what do you think this dinner party is going to achieve – how are you going to spot the murderer?"

"I haven't figured that part out, exactly," said Rosemary. "I just thought it would be a good idea to get everyone in one place and watch for clues."

"That is a very vague plan," Athena said. "I've got no idea what could go wrong because there are just so many possibilities. Inviting all the suspects to the very same house that the villain has been trying to break into...?"

"Exactly!" said Rosemary. "Someone is bound to sneak off, looking for the source of our power."

"Which is...? The box?" Athena asked.

"Perhaps," said Rosemary. "It certainly seems to be a big connection point for everything that's happened so far...maybe we should have brought it with us to keep it safe."

"Really, Mum? You think it would be any better protected with us in the car than in a big magical house? That's absurd. Plus – Granny's ghost is there to haunt anyone who comes in."

"I hope you're right," Rosemary said.

"Anyway, back to your dinner party," said Athena. "So, it's some kind of test? Oh – I have an idea – we hide the real box and have something similar on display, which we say is an important family heirloom that Granny left us, only we don't know why."

"Actually, that's brilliant. Good work, kiddo!"

"Don't call me that!"

Just then, Marjie returned, bearing a tray laden with eggs, sausages, and fried tomatoes.

"Oh Marjie – this is...a lot of food," Rosemary said. "Thank you. It looks delicious."

"I have to feed you up for your big journey," said Marjie. "Also, I couldn't help overhearing..."

Rosemary and Athena gave each other a worried look.

"Now, don't fret. You can trust me," Marjie said. "I want to get to the bottom of Galdie's death almost as much as you do. She was very dear to my heart, you know. Anyway, I think it's wonderful you're trying to solve the mystery. I'm only nosing in to make a little suggestion."

"What's that, then?" Athena asked.

"Well...I like the idea of the dinner party, but don't you think a little spell might be in order, you know, to help determine which attendee is the killer?"

"Go on," said Rosemary. "What kind of spell?"

"Perhaps something to reveal the truth?" Marjie said. "I'll look into it for you, though bear in mind that they might have armed themselves against magic and my spell might not work."

"Thank you, Marjie. That would be brilliant," Rosemary said.

Marjie's face lit up and then she bustled off, humming to herself, while Rosemary and Athena dug into the hearty breakfast spread.

The tea shop was buzzing with customers by the time they finished eating, and Rosemary didn't get a chance to properly say goodbye to Marjie, but she did slip some money under her tea cup to cover the meal, knowing full well that Marjie wouldn't dream of charging her.

"Stop doing that, Mum," Athena said. "People will think we're Americans."

"Oh, don't be silly," Rosemary said. "How else are we supposed to pay our way around here?"

"I thought we were broke."

"Well, I am rather short on cash, but I have a bit of wiggle room left on my credit card, which will at least get us enough petrol to make it to Burkenswood and back with aplenty for food along the way. When I get back, I seriously need to get a job as quickly as possible, even if that means competing with Ferg in the local taxi industry."

"If you do that, you'd better offer the luxury service. I don't think we can get by on 20p per minute."

"Deal," said Rosemary, putting her coat back on. "Let's go."

They climbed into Granny's car and made their way smoothly out of the town square and towards the main road, heading out of town.

"This car drives like a dream," Rosemary said. "Not that I'm a car person, but it's so nice. I'd love to keep it, if we can afford it."

"I do feel a bit like a member of the royal family, riding in this thing," Athena admitted. "Surely we can afford it once the inheritance comes through."

"I guess that depends on how successful Elamina's challenge is," said Rosemary. "And on whether I'm cleared in the investigation. Otherwise, the Crown might seize everything."

"How awful would that be?" said Athena. "Just when we're so close to a life of luxury – you'd be thrown in jail and I'd be sent to juvenile detention or something."

Rosemary shuddered. "Don't talk about it. We aren't guilty and we're going to do everything in our power to prove it. Wait – what's that?" Something was blocking the road up ahead. As they drew closer, Rosemary realised what it was. "Oh, crud!"

Constable Perkins's car was parked across half the road, and he was checking every car as it drove by.

"Just my luck!" said Rosemary. "The one time we're actually leaving town, he happens to be conducting a road block."

"Is it just luck, though?" Athena asked. "Or something more sinister?"

They grew quiet as they pulled up to where the officer was standing, hands on hips, glaring at them. Rosemary reluctantly wound the window down.

"And just where do you think you two are going when I've expressly forbidden you from leaving town?"

"Uh, good morning, officer. We were just popping back to Burkenswood since we need to pick up our possessions if we're going to be staying in Myrtlewood for a while."

"Oh...you are, are you?" Constable Perkins said. "Not on my watch!"

"But we need our clothes!" Athena cried. "I can't wear the same two outfits every day forever!"

"That is not my problem, missy," he replied sternly, then turned to Rosemary. "And you, Ms Thorn, should know better. How am I supposed to know you're not secretly skipping the country?"

"Because I promise I'm not, and because you have some magical truth-seeking power?" Rosemary suggested.

"Not good enough," the police officer said.

Rosemary sighed. "What are we supposed to do, then, sir? We have our whole lives, as they were, back at the flat in Burkenswood."

"Surely, someone who isn't one of you could fetch you any items you deem necessary," Constable Perkins suggested. "I have a right mind to arrest you just for attempting to breach my orders."

"No. Please don't," said Rosemary. "We'll turn right around and go back to Thorn Manor – and if there's anything else we're not sure about we'll check with you first. I promise. Actually, to make it up to you, why don't you come to our dinner party on Friday night?"

Athena glared at Rosemary from the passenger seat.

"It wouldn't do for me to muddy an investigation like that, Ms Thorn."

"Well...you'd actually be doing me a huge favour. You see...we've planned a little gathering – not much, just a kind of housewarming – but now Athena is worried that whomever is responsible for the attacks might be one of our new Myrtlewood friends. So...having you there – as a strong and competent police officer – would really set her at ease."

Rosemary wasn't looking, but she could feel Athena's glare intensify.

"You're really that worried about your safety?" Constable Perkins asked.

"Of course we are!" said Rosemary. "After the other night – the attack on the house. We both could have died, just like Granny."

"Let me think about your kind and generous offer to invite me to a party to be your personal bodyguard..." Constable Perkins said.

"It's not like that," Rosemary insisted as the officer waved a few other cars past that had backed up behind them. "I just wondered if it would be in your best interests, too. I mean, if the killer is there, you might be able to catch them red-handed, stealing whatever it was they wanted to take from Granny."

"How do you know they don't already have it?" the officer asked.

"Why would they keep coming back, if that was the case?"

"Fair point," he said. "Alright. I'll think about it. But I suspect I'll either come as a civilian, or I'll wear my uniform and patrol around outside waiting for any funny business – and that's only if other duties don't call me away."

"Thank you, officer," Rosemary said. "That sounds marvellous."

"And no more funny business from you two!"

"Absolutely not." Rosemary started the engine and began to turn the car around to head back to Thorn Manor.

"What was all that about?" Athena asked. "I am *not* the one terrified for my life – that would be you. Don't you remember he has the power to tell truth from lies?"

"It just kind of slipped out," Rosemary said. "But I don't think any of it was a complete lie – you should be fearing for your life after all."

"Why not just tell him the truth about the dinner – that we are deliberately inviting suspects?"

"Because he'll think we're being vigilantes and he'll put a stop to it," Rosemary said. "Remember, everything has to be *his* idea."

"And you wanted him there, why?"

"Well, I'm not a hundred percent sure that he's not the one who hurt Granny for one – I mean, that would be awfully convenient, wouldn't it? He could pin it on us. He has the power."

"What would his motive be, though?" Athena asked.

"Power? The same as everyone else?"

"I don't get that impression from him, though," Athena said. "I mean... he's a terrible communicator, and a grumpy old git – but he's not sinister or evil or anything."

"I'm glad you don't think so," Rosemary said. "But we are not basing the entirety of our investigation on your gut instincts."

Athena sighed. "Back to another important matter," she said. "How on earth are we going to get all our things collected from Burkenswood? It's not like we had any friends to speak of back there who could just run them a couple of hours down the road for us. We've moved around far too much to have any real friends."

Rosemary thought about that for a while. It was true – they didn't have any close friends in Burkenswood who'd likely be up for that kind of favour.

"The people in Myrtlewood are so nice they might well do it," Athena continued. "Though we've only really just met them, despite some family connections."

"Hmm," Rosemary said. "You're right. I bet Marjie or Liam would do it for us, if they could, or Sherry, when she's better, but it seems rude to ask when we hardly know them. Besides, any of them could be the killer."

"I thought we'd agreed that Marjie is definitely not the killer," Athena said defensively.

"Well, how else did Constable Perkins know to set up a road block right when we were leaving town?" Rosemary asked. "Marjie was the only one we told."

"That's true," said Athena. "But it could have just been a massive coincidence – or maybe he used magic...or someone else is watching our every move. All of those things seem far more likely."

"Even still," Rosemary said. "I'll be keeping an eye on her on Friday. She's the only one who knows about the test – so we'll have to create a slightly different test, just for her."

"Fine, but none of that helps us get our clothes and stuff, Mum."

"There's always Dain."

"Oh...no. No, no, no! We are not calling Dad. No way!"

"He's actually quite good in a pinch," Rosemary reasoned. "The amount of times I've had to call him to jump-start my car..."

"And then he sticks around for a week and eats all our food, and your money mysteriously goes missing..."

"Still, what choice do we have?"

"Mum!"

"What?"

"We cannot bring him back into our lives, just when things are starting to improve!" Athena said.

"Do you really call being attacked by demons an improvement?"

"No – not that part."

"Or being accused of murder?"

"Oh, don't be a drama queen," Athena said. "You have not been formally accused of anything."

"Still..."

"No, Mum. I was referring to the smallish fortune and the big fancy house we are in the process of inheriting. That is something we want to keep Dad about a million miles away from. It's just as well we've moved addresses already, so he doesn't know where we are."

"Well..."

"Mum! No, you didn't."

"I might have sent him a little text message."

"I can't believe you!" Athena cried, burying her face in her hands.

"He's your father. He deserves to know where you are. I'm pretty sure it's illegal for us to move house without telling him."

"So, now you're all concerned with the letter of the law?"

"As of recently, yes," Rosemary said. "If I'd thought about it properly, I wouldn't have even tried to leave town today. It only makes us look more suspicious."

They pulled up into the garage of Thorn Manor. Athena got out of the car and slammed the door in a huff.

"Tea?" Rosemary asked.

"No," Athena said, stomping into the house.

"Oh, don't be like that, sweetheart. I know he's got issues, but he's still your father."

"That's not my fault," Athena shot back.

"Still, he may be our only legitimate option right now. I might just give him a quick text and see is he's free. Don't worry, I promise I won't tell him about the inheritance – in fact, I won't even tell him about Granny passing, so he doesn't get any ideas. I'll just say we're going to need some things. I can even see if he'll sell that old bomb of a vehicle for us."

"Real smart move, Mum."

"It won't be worth much," Rosemary said. "In fact, he can keep the money in exchange for bringing us all our things."

"Fine," Athena said. "Suit yourself, but you're lucky we don't have anything else worth selling or he'd pawn it all before you could blink."

"Athena..."

"No! I've had enough." She stormed upstairs, slamming the bedroom door behind her.

Rosemary sighed. Of course, Athena had a point. She was rational to a fault, and her father was the total opposite. It was actually baffling to Rosemary how she managed to raise such a reasonable and astute daughter, given both her parents' obvious shortcomings in those particular areas. It wasn't that Rosemary was bafflingly irrational. It was more that rationality held little interest for her mind, which preferred to dart from one thing to the next, finding strange connections.

Having Athena around was balancing for her, grounding.

Dain, on the other hand, lived on a different planet entirely most of the time – figuratively, of course. But, as Rosemary had argued, he was good in a pinch, and he had gotten her out of many spots of bother over the years – though not quite as many as he'd gotten her into.

It was true that when he showed up, Rosemary had little in the way of defence against his charm, and he'd inevitably found his way back into her bed and into her heart, only to hurt her again, but not this time. Rosemary was determined – even if she had to look up a magic spell to protect herself from womanisers.

Spells...that's it!

She sent a quick text message to Dain asking for the favour and then decided that magic spells were exactly what she needed to learn about – to arm herself against the charms of her ex or any number of other predators.

She made herself tea and took it with her into the library.

The box was still sitting on the desk, innocuously, despite all the power it seemed to possess.

Rosemary chose to ignore it, seeing as she didn't know what other surprises it might contain. She thoroughly immersed herself in scanning the bookshelves. Befitting her character, Granny Thorn had been quite the collector of interesting reference material. Among the hundreds of titles here were several large volumes of *Material Medica* – detailing the botany and uses of healing herbs, and multiple encyclopaedias and histories of magic, which could definitely come in handy.

Rosemary practically kicked herself for not exploring the library earlier. It seemed obvious that the information they needed would be contained somewhere in these volumes. She got quite cross with herself, in fact, until she remembered it was only Tuesday in the longest week she'd ever experienced. She was only a couple of days into even believing in magic, let alone researching it.

Perhaps there's something about this house...or this town that makes time slow, Rosemary wondered, as she traced her fingers along the spines.

Her nail caught against something not-quite-book-like. On closer inspection, it was a rough piece of paper. Rosemary pulled at the large volume on mythical creatures behind. The paper slipped out and fell to the floor. It appeared to be an invitation of some kind.

You are cordially invited to the symposium of the Bloodstone Society, it read, followed by an address in Burkenswood with a time and date proposed for the sixth of June, though no year.

*The Bloodstone Society...*Rosemary thought. That's what Sherry was talking about the other night. And here they were, inviting Granny to some kind of fancy event.

It must be fancy, Rosemary reasoned. *There's even a wax seal on the back.*

The seal had mostly crumbled off, but the corner of it looked slightly like a shield. It reminded Rosemary of something, though she couldn't place exactly what it was.

"Peculiar and more peculiar," Rosemary muttered to herself, wondering if it was Alice or the caterpillar who had said something like that in the original story.

She carefully took the invitation and placed it next to the stack of useful-looking books she was collecting.

Madame Tuison's Collection of Spells and Incantations certainly looked promising, as did *A Magical History of Myrtlewood* by A. C. Twigg. *Twigg...*that sounded familiar, too.

She also stacked up several books on protective charms and a few volumes of *The Basics of Witchcraft*, seeing as she really was starting from ground zero, here.

It was a pity that Athena was in such a foul mood, Rosemary reflected; going through all these books was exactly the kind of thing the young Thorn would have loved.

Rosemary chose some volumes especially for Athena to look at when she was in a better mood. Perhaps she could even find a spell to repel a deadbeat ex.

Though the books were fascinating, Rosemary couldn't help but glance back at the little wooden box on the desk every few minutes.

It almost seemed to call to her, not in a creepy way, but in a familiar manner that had a hint of destiny about it.

"Oh, alright," she said to the box. "I'll bite – but no funny business. Nothing dangerous or deadly, only things that will help us solve the mystery and get our lives in order, *please*?"

She left the piles of books on the floor and approached the desk.

The box seemed to be glowing slightly, and Rosemary had second thoughts about touching it, especially with Athena upstairs and blissfully ignorant of her mother's antics. She thought about turning away, taking the books, and shutting the door, ignoring the stupid box, but her curiosity got the best of her.

Rosemary reached out for the small wooden chest and braced herself as her fingers brushed against its surface.

Nothing happened.

She was still standing in the library, holding the box, and then the world around her seemed to fall away in pieces like those of a broken mirror, cascading into darkness and emptiness. The box in her hand glowed brightly in the dark. She glanced down to see it had transformed into the crystal she had seen before.

"Hello?" she said into the darkness. There was no reply.

Rosemary cleared her throat. "Uhm...elder woman?"

Still nothing but stillness and darkness. Then she heard something...a subtle thud in the distance, echoing like a heartbeat.

There was nowhere else to go and nothing else to see, so Rosemary stepped forward, towards the sound that continued, intermittently, to thud gently.

She could see a soft glow in the distance, which, as she approached, became clearer. The first thing she could make out was a rock face, and she wondered whether she had reached the same place as last time, even though the elder was nowhere to be seen.

As she stepped closer, she recognised creeping green vines, which clung to the rock. And the further she walked, the thicker they grew until they were all around her – a forest of vines.

The thud became louder and louder, leading Rosemary on until she saw a bright white light shining through the dense green foliage.

Rosemary had thought the vines were friendly, or at the very least that they were harmless. But, by and by, she realised that they were holding tight to the bright light, that looked more and more like a larger version of the crystal she held in her hands, suffocating it, choking it. The thrumming sound was the light crystal fighting back or crying out for help.

She reached up, hoping to free it. A voice sounded behind Rosemary, startling her. "No, stop. Don't touch them."

Rosemary turned to see the same woman as before – the elder. Rosemary hesitated, looking at the vines. They seemed malicious now, as if they were watching her, waiting.

"You must release the binding," the woman said. "Before it's too late."

Rosemary glanced back at the vines...

The vines are the binding, she realised. *Not an evil force, on their own, but something created to protect, which has now become too restrictive and is starting to strangle the very thing it's supposed to keep safe...*

"But how?" Rosemary asked. "How can I release it if I can't touch the vines?"

"You must look within," the elder said infuriatingly.

"What is that supposed to mean!?" Rosemary asked. "I want a simple answer about what to do – none of this cryptic and vague rubbish! Look within? A fat lot of good that's going to do me!"

The elder blurred in front of Rosemary's eyes, along with the vines and the light and blackness around them. Everything faded to grey, and Rosemary woke to the sound of Athena telling her off again.

"What the!? Mum! What in blazes do you think you're doing getting yourself knocked unconscious again! You scared me half to death!"

"Oh...sorry," Rosemary said, opening her eyes to see she was back in the library. She felt a heavy sense of dread and a desperate yearning to see Granny again, to talk to her and ask her to explain herself.

"It looks like a tornado came through here," Athena said. "What happened?"

"Well, I was looking through the books to see if there was anything useful – you know – like a spell to protect me from your dad's charms or a recipe for some anti-vampire repellent or something, and then I decided to try the box again."

"You're saying you threw the books all around the room?!"

"No," Rosemary said, coming to her senses to see that the books had, indeed, scattered. "I put them in piles. They must have been knocked over when I passed out."

"Honestly!" Athena said. "You just don't think things through."

"I think we've covered that already," Rosemary said. "Plenty of times, in fact. Now help me take these books to the dining room table. There are some great ones in here – maybe there's even something that can help us contact Granny and talk to her again."

Nineteen

"Here's another option, look," Rosemary said. "But it requires a Ouija board. Do you think we could make one?"

"You really won't give up on this contacting the dead thing, will you?" Athena asked. "I told you it was a bad idea."

They sat around the dining room table, which was piled high with books, sipping tea and leafing through the large number of volumes that might have useful information contained within.

"Oh, come on," Rosemary said. "I really have to figure out what's going on with the Thorn magic binding and how to break it. You should have seen what it was like in there."

"Mum, you weren't *in* anything. You were passed out on the floor hallucinating about that elder again."

"I think we're well beyond hallucinations at this point, Athena."

"That might be so, but we can't tell if what you saw was a fair and accurate representation of the truth."

"Don't use legal jargon on me. You know it upsets my allergies," Rosemary said, taking a big sip of tea to calm her nerves.

"No, Mum, your imaginary allergy is to estate agents, remember?"

"Legal jargon is just as bad. Oh, bother. I'm going to have to invite that lawyer over on Friday, too, aren't I?"

"Your special friend, Mr Burk...or should I say, *Perseus*?" Athena teased, picking up another book from the piles in front of them on the table and scanning the table of contents.

"Don't start that again."

"Look," said Athena. "All I'm saying is that we don't know if what you saw is real. It might be a trick...or you might not fully understand it."

"Exactly!" Rosemary said. "And that's why I need to talk to Granny again. She's the only one I can really trust to explain all this."

Rosemary still had absolute faith in Granny Thorn, despite everything. Even though Rosemary now had more questions than ever, she needed to believe that her grandmother had a good reason for her secrecy. If only they could talk to her again to figure it all out.

"Mum," said Athena. "I've seen way too many horror films to ever attempt a séance."

"But we aren't trying to raise the dead or contact anyone creepy," Rosemary insisted. "This is Granny we're talking about."

"At least six of these books warn us to never attempt contacting the dead unless we know exactly what we're doing, and most of the rituals I've found require it to be the festival of Samhain...which I think is in the autumn. Almost the opposite time of year!"

"Still, we know Granny, and we know she's around here somewhere. She seems to be the most likely candidate for us to contact, and I'm not bloody waiting until autumn. That crystal wrapped in vines was pulsing in an unnerving way. It looked like that whole thing was going to blow!"

"You mean explode?"

"Explode or implode...I don't know. It just felt to me like time was running out, and the elder implied as much."

"Oh fine," Athena said. "We'll try your Ouija board idea – but just this once, and..." She hesitated.

"And what?"

"You have to make this protection charm first, to ward off Dad."

"Fine!" said Rosemary, grasping the book that Athena shoved her way. "*Altazar's Compendium of Enchantments*?"

"You just need a little black square of cloth and salt and..." said Athena, pointing to the ingredients list. "Rosemary...well, that's convenient."

"Convenient that it's my name?"

"No, that's just a coincidence. Rosemary is apparently known for its protective properties. It's convenient because I spotted a big bush of it right by the front door."

"Since when are you the expert in herbology?"

"It's herbalism, Mum, and I'm not an expert. It used to grow at my old school along with lavender. The bees love it."

"Well in that case..." Rosemary said, letting her words train off into thin air.

"Hmm. It says you need some black onyx for this one. Where can we find that?"

"Maybe in one of these cupboards," Rosemary said, putting the book down and opening up some of the cupboards in the various sideboards on which gran kept her paperweights and doilies and other odds and ends. The first two cupboards only contained various old china dinner sets, but the third one Rosemary tried had a whole lot of interesting things. Her eyes fell on a large, smooth wooden board. "Hey look!" she said.

"Did you find onyx?"

"No, but I did find a state-of-the-art Ouija board," Rosemary said, pulling it out of the cupboard and waving it around.

"Be careful with that thing," Athena said, ducking out of the way as it swung towards her.

"Can we use it?!" Rosemary asked, excitedly. "Can we? Can we?"

"Sure, after you've made the charm."

"Oh, fine." She crossed her arms and pouted a little for good measure.

Athena began rummaging through some drawers nearby. "This one's full of crystals!" she said. "Look!"

Rosemary did look to see an entire drawer of sparkly stones. "Very pretty," she said. "You know. I really don't remember any of this from when I was a kid. I wonder if I played with those. I bet I would have loved them."

"I think Granny Thorn kept them as important magical items," said Athena. "Not children's playthings."

"Granny wasn't like that," Rosemary said. "She let me play with anything – and she never treated me like a silly child – everything was for learning about and exploring the world."

"It's a bloody shame she addled your memory then, isn't it?" Athena said. "You might have been a brilliant scientist or inventor or something."

"I've never thought of that," Rosemary said. "Gosh...I hope not."

"Why not?"

"Well, for one, it would mean Granny took away a great opportunity for me to do something important with my life, and secondly, because working in a lab all day sounds dead boring!"

"You're a walking contradiction, you know that?" Athena said. "Look, that black one at the back is probably onyx."

Rosemary picked it up. The small black opaque stone was shiny but unremarkable in her hand, like a polished pebble. "It looks like the picture in the Gem Index. Is this all we need, then?"

"No, let me see. Oh, you also need black pepper – though there's plenty of that in the kitchen."

"Salt and pepper and rosemary. Sounds like we're roasting lamb," Rosemary said. "Ooh, actually, that's a great idea for Friday's dinner. Especially if rosemary does have protective properties."

"I'm not sure it works like that," Athena said.

"I'm sure I can find a way to spell the food to our advantage," said Rosemary. "Anyway, a roast lamb is an easy meal to chuck in the oven and then ignore for a couple of hours while I do other things."

"Suit yourself," Athena said. "But you know I don't eat baby animals."

"Roast mutton it is then!" said Rosemary. "Even better, I'll roast it on a lower temperature for longer so that it's nice and tender. That will buy us plenty of time to get everything sorted for dinner."

They found a piece of black fabric and some black twine in amongst Granny's sewing things which were stored off to the side of the parlour, and then Athena ducked out of the front door to cut a few twigs of rosemary from the bush.

"That's everything!" Rosemary said. She gathered all the ingredients together on the kitchen bench and said the protection chant over and over again as she combined the salt, black pepper, and rosemary leaves inside the black cloth with the onyx.

Earth and air, fire and water, may I be protected from Dain.

She tied the bundle together and waved it over a lit candle, three times, while picturing Dain and what she often thought of as his stupid, handsome face. Then she sprinkled salt water over herself and the bundle, and flicked some at Athena, while picturing calm, tranquillity, and peace, which, in her mind, looked like a windswept beach.

"Hey!" Athena said.

"Quiet – I'm being tranquil here. I want to hear only the sea."

Athena sighed. "Are you quite finished?"

"I think so," Rosemary said. "Now I just have to wear it around my neck for days on end. Lucky black goes with everything."

"That's the spirit," Athena said. "I hope it works."

"Ooh, can we do mine now?" Rosemary asked. "I'm dying to speak to Granny."

"After dinner?" Athena suggested. "I'm starved, and I assume it's not the best idea to contact the dead on an empty stomach."

"Oh, very well then," said Rosemary. "But after that there's no more stalling."

She whipped up a quick dinner of tinned tomato soup and toast, marvelling at how the half-loaf of bread they'd brought with them and the other modest supplies in the kitchen seemed to be lasting so well.

This is the kind of magic I can get behind, Rosemary thought, smiling at the house and patting the kitchen bench in appreciation.

They ate their soup in silence.

Rosemary assumed Athena was thinking about Finnigan, while Athena assumed Rosemary was thinking about contacting Granny, meanwhile they were both actually worrying about each other, and about a potential impending visit from Dain, with their possessions, if he actually came through this time.

After dinner, they cleared the kitchen table and laid out the Ouija board.

"Alright," said Athena. "What do we do now?"

"How should I know?" Rosemary asked.

"You're the one who was reading about all the séances, remember."

"Oh, yes. That's right. So, I think we light a candle, with a clear intention in our minds and then hold hands, thinking of the person we want to contact."

Rosemary retrieved a candlestick and lit it, focusing on getting a clearer understanding of the binding and how to free their powers.

Then she stood back and reached for Athena's hands as they stood over the board.

"Are we supposed to close our eyes?" Athena asked.

"Of course not," said Rosemary. "How on earth would we see the letters Granny spells out if we have our eyes shut?"

"I just meant at first, to focus."

"Will you two stop bickering for just one moment and give an old woman some peace?"

Rosemary and Athena both glanced down at the Ouija board to see Granny's face materialising there.

"Oh, gosh!" said Rosemary.

"This is way more effective than in the movies," Athena admitted.

"You know you can just summon me by calling my name loud enough?" Granny Thorn said. "You don't need to resort to all this codswallop."

"Hey. It's your board," Rosemary pointed out. "And no, I did not know that. It would have been a really useful thing to tell me last time you appeared to us, just like you could have told us who your killer is."

"Oh – I'd love to!" Granny said.

"Great," said Athena. "Who did it?"

"I'd love to," Granny said, frowning. "But I'm afraid they bound me from doing any such thing – those gormless gits!"

"I see," Rosemary said, her mood sinking in disappointment. "And I suppose ghost testimonies don't count anyway, even in Myrtlewood."

"I'm afraid not. I'm sorry I can't be of more help to you."

"But there's more than one of them – the attackers," Athena said. "You used plurals."

"A smart lass you are, dear," said Granny.

"Thank you," said Athena. "Granny Thorn, is there anything else you can tell us about them?"

"I'm afraid not, love, but I did leave you clues, and I can tell you a smidgeon about *that*."

"Please do," said Rosemary, perking up. "And then also, if you can, tell us about the binding and how to break it."

"The clues are: Blue. Lace. Dance."

"That's it?" Rosemary asked. "Those are the clues?"

"Well, not exactly. They're the clues to help you find the actual clues that I've hidden."

"What is this tosh!?" Rosemary said. "Can't you just tell us?"

"No, dear, I cannot. Mind your tongue."

"Why not?" Athena asked in a much calmer voice.

"The reason is perfectly obvious," Granny said. "I told you, they bound me from revealing who they are. Also, they might well be listening. I've done everything in my power to protect you, including hiding the information that others might use against you."

"You really think they're listening to a conversation in our kitchen?" Rosemary asked.

"It's possible to listen in when people are communicating between realms," said Granny Thorn. "Think of it like radio-waves."

"Well, that's just perfect," said Rosemary, scowling in frustration. "I suppose you can't tell us how to break the binding, either."

"Actually...no. But find the clues and you will figure it all out rather quickly."

"Well, you're a great help," Rosemary muttered, a caustic edge to her voice.

"I'm sorry, Rosemary dear. You did always have a short temper, and patience is not your forte, but please try to push through the frustration. You're going to need to do that in order to break the binding."

"Next, you're going to tell me I have to look within, like that elder," Rosemary scoffed.

"Oh, you absolutely do," said Granny. "But clearly you're not quite ready for that."

"What's that supposed to mean?!"

"Shush, Mum," Athena scolded. "We only have Granny here for a short time – remember – it uses up lots of her energy. Stop getting so cross and be practical."

"Fine, I'll hold my tongue," Rosemary said.

Granny stuck her own tongue out at that.

"Behave yourself, Granny Thorn!" said Athena. "We can't have Mum getting wound up again."

Rosemary glared at both of them.

"Okay," Athena continued. "Granny, you can't tell us how to break the binding, but can you at least explain more about how the whole thing happened – and how you came to bind our powers in the first place?"

"My dears – they've been after us for years. I only wish I saw this coming before it was too late. The binding is very old magic, and I daresay you'll find bits and pieces about it in the books in my library, but casting it is a very different process from breaking it, so don't worry too much about what I did. The main thing you both must focus on is yourselves. Think not too much on the past. Dwell not too much on the future. The answer is in the present. That is very important."

"In the present, I'm talking to a dead woman whom I'm very cross at," Rosemary said.

"Shh," said Athena.

"And with that, my energy is ebbing," said Granny. "I must bid you farewell. Remember that I love you very much, my sweet girls."

Granny faded back into the Ouija board. Rosemary sighed and dropped Athena's hands. "Well, a fat lot of good that did us."

"I think it might have actually been quite useful information," Athena said. "We just have to work it out."

"Always more cryptic messages and riddles!"

"Hey, you were the one who insisted we try to contact her," said Athena.

"That was before I knew she was going to be so infuriating."

"She tried to be helpful – I'm not sure why you threw a wobbly like that."

"I was...I suppose I got overwhelmed. This whole situation is intense and scary. I can't believe what Granny did to me, but also I missed her so much. I still do, and I just want to figure out who is responsible for her death. I was feeling too many things at once and then I got so brassed off when she wouldn't be straight with us"

"Through no fault of her own."

"Sure, take her side," Rosemary was half-joking.

"We are all on the same side here," Athena said. "And when you're ready to behave like a grown-up, you can come and join us."

"I'm going to bed," Rosemary announced. "I'm too tired for adulting."

"Aren't you going to help me look for the clues? Something blue...lace... dance. It's a bit like a wedding, isn't it?"

"It's silly is what it is," Rosemary said. "I don't want to play games."

"Says the woman with the Ouija board!"

"Bed!" Rosemary said, storming upstairs. "Goodnight," she called down from her childhood bedroom before throwing herself on the single bed. It was silly, she knew that. She was behaving like a child, but surely all adults did that sometimes. Rosemary oscillated between rage that Granny had stolen a piece of her mind from her and sadness that she had been magically excluded. All of this burned above a deep-seated guilt. She hadn't been there for Granny, spell or not. Was that why Granny hadn't let her in on the secret? Everything had happened so fast that she'd barely had a chance to process any of it, and the impending danger only made it that much worse. *We will get out of this mess,* she vowed. *I'm going to kick the arse of whoever threatened my family, and then I'm going to live a life I'm actually in control of.*

Twenty

Rosemary lay in bed the next morning, feeling slightly better. She had processed a lot of the anger from the previous night, but still felt a keen sting of betrayal regarding Granny and being deceived for all those years by the person she most trusted.

Is this what looking within is like? Rosemary wondered, swallowing the bitter truth. *I don't much like it.*

She had no idea what the somewhat vague message meant, or how far she'd have to look before things finally made sense and she figured out how to break the binding.

Rosemary flinched at the sound of a knock.

"Yes?" she asked.

Athena pushed open the door, fully dressed and energetic-looking. "Come on sleepy head. Are you ready to help me look for clues yet?"

"Oh, alright."

"Good, because I've already made breakfast and tea."

"Really?" Rosemary asked, pushing herself out of bed and following Athena downstairs. "What did you make? It smells good."

"Just bacon and eggs."

"I can't believe that bacon's still good," Rosemary muttered. "Did you check it?"

"Oh Mum – when are you going to get used to having a magical refrigerator? Of course, I checked it. The food here seems to replenish itself somehow. We might be broke, but we're not going to starve."

"That's great," Rosemary said. "For as long as it lasts, anyway."

"You're such a cynical old lady."

"Well, either we release the binding and who knows what happens to the magic then, or we don't figure out how to and the whole thing implodes...or explodes. I'm not sure which is worse."

"Depends on where you're standing, perhaps," Athena said, serving her mother a plate of fried eggs and bacon on toast.

"Thank you," Rosemary said. "This was very thoughtful."

Athena shrugged. "I was hungry," she said. "And besides, I figured we needed a good meal after yesterday, when we didn't have a proper lunch and just had soup for dinner – and both got so cross at each other."

"You're very wise," Rosemary said.

"Remember that next time we argue," said Athena.

"So, what's your grand plan for today?" Rosemary asked. "Since you're already up and dressed and organised so early in the morning."

"It's nine o'clock, Mum," Athena said. "And my plan for the day is to find those clues that Granny hinted at. Yes, I do expect you to help me."

"Oh, very well," said Rosemary, finishing off her breakfast. "Where do you suggest we start?"

"Granny's bedroom, I think," Athena replied.

"Do we have to? It's all so intimate, going into someone's personal space like that."

"Personal space is something different, Mum, and it would serve you well to get a better grasp of it!"

"You know what I mean," said Rosemary.

"Yes, and yes, we do have to," Athena replied. "It makes sense that Granny would keep something important within reach."

"Or that she'd hide it far away, in the conservatory or something, so that people wouldn't guess."

"People like you would guess that," Athena pointed out. "You just did."

"Okay, fine. We start upstairs, but then I'm checking the conservatory."

"Blue. Lace. Dance," Athena repeated the clues Granny had given them. "Something blue, or lacy, or both – or something that dances?"

"Mmm, hmm," said Rosemary, getting up from the table and following Athena upstairs. "Could be anything, really."

"I'm hoping it will be obvious once we find it," Athena said. "Do you think it's one thing with three clues or three things that make up one clue?"

"How should I know?" Rosemary asked. "Nobody tells me anything useful."

"Oh, stop sulking, Mum," Athena said. "Granny Thorn had her reasons." She turned the handle and opened the door to Granny's bedroom.

Rosemary was taken aback by the nostalgia of it. Everything about this room reminded her of Granny, and it stabbed at her heart, painfully.

Why wasn't I trusted? Why couldn't she have let me in on her big secret instead of robbing me of my memories and keeping everything from me? Even Elamina knew about our family's magic...

Rosemary had always thought she was Granny's favourite, which made it hurt even more that she'd been kept in the dark. Her memories were so personal – her whole sense of self hinged on what she could remember of life, and a part of that had been stolen, which also meant the other parts made less sense. It was no wonder she had felt so fragmented. *It's like my whole childhood was a lie...and my adulthood too.*

She didn't share her lamenting thoughts with Athena to avoid being told off again.

"Look, here's the wardrobe," Athena said, pulling it open and examining the contents. "Lots of black dresses. Did she have lots of funerals to attend?"

"Granny just liked wearing black," Rosemary said, swallowing some of her own bitterness in order to focus on the matters at hand. "She said it goes with everything, so why wear anything else?"

"You do realise that second part defeats the purpose of the first part," Athena pointed out.

"I suppose you're right," said Rosemary. "Granny also said she liked black because it didn't stain easily."

"Very pragmatic. Look there are a bunch of other bright colours in here too: red dresses, green dresses, even purple. Lots of solid colour. I gather she wasn't a fan of prints or pastels."

"She certainly wasn't," Rosemary smirked. "Granny said pastels were what happened when colours gave up the will to live."

"I can't argue with that," said Athena. "She and Marjie must have made a funny pair – Granny in black and Marjie in pastel florals."

"They always said they were like chalk and cheese," Rosemary said.

"There's some black lace in here, but only one solid blue dress."

"Why are you fixated on the wardrobe?" Rosemary asked. "Those clues were so vague they could mean anything."

"Sure, but I figured it might have been a blue lacy dress – you know – the kind she might go out dancing in?"

"Granny did like to go to the local cèilidh dances," Rosemary recalled. "She said they were a whole pile of fun and good energy."

"There you go," said Athena. "But there's no blue lace in here. Hmm. Maybe we're on the wrong track entirely."

They scanned the rest of the room, but there weren't many blue objects, or much lace either, though Athena did discover a rather extensive shoe collection.

"Doilies are lacy," Rosemary said. "You know – like the ones downstairs...and there are blue paperweights around there, too."

"Worth a try," said Athena. They retreated back down to the ground floor and looked at the items sitting on top of the cabinets.

"This one has a little blue," said Rosemary, holding up a blown glass paperweight. "And it was sitting on top of a doily."

"But what about the dancing?" Athena asked.

Rosemary shrugged. "We could check inside the cabinet?"

They sorted through the contents of the cupboard directly below the blueish paperweight, but all they found was a collection of silly hats.

"Granny Thorn might have worn them out dancing?" Athena suggested.

"Only if it was a fancy dress ball," said Rosemary. "It seems like a weak connection...but even if this was what Granny was alluding to – how are we supposed to find the hidden clue from a bunch of old junk?"

They sorted through the hats for possible leads, and then checked the doilies and the paperweight again, but nothing stood out as obvious.

Rosemary sighed and got up, brushing some dust from her jeans. "I'm going to check out the conservatory," she said.

"What's your obsession with that?" Athena asked.

Rosemary shrugged. "It's where I'd hide things. The conservatory was always such a lovely, lush place when I was growing up. I loved it in there."

"Fine," Athena said, following behind her mother as they left the house through a side door and made their way around the outside.

"It looks a bit rough," Athena said, looking up at the old octagonal glass conservatory adjacent to the west wing of Thorn Manor. It did appear to be covered in a heavy layer of mildew and moss.

"Clearly the magic that maintains the house doesn't stretch all the way out here," Rosemary said.

"I know, it's just...would Granny Thorn really come all the way out here to hide something? She was old and frail."

"Granny was always active," Rosemary said. "If she was still making it up the stairs to use her bedroom, right to the point of leaving me a note there before she died, I'm sure she could have put on her Wellington boots and clomped out here easily enough.

"Wait, that's right...the note," said Athena.

"What about it?"

"Do you think it might contain any clues or useful information that might help us decipher this puzzle?"

"I don't know," said Rosemary. "I'll have a look at it when we get back inside."

She pushed open the door to the conservatory and winced at the sound of many insects scuttling away to hide.

"Not much in there," said Athena. "Unless you count rather a lot of moss, and what's that fuzzy plant?"

"Asparagus fern, I think," said Rosemary.

"It's...kind of lacy...Oh...that's right!"

"What?"

"Isn't there a plant that grows wild called something-lace?" Athena asked.

"Queen Anne's lace?" Rosemary suggested.

"Yes, that one. Do you think...?"

"Too vague," said Rosemary. "It grows all along the roadsides around here."

"Maybe that's part of the clue," Athena suggested. "Like we're supposed to follow the road with that plant growing along it to find something blue and then do some kind of ritual dance?"

"Are you serious?" Rosemary asked. "Granny was odd, but she wasn't completely potty! Anyway, you'd have to follow every single road, just about."

"Hey – I'm just trying to come up with ideas," Athena said defensively. "Your only idea was to look in here – where there's nothing but old pots and ferns. Nothing blue. No lace. No dancing."

Rosemary looked under a few pots, but as the centipedes and spiders scurried away, she thought better of it and retreated back outside.

"It used to be beautiful in there," Rosemary said sadly. "It was glorious, with all kinds of tropical plants. Granny even grew bananas!"

Athena gave her mother a sympathetic look and patted her arm. "Maybe we can restore it to its former glory," she suggested. "Once the inheritance comes through."

Rosemary smiled at her daughter. "I'd like that," she said as they made their way back to the house. There was so much potential in their lives now. If only they could get through the pressing danger.

Twenty-One

They searched the house from top to toe, trying to make connections with the prompts Granny had given them.

"It's all so exhausting," Rosemary said as they sat down to a light lunch of kippers on toast.

"Really?" Athena asked. "We've only been looking at old stuff."

"Maybe for you," Rosemary said, "but everything I come across seems to jog my memory, and bring back old feelings – both good and difficult. It all makes me miss Granny, and then I keep remembering that I'm still cross at her."

"That does sound like a rollercoaster," Athena said.

"I'm emotionally exhausted. I might need an afternoon kip."

"Go on, then," Athena said. "I'll keep looking down here, and you go upstairs to have a rest – you poor old thing."

"I'm only as old as I feel," said Rosemary. "Which is about a million years old right now!"

She gave Athena a quick hug and made her way upstairs. Afternoon sunlight was pouring in through her childhood bedroom, warming the air up to just the right temperature. Rosemary got into bed, wondering if she would ever move into Granny's larger room. It seemed wrong to do that, and eerie. Granny's room was Granny's room. Besides, her ghost might want to hang out in there when she built up a bit more strength.

Rosemary yawned, closed her eyes, and drifted off to sleep. She dreamed of the vines – thick vines – choking the light, choking the life right out of her. Rosemary tried to scream and cough at the same time, waking herself up.

She lay in bed, her heart racing, reminding herself that she was fine. Everything was okay.

As her heart-rate slowed, she looked around the room, at the things she had collected as a child – her colourful silk scarves; the shells she had picked up on the beach as a child, sitting in a bowl on the windowsill; the pictures of fairies she'd pinned to the wall.

Her eyes fell on an object on the dresser. It was a music box that Granny had given her as a present, much to eight-year-old Rosemary's delight.

It was a long time since she'd looked inside, but she recalled the box contained a tiny ballerina that danced on a mirror as if by magic – though actually by magnets. She remembered keeping special stones and knick-knacks in there, things she had hoped would one day be valuable, but in all probability were not.

The memory struck a chord.

Dance…

Rosemary got up and opened the box, disappointed to find it empty except for the ballerina. She picked it up and placed it on the mirror in the centre of the box, and then she gasped.

"Athena!" she called out.

Athena came running.

"What is it? Are we being attacked again?"

"No," said Rosemary. "Look at what I found."

"It's…a toy jewellery box?"

"Look closer."

"What am I looking for?"

Rosemary pointed to the lace skirt, worn by the tiny ballerina, then to the blue velvet lining of the box. "This must be it!"

Athena looked sceptical. "Was that Granny Thorn's or yours?"

"It was mine. Granny gave it to me," Rosemary said. "Remember what she said – the answer is in the *present*!"

"But it's empty," Athena pointed out.

"It's really cool. Watch this," said Rosemary, twisting the latch to wind it up. The box immediately began to chime out a song, and Rosemary set it down on the dresser. They watched as the little ballerina started to dance, propelled by her own magnetic stand and the inner workings of the box.

"Granny used to always sing this to me," Rosemary said.

Come away my little child,
through the forests of the wild.
Feel the pulling deep within,
Trees will dance and trees will sing,
until they die and fall
elemental magic calls,
until we let the light shine though, rise up and seize it all.

"You know that's not how the original poem goes," Athena said as Rosemary stopped singing.

"What poem?"

"You know? The Yates poem. It's really famous – about faeries and stuff."

Athena had a strange, unreadable expression on her face.

"It's funny. I can't remember that either. It might be part of Granny's spell."

"Or your memory could be bad in a perfectly ordinary way," Athena said.

"You're suggesting Granny made this version up?" Rosemary asked. "I wonder why?"

"Maybe she was teaching you how to break the binding this whole time!"

"You mean – that song is the key – like a magic chant?"

"Could be – either that or its instructions."

"What kind of instructions?"

"Like - go into the forest and find an old fallen tree and, I don't know, meditate?"

"Meditate?! What are you, a yoga guru?"

"Yes, meditate," said Athena. "Remember – the elder said to look within, and I'm pretty sure that song says the same thing."

"Oh, bother!"

Despite her resistance, Rosemary felt somewhat buoyed by their discovery.

"You're in a much better mood," Athena commented as they sipped their afternoon cups of tea.

"It's just nice to know that Granny has been teaching me this stuff...all along...leaving me clues for how to break the binding. I wasn't just an afterthought."

"She really went to great lengths to keep all this stuff hidden, didn't she?" Athena said. "Which isn't exactly reassuring. It means that whoever was after her was very bad news."

"It was all so long ago," Rosemary said. "Does that mean we can cross off a whole bunch of suspects who would have been too young a few decades ago?"

"No," said Athena. "They might still be involved. Those guys who attacked us looked relatively young."

"Blast, you're right," Rosemary said. "And here I was, trying to find a way to avoid inviting a bunch of people to dinner."

"You still haven't invited everyone?!" Athena cried. "You'd better get a move on. Friday is only two days away."

"Oh fine," Rosemary said. "I'll do it after I've finished my tea."

And so she did. Rosemary spent a good chunk of the rest of the afternoon sending out messages and making phone calls to the remaining people on their list.

"I hope it's not too short notice," Rosemary said, finally putting her feet up after sending the last message.

"Like you said before," said Athena. "The real culprit is sure to come if they are keen on another look inside the house and a chance to steal the family magic."

"Speaking of that...we need a decoy box."

"Way ahead of you," said Athena. She wandered over to the cabinet and retrieved a small wooden carved box of a similar size to the one in the library.

"Brilliant! When did you find that?"

"While you were off having your nanna nap earlier."

"It's perfect," said Rosemary, examining the empty box.

"Maybe we can sprinkle some gold powder over it to make it look more magical," Athena suggested.

"Oh, yeah?" said Rosemary. "And where are we going to find that? You know all about my aversion to glitter."

"Don't remind me about my school production disaster," Athena said. "But I know where Granny kept a whole lot of strange, coloured powders."

"What? Why would she do that?"

"I suspect they're a magical ingredient," said Athena. "I think I saw something about using powders as a base for charms."

She wandered over to the dining room where piles of books were still stacked up and returned with *Altazar's Compendium of Enchantments.*

"Your favourite book," Rosemary muttered.

"Look – it says here that powders are an effective vehicle for spells, especially those directed at other people. Hmm...that gives me an idea..."

Athena scanned the following three pages of the book. "This might work."

"What?" Rosemary asked.

"It's a green powder...a spell that reveals malicious intent...only you have to blow it directly into people's faces."

"Sounds delightful," Rosemary remarked.

"It could be a useful tool to have on Friday," Athena insisted. "Especially if your rather vague plan turns out fruitless."

"It does sound like something that might come in handy," Rosemary said. "Though we are not going to make many friends if that's our way of welcoming them!"

"No," Athena admitted, reading on. "It's best left as a backup plan, especially considering its potential side effects are eye burns and vomiting."

"Definitely not my first choice," Rosemary agreed.

The sky outside had darkened by this time, and Rosemary began thinking about what to eat for dinner. She went to the fridge, only to find it stocked with a leg of mutton and half a dozen other new ingredients, which she was certain hadn't been there before.

"Hey Athena!" she called out, waving the large cut of meat around.

"What on earth?"

"I love having a magical refrigerator!" Rosemary crowed.

"How...?"

"Remembered how I mentioned making roast mutton yesterday?"

"No way!" Athena said, bounding over to the kitchen. "Ooh, and look! Cornish Pasties! I was craving them this morning."

"Splendid. This brings the term 'smart-appliance' to a whole new level! Cornish pasties for dinner?" Rosemary said.

"Not sure they're a traditional dinner food," Athena said. "But who cares!"

Rosemary turned the oven on to heat up the pasties and then looked in the pantry for something appropriate to serve on the side. She was interrupted by a knock at the door.

Startled, Rosemary looked at Athena, whose eyes were wide.

"What do you think that could be?" Rosemary asked.

"Nothing good, that's for sure," Athena replied.

"Do you think they'll go away if we don't answer?"

"Actually, I think they'll probably break in..."

"Oh, fine," Rosemary said. "I guess I should go and check to see who it is, at least."

"Wait," said Athena, grabbing Rosemary by the Arm. "What if it's Dad?"

"Why would he be here?"

"You asked him to bring all our stuff, remember?"

"Oh, yeah...That's right. Well, if it's Dain, then we should definitely answer the door and help him to bring things in."

"I don't want you going near that man," Athena insisted.

"Even after the protection charm?"

"We don't know if it works," said Athena.

"So, what do you propose?" Rosemary asked.

"I'll answer the door and tell him you're occupied."

"He's not going to buy that."

"You're sick with terrible di—"

"Enough!" Rosemary said. "I'm not letting you answer the door in case it's someone dangerous."

Athena crossed her arms and pouted as Rosemary pushed past on her way towards the front door. She checked the side windows, just to make sure it wasn't anyone too dodgy looking.

"Well, that's strange," said Rosemary.

"Who is it?"

"It's just...a pile of boxes." She opened the door and looked around. "Yep, all I can see is boxes, which I really hope are our things."

She lifted the lid on one of them to find a pile of her old shoes. "Yep – it's our stuff...but where is Dain?"

"Is he over there in the car, maybe?" Athena asked.

Rosemary squinted into the darkness to see the vague outline of their old rust-bucket. "Dain?" she called out.

There was no answer, and so Rosemary approached the car, looking around warily, in case of attack.

The doors and car boot were open, and the key was sitting in the ignition, but there was no sign of Rosemary's deadbeat ex.

"Dad?" Athena called out into the night, but only an owl answered back. "That's just creepy," she said.

Rosemary locked up the car, and the two Thorns picked up the boxes and brought them into the foyer of the house, quickly closing and locking the front door behind them.

"Dad must have been here...surely," Athena said.

"But where did he go?" Rosemary asked. "Did someone attack him? Kidnap him?"

"Seems unlikely that they'd do it silently without disturbing us," said Athena. "Maybe your charm actually worked."

"What? You mean it teleported him somewhere else like in the space films?"

"Or...like it made him run away – very quickly?" Athena suggested, with more than a hint of doubt in her voice.

"Oh, well..." said Rosemary. "I guess that's for the best, as long as he's okay."

"I do not care if he's okay. He can rot."

"Athena!"

"Look – you're cross at Granny when she was actually pretty decent for the most part, albeit secretive and odd."

"That's different—"

"And you don't even talk to your parents."

"Because they only ever want to chat about saving my immortal soul and sending you off to bible camp!"

"So?! Imagine what it's like to have Dain for a father. I'd take bible camp and a secure, loving home any day over Dad nicking off with your wallet again."

Rosemary sighed. "Okay. Point taken."

"Great. So, you're not going to try to pretend he should be in my life anymore?"

"I guess I'll have to leave all that up to you," Rosemary replied. "You're the expert on your life, after all."

"And it's time you started treating me like I am!" said Athena.

Twenty-Two

Both to Rosemary's satisfaction and dismay, every single person she had invited on Friday had RSVP'd as attending. It was good to know that all the likely suspects would make it, as she'd woken in the middle of Wednesday night worrying that the real perpetrator might decline, and instead, use the distraction of the dinner to attack them.

On Thursday morning, Rosemary sat at the kitchen table, making lists of all the things she needed, while Athena painted her nails a deep aubergine purple.

"Do you think the fridge is reliable as a source of ingredients?" Rosemary asked. "And how fast does it even work?"

"How should I know?" Athena asked. "Why don't you test it? Fridge! I want Hobnobs! – Now go check."

"Okay," Rosemary got up and opened the fridge to find that the mutton roast was still there, however Hobnobs had not appeared. She looked at Athena and shook her head.

"Drat," Athena said. "Maybe it only does non-branded foodstuffs."

"You mean, like real food?" Rosemary asked.

"What even is *real*, anymore?"

"I wish I knew the answer to that," said Rosemary. "I might need to go into town and do a quick shop, just in case the magic falls through. Do you want to come?"

"Don't even think of leaving me alone in this house," Athena replied. "Plus, I can't trust you to remember to buy me Hobnobs."

They got ready. Even though the weather was fine for walking, they made their way into town in Granny's car, since they needed to carry all the shopping back somehow.

Myrtlewood village was bustling with people and cars. Rosemary managed to find a park near Burk's office, but deliberately avoided glancing at the old stone building as they made their way through the town square towards the local grocery shop.

"Oh, hello there?" Ferg's distinctive voice rang out from behind a tree.

"Hello...tree-Ferg," Rosemary said.

"I'm just regular Ferg," he said, stepping out from the tree holding old wilted blossoms. He reached down to the large box at his feet and drew out some fresh flowers.

"What are you doing there?" Athena asked.

"I'm replacing the old drooping blossoms in the displays with fresh ones," Ferg explained.

"Why do you start decorating so early if you just have to replace them?" Rosemary asked.

"It's just the nature of this season. It's tempestuous like that," said Ferg. He shook his head sagely. "But you have to do what you can to please the Gods. We must feast for Brigid. Demeter must return to put the world to rights!"

"You really believe in the gods, across multiple pantheons, huh?" Rosemary asked.

Ferg lowered his voice. "Shh. Of course I do! And if you aren't careful, they'll show you exactly how real they are. Now get out of here before they hear your lack of faith and send a lightning bolt this way."

"You're serious," said Athena, shaking her head in disbelief.

"Or seriously superstitious," Rosemary muttered under her breath, only to receive a sharp kick from her daughter.

"So," Ferg said. "I hear you're planning a bit of a get-together tomorrow night."

"Oh..." said Rosemary.

"Did we invite him?" Athena whispered.

"Was I supposed to? I can't remember," Rosemary hissed. "Did we suspect him?"

"I think we suspected just about everyone," Athena whispered back.

"Maybe we'll just invite the whole town and see what happens."

Athena gave her a tense look.

Rosemary turned back to Ferg to see he was clearly awaiting his invitation awkwardly.

"Won't you join us?" Rosemary asked.

"Excellent," said Ferg, skipping up and down on the spot like a fawn. "I'd be delighted to accept."

Rosemary and Athena walked away, slightly disconcerted.

"It'll all end in a flaming pile of eye burns and vomiting and we'll be banished from Myrtlewood forever," Rosemary grumbled.

"That's way more likely than it should be," Athena said.

"We haven't mixed up that powder charm yet," said Rosemary.

"Actually, I did it this morning while you were having a lie in."

"Athena!"

"What? It's a backup plan."

"A terrible one."

"It could come in handy," Athena insisted.

"What *would* come in handy is some kind of defensive spell, like a charm to banish your enemies," said Rosemary.

"I cooked up a couple of those too..." said Athena. "Though I don't know if any of them will work."

"That's excellent. Well done, you," Rosemary said.

Their grocery shopping took longer than expected, as every second person seemed to want to introduce themselves and chat and mention they'd heard about the dinner party on Friday night and then pause awkwardly, waiting to be invited, but Rosemary was onto them and waited out the silence before saying a cheerful. "Got to dash! Nice to meet you," and continuing on her way.

Athena did manage to con her mother into buying a packet of crisps as they made their way around the aisle of the small and independent grocery shop, which was surprisingly well-stocked for a small town.

By the time they made it back to the car, they were both starving.

"Quick stop at Marjie's?" Rosemary suggested. "I'm sure it's dangerous for me to drive with low blood sugar."

"Agreed," Athena said. "I'm sure it's dangerous being in your presence with low blood sugar."

"Dangerous for you, or me?"

"Both," said Athena.

Marjie's tea shop was bustling, and they were lucky to find a table, but as soon as they sat down, Marjie was on her way over with two large roast beef sandwiches and a pot of tea.

"Is this for us?" Rosemary asked.

"Of course it is," Marjie said. "I saw you coming from across the square and thought I knew just what you needed."

"It actually is exactly what I feel like," Athena said. "How did you guess?"

"I have a knack fer these things," said Marjie proudly.

Marjie left them to attend to other customers, and Athena gave Rosemary a pleading look. "See, she can't possibly be one of the suspects. She's way too nice. We have to take her off our list."

"Niceness does not preclude murder," Rosemary said. "Besides, it's not doing her any harm. She doesn't even know about it."

"But what if she finds out?" Athena asked. "It'll break her poor old heart. And I'd feel rotten for going along with all this – accepting her hospitality."

"It's impossible not to," said Rosemary, holding up a wad of cash she found stashed under the teapot. "I tried to pay her the other day, but she's given our money back – with interest!"

"She *can't* be the culprit," Athena insisted. "She's had plenty of opportunities to poison us, plus she could have come to the house any time, and we'd have let her right in, but she hasn't even tried."

They started eating, enjoying the soft fresh bread and tender beef, the tang of pickles and crisp salad.

"How's the lunch?" Marjie said, having clearly just returned from serving other customers.

"Great, thanks!" said Athena, taking another big bite of her sandwich.

"Listen," said Margie, lowering her voice. "I've been meaning to pop in and see you. I have a wee charm prepared that you can use when people arrive tomorrow. It should track their movements through the house, so you'll be able to see anything out of the ordinary. I can bring by the components and show you how it works later on."

"Thank you," Rosemary said. "That sounds perfect."

Marjie beamed at them and then left them to it.

"See..." Athena said.

"She just invited herself around to the house," Rosemary pointed out. "And you said that was perfect."

"Well, what was I supposed to say? Stay away, foul demon?"

"You obviously don't want her to think we were suspicious of her, because you care about her feelings."

They finished up their meals and drove somewhat solemnly back to Thorn Manor.

Rosemary began the preparation for the following day's dinner party almost immediately, leaving Athena to pour over the books still cluttering the dining table. It was rather peaceful, chopping onions in Granny's lovely wooden-panelled kitchen. It had been a long time since Rosemary properly cooked a meal. She used to love it, but life and stress and being strapped for cash had gotten in the way.

As she began to sauté the diced onions with spices she was reminded of the year and a half of cheffing school she'd gotten through before her pregnancy with Athena and tight finances had forced her to drop out. She'd wanted to specialise in pastry cheffing and become a chocolatier, for surely there had been nothing better in the world to young Rosemary than good chocolate.

Chocolate... Even her very favourite thing had lost its appeal over the years of struggle for survival. Rosemary hardly ever indulged in it these days, though in her occasional daydreams, she was stirring up her own truffle blends and inventing interesting flavour combinations like passionfruit and coriander, or quince and sage, or blackberries and thyme.

Why does life have to always get in the way of dreams? she lamented.

A knock at the door disturbed Rosemary's truffly dreams.

"Marjie!" Athena called out from the next room.

"Let her in," Rosemary called back.

"Of *course*, Mum!"

A moment later, Marjie bustled into the kitchen with a tray of unusual objects, followed by Athena.

"Hello dear," Marjie said, kissing Rosemary on the cheek. "Now, I won't keep you long. I see that you're busy there." She nodded to the pan of onions that Rosemary had been occasionally stirring as they caramelised.

"No worries," said Rosemary. "I can just turn this down."

She adjusted the heat to very, very low and stepped away from the stove as Marjie placed her tray down on the kitchen table.

"Now," Marjie said, picking up two clear crystals. "You place these two on either side of the front door...like so." She took them over to the door and put them down near the bottom of the doorframe on both sides.

"This one hangs above the door." She held out a little pink bouquet, disguising a bundle in its midst. "I've tried to camouflage it in the flowers to make it less obvious." She passed the bouquet to Athena.

"Clever," said Athena.

Rosemary merely nodded.

"I'll let you hang that up, dear," said Marjie. "I wouldn't want to put my back out, trying."

"Sure thing," Athena said and skipped off to hang the bundle.

Marjie returned her attention to her tray. "And this—" She produced another bundle, which was black this time. "This goes in your pocket when you're welcoming them in. Be sure to shake hands or make some kind of skin contact with every single one of them."

"Very well," said Rosemary. "What's the rest of it for?"

"Oh, the other bundles are to be placed in the key corners of the rooms where the guests are likely to be. I'll let you do that part, too. After the working, we'll be able to see trails for every one of them and where they've been."

"Thank you for going to all this trouble," Rosemary said.

"Oh, it's nothing, dear," said Marjie. "My only concern right now is keeping you both safe."

Rosemary felt a stab of guilt. She badly hoped this wasn't all an act on Marjie's part, but even if it wasn't, it felt wrong to suspect her.

"I'm back!" said Athena, bounding back into the room. Rosemary marvelled at her ability to behave like a sullen teenager one minute and like an excited eight-year-old the next. "Hey, Marjie, won't you stay for a cup of tea?" Athena asked.

"Oh, I wouldn't want to trouble you," Marjie said.

"It's no trouble," said Athena, putting on the kettle. "Take a seat."

Rosemary gave Athena a puzzled look. It wasn't that she minded Marjie staying for tea. Indeed, she was slightly embarrassed that she didn't think to offer herself. It was more that Athena was acting out of character. She was clearly up to something.

"While the kettle boils," Athena said. "I just want to try something..."

"Athena," Rosemary said with a hint of warning in her voice. She reached out for her daughter's arm, but Athena shook her off.

Rosemary noticed an instant later that Athena had something hidden in her closed fist.

"Marjie, will you close your eyes for just a moment?" Athena said, walking over to the kitchen table.

"Oh course, dear."

"Athena!" Rosemary whispered urgently, but it was too late.

Athena raised her palm to reveal a sparkling green powder and blew it gently towards Marjie. The powder moved, slower than seemed physically possible, creating a small dust cloud around Marjie, who sneezed. The green turned to orange, and then the powder vanished. She opened her eyes in surprise. The colour was quickly fading back to normal.

"Athena!" Rosemary said sternly.

"What was that?" Marjie asked, surprised.

"Just something I was practicing," Athena said with feigned innocence.

"Trying to prove a point, more like," said Rosemary.

"And it worked! I was right!" Athena crowed.

"Just as well we didn't see any of those side effects!" Rosemary hissed.

"That's why I told her to close her eyes," Athena insisted. "The side effects are more likely if it gets into people's eyes or mouth."

"Oh, come now, you two," Marjie said. "I think I've worked out what that just was."

Rosemary and Athena looked at each other, hoping Marjie was assuming something else.

"Did you really suspect me?" the older woman asked sadly.

There was a moment of tension in which Rosemary felt a great rush of guilt.

"I didn't," Athena insisted. "Which is why I had to show Mum that you're innocent." She scampered back to the kitchen towards the tea things.

Another moment passed where Rosemary thought of a hundred ways to apologise to her grandmother's closest friend for suspecting her of her murder, and all of them fell flat in her mind.

"Well, I suppose you can't be too careful these days," Marjie said cheerfully, sipping the tea that Athena had just brought her.

"You're not cross?" Rosemary asked.

"I don't see why I should be," said Marjie. "I think it's grand that you clever girls are doing such a good job of looking out for yourselves – I can't fault you for that! I care very much about the both of you."

Rosemary smiled. "I *am* sorry," she said.

"No need to apologise, dear. You're doing a great job – and I'm glad I passed your test! Now I'll leave you to your preparation, but do give us a bell if I can help with anything else."

Twenty-Three

Rosemary slept fitfully that night.

She dreamed of walking in the forest surrounding the house, searching...searching for the source of their power.

I've got to release the binding...

The music from the ballerina box started to play, and Rosemary began dancing – dancing...she couldn't stop, even though the dancing was making her younger and younger until she was just a small child screaming out.

Noooo!

Rosemary awoke to twisted, sweaty sheets.

"Mum? Are you alright?" Athena was there, in the doorway.

"Just a bad dream, love," Rosemary said.

"It's the magic, isn't it?" said Athena. "It's getting to you."

"Some kind of tension does seem to be building," Rosemary admitted.

"The whole house feels like it's humming slightly," said Athena.

"It does, doesn't it? But don't worry. We're going to work this out."

The day was taken up by preparations for dinner. Rosemary stuffed the mutton leg – which was thankfully still in the fridge – with garlic and rosemary sprigs, and smothered it in olive oil and sea salt. Then she set to work on an enormous pot of her ratatouille soup, a favourite recipe that she hadn't bothered to prepare in years. Later, when the mutton was roasting slowly in the oven, she peeled potatoes to be served with it, and then prepared several large chocolate treacle tarts, enough for all the guests. Finally, she got to work on the salad course of delicately sliced pears with toasted walnuts, rocket, basil, and parmesan with a mustard and lemon juice dressing designed to protect the pears from oxidising. She kept the rocket and basil aside to add right before serving, lest they wilt.

"This is all very swish," Athena said, coming into the kitchen to see dozens of matching plates and bowls stacked up, ready for the servings of food. Rosemary was toasting the walnuts in one of Granny's many large cast-iron pans.

"You're going to help dish this out, aren't you?" Rosemary said. "I'll have to keep an eye on the guests the whole time."

"Marjie and I have got you covered," said Athena.

"When did that happen?"

"When I walked her out to her car. She insisted on coming back here early to help out with dinner, and I accepted of course – now that we know she's definitely not a baddie."

"But she's already helped us enough," Rosemary said. "I'm going to forever be in debt of gratitude to that woman...and thank you," she said, hugging Athena. "That has actually given me a lot more peace of mind. I'm not sure how else I would juggle all this."

"What are daughters for?" said Athena, hugging her mother back.

"Winding me up and driving me batty?" Rosemary suggested.

"I think you do that well enough on your own."

Marjie did indeed arrive about an hour early, and headed straight to the kitchen to help Athena plate up the salad while Rosemary did a last-minute sweep around the house to check that everything was in order.

She couldn't very well move the box from the desk in the library to hide it, since touching it sent her somewhere else. Instead, she found the key for the library door and locked it, along with several other doors on the ground floor – just so it wasn't suspicious as the only locked door.

Athena had carefully placed the decoy box on the mantlepiece in the parlour. It stood there, gracefully dusted with a little gold power for magical effect and surrounded by sparkling crystals from Granny's drawer.

Satisfied that everything was as orderly as it could be, Rosemary headed upstairs to change into something less covered in food. She didn't have many nice dresses, being someone who preferred to live in jeans, but she had a simple black dress that looked okay if she paired it with a nice necklace and earrings. She chose the amethyst necklace that Granny had given her for her sixteenth birthday and a set of purple dangly earrings to match the colour, and even slipped on some simple black ballet flats instead of her usual boots, sneakers, or bare feet.

By the time Rosemary made it back downstairs, the salad course was resting on the kitchen table and the soup was being ladled into bowls, ready to be kept warm in the oven after she removed the lamb roast.

"Everything's in order!" Rosemary announced, sounding somewhat surprised.

"And don't you look lovely!" Marjie cooed.

"You clean up alright," Athena commented.

Rosemary shrugged. "That's high praise coming from a teenager."

"Stop stereotyping me," Athena said.

Just then, the doorbell rang.

"Now, have you got all the parts of my enchantment sorted?" Marjie asked.

"Yes," said Rosemary, picking up the key bundle from the kitchen sideboard and tucking it into the pocket of her dress. "The number one lesson here is to always buy dresses with pockets," she said sagely.

"Very good."

"Oh...music!" Rosemary cried. "I forgot."

"I've got that sorted," Athena said, bringing up the music app on her phone. "This is hooked up to the surround sound."

Rosemary smiled and then frowned. "What kind of music do you have lined up, exactly?" she asked. "And since when does Granny have surround sound? She doesn't even have a telly."

"Of course she does, silly," Marjie said. "It's behind the big tapestry in the parlour."

"And I made a playlist for exactly this occasion," said Athena, pressing play. Mediterranean acoustic music flooded through the house and Rosemary smiled.

"Now go get that door before everyone gives up on us!" Athena said.

To Rosemary's displeasure, the first guests to arrive were her not-so-dear cousins. Elamina looked resplendent, if icy, in a glittering midnight-toned gown, and Derse was in a three-piece suit.

Rosemary made a great effort not to breathe in Elamina's signature overly sweet floral perfume. She tried to smile, but it turned out to be more of a grimace. "Welcome," she said as she awkwardly reached out to shake her cousin's hands. It wasn't something that she'd normally do, but it was required for Marjie's enchantment to work and Rosemary figured they needed all the magical help they could get.

"Are we quite on time?" Elamina asked, looking at Rosemary's hand as if it was a days-old dead thing, but begrudgingly taking it and giving it a pathetic little shake.

"You are actually a little early," Rosemary said as she grimaced again, this time from the painful force of Derse's handshake. "Uh, haven't you ever heard of being fashionably late?"

Elamina gave a funny little laugh and muttered "fashionably" a few times, as if she was struggling to reconcile the concept with Rosemary's presence.

"Erm, come in, I guess," Rosemary said, taking their coats and leading them through into the parlour where Athena was now waiting as planned to offer them drinks and keep an eye on the general goings on.

"This is your…offspring?" Elamina asked, giving Athena a faint but vaguely genuine smile as she eyed her curiously.

"Yes, I suppose you haven't really met her properly," Rosemary said. "This is my daughter Athena."

"Charmed," Elamina said, holding out her dainty hand for Athena to shake. Derse merely nodded at the girl and accepted her offer of sherry. Elamina opted for straight whiskey.

The next to arrive was Constable Perkins, dressed in a bright blue blazer and a red bowtie.

"You made it!" Rosemary exclaimed, shaking his hand enthusiastically as she tried to suppress a giggle at his unusual outfit. "Right this way."

She led Constable Perkins into the parlour, enjoying the sight of her cousin's mortified faces as they surveyed their fellow guest. She deliberately introduced him with his police title to ensure they were on their best behaviour, hopefully for the entire evening.

"The cousins, eh?" the police officer in not-so-plain clothes said. "I've been meaning to have a chat with you both concerning your grandmother. Perhaps we can schedule an appointment now."

Elamina glared at Rosemary, who smiled with satisfaction, which was short-lived as another knock sounded at the door. She raced off to let in Liam who arrived with a well-recovered Sherry.

"Sorry, I didn't call or drop by," Sherry said, handing Rosemary a bottle of red wine. "I had so much to catch up on after a few days in bed!"

"No worries," said Rosemary, vigorously shaking their hands.

"So formal," Liam said as he shook back.

"Just being polite," said Rosemary, leading them over to Athena in the Parlour.

Perseus Burk arrived a few short minutes later in a silk shirt and black jacket, no tie. He held a bunch of white roses and another bottle of red wine, which he handed to Rosemary, who quickly put the bouquet down on the sideboard before Athena could see and make fun of her.

"Thank you," Rosemary said, not wanting to make eye-contact for very long with the handsome, yet very suspicious man – if he indeed was a man and not some other kind of creature entirely. She reached for his cold hand, which gave hers a little squeeze. Rosemary pulled back from the intimacy and waved Burk inside. Don June, the mayor, in his usual black and purple outfit was hot on his heels, arriving before Rosemary even had a chance to close the door.

"Thank you for coming at such short notice," she said.

"Nonsense! I'm always keen to socialise with the constituents – do keep me in mind for all future events," said Mr June. "It's just a shame that my husband couldn't make it tonight. He's out of town on business."

"Your husband?" Rosemary muttered absentmindedly.

"Yes, Zade. You'd love him."

"Maybe next time we'll get to meet him," said Rosemary, smiling.

No sooner had Rosemary shaken hands with the mayor and ushered him to the parlour when the door knocker sounded again.

This time, Despina and Geneviève stood on the doorstep, both frowning slightly, flanked by Ferg, who was grinning ear-to-ear.

"Beautiful night for a party!" Ferg said. "I was just pointing out to these two what an odd pair they make; the big one dresses young and the little one dresses old!"

Rosemary smiled apologetically at Despina, who was wearing pastel pink, and Geneviève, who was dressed entirely in black, wearing a long cocktail dress and coat, her chestnut hair falling in carefully tamed ringlets.

Rosemary managed to shake all of their hands and usher them into the parlour.

"Right, that's it then," she said to Athena, who had almost finished handing out drinks.

"Well..." Athena said.

The house seemed to hum at a stronger frequency than before.

Athena's eyes went wide. "Did you just feel that?"

Rosemary nodded and glanced around, but none of the guests seemed to notice the building intensity. They were all engaged in polite, impolite, or odd conversation. "What do you think it could be?" she asked in a whisper. "Is the house reacting to Granny's attacker being here?"

"Well, in that case, why did it start humming earlier before any guests arrived?" Athena asked. "And why did it build up now, after everyone is already inside, rather than when someone in particular entered?"

"You have a point," Rosemary said. "Maybe it's just reacting to having so many people – magical people – inside."

"Or maybe it's to do with the binding," Athena suggested quietly. "You said the energy was building up, and it was going to explode."

"Or implode," Rosemary reminded her.

"I don't much like the sound of either, especially when we're all inside."

"We can't very well conduct a dinner party out in the cold," Rosemary said.

"You could call it off," Athena pointed out.

"And waste all the effort we've put in just because the house is humming? I don't think so."

Rosemary turned back to the group and cleared her throat. Heads turned towards her, but then the door knocker sounded again, and she had to excuse herself once more.

Who on earth could that be?

Covvey Dunne and Agatha Twigg from the pub stood in the doorway, dressed in what Rosemary assumed were their fancy going-out clothes. Agatha wore a green sequined dress and Covvey had on a smoking jacket over a t-shirt and jeans.

"Erm, hello?" said Rosemary. She certainly did not remember inviting them.

"We're here for the party," Agatha said, bustling past.

"Oh..." Rosemary said. It was too late. They were both inside, and she hadn't managed to shake their hands. She thought about trying to turf them out, but then wondered if they'd come because they were involved with the sinister plot to steal the family magic. Of course, under normal circumstances, that would be more than enough to send people packing, but Rosemary felt some urgency in getting to the bottom of the mystery, since her freedom was at stake. She was not going to be jailed, especially for a crime she'd never ever want to commit. She shook hands with them, hoping that the charm worked once people were already inside, and led them to the parlour where they proceeded to glare at many of the other guests.

Rosemary rushed back to the kitchen.

"Any chance of adding a couple of extra plates?" she asked Marjie who was setting the mutton to rest.

"You can't count?" Marjie asked, smiling cheekily.

"More like gate-crashers," Rosemary said.

"Who are they?" asked Marjie.

"That Covvey man and Agatha Twigg."

"Typical trouble makers," Marjie said. "I love them both, but they can't manage to mind their own business. Always sticking their heads in where they're not welcome."

Rosemary shrugged. "Is there enough food to go around?"

"I think you're forgetting I have a certain knack for this thing," said Margie. She twiddled her fingers and two more bowls filled with soup and salad appeared.

"You just made that?"

"I replicated them – making them from scratch would be too hard, but a little replication is easy as pie. Now, get out there and attend to your guests. Poor Athena is in there all alone with that lot!"

Rosemary gave Marjie a quick hug. "Thanks so much for all your help."

"It's nothing, dear. Now go!"

Upon returning to the parlour, Rosemary picked up a glass and teaspoon and tinkled them together in the universal sign for making a speech.

"Thank you all for coming," she said. "In a moment, we'll go through to the dining room for dinner, but I just wanted to say a few words first."

She had practiced the carefully designed speech, but was sure it would come out garbled. The important thing was creating the right level of intrigue about The Box.

"Granny Thorn was very dear to me," Rosemary said. "And though I miss her very much, it's an honour to be here, in her house, surrounded by many of her friends and loved ones."

Rosemary noticed that Elamina and Derse were glaring at her, but she pushed on. "When we first came to Myrtlewood, it was just for a meeting. We only packed for one day – that was almost a week ago, though it feels much longer and not entirely in a bad way," she smiled warmly. There was a small murmur of laughter from the group.

"But Myrtlewood has won our hearts over in this short time, and we are delighted to stay here as caretakers of Granny's house and all her unusual things."

Another little murmur of laughter, though none of it from the cousins, who looked even angrier than before.

"For example, the refrigerator seems to fill itself, quite as it pleases, and we've hardly had to do a lick of housework. Trust Granny to find a way out of dusting!" Slightly louder laughter rang around the room. "Or this box," Rosemary said, gesturing towards the mantlepiece. "Granny told us it was extremely important, yet she didn't even say why, so we just keep it here on the mantlepiece, hoping it does whatever it needs to do."

There were many curious looks towards the decoy box sitting innocently between the crystals.

"Anyway, I'm sure you're all starved," Rosemary said. "So, without any further delay, come through and eat!"

She opened the side door to the parlour, which led directly into the dining room. The big wooden table had been beautifully laid out with dark blue cloth napkins, polished silver cutlery, and Granny Thorn's special crystal glasses.

Everyone took their seats as Rosemary and Athena poured wine they'd found in Granny's cellar for those who wanted it, and offered grape juice as a non-alcoholic option.

When Rosemary got to Geneviève, she didn't bother offering her wine, but went straight to the grape juice. The girl scowled at her. Rosemary gave her a cheeky grin. "Maybe in a few years, I'll be offering you wine," she whispered.

"If you survive that long," Geneviève said through gritted teeth.

Rosemary looked at the girl, who flashed her a charming smile and giggled, and Rosemary giggled back, slightly baffled by the joke.

As she continued round the table, there was another knock at the door.

"Oh no!" Rosemary said under her breath to Athena. "What now?"

"It's probably just Finnigan," Athena said. "Don't worry. I'll get it."

"I forgot about him!" Rosemary said.

"I wish you forgot about him earlier and stopped giving me a hard time," Athena hissed and bolted towards the door. Rosemary stuck her head out of the parlour to check if the new arrival was indeed Finnigan. The broody teen stood in the doorway, eyes locked on Athena.

Satisfied that it wasn't any other uninvited guests, Rosemary ducked back to the kitchen to tell Marjie it was time to serve the salad.

"Way ahead of you," Marjie said, holding a big tray of salad bowls.

Rosemary picked up a second tray of salads and headed back to the dining room, passing the teenagers, who seemed to be hovering by the door.

"I have to leave," Finnigan said.

"But you only just got here."

"Sorry." He turned to Rosemary, looking awfully pale. "Thank you for your hospitality, uhm, be careful."

"I'll...see him out," Athena said.

Rosemary shook her head in astonishment. "Teenagers are so peculiar," she muttered to herself, but as she wandered back towards the dinner party, she felt a creeping suspicion about The Boy.

Twenty-Four

Athena was relieved to escape the noise and bustle of the dinner party, even if it was only for a few minutes. Despite the comparative peace outside, she walked Finnigan out with a jumble of questions circulating in her mind.

"What was all that about?" she asked when the front door was closed.

"Shh," Finnigan whispered. *Not here. Some of them have powerful hearing*, he added in her mind.

He took Athena's hand and led her around the side of the house. She felt even more perplexed and slightly concerned.

"This should be far enough away," Finnigan said, still keeping his voice low. They had passed the conservatory and were almost at the back of the house, near the forest.

"What is going on?" Athena asked. "And why do we have to keep our voices down, can't we speak telepathically?"

"It doesn't come easily to you yet," said Finnigan. "There's too much of a risk of getting things mixed up, and I want to make sure that doesn't happen."

"Things are about as clear as mud," Athena said. "Why couldn't you stay for dinner? What's wrong?"

"There are enemies in your midst," Finnigan said.

"How can you tell?" Athena asked suspiciously. "Actually, there are supposed to be enemies at the dinner party. That's all part of the plan."

"You plan to dine with evil-doers?"

"Why do you speak in such an old-fashioned way?" Athena asked.

Finnigan shrugged. "Athena, they are our mortal enemy."

"I still don't understand what you're talking about," said Athena. "Can't you tell me? Who are the enemies? We've just invited all the suspects who might have killed Granny Thorn, but we don't know which one it is."

"They are not one," said Finnigan cryptically. "They are many."

"Why are you speaking in riddles? It's almost like you're not even able to tell me the truth." This thought upset Athena so much that tears pricked the corners of her eyes. After all, this was a life and death situation – not a time for playing games.

"The truth is bound," Finnigan said, just as a gust of wind blew his hair away from his grey-blue eyes. He turned as if responding to a sound that Athena could not hear and stared off into the forest as a thick mist started to descend over the trees.

"Come with me," he insisted. "I can keep you safe from them."

"No," Athena said. "I can't. My mother would kill me, and anyway, I hardly know you."

There was a moment of silence, and then Finnigan spoke. "I must go now. I wish I could protect you. Please be safe. Do whatever you can to get them out of your house. You're much more powerful than you realise."

"Finnigan..." Athena reached out for him as he walked backwards into the forest.

"Goodbye, Athena. Take care."

"Wait!" Athena said, but it was too late.

Finnigan had slipped away into the mist. She watched as it curled around him, and for a moment, Athena could have sworn his features flickered into something more ancient and beautiful and slightly frightening.

As he disappeared, his voice echoed inside her mind.

You are one of us. Stay away from the enemy. They will only do you harm.

Twenty-Five

Rosemary walked into the dining room to start distributing the salads with Marjie right behind her.

"Psst! Rosemary!" Marjie hissed from the side of the room, where she'd put her tray down on a cabinet.

"What?"

"Come with me for a minute."

Rosemary followed Marjie just outside the door and out of earshot of the guests.

"I can't believe you're trying to feed vampires human food!" Marjie said quietly but urgently.

"What?" Rosemary said. "I realise my cousins are very pale, but I don't think they're vampires."

"Oh, not them!" Said Marjie. "But several of the others!"

"Who?!" Rosemary asked.

"It's not polite for me to say," said Marjie. "They get rather cross if you start telling people about their...condition. Vampires are very private."

Rosemary frowned. "Honestly, Marjie – how was I supposed to know?! It's not like I'm asking about their sexuality or anything," she said. "I simply want to know which of my guests want to drink my blood." Rosemary gulped, trying to ward off her own rising panic. There was too much new information to process, and she felt flustered. Athena was nowhere in sight, and the guests were no doubt getting hungry.

"Leave it to me," Marjie said. "I'll just enchant a few of these bowls so that they're vampire-friendly and everyone will be none the wiser."

"What happens if they just eat regular food?" Rosemary asked.

"You don't want to know," said Marjie. "It gets very messy. You just go and check on the chocolate tarts, and I'll sort this out."

Rosemary headed off to the kitchen, feeling flustered. The chocolate tarts were cooked, so she removed them from the oven to set and then headed back to the dining room, where the salads were all laid out. All of them looked completely normal, and Rosemary eyed the guests warily, wondering which of them were vampires.

Athena was still mysteriously missing, but reappeared moments later, blushing slightly. Rosemary was too relieved at her return to be cross about her temporary vanishing act. It had probably only been a few minutes, but still she wasn't too happy about the short time she'd spent not knowing where her daughter was.

Get used to it, Granny's voice said in the back of Rosemary's mind.

What? Granny? Is that actually you?

O'course it is, Granny replied. *Now eat something before you get low blood sugar and completely lose it.*

Rosemary scoffed down her salad, wondering how much Granny knew, or how much she could reveal about the present situation.

Which ones are vampires? Rosemary asked in her mind.

It's rude to say, Granny replied. *But you can probably work it out easily enough.*

I cannot tell. They all look perfectly normal to me. Rosemary surveyed her oddball guests. *Well, not normal, but not evil.*

Don't stereotype vampires like that, said Granny. *That's also rude. They're no more evil than human beings...well, most of them.*

Granny's assertion was slightly reassuring to Rosemary, who had felt rather prickly about having vampires at her dinner table. She surveyed the guests to see if she could tell which ones weren't breathing.

They certainly were an odd bunch. Constable Perkins was getting slightly sloshed, looking even more clown-like and attracting disturbed glances from Elamina and Derse, who had only just recovered from their shock when Marjie – who they must have assumed was a servant – sat down on the other side of them to eat. Burk appeared to be wrapped up in a conversation with Liam and Sherry.

Rosemary thought about it for a while. She hadn't seen Sherry during the day, only at night at the pub. Did that mean...? The only other two guests she'd never seen during the day were the gate-crashers, Covvey and Agatha, who both seemed harmless, if a bit rough around the edges.

Rosemary wondered if that meant that they were the vampires here. *Is it common for vampires to invite themselves to dinner? Don't they need to be invited in?*

She would have appreciated a reply to these questions, but Granny seemed to have vacated the space she'd been occupying in Rosemary's mind.

Of course, there was still Burk with his cold hands and his supernatural speed, though Rosemary had seen him in his offices during the daytime and in the pub at lunch. She really knew so little about vampires outside of fiction and wished she could ask Marjie or Granny more questions.

As Athena and Marjie served the soup course, the whole house seemed to tremble, making some of the glassware tinkle subtly. The guests looked at each other and then at Rosemary, who merely shrugged, though a concerned glance passed between her and Athena.

What's going on with the house?!

Rosemary watched the guests carefully for anything suspicious. Just as they were finishing up the soup, Burk excused himself and got up from the table, saying he needed a pit-stop.

Rosemary had been waiting for just such an occurrence.

Aha! she thought. *He's trying to steal the decoy box!* She got up from the table a moment later, saying she was going to check on the main course, leaving Athena to keep watch over the other guests. Instead, she made her way directly to the parlour, only to find it empty. The box was still exactly where it ought to have been, undisturbed.

Panic shot through Rosemary. She felt an urgent need to check the library, but as she headed in that direction, she noticed a tall, dark figure standing by the stairwell. She froze, her mind darting back to the crow man, but as her eyes adjusted to the lack of light, she realised it was Burk standing there.

"Uh, hello?" Rosemary said. "The loo is the other direction."

Burk turned towards her, a pained expression on his face. "He was here, wasn't he? This was where it happened?"

Rosemary gaped as an entirely different kind of panic floored her. *He knows!*

"I don't know what you're talking about," Rosemary said, trying to play dumb.

"My brother..." Burk said. "He's been missing for days, which wouldn't normally be too unusual. But I was wondering after the attack on your house..."

"Perseus..." Rosemary tried to think of a million reasons why she couldn't possibly have killed his brother, but none came.

"I can sense his essence," he said. "It was here that he...that he died. The dusting, it leaves a residue, you know."

Rosemary coughed. "Oh...gross..."

"Tell me the truth," Burk said, his voice steady and even, but chafing around the edges. "It was you who did it. You killed him, didn't you?"

There was nothing for it. "Yes," Rosemary said. "He attacked us. He went after Athena..."

Burk's eyes were dark as onyx and Rosemary wished she could take back her confession for fear of retribution. What was she thinking, incurring the wrath of the Burk family so openly and readily? They'd surely come after her and make the rest of her life a living nightmare, for as long as it lasted, anyway.

But Burk just grimaced, tears gleaming in corners of eyes. "I suppose he had that coming," he said.

"You—you're not mad at me?" Rosemary stuttered.

"He would have killed you," said Burk. "You know what we are, don't you?"

"I knew what he was, but..."

"You must have known. You fed me blood-enchanted food."

"That was Marjie," Rosemary insisted. "She told me there were vampires here, but that it would be rude to tell me who they were."

Burk gave a dry chuckle. "People in this town are so polite. But you must have suspected me."

"I didn't think it was genetic," Rosemary said.

"It's not," said Burk. "It's a long story as to how we both got turned."

"I have all night, I guess," said Rosemary, only to be interrupted by a loud scream from the direction of the parlour, followed by another great tremble from the house. "On second thought, maybe we can save the story for another time!"

Rosemary ran back to the dining room to see the guests dispersing out into the hallway. Her eyes widened as she looked through the open door at the carnage as she was buffeted back by strong winds.

Terrifying darkness quaked from the centre of the room in the form of a vortex. This one was even more intense than the one that had appeared at the front door days earlier, and it seemed to have opened up in the centre of the table. An ominous, low vibration underscored the swirling black darkness inside. Gales of wind blew in both directions at once, sweeping out of the room, around the sides of the chasm, and pulling in through the centre. Rosemary braced herself against the strong currents of air, checking for everyone's safety but mostly looking for her daughter.

"Athena!"

Several of the dinner guests clung to the side of the room. Elamina and Derse gripped tensely onto the windowsill, and Constable Perkins was wrapped around the cabinet on the other side of the room, groaning softly.

"Athena!" Rosemary called.

Suddenly, her daughter was at her side.

"The house can't hold all these people!" Athena called out. "I knew this was going to happen!"

"It's the family magic," said Marjie, from behind them. "You've done something to start the unbinding process, but it's only partially complete. It needs to be released fully or..." Marjie's words trailed off.

Rosemary didn't want to know what came after the "or". She could guess well enough that more chaos and danger would ensue.

"You can do it, Rosemary," Marjie said. "You're the one with the power here."

"Yes, Mum, you can. This is our magic – and you're the one Granny Thorn chose to inherit it after all."

"But I don't know what to do!" Rosemary shrieked, beside herself with panic. Suddenly the burden on her shoulders was overwhelming, and she felt shattered, as if the disconnected parts of herself would never reunify into a cohesive whole. Anxiety was a vice in her chest, tightening her breathing.

"Just calm down dear," said Marjie. "It will come to you."

"Yes," Athena said. "Calm down and look within. Remember?"

"You know I hate that," Rosemary said, trying to breathe deeply, though the tightness in her torso made it impossible.

"There's no time like the present to change your mind and become its biggest fan," said Athena. "What did Granny Thorn's song say? Meditate in a forest of something?"

Rosemary wanted to argue and kick and scream, but there was no time for regressing to her childhood state and throwing the tantrum she felt was warranted. She had to take action. All her defence mechanisms were to run and hide, but that wouldn't work now. She had to take back control. She couldn't waste any more energy feeling panicked. Instead, she closed her eyes.

She listened to her own heart beat in her chest.

Calm, she instructed her body. *Calm down. Focus.*

She waited a moment longer until she felt a gentle easing and then took several deep, slow breaths. It was time to focus. There was no time to go to the actual forest now, like the song implied, but everyone kept telling her to bloody well look within, so, keeping her eyes closed she imagined she was in a forest.

The sounds around her faded to birdsong with a distant rumbling. The gales softened into a summer breeze. Rosemary wandered deeper into the forest.

It was so beautiful, so peaceful she could stay there all day, but an urgency tugged at her. She followed the humming sound into the darker and darker wood all around her, with barely any light filtering through. Then, up ahead, she saw it.

The giant light crystal shone through the vines from which it was trapped.

What do I do? Rosemary asked in her mind, seeking guidance from anyone who might hear her, but particularly from Granny.

You must have confidence in yourself, Granny's voice responded.

Thank goodness you're here with me, Rosemary thought, relieved.

I'm always with you, my dear. You just need to connect with your true self and you'll sense my presence. I'm always watching out for you.

Rosemary quashed her frustrations with Granny for the moment, figuring this wasn't the time to relitigate the 'why didn't you just tell me?' line.

Please give me solid instructions on what to do next, Rosemary replied.

First, trust in yourself. Have confidence...then, when you're absolutely sure of yourself, reach out and touch the crystal – not the vines and say the words I taught you.

What words? Rosemary asked frantically.

But Granny's presence had vanished again.

"Infuriating old bat!" Rosemary muttered. *Okay...so I just have to be confident. Rosemary. You are awesome. You've got this. Everything is coming up roses. This will be a piece of cake. The right words will come. It's obvious. Just go for it!*

She reached out towards the crystal, careful to avoid the vines. She managed to only hesitate slightly as her arm extended.

Her hand connected with the light crystal. A great jolt of energy coursed through her, making her feel powerful, indeed...and slightly high.

"Wowee! Okay. The words are...Blue, lace, dance?"

Nothing happened, except the vines began to bulge and creep tighter around the crystal, slowly inching closer to her hand.

"Oh, crud!" said Rosemary, then wished she could take it back, as "crud" clearly wasn't a magic word either.

She closed her eyes and took a deep breath.

I'm looking within...I'm being confident...I'm unbinding the family magic...

A shimmer of light swirled in the darkness in front of her. She could feel her wildness growing, blooming, breaking free from the cage it had been locked in.

Another voice broke through her thoughts, and this time it wasn't Granny's. It was an ancient voice, but light and airy and fresh at the same time.

You are not ready. You must connect to your elemental core to free the Thorn family magic.

"Drat!" said Rosemary as she was immediately jolted out of the forest in her. She found herself staring up at the ceiling of Thorn Manor.

Twenty-Six

"Blasted bloody Hades!" Rosemary yelled.

Liam and Marjie stood over her, looking concerned.

"What's going on?" she asked. "Where's Athena? What happened to that massive chasm in the dining room?"

"I'm here, Mum," Athena said from behind Marjie. "And things seemed to have settled down in there."

Rosemary propped herself up, relieved to see her daughter, and doubly relieved that the chasm, along with its vortex of doom, had disappeared. "Well, I can't say that was a rollicking success," she said.

"What happened?" Athena asked.

"I was about to ask you the same thing," said Rosemary. "Not much at all happened on my end – I'll tell you that!"

Rosemary felt light and agile following her encounter with the huge crystal. She jumped up and gave Athena a big hug before attempting to assess the damage. The dining room was in chaos and the few remaining guests were keeping well clear. Some of them were even milling around outside the house. She checked the parlour to find that the decoy box was, indeed, missing, though she was pleased that the door to the library remained locked. When she opened it, the real box was still firmly in place on the table.

I hope Marjie's spell worked, Rosemary thought. *Otherwise, we're back to square one.*

She was even more furious with Granny Thorn than she had been earlier. *Couldn't she have thought to mention me needing to connect with my elements or whatever?! Perhaps left me a handy instruction manual?*

It was a strange thing for Rosemary to ask for, seeing as she never read the instructions properly on anything, preferring to just muddle through on intuition and blind luck. But this particular situation clearly called for a detailed set of guidelines.

She apologised profusely to the remaining guests and told them she'd invite them back another time, though most of them looked at her as if they'd rather not chance it.

She noticed some distinct absences, too. Elamina and Derse were gone, as were the gate crashers. Ferg was nowhere in sight, and neither was Mr June. To Rosemary's slight disappointment, Burk had also made himself scarce. She'd been wanting to find out more about the mysterious vampire.

Despina and Geneviève were also understandably absent. Rosemary had some sympathy for them. She certainly wouldn't want to have any child in her care near a nightmare like the one that just appeared in the dining room.

Constable Perkins, his cheeks still flushed from wine and sherry, insisted on sticking around to investigate. He promptly fell asleep at the kitchen table, snoring slightly.

Marjie discreetly informed Rosemary that there was no hope of her tracking charm working since the vortex had scrambled all the energetic traces in the house.

"It looks like spaghetti," Marjie said.

"Oh, bother," Rosemary replied, disappointed that the evening she'd planned had been such a dismal failure.

Marjie insisted on sticking around. She and Athena had started on the dishes. Their clanking and chattering in the kitchen did not seem to disturb the police officer, who was clearly out of it. Rosemary made a note to ask Marjie what her secret was with getting teenagers to do chores so easily.

Aside from that, the last guests to leave were Liam and Sherry, who both kept offering to help clean up. Rosemary told them there was no need to do anything now, assuring them that if she needed help, she'd call them tomorrow. Sherry gave her a tight hug on her way out. Liam, however, lingered a little longer, his muscular frame taking up most of the doorway.

"Err, Rosemary?" he said, keeping his voice low so as to be out of earshot of the others.

"What is it?

"This might be a bad time, but...I was wondering, when things have settled down a bit...would you like to go out for a drink?"

Rosemary shrugged. "Of course," she said. "It'll be nice to have a bit of a catch up."

She was perplexed as to Liam's obvious discomfort and seriousness until, after a bit more erming and ahhing, he mentioned the word 'date.'

"Oh!" said Rosemary, taken aback. "Erm...What about Sherry? I thought you two were..."

"Sherry?" said Liam, his eyes widening in surprise. "Sherry's my cousin!"

"Oh...I didn't realise. I don't remember meeting your family. Thanks for...err, thinking of me," Rosemary said. "This is a really terrible time, and also, I don't date."

Liam's handsome face fell, and Rosemary felt a twinge of regret.

"But...if I ever do want to...err, go out, I'll give you a bell."

Liam smiled, slightly sadly, and left without a goodbye.

Rosemary closed the door, baffled and embarrassed. There wasn't any space in her life for romances – despite Liam's sweetness and the good times they'd shared as teenagers. Rosemary was even more confused by the small candle she might be holding for a certain...vampire! Sure, both of them were charming and good-looking, but life was far too complex to add dating to the mix. It didn't seem like things would get any simpler in the foreseeable future, either.

No thanks to Granny! Rosemary thought sharply, daring her grandmother to respond.

What is it now, pet? Granny responded.

You didn't think to tell me I had to connect with the elements or whatever?

Oh, Rosemary, Granny replied. *You did more than enough of that when you were younger.*

Did I? Really? Before you addled my memory, you mean?!

It's all still there, silly. You just have to connect with your inner self.

"Aghhh! This is infuriating!"

"What is, love?" Marjie asked.

"Yeah, Mum, we've been watching you pace around the house, making funny faces, for the last ten minutes. Are you finally losing it?"

"Granny is in my head. Only she's being just as infuriating as she was before!" Rosemary grumbled.

"That is super weird," said Athena.

"Say hi to Galdie for me!" Marjie said, as if it was all perfectly normal to her.

"I'm starting to feel like I never really knew her," Rosemary said, sighing. "It's like the version of her in my head was just a tiny fragment of who she was, and I don't really remember her properly. Who was she? What did she even like doing?"

"Oh, Galdie was enthusiastic about so many things," said Marjie. "She was right into crafts. Loved embroidery. She spent a lot of time hiking in the bush, collecting wild herbs for her various magical workings...Oh, and the dancing of course."

"I remember the crafts and the dancing," Rosemary said.

"Oh, yes, Galdie loved a good cèilidh," said Marjie. "She'd get on her yellow dancing shoes with the bright blue laces..."

"Wait a minute!" said Athena. "What did you just say?" She shot Rosemary a sharp look.

"She'd put on her favourite dancing shoes," said Marjie. "That's all dear."

"Blue. Lace. Dance!" Rosemary made the connection, and a second later, she and Athena had bolted upstairs to check Granny's room again. Sure enough, in the top row of shoes in the wardrobe sat a pair of yellow suede shoes with electric blue laces.

"Interesting choice of colour combination," said Athena, as Rosemary reached up to grab the shoes.

"What now?" Rosemary asked.

"Look inside, silly!" said Athena.

Rosemary reached inside the soft suede of the shoes to find a small silver key.

"So, this was really what Granny meant?" Rosemary asked. "I wonder what it's for?"

"It's a double clue!" Athena cried, taking the key from Rosemary's hand and rushing to the small bedroom. "I bet there's a keyhole on that box somewhere. It's really clever of Granny Thorn, don't you think?"

"I've never seen a keyhole on that box in my life," said Rosemary dismissively, as Athena picked up the music box and spun it around, examining it.

"Look – here, it's just at the back next to the wind-up-thingie." Athena pointed to reveal that there was, indeed, a tiny keyhole.

"Okay, Miss Smarty Pants. What do we do now?"

"What do you think, Mum? Here." She held out the key for Rosemary to take.

Rosemary felt a tingle of nervousness and excitement. Clearly, Granny Thorn had put a lot more thought into this than she'd previously realised, not that Rosemary was ready to completely forgive her just yet.

She cautiously fitted the key into the lock and turned it, expecting sparks to fly and magic light to beam out all over the place. However, it was a perfectly ordinary latch.

It clicked open, revealing a false bottom to the jewellery box.

Inside was a stack of paper, an inch thick, covered in Granny's cursive scrawl.

Rosemary reached forward, but Athena was too quick.

"Hey!" Rosemary said as her daughter began scanning the pages. "Give that here!"

"You hate reading the manual!" Athena said in an accusing tone.

"It's a...manual?"

"Well, not exactly," said Athena. "But from what I can tell it's a whole lot of useful details."

Rosemary and Athena spent the next couple of hours poring over the notes Granny had written, interrupted only by Marjie, who seemed to know better than to ask questions, but delivered a tray of re-heated mutton and roast potatoes to the door before she left to head home. Rosemary and Athena gratefully scoffed the food while continuing to read.

As for the information they'd discovered, some of it was perfectly self-explanatory – like 'this is where I keep the keys to the car – make sure you get it serviced regularly. Take it to Daisy's on the west side of town, and whatever you do, don't let Ferg try to do it. He is not a trained mechanic!'

"Why did Granny Thorn keep that kind of thing locked up so secretively?" Athena asked. "It seems like basic useful information."

"Maybe because she thought it would be sensible to keep all the useful information in one place where we couldn't find it!" Rosemary said, exasperated. "And while it would have been great to know about the car keys when we first arrived. I haven't found anything remotely useful for our current situation yet. Half of these pages are gobbledygook."

"Look!" Athena said. "This page is all about the binding – there are little drawings of the vines and...ooh, it doesn't tell us anything we haven't already worked out."

"Let me guess? It says 'look within?'"

"Pretty much," said Athena, handing Rosemary the page. "Ooh – but this is useful!"

"What?!" asked Rosemary.

"It describes how the house and the Thorn family power are connected via another secret dimension – that explains where you've been popping off to when you lose consciousness."

"Great," said Rosemary. "If only knowing that helped us figure out how to break the binding. You know it's strange, when I touched the crystal before, I felt so...energised, and I still feel it a bit, now. It's like I'm buzzing with energy."

"That's funny," said Athena. "When you hugged me after you came to, it felt...well, it felt pretty wild actually."

"Wild how?"

"Kind of as if a wave of golden energy washed right over me," said Athena. "Maybe it's the Thorn magic, trying to get back to us in any way it can. I wonder if that's what settled the energy in the parlour down and closed up that cavern. Do you think that if you just went back in to the netherworld, or whatever it is, that you could just stand there and draw the energy out until it was all released from the binding?"

"I'm not a bloody car!" said Rosemary. "It's not as simple as fuelling up, you know. The crystal told me I wasn't ready, and besides, I didn't like the look of those vines. I was terrified they were going to come after me and choke me or something."

"It was worth a shot." said Athena. "I wish that more of this made sense." She held up some indecipherable pages.

"What's that one?" Rosemary asked, pointing to another page in Athena's lap. "Look! It says The Bloodstone Society on it!"

She grabbed hold of the page along with those immediately following it.

"What does it say?" Athena asked.

"The Bloodstone Society is an ancient secret society, blah-blah-blah."

"Mum – that actually sounds useful to know."

"You're right," Rosemary said. "It says here they grew powerful not only by drawing on the power of their members but also by stealing the power of old magical families."

"Like ours!" said Athena.

"Exactly. It says they were once the terror of the magical community – worldwide. The members bound their souls to the Society in exchange for power and are forever at the mercy of their tyrannical leader. Apparently, many old witch families went into hiding to escape them, including through resorting to the desperate measure of binding most of their own power so that it was undetectable. That way they just appeared to have the same level of power as regular magical people."

"So that's what Granny Thorn did?"

"It seems likely," said Rosemary. "It says here that the clan's power has been waning, which only makes them more desperate and dangerous. They must have come after Granny – figured out about the old family magic. That's probably what Granny's letter was talking about. Remember the one she left for us when we first arrived? They come by tooth, claw, and fang. It says here that some members are vampires and shapeshifters. I guess granny was cryptically alluding to it while trying to keep this secret."

"Why would she want to do that, though?" Athena asked. "If someone was trying to kill me, I'd be shouting their identity from the rooftops."

"I guess it's possible that the Bloodstone Society has ways of tracing the people who talk about them," Rosemary said and shuddered.

"But I guess they already know all about us now, so we're in no more danger by saying their name or anything," Athena said, though her tone was anxious and doubtful.

"Or maybe...the authorities are in on it," Rosemary said, feeling uneasy about the police officer supposedly asleep downstairs.

"Or that they are so powerful they make it impossible for people to talk about them – remember how Granny Thorn couldn't tell us who killed her?" Athena said.

"That's true. But don't you think we should check on the sleeping cop in our kitchen, just in case?"

"He's harmless," said Athena. "I'm sure of that – aside from his suspicions of us!"

Rosemary was about to argue, but then her eyes landed on something else. "Athena, look!"

"What is it?"

"It's a piece of a waxed seal that Granny must have stuck on here – and I know where I've seen the other part of it." She got up and raced to the library with Athena following close behind.

Rosemary unlocked the door to the library, relieved to see everything in the room was in place. She dashed in and began frantically searching the shelves. "It must be here somewhere!"

"The box is still on the table," Athena said.

"Good! But I'm looking for something else."

"What?"

"Hmm..." Rosemary ducked behind the desk and emerged triumphantly a moment later, clutching a piece of paper.

"What is it?" Athena asked.

"Look," Rosemary said, matching the substantive part of the seal she had just found with the piece remaining on the invitation.

"So, we have...a little coat of arms thing?"

"Yes! With a crow, snake, wolf, and a Celtic knot."

"Tooth and claw and so on?" Athena asked, sceptically.

"I've seen it before," Rosemary said, squinting at the shield. "I just know that I have..."

"Oh, no...not your memory again!" said Athena. "Anyway, enough about the stupid seal. How do we stop this awful secret society from killing us for our power?"

Rosemary took a closer look at the scrawled writing on the other page she was holding, on which Granny had taped the piece of seal.

"From what it says here, it seems like their power has been depleted slowly over the years, while ours only builds up more because it's connected to the earth. So, Granny was anticipating that our magic would have surpassed theirs very soon. In fact, it seems from this, like she was just about to try to release the binding herself and go after them when they snuck up on her!"

"I couldn't help but overhearing..." a voice boomed from the doorway.

Rosemary jumped, turning quickly to see Constable Perkins standing there in a posture clearly intended to bar their exit.

Was he actually asleep this whole time? Rosemary wondered. *Is he part of the Bloodstone Society, coming in here to finish what they started?*

The officer took a step towards them and reached into his pocket.

Rosemary flinched, terrified he was reaching for a gun or some kind of magical weapon.

Instead, he pulled out a large handkerchief and blew his nose loudly. Rosemary and Athena gave each other grossed-out looks.

"You're one of them, aren't you?" said Rosemary. "The Bloodstone Society."

"I take offence to that!" said Constable Perkins, stuffing his soiled hankie back into his pockets. "I happen to have been after that society for decades."

"So, you know they were the ones who killed Granny and not us," said Rosemary.

"I'm jumping to no such conclusions," he said. "After tonight's fiasco, it's hard to know what to believe. This whole thing could have been a set-up, staged by you two, including the conversation I just overheard."

"Are you meaning to tell me you've been after them for decades and that's the only hypothesis you've come up with?" Rosemary asked, flabbergasted.

"I'll have you know I have a number of suspects!" the officer said. "And they are a tricky bunch to catch. They all keep changing their identities, and no one – not even those in the society who I have apprehended over the years – knows who the leader is."

"Oh, yeah?" Rosemary asked. "Who are your suspects then?"

"Mum!" Athena whispered, trying to kick Rosemary, who stepped out of the way to avoid her daughter's foot.

"Proof," Rosemary demanded, "– or you're just making it up."

Constable Perkins glared at Rosemary, then fished inside his blazer pocket and pulled out a notepad. He flicked through a few pages then held it up for her to read.

POSSIBLE BLOODSTONE MEMBERS

Ferg – always involved in every little thing.

Mr June – power seeking.

Perseus Burk – nocturnally inclined and wealthy.

Rosemary was blown away by the banality she saw on the page, but before she could react, Constable Perkins stepped further into the office.

"I'm taking this box as evidence," he said, reaching out for The Box.

"No!" Rosemary cried, trying to get in Constable Perkin's way.

She was too late to stop him.

A sudden bang sounded, and a bright flash of light filled the room. It quickly faded to reveal the unusually dressed police officer lying on his back on the floor.

Athena gasped.

"He's alive," Rosemary said, checking his pulse. "But it looks like he's out cold. Oh, my goodness. This is not a good look! Quick, help me drag him out of here. I want him as far away from the box as possible when he comes to."

"We can't just drive him somewhere and leave him by the side of the road, can we?" Athena asked.

"I don't think that's wise," said Rosemary. "He's suspicious enough of us as it is."

It was tough work, but they managed to get him out to the lobby and then spent several minutes wondering what to do. Eventually, they decided there were no good options.

"We'll figure it out in the morning, I guess," said Rosemary. "It's well past midnight; why don't you get some sleep."

"What? With him down here?" Athena asked. "I don't think so. It's too creepy."

"Well, let's have a cup of tea to settle our minds, and maybe we'll think of something brilliant."

Brilliance wasn't required. As Rosemary and Athena sat on the window seats sipping their tea, they heard a cough from the lobby. On further investigation, Constable Perkins had gotten himself up off the floor, and seemed to be blushing, as if he'd quite embarrassed himself. He thanked them for a lovely evening and left, seemingly forgetting about the whole incident earlier.

Rosemary sighed in relief, then looked slightly concerned. "Do you suppose he's alright to drive? He looked a bit tipsy earlier."

"What? Him?" Athena asked. "He only had a tiny glass of sherry and another of red wine the whole evening. What a light-weight."

"Maybe the drunkenness was an act," Rosemary suggested. "People probably tell you all kinds of strange things when they think you're too drunk to remember."

"Do you think he's a double agent?" Athena asked. "He could be part of the Bloodstone Society and just pretending to investigate them. Maybe his idiocy is just an act."

"Could be," said Rosemary. "And what about The Boy?"

"Who, Finnigan?" Athena asked, rubbing her eyes.

"The very same," said Rosemary. "Don't you think it was suspicious how he showed up and then just disappeared? He could be one of *them.*"

"Mum," Athena said, frowning. "Don't start."

"Seriously," said Rosemary. "That boy is a bad egg, I can tell."

"He's not an egg at all," Athena grumbled, but they were both too tired to have a proper argument about it.

"He did try to lure you away," said Rosemary half-heartedly, as she checked the front door to make sure it was locked. "I bet he was trying to abduct you. What is he, a shapeshifter?"

Athena had a strange look in her eyes that only made Rosemary more concerned than she had the energy to be.

"Don't be ridiculous," said Athena.

"How did he even know to come to dinner?" Rosemary asked. She took out her earrings and yawned.

"I invited him, remember? You said I could. I texted him, but he didn't reply."

"Unreliable, or too busy plotting against us?"

"You're wrong about this," said Athena. "I'm a good judge of character."

"Yeah, well so was I before I met your father."

"See, this is all really about you and your questionable life choices," said Athena. "My brain's broken. Need. Sleep." She zombie-walked upstairs, followed by her similarly exhausted mother.

Rosemary slipped into her pyjamas and into bed. As she drifted off to sleep, a connection flared in her mind.

Despina! she realised. *It was Despina who wore that same emblem on the seal on her badge the first time she came to the door. She must have been trying to send us a message – to show us she was powerful, even though we had no idea.*

"I knew she wasn't to be trusted. Estate agents are trouble," Rosemary muttered to herself as she scrambled up and wrote herself a hastily scrawled note so that she absolutely did not forget. After all that, she slept like a newborn baby – which is to say, she slept fitfully and woke several times in the night – but at least, she did get a little sleep.

Twenty-Seven

Rosemary woke to the sound of clanking in the kitchen. The sun was already high in the sky, and though she was grateful for the sleep in, her entire body was filled with the lead-weight of dread. She dragged herself out of bed immediately.

Athena's bed was empty. Rosemary rushed downstairs in terror, only to find her daughter making pancakes on the griddle.

"You scared me half to death!" Rosemary said.

"Don't be so paranoid then," Athena replied.

"Don't I have a right to be paranoid after all that's happened recently?" Rosemary asked, sitting down at the table and pouring herself some tea. She was still halfway through processing all the events of the past day. One memory in particular, as it flooded back, was enough to make her snort her tea in accidental laughter.

"What is it?" Athena asked.

Rosemary coughed and tried to clear her sinuses. "Oh nothing," she replied. "Did you know that Liam and Sherry are cousins?"

"Gross!" Athena cried. "I knew this was a small town, but that is *sordid*!"

"No," said Rosemary. "Not like that. They're not together."

"How do you know?" Athena asked.

Rosemary was silent for a moment, thinking back to the conversation she'd had quietly with Liam.

"He asked you out!" Athena shouted from across the kitchen.

"How did you know that?" Rosemary asked. "You're not that good at guessing."

Athena blanched. "I sort of...sensed it inside your head."

"How rude! Give a woman some privacy!" said Rosemary. "Wait a minute – how on earth...?"

Athena smiled at her mother, a slightly guilty expression on her face. "I think my powers are coming in."

Rosemary got up from the table and wrapped her daughter in a big hug, and then stood back and pinched her cheeks. "My little witch is all grown up."

"Shut it, Mum!" Athena complained, pushing Rosemary away.

Actually, let me try something.

"Try what?" Rosemary asked.

"Oh, my gosh! It worked!"

"What worked," Rosemary asked.

I said that only in my mind.

"You did?"

You see, my lips aren't moving.

"Wow!" said Rosemary. "Wait, let me try." *Bananas are pink,* she thought.

"They tend to be kind of yellow," Athena said.

"It worked!" Rosemary crowed. "I'm telepathic!"

"No. I am," said Athena. "I can read your mind. I don't think you can read mine."

Rosemary paused and tried to concentrate on Athena's thoughts. "Unless you're really thinking nothing, my telepathy isn't working, after all!"

"Maybe you don't have it," said Athena, shrugging.

"Not fair," said Rosemary, then she narrowed her eyes at Athena.

"Not that look. Wait, are you worried or suspicious?"

"Both," said Rosemary, her mind racing at the new revelation. "Firstly, are you okay? Do you think this could be dangerous?"

"I'm fine," Athena said, clearly downplaying the situation to calm her mother's fears.

"I'll take you word for it, for now anyway," said Rosemary. "But secondly, you've been keeping this a secret from me, haven't you? When did all this start?"

Athena lowered her gaze towards the pancakes and focused on flipping one, then murmured. "Actually, it first started around the time I met Finnigan."

"What! Not him again. I told you he was suspicious," said Rosemary. "I can't believe you didn't tell me. That was days ago!"

"At first I thought it was just him I could read and who could hear my thoughts. He said we were the same in some way."

"Both telepaths, eh?" Rosemary asked, feeling even more apprehensive.

"I guess," Athena said. "That's kind of how we got to be friends so quickly. But I never heard anyone else's thoughts, well, not clearly."

"But you heard something?"

"Yes...but it was blurry, like little murmurs or tones, but nothing clear enough to understand. I felt a bit crazy, like my head was becoming an out-of-tune radio, picking up on all kinds of things, but nothing made sense. Last night, after you hugged me, it became a bit clearer, but it's still really annoying."

"And *why* didn't you tell me?"

"You seemed to have enough on your plate already, without having to look after a daughter who was losing the plot," Athena said. "I didn't want to worry you."

"Or share about your private interactions with a boy!"

"Or that," Athena admitted, walking over to the table with a big plate of pancakes.

Rosemary sighed, taking a pancake and squeezing the juice from a slice of lemon over it and then sprinkling on brown sugar in the traditional way. She then rolled it up and scoffed it, just like she always did.

"These are really good. Thanks," Rosemary said.

"You're mad, aren't you?" said Athena.

"Only a little. You know I want to know what's going on with you."

"Yes – and you also want to know where I am at every single moment. It's getting a bit much, Mum. You're smothering me."

"It's dangerous here!" Rosemary insisted.

"So what? The world's a dangerous place and I'm a teenager. I need my freedom."

"Give me a while to adjust, okay?" said Rosemary. "I've only known about magic and all this other scary stuff for a week. It's going to take me a while to let you wander in the woods alone."

"You're the one who's supposed to be wandering in the woods," Athena reminded her. "Chillin' with your inner self and all that."

"Don't remind me!"

"You really should do it, though," Athena said. "It's the only lead we've got at the moment, and things are looking dire. Who do you think is responsible for all this? And don't say Finnigan!"

A knock sounded from the front door.

Rosemary answered it to find there was no one in sight. A note sat on the doorstep, written on a pink card.

Despina!

Rosemary suddenly remembered her realisation from the night before. She rushed upstairs to check her hurried scrawl.

"Are you alright?" Athena asked, still seated at the table as Rosemary clomped back down the stairs.

"It's Despina!" Rosemary cried.

"The estate agent? Are you being prejudiced again?"

"No. I remembered it last night. Despina was wearing a strange brooch when I first met her. It was the exact same pattern as what was on that seal!"

"Really?" Athena said. "If that's true, why would she wear the Bloodstone Society crest in public? Wouldn't that be too obvious?"

"Except that it's a super-secret logo!" Rosemary said. "So secret that Granny had to hide it and give us silly clues. Or maybe she's just so confident because she's in the upper echelons of the society. She doesn't need to hide because she's so powerful. She was sending us a message, but we didn't understand what it was."

"True," said Athena. "I couldn't find anything about them online, not even their stupid logo, which means wearing it only sends a message to people who are in the society or already know about them. If she's the leader, she can be as bold as she likes."

"And look – this note was just left on the door on pink cardboard. Can you think of a single other person who'd do that?"

"Erm..." said Athena.

"No! See. I told you! Despina's awful. That poor little niece of hers. Imagine having to put up with an aunt like that?"

"What does the note say then, Nancy Drew?" Athena asked.

Rosemary opened the card up and read it.

"Oh, no!" Her face fell.

"What?"

"Oh, no, no no!"

"Mum?"

"The Spring Festival!"

"I thought we'd decided to skip it in light of everything going on here," said Athena.

"Read this," said Rosemary, holding out the note.

See you at the Imbolc Festival...or else everyone there will burn!

"Well, that's obviously a trap," said Rosemary. "There is no way I'm falling for it. Estate agents are not telling me what to do and neither are secret society leaders. Certainly not anyone who is both!"

"Maybe she knows we'll think like that," said Athena. "It's too obvious, otherwise."

"Then you think we should go?" Rosemary asked. "She's just going to sneak into the house and steal the magic!"

"If she was going to do that, why not try at any other time when we were out?" Athena pointed out. "They obviously need us for something."

"We have to go!" said Rosemary. "She won't suspect that. Ooh, unless she thinks we'll think that, and so she really does want us to go. Ugh, I hate being manipulated when I don't even know in which direction! Let's just go."

"And walk straight into a trap? Besides, what will we do? We don't really have any controllable powers."

"If they are planning something terrible, we can warn the people – get everyone out of the way. Children will be part of the festival, remember? Remember all those young, innocent faces? If they're at risk, they must be protected."

"Okay, fine," Athena said. "Let's go save the children, but don't say I didn't warn you."

Rosemary checked the box on the table in the library one more time. It looked innocent, but it was apparently powerful enough to protect itself from every other threat so far. It stood to reason that it – and the family magic – would be safe if they left the house.

They hurriedly got dressed and then jumped into Granny's car and drove to the town square. The whole place was packed with people, most of them wearing robes and carrying boughs of spring blossoms. Clearly, the entire town attended these things.

Once parked, they ran towards the circle within the square where everyone seemed to be gathering for the Imbolc ritual.

Rosemary looked around frantically for anyone who looked suspicious. She could see the young children in their little blossom costumes, all lined up and ready for the ritual to start. Ferg seemed to be instructing them on what to do next.

"Over here," Rosemary said, guiding Athena around the circle of people towards Ferg, who was wearing brown robes draped in a cherry blossom printed shawl.

"Should we warn Ferg?" Athena asked. "He seems like he's in charge. He could get everyone out if there's danger."

Rosemary looked at Ferg, suspicious. "No. We have to keep an eye on him."

"Do you suspect him?" Athena asked.

"Well, Constable Perkins does."

"I'm not sure that's an adequate reason," said Athena. "Besides, aren't we supposed to be warning people?"

"Change of plans," said Rosemary. "Let's be stealthy. Just watch for anything suspicious."

"Ah!" Ferg said, turning towards them. "Perfect timing. My spring maidens!"

"Your what, now?" Rosemary asked.

"You're not exactly dressed for the occasion," said Ferg, eyeing their jeans and dark coloured coats. "But you'll do. Here!"

He held out two flower crowns, adorned with ribbons and spring blossoms.

"What...?" Rosemary and Athena both said.

"Put these on and go and stand by the children. You don't have to say anything – just walk around the circle when it's time. The kids know what to do."

Rosemary tried to argue, but Ferg insisted, and besides, she reasoned they'd have a better view of the ritual from inside the circle, so she gave up and agreed despite Athena's glaring.

They put on the flower crowns and stepped inside the circle, next to the row of children.

"I feel ridiculous!" Athena hissed.

"Welcome to my world," said Rosemary. "I feel like this often."

"If you're suspicious of Ferg, why are you doing what he says?"

"I'm suspicious of a lot of people," said Rosemary. "I don't know who is helping Despina, but she's clearly the ringleader. Besides, he's right. It's much easier to see everything from inside here." She squinted at the crowd, trying to find the estate agent among the many faces there, but saw no sign of her.

"There must be two hundred people here!" Athena said. "Surely they can't all be in on the secret society, or it wouldn't be a secret."

"They all look pretty innocent to me. Just keep an eye out for that estate agent, or anything dodgy," Rosemary said.

The crowd hushed as the ritual began. Rosemary felt a stillness descend around them, a peacefulness. A few weeks ago, she would have assumed it was just in her mind, but now she was sure it was part of the magic of the ritual, drawing on the power that seemed to hang in the air above the town. Though she had always known Myrtlewood was special, she had never felt so aware of the town's magic as she did now. She could almost see it, the sparkle in the air, the shimmer, as a light breeze whipped around the circle.

Mr June, wearing a long blue-grey cloak strode into the centre and waved his arms dramatically in the air. He performed a poem about the end of winter and the beginnings of spring. Despite his theatrics, Rosemary could feel the truth in his words, feel the natural environment surrounding the town as it willingly gave way to the seasonal change.

She allowed herself to close her eyes briefly, searching for something inside, her wildness, the disconnected parts of herself, perhaps even her magic.

Mr June stepped out again, and three women took his place, summoning in the new energies of warmth for the year and asking for the blessings of the goddess Brigid. Two of them held baskets of flower petals, which they began to scatter while the other one walked around, holding a large wand with an amethyst crystal at the end and "cast the circle" around everyone.

Rosemary could feel the energy condense around them, bringing them closer into the experience as many around the circle echoed her words. "This is sacred time, this is sacred space. I am fully present, here and now."

Rosemary knew she should be on the lookout for danger, but instead she found herself focused on the present moment, the feel of her body, and the energy around them.

The women stepped back again. Other people standing at the four direction points announced they would summon the four elements.

"Pay close attention," whispered Athena.

"Why, is there something suspicious?"

"No, this is elemental magic. Remember? You have to learn it."

Rosemary took note as the directions were called. Air from the east felt light and refreshing; fire from the south brought a burning warmth into the circle; water from the west a cool, soothing connection, and earth from the north was stable and solid.

"Now," Ferg said, stepping forward. "We all know the best way to bring in the warmer months is by dancing! The children and spring maidens will lead us in this dance! Go on!

Rosemary and Athena looked at each other and gulped.

"Err..."

"Come on!" one of the children said, grabbing Rosemary's hand and leading her and Athena into a free and frivolous dance. The children began skipping and twirling. Rosemary, Athena and the entire crowd followed suit, imitating the uninhibited way the children spun and jumped, gradually leading them all in a spiral towards the centre of the circle.

The dancing was tremendous fun. Even Athena seemed to be enjoying it, but Rosemary was keeping her eyes peeled for suspicious behaviour all the while. As the dancers made it to the centre of the circle and then turned around to spiral out again, she caught a glimpse of someone in a dark hood – someone ominous looking. Rosemary grabbed Athena's arm and pulled her in the direction of the dark hooded figure. They followed, ducking around various villagers as they ran.

The figure was headed out towards the boundaries of the circle.

"Rosemary!" Marjie cried, wrapping her in a big hug. "I didn't expect to see you here after such a late and troubling night, but I'm so glad you could make it."

Rosemary tried to reciprocate Marjie's smile, but kept her eyes trained on the figure, as did Athena.

"Excuse me," she said and continued to hurry after the suspicious character, only to lose sight of them near the lawyer's office building.

"Well, that was a dead end," said Athena. "You don't suppose they just vanished into thin air, whoever it was?"

"I bet it was Despina," said Rosemary.

Athena sighed. "It was too tall to be Despina."

"One of her cronies, then."

"Look, Mum. The ritual is wrapping up now with no incidents. The children are fine. You don't suppose this whole thing of making us come here was just a—"

"You're right," Rosemary said as dread condensed in her gut. "It was a triple trap, or maybe just a regular old trap. This was all a ruse to get us away from the house!"

"I thought so!" said Athena.

"Well, if you were so sure you should have told me," Rosemary replied. "Come on. Let's sneak away before someone else tries to chat to us and get back to Thorn Manor as fast as possible."

Twenty-Eight

As Rosemary and Athena neared the house, dark storm clouds were brewing in the sky directly over the property, despite the late afternoon otherwise looking rather clear and sunny.

Rosemary drove up the driveway to see dozens of dark-hooded figures, black masks obscuring their faces, surrounding the house. The shadows in the sky seemed to be growing above them, spreading out to cover the area around the house. They blocked out the sun, making it seem like night.

"This is bad!" said Rosemary. "This is very, very bad. Do you think we can just turn around and run away?"

"No," said Athena. "I think we're well past that."

Rosemary's heart raced as she realised it was true. Running away now would only result in more problems, which was annoying, because running away was by far her most preferred option. She continued driving, passing some of the figures, who turned to watch as the car pulled closer to the Thorn Manor.

"Mum...what are you doing?" Athena asked, fear rising in her voice.

"You're right," Rosemary said. "I need to confront this head-on. Stay in the car. I'll try to talk to them."

"I don't think they're here to talk, Mum. Besides, if you are going to talk, I think it's safer if I come with you to stop you putting your foot in it," Athena said.

"Not in a million years, kid," said Rosemary. "Stay right here. If talking doesn't work then at least the closer I get to the house the more likely the family power is to kick in and give me super strength."

She got out of the car, shivering from both the chill in the air and from the fear that pricked the skin on her arms, giving her goosebumps. As she turned towards the house, trying to maintain her composure, the hooded figures began chanting in low voices, uttering words in a language Rosemary did not understand but suspected was Ancient Greek or Egyptian, perhaps.

"Hello!" Rosemary called, trying to sound cheerful to dilute the atmosphere of tension and fear. "Err, is Despina about? I'd like to have a few words..."

A dark swirling vortex appeared above the house, as if summoned by the chanting. Rosemary watched, horrified, as an enormous shadowy beast emerged from the vortex. It was shaped like a huge Celtic dragon. Its scales glinted gold and red as it circled in the sky, and then, looking directly at Rosemary, it began flying straight for her!

Rosemary turned back to the car to see her daughter's expression of terror, mirroring her own.

"Athena! Run!"

Athena shot out of the car, and they both ran for the woods surrounding the house, jumping over brambles and dodging through thickets. The hooded figures were after them – chasing them through the trees. Rosemary tried to keep an eye on Athena as they ran, though it was a difficult task with all the obstacles in their way.

Rosemary shrieked as a bird swooped from the sky, transforming mid-flight into a hooded man, and falling into a nimble crouch on the ground.

"We meet again," the man said, pushing back his hood to reveal his scarred face. Rosemary recognised him as the crow man who had appeared unconscious in the house a few nights before. Verikus.

Athena shot her mother a terrified look as the sound of footfalls caught up with them.

"I've got no time for this," Rosemary said.

"Mum, duck!" Athena cried. Rosemary dived to the ground just in time as Athena hurled one of her home-made concoctions she'd stashed in her pockets towards Verikus, who screeched as a cloud of grey smoke burst from the charm, sending feathers flying.

"Nice one," Rosemary said as they kept running. There was no time to stop and assess the damage, as the rest of the Bloodstone Society were still hot on their heels.

Rosemary was almost out of breath. She tried to keep her eyes on her daughter, but Athena was too fast. She disappeared into a dense cluster of bushes.

Through here!

Rosemary heard Athena call out telepathically. She shot through the bushes, only to find a small clearing.

Athena was nowhere in sight, and neither were the hooded beings.

"Athena!" Rosemary yelled, and then held her tongue, not wanting to attract any more attention. Her heart thudded so rigorously in her chest that she felt it might leap right up into her throat.

She looked around the clearing, unsure of which direction to head. One path among the trees seemed lighter, as if it were glowing somehow.

I'll take that as a sign.

Rosemary followed it as it wound through the trees, her eyes darting all around for her daughter, fearing she had been taken by the enemy, hoping against hope that Athena was okay. She ran quickly at first and then slowed as the air began to feel unusual – lighter and denser at the same time, as if it was carrying more energy, laden with magical charge.

The further Rosemary progressed down the path, the brighter the air around her seemed to be, as if it was itself glowing. Golden.

This is a special place, she realised. *One of Granny's special places in the woods.*

At the end of the path was another smaller, circular clearing with a large boulder in the centre, a perfect size for sitting on.

Rosemary perched on the boulder. She took a deep breath and tried to calm her mind.

I need to find Athena and somehow stop Despina and her cronies – in that order, but I don't know how to do either of those things.

She closed her eyes and tried to listen out for Athena's telepathic voice – but there was only silence. Then a memory of Athena came back to her instead, urging her to meditate.

*Well. There's no time like the present...*Rosemary thought. *And at this point, what else can I do?* So many of Granny's words pointed to looking within, and to the forest, after all.

She sat cross-legged on the boulder and closed her eyes, just relaxing and breathing, listening to the sounds around her and allowing her mind to go blank, and from that blankness, she fell into darkness.

Rosemary found herself in the void again. Just like before, she held the crystal in her hands, but this time, it glowed brighter. She held it up above her head, allowing the light to shine over her. Then, intuitively, she held it to her heart.

As the cool glassy surface connected with her chest, Rosemary felt something shift inside her mind – an opening – and with that opening came a tidal wave of energy – a flood of memories and feelings; her childhood time spent wearing a bright-red felt cape, following Granny in the forest down the special path as Molly the cat wandered stoically behind them; learning about herbs, mixing potions in the kitchen, summoning the forces of nature; playing in the water, in the sea and streams, dancing with the wind; carefully lighting the sacred fires, lying on the very boulder that she now sat on, and connecting with the earth.

Granny was right – I do know this. I did all the elemental training I needed when I was a child.

She felt a strong sensation of unravelling in her chest.

Whatever had pulled her into pieces and bound those pieces to keep them apart all those years ago loosened. She leaned into the feeling as if unwrapping treasure, buried deep inside.

To her great satisfaction, the disparate parts sprung together like magnets.

From within came a purposefulness, a deep knowing. She was still that wild little girl that danced in the rain, even though the world had done its best to beat the joy and freedom out of her. She was sick of being a victim, at the mercy of fate, and now she understood that she didn't have to be. Not anymore. It was time to wake up and take control of her life. It dawned on Rosemary that she was unleashing a great power – not the old family magic, as yet – but her own power, which had been carefully bound along with it.

She was re-claiming a part of herself that had been taken away, and with that, all the walls and blockages of insecurity inside her came tumbling down. Rosemary connected with her own powerful confidence – her true self.

A huge wave of light rushed out from her. In her mind's eye, it swept across the surrounding land, vast and powerful, sweeping away the shadows, clearing the sky.

The dragon reared up. Rosemary could sense it above her body, seeking her out, just as she watched from the sky. It circled the house and then flew over the forest, diving towards the clearing in which she sat.

Oh, no, you don't.

From her aerial vantage point, she gathered the energy around her, the life force of the forest, the hum of magic from Thorn Manor, the new pulse of power inside her. Weaving all this together, Rosemary could feel her bond with Athena, feel her daughter reaching out with her mind, joining in with her own energy.

Rosemary pulled all these forces together into a powerful ball of energy and hurled it with all her mental might towards the dragon.

A wave of energy blasted through the air, sending Rosemary careening back into her body. She opened her eyes, raising her arms over her head. Above her, the light shone brightly through the trees. A feminine shape hung in the clouds above, somehow reminding Rosemary of the spring goddess Brigid. Rosemary smiled, and though she was sure it was probably an illusion, she issued a silent prayer just in case.

Thank you for your blessings, Goddess.

As Rosemary lowered her arms, the trees around her seemed to murmur in awe, rustling their branches.

She stood up, glowing with energy. She could feel Athena's presence now and knew exactly where to find her. Rosemary walked back along the forest path, heading directly for the house. The trees seemed to part for her, because there surely were no obstacles in her way as, with a flicker of gold in her eyes, she approached Thorn Manor.

Twenty-Nine

All was silent as Rosemary neared the house. The sky above had cleared and there was no sign of the black-clad beings or the beast, or even of any birds or insects for that matter. The wave of energy from Rosemary's mind really had swept them all far away just as she'd imagined.

There was no sign of Athena either. Rosemary's heart beat a drum in her chest, determined to find her. With magically enhanced senses, she could tell that her daughter was somewhere inside – taken by the Bloodstone cronies to use as leverage.

Rosemary entered through the front door. The house felt almost empty. Eerie. But she could feel her daughter's presence, and something else that set the hairs on her neck standing on end.

Mum! Get away! It's a trap! Athena's voice rang out in Rosemary's mind.

Rosemary walked directly to the library to find Athena there, sitting in the chair behind the desk, her wrists tied to the armrest. Rosemary felt equal parts relief that Athena seemed to be okay and horror that someone had restrained her like that, but both feelings were quickly overruled by a righteous rage.

"What are you doing here?" Athena cried, tears streaming down her cheeks. "I told you to get away!"

"I'm not leaving you," Rosemary said.

"Don't you see? She's got you right where she wants you..."

Athena's words trailed off as footsteps sounded outside the door.

Rosemary braced herself, still awash with her newly released magic, but cautious.

The door opened and little Geneviève walked in, wearing a silver pantsuit, her hair tied back in a tight bun.

Rosemary let out the breath she was holding. "Are you okay?" she asked. "Are you lost? Can you tell me where your aunt is?"

"Mum!" Athena said. "She's..."

"Cut that out," Geneviève said, her voice deep and gravelly. "I'm six thousand years old and I'm tired of being treated like a child."

Rosemary was stunned. "You're a..."

"A vampire, of course," said Geneviève. "I thought you figured that out already, despite being so dense. I must admit it did surprise me when you fed me blood-enchanted food. I suppose that was just Marjie getting things to run smoothly. Little did any of you know that I had other plans."

"You...?"

"The magic in the house already made it volatile. I just gave it a little nudge to generate that vortex. I needed to get rid of all those people and get you back on track towards unbinding the magic," said the very small, very young looking, very old person.

"You can do magic?" Rosemary asked.

"Being the leader of the Bloodstone Society has some advantages."

"The leader? It was really you driving all this!" Rosemary said, aghast.

"Yes, I think we've covered this," said Geneviève, sounding bored. "You've done exactly what I planned you would do. Everything is working out exactly as I intended. Now give me the box or the girl dies." She pointed a finger at Athena, who shuddered.

"No, Mum. Don't do it."

"I think you're mistaken," said Rosemary. "It's just an ordinary box. Go ahead. Pick it up and see for yourself."

"Nice try," said Geneviève. "I knew full-well that that box in the parlour was a fake."

"So, it wasn't you who stole it?" Rosemary asked.

"Of course not. That would have been silly and pointless. I know all about this box, and I know you are the only one who can touch it."

"Except that I can't," said Rosemary. "Every time I've touched it, I get transported to who knows where."

"Try it again," Geneviève instructed. "I do believe that now you've unlocked your own magic properly – which that dragon gag was designed to do – it will work just fine."

"That was just an illusion?" Rosemary asked.

"Oh no," said Geneviève. "It was a manifestation of the Bloodstone power – which is much greater and vaster than you can imagine." Her expression was pointed, and her tone was cold and impatient. "So, you should be very afraid and do as I say. Now, if you'll just pick up the box and hand it to me – officially giving me the Thorn family's magic – I'll leave you alone, to rot, in peace."

It sounded a lot like a rather flippant business transaction.

"Erm..." Rosemary said.

"No! Mum! Don't do it!" Athena cried.

"Shut it, sweetie," said Geneviève, pointing her finger threateningly at Athena.

"I knew I didn't like you from the start," Athena said, glaring. "Mum, whatever you do, don't listen to her."

"Rosemary," Geneviève said with an edge in her voice. "Do exactly as I say if you want your daughter to live."

"You expect me to trust your word after you killed my grandmother?" Rosemary asked, as conflicted rage and the urge for vengeance clashed with fear and the absolute need to protect Athena.

"What choice do you have?" Geneviève asked. "Sure, I admit it. I killed the old bat. It took years of planning, and it was hard to even track her down, but once I set my mind to something, I achieve it. Always. It's not easy being trapped in such a young body. No one takes me seriously, but it does have its advantages. I laid a trail to throw her off the scent. She knew someone was after her and I knew she suspected my 'aunt' just like you did. I was careful to use magic to mask what I truly am, so she never suspected me. And when I showed up looking distraught one night with my hair all tangled, she let me in and made me a cup of tea. When her back was turned, I set a trap and brought the whole clan in to make sure she didn't have a chance of getting the upper hand. She held us off for a while with her magic, but in the end, we broke through. I used a binding charm with my final blow to make sure she couldn't come back as a spirit and blab about me or the Society."

Rosemary took a deep breath. "Thanks for your honesty, I guess," she said. "But nothing you've said makes me trust that you'd let us live, so why should I hand you the box?"

"Stubborn." Geneviève gave a tired sigh and pouted. "Your Granny could have lived too if she hadn't been so stubborn."

"I don't believe that, Mum, and neither should you," said Athena. "Don't do anything she says."

"I don't have all day," said Geneviève sternly. "The box, Rosemary. Give it to me now or the girl gets vaporised!"

The gleam of gold flashed again in Rosemary's eyes. Only Geneviève was too fixated on the box to notice.

Rosemary felt the confidence of her own true power course through her in all its gleaming wildness, and in that moment, she knew exactly what to do. She walked over to the desk and picked up the box to find that Geneviève was indeed correct. She didn't black out or find herself on another plane this time.

Mum...no!

Despite Athena's continued telepathic urging for her to drop it, Rosemary did not, nor did she hand it to the very young-looking old vampire.

Instead, urged on by the centre of energy within her, she opened it.

Rosemary found herself back in the other world – but this time it was on her own terms.

Darkness still surrounded her, though the light crystal she held shone much brighter. The space around her was no longer a total void but was illuminated, revealing shimmering cave walls all around.

She knew instinctively where to go. She walked purposefully through the cave to see the elder standing before her.

"You have arrived," the elder said, her silver hair shining brighter and her eyes glinting with pride. She gestured for Rosemary to walk ahead towards the familiar sight of the thick dark green vines wrapping around the huge, shining crystal.

This time, Rosemary did not hesitate. She moved forward with self-assurance to stand before the centre of the Thorn family's bound magic. She reached out and confidently took hold of the elder's hand, lifting her other hand to connect with the crystal.

A wave of light rushed through her.

You are ready, the power said, light and bright in Rosemary's mind. She closed her eyes and sang the words she now knew intuitively were the ones she had been taught for this very purpose all along.

. . .

Come away my little child,
through the forests of the wild.
Feel the pulling deep within,
Trees will dance and trees will sing,
until they die and fall
elemental magic calls,
until we let the light shine through, rise up, and seize it all.

As she sang, the elder's voice joined hers in harmony. The song reached deep into her heart, into her soul, into their shared genealogy and twisted like a key.

Around her, the sounds of a thousand voices rang out in harmony. Her ancestors were around her, behind her, supporting her. The newly reunited parts of Rosemary Thorn breathed a collective sigh as the old family magic flooded in, coating her from the inside out in strength and grace, nourishing the neglected parts of her spirit and psyche.

This was it. This was her destiny.

Rosemary let all her elemental memories flow through her mind, and her magical recollections of Granny, of being in the forest, of being connected to nature and to the old family magic.

A cracking sound pierced the air.

They watched as the crystal shattered, the vines shrivelled up, and everything around them seemed to break apart into pieces.

Rosemary opened her eyes to find she was in the library, still standing this time.

"What happened?!" Geneviève demanded, clearly flummoxed. "There was a bright light and I couldn't see. I thought I would melt! What was that?" She stepped forward to take the box from Rosemary's hands, only to find it empty. The power was no longer contained. It was hovering in the air, throbbing through the house, pulsating in the veins of the Thorns.

"No!" Geneviève shrieked, her eyes glowing red just as smoke began to coil up from her shoulders.

"The Thorn family magic has been released," said Rosemary, her own eyes glowing golden. "And it's more powerful than the Bloodstone Society's."

"It is not!" cried Geneviève. "You'll pay for this, Rosemary Thorn!"

A torrent of flame burst out from Geneviève's small frame. It built up into a furnace, and another dragon emerged, smaller than the one summoned by the group of Bloodstones, but somehow fiercer. Some books caught alight and others fell to the floor as it circled in the air, stirring chaos through the room, before roaring towards Rosemary.

But Rosemary was prepared. She let the power surge up inside her, even stronger than before, now that she had unbound the Thorn magic. She did not falter, did not waver as the flaming beast shot towards her. She simply raised her hands confidently and released her power. A wave of magical water burst out, cool and refreshing, dousing the flames in the room, but not dampening anything.

Geneviève shrieked and blasted another wave of power out towards Rosemary. It was black as night this time. Rosemary met it head on with a bright beam of golden light, blasting Geneviève's own magic back at her.

Rosemary and Athena watched as the small, ancient, innocent-looking evil being burst into dust, leaving the box to tumble to the floor where it lay open. Silvery particles, which had once belonged to the ancient evil being floated in the air and then moved swiftly towards the empty box as if being sucked in. The lid swung shut with a click.

Rosemary ran to Athena and untied her, then wrapped her in a big hug that her teen didn't even try to push away.

After a moment of silence, their eyes flicked towards the box.

"Do you think she's dead?" Athena asked.

"I suspect so, seeing as she was vaporised," said Rosemary.

"Good riddance," said Athena.

"I know she wasn't really a child, being six thousand years old and all," said Rosemary. "But it still feels wrong."

"She kind of had that coming, though," said Athena. "You did well, Mum."

"Thanks," said Rosemary. It felt odd accepting the praise, but she'd take it, as positive feedback was rare from her teenager. "Ick..." said Rosemary. "It feels so wrong. I'm glad that box did the clean-up. I would hate the idea of having to get her essence out of the carpet!"

Thirty

Rosemary and Athena made their way out of the library towards the kitchen, clearly in need of a cup of tea, but a humming sound distracted them.

They checked the front windows to see a small crowd appeared to be gathering outside Thorn Manor in the evening light.

"What's all this?" Rosemary asked warily.

"It looks to me like...friends," said Athena. "Look. There's Margie and Sherry...oh, and Constable Perkins!"

"I suppose we'd better go and see what this is all about," Rosemary said with a fleeting glance of longing in the direction of the tea kettle.

She opened the door and stepped out towards the group, ready to meet them.

Constable Perkins approached.

"You're both under arrest!" he shouted.

"What?! What for?" Rosemary asked, surprised.

"For...for...disorderly behaviour and...and...disturbing the natural order of things, that big flash of light and all them clouds and the blimin' dragon came from here, they did!"

"Stand down, Constable," said a cool and confident voice.

Rosemary looked over Perkins's shoulder to see a woman with arrow straight black hair and flawless porcelain skin, wearing a sleek black suit.

"Err, Neve," Constable Perkins said, looking disgruntled. "It's okay, love. I've got this."

"I said, stand down. And as your superior, you'd best obey me," the woman said, stepping forward to shake hands with Rosemary. "I'm Detective Constantine Neve," said the woman. "But everyone just calls me by my surname, Neve."

"Constantine is your first name?" Rosemary asked.

"Indeed, it is. My parents had a strange sense of humour. Anyway, I apologise for my colleague's behaviour. He likes to think he runs the roost, especially when I'm out of town on business, but he knows I'm also the acting head of the local police station since Captain Sledge retired."

"Oh...erm...nice to meet you," said Rosemary, trying to make a good impression.

Detective Neve, in her sleek black suit, seemed rather normal, aside from her name, and for a moment, Rosemary wondered if she actually knew about all that magic stuff...until she opened her mouth again to explain.

"I've been on the case of the Bloodstone Society for months. Only they led me on a wild goose chase half way around the country. I knew Despina Crepe was involved, but I figured she was a minor level member. I had no idea about Geneviève."

"I suppose someone so powerful and experienced would have a habit of staying off the radar," said Rosemary empathetically. "I thought Gen was a sweet little girl."

"What happened to Despina?" Athena asked.

"There's no sign of her, I'm afraid," said Neve. "Or of the others."

"I suppose that's a good thing," said Rosemary. "If I never see them again, that will be just fine. But how did you know what just happened up at the house?" she asked, narrowing her eyes a little.

Neve laughed. "You're shrewd. I don't blame you. Like I said, I was travelling all over the place, trying to follow the trail, which was clearly all a set-up. Only it took me two weeks to realise it. They clearly wanted me out of the way. I came back in time to consult my scrying mirror and see what happened up at the house just now. That was brilliant. Thank you for what you did today. Congratulations on a job well done!"

Rosemary and Athena both beamed, delighted by this turn of events, while Constable Perkins scowled.

"Alright, Gerry," she said, putting a hand on Perkins's shoulder. "Let's get you back to the station before you end up red-carded again." She led him away, making space for Marjie to rush forward and wrap both Rosemary and Athena up in a big warm hug.

"You both did your Granny proud today!" she cried. "Now, if you don't mind, I'll pop inside and put the kettle on and rustle you both up some dinner since you missed the Brigid's Day feast."

"There was a feast?" Athena said. "Why did no one mention that?"

"Of course there was!" Marjie said. "There's always a feast after a ritual. But don't worry. I brought plenty of leftovers and lemon cake for dessert!" She held up a big cloth bag bulging with cake tins.

"That sounds perfect," said Rosemary. "I'm starved."

No sooner had Marjie bolted for the front door, then Sherry came forward and hugged them, too. "I knew you could do it. Excellent work – all round. Come over to the pub tomorrow for lunch or dinner on me!"

Athena nodded enthusiastically.

"Thanks, that would be lovely," said Rosemary, noticing Liam hanging back behind Sherry, rather than coming forward to chat. She wondered how long it would be before he was comfortable speaking to her after that previous awkward conversation, but she didn't have much time to think about it before Ferg stepped up, holding a small box wrapped in a yellow bow.

"What's this?" Rosemary asked, taking the box cautiously.

"A small gift of my own homemade fudge," Ferg said. "I heard through the grapevine that you were quite the connoisseur of confectionary in your youth."

"Ooh...how thoughtful," Rosemary said. "Thank you."

"Thank *you*, madam." He lifted his brown Saturn-day cap and tipped it to Rosemary and then to Athena. "Mademoiselle. Good day to you both."

Rosemary and Athena looked at each other, slightly puzzled, but smiling warmly.

"Excuse me," a familiar deep and silky voice said. Rosemary was pleased to see that it was Burk. "I came here to apologise," he said.

"For what?" Rosemary asked.

"For disappearing during your dinner party. I wish that I could have helped you more, only...I was trying to lay low. I've been on the run from the Bloodstone Society, and I knew they were after you."

"Oh...why?"

"I used to be a member...a long time ago, I had to earn back my soul, only they weren't happy about it. They came after me and I had to magically obscure my identity from them. I didn't want to get too involved here, in case they found me out. It's a strange sect, you see. None of the members know who each other are, unless they choose to reveal themselves. Only the leader knows who all of them are...I only tell you this to keep vigilant. There are bound to be society members lurking around Myrtlewood."

"You were a part of them?" Rosemary gaped.

"I was," said Burk. "But I left over two hundred years ago."

"You're really...old," said Rosemary, and then blushed as she realised that had sounded quite rude.

"I told you, it's a long story," said Burk.

"I hope to hear it sometime," Rosemary said, smiling before she was whisked away to be greeted and thanked by Mr June in his official capacity as Mayor.

Mr June gave a speech in which he declared that even the Goddess Brigid herself had blessed the town with her presence and was spotted in the air above Thorn Manor.

Athena gave Rosemary a questioning look.

"Ah, so that's possibly what I saw in the woods..."

Athena shook her head, incredulous.

Mr June ended his speech and then bowed and proclaimed Rosemary and Athena as both VIM's – Very Important Myrtlewoodians. He even handed them little gold brooches depicting an M with a myrtle tree growing behind it.

"Uh, thank you," said Rosemary, surprised by all the spontaneous gratitude as the crowd around them cheered.

A few people scampered out of the way as a shiny Rolls Royce pulled up the driveway, driven by a chauffeur.

"This can only mean one thing," Rosemary muttered to Athena.

Elamina wound the back window down and beckoned Rosemary and Athena over with her index finger. Rosemary kept a safe distance from the clouds of lily of the valley perfume that wafted out of the car.

Burk came over to stand with them, too, though whether out of curiosity or protectiveness Rosemary couldn't tell.

"The family magic is flooding back," Elamina said, a look of astonishment on her face. "I don't know how you did it, but it worked."

“Great,” said Rosemary.

“You exceeded my expectations,” said Elamina coolly, while Derse maintained his usual sneer on the seat beside her.

“When I discovered Granny had left you the house, I was beside myself,” Elamina continued. “My apologies regarding your Burkenswood office, by the way,” she said to Burk. “I didn’t mean to set it on fire. I just lost control of my power when I heard about the house going to Rosemary. I didn’t believe she would have what it takes to release the family magic. Oh, and about this...”

Elamina reached out and handed Rosemary the decoy box. “Here,” she said. Clearly, she’d been the one to steal it from the party.

Rosemary glared at her cousin. “Thanks,” she said flatly.

Elamina gave a little shrug. “I didn’t think you’d have what it takes to release the binding,” she explained. “I tried to take matters into my own hands, but you tricked me.”

“I’m not going to apologise for that, you realise,” Rosemary said. She certainly wasn’t planning to grovel for forgiveness when Elamina hadn’t apologised to her.

“Very well.” Elamina turned to Athena. “Aren’t you charming?” she said. “Sorry about all this fuss. Goodbye, sweety.”

Rosemary balked as Elamina gave a little wave and the window slid up.

The Rolls Royce retreated back down the driveway and Rosemary grumbled. “She apologises to everyone but me! Typical...Still, at least I was right about one thing. I was sure Elamina was responsible for that fire!”

“I’ll give you some credit for that one,” said Athena.

They looked around at the somewhat dispersed crowd.

“Well, this was all kind of...grand!” said Athena. “I suppose we can get back to normal, whatever that means now.”

“That’s right, school starts next week!” said Rosemary. “Which is the day after tomorrow.”

Athena groaned. “Just when I was starting to relax.”

“Clearly, the fun never stops around here!”

Just then, Athena turned her head in the direction of the driveway. Rosemary followed her gaze to see Finnigan, looking like a perfectly innocent teenager.

Athena shot her mother a pleading look. “It clearly wasn’t him,” she said. “You had no right to be suspicious.”

"You never know," said Rosemary. "It *was* another young-looking person, but okay, fine, I'll admit you are a much better judge of character than me."

"Can I hang out with him, then?"

"Oh – go on then," Rosemary said.

"Really?"

"Yes. Go and spend time with your friend for a little while before dinner, but stay within shouting range of the house and be sensible!"

"I'm always sensible," Athena said, flicking her flaming red hair over her shoulder as she walked off towards The Boy. "It's you who should be following that advice," she muttered.

"I heard that!" said Rosemary and smiled as she turned and headed back for Thorn Manor, and tea, and dinner, and cake.

Later that evening, Rosemary and Athena sat on the window seats, drinking tea as they looked out the windows towards the forest.

They were feeling full and satisfied after eating more of Marjie's wonderful pasties and cake, and they'd even opened the fudge Ferg had given them as a gift which was surprisingly delightful.

"This is really good," said Athena.

"Yes," Rosemary agreed. "Smooth and rich with a hint of elderflower."

"Who would have thought Ferg was an excellent confectioner?"

"I wish *I* was a confectioner," said Rosemary. "You know how much I love chocolate."

"Well, you can be whatever you want now, Mum," said Athena. "Your destiny is in your hands."

"Thanks," said Rosemary. "I'm not sure if that's wise, epic or just an incredibly cheesy thing to say."

"Why not all three?" Athena asked. "And while we're at it, I think we've learned something today."

"Like don't trust innocent-looking tweens?" Rosemary suggested.

"Yes, that, and also you learned to use magic on purpose, not just by accident, which makes you at least thirty percent less ridiculous than usual."

"Gee, thanks," said Rosemary. "Do I get an award?"

"Smugness is its own reward. You should enjoy it. Besides, you have nothing to complain about. Your magic actually works, whereas I still don't have any cool powers apart from a buzzing brain with occasional telepathy."

"It's probably a good thing," said Rosemary, taking another sip of tea and smiling at her daughter. "I'm not ready for you to be all-powerful yet. You're already enough of a know-it-all."

"Hey," said Athena, laughing and giving her mother a playful shove.

"I wonder where Dain is," Rosemary said, becoming more serious. "It's strange how I still keep forgetting him, even though I've remembered almost everything else...at least I think I have."

"I'm trying to forget he exists, actually," said Athena. "Seriously, Mum, we're better off without him."

An owl hooted, and they looked back out into the garden.

"Do you think they're out there, watching us?" Athena asked.

Rosemary shook her head. "No. Neve thinks they've cleared out of town. After that performance, it seems like Despina won't be showing her face for a while."

"But the others," Athena said. "We don't even know who they are."

"True," said Rosemary. "And now that their power has diminished, they'll want to keep it that way. Besides, from what Burk said, a bunch of them will be relieved to be able to cut ties with the Bloodstone Society."

"Burk *and* Liam, hanging off your every word," Athena teased.

"Don't start that again," said Rosemary. "Anyway, back to the subject at hand. What did you learn today?"

"I've learnt..." Athena started, and then her eyes went wide. "Mum!"

"What?"

"Something is watching us again!"

Rosemary looked out the window to see a pair of glinting eyes in the darkness, reflecting the moonlight. "An animal...?" Rosemary started, but whatever it was began moving closer, a dark shape, low to the ground, darting towards the house.

"What?" Rosemary started, but Athena had already run towards the door. "Don't open it!" Rosemary cried, but it was too late. "Athena!"

Athena opened the door and bent down to retrieve the creature. She turned back towards Rosemary, holding a fluffy black kitten with dazzling green eyes.

"We're witches, right?" Athena said. "Apparently, that means we attract cats."

Rosemary stepped closer, and the little black floofball leapt into her arms. "What in Brigid's name!?" she said, cradling the adorable purring creature.

"You've done well, dears," said a kind and familiar voice, coming from the mirror across from the door.

"Granny!" said Rosemary, realising the resentment and anger she had felt for the old woman had evaporated, most likely over the course of unlocking her magic.

"You've done well and I'm proud of you both."

"Ahh, thanks," said Rosemary, stroking the cat. "I think I get it now; why you had to do what you did."

"I'm not perfect," said Granny. "I could have done a thousand things differently and possibly better, but it was the only way I could think of at the time to keep you both safe until you were ready, and now you clearly are." She smiled warmly.

"Can you explain this, then?" Athena asked, nodding towards the kitten.

"It's Rosemary's familiar, dear," said Granny.

"Familiar?" Rosemary asked. "It really is just like fiction."

"Why does Mum get a familiar?" Athena asked, scratching the kitten's head. "Where's mine? I've always wanted a cat."

"We can share," Rosemary suggested. "I've always been afraid to get a pet in case I can't look after it properly. It's hard enough keeping both of us alive, clearly."

"Don't worry, Athena," said Granny. "Yours will come in time, as soon as your powers properly kick in."

"Molly was your familiar, wasn't she?" Rosemary asked, remembering Granny's old mottled cat.

"Indeed, she was, and she was with me right until the end. Familiars last as long as their witches, all going well."

"I can't wait!" Athena said. "I really will get cool powers *and* get to have a cat. Livin' the dream!"

Granny nodded sagely. "Indeed. But for now, just look after your mother. I think she's going to need it in the coming weeks." She winked.

Athena laughed and Rosemary gulped.

"What's that supposed to mean?"

"You'll soon see," said Granny. "I'm fading now, but farewell, my lovelies. I'll see you again soon!"

"That woman!" said Rosemary. "Exasperating."

Athena laughed again, taking the cat from Rosemary. "It must run in the family," she said.

Rosemary smiled and wrapped her arms around Athena and the small purring kitten. It might be bizarre and dangerous, but their lives had also changed so much for the better in such a short space of time. It would be remiss of her not to appreciate it.

Experimental Magic

MYRTLEWOOD MYSTERIES BOOK TWO

Prologue

Dain pulled up to the old house. It was just as he remembered it, though it had been years since he'd been there. Rosemary's grandmother had warned him off, and he wasn't fool enough to mess with someone as powerful as Galderall Thorn.

Even now, he was wary of ringing the bell in case she answered and blasted him to another realm.

He parked the car and began unloading boxes.

His daughter's things.

Rosemary's things.

He knew he didn't deserve them – these women who had somehow become the most important part of the tornado of his life.

He had wronged them too many times – stole from them, lied to them, left them, only to return again and start the whole cycle over. Dain had wanted things to be different, every single time, and yet there was only so much he could control.

This was the least he could do – pack their things into boxes and drive them over here. Rosemary even said he could keep the car and sell it. She knew him too well – knew he would need the money. Dain sighed.

The last box was loaded onto the porch and he could hear them inside – Rosemary and Athena – talking. Their voices were soothing to him. They anchored him here in this world where he had no real place.

He wanted to see them, but he was afraid of the old woman, and something seemed to be holding him back.

It must be Galderall's power. She's trying to keep me away from her family...from my family.

It wasn't strong enough to stop him and his instinct was to push through, but he hesitated again, unsure whether they would want to see him or not.

Hesitation was unusual for Dain, who'd never had any particular form of self-control. *It must be the magic making me hold back,* he thought, and that was enough to get him to push through, no matter how scared he was of Granny Thorn.

He reached up to the door and knocked. Then he turned around. He could hear it. From far away, a familiar sound, roaring towards him faster than anything of this world.

Oh no...they've found me.

A swirling mist appeared, enveloping Dain in white, and he disappeared from the human world.

One

"Mum!" Athena yelled down the stairs. "Where's my green jersey?"

"How am I supposed to know?" Rosemary called from the kitchen. "Come and have your toast before it gets cold. We're running out of time!"

Athena clomped down the stairs. "I have absolutely no good clothes and this school doesn't have a uniform like St Maria's did."

The black fluffy kitten that had been hovering around Rosemary's feet crossed the floor to greet Athena, who immediately went to the fridge to feed her.

"Little fuzzball is taking a liking to you," said Rosemary.

"When are you going to give her a proper name?" Athena asked. "She's supposed to be *your* familiar, but she definitely likes me more. Maybe I'll name her...hmm, how about Serpentine?"

"Eat some breakfast," said Rosemary, brandishing toast. "The cat can wait."

"Fine," said Athena, grabbing a piece. "What can't wait is finding my jersey. Can't you do a magic summoning trick or something?"

"You know that has only worked a few times," said Rosemary. "And only by accident when I was actually looking *at* the thing."

"Please? Just try. You should be experimenting with your magic – learning it properly."

"Oh, fine."

Rosemary closed her eyes and imagined Athena's forest green jumper. She held out her arms and willed it to come to her.

There was a rustling sound and Rosemary felt quietly optimistic for a moment, until a pillowy force smashed into her, knocking the plate of toast off the bench and sending her hurtling to the floor.

Rosemary opened her eyes in shock. "What the—?" She looked around. "Don't tell me I was just bowled over by a wall of fabric?!"

"That was kind of awesome," said Athena, peering at her mother over a pile of blankets, cushions, and throws. "I mean, I know you didn't intend to do that, but it's a bit like those really random super powers – you have control over all cloth-based materials or something."

"Oh, stop it. I do not," said Rosemary. "I just don't know what I'm doing with this magic stuff. Although it's just as well my super-strength seems to be only in response to danger or I'd have broken all the tea cups by now."

Athena sighed. "It's *so* not fair that you have all the power and can't be bothered learning to use it."

Rosemary looked around at the pile of fabric and shrugged.

They both laughed.

"You know that feeling," said Rosemary. "When you're riding high, confident and full of a sense of empowered purpose?"

"Not really," said Athena, offering her mother a hand and pulling her up. "Is that how you're feeling? Because if it is I want whatever is in your tea!"

"No," said Rosemary with a frown. "That's how I felt after I unleashed the family magic and defeated that vampire brat. I want it back. It's like just when I'm starting to think I've finally mastered this life business, I'm suddenly back to square one and Monday mornings. Why is that?"

"Neuropsychology?" Athena suggested. "But at least you don't have to go to work. You got fired, remember?"

"Don't remind me! I need to start applying for jobs. Who knows when this inheritance business will get sorted. *And* I really need to master this magic stuff before it all backfires on me in a much worse and less fabric-oriented way."

"You'll get the hang of it," said Athena with a giggle. "Besides, it worked." She held up her jersey, lifting it out of the pile. "It must have been in the parlour with all these cushions and throws."

"Well, that's something, I guess. Next time I need a wall of fabric to smash into me, I know what to do." Rosemary glanced at the wall clock. "Oh no."

"What?"

"Look at the time!"

"Let's go then," Athena said, picking up another piece of toast from the plate that had clattered very gracefully to the floor, right-side up, no doubt supported by the delightful magic of Thorn Manor.

They raced to the car. Granny's old and elegant Rolls Royce started with a purr and Rosemary drove them quickly towards the school, instructed by Athena who was following the directions on her phone to avoid her mother getting them lost *again*.

Rosemary pulled up in front of the old castle-like stone buildings.

"Seriously?" she said.

"What?" Athena asked.

"It's like you're about to join Miss Cackle's Academy or something."

"What did you expect in Myrtlewood?" Athena asked. "Because this is pretty much what I was anticipating."

"I hope you don't have to make potions with gross newt's eyes," Rosemary said. "Do you want me to come in with you?"

"I'd rather gnaw off my own arm," said Athena.

"Harsh!"

"Mum, you do realise this is my opportunity to make a first impression at a new school, right? Parents are *not* cool."

"Fine," said Rosemary. "But don't blame me if you get lost and can't find anything."

"I don't think you have a good track record when it comes to senses of direction," said Athena. "I'm probably better off without you!"

"You have a point," said Rosemary. She reached over and hugged her daughter goodbye from the safe distance of the car, so as not to tarnish Athena's reputation. She watched as the sixteen-year-old made her way towards the ornate building, sporting a significant number of towers and clad in large swathes of ivy.

She had a pang of pride, watching her daughter waltz confidently into her new school. This was followed by the sting of longing for the life Rosemary could have had if things had been different.

What if I'd grown up in Myrtlewood with Granny, rather than with my extremely religious parents in St Austell?

What if I'd gone to school here? What would my life have been like?

With a strange sense of emptiness, Rosemary drove the few blocks back into Myrtlewood village, parking next to the tea shop. She was more than ready for a pick-me-up. What she wasn't prepared for was seeing a certain gentleman sitting inside, watching her arrive as if he'd been waiting for her.

Two

"Mister Burk," Rosemary said as she entered the tea shop.

Burk put down the newspaper that he was clearly no longer reading.

"Rosemary," he responded.

It took a moment for it to dawn on Rosemary that Burk, as a vampire, should surely be fizzling up into dust. She stared at him in horror. "But it's day time!"

"Indeed it is."

"Wha—" Rosemary stuttered, panicking, as she expected Burk to disappear at any moment.

"Marjie has UV resistant glass," Burk explained. "And an underground entrance through her cellar."

"Oh," said Rosemary in relief. "Of course she does,"

She looked around for Marjie, who was nowhere to be seen.

"Do you have a minute to talk?" Burk asked.

Rosemary blushed, remembering the few fleeting moments of intimacy she'd shared with the elegant vampire. Nothing had happened, and Rosemary didn't date – not with her track record. She was worried Burk was about to suggest they start something.

Her mind raced with excuses and possibilities as she recalled the awkward conversation she'd had a few days before with Liam, her old teenage flame, where he'd asked her out and she'd had to decline. Things had been weird with him after that. Liam had been distant and awkward. The last thing she wanted was additional weirdness – from her lawyer!

"Uhh...umm," said Rosemary. "I'm kind of busy."

It was a total lie. Now that she'd dropped Athena off at school, the only things occupying her were the utter emptiness of her day, her challenging financial situation, and how to get control of her magic...All things that were not as immediate as her desire for a nice cup of Marjie's special tea and a slice of lemon cake.

"It won't take long," Burk assured her. "But you could make an appointment to see me at my office if you prefer."

"Your *office*?!" Rosemary asked, shocked at what she assumed he was suggesting.

"Yes," said Burk wryly. "You know, my office, across the square where I practice law, including administering your grandmother's estate. Remember that?"

"Oh," said Rosemary. "Of course. You want to talk to me about *that* stuff."

"That stuff," said Burk, his voice dry yet amused. "Yes. I have some updates for you. It would be more professional to meet in my office, but I reasoned that since you're here..."

"So what's the news?" Rosemary asked, blushing even more at her arrogance for assuming that Burk must surely be asking her out. He was a gorgeous, educated man who wore nice suits. He had a very, *very* long undead existence ahead of him – not to mention the age gap!

Burk probably thinks of me as a little child, Rosemary thought, *her blush deepening.*

"Are you quite alright?" he asked. "You look flushed."

"Yes, just feeling a bit warm."

"You're not coming down with a fever, are you?" Burk said, raising his cool palm to her head in a slightly paternal gesture.

"No, really," said Rosemary. "I'm fine."

"There you are!" said Marjie, bustling over to give Rosemary a kiss on the cheek. "I was busy out the back. You know, now that it's spring and wedding season, I'm overrun with catering orders!"

Rosemary smiled at her Granny's old friend with the wild curly red hair, who had quickly become one of her and Athena's closest friends in Myrtlewood.

Beeping sounded from the kitchen.

"Help yourself to anything from behind the counter, dear," said Marjie. "I need to get the jam tarts out of the oven before they burn! And then I need to ice the cupcakes!"

Rosemary looked back at Burk as Marjie disappeared into the kitchen.

"You were saying?" she prompted. "What lawyerly things do you have to tell me? Please say it's good news."

Rosemary was dreading what might happen if the money from Granny didn't come through soon. She was up to her neck in debt, due almost entirely to Athena's father, Dain.

"It is, I'd say," said Burk. "The estate of Galderall Thorn is being processed now. A significant sum of money will be incoming shortly."

"Oh my gods! That's fantastic!" said Rosemary. "There seemed to be such a big delay before, I wondered if it was ever going to come through."

"Well, you've now been cleared of murder," said Burk. "That helped."

"And how exactly do you clear someone of murder when an ancient child vampire, a secret society of supernatural beings, and a giant apparition of a dragon are involved?" Rosemary asked.

Burk shrugged. "The Myrtlewood authorities have their way of doing things. It's slightly...different from the way mundane society functions, but it works."

"Well, to celebrate, I'm having cake!" Rosemary announced. "Do you want anything?" she asked Burk.

"I'm fine here," he said, waving his hand over his coffee.

"Oh, that's right, I forgot. You can't eat normal food. Erm, by normal I mean human, uhh...do you count as—never mind. It's just as well Marjie can whip up those enchantments to make things err...palatable for you. Though I wouldn't have the faintest idea how—"

Burk cleared his throat.

"Sorry," said Rosemary, aware she had been growing redder in the face as the rambled. "I really need Athena around at times like these to stop me."

"It's fine," said Burk, looking amused. He took a sip of his beverage and Rosemary wondered briefly if his coffee had to be enchanted too, but decided it might be rude to ask. After all, vampires were very private beings.

"I'll just..." she said and got up to help herself to a large slice of lemon curd sponge from behind the counter.

She was still behind the counter, about to head back over to the table to sit with Burk and maybe convince him to divulge some more information about the timing of the aforementioned great pile of funds, when the door opened. Mr June, the mayor, waltzed in, his oily hair sticking to his forehead and his long purple cape looking slightly more crinkled than usual.

"A large slice of carrot cake if you please, love," he said, tipping his hat to Rosemary. "I didn't know you'd been hired."

"I haven't," Rosemary said, raising her hands in innocence. "Marjie just told me to help myself while she's busy icing cupcakes."

Marjie popped her head around the kitchen door at that moment. "You could help Mr June as well, dear, if you don't mind."

"Sure," said Rosemary, fetching another plate so that she could serve the Myrtlewood mayor a slice of carrot cake. She took it over to his table, and then carried her own cake back to where Burk was sitting.

"So," she said, after savouring a few mouthfuls of the delicious light, tart, and creamy sponge. "What kind of timing are you expecting?"

"Excuse me?" Burk asked.

"For the estate to be fully processed."

"It could be weeks," Burk said. "Two months, tops. It just needs to be checked by a handful of lawyers and bureaucrats. These things tend to take an unreasonable amount of time."

Rosemary nodded, feeling her heart fall. She was already skint and Athena needed new clothing, especially as Myrtlewood Academy didn't have a uniform and teenagers needed to have at least a few decent outfits to cycle through.

"Are you sure you're alright?" Burk asked.

"What are you, my mother?" Rosemary retorted. "I'm fine."

"Ten minutes ago you looked flushed and now you look pale. Humans as so changeable and so...fragile."

"Don't be ridiculous," said Rosemary. "I may be many things. Changeable, sure, but fragile? Certainly not. I've been through a lot in my life and I'm tough as nails."

Burk smiled and returned to reading his paper.

Rosemary tried to stifle her sigh. She wasn't fragile, exactly, but she was broke. The debt just kept piling up and her credit was so bad she couldn't even hope to get another loan to tide her over for a few months.

It took Rosemary a while of dwelling on her financial woes before she remembered she still had a few questions to ask the lawyer.

"Burk," she said, trying to be polite and maintain distance all at the same time.

"Yes?"

"When we first met...Umm, how do I say this?"

"You suspected me of killing your grandmother?" Burk suggested.

Rosemary blanched again. "Well, kind of. The thing is, you seemed to want me to sell the house – at our very first meeting. Later on, that seemed suspicious. I just wanted to know why."

Burk looked slightly embarrassed. "I simply thought you were so young and metropolitan compared to the old country lifestyle we have around here. I assumed you'd prefer to live in a city. That's all."

Rosemary spluttered as she sipped her tea. "It's funny," she said. "I don't feel young at all, but I guess by comparison..." Her words trailed off, as she wasn't sure it was polite to refer to a vampire as excessively old, even if he was. "Is that really the reason?" she asked, raising an eyebrow quizzically.

Burk sighed. "Not entirely. I also suspected there was danger connected to the house and that the Bloodstone Society was involved. I suppose I felt... protective of y—your family and wanted you and your daughter to be safe."

"That's kind of you," said Rosemary, wondering if Burk had boundary issues.

"I also suppose I felt guilty," Burk said.

"Guilty?"

"Yes. That something had happened to my client, Madame Thorn, at what I suspected was the hands of my old enemy."

Rosemary smiled in what she thought was a reassuring way.

Yes, definitely boundary issues.

Three

Athena was relieved her mother hadn't insisted on coming in with her. High school was hard enough without parents there. They'd managed to sort out her enrolment the week before, over the phone, despite the school apparently being closed for the spring festival of Imbolc. Strangely, they hadn't needed any documentation of the kind that Rosemary had been required to provide at other schools. In fact, Myrtlewood Academy had all the documentation of the Thorn family they'd needed. All Athena had to do was turn up and make herself known at reception so that she could be shown to her class.

It sounded simple, but it really wasn't.

Athena had experienced so many awkward, isolating, humiliating, and generally uncomfortable things at the various schools she'd attended over the years, as they'd moved around so much.

Every one of those bad school memories seemed to be haunting her as she walked through the courtyard between the big old stone buildings, following signs for reception.

To make matters worse, she hadn't figured out how to turn off the buzzing in her head which was interrupted occasionally by the errant thoughts of people around her. This made her paranoid that she would seem utterly bonkers to her new classmates. She'd asked Finnigan to help her master the telepathy that he seemed to understand so well, but nothing he'd said had made a difference so far.

Finnigan...

That was the other thing plaguing her mind. She kept thinking about him – the boy who had appeared in her life out of nowhere, only to make a very deep and lasting impression.

Athena wasn't used to having *feelings* for people. Indeed, she'd sometimes wondered if it was a part of her that was missing. While her peers had often talked with dazed expressions about their crushes, including celebrities they'd never met, Athena had never liked anyone in that way. She barely even had any friends, let alone romantic relationships. It had niggled at her for a long time that there must be something badly wrong with her, and the voices she heard only added to that concern.

But Finnigan understands. He's got the same ability – or curse – or whatever it is.

She wished that he attended Myrtlewood Academy, but alas, he'd informed her that his education was carried out somewhere a little further afield.

So here she was, starting a new school yet again, knowing no one, and to make matters worse, this was clearly a magical school in a magical town and she had the magical aptitude of a broken radio.

Athena entered through the doors marked 'reception' to find a big carved wooden counter. Behind it sat a rather small woman wearing a sage green cardigan over a pale-pink-and-cream polka-dotted dress. The dress had a Peter Pan collar, making the woman appear even more childlike, despite the obvious lines on her face and her grey hair. She appeared to be so busy with the papers on her desk that she didn't notice anyone come in.

Athena cleared her throat. "Excuse me," she said.

The receptionist looked up, over her horn-rimmed spectacles. "Greetings. How may I help you?" she said in a high and croaky voice, flashing a reptilian smile.

"I'm Athena Thorn. It's my first day. I was told to come here."

"Thorn...Thorn..." the woman muttered, licking her index finger with a rather long tongue and rifling through a stack of papers. "Ah yes. Here you are. Nice to meet you. I'm Marla Twigg – Ms Twigg to the students."

"Twigg?" said Athena. The name sounded familiar.

"Yes," said Ms Twigg, batting her eyelashes. "You're probably wondering whether I'm related to the famous historian, Agatha Twigg."

"Oh, Agatha. That's right," Athena said. "We met her down at the pub."

Ms Twigg looked slightly ruffled at that response, clearly expecting more awe in the recognition.

"Oh...umm," Athena continued. "She's a historian? Actually, come to think of it, I was looking at a book by A. C. Twigg the other day...and...err she came to our house for dinner once, but I didn't realise..." Athena stopped, realising she was rambling like her mother. "Uh...Are you related?" she asked.

"She's my aunt," said Ms Twigg proudly. "She's quite well known, you know. But I suppose your family is too. The Thorns are infamous in these parts."

She said all this with a generous smile, but her words only increased Athena's sense of dread.

The family is famous...but I'm utterly useless. Mum is the one with magic and all I have is a buzzing sound in my head!

"Follow me," said Ms Twigg, hopping off her rather tall chair and gesturing out to the foyer. Athena was startled to find the woman was even smaller than she'd realised, and only came up to just above her waist. She followed her along the wood-panelled hallway.

"You're very early, you know," said Ms Twigg.

"I thought I was late," Athena said. "Why are there no other students around?"

"We start mid-morning, usually."

"But the website said..." Athena stared.

Ms Twigg gave a small, shrill, laugh. "I forget we have a website. It's compulsory for all schools in the district or the country or something. It has standard information so that we don't look suspicious to the mundane folk."

"Oh," said Athena, nodding. "Of course. Does that mean school finishes late, too?"

"No, it simply means we bend time if we have to – to get through the lessons. School must finish promptly at 3:15 p.m. or we'd all be late for our afternoon tea, wouldn't we?"

"But why—?"

"Nobody likes mornings," said Ms Twigg, as if it was all perfectly obvious. "Here is the library."

Athena peered into the large high-ceilinged room filled with enormous old wooden bookshelves laden with books.

"Wow," Athena said. "That's awesome."

Ms Twigg smiled at her, clearly savouring the response. "Thank you. It is my library. I am also the librarian here."

"Cool," said Athena.

"Is it?" Ms Twigg asked. "It actually feels rather muggy in here, for February anyway."

Athena thought Ms Twigg was making a rather naff joke at first, but quickly realised there was no humour involved. The response reminded her of Ferg and other odd characters she'd met around Myrtlewood. For a moment Athena felt like she was on another planet. She chose not to explain her remark, as it clearly wasn't worth her effort. Instead, she silently followed Ms Twigg around the school, baffled by half the things the small woman said.

"The planetarium is through that way, along the eastern corridor, and I'm sure, being a Thorn, you'll be keen on the herbarium – it's around the back of the building on the southern side. Your grandmother was a maverick with herbs."

Ms Twigg continued on, gesturing around and naming half a dozen other "arium" type places Athena did not quite comprehend and immediately forgot.

"Here is your hearth room," said Ms Twigg, leading Athena to a particular door, though by this time she had no idea where in the sprawling building she was or how she'd gotten there.

"My what?" Athena asked.

"You know – the room you start the day with. Your main classroom."

"Oh...great," said Athena. "Kind of like a form room or homeroom?"

Ms Twigg gave her a blank look and then turned on her sage green heels and strode away.

Well, that was rather abrupt, Athena thought, worried that she'd somehow disappointed the receptionist-slash-librarian and dreading that there was only more embarrassment to come.

ATHENA PUSHED OPEN the hearth room door to find the room empty. It could have almost been an ordinary classroom at an ordinary school, except there were only a handful of desks arranged in a semi-circle, facing towards a large oak table laden with books, unusual vessels, and all sorts of objects bearing a vague resemblance to bizarre chemistry equipment. Behind the table there appeared to be a large pile of rags, but when Athena's eyes came to rest on them she could have sworn they were moving.

No. They were definitely moving.

The rags roared loudly, making Athena jump. She lost her balance, knocking over a desk. It clattered loudly to the floor and Athena felt creeping panic. Surely, whatever the creature in front of her was, it must have heard her.

Finding her balance, she looked back in horror at the unknown beast and watched as some of the rags slid back in the form of a hood. A very old face with a very large white beard emerged, with little bright blue eyes, blinking up at Athena in surprise.

"Oh, sorry," Athena said.

The old man cleared his throat. "Hello there," he said in a kindly voice. "And who might you be?

Athena stuttered for a moment before muttering, "I'm Athena Thorn."

He gave her a serious, squinty look and then rummaged around on the chaotic table in front of him, which Athena realised must surely be his desk, until he found a small pair of round-lensed spectacles that reminded her a little of the Beatles.

He put these on and squinted at Athena again.

"Thorn. Hah! Indeed you are. Related to old Galdie, rest her spirit."

"That's my great grandmother," Athena said, nodding. "And I don't think her spirit is getting much rest. She's up to mischief in the spirit world, I'm sure of it. That's when she's not popping in to Thorn Manor for deep and meaningful chats."

Athena clasped her mouth, recalling that Granny Thorn didn't want people to know about her ghostly apparition.

"Is she now?" the old man asked, smiling with such warmth that Athena stopped worrying. Then his smile shifted into a slight frown. "Oh, bother. How rude of me not to introduce myself. I'm Aventurine Spruce. And I suppose I am your new hearth teacher."

"I suppose so," Athena said. "I think I'm a bit early. Oh, and I'm sorry I knocked over the desk."

"Never mind that," said Mr Spruce. "Take a seat and make yourself at home."

Four

Rosemary stayed for too long at the tea shop. The early rush of guests had cleared out and they were well into the pre-lunch lull. She didn't feel in the mood to go home to Granny's house and be all by herself or have to confront her unpredictable grandmother's ghost. Not today.

Burk had long left for his office. Rosemary borrowed his newspaper so that she could look at the job listings. There were a few options in the next town over, but that would require driving there, probably at the exact same time she needed to be getting Athena to school. Still, she needed a job.

The money from Granny's estate would help, whenever it happened to come through, but even then it wouldn't last forever. The problem was, she didn't have any qualifications or much experience. She circled a request for grocery check-out attendants and then slumped down onto the table, not even attempting to conceal a loud sigh.

"What is it, love?" Marjie asked, coming over.

"It's nothing." Rosemary straightened up and plastered on a smile.

"Looking for work?" Marjie asked, gesturing to the newspaper.

"To be honest, I'm a little short on cash," Rosemary admitted. "I can't see any postings for jobs in Myrtlewood though."

"Oh, no one bothers with that," said Marjie, gesturing at the paper. "That's all for the mundane world, you see. If we posted help-wanted ads in the county newspapers we could get people showing up who screamed at the first sight of magic. No...here we just ask around if there's a job needing doing or a person needing work."

"Oh," said Rosemary. "So if the newspaper isn't even relevant to Myrtlewood, why would anyone want to read it?"

Marjie shrugged. "Just keeping up to date with the state of the world, I s'pose. It's good to be informed. But don't change the subject. Tell aunt-Marjie your troubles and I'll see what I can do."

Marjie came and sat down at the table, bringing Rosemary cream and jam scones and a pot of tea with her special pick-me-up charm added in for good measure.

Rosemary took one sip of the brew and instantly felt better. The shame she'd been carrying about her money problems seemed to evaporate and she filled Marjie in on the whole sorry state of affairs.

"So you'll be fine soon," Marjie said. "Galdie's money will come through and sort you out."

"Sure, for a while," said Rosemary. "But for now, I'm totally skint. Even after the money comes in, it's not going to last, is it? I'll need some kind of job, some income, to be self-sustaining. I don't want to squander my inheritance and go back to being broke again."

"Take another sip of tea, love," said Marjie.

Rosemary did as she was instructed and watched Marjie's face furrow into intense concentration.

"It seems to me," Marjie said, "that you have two problems here."

"Not just one big gaping one?" Rosemary asked.

"No," said Marjie. "You've got the problem of what to do with yourself right now, and for the next few weeks, just to get by – which is the easy problem to solve."

"Easy?! How is it *easy*?" Rosemary asked. "Do you know something I don't?"

"Oh Rosemary, we love you in this town, and I'm sure there's plenty of work. Ferg's got plenty of jobs, I'm sure he has a few he can spare. What are you keen on?"

"Honestly, I'll do anything," Rosemary said, feeling her problem halved already, simply by sharing it with Marjie.

"How about here?" Marjie asked.

"The tea shop?"

"Sure," said Marjie. "It's the busy season for me – like I told you before. If you don't mind donning an apron then I'd love to have you here to keep the customers served while I potter around out the back. You could even help me cook if you like. I know you're gifted in the kitchen."

"Won't it be a bit crowded out the back with Herb around?"

"Oh pish," said Marjie with a dismissive wave. "Herb has been too busy with his blighting model train club. They're staging an exhibition. He's been of no use to me. You'd be perfect."

"Really?"

"O'course," said Marjie. "You've already served the mayor, and I've seen what you can do in the kitchen. You can start tomorrow, if you like. Simple as that."

Rosemary sighed – but this time in relief and delight. "That's wonderful. Thank you!" She threw her arms around Marjie. "You're a lifesaver, and I couldn't think of a lovelier job."

"See – that speaks to your second problem," said Marjie.

"What's my second problem?" Rosemary asked, baffled.

"You might not be ready to hear this," Marjie warned.

"Oh no. You can't do that! You can't tell me I have a problem and then keep me in suspense. What is it?"

"Long-term thinking," Marjie said sagely. "You're too used to living week-to-week – never risking getting your hopes up about the future."

Rosemary nodded. "I haven't had that luxury."

"True, but it's also something you're afraid of, I'd wager."

"You're probably right," Rosemary replied, resting her cheek in her hand, elbow leaning on the table in a manner in which her conservative parents would have told her off for. "It's easier not to think about the future. When I do, there's just this big scary void of unknowns and potential failure."

"You can put that in the past now," Marjie said, gently patting Rosemary's shoulder. "You're home with us, in Myrtlewood, and we take care of our own."

Rosemary smiled. "Thanks. That's lovely of you to say."

"It's just the truth, is all," said Marjie matter-of-factly. "Now, you can stop worrying and start asking yourself, like that famous poet says: What is it you want to do with your one precious life?"

Rosemary groaned. "I've been asking myself the same question. For years, actually. It all just seemed so impossible before, but you're right. Now that I finally *do* have enough freedom in sight, it's terrifying!"

It was Marjie's turn to sigh. "That it is, love. To be sure, not feeling we have any choice in our destiny is tough, but having the power to choose, well that can be even harder."

"It's a lot better, though," said Rosemary. "Having a choice over my life is far more preferable over not having any power."

"But…?" Marjie prompted.

Rosemary rested her head in her hands. "But I'm scared that if I do try to do something new I'll just mess it up and get into more terrible debt and we'll be back to square one. Or I'll make the wrong choice and miss out on what I really should be doing. Or…or…"

"I understand, love," said Marjie. "You have an enormous case of what the young people call FOMO – fear of missing out."

"Athena says young people don't use that anymore," said Rosemary. "Now that older people know about it. Perhaps it's more FOF."

"Foff?"

"Fear of failure," said Rosemary. "Though I'm not sure anyone calls it that. But yes…a bunch of fears and a bunch of unknowns."

"Well, you know what the good thing is?" Marjie asked.

"What?"

"You're safe, and well, and you have Athena who's just going to flourish here, I know it. You don't have to figure it out all at once, and in the meantime you can help me out at the shop."

"You're right," said Rosemary, smiling again. "Thank you, Marjie."

"It's no bother, dear. I'm just so chuffed to have you home in Myrtlewood after all these years." And with that, Marjie got up to serve a customer, humming happily to herself as she did so, leaving Rosemary to ponder her hopes and fears.

Five

Athena sat anxiously behind a desk, examining her dark purple chipped fingernail polish. Mr. Spruce had fallen back to sleep and was snoring rather loudly. She didn't want to disturb him and she didn't know what else to do.

She kept her head down as the other students started to arrive.

"Who in Hades are you?" A shrill voice interrupted Athena's thoughts.

She looked up to see a blonde girl with a long neck and pointy nose, her hair pulled tightly into a high ponytail.

Athena glanced around the room to see a few more faces. All eyes were on her.

"I'm Athena Thorn," she said.

The girl's blue eyes bulged in recognition.

Apparently everyone knows our family name. Athena felt the weight pressing down on her, of all the expectations that the name seemed to carry with it.

"I'm Beryl Flarguan," the girl said in an icy tone. "I come from an old witching family, and I'm top of the class."

Athena gave her a puzzled look. "Okay."

"You might come from a well-known family, but I'm better," Beryl continued. "You're not going to beat me." She then turned, with her nose high in the air, and stormed to the other side of the class, taking the desk closest to Mr Spruce.

Athena looked around to check how the other students were reacting to Beryl's display.

Are they all going to be that horrid?

She was relieved when the cool-looking kid next to her wearing an oversized hoodie shot her a sympathetic look. Meanwhile, a couple of others in the room burst out laughing. Athena eyed them warily, unsure if they were laughing at her or Beryl.

One girl had bright blue hair in a pixie cut. She smiled warmly at Athena. The guy next to her, who was also laughing, was tall with rather a lot of black hair. Athena wished she could tell what either of them were thinking. Her head was buzzing with static, but there were no clear thoughts coming through, which was the usual case when she was surrounded by people.

Athena cursed her power, which was literally more of a headache than an asset. It would be much more useful if she could hone it somehow so that she could hear specific thoughts. She made a mental note to ask Finnigan about this.

A tanned boy with dark red hair and a slight build entered the classroom. His eyes fixed on Mr. Spruce.

"Sprucey's asleep again," he said mischievously.

"No way, Felix," said the girl with the blue hair. "Don't you try anything."

"Just a little charm," he replied, taking a glowing blue ball from his pocket and setting it on the desk in front of Mr Spruce.

Athena looked around, anxiously wondering what was going on. All eyes were on Felix as he bent to whisper something over the ball and then stepped two large paces back. The charm whirred and fizzed, and blue smoke burst from it, causing Mr Spruce to sneeze and stand up in alarm.

"Huh! Emergency! Emergency!" he cried.

The class giggled and clapped and laughed, all except for the blue-haired girl and the kid in the hoodie next to Athena, who seemed to be taking this all much more seriously.

"Felix!" Mr Spruce bellowed. "I take it this was another one of your pranks."

"Guilty as charged," said Felix with a twinkle in his eyes.

Athena breathed a sigh of relief. At least the prank was just for show, no real harm done.

"A new kid, eh?" said Felix, swaggering over to Athena and sitting down next to her. "Well, fancy that. Fresh blood."

Athena blanched, feeling slightly queasy, and looked at her hands again.

"Order! Order!" Mr Spruce said.

"We're not in court, sir," Felix said casually.

"Felix, do I *have* to give you detention again?"

"It's not detention if I don't show up," Felix replied.

Mr Spruce's voice took on a tone of authority. "Alright. I'll send you to Ms Twigg."

There was a hush around the room.

"Please don't!" Felix said, sitting up straighter in his chair and crossing his arms. "I'll be good. I promise."

Athena wasn't sure if Felix was playing the clown, but from his tone she sensed he was genuinely scared of the tiny librarian.

"Very well. Class, let's get started," said Mr Spruce. "Take out your homework. If I recall correctly, you were to memorise a chant to the Moon and then write three paragraphs on what it meant to you. If you'll all begin..."

The class began reciting a chant that, of course, Athena had never heard before. She felt incredibly out of place.

She'd never been particularly good at ordinary schooling, but now she was so totally out of her depth that she didn't know how to respond.

She felt perplexed about how any of this could possibly fit into the national curriculum or qualify as a useful education.

The buzzing in her head had become a right headache, and her sense of dread only worsened. The next class was History and Folklore, taught in the library by none other than Ms Twigg, who, like Ferg, appeared to have far too many jobs for one person, although unlike Ferg, hers all seemed to revolve around the school.

Athena didn't know where to start with ancient fairy texts. The other students all seemed to know exactly what was going on. She kept to herself and tried not to interact with anyone, though Beryl kept shooting her sly looks, clearly enjoying Athena's obvious discomfort.

It was painfully clear that Athena had no clue what was going on and the teachers were far too odd and unsettling to be of much help.

The other kids didn't seem to be quite so awful, but Athena didn't want to take any chances with them either. Though some of the students seemed helpful and even friendly, she felt safer keeping to herself. There were too many unknowns.

At lunchtime she hung back in the library and tried to make sense of the thirteenth century texts written by visiting Welsh nuns about the local pixies.

She was tempted to pull out her phone and search online to see if she could find an explanation for some of the concepts that made no sense to her, though she doubted Wikipedia would have anything so obscure. Besides, she doubted Ms Twigg would approve of phone use in the library.

Ms Twigg stood behind the desk keeping a close watch on everyone in the room and looking mildly threatening. Athena was still slightly unnerved about why Felix the prankster was frightened of the small woman.

After lunch was art class. At least that one was relatively similar to the kind of curriculum Athena was used to. The teacher was old and petite, wearing a tartan suit. She introduced herself to Athena as Ms Tabitha Coin. "But please call me Tabby," she added.

The class began and Athena was paired with Sam, the kid in the oversized hoodie, who had a nose ring, and shortish scruffy dark hair streaked with purple.

Athena smiled awkwardly. "Hi," she said. "I'm Athena."

"I'm Sam, but you already knew that from Tabby...Err, but before we start, you should probably know that I...err, I don't have a gender. Like pixies."

"Pixies?" Athena asked, baffled.

"Let me try this again," said Sam. "What are your pronouns?"

"Excuse me?" Athena replied as they sat down, wondering if this was another magical thing she was oblivious to.

"Your pronouns. You know...? I prefer people to call me 'they' or 'them'."

"Oh!" Athena said. "You're non-binary?"

Sam looked slightly surprised. "I suppose I am," they said.

"That's the term people use in the non-magical world," Athena explained.

"Non binary," Sam repeated. "I like that. I normally just explain it to people in terms of the faerie creatures that are genderless, like pixies, though

I hear they prefer "it" pronouns, which they use for everything... which of course is *not* an okay thing to call most people."

"I...have no idea about pixies, but in terms of pronouns, she/her, I guess," Athena said. "I haven't thought about it that much."

Sam shrugged. "Most people don't if they don't have to." They gave Athena an uncertain look, as if trying to gauge her reaction.

"Thanks for telling me about your pronouns, and also about the pixies. That's all good to know," said Athena. "It's kind of cool that the magical world understands."

"For the most part," said Sam. "I mean, there are also plenty of gods who change their genders all the time, and other creatures too. But some humans are still strange about it."

"I'd never thought about gender-fluid gods," said Athena.

"Gender-fluid!" Sam crowed. "I love it!"

Athena smiled. She hadn't previously been particularly aware of Sam's gender. But unlike magic, this at least was something Athena understood. There had been several diverse gendered students at her old high school.

Sam beamed at her. "We've got to draw each-other," they said.

Athena and Sam sat on opposite sides of a desk, each trying to capture the other's likeness on the canvas boards they'd been given by the art teacher, Tabby.

Sam was quite friendly, if a little timid, but Athena could relate. She didn't feel particularly boisterous herself.

Felix kept interrupting the class, making jokes about the blue-haired girl, Elise, whose locks progressively changed colour to red as he drew her.

Athena tried not to stare at Elise's flame-coloured hair.

"She's like a mood ring," Sam said.

"What?" Athena asked.

"You know, her hair changes colour depending on how she feels."

"Oh, wow!" Athena said, surprised. "I'm...I'm not really used to the magical world."

"I can tell," said Sam. "Don't worry. You'll get used to it. Like Ash."

"Ash?"

"Ashwagandha, over there," Sam gestured to a beautiful dark-haired girl who Athena guessed was of South Asian descent. "She moved here from Surrey with her parents last year after they discovered her powers. They heard Myrtlewood was the best place for a magical education."

"Oh, that's interesting," said Athena, feeling more confidant as the conversation progressed.

"At least you *have* power," said Sam.

"Not really," said Athena. "My mum does."

"You've got loads of it. I can tell," Sam insisted. "Even if it hasn't manifested yet. I'm probably the only one at the school who doesn't have much of anything. I just live here. My family practice folk magic, but I'm nothing special, not like these other kids."

As they continued to draw each other, Sam became flustered, using the eraser more and more frequently.

"What is it? Athena asked.

"I just can't seem to capture you. It's like...you're not even there." Sam's words shocked Athena.

She was even more surprised when Sam showed her the vague and blurry face they'd drawn of her in comparison to the very lifelike sketches in their notebook of other faces and animals.

"There's something strange about you," Sam said. "It's not just the power. There's something else."

Athena felt herself withdrawing back into her shell again. Even at a magical school there was something wrong with her. Even among freaks, she didn't fit in.

To make things worse, the trouble maker, Felix, wandered across to them at that very moment, staring at Sam's sketch and then at Athena.

"I wouldn't say the likeness is uncanny," he said. "But there is something odd about you, new girl."

Six

Rosemary made her way home to Thorn Manor a little before midday, buoyed by several additional cups of Marjie's special tea.

As she drove up the driveway, admiring the glimpses of the sea along the Cornish coast, she felt slightly more confident about her future. She had a temporary part-time job to tide her over, after all. Working in Marjie's tea shop would be a lovely way to get to know more people around town, and she'd get to spend time around delicious food all day which meant she'd be in her element.

She parked the car out front, and looked up at the house. It was her home and that felt wonderful after so long hopping between different terribly run-down flats and shared houses without any real sense of grounding.

She stood back and admired Thorn manor. The old stone building held a certain presence, with its excessive (and dusty) rambling wings and its romantic (but inaccessible) tower. They had searched again but still had been unable to locate the entrance to the mysterious tower. An odd feeling came over Rosemary as she looked up at the house. She had the sense there was something different about it. Something had changed since she'd last been home, a few short hours before.

The last time Rosemary had had a feeling like this, there had been a giant gaping void inside the front door, and that was enough to made her gut tighten.

For the past few days she hadn't been thinking about the dangers they still likely faced. She'd been avoiding worries – as much as possible, anyway – about that blasted secret society and their ploy to get hold of her family magic.

It was hard to believe how much had happened in the short time Rosemary and Athena had been back in Myrtlewood. The Bloodstone Society's attack had only been a few days ago, and though Rosemary had managed to vanquish their small vampiric leader, she couldn't help but wonder now, what about the rest of the group? Had they really dispersed as she had hoped, their power depleted?

Her own power had surged during the confrontation when she'd finally unlocked it, along with the previously bound Thorn family magic, but since then it had ebbed and only seemed to work quite randomly, with unintended consequences like that morning's fabric avalanche.

She eyed the house suspiciously, wondering if there might be intruders lurking inside.

Even if I don't have complete control of my power yet, I'm sure it will come to me if I need it, Rosemary reassured herself. *No one busts into my house without consequences!*

She got out of the car and stormed towards the house. She heard an anxious mewl and saw the kitten emerge from a cat door that the house had graciously added of its own accord. Fuzzball the yet-to-be-properly-named ran for a little while and then paused before stalking off into bushes nearby. Clearly even the cat didn't want to be inside the house at this point.

"If you're in there – whoever you are – you've got another thing coming!" Rosemary called out as she tried the door handle. It was still locked, so she used her key, fumbling clumsily with it in a way that was not as intimidating as the impression she was trying to give off.

The door opened and everything looked...normal.

Rosemary wondered if she had just been paranoid, moments before. It was understandable to be a little on-edge, given everything they'd faced in the past week and a half, but she had been sure *something* was different about the house.

She checked the main living area and upstairs for signs of intruders, but everything seemed to be in order. She was tempted to examine the entire house, but that would take quite a long time and she was already in need of another cup of tea to calm her nerves.

She sat down at the kitchen table while the kettle boiled and rested her head in her hands. Now that the sense of danger had passed, she was back to feeling unnerved about the future again. A part of her even wondered whether she had unconsciously imagined something being different about the house just to distract herself from that empty unknown.

Rosemary didn't make tea, after all. She turned the stove off, removed the kettle, and went upstairs feeling utterly exhausted at the prospect of having to think seriously about what she really wanted.

Myrtlewood had been so welcoming to her and Athena, but she had big shoes to fill, left by Granny Thorn, a notorious witch, highly involved in the community, and generally well-liked.

Rosemary had no control over her magic, so she could hardly offer magical services to the town, and she felt half her life had already been wasted. All of these circular thoughts just added to her tiredness and sense of uselessness.

To deal with this proactively, she decided to have a nap, but she only made it as far as the upstairs hallway.

Something *was* different. Only, it wasn't an intruder.

It was a *door.*

Right next to the hall table, laden with its usual doilies and decorative plates, ornaments, lamps, and crystals, was a door Rosemary had never seen before.

It might well have been there when she did a quick sweep of the main part of the house, scanning for potential assailants from the Bloodstone Society, but it surely hadn't been there earlier on. It was a smallish door, made in the same oak wood as the panelling that lined the walls. It had a large rose carved on the front and was edged with gold leaf.

Surely, I would have noticed a door edged in gold leaf, sitting right outside my bedroom! Rosemary approached the door cautiously.

It wasn't overly surprising that something in Thorn Manor would change by itself. The house had a wonderfully convenient habit of fixing and cleaning itself, after all, at least in the main living areas. But this, she had not expected.

A door has to lead somewhere...and a door like this has to lead somewhere interesting!

It bore a tarnished golden lock, one that would fit an old-fashioned style of key. Just like many of the keys on the keyring of her master set.

Rosemary felt a lump of tightness in her gut. She *needed* to know what was behind that door, as if called towards it by fate itself.

She reached out to touch the golden lock. It shimmered, the tarnish disappearing, just like the front door lock had when Rosemary and Athena first arrived back at Thorn Manor.

She ran downstairs to fetch her keys, hoping the door wouldn't disappear. She returned moments later, relieved to find it was exactly as she'd left it.

Rosemary fumbled with the keys until she found a small old-fashioned golden key with a rose stamped into its end.

This must be it!

Rosemary took the tiny key and placed it into the lock. As she turned it, she sensed something click into place, internally.

It felt a bit like levelling up in a video game, the kind she used to play with Athena to pass the time when they'd had nothing much else to do in one of the old shared houses they'd lived in.

The door swung open and Rosemary hesitated. The house had always looked after her and Athena so far...but was this the house's doing or something more malicious? She took a deep breath, trying to sense through her magic to see if she could intuitively tell if she was walking into some kind of trap or not.

She wished her grandmother was around to ask, but even Granny Thorn's ghost seemed to be keeping her distance recently.

Nothing *seemed* evil in the air around her. Nothing about the door seemed out-of-place, despite its sudden appearance.

And besides, if it was bad, why would Granny have given me a key?

She took a tentative step through the open door to find a spiral staircase.

The tower!

Rosemary felt a thrill of excitement. She and Athena had searched for the entry to the tower when they'd explored the house to no avail. Rosemary had assumed it must be somewhere in the dusty west wing of the house, but she'd given up looking for it after too many sneezing fits.

She felt slightly guilty, coming up here alone for the first time. Athena had gotten all misty-eyed at the romantic idea of the tower when they'd first arrived and insisted it would be her bedroom, but Rosemary figured she might as well check it out and therefore, be better able to manage Athena's expectations, as it was likely the tower would be quite dusty and small, and in some state of disrepair.

Rosemary made her way up the staircase to find that the top room of the tower was actually huge – at least double the size of the parlour, with panoramic views out to sea, over the forest, and across to Myrtlewood village. Rosemary had never tried to look for Thorn Manor from the township and she wondered whether it would be visible. Or was it perhaps magically disguised?

This room certainly *was* magical.

From the outside, the tower looked tiny.

It wasn't dusty as she'd expected, either. The wooden panelling under the windows gleamed, carved with rosebushes, and edged in more gold leaf. The velvety blue ceiling was painted with gold and silver stars to look like the night sky. The dark hardwood floor beneath her feet seemed to be etched with gold to resemble a map of the earth.

Rosemary took a deep breath and admired the beauty of the room, but she could tell it wasn't here for show. This was a working room. A large cauldron sat in the centre, surrounded by an assortment of green velvet chairs. A bookcase stood to one side bearing a collection of books that looked to be very old. There was also a large ornate wooden desk and a table covered with interesting looking potion bottles and contraptions.

So this was where granny did her magic!

Rosemary had never been up here before, even as a young child, and now that she saw the space she felt she understood her grandmother a little better. Granny Thorn was an enigma, a secret hidden within another secret like stacking boxes.

She walked the circumference of the room, examining things, and then flopped down in one of the armchairs and sighed.

She was delighted to find the tower room, but after the initial wonder wore off she found her previous exhaustion creeping back in.

"Oh bother," she muttered. Myrtlewood had been so welcoming, but was that because they expected Rosemary to be some kind of amazing witch? The Thorn magic was legendary in this town, for good reason. Whatever Rosemary did, she'd be in Granny's shadow, and if she failed...Well, she could lose everything.

"What's that dear?" Granny's voice asked.

Rosemary jumped.

She looked across the room to see a large standing mirror, framed in dark wood, next to the bookshelf. She hadn't noticed it there before. Whether it had merely escaped her notice or had suddenly appeared was anyone's guess. What *was* clear, though, was that Granny Thorn was in the mirror glass, reflected as plain as day, wearing one of her signature black dresses and with her wild white curly hair tied up in a bright red scarf.

"Granny?"

"Of course. Who were you expecting? Dolly Parton?"

"Not in particular," said Rosemary. "But I haven't seen or heard from you for days. I thought you might have..."

"Moved on?" Granny Thorn asked, with a little cackle.

"Yes," Rosemary admitted, wondering if that was a rude thing to assume about a ghost. Supernatural creatures had their customs, after all, and though she was largely unfamiliar with them, she was trying her best to show respect. "I did wonder whether releasing the binding might have..."

"Sent me packing?" Granny cackled again.

"Something like that."

"It'll take more than a gigantic blast of magic to cast me off into the nether regions."

Rosemary laughed. "Well, you certainly haven't lost your sense of humour. You look much clearer that you did last time. Your cheeks are even rosy!"

"Why, thank you, dear."

"What have you been doing?" Rosemary asked. "I mean, what's it like over there?"

"Oh, well I've had meetings with the Counsel of Elder Souls, and I have business with a few spirit guides who want my opinion on some documents in the Akashic Records. Quite busy, really. I'm glad you released that family magic though. It's given me a real boost. I'm so proud of you, dear."

"Thank you, Granny," Rosemary said, flushing with pride, which only reminded her of how little praise she'd received before in her life. Much of that had come directly from the woman in ghost form she was currently speaking to.

"So, dear, I've been meaning to ask. What are your plans now?"

"If only I knew!" Rosemary said, flailing her arms in the air dramatically. "Marjie has offered me some part-time work in her tea shop to tide me over."

"Tide you over?!" Granny asked, outraged. "I left you plenty of money. It's a shame you always refused to take it while I was alive."

"It hardly seemed fair to scrounge off a pensioner," said Rosemary.

"Hah!" said Granny. "That's where your poor judgement gets you. So what's happened to my fortune?"

"Well, your – I mean my – inheritance is apparently coming through shortly."

"Tell that stud muffin vampire of a lawyer to get a move on," Granny said. "I don't pay him good money to muck around. What's the big delay?"

"It didn't help that we were caught up as potential suspects in your murder," Rosemary said, glaring a little. "You didn't exactly make it easy for us to figure it all out."

"I did what I could," Granny said dismissively. "Oh well, you'll get by, then. Make some tea and serve some cake until the money comes in. Then what?"

"Why does everyone keep asking me that?" said Rosemary. She slumped back down in the chair. "Actually, that's what's got me into a funk. I'm scared of finally trying to do something with my life and then failing. Everyone knows our family here – knows you were a magnificent witch. And me? I can't even summon a jumper without creating chaos."

"You'll grow into your powers, dear," said Granny reassuringly.

"I don't know if that's who I am, though," said Rosemary. "I can feel my power – even though I can't control it yet. But I feel like a teenager at the career counsellor's office: totally lost on what to do, but with magic thrown in! Plus, I'm already middle-aged."

"Hah! Thirty-nine is *not* middle aged. If that blasted vampire child hadn't snuck up on me with her stupid dragon I'd have lived well past a hundred and seven."

"You were a hundred and seven?" Rosemary asked. "But you were so spry."

"Give or take a few decades," said Granny. "You lose count after a while. I'd probably been a hundred and seven for a few years, come to think of it."

Rosemary sighed. "At least we have longevity in the DNA. So what you're saying is, I may well have a whole lot more time in which to not know what to do with my life?"

"Pish posh," said Granny. "First, you complain you're too old, now you complain you're too young. Age is a mere figment of the limited physical concept of time. It's no big deal."

"Oh, and I suppose stretch-marks are just organic tattoos?"

"If you like," said Granny with a grin.

"Can't you see I'm trying to mope around to avoid making hard and scary decisions about my future?" Rosemary said, only half joking. "Everything has changed for us within the last fortnight and I'm taking a while to adjust. All I need is my dead grandmother telling me to pull my head in!"

"Good, pull your head in!"

"Fine!" said Rosemary, folding her arms in a mock huff. She couldn't stop herself from smiling at her Granny. "I've missed you."

"I've missed you too, poppet. And come to think of it, I have a little gift for you."

"Really?" Rosemary said, and then frowned. "Please tell me it's not something cryptic, like a music box with a very secret manual locked inside which can only be accessed through a key hidden inside your smelly old dancing shoes!"

Granny laughed and clapped her hands. "Oh, you!" she said affectionately. "You always were my favourite. And no, it's not cryptic this time. It's really quite simple."

"What is it?"

"Look inside the box."

"What box?" Rosemary asked. "Not another mystical object that will transport me to a disorienting alternate dimension where an ancestor will give me lessons in how to unlock family magic, because I've had quite enough of that!"

"It really has been a busy fortnight, hasn't it?" said Granny. "But no. The box on the desk, silly."

"There is no..." Rosemary said, glancing at the old writing desk, which now did indeed have a small metal box sitting on top. "That wasn't there before."

Granny gave her a mischievous look.

"This better not be a trap," said Rosemary.

"I promise it isn't," said Granny excitedly. "Just look inside."

"Oh, alright."

Rosemary walked over to the desk and reached for the box. She opened it and breathed a sigh of relief when nothing unusual happened. Then she gasped in wonder at what was inside.

"For me?" she asked.

"That's what I told you," said Granny.

Rosemary admired the gleaming emerald pendant, set in gold, that seemed to glow with its own light.

"Can I...touch it?" Rosemary asked.

"Of course you bloody well can," said Granny. "Put it on. What else do you think it's for?"

"What I mean is, will it do anything weird?"

"If by weird, you mean magical – which is quite offensive, actually – then yes, it certainly will do something *weird*."

"Haven't you ever heard of informed consent?" Rosemary asked. "Oh, and I'm sorry, I didn't realise calling magic weird was offensive."

"Actually it isn't," said Granny.

"What? But you just said."

"Weird comes from 'wyrd'," Granny explained. "It is a sacred word, speaking to the mystic interconnectedness of all things, and it's offensive to use it in a non-magical way."

Rosemary sighed. "Oh, whatever."

"Just put the necklace on, dear," said Granny.

"Not without knowing exactly what it'll do," Rosemary insisted.

"This is the pendant of Elzarie Thorn."

"Who?"

"Your great, great, great, great grandmother," said Granny.

"That's lovely," said Rosemary. "So, it's a special family heirloom. And it does what, exactly?"

"It'll help to stabilise your powers – that's all," Granny said. "It'll make you feel more centred, more comfortable in your own skin. That way, it'll help with mastery."

"That actually sounds pretty good," said Rosemary.

"Put it on then, my dear, go on."

"It's not going to make me breathe fire or poo chocolate buttons or anything?"

"No – it'll just centre you. I promise."

"Alright," Rosemary said, tentatively.

She picked the necklace up and felt her fingers instantly tingle in a pleasant way that made her giggle.

"It's lovely, isn't it?" Granny said. "I wore that necklace every day for many years. It passes on the maternal wisdom of our line, you see."

"I thought you said it would centre me," said Rosemary.

"Exactly," said Granny. "Go on. Put it on. Stop dawdling."

Rosemary lifted the necklace up, carefully placing it around her neck. The pendant was drawn to her, like a magnet, lighting on her sternum. The clasp practically fastened itself.

"How does it feel?" Granny asked.

"Good," said Rosemary, drawing in a breath that felt like refreshing mountain air.

"Is that all?"

"It's...it's like I'm more...all in one place instead of feeling scattered from worrying about this or that. I'm...I'm present."

"See," said Granny. "I told you I had a present for you!"

"Very clever," said Rosemary, rolling her eyes at her grandmother's ghost.

"And with that, it's time for me to go," said Granny.

"Sorry," said Rosemary. "I mean, thank you. I promise to behave myself and stop being cheeky and sarcastic."

"Oh no you don't!" said Granny. "You keep being your vivacious self. As for me, I only have so much energy to expend in the physical plane and I have other matters to attend to. But do give us a yell if you need anything. I'll pop in if I can."

"Thanks Granny. There's...there's so much more I wanted to talk to you about. To ask you. Like, what's going on with Athena. Why is it she can hear thoughts?"

"Oh that," said Granny, though her voice was growing quieter as her image began to fade out. "That's something you should talk to her father about."

"Dain?!"

"Yes – that troublemaker. He knows a lot more than he ever told you, I'd wager."

"Seriously."

"Seriously. The only trouble is, he's missing, isn't he?" Granny said, barely visible as she continued to fade.

"What are you talking about?"

"You'll figure it out, soon enough," said Granny, and with that, she disappeared.

Seven

Rosemary returned downstairs, locking the special door to the tower behind her, as it seemed prudent to protect Granny's special space.

Little fuzzball yawned from the window seat and then stretched and lazily made her way over to Rosemary for a pat.

Rosemary scratched the purring animal behind the ears and then made her way to the kitchen to finally sort the tea she'd been planning on having earlier. She also made some simple toast with sliced tomatoes, black pepper, olive oil, and basil for lunch, to compensate for the overly rich cake she'd had quite a lot of earlier.

She sat on the window seats, sipping her tea and nibbling her toast, looking out at the light drizzle that had started falling outside. Wearing the necklace did make her feel better – not in the bubbly way Marjie's tea did, but calmer and more centred, just as Granny had described. It did not, however, remove all her worries or her errant thoughts, which her grandmother had only added to.

What happened to Dain?

The last she'd heard from her wayward ex, he'd agreed to deliver all their measly worldly possessions from the run-down flat in Stratham to Thorn Manor. Rosemary had asked for the favour as Constable Perkins wouldn't let her leave town while 'under investigation'.

Dain had come through, despite generally being unreliable. In the past, he'd had a bad habit of erratic behaviour, such as taking off with the contents of Rosemary's wallet.

It had always puzzled Athena that her mother never properly got angry at Dain, considering everything he'd done. Rosemary's frustrations with him never seemed to last. Athena had often commented that he must be possessed with a strange power over her – and indeed, over almost every woman he met, but Rosemary never considered the possibility that it was a magical ability of any sort.

She wanted to text him, to see if he was okay...to check whether Granny was right about him being missing, but Athena would hate that.

Athena had no time at all for her father – to the point where she'd gotten Rosemary to make a protection charm to ward him off, lest he weasel his way back into their lives.

Is that why he's gone missing?

A lump of guilt formed in Rosemary's abdomen. They'd intended for the charm to ward him off and stop him from getting his slippery hands on the Thorn family fortune.

Had they, instead, sent him somewhere else entirely? Or addled his brain so that he couldn't make his way back to wherever it was he was living these days in the general vicinity of Stratham?

Two weeks before, Rosemary would've scoffed at all these ridiculous thoughts, but now they seemed common sense. Magic was real. She did not yet comprehend how it worked or what the boundaries were, but she had accepted it as the only possible explanation for all the unusual things that had happened to them in Myrtlewood.

Had their attempt at warding against him made Dain disappear entirely?

How stupid of me to meddle in something I don't understand!

She clutched the necklace, which sent a ray of reassurance through her, but it did not entirely quell her anxiety.

Rosemary texted Dain, knowing that her daughter would be mad about it. Perhaps Athena didn't need to know about that little detail, but someone certainly needed to check to see if something had happened to her father.

She waited until the tea went cold, but there was no response.

Rosemary kept checking her phone as she paced around the house. The rain was falling more heavily outside, which gave Thorn Manor a sense of tense ambiance.

Though Rosemary felt more certain of herself, she was unnerved by

Granny's final words to her upstairs. Her phone remained dormant, until a phone call came through.

Athena calling.

"Bollox!" Rosemary cried, checking the time. She answered the call. "I'm so sorry, love."

"Sorry...as in you totally forgot about your only child on her first day of school and left her to wait in the rain?"

"Pretty much. I've uhh...I've had some distractions."

"That's just great," said Athena darkly. "And are you going to distract yourself from those distractions and come and get me RIGHT NOW?!"

"Yes," said Rosemary, grabbing her jacket. "I'm on my way."

"Good, because my only half-decent outfit is getting soaked!"

Rosemary ran outside through the rain she hadn't noticed earlier. She jumped into the Rolls Royce, grateful that it was a hundred times more reliable than her rusty bomb of a car. *The one that Dain had driven over here...*

Come to think of it, what happened to the old car?

It had been there one night and she hadn't seen it since.

The spectre of her old vehicle plagued Rosemary's mind all the way to Athena's school. *How could I possibly have forgotten about it? How did I not realise it was missing?*

Her anxiety was so strong, edged with shame about forgetting to pick her daughter up on time, that it counteracted any calming balancing affect the emerald pendant might've otherwise had.

By the time she pulled up outside Myrtlewood Academy, Athena looked thoroughly soaked. The tree she was standing under had not been sufficient protection from the downpour.

Athena did not make eye contact with her mother as she got into the car.

"I'm sorry, love," Rosemary said.

"Don't talk to me," said Athena. "I'm not in the mood."

Rosemary sighed, her guilt swallowing up all her other scattered thoughts for the moment. "Do you feel like going to the pub for some mulled mead?"

"No."

"Marjie's for hot chocolate?"

"No. I want to go home."

"Okay," Rosemary said, giving up on peace offerings and guiding the car back towards Thorn Manor.

Once home, Athena went straight to her room.

Rosemary had been looking forward to telling her about the mystery door, and showing her the gorgeous – and unexpectedly large – tower room, but she decided to let the teen cool off first.

Rosemary decided she, too, needed to relax. She went upstairs and ran a bath in the large claw-footed tub, adding in Granny's rose geranium bath salts and a splash of bubble mixture.

Before she got in, she remembered to take off the special necklace so as not to tarnish it. She draped it carefully over the bench.

As soon as it was off, Rosemary's energy lapsed, and she felt scattered. The psychological disturbance of returning to her normal state of mind, however, was temporary. As soon as she got into the bath, her anxieties melted away and she was left feeling lovely and serene amid the sweet rosy scented bubbles.

Everything will work out, Rosemary told herself, feeling more optimistic than she had in a long time.

Things have already gone so well...Apart from the secret society coming after us, and the murder investigation, and that giant dragon thing, and the break-ins, and the ancient tiny vampires...and...actually all of that went surprisingly smoothly, considering.

We're at home here, and we're settled for the first time in a long, long time. And I even have a job.

I don't have to worry about money. Athena might be mad now, but she'll come around.

There was a loud knock at the bathroom door.

Rosemary rocketed out of the bath and almost slipped over on the tiles, reaching out for the towel rack for support. *Did I forget to lock the front door?* she wondered. *Has someone just wandered in, looking for me?*

"What is it?" Rosemary asked.

"How long are you going to be?" Athena asked, her voice taking on a demanding tone. "I should be the one having a bath. After all, it was your fault I got soaked. Didn't you even think to run one for me?"

"Actually, it did cross my mind," Rosemary replied. "But you'd already refused all my other offers and told me not to talk to you...so."

"Fine!" said Athena.

"I won't be long," Rosemary promised. "I'll run you one as soon as I'm done."

"Never mind," Athena said, retreating back down the hallway.

Surely, this bad mood isn't just because I forgot to pick her up on time,

Rosemary thought with a sinking feeling. *I bet the first day at school did not go well.*

She got back into the tub and washed her hair, contemplating what kind of thing she might say or do to support her daughter who was clearly having a very bad day.

Rosemary decided she would run Athena a bath, after all, and then make her a special meal. She quickly finished up in the tub and then ran a fresh bath with extra bubbles. It seemed to take quite a while for the water to fill up, and Rosemary wished it was faster because her mind began to race with great ideas to help Athena feel better. While the water was still running, she popped downstairs to get started on a special spiced hot chocolate.

She hummed to herself as she blended the herbs in the mortar and pestle, and then mixed them in a saucepan with milk, cocoa, and dark chocolate, which she put on to simmer.

"Ah, Mum?" Athena called from upstairs.

"What, love?"

"Why is the hallway wet?"

"Oh drat!"

Rosemary raced back upstairs to see water flooding out from under the bathroom door.

"You left the bath running!" Athena shrieked.

"It was for you," said Rosemary. "It was filling so slowly. I wasn't gone long."

"I told you I didn't want one. Uhh..."

A STRANGE GURGLING sounded from behind the door in question. Rosemary tentatively tried the handle and the door swung open to reveal a wall of warm, bubbly, rose-scented water which immediately rushed towards them, sweeping them along the hallway and all the way down the stairs.

Athena spluttered, wiping bubbles from her face. "What was that?"

Rosemary was so shocked, all she could do was laugh. To her great surprise, Athena joined in and they both lost themselves in cackling giggles for at least ten minutes. They laughed until their abdominal muscles ached and then they lay there, slumped at the bottom of the staircase.

Fuzzball approached them to investigate, took one sniff of the water, and strode away with an unimpressed look on her face.

"That was so weird," Athena said. "There's no way all that water came from overfilling the bath. It must have been your magic."

"Or yours," Rosemary suggested. "You sounded quite mad before when you demanded a bath."

"I don't really have magic, remember," said Athena. "I just have annoying voices in my head that belong to the minds of other people."

"About that..."

"What?"

"I spoke to Granny Thorn today," Rosemary said, relieved Athena seemed to be feeling much better so that she could finally talk about the matters at hand. "Well, I spoke to her ghost, anyway. She told me something strange and troubling that you probably should know about."

"Why didn't you tell me earlier?" Athena asked, sounding concerned.

"You didn't want to talk to me," Rosemary replied. "And you hardly seemed to be in a mood for any more troubling news."

"What's that?"

"Well, the news is..."

"No, wait, what's that you're wearing? That necklace. It's gorgeous." Athena pointed to Rosemary's neck.

Rosemary reached up to feel the shape of the emerald pendant there.

"That's strange," she said. "I could have sworn I took it off before I had my bath."

"Can I have it?" Athena asked.

"Maybe one day," said Rosemary. "Granny Thorn gave it to me. It's supposed to centre my energy and make me more present."

"And how's that going for you?" Athena asked with a cheeky grin.

"Well, I'm...here," said Rosemary. "It's been a heck of a strange day."

"Tell me about it," said Athena, pushing herself up off the floor and pulling her mother up too.

"I'll tell you all about it over cocoa," said Rosemary. "Oh blast! I forgot I left the cocoa on!"

She and Athena raced to the kitchen to find the oven had been turned off and two cups of perfectly brewed cocoa sat on the bench next to a pile of fresh, clean clothes for each of them.

"Thank you, house," Rosemary said, chuckling.

"Hey, you don't suppose the house was to blame for that whole bath-water incident, do you?" Athena asked as they wandered back up the noticeably dry staircase to go to their rooms to change.

"It wouldn't surprise me," said Rosemary. "Maybe it was trying to shake you out of your grump."

"I guess it was successful then," said Athena. "There's nothing like a bubbly rose-scented tsunami to blast away a foul mood."

They came back downstairs in fresh, dry clothes, and headed to the parlour with their hot chocolates, to sit on the comfy sofas there. The fireplace spontaneously lit itself as they walked in, creating an even cosier atmosphere.

Rosemary patted the wood-panelled wall in appreciation of the house and then sat down to enjoy her hot chocolate.

"So, tell me what this news is, then," said Athena.

"Well, the troubling part is..." said Rosemary, and then hesitated, wondering how much her daughter needed to know.

"Dad's gone missing?" Athena asked.

"Hey, stop reading my mind," said Rosemary. "I'm trying to be a good parent and censor things for you."

"Really, Mum," said Athena. "I'm almost an adult. I think I can handle it. Besides, I need to practice using this stupid telepathy and your mind is the only one simple enough for me to read."

"Simple?" said Rosemary. "Who are you calling simple?"

Athena laughed.

"It's a serious situation though," said Rosemary. "Your father—"

"So he's gone and got himself into trouble. Big deal. It's hardly out of character for him, is it?"

"Only...the car disappeared too."

"What car?" Athena asked.

"Our old car," said Rosemary. "Remember, it was parked outside when the boxes turned up on the doorstep, and then...well, it must have vanished."

"Or someone drove it away," Athena suggested. "That's strange. I forgot all about the car."

"Don't you think it's weird we didn't notice?" said Rosemary. "And Granny knew about it, somehow. I have a feeling it was magical. I can't help worrying that our charm to ward him off backfired and blasted him into a different dimension or something."

"I don't think that's likely," said Athena. "But even if it is it's probably a good thing not to have to worry about him anymore."

"Athena! I know you have no time for him, and I accept that, but he's still your father. And here's the thing – Granny said he knows something about your mind-reading ability."

"What?!" said Athena, looking livid. "Did you tell him?"

"No. Not like that. Granny wasn't exactly detailed in her description, but she implied your power is to do with *his* side of the family."

"But he's not magical," said Athena.

"Not to our knowledge. But it kind of makes sense when you think about it. He always had a strange power over people – specifically women – and that's not all. Remember how I never even got mad at him no matter how many times he messed me around or stole from me? That's not normal."

Athena was silent for a moment, then said, "I don't want it."

"What?"

"This gift – or curse – or whatever it is in my head. I don't want it if it's from him."

Rosemary sighed. "You may not have a choice if it's genetic."

"But Finnigan..."

"Finnigan what?"

"Finnigan is like me. He can do it too. I don't need to ask Dad about it. I can just ask him."

Rosemary gave her daughter a curious look. "Don't you think it's a bad idea to get involved with someone like your father?"

Athena glared at her and threw a cushion, which narrowly missed Rosemary's head.

"Hey! Watch it!"

"Don't ever say anything like that to me again," said Athena. "Anyway, we are not *involved*. That's such an old-person way of thinking. I haven't even seen him since after that...that incident with the dragon and the nasty little girl vampire on Saturday."

"But have you heard from him?" Rosemary asked.

Athena was silent.

"I suspected as much."

"Stop it, Mum. Let me have some privacy."

"Fine," said Rosemary. "But I do want to know about your first day at school – at least the basics. Whatever you want to tell me without invading your privacy."

"It sucked."

"That bad?" Rosemary asked. "Was it the kids or the teachers?"

"The teachers are fine, the kids are nice...mostly."

"So what's the problem then?"

"I am!" said Athena. "It's all magical and I know nothing. I suck."

Rosemary sighed. "Don't be so hard on yourself, love. It's your first day. You'll catch up in no time."

"Easy for you to say, you don't have to go to school. You don't even have a job. Speaking of which, how are we going to get by? I need new clothes urgently!"

"Actually," said Rosemary, "I have some good news on that front."

"Really?"

"Marjie offered me some part-time work in the teashop while she's busy catering spring weddings, so we'll have some cash to tide us over until the inheritance clears. I also ran into Burk there, who said it might only be a matter of weeks..."

Rosemary didn't want to bother her daughter with the other thing that had been troubling her – the uncertainty and fear of failure she felt regarding what to do with her life.

"That's great!" Athena said. "And don't worry about that other stuff, Mum. You'll figure it out soon enough."

"I told you to stop reading my mind!" Rosemary said. "Didn't you just say you value privacy?"

"You're my mother. You have no privacy. Anyway, whatever you do – it has to involve food. Marjie's tea shop is a great place to start figuring things out."

"Why are you so sure about that?" Rosemary asked.

"Food was your first love," Athena said, batting her eyelashes at her mother. "You always wanted to be a chef, didn't you?"

"I suppose I did, once upon a time. But now that I've inherited all this from Granny, including the family magic, I feel like I need to become some kind of epic witch so that the town isn't disappointed in me."

It was Athena's turn to sigh, or at least groan and roll her eyes. "Mum, that's silly."

"Is it, though? I would love to be able to go to magic school. Do you think they take adult enrolments at Myrtlewood Academy?"

"Don't even think about it," said Athena. "I'm already embarrassed enough about being a total newbie without having to worry about having a parent at school! Anyway, Granny wouldn't want you to try to become like her or anyone else, and neither does the town expect that. Just be yourself and stop being so neurotic."

"I'll stop being neurotic if you stop being such a wise-arse," said Rosemary.

"Deal," said Athena. "Actually, you already seem a bit less neurotic – your thoughts are clearer to read too."

"It must be the necklace," said Rosemary. "And hey! I told you to stay out of my head!"

"Not going to happen."

Eight

Athena smiled across the table at her mother, feeling much better after all the laughter earlier, and enjoying the home-cooked meal of spaghetti Bolognese that Rosemary had managed to quickly whip up for dinner.

Rosemary was thinking about culinary herbs, and occasionally her mind darted to her new job in Marjie's tea shop or concerns about her daughter's new school. Athena listened to all this with quiet interest, not wanting to show her mother exactly how much mind-reading she was now capable of.

"This is good," Athena said. "You should cook more often."

"While I was making dinner I was thinking about what you said before," said Rosemary. "I do love food. Do you really think I should go into the restaurant business?"

"Maybe," said Athena. "Though that does sound rather stressful. Isn't that what they say about chefs – they're always so stressed that they swear a lot and throw plates?"

"Hmmm, true. Maybe it's good I never finished culinary school, then," said Rosemary. "The last thing I need right now is more stress."

"You seem pretty calm actually," said Athena.

"The necklace must be helping."

"How did you get it, again? Did Granny's ghost just pop up and hand it to you?"

"Funny you should ask," said Rosemary, setting down her cutlery on her empty plate. "I got home and there was something different about the house."

"Oh no, not again!" said Athena.

"It wasn't actually a bad thing," said Rosemary. "Though, I was suspicious at first."

"What was it then?"

"There was a new door."

"A what?"

"A new door, upstairs. Come on. I'll show you."

Rosemary got up from the table and led Athena upstairs.

"Wait," she said, looking at empty wall space. "It was right here."

"Are you sure?" Athena asked. "Is it hidden or something."

"It was glaringly obvious before – all carved and gleaming, and edged in gold leaf. But come to think of it, I didn't notice it again when we got home."

Athena gave her mother a sceptical look. "I've never seen anything like that around here."

"Neither had I, but believe me – it was here."

"So there was a door," said Athena. "And...?"

"It led up to the tower."

"No way!" said Athena. "Not fair. That's supposed to be my new bedroom."

"I think Granny's still using it," Rosemary said.

"What do you mean?"

"It's huge, for one thing – way bigger than how it looks from outside – and there are all these special-looking magical things, including a big cauldron. Anyway, Granny appeared to me in a mirror up there. We had a good long chat and she gave me the necklace."

"As in, handed it to you?"

"As in, the desk was empty one minute, and the next thing I knew a box was sitting there with the necklace inside. Apparently it belonged to my great, great, great times a million greats ancestor Elzarie Thorn. That was how Granny gave it to me. She insisted I put it on right then and there."

"Interesting," said Athena. "You know, if you'd told me all that a couple of weeks ago..."

"I know, I never would have believed it either."

"It's weirding me out to think that Dad might know about all that magic stuff – that he might have known about it for years."

"It is a strange thought," said Rosemary. "Granny also told me off for misuse of the word 'weird', which is apparently a sacred term or something."

Athena shrugged. "Who would have thought?"

"Anyway, it does bother me if your father is missing, even if you don't give a bat's claw about it."

"Do bats even have claws?" Athena asked. "I mean...sure, I don't want him to come to any serious harm, just like anyone else. But he's hardly even a father to me, is he? What has he done for us other than cause trouble?"

"I get it, kid," said Rosemary.

"Don't call me that," Athena grumbled, then yawned. The day was catching up to her and so was her curiosity, but she didn't want to tell her mother what she planned to do next. "I might go to bed," she said. "It's been a long day and it's only Monday!"

"Fair enough, love. You go to bed and I'll go downstairs to clean up, if the house hasn't beat me to it."

Athena hugged her mother goodnight, picked up the kitten which she was clearly trying to claim as her own, and made her way to bed. It was nice having a whole large room to herself with a big queen-sized bed. She put the purring kitten down near her pillow and made her way directly across the room to what had – that very morning – been a large window, only to find it was now a set of French doors, leading out to a small balcony.

"Thank you, house," Athena whispered. The house had clearly been reading her mind. Athena had been daydreaming earlier about sneaking out the window, wondering whether the thick ivy that clung to the side of Thorn Manor was sturdy enough to hold her.

The doors opened easily and a crisp breeze blew into her bedroom. Athena grabbed a soft woollen blanket, scuffed on her slippers, and slipped outside into the cool, dark night.

Finnigan, she called out. *Finnigan, if you can hear me, please come here. I need to talk to you.*

Athena looked out into dark forest surrounding the Thorn Manor. She could hear the hoot of owls and the swish of ocean waves. The moon was beginning to peek above the horizon over the sea, in the distance. It was possible she was simply talking to herself in her head. Finnigan could be miles away, and yet, he'd told her that he'd come if she called. She'd thought of him often, but had resisted the urge to call until now. Now, she had a good reason. She needed to understand what was going on inside her head –

regardless of what her father had to do with it. She needed to understand herself.

Athena. Finnigan's voice rang through her head. *You called.*

I wanted to talk to you, Athena replied. *Can you come?*

Not tonight. I'm...far away.

Athena wondered how far their telepathic voices could possibly be travelling.

I'll be back soon, he continued.

How soon?

Tomorrow night or the night after.

But, wait...

I have to go. Take care of yourself, Athena. Until next time.

Athena frowned. Finnigan obviously had more important things to do than talk to her. She felt a bit confused and cross, not because he was busy, but because he seemed so aloof.

What's really going on? she wondered.

Nine

Rosemary woke up bright and early the next morning and rose from her little single bed in the room Granny had kept for her as a child. She knew it was odd, a fully grown woman sleeping in a child's room, but it was *her* room and she hadn't gotten around to redecorating, given the chaos of the last few weeks. She prepared herself mentally to ferry Athena to school and get herself to work, only to find her daughter still fast asleep in bed.

"Come on, love. You'll be late if you don't get up soon."

Athena yawned and groaned. "School doesn't start until mid-morning," she grumbled, and pulled the covers over her head.

"That's ridiculous!" Rosemary said.

"No, it's true. You can even call them to find out."

Rosemary did, in fact, call them, only to be told that Athena was right.

"I told you so," Athena said, clomping downstairs in her dressing gown.

"Sure," said Rosemary. "But it sounded like wishful thinking to me. How am I supposed to get you to school now? I told Marjie I'd be in at nine. I suppose I can call her and tell her it will be more like ten thirty."

"Don't be silly, Mum," Athena said as she poured herself some tea. "I can just walk. It'll only take about twenty minutes."

Rosemary handed her daughter a plate of toast. "I suppose that'll be alright. Don't get into any strange cars or talk to any wolves in the forest or anything like that, though."

"I'm old enough to walk across the village unchaperoned," Athena said.

"It seems like you're feeling better about school, too. I haven't heard any more complaints."

Athena shrugged as she sat down at the kitchen table. "I *want* to feel better about it. Anyway, it's not the school that's the problem. It's just that I don't know the first thing about magic and the whole curriculum is based around it."

"How do they get you ready for national testing, you know A-levels and so on?" Rosemary asked, emptying the teapot into her own cup.

"They said they have their way of helping us learn the basic mundane curriculum without actually studying it specifically," Athena said, between bites of toast. "The qualifications carry across in case we want to go on to other non-magical academic pursuits. But I have no idea how that works."

"It sounds fabulous," said Rosemary, feeling a little envious. "Much, much better than the strict religious school I had to go to when I was your age."

Athena put down her piece of toast and sighed.

"It *would* be fabulous if I had even an ounce of your magic. It's so not fair."

"I can try asking Granny about that," Rosemary suggested. "Next time she pops in, whenever that is."

"Please do," said Athena with a pleading look. "I need all the help I can get."

Rosemary left for work while Athena was still eating toast in her dressing gown, complaining she had nothing to wear. Promises were made regarding a weekend shopping trip.

As she drove the short distance to Myrtlewood, Rosemary hoped the second day at school went much better than the first. Athena had always struggled with school. She wasn't particularly interested in a lot of the curriculum and making friends had been hard in the past, especially as they'd moved around so much. This school was particularly important, as it seemed they would be in Myrtlewood for the foreseeable future.

Rosemary parked up near the tea shop and found it buzzing with activity. Three people stood waiting at the counter to be served and most of the tables were already full.

"Thank goodness you're here!" Marjie called out.

"I've never seen this place so packed," said Rosemary, making her way around the shop and behind the counter.

"I suspect you have a little something to do with that," said Marjie as she served a piece of chocolate orange torte and a beef pasty to a vaguely familiar looking woman with dark hair and a red coat.

"Me? Why?" Rosemary asked.

"News travels fast around here. Everyone wants to come and meet the descendant of Galdie Thorn, especially after what we all saw in the sky over your house!"

Rosemary stifled a groan as the customer smiled at her. When the woman left for one of the few remaining tables and the other customers' orders had been taken, Marjie gave Rosemary a big hug and handed her a bright green apron covered in red roses.

"This one's for you," said Marjie. "It will bring out your eyes."

Rosemary smiled. She put the apron over the plain black-on-black t-shirt and jeans combo she was wearing and instantly felt at home. Working in the tea shop and serving the customers was easy, though she had to pay careful attention to the money side of things. She'd never been particularly strong with numbers and Marjie's system was much more manual than the automated grocery store checkout she was used to.

Many of the customers did, indeed, want to meet Rosemary and introduced themselves to her enthusiastically, telling her all about how marvellous her grandmother had been. She heard numerous stories of how Galdie had helped them out with a wayward pet or a mysterious ailment. This was a little overwhelming for Rosemary as she already felt a weighty burden to fill Granny's shoes and had no idea how to. She clutched her emerald necklace for a little extra centredness.

The necklace itself did not go unnoticed. Marjie was the first to remark on it – remembering that Granny had worn it for years.

"I always envied that pendant, I did," said Marjie wistfully.

Various customers remarked on the emerald, as well. There was quite a mix of clientele that day. Some only wanted take-away tea and cake, whereas others seemed to while away the morning, much like Rosemary had done the day before. One of these customers was the dark-haired woman with the red coat that Rosemary had noticed multiple times before.

As Rosemary was clearing one of the tables, the woman caught her eye and smiled again. Rosemary smiled back.

Just then, a familiar face entered the tea shop. Detective Neve wore a smart navy jacket over a plain cream silk shirt and dark blue jeans. The stylish outfit complemented her perfectly straight jet black hair.

"Rosemary," Neve said, grinning.

"Hi," said Rosemary, smiling. "Thanks so much for your support last week. It made a huge difference to us."

Detective Neve had helped to resolve the rather outrageous issues with Granny's murder investigation, the secret Bloodstone society, and the tiny-but-ancient vampire who had tried to steal the Thorn family magic.

"You are the one I should be thanking," said Neve. "I'm so pleased we got to the bottom of things, but I'm not sure how far I would have gotten without you stopping Geneviève."

Rosemary smiled. "I just did what I had to do at the time. But really, thanks for getting Perkins off my case." Rosemary hesitated, then asked, "Do you think it's safe now? I mean, the other members of the Bloodstone society are still out there somewhere." She looked around the tea shop suspiciously.

"There's no sign of Despina," said Neve, lowering her voice. "And it seems the other members have disbanded for now, since the society's power has waned, but stay vigilant."

Rosemary frowned, worrying that she perhaps shouldn't have let Athena walk to school alone. The threat from vampires seemed less severe in broad daylight at least, but the evil secret society seemed to have all kinds of other magical members who were perfectly comfortable in the sun, including animal shapeshifters.

"It's just as well," said the woman with the red coat as Neve took a seat next to her at the table.

"Oh, excuse my manners," said Detective Neve. "This is my partner, Nesta Divine. Nesta, meet Rosemary Thorn."

"It's nice to finally meet you properly," Nesta said.

"Nesta Divine!" Rosemary said. "What a wonderful name. Are you another kind of police officer, then?"

"Hah! No," said Nesta. "Not that kind of partner. We live together."

"Ohhh, sorry!" Rosemary said, blushing a little at her error.

"It's a common mistake." Nesta smiled warmly. She began pulling her long, wavy black hair into a tight bun as Rosemary went to clear a table.

As Nesta went to lower her hands, her fingers collided with the tea tray Rosemary was attempting to carry to the kitchen, knocking over a tea pot and sending a half-full cup of oolong careening over. The contents spilled all over Rosemary's apron.

"I'm so sorry!" Nesta said.

"It's no problem," said Rosemary, mopping up the spill with a spare napkin.

Nesta looked embarrassed. "Really, I'm mortified. How clumsy of me not to see you there."

Rosemary smiled at her reassuringly. "I'm usually the clumsy one, so it's actually a refreshing change. I'm not sure how I managed to last all day without spilling something on myself."

"I'm sure that's not true, you seem so comfortable in the kitchen," said Nesta.

"I do love food," Rosemary admitted gleefully.

Nesta and Neve both nodded enthusiastically. Rosemary was enjoying their company so much that she didn't really want to go back to cleaning up behind the counter, and fortunately there was a lull in customers, so she decided to take a break. It struck her that she missed hanging out with women roughly in her own age bracket.

"That's a lovely necklace you're wearing," said Nesta. "It looks special."

"Thanks," said Rosemary. "It's a family heirloom. I quite like it.

"I hear you're new in town," said Nesta. "And you've already been through so much! I bet that's a tough adjustment. It's a very welcoming town, but it takes a while to make new friends anywhere. Why don't you come over for dinner sometime?"

"That's nice of you to offer," said Rosemary. "Sure, why not? As long as I can bring my teenage daughter, she's sometimes grumpy but is often good company."

"Of course," said Nesta and Neve at the same time.

"Neve was saying she wanted to invite you both over anyway," Nesta continued. "She's always trying to get me to socialise more. I work over in Burkenswood or from home. It's a long commute when I do go into work, whereas when I'm at home I tend to be quite isolated, so I don't have too many friends here either."

Rosemary could empathise with that. She hadn't had many friends, either, until recently.

"Just let me know a day and time," said Rosemary. "We don't have a lot of other plans at the moment, so I can probably make it anytime."

"How about a Thursday later this month?" Neve suggested. "Nesta works from home Mondays and Thursdays, so she won't be too exhausted from the commute that day."

"Sounds good," said Rosemary. She thanked both women and then left to carry the dishes to the kitchen and do some more tidying up.

As Nesta and Neve got up to leave the tea shop, Rosemary felt happy about the possibility of making new friends. Detective Neve was brilliant and smart and exactly the kind of person Rosemary would want to have as a friend, and Nesta seemed lovely. She hoped Athena didn't mind her accepting a dinner invitation without discussing it first.

She felt another pang of guilt about Athena walking alone, but when she called the school on her break to check if her daughter had arrived safely, the receptionist only gave a little laugh and said, "Of course she did," in a slightly mocking way.

Rosemary put down the phone and sipped her tea, painfully aware that Athena would be mad at her for that little intrusion into her school life. She decided to stop being quite so over-protective of her daughter, but it was hard to let go, knowing that members of the Bloodstone Society might be lurking out there somewhere, no doubt biding their time before launching another attack.

Just then, the door burst open and a small bundle of energy bearing blonde ringlets raced in.

"Mum, Mum, Mum! Ooooh, look at the cakes! Look at all the cakes!"

"Yes, dear," said the harried looking woman, following tightly behind the child. "Which one do you want?"

"Just one?" The child sounded seriously disappointed.

"Yes, of course, Gretchen. You are always allowed just one cake. What do you think we'd do with more than one?"

"Eat them!"

"Just a minute, Prue," Marjie called from the kitchen.

"Nooo!" said little Gretchen.

"It's alright. I'll help," Rosemary said, getting up from the table. "I'm about finished my break anyway."

"It's fine," said Prue. Though she did seem slightly relieved when Rosemary insisted it was no trouble to serve the energetic young Gretchen who Rosemary guessed to be about four or five years old.

"Which will it be?" Rosemary asked in a tone that she hoped matched the child's enthusiasm.

"Chocolate!" said Gretchen. "No...strawberry! Oh please, can't I have both?"

"How about half a piece of chocolate and half a piece of strawberry?" Rosemary asked.

"Yes!" said Gretchen. "Then I really get two pieces."

"You don't mind?" Prue asked.

"Not at all," said Rosemary. "I'll take the other halves home to share with my daughter."

Gretchen smiled. "Can she come over to play?"

"I'm not sure," Rosemary asked. "She might be a little bit too grown up."

"Oh bother," said little Gretchen, causing Prue, Rosemary, and Marjie to all laugh.

"What's so funny?" Gretchen said suspiciously.

"You're just a bit clever," said Rosemary. "Aren't you?"

"I am," said Gretchen. "I know all my alphabets."

"How remarkable," said Rosemary. "Here you go."

She handed over the slices of cake to Prue, who helped Gretchen carry the plate safely to a table. As Rosemary watched them walk away she could have sworn she felt a tingling sensation in her necklace. It came with a feeling of foreboding, as if something big was about to happen.

Ten

Athena arrived at school later in the morning for her second day. There were more students of various ages milling around the courtyard, though not very many overall. As the only school in the village, Myrtlewood Academy started with young children and went all the way up to the end of high school.

For the size of the old school grounds there didn't seem to be many pupils on the roll. When Athena had mentioned this to Miss Twigg the previous day, the tiny reptilian-like teacher had merely shrugged and muttered something about "ebbs and flows."

Athena pulled out her timetable. First up was Alchemy, which she guessed was supposed to be the equivalent of chemistry. The class was in the East Wing of the main building. She put her timetable back into her bag and tried to orient herself.

Her sense of direction wasn't quite as bad as Rosemary's, though it was a close second.

"Hey," a voice called out. Athena continued on, hoping it wasn't directed at her.

She was intending to avoid as many people as possible.

"Hey, new kid. Athena, is it?"

Athena couldn't very well avoid such a direct address. She turned to see the blue-haired girl from yesterday who she recalled was named Elise.

"Hello," Athena mumbled as the girl approached.

"I just wanted to apologise for yesterday."

"What for?" Athena asked.

"Well, mostly for Felix," Elise said. "He's out of control. He can be such a cad sometimes."

"Why are you apologising for him?" Athena asked.

Elise shrugged. "I'm just sorry if you had a hard time. It must be strange starting a new school, especially when it's as bizarre as Myrtlewood Academy."

"It is a bit strange," Athena admitted, allowing herself to smile. Elise seemed friendly, at least a lot friendlier than Beryl, who appeared to be glaring at the pair of them from across the courtyard.

"Don't mind her," Elise said, giving a little wave in Beryl's direction. "She's so stuck up, she's practically on the ceiling."

Athena laughed. "What's wrong with her?"

"Her family are all a bit like that, I think," said Elise. "They have high expectations and Beryl's always trying to impress them by being top of everything."

Athena smiled. "She's not going to have much competition from me. I've never been top of the class in my life."

"You never know," said Elise. "It's a different school and by the sounds of it you've got loads of magic."

Athena blushed. "I really don't. My mum does, even though she doesn't know how to use it."

Elise gave Athena a quizzical look. "You're not just human. Are you?"

"What?" Athena responded. "What do you mean?"

"You must have something else in you, something otherworldly."

"I don't know about any of this stuff," said Athena dismissively. "Weird things have been happening over the past couple of weeks and I have no idea what's going on, but I'm pretty sure I'm just a mostly-regular human."

"Well, I'm happy to be your friend," Elise said, holding out her hand to shake. "If you'd like."

Athena smiled, not detecting anything nasty in Elise's demeanour or indeed in her thoughts. She shook Elise's hand.

"Is this normally how you make friends?" Athena asked. "It seems awfully official."

Elise giggled. "I don't know. I just do whatever I think makes sense at the time, really." She held up her hands and waved them playfully in the air. "Come on, it's Alchemy class now, right?"

Athena smiled and walked with Elise towards the classroom. Maybe, just maybe, school wasn't going to be as bad as she'd previously thought.

Athena sat next to Elise in Alchemy class in rapt attention. The class turned out to be loads of fun. The teacher, Perran Graveolum, seemed young and energetic and liked to make bold statements about the nature of the universe and then back them up with magical experiments which he then got the class to replicate.

Today's activity was creating a tiny galaxy in a cup of tea. There was a particular spell involving what Mr Graveolum referred to as *cosmic dust* which one sprinkled into a pot of freshly brewed English breakfast tea and then recited a chant over.

Athena partnered with Elise and Sam and they had a lot of fun. First they blended the cosmic dust in the mortar and pestle. It made a funny clicking sound which was oddly satisfying. Then they brewed the tea, which Athena was an expert in by now given her family's excessive tea habits.

By the time they'd turned the teapot three times and poured the tea out into the glass teacup, theirs was the sparkliest galaxy.

"Perfect grade," Mr Graveolum said. "A microcosm of the macrocosm." He held up his hands. "I present you a prime example of how we're all both very, very big and excessively small at the same time." He crowed with laughter.

Beryl glared at the three of them. In comparison, her galaxy hardly sparkled at all. In fact, it looked simply as if she'd dropped a thimble of milk into a weak cup of tea.

"She's not going to be happy about this," Sam said quietly.

"Don't worry about her," said Elise. "She can't be the best at everything all the time. Nobody is."

"Well, Beryl is, most of the time," said Sam. "She doesn't like competition."

"She's gonna have to learn to live with it," said Athena. "The three of us combined are obviously fabulous at magic."

Elise laughed. "I told you, you're powerful."

"It's the magic of teamwork," Athena said sarcastically.

Sam giggled.

"What's so funny?" Beryl asked, walking towards them with a cold expression.

"We were just talking about teamwork." Elise flashed Beryl a sassy smile.

"And how wonderful it is to work with people with such a sense of camaraderie. Wouldn't you agree?"

"Absolutely," said Mr Graveolum. "Sensational. I'm so pleased you're getting on board with a bit of collective spirit."

Beryl blanched and returned to her own desk. She'd refused to work with any of the other students, saying they'd only ruin her experiment.

"What are you doing for lunch?" Elise asked.

Athena shrugged. "Maybe the library...reading?"

"Nonsense, come and hang out with us," said Elise. She gently pulled Athena by the wrist of her cardigan as they walked out of the class and towards the far corner of the courtyard.

Felix and another boy were already sitting there.

"Not them, really?" Athena whispered.

"Felix isn't that bad when you get used to him, and Deron is lovely," Elise insisted.

Athena eyed the taller dark-haired boy sitting next to Felix. He was built like a thug, but he did have a warm, friendly smile on his face.

"But if you really don't want to we could sit somewhere else," Elise continued.

"It's fine," Athena said and followed Elise and Sam over to the corner of the courtyard.

"New girl!" said Felix. "Come to hang with the cool kids?"

"I think you should apologise to her actually," said Elise.

"What for?" Felix lowered his eyebrows.

"For subjecting her to your idiocy,"

"Hey," said Felix, scowling and then grinning. "Oh fine. I apologise for my immense wit and wisdom, my sparkling personality, my strong character, and my excellent tenacity."

"Felix, what kind of apology was that?" Deron asked.

"It's fine. You don't owe me any kind of apology," said Athena.

"See, I am perfect." Felix raised his arms in triumph.

Athena sighed and sat down next to Elise. She pulled out the lunch she'd brought from home. It was a sandwich made with bacon and eggs.

"That looks good," said Sam. "I bet it doesn't to Elise though. She can't eat animal products."

"Are you a vegetarian or a vegan or something?" Athena asked.

"No, it's more like an allergy," Elise said.

"Elise is a dirty rotten pixie," Felix teased, scrunching up a piece of paper bag and throwing it at the blue-haired girl.

"I'm nothing like a pixie," said Elise.

"Close enough," Felix replied. He opened his own lunch box and began scoffing food. Athena watched in astonishment as he gobbled down several large pork pies.

"He always eats like that," said Elise.

"Not a pixie," said Felix, returning to the subject after abruptly finishing his enormous lunch. "That's right you're a water nymph or something."

"I told you," said Elise. "My mother is a naiad. That is all."

"A what?" Athena asked.

"Similar to a water nymph...I guess," Elise conceded.

"Nympho," said Felix, giggling.

"Shut up." Elise glared at him. "Nymphs and Naiads are nature spirits, a bit like faeries. Mum comes from the family that creates rainbows. That's what's wrong with my hair."

"Your hair's cool," Athena said. "And that's amazing. I don't know about anything like that. I have so much to learn."

"Don't worry," said Felix. "I'll show you all there is to know about being magical."

He put down his lunch box and stood up. Immediately, red fur started sprouting from his face.

Athena gasped in horror as the beard spread to his hands and he shrunk down to the ground, transforming into a large fox and running around in circles in the courtyard.

"He loves to surprise people with that trick," Sam said.

Felix turned back to his human form. "It's not a trick," he said.

"You're a shapeshifter?" Athena asked.

"So you do know about my kind?" Felix seemed disappointed that Athena wasn't impressed or amazed.

"We did have an encounter with a particularly bad seed up at the house..." Athena said.

"We heard something about that," said Elise. "What really happened?"

"It's a long story," said Athena. "Too long for a lunch break."

She turned back to Felix. "I was wondering about something. What happens to your clothes when you change forms?"

"You mean, why don't I lose my clothes and end up naked somewhere?" He winked at her. "I guess it's part of the magic. It kind of absorbs anything

I'm wearing and then spits it out again when I change back. It's quite handy really, so I don't get caught out butt naked in public."

"That's really just as well," Athena said, laughing.

"Of course. I wouldn't want to blind everyone with my outrageous beauty," said Felix.

The bell rang and they made their way to Folklore and History. Athena walked down the passageway lined with eclectic paintings and old black and white photographs. Her eyes came to rest on a familiar face.

"No way," she said, approaching.

"Someone you know?" Elise asked.

Athena nodded. She couldn't tear her eyes away from the face. It was Finnigan, his dark hair falling across his forehead in the way it always did, his eyes sparkling.

"An old family member?" Sam asked.

"No, a friend, but I'm surprised to see him here. He goes to another school."

"It can't be. That was one of the students who disappeared over eighty years ago," said Sam.

"What?"

Sam pointed to a plaque sitting next to a row of portraits.

In commemoration of our cherished pupils, Eloise Staggart, Ferin Soot, and Finnigan Marsh, who went missing on the 21st of March 1938.

Chills ran down Athena's spine and she glanced back to the photograph of Finnigan.

"Maybe your friend is a relative?" Sam suggested.

Athena shrugged. "Maybe," she said. Though, examining the portrait even closer only made her surer that it was really him. She sighed.

Finnigan, you have some explaining to do.

Eleven

By the time Rosemary finally sat down for a bite of lunch, she was famished. Her first day working at the tea shop had been incredibly busy, and it wasn't over yet.

The bell above the door tinkled as she took the first bite of the beef and mustard roll that Marjie had made her especially. She looked up to see Ferg enter the shop wearing a bright orange jumpsuit that somehow suited his wire-rimmed spectacles.

Orange must be his colour for Tuesday, Rosemary thought, recalling Ferg's odd insistence on wearing set colours for each day of the week.

"Ah! Rosemary," he said. "Just the person I wanted to see."

Rosemary looked up at him, perplexed, then narrowed her eyes. "Really? Why?"

"I'm looking for volunteers to help organise Ostara."

"Organise what?"

"The Spring Equinox, of course," said Ferg. "Traditionally it was called Ostara, the celebration of the Goddess, Eostre. You may be more familiar with the term 'Easter'," he said, making the double quotation marks with his fingers in the air.

"Easter, as in when Jesus died?"

Ferg chuckled in surprise. "What do you think he died from? Eating chocolate eggs...or did he lay chocolate eggs? That's a trick question, by the way."

"You're saying that chocolate eggs are an ancient pre-Christian religious thing? Because I don't think cocoa was even on this continent until the end of the Middle ages," Rosemary said.

"No, traditionally they were proper chicken eggs, but painted."

"I'm no good at crafts," said Rosemary. "Just ask Athena. I'm sure I'd sooner break the eggs than paint them."

"Children paint the eggs, Rosemary," said Ferg in a very serious tone. "I need your help with the ritual. I reasoned that since you're new in town it would be the perfect opportunity to get to know people and dive into something exciting."

"Oh," Rosemary said. "But didn't we just have the spring festival?"

"We had Imbolc," said Ferg. "That's the festival to signal the end of winter. Next is the Spring Equinox and after that there's Beltane, which is more about the beginning of summer."

"Why so many festivals?"

"Because they are magnificent," said Ferg simply.

"Umm, thank you for thinking of me," Rosemary said. "But I've got rather a lot on my plate at the moment with starting a new job here and supporting Athena with her new school. I don't think I can take on anything else right now."

"Nonsense!" said Ferg. "You'll be perfect. There's not all that much to do – if you know how to delegate, that is. Here."

He held out a small booklet entitled: *How to Celebrate the Spring Equinox*, by A. C. Twigg.

"Ferg," said Rosemary. "I said no."

"Oh," said Ferg, hanging his head. He looked dreadfully disappointed. "I see."

"Sorry," Rosemary said. "I might be able to help a little bit, but I'm not signing up for any more responsibility just yet."

Ferg looked up at her, an innocent expression on his face. "What is it about responsibility that scares you?"

Rosemary was floored. She didn't know how to respond. She only knew that his words had cut straight to the heart of her current struggle regarding what to do with her life and that her emerald pendant had started humming.

"That's a lovely necklace," Ferg said after a while.

"Thank you," Rosemary replied, attempting to return to her lunch. She took a big bite of her roll, hoping it would help to end the rather awkward conversation.

"How about I'll just leave the book here, and you can think about it?" Ferg said. "Have a read and let me know if you change your mind."

Rosemary was still chewing her food and didn't get a chance to respond before Ferg skipped away.

She sighed and picked up the booklet. At least it would give her something to focus on while she ate to distract her from other more serious worries.

The equinoxes, when the night and day are equal, are about finding balance. They are the times of year when the veil between the worlds is the thinnest, it read.

"What have you got there?" Marjie asked, coming over to the table, her white apron covered in chocolate stains from the hundreds of cupcakes she'd been icing – and then magically duplicating – for a very large wedding party. "Oh, it's Aggie's wee booklet."

"It is?" Rosemary asked.

"Yes, Agatha Twigg. You know – she gate-crashed your dinner party."

"I didn't know she was a writer."

"Actually, Aggie is a very famous historian," Marjie said. "She knows all about Myrtlewood and magical histories around here. Has Ferg roped you into helping with the equinox, then?"

Rosemary smiled. "Ferg is trying his best, but I said no."

"Oh bless!" said Marjie. "Good on you for having boundaries. I know he can be a demanding chap."

"So demanding that he left this book here so I could have a read and think it over," said Rosemary.

Just then, the bell sounded above the door and the mayor walked in, looking ruffled. Even his hair was somewhat scruffier than usual and his customary black and purple cape looked like it had been dragged through a bush backwards.

"The usual, please, Marjie," he said, sitting down at a table by the window and glancing around suspiciously.

"Are you alright there?" Marjie called as she bustled back to the kitchen.

"Fine, fine," Mr June said. "Why wouldn't I be?"

Marjie shot Rosemary a puzzled look from the kitchen. "I'll make your tea," she called out. "Rosemary, can you get Mr June a large piece of carrot cake with extra cream on the side?"

"Sure," said Rosemary. She had finished her lunch and was ready to get back to work anyway.

"Oh, you're properly working here now?" Mr June asked, taking in Rosemary's apron and raising an eyebrow.

"I'm helping Marjie out, since it's her busy season," Rosemary said. "I just started today."

"Interesting." Mr June stroked his goatee. He turned his attention to a small notebook which he fished out of his pocket and began writing in, occasionally glancing around to check if anyone was watching.

Rosemary served the carrot cake and carried it over to the table. As she placed it down in front of the mayor, he glanced up and his eyes locked on her necklace.

"That!" he said, pointing at the emerald pendant that hung from Rosemary's neck. "Where did you get that?"

Rosemary was taken aback. The pendant had drawn a lot of attention, usually from people who commented on how nice it was, but there was an entirely different tone in Mr June's voice that she couldn't quite place. Was it anger or fear?

"My grandmother gave it to me," Rosemary said, clutching the pendant reflexively.

"She did, did she?"

"Yes."

"I'll have you know that pendant is property of the town of Myrtlewood and belongs in the museum!"

"Err...well, it was in my house, and Granny said it was hers."

Mr June gave her a dubious look. "How much do you want for it?" he muttered, lowering his voice.

"I...I don't want anything for it," Rosemary said. "It's a family heirloom. Granny said it belonged to my great, great, great, great grandmother or something. Maybe you're thinking of a different emerald necklace?"

He narrowed his eyes at her. "There is no other like it. Come on. Five thousand quid. I'll write you a cheque right now."

Rosemary was flummoxed. She'd assumed the pendant was worth money, being old and made of gold and emerald, but she'd never thought of selling it. And even though it might be tempting to have a bit of extra cash, Mr June's reaction to seeing the family heirloom was so bizarre. His whole manner seemed off. She simply couldn't take the offer seriously.

"Here you are," Marjie said, bringing the tea over to Mr June's table. She caught Rosemary's eye and added, "Dear, can you come out the back and help me with something?"

Rosemary gladly followed Marjie back to the kitchen. "What was all that about?" she asked.

"Something is not right with him today," Marjie said.

"You're telling me!" said Rosemary. "He seems to be so obsessed with my necklace. I'm actually worried he's about to try to fight me for it."

Marjie sighed. "It happens from time to time."

"What happens?" Rosemary asked. "The mayor picks fights over necklaces?"

"He just goes a bit...well, a bit strange. My theory is that he has an obsession with eternal youth, you see. He's always off to see one quack doctor or another, filling himself with potions. He's even tried to get *turned*."

"Turned?" Rosemary asked.

"Into a vampire," Marjie explained in a whisper. "Only it's not so common, these days. Vampires don't tend to like the idea that they might crowd out the world too much, living so long and all. They're very selective about who they'll turn. It's usually only a desperate act of love. You know, if they can't live without someone."

"Oh," Rosemary said, taken aback. "I'd never thought of that. It must be lonely, outliving almost everyone else."

She wondered about Perseus Burk and how lonely he might have been over the decades or centuries...however old he really was.

"Anyway," Marjie continued. "The potions make him a bit wild, sometimes. And he's always wanting to collect special magical talismans, like your necklace."

"He said it's property of the town," Rosemary said.

"Oh, pay him no mind," said Marjie. "He's a babbling lunatic when he's like this."

"Isn't that offensive, to call someone a lunatic?" Rosemary asked.

"Not around here, it's not," said Marjie. "The moon does things to people. Especially shifters. We all know it."

There was a lot more Rosemary wanted to ask about shifters and vampires and all sorts of other magical things, but Marjie looked busy wrestling an enormous piping bag over a large chocolate wedding cake. She glanced back out to the main part of the shop to see Mr June walking out.

Rosemary decided to get on with her work. The mayor had hardly touched his carrot cake, but he'd left no sign of coming back either. She tucked it behind the counter, just in case, and wiped down his table.

The bell sounded again. Rosemary looked up, expecting to see Mr June back to re-claim his cake. She was startled when Athena bounded in instead.

"Oh no!" Rosemary said. "What's the time? Did I forget to pick you up again?"

"Relax, Mum," said Athena. "You're fine. They just let us out early from school."

Rosemary breathed a sigh of relief, but as she inhaled again potential dangers flooded her mind. "You should've called me to come and get you."

"Don't be silly," said Athena. "It's hardly a ten minute walk into town, and the weather is nice today."

"The weather might be nice, but I spoke to Detective Neve earlier. They still don't know what's happened to the Bloodstone Society members. They could be back at any moment."

"Mum, I can't live my life in fear just because of some stupid secret society. Anyway, it's bright daylight. At least the vampires won't be around to get me."

Rosemary was silent for a moment looking at the floor, considering this, then she glanced up at her daughter to see her smile.

"You're in a good mood," Rosemary said. "I take it today went better than yesterday?"

"It did!" Athena said.

"Marvellous!" said Rosemary. "How about a piece of cake, to celebrate?"

Athena's eyes scoured over the cabinet. "I want that chocolate orange one,"

"Blast," said Rosemary. "There's only one piece left and I was hoping to have that myself."

Athena smiled. "Get two forks, then. We can share it."

"Are you sure?"

"I don't need the whole piece by myself," said Athena, warmly. "And if I'm still hungry afterwards I could always have that strawberry torte. I hope Marjie doesn't mind us tucking into her cake cabinet, though."

"Tuck away!" Marjie called out from the kitchen. "It all needs to be eaten."

Rosemary made a pot of Earl Grey tea and carried it to their usual table, along with the last slice of chocolate orange cake and two forks. She also brought over the two half slices of cake left from little Gretchen's earlier appearance, for good measure.

Though the danger was still tugging at Rosemary's mind, she couldn't help but smile at Athena's especially good mood. While she waited for the tea to brew she took a little bite of the chocolate orange cake.

"Ooh...this is delicious," she said, closing her eyes to savour the rich, tangy aromatic flavour.

"See," said Athena.

"See what?" Rosemary asked.

"Whatever you decide next, it has to be focussed around food. You *love* food – especially chocolate."

Rosemary took another bite of cake and sighed in delight. "Maybe you're right," she said. *I should put that cheffing training to good use, one way or another.*

She closed her eyes to better experience the taste and texture of the wonderful cake. As she did, an image popped into her mind: a little chocolate shop with a red-and-white-striped awning, its front window display filled with fabulous confectionary, including an enormous mermaid made of chocolate.

Rosemary pictured shelves lined with all kinds of hand-made chocolate bars of different varieties, a cabinet of speciality truffles, and a hot-chocolate bar where she could whip up her favourite indulgent recipes.

As her fantasy ran away with her she imagined that she could refine her magic for delicious purposes – that each confection she invented could have a distinct property. She could serve customers a pick-me-up orange bergamot cream if they came in feeling down, a spiced dark chocolate truffle for a little boost of energy, or a chocolate dipped Turkish delight if they needed something soothing and heart-warming. The possibilities were endless.

"Earth to Mum," Athena said, jolting Rosemary from her daydreams.

"Sorry," Rosemary said, "I was just imagining... Well, it was nothing really."

Rosemary was suddenly embarrassed by everything she'd just dreamed up. It was impractical, of course. She had no control of her magic, and though she could make a fine hot chocolate and was a dab hand at basic truffles, she had no mastery over proper chocolate making.

"It can't have been nothing," Athena said, her voice lilting. "Not with that smile you had on your face. Were you thinking about that handsome vampire?!"

"Shhh," Rosemary said. "And no, I absolutely was not. If you must know I was just indulging in a little daydream about what it would be like to have my own chocolate shop."

"That's perfect!" Athena said, her tone both excited and deadly serious. "You have to do it."

"Don't be ridiculous," said Rosemary. "I'm no chocolatier."

Athena beamed at her. "You make the best hot chocolates. I'm sure you'll get the hang of the other stuff. How hard can it possibly be?"

"Quite tricky, I think," said Rosemary, taking a sip of tea. "It's an artform – an entire culinary specialty!"

"So learn," said Athena. "Or simply buy in all the things from other chocolate makers that you don't know how to make yourself."

"That would defeat the purpose a bit. In my fantasy I was making chocolate with magical properties."

"Even better." Athena took another bite of cake before adding, "you'll figure it out."

"Figure what out?" Marjie said, coming out from the kitchen, covered in chocolate stains.

"Oh, nothing," said Rosemary, not wanting Marjie to worry about the possibility of an imaginary chocolate shop as competition.

"It's not nothing, actually," Athena said.

Rosemary tried to kick her gently under the table to get her to be quiet, but Athena simply moved her legs and continued.

"Mum has figured out her true vocation...as a magical chocolatier!"

"Marvellous!" said Marjie. "That's perfect, that is! When will you get started?"

"Hold on," said Rosemary, though she couldn't help smiling at Marjie's enthusiastic support. "I don't even know what I'm doing yet. Any potential shop would be a long way off."

"Well, you just tell me what you need, dear," said Marjie. "And I'll do whatever I can to help."

Athena grinned at Rosemary from across the table as they both took another big bite of the delicious cake in front of them. Rosemary closed her eyes again and allowed herself to dream just a little more about the possibilities her future might hold – a little chocolate shop where the flavours make people feel things – feel better.

That's my kind of magic.

Twelve

Rosemary arrived home, tired but happy, with Athena in tow. Work was more fun than she'd anticipated. The teashop was a great way to meet people and keep her finger on the pulse of the town. She even felt safer, knowing that whatever nefarious things the members of the Bloodstone Society might be up to, she was sure to hear about them through the gossip that happened all around her during an ordinary day.

"I'll make tea," Athena said as soon as they got in. Her good mood seemed to be continuing. "What's for dinner?"

"I thought I'd be too tired to cook after a long day. So Marjie gave me a couple of beef pies and some coleslaw."

"Sounds good," said Athena, smiling.

Despite Athena's recent positivity, Rosemary had a distinct feeling her teen was hiding something again.

Athena had been silent on the drive home and Rosemary wondered if whatever was occupying her was just an ordinary teen issue, like a crush, or whether it was more magical in nature. Whatever it was, Rosemary hoped it wasn't dangerous. They'd already had more than enough danger in their lives recently.

"Aren't you going to tell me about school today?" Rosemary asked. "What happened that significantly lifted your spirits?"

"Do I have to tell you every little detail of my life?" Athena asked, her voice teasing.

"No, just the highlights and lowlights," Rosemary replied. "And the bloopers reel, please. I need some light entertainment."

"Actually, it's been surprisingly less embarrassing than I'd feared," said Athena. "And...most of the other students were nice to me. I don't want to jinx it but I might even be making new friends."

"That's wonderful, love," said Rosemary. "Tell me about them."

"Oh fine. If you must know," said Athena. "Sam is quite shy, and really cool! They are non-binary, you know? And they have a nose ring. They come from a less magical family than lots of the other students. Sam says their parents practice folk magic – like home remedies and little charms and things, but nothing powerful. It kind of makes me feel less alone because I don't seem to have any kind of magic aside from the annoying head radio. Lots of the other students are amazing with magic. Elise is really talented – and her hair changes colour with her mood!"

"Amazing," said Rosemary.

"I know. I'm quite jealous of that," said Athena. "She's some kind of Naiad, like in a fairy tale. She's really nice, though. She invited me to sit with her friends at lunch, and it was pretty good actually, even though Felix was there."

"What's wrong with Felix?"

"I guess he's like the class clown, really over-the-top and chaotic. He likes to play tricks on the teachers and he's so full of himself it's nauseating."

"Sounds like a real charmer," Rosemary said, rolling her eyes. "I know the type."

"Elise says he's not that bad when you get to know him. But guess what he did at lunch?"

"What?" Rosemary asked tentatively.

"He turned into a fox!"

"No way!"

"Yes. One minute he was standing there and the next, he just...was a fox!"

"So he's a shapeshifter, like that crow guy?" Rosemary asked.

"I guess so," said Athena.

"Maybe keep your distance from him, then."

"Mum, just because we met one dodgy shifter it doesn't mean they're all like that. You told me vampires aren't all bad. Like Burk – you trust him, right?"

"I suppose I do, to an extent," said Rosemary.

"Or is it just that you *like* him?"

"Athena! No, that's not it. He's like a thousand years old, and plus, he's a lawyer. That's uncomfortably similar to being an estate agent, don't you think?"

"Excuses, excuses. I know you like him," Athena said, batting her eyelashes.

"Even if I did like him, I don't date and I don't intend on starting any time soon. Besides, if I did date, then Liam has already asked me out and he's much closer to my age, and more...normal. Given how bizarre my life has become, I think I'd hypothetically be looking for a nice *normal* relationship."

"Mum, you can't use me as an excuse not to date much longer. You'll become one of those old people with tons of cats and a house full of old junk."

"That's fine by me," said Rosemary, taking a seat at the kitchen table. "I already have *one* cat. That's progress!"

"Seriously," Athena continued, as she rinsed out the tea pot and began to fill it with fresh leaves. "I'm practically an adult now and I don't care if you see people."

"I'm surprised you'd say such a thing when you know about my terrible taste in men. Anyway – we were talking about *you* and *your* social life."

Athena carried the tea pot to the table along with their favourite cups. "It's actually nice to think I might *have* a social life for a change."

"What about Finnigan?" Rosemary asked carefully. "Is he no longer in the picture? I thought you were going to ask him about the head voices and try to find out more?"

"He's...well, he's away, I think. But I'll try again tonight. And I guess I should ask him what he knows about Dad, too, even though it might not be a totally terrible thing if he's magically disappeared."

"That's right, Dain!" said Rosemary, as Athena passed her a cup of freshly brewed Earl Grey. "How did I forget about him again!? It's like there's a mysterious hole in my brain when it comes to him. Granny said he's disappeared...and I just forgot all about it!"

"You're not exactly known for your stellar memory."

"Maybe not, but that is the kind of serious thing I would normally remember and worry about at every opportunity, and it just kind of fell out of my head. It's a bit like the car vanishing. How did I forget about that? It must be something magical."

"It could be," said Athena, shrugging. She took the last sip of her tea and her tummy grumbled. "Can we have dinner already?"

"Of course," said Rosemary. "But I'm still worried about Dain and the possibility that my memory is being magically interfered with...again! I think I should tell Detective Neve."

"Alright, fine," said Athena. "You call the cops, I'll get dinner heated."

Rosemary went upstairs. She intended to make the phone call straight away but, upon realising how filthy she was after a day in the kitchen, she decided to shower first.

She turned on the shower faucet to heat up while she undressed and took off the emerald pendant, placing it on the bench by the bathroom sink. Then she stepped into the shower and let the warm water run over her, easing away the worries of the day and cleaning her mind just as she cleaned her body.

A LOUD CLANGING noise startled Rosemary from her shower trance. She turned off the faucet and immediately smelled smoke.

"Athena!" she called out, wrapping herself in a towel and racing downstairs.

A large plume of smoke bulged out from the oven. Athena was racing around, opening the windows.

"I burned dinner!" she cried. "The oven must be magically fast. I thought it would take ages to heat them. Sorry!"

"It's alright," Rosemary said, extracting a tray containing two very burnt pies from the oven and throwing them out through the open front door so that they landed, gracelessly, in an overgrown flowerbed. "Have a look in the fridge and see what's there. We can always just have beans on toast again if all else fails."

Athena went to the fridge, only to find it completely bare. "What?" she said. "It's almost always full of food. How is this possible?"

"She moves in mysterious ways," said Rosemary, patting the house kindly.

"Mum!"

"What? The last thing we need is to lose favour with our sentient abode. Check the pantry."

"The only thing in here is Jaffa cakes and the packet of crisps I made you buy the other day," said Athena. "Do you think she's glitching or something?"

They looked around at the house. Everything else seemed to be in order.

Rosemary shrugged. "Dinner at the pub, then?"

"Sounds good," said Athena. "But you'd better get changed first."

"Oh...yes." Rosemary clutched her towel. She ran back upstairs to her bedroom and threw on the first clean items of clothing she could find. Not only was she starving at this point, but she didn't want Athena getting hangry because that only ever ended in tears.

She was on her way back downstairs when she heard voices, which only made her rush faster, and that, in turn, meant that she tripped on the stairs and landed painfully on her knees.

"Gah!" Rosemary cried.

"Mum, what's wrong?" Athena asked, running towards the staircase.

"I'm fine." Rosemary groaned as she pushed herself up. "Just a little accident. I heard voices. Who's here?"

"It's only me," said Sherry, coming over to help Rosemary as she hobbled down the last few stairs. "I thought you two might need a break from cooking, so I brought over some of my famous Guinness stew and rye bread. Liam's minding the pub tonight because it's my night off."

"How sweet of you," said Rosemary, smiling. "You actually have no idea how well-timed this is."

"That's right," said Athena. "I just managed to burn our dinner and we were on our way to the pub anyway."

"Well, let me bring the pub to you!" said Sherry. "Though I didn't bring any drinks with me or anything."

"We'll supply the wine!" Rosemary eyed the big containers of delicious smelling food Sherry was carrying. "Won't you join us for dinner?"

"That would be lovely," said Sherry. "I brought more than enough to go around and it saves me having to dine alone at home with only the cat for company."

As they sat down for dinner, Rosemary had the disconcerting feeling that she'd forgotten something important, but she couldn't remember what it was. She made a mental note to ask Athena about it later, but as she chatted with Sherry she managed to forget that too.

Sherry was full of the best kind of town gossip – not malicious, but fun and interesting news and titbits about the goings on that she'd picked up by osmosis just from working at the pub.

They learned about rumours that Neve was about to propose to Nesta – or was it the other way round?

"How exciting!" Rosemary said. "I met Nesta today and she's great. They both seem so good together."

"They do make a great pair," said Sherry. "Not all is well in town, though. Mr June is having issues!"

"He was in at the tea shop today and behaved very strangely," said Rosemary. "Marjie said he's on a quest for immortality."

"There was a rumour floating around that he's also being investigated for embezzlement, something to do with his tax return," said Sherry.

"What? Oh dear, I didn't know Myrtlewood had to follow the same laws as everyone else in the country," said Rosemary. "It feels like such a cloistered little bubble here."

"Of course we do," said Sherry. "We've all got to pay our taxes and do our bit. Anyway, Mr June is a bit of a worry. No one else wants to be mayor, but no one particularly wants him to be, either."

"He certainly is an odd character," said Rosemary. "Though there are plenty of them around. Ferg, for instance. Has he always been so strange?"

"Of course he has," said Sherry.

"Is he married or anything?" Rosemary asked. "I can't picture it."

"Why. Are you interested?" Sherry asked.

Rosemary laughed. "No. It's not that he's bad looking or even unkind. It's just he's..."

"He's Ferg," said Sherry. "The whole town actually assumes he's not the romantic sort. He doesn't seem to have relationships at all."

"He's probably asexual or aromantic," said Athena. "There's a whole spectrum of that kind of thing. You shouldn't judge."

Rosemary smiled. "I suppose I should stop being so nosey."

"You're so knowledgeable!" Sherry said to Athena. "Tell me, how is school going?"

"It's actually not too bad," said Athena. "Surprisingly. Though I don't understand much about magic and that's the entire curriculum."

"I'm glad it's not too bad, then!" said Sherry. "Who's in your class?"

"I don't know all the names yet," said Athena. "There's a kid called Sam."

"Oh yes, little Sammy Jenkins," said Sherry.

"And there's Elise – with the blue hair."

"Elise Thornton?" Sherry asked. "I didn't realise she went to school here."

"What do you mean?" Athena asked.

"Oh, you know, her mother's a Naiad. They often have different ways of doing things. Like other fae folk, they aren't from this realm, originally."

Athena and Rosemary looked at each other.

"No, we don't really know," said Rosemary.

"Are you saying there's another...world?" Athena asked.

"Sort of," said Sherry. "It's here, but not here. Kind of like the layers of a cake. All the layers are on top of each-other and happening simultaneously, but they're also at different vibrations of energy or something, so we don't see those that are beyond the veil unless they come through into the physical plane."

"That's fascinating," said Athena.

"It is," said Rosemary. Hearing Sherry speak of different planes of existence was reminding her of something that felt urgent and important but she couldn't remember what it was. The effect was infinitely frustrating.

"Myrtlewood is located across ley lines," said Sherry. "That's why there's so much magical energy here and why otherfolk flock to these parts."

"Otherfolk?" Athena asked.

"Yes," said Sherry. "People like us. People who don't fit in, in the mundane world."

"Oh," said Rosemary with a sense of recognition. "I didn't realise that's how I'd always felt. No matter where we lived, I couldn't make things work. We never seemed to fit in."

"I never made any proper friends," said Athena. "Even in Stratham where I had a few friendships – none of them were really close."

"Well, you're here now," said Sherry. "And this is where you belong."

Rosemary felt her frustrations ease at Sherry's words. It was nice to finally belong somewhere.

"I've been meaning to ask you," Rosemary said. "What do you think has happened to the other members of the Bloodstone Society? There seemed to be so many of them when they attacked us, but they were all wearing dark hoods. I wish we knew who they are. Do you have any ideas?"

Sherry exhaled slowly. "There are lots of rumours about that. But it's hard to tell what to believe. It seems like every second punter at the pub has said something or another – usually the accusations are baseless. They're just trying to dob in someone they don't like."

"How do you know they're baseless?" Athena asked.

"Well, if I believed every rumour I heard, just about the whole town would be a member of that society and up to no good."

Rosemary sighed.

"If it's any consolation, the rumours are pretty consistent on one thing," said Sherry. "Everyone is saying that now the Bloodstone power has dispersed, all the members are free. Apparently, many of them are glad to be free of it and have gone off to do their own thing now that they aren't under Geneviève's thumb anymore."

"That is good news," said Rosemary.

"Let's hope none of them bother coming after us, then," Athena added.

"You shouldn't totally let your guard down," Sherry said. "But remember, your family power is massive compared to theirs right now. You're like a lion and they're an itsy bitsy spider."

"That would be a great analogy if you'd used an ant or something instead of a spider," said Rosemary. "I don't fancy any venomous bites, metaphoric or otherwise."

"That's what I mean by keeping your guard," said Sherry. "You're much more powerful, but there are still risks."

"It's good to know that their power is so depleted though," said Rosemary.

Sherry smiled and took a big gulp of her wine, then excused herself to use the bathroom.

"See, there's nothing to worry about," said Athena once Sherry had left the table. "The Bloodstones have all gone off to do their own thing. I can walk to school. I'm safe even with no real magic."

"You have magic," Rosemary said. "Remember, you made those charms? They were powerful – one took care of the creepy crow man."

"Anyone can follow a recipe," said Athena.

"Not everyone can," Rosemary reminded her. "You know I'm no good with instructions. Besides, if a non-magical person followed those recipes I doubt they'd get anywhere near that kind of result. Actually – that's an idea. Mix up some more charms. I'll feel a lot better about letting you go off to school with those in your pockets."

"Fine," said Athena. "As long as you write me a note to explain my magical pocket arsenal."

"Done," Rosemary replied. She gave her daughter a quizzical look. Something was not right. "Wait. What is it you're not telling me?"

"I don't know what you're talking about," said Athena, taking a bite of food.

"Don't lie," said Rosemary. "Want to swap powers so I can read your mind?"

"I gladly would if I could," said Athena. "It's a crappy power." Then she narrowed her eyes at her mother. "Although I don't want even more invasions into my privacy!"

"Am I interrupting something?" Sherry asked.

Rosemary and Athena both looked to where Sherry was entering the room. "No!" they said simultaneously.

"I best be going, anyway," said Sherry. "Thank you both for a lovely evening."

Rosemary and Athena bid Sherry a good night and started cleaning up.

"You know what's funny?" Athena said, standing at the open fridge, ready to put the leftovers in.

"What?" Rosemary carried a pile of plates in from the dining room.

"The fridge is fully stocked again," said Athena. "And the pantry is too."

"That is very odd," said Rosemary. "I'll have to ask Granny about that the next time I see her."

Athena yawned.

"You go to bed, love," said Rosemary. "I'll finish the washing up."

"Okay, good night," Athena said and gave her mother a quick hug.

Rosemary watched her teen disappearing upstairs and frowned.

Her spidey-sense was tingling. There was definitely something else going on with Athena, but for now, it remained a mystery.

Thirteen

Finnigan, Athena called out in her mind. She was standing on the balcony outside her room which the house had mercifully kept intact.

Finnigan! She tried to call louder. *He said he would come tonight.*

She shivered into the night, wondering if she should go back inside to wait. Surely, even if he could hear her, it would take him quite a while to get here. She might as well be wrapped up in her warm bed, napping, since she was actually feeling quite tired.

She turned towards the house only to jump at the sight of a shadowy figure standing right behind her.

It was all Athena could do not to scream as arms reached out for her, resting on her shoulders, reassuring her. She looked up into a familiar face.

"You called?" Finnigan asked.

"You!" she said in a shrill whisper. "You scared me!"

"My apologies," he replied. "I came as quickly as I could."

"You were very quick," Athena admitted. "Almost as if you were waiting out here for me to summon you." She gave him a suspicious look.

"I promise you, I was not," said Finnigan with a cheeky grin.

"So you used magic, then?"

"Something like that."

Finnigan raised his arms for a hug.

Athena allowed herself to lean into him – allowed his arms to wrap around her. He smelled like peppermint and fennel and jasmine all mixed together. Sweet and spicy and fresh. She savoured the hug, even though she wasn't sure she should.

If Finnigan is like my father, how can I possibly trust him?

"I can assure you, I'm nothing like your father," he said.

"Don't poke around in my head," said Athena. "Anyway, how do you know my father?"

"I don't, personally," said Finnigan. "But I've heard of him. Is that why you called me? To ask about your father?"

He took a step back, a guarded look crossing his face.

"Not at all," said Athena dismissively. She walked to the edge of the balcony and leaned on the railing, looking out to sea. "I don't want to talk about him at all, unless you can tell me how he disappeared. But what I really want to ask about is the telepathy. I need to learn how to use it... And there's something else."

"What is it?" Finnigan asked.

"I'm going to school at Myrtlewood Academy, and there's a picture on the wall. An old-fashioned picture which was from the 1930s. The boy looks exactly like you. The plaque said he went missing."

Athena had been thinking about this all evening. She'd been sure the photo was of Finnigan when she was looking at it, but since then she'd had second thoughts.

"Was it...a relative maybe?" she asked.

"No. Not exactly," said Finnigan.

"Then what...?" Athena asked.

"It's a long story."

"Don't tell me. You're a changeling or something?"

Finnigan's expression darkened, as did his tone. "No. Who told you that?"

"Sorry," said Athena. "I don't mean to offend you. I don't understand any of this stuff. You're implying that changelings do exist, whatever they are? People have mentioned fairies around here, but I still can't quite believe..."

Finnigan laughed. "I assure you that I'm no changeling."

"Then what?"

"You'll find out," he said with a wink.

"But it doesn't make sense. People must see that photo all the time at school and then see you. You're around town all the time, surely someone would have noticed the uncanny resemblance?"

"They can't see my true face," said Finnigan.

"They can't?" Athena asked. "So what can they see when they look at you?"

"It's like an impression of me, but not me, exactly. They match my features up to other features that they're familiar with and they see something a little different, depending on who they are."

"But they don't see you? Is that what's happening with me too?" Athena asked sceptically. "I'm looking at you but only seeing an impression that just happens to look like that boy in the old photo."

"No, Athena. That boy in the photo was me, a long time ago."

Athena felt goosebumps raise on her skin that had nothing to do with the cold night air.

"So...you were alive all those decades ago. Doesn't that make you very old?"

"It does not. I wasn't really in this world most of that time."

"Now you're talking about another world? Wait a minute," said Athena. "You're saying I can see your real face and other people can't?"

"That's exactly what I'm saying. Just like you and I can read the minds of other people."

"We're the same?"

"Similar."

"What are we?"

Athena turned back towards Finnigan, only to find him gone. As she glared in frustration at the empty air a single word echoed through her mind: *Fae.*

As Athena lay in bed that night, her head swam with the revelation and all the possibilities that came with it. The word had come to her, not from Finnigan himself, but from somewhere else. Still, it could not be dislodged from her mind and she was certain it was true.

I'm fae...

I am fae...

What does that mean?

There were so many things that didn't make sense to her. Finnigan hadn't been in this world, so had he been in the realm of the fae? Where was it and how did he get there?

Then, there were the questions about her heritage. She was sure whatever faery genetics she might have couldn't come from Rosemary's side of the family, which could only mean one thing. Athena wasn't quite ready to think about that. Though it was true she didn't know anything about his family of origin, she refused to have anything to do with her father. Given his utter uselessness and inability to function in life, she was wary of what being fae might say about her...or Finnigan.

If Finnigan is fae too, why did he disappear all those years ago? What does that mean for me?

There were too many questions, the answers to which evaded her. She didn't have enough information to make sense of any of it, but she knew someone who might be able to help.

Fourteen

Rosemary awoke the next morning feeling as if she'd had one too many glasses of wine the night before, though she'd only had one and a half over dinner with Sherry.

She groaned. Why does getting older mean I can barely have a drink without earning myself a hangover?

She looked around at her childhood bedroom, noticing how sad-looking the peeling wallpaper was. She wanted to go back to sleep, more than she wanted almost anything in the world at that moment, but as her mind became clearer and she remembered all her obligations, she resigned herself to the fact that she had to get up. She groaned again and pulled herself out of bed.

She could hear Athena clattering around in the kitchen downstairs. The realisation that she'd out-slept her teenager on a school day made Rosemary check the time.

She groaned for a third time.

"So late!"

She threw on the first clean items of clothing she could find – drawing on an even more limited selection than she'd found the night before – and clambered downstairs.

"Why didn't you wake me up?" Rosemary grumbled as she entered the kitchen.

"That's not my job. Oh gosh. What on earth are you wearing?" Athena asked.

Rosemary looked down at her outfit – a pink ruffled skirt with a red halter and a bright green cardigan.

"Go and change this instant!" said Athena.

"No time! I'm late for work," said Rosemary, scoffing down a piece of buttered toast from the plate in front of Athena.

"Hey – that was mine!" Athena said.

"Thanks," said Rosemary. "I hope you don't mind too much seeing as you start so late and I'm insanely jealous of that fact right now."

"It's fine," said Athena with a sigh. "Though I really do wish you'd change out of that clashing nightmare."

"The apron will cover most of it," said Rosemary. "Got to run!" She kissed her daughter on the cheek and scampered out the front door.

"We are *so* going shopping for clothes as soon as you get paid!" Athena called after her.

Rosemary drove to Marjie's tea shop as quickly as she could, without breaking any obvious laws, though she wasn't exactly sure what those were in Myrtlewood. She suspected they might be somewhat different from anywhere else, but she decided to err on the side of caution. She had already gotten on Constable Perkins' bad side too many times, and the last thing she wanted was that bothersome and suspicious old copper breathing down her neck again.

She was already parked outside Marjie's shop by the time she remembered she wasn't wearing her special emerald necklace.

Oh bother. Well, I guess I'll see how I do today without it.

Marjie greeted her, full of smiles as usual. She clearly didn't care a jot about Rosemary being late but did eye her outfit with a curious expression before handing her a bright green and red floral apron.

"Are you sure?" Rosemary asked, looking at the apron.

Marjie sighed. "It sort of matches your outfit. As well as anything possibly could, anyway. Interesting look you've got there."

Rosemary looked down at the hot pink, red, and green assortment of clothing she wore. "Laundry day, I guess," she said. "Plus, Athena and I both need to go clothes shopping when we can afford it. We're badly in need of new clothes."

"Why didn't you say so?" Marjie asked. She walked out the back and came back with a floral printed envelope. "Here!"

Rosemary examined the envelope to find it filled with crisp cash. "Oh... no I couldn't," she said.

"Nonsense. I was going to pay you on Friday," said Marjie. "But you might as well take it now."

"Really, I can wait," said Rosemary.

"Take it now. I don't want you scaring the customers off with whatever your next even-more-desperate outfit is! Besides, I'm sure I can count on you not to skip town before you've earned it back."

"Of course you can," said Rosemary. "It's just..."

"What is it, dear?"

"You've been too kind to us. I already feel as if I'll never be able to pay you back for all the lovely things you've done."

"Your happiness is compensation enough," said Marjie. "Stop feeling guilty about generosity and accept it in the spirit in which it is given. Which is freely!"

Rosemary smiled. "Thank you, Marjie."

"I'm serious," said Marjie. "I don't do nice things for people just to make them feel bad. I expect the opposite, in fact."

Rosemary kissed Marjie on the cheek and handed her back the envelope. "Give this to me on Friday," she said. "I'm determined to maintain as much self-respect and integrity as I can, and if that means waiting until payday to go clothes shopping, so be it."

"Self-respect and integrity in that outfit?" Marjie asked, giving Rosemary a cheeky grin.

A velvety laugh sounded behind them. Rosemary turned to find Burk at the counter. She hadn't realised her conversation back in the kitchen had been in earshot of any of the customers.

I guess it is true that vampires have super hearing.

She glared at him as she approached the counter.

"Sorry," he said. "I didn't mean to butt in."

"You both should be sorry," Rosemary said. "Athena is usually the only one who makes fun of my outfits. But I suppose it's warranted this time."

"You look...great," Burk said.

"Don't lie," said Rosemary. "Now how can I help you, need a cup of blood-enchanted coffee or something?"

"Keep it down!" said Burk in a rushed whisper.

Rosemary blushed. "I guess it's my turn to be sorry. I keep forgetting it's rude to...out your kind."

"It's just private information," said Burk, shrugging. "I'm sure no one wants details about their health or personal activities spread around town. Besides, there's still a lot of prejudice against...our kind. And no, I'm not in for refreshments. I came to tell you that the money has come through."

"Really?!" Rosemary asked. She stepped out from behind the cover and threw her arms around Burk, who didn't seem to quite know how to receive a surprise hug. He stood there awkwardly, patting her on the back.

"Yes, really," he said. "Well, a big lump sum has gone through, the rest of it is in a trust belonging to you and Athena. She will get a sum when she turns seventeen, and you can draw on the trust for a range of different things. Galderall Thorn set specific criteria so the money can only be used for education and investments in your future."

"Why didn't I hear about this trust before?" Rosemary asked.

"It was all in the fine print," said Burk. "Something tells me you're not one for details." He grinned.

"I suppose not," Rosemary admitted.

"It seems your grandmother didn't have confidence in everyone in your life and wanted to ensure the bulk of the money was protected from them."

"She had a point," Rosemary said. "But...well, that's wonderful! Athena and I can go shopping for clothes today after all."

Burk nodded solemnly. "I can see why that might be necessary."

"Won't everyone just stop making jokes about my outfit already?" said Rosemary in mock exasperation. The truth was, she didn't care if she was wearing a fully-fledged clown suit right at that moment.

She was free of the crushing weight of debt she'd been carrying around for most of her adult life. The sense of lightness made her feel rather high. Rosemary was so excited that she had to restrain herself from flinging her arms around Burk again.

"Thank you!" she said.

"I'm just doing my job," he replied, but his expression revealed that there was more to the story. Instead of wondering what that might be, Rosemary went to find her phone and check her bank balance.

She gulped.

A sizeable sum had indeed been deposited. It was more than enough to cover her debts, and there was a tidy amount left over that sent a tingle of anticipation through her. Suddenly her dreams didn't feel so fanciful.

I could really do it...

I could have my own chocolate shop!

Fifteen

Athena arrived at school early, hoping to catch Elise before class. Her blue hair was easy to spot across the courtyard. Elise was standing next to Deron, holding a stack of old books. Athena waved her over hoping to talk to her alone.

"Hey," said Elise, smiling as she approached. "How's it going?"

Thankfully Deron hung back.

"I'm alright," said Athena. "I just...I wanted to ask you..."

"Ask away."

"The other day, you told me there was something otherworldly about me, and I think I know what it is."

"Oh really?" Elise said. "You were so sure I was wrong."

"I was then," said Athena. "But something happened. I won't go into the details. The thing is, I think..."

"Go on," said Elise.

"I think I might be fae, at least partly."

"Interesting," Elise said, looking at her with curiosity.

"Why is it interesting?" Athena asked.

"Well, it's very rare for the high fae, at least, to...to breed—"

"Gross!"

"You know what I mean – with humans. I think it's forbidden."

"That doesn't sound too good," Athena said. "And what does it mean 'high fae'?"

"Well, fae encompasses a whole subset of existences, even my family are considered part of the fae kingdom, but usually when people talk about the fae, they mean one particular species. I suppose they are kind of the rulers of the fae realm," Elise went on. "I don't know much about them and they're very secretive. I'm not sure exactly why they can't br—"

"Do you think I might have been lied to?" Athena interjected, thinking of Finnigan and hoping it wasn't true.

"Probably not," said Elise. "I've heard that the fae can't lie. So unless somebody else is tricking you into believing that..."

"But I can lie," said Athena.

"That's a good point," Elise replied. "Though you've never gone to the fae realm, so you're not fully under the grip of their magic. I'm actually not sure if humans with fae heritage can lie, anyway."

Athena wondered whether Finnigan always told the truth. He hadn't told her very much to begin with.

"How did you find out about this?" Elise asked.

"I have this friend...I guess he's a friend," said Athena. "I was talking to him last night and I got this idea in my head that he...we might be fae. He couldn't tell me much."

"That's probably because of the vampires," Elise said.

"The what? Why we talking about vampires now?"

"They've been at war with the fae for thousands of years. The vampires hunted them to the point of endangerment, at least in the human world. Fae have come up with a lot of magical protection mechanisms in response."

"What kind of protections?"

"All sorts," said Elise. "But they're really not obvious. I've heard there are some clever disguises in fae DNA that will stop them from being recognised for who they are."

Athena felt a tingle of recognition. That must be why Sam couldn't draw me.

"What about humans? Do the protections work against humans?"

"Probably some of them," Ellie said. "Humans might be a risk too. They could be in league with vampires, or under their control. I'm not an expert about fae, so don't take my word for it. Nobody really talks about them. There's not much in the library either, not about high fae, just catalogues of local pixies and dryads and so on. Wait, so you think one of your parents...?"

"Well, it's clearly not from my mother's side, and I don't really want to think about my dad at all."

Elise gave her a sympathetic smile. "Let me know if there's anything I can do to help," she said, just as the bell rang for class.

Sixteen

Rosemary sat at her favourite table by the window, browsing a list of chocolatier courses to find one she might be able to enrol in online. The tea shop had reached its post-breakfast lull and there were only a few quiet customers left.

That morning, she'd helped bake the Ostara buns and Marjie even let her have a go at making chocolate eggs. It took a few attempts to get the luxury compound chocolate in and out of the moulds, but it was rewarding, and delicious too. The experience had given her more motivation to make progress towards her dream.

"Why are all the best courses in London?" she muttered to herself.

"What's that, dear?" Marjie asked from the kitchen. She was holding an enormous pink piping bag.

"Nothing," said Rosemary, not wanting to reveal anything to Marjie just yet.

The door burst open and all eyes turned to see the woman standing there, tears running down her cheeks. It took Rosemary a moment to recognise Prue, the slightly harried mother she'd met the day before.

"She's disappeared!" Prue said.

"What's that, dear?" Marjie asked, coming out from the kitchen with a smear of pink icing on her cheek.

"My little girl. Gretchen. She's gone!"

"What happened?" Rosemary asked, her mouth suddenly dry.

She got up from her table and gently led the trembling Prue back to sit down, as the woman was clearly too upset to speak readily.

Marjie brought over a tray of her special tea, with shortbread. After a couple of sips of the enchanted brew, Prue began to explain.

"We were just at home, this morning. I was busy putting the washing out and Gretchen was playing in the back yard, over by the rosebushes."

Rosemary and Marjie nodded encouragingly.

"One minute I could hear her," Prue continued, "and the next it was silent. So, of course I looked around wondering what kind of trouble she'd gotten herself into. Only she was...she was gone!"

"Oh," said Rosemary, not knowing what else to say.

"Of course I looked for her, high and low, all around the garden. I knocked on all the doors nearby and no one had seen her. I even went out back to Fin's Creek to see if she'd wandered away down the valley, but there was no sign of her. None at all."

"Have you called the police?" Rosemary asked. "And if not, would you like me to?"

"I tried," Prue said. "But Constable Perkins said it wasn't an emergency until she'd been missing a whole day. Fancy that! A child? Children of that age don't just go off partying."

Rosemary bit her tongue to protect the poor distressed woman from the string of expletives at risk of coming out over her rage at the incompetent police officer.

"Let me call Neve," Marjie said. "She'll give him what for."

"Thank you," said Prue. She took a big gulp of tea, draining her cup. Rosemary immediately filled it again, unsure how else to help the poor woman.

"Just let us know if there's anything else we can do," Rosemary said.

"I don't even know you," Prue replied. "But thank you for your kindness."

"It's nothing," said Rosemary. "I have a daughter too and I can't imagine what it would be like to lose her."

Prue gave a big sob and tears began pouring down her face again.

"Sorry," said Rosemary. "I didn't mean to upset you...Just know that we'll do whatever we can to get Gretchen back."

"Neve's on her way," said Marjie.

Several minutes later, Detective Neve arrived and led Prue away.

"Let us know if we can help with the search party," Rosemary said as they walked out the door. Detective Neve gave her a curious look and then turned her attention back to Prue as they walked away.

Rosemary returned her attention to Marjie who had gone oddly silent.

"What's going on, Marjie?"

Marjie had a distant look in her eyes. "I think I'll just close up the shop early, for today."

"What?" Rosemary asked, but Marjie was busy closing up and seemed to be in no mood to talk.

Seventeen

It was as if a strange spell had fallen over the town of Myrtlewood. People's expressions became grim or vacant. No one spoke. Rosemary helped to wipe down the counters and sweep up, but by the time the tea shop doors were locked and she'd made her way back to her car, she was feeling deeply unsettled.

It was too early to pick Athena up from school, so Rosemary drove around in circles, thinking far too much for her own good.

Why is everyone acting so strangely? Is it just the news about the little girl going missing, or could it be that they've been bewitched somehow? Why aren't we all out looking for her?

None of it made sense and Rosemary couldn't help but think it must be part of some grand magical conspiracy. Has the mayor started abducting children to use in his magical pursuit of eternal youth? Or is it something even more sinister? Could the mayor be a member of the Bloodstone Society? Does he have the whole village under his spell?

Rosemary couldn't take it anymore. She didn't know where the mayor lived, and she was sure that the local law enforcement would be of no use, after Neve's odd reaction. She decided her best bet was to find Marjie again and get her to snap out of whatever spell she was under and tell the truth about what was going on.

It had been decades since Rosemary had visited Marjie's cottage, but she managed to navigate to a place that looked like the correct address, using sheer stubborn intuition.

Rosemary parked in front of the small whitewashed stone building, complete with red shutters and a rambling garden. She wandered up the driveway towards the front door past masses of over-grown rose bushes, only to find a sign that read: 'go 'round the back.'

Rosemary wandered around the side of the house, feeling somewhat less determined and more confused than she had moments before.

She passed a shed with the eclectic remnants of Marjie's former businesses in the window, including boxes of recyclable toilet paper that had not been the hit their creator had expected.

Rosemary couldn't help but smile at her quirky but unflappable family friend. Surely Marjie would be able to explain things.

"Oh, hello," said a familiar voice, decidedly unlike Marjie's.

Rosemary was startled, especially since the voice didn't appear to be coming from anyone. The back garden was full of vegetable plots without a person in sight.

"Ferg?" Rosemary asked, sure it had been his voice.

"Correct," said Ferg, saluting as he popped up from behind a trellis of vines that looked suspiciously like beans, despite it being far too early in the year for them. He was wearing purple overalls so violently neon that they almost hurt Rosemary's eyes.

"What are you doing here?" she asked.

"My job, of course," said Ferg.

"Another job?!"

"Yes," Ferg said simply. "I take it you didn't come here just to distract me from the brassicas."

"Oh no," said Rosemary, taken aback. "I'm after Marjie."

"Rosemary?" Marjie's voice said from the back door of the house. "What a nice surprise. Come in, dear!"

Rosemary wandered in to find Marjie in the kitchen, looking a lot more lively and less vacant than she had done earlier. This helped Rosemary to feel more at ease. She joined Marjie for a cup of tea in her doily-filled living room, while Herb dozed in a stuffed armchair, snoring rather loudly.

"Pay him no mind," said Marjie. "He's always like that after a train expo."

Rosemary smiled and took a sip of tea.

"So, to what do I owe the honour of a visit from Rosemary Thorn?" Marjie asked.

Rosemary took a deep breath, telling herself to be calm and level-headed and to speak deliberately and concisely. Instead, she blurted out the entire contents of her rambling and slightly paranoid thoughts.

Marjie looked troubled. "I'm so sorry to have caused you worry. You must understand that Gretchen going missing is painful for us. For the whole town, in fact."

"Are you saying that's what explains it?" said Rosemary. "That's why everyone went quiet? You're sure it's not a spell?"

"Quite sure," said Marjie with a patient smile.

"But everyone was just so strange. And Neve just looked baffled when I mentioned the search party."

"That's because there won't be a search party," said Marjie.

"What? Why not?" Rosemary asked.

"Half a dozen of Prue's neighbours would have already performed seeking spells by the time Prue even arrived at the shop. I even cast a quick one, myself, in the kitchen."

"Oh gosh," said Rosemary. "You're not saying the girl is dead?"

"Of course not!" said Marjie. "If she was dead we could find her."

"Why can't she be found then?" Rosemary asked. "Why aren't your spells working? Why would a search party be no good? Ohhh..."

"She's not *here* anymore," said Marjie, her eyes clouding over with grief. "She's gone somewhere else, beyond the veil."

"This has happened before, hasn't it?" Rosemary said.

"It has happened before, yes, to other children. Fin's Creek is known for disappearances," Marjie replied.

"Sherry told us about the fae and the other planes of existence."

"Sherry would know," said Marjie. "She was one of the ones who disappeared, once upon a time."

Rosemary gasped. "She did? When was that?"

"I don't recall exactly. A few decades ago, when she was a wee lass."

"And she just came back somehow?" Rosemary asked.

"I don't recall all the details, dear," said Marjie. "You'll have to ask her yourself."

Eighteen

Rosemary's head was spinning after the upsetting disruptions to her day. She was definitely not happy for Athena to walk home alone, and had rung the school to check in about what time they'd be finishing that day.

"You're very fixated on time, aren't you, dear?" Ms Twigg had said.

"I'm afraid so. Sorry for the inconvenience," said Rosemary, barely masking her sarcasm.

"It looks like they'll finish up around three."

"Thank you," Rosemary said. "Can you please get a message to Athena? Tell her to wait out front for me, where everyone can see her."

"Very well then," said the prim voice.

Rosemary arrived outside the school just after 3:00 p.m., relieved to find her daughter standing there.

"Ms Twigg told me to wait out here. What's this all about?" Athena asked. "Did someone die?"

"Not yet," said Rosemary.

"Uhhh?"

"Get in. I'll explain on the way."

"Where are we going?" Athena asked. She sounded miffed.

Rosemary hesitated and then remembered about the money coming through. *That should surely lift any teenager's spirits. Before I have to tell her about everything else!*

"Clothes shopping," said Rosemary.

That was all the persuasion Athena needed to jump quickly into the car. Rosemary drove them to the nearest shopping centre, which was in Cobbleston, the next town over. On the way, she filled Athena in on the missing child.

"That's awful," said Athena. "But I don't see what that has to do with me."

"You're a child," said Rosemary.

"I'm hardly a child, Mum. I'm almost an adult."

"Well, you're my child and I'm not taking any chances."

"Come on, Mum!" Athena said, crossing her arms.

By the time they got to the shopping centre, Athena was clearly fuming, but Rosemary was insistent that there had to be stricter rules, at least while children were going missing around town.

Athena was only distracted from her huff when she found out that the money had finally come through, meaning they could afford whole new wardrobes. Athena's mood brightened, but she insisted Rosemary keep her coat on the whole time at the mall, to hide her bright and clashing outfit from innocent bystanders.

"This is the best!" Athena said as they walked through what Rosemary considered a young-people-looking-cool shop. Athena was delighted that she could choose any item of clothing she wanted for a change, rather than being confined to absolute bargains and second-hand stores.

"We can afford a little splurge now," Rosemary said cautiously as Athena loaded herself up with black jeans and floaty-armed tops in a range of different colours. "But we will still have to be careful not to waste all our money so that we're okay in the long run."

"As long as you don't talk yourself out of doing something important with the money," Athena said. "You *have* to start that chocolate shop. It would be such a shame not to."

Rosemary sighed. "I do really want to. I even found a few courses I could enrol in to learn to be a proper chocolatier."

"Great!" said Athena. "Ooh, this one's for you. Try it on."

She held up a black velvet lace-up top that looked a bit like a corset with long droopy sleeves.

"It's too low-cut," said Rosemary. "Besides, where would I wear something like that?"

"It is not, and anywhere," said Athena. "Come on. At least see what it looks like when you wear it. You're a powerful witch and you should start looking the part."

"Shh," said Rosemary, looking around the shop.

Athena grinned at her. "You really think we'll get ourselves in trouble for talking about magic when no one here will believe in it at all?"

"Fair point," said Rosemary. "Fine!"

She grabbed the top and stalked off to the fitting rooms, feeling like she was the teenager in the situation.

By the time they finished shopping, Rosemary had bought not only the black velvet top but a number of other items that Athena had suggested along with several things the teen had pronounced frumpy or tasteless but Rosemary considered practical. Athena had selected double that amount of clothing for herself and seemed to be in a much more cheerful mood than earlier.

Rosemary, however, was still feeling shaken by the situation with the missing girl. Her mind spun with awful possibilities. She tried to call Sherry as soon as they arrived home but only got the answer phone.

Of course, she's probably busy at work.

"How about we go to the pub for dinner?" Rosemary suggested to Athena, who had spread out her clothing haul on the window seats and was busy matching outfits.

"Sounds good," Athena replied.

Rosemary went upstairs to change out of the clashing clothes she'd worn to work and into something new and clean. She put on the black lacy top that Athena had chosen and a new pair of jeans, then she washed her face and reapplied her lipstick. All the while her mind raced around in circles about the missing girl, trying to figure out some way she could help.

It took Rosemary a few more minutes of circling inside her own mind before she remembered the pendant. Surely that would make her feel better. She glanced down at the bathroom bench, recalling that she'd left it there when she'd showered the day before.

The bench was empty.

Rosemary stared at the clear marble surface, puzzled.

My memory might be terrible, but I'm sure I left it right there.

She looked around the bathroom floor, hoping that it had just fallen somewhere, but it was nowhere in sight.

Someone must have taken it.

"Athena!"

Rosemary stormed back downstairs.

"What?" Athena asked.

"Have you taken my special emerald necklace?"

"No," said Athena, somewhat defensively. "Why would I?"

"You were admiring it the other day. You said you wanted it."

"Sure, I was admiring it," Athena said. "But I'm not a bloody thief! If I'm going to take your stuff, I'll tell you first."

"Then what happened to it?" Rosemary asked.

"Stop getting so wound up," said Athena. "It'll turn up."

"You know, I am actually feeling *quite* wound up that an irreplaceable and valuable, not to mention useful, family heirloom given to me by my dead grandmother's ghost has somehow vanished."

"Well, how do you think I feel being accused of stealing a stupid family heirloom by my *own* mother?!" Athena yelled and stomped upstairs.

"Athena, I'm sorry," Rosemary said, following after her.

"I don't care," Athena said.

"What about dinner?" Rosemary called, but Athena didn't reply.

Rosemary sighed and collapsed on the window seats, feeling a pang of guilt about the argument. Athena's moods were all over the place recently. Rosemary had put it down to regular teenage moodiness. Throw in magical powers coming in and the mix was far too chaotic to comprehend.

She pulled herself up and went to the pantry to find a tin of tomato soup to heat up for dinner, humming to herself as she prepared the simple meal with a side of buttered toast.

She served some for Athena and set it on one of Granny's silver trays, but when she took it upstairs and knocked on the door, Athena still apparently wasn't speaking to her and didn't respond. The soup was left to go cold in the hallway instead.

Rosemary ate her own dinner in silence at the kitchen table, her thoughts circling around the things she could not control until she felt utterly frantic. She longed for the centring power of the emerald pendant, but clearly, she was going to have to calm herself.

Rosemary decided to focus on the things that were within her power, or would be soon: the plans she could make towards the chocolate shop. She went up to bed, dreaming dreams of cardamom apricot swirls that soothed the nerves and peppermint crisp bites that refreshed the mind.

Chocolate makes everything better.

Nineteen

Athena stood on her balcony, taking in the cool night air and the atmospheric clouds brewing on the dark horizon. This time when she called out to Finnigan, he arrived straight away.

"You have a lot of explaining to do," she said.

"I do?" Finnigan asked.

"Why are you always being so cryptic? Don't I have a right to know about what I am?" A pang of unfairness hit her, and she held back tears.

"Yes, of course you do."

"Then tell me. What am I?"

"You already know," Finnigan said.

"Fae..."

He merely nodded in response.

"What does it mean to be fae?"

"You deserve to know," Finnigan said. "But all I can give you here are words, and words can't explain it. You have to come with me."

Athena's neck prickled with fear. "Come with you, where?"

"I think you know where," Finnigan said, turning away from her.

"I can't just leave my mother," said Athena. "And what about school?"

"It's not like we're going away forever. You'll be back before you even know it."

"Can you guarantee that?" Athena asked. "Clearly, time works differently on the other side of the veil, or you'd be ancient. What if I disappear for twenty minutes and come back in fifty years? I'm not just going to leave my entire life behind."

"It's not like that," Finnigan said. "Once you know how to work things you can come back and forth like I do."

"Can't you at least tell me more? I'm pretty sure this is nothing to do with Mum's side of the family. It's my dad isn't it? He's one of them, one of you."

"In a manner of speaking," said Finnigan.

"So I'm half..."

"Wow."

"What?"

"Athena, you're fae. You're not half fae. It's not like a percentage thing. It's more universal. You are human and Fae."

"And you?" Athena asked.

"Yes, me as well. My father was human. He had a relationship with my mother which was forbidden. She had to return when I was a baby. I never knew her when I was a kid. My dad raised me until...well. It was an equinox a long time ago."

"But not a long time for you, then?" Athena asked.

"Yes and no," said Finnigan. "I suppose I've only aged about a year. Maybe two. It feels like a lot longer though. I come back here to visit, to check on things...when I'm asked."

"Does that mean you are on reconnaissance or something?"

Finnigan looked away.

"You're a dirty spy!" she said, not bothering to hide the accusatory tone.

"So what if I am?" Finnigan asked.

"I honestly don't know," said Athena. "I know so little about any of it."

"There are things you are better off not knowing. Your father..."

"I don't want to know about my father. I told you."

"That is probably for the best for now," he said with a dark look.

"See – so cryptic!" said Athena, stepping away from the boy and looking out over the balcony towards the horizon.

"You just told me you don't want to know."

"Not about him." She crossed her arms.

"But you do want to know about yourself," said Finnigan, taking a step closer to Athena.

"Of course I do," she said.

"I've told you just about all I can in words."

Athena sighed in frustration. "Can you at least explain to me how to use this stupid brain psychic radio power?"

"I can show you if you come with me."

"That's not fair!" Athena said, gripping her elbows, tightly.

"Athena, believe me when I tell you the fae do not reveal their secrets in this world."

"Not even to me?"

"Not even to our own kind if they live in the earthly realm."

Athena's frustration was quickly turning into anger. "Why not?"

"We simply can't," he said. "It's a magical bind. Surely you understand that."

"I don't understand anything right now," said Athena. "But sure, I've heard of magical binds if it's like when Granny couldn't tell us who killed her."

"Similar," said Finnigan. "It causes me pain, even to have this conversation."

"Pain?"

Finnigan grimaced. "This is at the very edge of what I'm capable of revealing."

Athena looked at him more closely, noticing how tense his muscles were.

"I'm sorry," she said. "I didn't mean to cause you pain."

"I'm aware," said Finnigan. "I must leave now. Call me if you want to take up my offer."

Athena sighed and glanced back towards the house where her infuriating mother was sleeping. By the time she returned her gaze to Finnigan he was gone without so much as a "goodbye."

As Athena lay in bed, later that night, her thoughts drifted into dreams of what it could be like to leave the mundane world behind and embrace her fae heritage. Some of the dreams were frightening, but some...were delightful.

Twenty

Rosemary arrived at work the next morning, her whole body aching with exhaustion. Athena had been silent, barely speaking all morning. She hadn't even protested when Rosemary insisted on driving her to school early so she could get to work, and didn't say goodbye.

Silence was exhausting.

As Rosemary entered the tea shop, Marjie looked up from behind the counter where she'd clearly been going through the ledger.

"Oh, you're here!" Marjie said, sounding surprised.

"Of course I am," said Rosemary, smiling. "I work here, remember."

Rosemary had a moment of panic. Had Marjie subtly fired her yesterday when she'd paid that impromptu visit to her cottage? She'd seemed fine about Rosemary's appearance, but perhaps she was just being polite.

"Don't get me wrong," said Marjie. "I'm happy to have you here. I just thought that now, with the money coming through and all–"

"I didn't think you knew about that," said Rosemary. She hadn't told anyone except Athena, mostly because she'd been so distracted by her own worries.

"Hard not to overhear things in here," said Marjie with a sad shrug.

"Actually, I'd almost forgotten in the chaos of yesterday," said Rosemary as she went into the kitchen to find her apron.

"Yes, with poor Prue. And little Gretchen."

"Yes," said Rosemary, frowning. "That's my main concern. And my necklace has also gone missing."

"Don't fret, dear. It's just a necklace," Marjie said sadly. "Enchanted or not."

"You don't understand, Marjie. Without that necklace my head's a mess. Granny wanted me to have it because she knew it would help."

"Be that as it may, you are perfectly capable of sorting out your own head. You don't need to rely on magical props for that. In fact, it's all the better if you get there on your own."

"Sure, in an ideal world," said Rosemary, worrying again about Marjie's mood. "But in reality I don't know how to deal with my own brain, let alone learn how to use my magic properly. I'm a hopeless case."

"Nonsense," said Marjie. "Magic is second nature to you Thorns. After you get over the speed wobbles you'll be right as rain."

"It doesn't feel that way," said Rosemary. "I'm totally overwhelmed."

"Oh dear," said Marjie. "Is there anything I can help with?"

"I don't think so," said Rosemary.

Marjie had a slightly pained expression. "Well, you just do what you need to do, dear. Don't let me hold you back."

"What is it, Marjie?" Rosemary asked. "You seem out of sorts. Is it about the girl going missing or something new?"

"It's nothing, dear."

"Marjie?"

"Oh fine. It just sounds so petty, is all."

"What does?"

"Well, yesterday I was happy for you when you found out Galdie's money had come through...and you came over to the cottage."

"Sorry about that," said Rosemary. "If I was intruding–"

"Nonsense," said Marjie. "You actually cheered me up."

"I don't understand," Rosemary muttered.

"After you left I was feeling a little brighter," said Marjie. "Then I remembered what I'd heard about your inheritance and it hit me – you won't need to hang about here anymore. And you know Herb is too busy to help out at the moment. Too busy with his bloody trains, and besides, he's not the best conversationalist. We were getting on so well with you here."

"Marjie..."

The older woman turned toward the cake cabinet, her eyes downcast. "You don't have to stick around just on my account. You're young and I'm sure you have much better things to do than spend all your time with a lonely old woman like me."

"Don't be silly," said Rosemary.

Marjie gave her an unimpressed look. "Well, you don't have to be rude about it."

"No, I mean, I really like hanging out with you and helping at the shop. Right now it feels like it's the only thing keeping me sane!"

"Is that so?" Marjie asked, a smile twitching at the corner of her mouth.

"Of course it is," said Rosemary. "I want to stick around here for a while and help you out, but also, I'm learning a lot about how to run a food business, so all this will help me with my long-term goal."

"You mean the chocolate shop?" Marjie asked, beaming. "You're really going to do it?"

"Yes," said Rosemary. "That's the plan, anyway. I have a lot to learn about how to be a chocolatier and also, how I can use my magic – deliberately – so that my chocolates are special, a bit like your charmed tea."

"Well, that's marvellous, dear."

"I might have to slowly cut back my hours here if I start studying," said Rosemary.

"Of course! Not a problem," said Marjie. "Oh! I just had an idea. You know the shop two doors down is empty?"

"Is it?" Rosemary asked. "I hadn't noticed."

"Well, why don't we go and check it out when business quietens down here. The lease hasn't been filled for months, maybe even years, so there's no rush, but wouldn't it be lovely if your shop was close to mine?"

"It certainly would!"

"Oh!" said Marjie, bursting with excitement. She rushed over to Rosemary and wrapped her up into a big warm hug.

Rosemary hugged her back, but as she pulled away another thought tugged at her mind. "Marjie, you don't happen to know how I can track down my emerald pendant, do you? I'm sure I left it on the bathroom bench at home but maybe it's been stolen. I wondered whether you had a clue as to where it might be."

"I've no idea, sorry," said Marjie. "I can try a finding spell for you later if you like, though it may not do much good if the blighters were careful."

"Yes, please," said Rosemary. "I'd appreciate that very much."

THE MORNING at the tea shop went past in a flurry of cakes and customers and cups of tea. They didn't even experience the usual pre-lunch lull, and Rosemary had to scoff down a few mince savouries just to stop herself from getting hangry. Despite the business, the disappearances were weighing heavily on her mind.

It seemed everyone in town wanted to come in and talk about the missing girl and lament about her poor mother and what she must be going through, and share rumours about the upcoming equinox, and most of them wanted to do this over cup of tea and a piece of cake or a pasty.

At first, the hum of gossip had interested Rosemary but, by and by, she realised there wasn't a ring of truth to much of what was said. A woman with a blonde bob who introduced herself as Crystal Cassandra 'the town psychic' enthralled a group of older men and women, clustering around the table at the front of the shop. Apparently, she sensed Prue was really at fault and that all would be revealed soon.

Marjie rolled her eyes at that, and Rosemary shut off from the spurious rumours that followed, as they had a toxicity to them that made her skin crawl. Marjie had been so sure that the girl had been taken to another realm, but still, Rosemary wondered whether that was really the case, or could it be a cover for something else entirely? After all, it struck her how convenient it was for kidnappers that everyone here believed in rumours of the fae stealing children.

Most of the customers had cleared out by a quarter to two in the afternoon, and Rosemary sat down for a cup of tea and a lamb, mint, and potato pasty.

"Finally," said Marjie. "I told you to go and take a break earlier."

"I know you did," said Rosemary. "But I didn't want to – especially when the whole place was full of all that nasty gossip."

"Oh, that crowd have nothing better to do with their lives than bicker about other people and make up vicious lies."

"That was my take, exactly," said Rosemary. "Poor Prue. It's bad enough that she's already suffering just about the worst thing imaginable, let alone having a bunch of gossips spreading fake rumours like that. I thought Myrtlewood was different from other places. I didn't realise that kind of mean behavior happened here."

Marjie sighed. "It happens everywhere, I'm afraid. Anyway, let's change the subject. How about we go and have a peek through the window of that empty shop two doors down and see how you like it."

"Oh yes?" said Rosemary, feeling herself perk up immediately. "That sounds like fun, umm, window shopping?"

"In a sense!" said Marjie. "Come on, get your coat."

Rosemary didn't initially think her coat would be warranted for a walk one third of the way down the block, but the biting wind made her grateful that Marjie had insisted on it. They walked past the hair salon next door and arrived outside an empty shop. Rosemary had never noticed it before, probably because there wasn't much to see.

A drab canvas awning extended above door and windowfront, covered in mildew. The shop's exterior had peeling paint in an unappealing slate grey, with speckles of a putrid green peeking through that Rosemary recognised as a '90s 'avocado' design fad. The interior didn't look much better.

Rosemary held her hand up against the glass to cover the reflection of the glaring overcast sky above. She saw what looked like several broken chairs, and a big corner booth upholstered in torn yellowy-brown fake leather. Towards the back sat an old juke box and a big wooden-panelled bar.

"What was this place?" Rosemary asked. "A dive bar?"

"Something like that," said Marjie. "It was frequented by a rough crowd and served as both a watering hole and a barber shop."

"Multi-purpose," said Rosemary. "Do you really think I should be setting up shop somewhere with a sordid past?"

"The rent will be low enough to be worth it alone," said Marjie encouragingly. "Besides, this place needs someone like you to spruce it up and show it some love."

"It is a great location," said Rosemary, looking around at the other shops on the street. "Oh, except for..."

The door of the shop on their right opened and Liam walked out, his sandy hair ruffling in the wind, his blue-green eyes widening in surprise.

It's right next to Liam's bookshop.

Rosemary had never been into Liam's shop, largely because of that awkward incident where he'd asked her out on a date and she'd had to turn him down.

It wasn't personal. Liam was a genuinely good man, and he was rather good looking too, and a far more suitable match than a certain vampire would be. In fact, he and Rosemary had once had a sweet and fleeting fling when they were about sixteen while she was in Myrtlewood staying with Granny for the summer. But Rosemary had sworn off dating.

Liam didn't take rejection very well and had managed to avoid her since the uncomfortable incident, but now, standing three feet away from each other, he could no longer pretend she didn't exist.

"Uhh, Rosemary."

"Hi, Liam," said Rosemary with a friendly smile and a little wave.

"Marjie," he said with a nod.

"Good day, dear," said Marjie.

"Uhh...yes. Got to run!" Liam said and indeed began running in the opposite direction.

"What was all that about?" Marjie asked with raised eyebrows.

"It seems rather childish, doesn't it?" Rosemary said. "Liam asked me out and I said no. Surely we can be adults about it."

"It must have hurt his pride, dear," said Marjie. "Either that, or he's madly in love with you and doesn't know how to face the fact that you don't feel the same way."

"Don't be ridiculous," said Rosemary. "He hardly knows me."

"Haven't you ever heard of love at first sight?" Marjie asked.

"I've heard of a lot of nonsense. It doesn't make it real. Anyway, enough about Liam. We're not here for him, we're here for this." She gestured towards the shop again.

"What do you think, then?" Marjie asked. "Do you want to be my almost-neighbour?"

"It's going to be a heck of a lot of work!" said Rosemary. "But I think it might just be perfect!"

LATER THAT DAY, Rosemary got out of the car to find the street near Fin's Creek was deserted, although she saw a few faces peep out of the windows of the houses nearby.

She wondered if they were afraid to go outside after the incident.

She walked through some long grass towards the creek. She'd managed to find the location using the map app on her phone, though she'd had to drive around several times because of her lack of sense of direction before getting to her destination.

The breeze through the trees was making whispering noises. The willows bent and boughed and the tall poplars creaked above. It would have been beautiful without the sinister feeling in the air.

It seemed strange to Rosemary that despite the child's disappearance there was no tape or any signs of a police search party. They must really be sure that Gretchen was gone from this world. Rosemary wasn't taking any chances. She couldn't bear to think how she'd feel if Athena disappeared.

The air felt oddly thick around her, and though she tried to breathe normally, it felt laboured.

"So, this is it," she said to herself. "This is where children go missing."

It was some comfort to know that they weren't presumed dead. That they were hopefully alive in some other world.

She wondered whether they missed their parents as much as their parents surely missed them or whether they would end up feeling okay about it, forgetting their families, and going on an adventure like the children in Peter Pan.

Rosemary paced the area, feeling as if she was being watched. There was nothing out of the ordinary that she could see. She walked down one side of the creek, crossing over some stepping stones to check the other side. Aside from the heaviness in the air and the uncomfortable feelings, it was just like anywhere else.

She walked back across the water and down the bank. Something caught her eye. A bright purple feather lay on the damp earth. It certainly hadn't been there before when she'd walked past. It did seem otherworldly. Rosemary reached forward to pick it up, but then she hesitated. It was possibly dangerous and certainly some kind of evidence. Instead, she pulled out her phone and took a photo that she could pass on to Detective Neve.

As she straightened up she had the sudden feeling she should leave as soon as possible and so, quickly, she did.

Twenty-One

The following day, the eerie experience at Fin's Creek was still playing on Rosemary's mind. Rosemary had texted Detective Neve the photo she'd taken of the feather and received a message back that it did look like something the fae would leave behind. She had thought about reporting her missing necklace too, though she decided to wait for a bit. The police obviously had enough on their hands with the missing child. The tea shop was still over-crowded and filled with spurious gossip. Hardly any of the customers were even there for food or beverages.

Rosemary decided to take a quick walk on her break, to take her mind off her numerous worries.

She peeped through the window of the empty shop, imagining what it would be like with a lovely bench and display cabinet filled with delicious chocolates. It still seemed like a pipe dream, though now, with her inheritance coming through, it was so close to her reach that she could almost taste the cocoa and vanilla.

She glanced next door towards Liam's Bookshop feeling a pang of regret.

I really should go in there and try to smooth things over with him.

It would be hard to avoid Liam if they became neighbours. Rosemary wasn't looking forward to talking to him, since he'd clearly been avoiding her. She gritted her teeth and rolled her shoulders back, then made her way through the door of the bookshop. A little bell rang but she could see no one inside. She looked up, over the stacks of books and shelves.

"Hello," she called.

A crashing sound startled her and she assumed Liam must have knocked something over, out the back.

She wasn't sure whether to just leave now before things got more awkward. Maybe this wasn't a good time, and he wouldn't be in the right mood to see her.

Then she heard the growl. A low deep sound like some kind of wild animal.

"Uhh, Liam?" she asked.

Rosemary felt her heart pounding in her chest. Something inside her was telling her to run. She began to turn around but movement caught her eye.

She froze.

A great hulking beast prowled slowly towards her. It was at least twice the size of a human and covered in fur like a dog.

"Uhh, hello? I'm going to hope that you're just a very large...and friendly shifter," Rosemary said.

The beast growled again.

"Maybe not so friendly," she muttered, slowly backing out towards the front door.

The beast sprung at her. She raised her arms, feeling her magic sizzling, but the beast was too quick. It flung her to the floor. Rosemary rolled and then ducked behind a shelf, hoping that her powers wouldn't fail her now when she actually needed them.

She blasted a bookshelf towards the beast, intending to knock it out. No such luck. It was already on its feet again, pacing slowly towards where she crouched.

I've got two options, Rosemary thought. *I can stay very still and see if it leaves me alone or I can just hope my magic is going to do its job and protect me.*

She cursed herself for not practicing her magic more in non-life-threatening situations. She slowly raised herself up, holding her arms out in front. This time she focused on aiming her magic more deliberately at the beast.

He growled again and sprung at her.

Rosemary braced herself, visualising her energy pulsing out towards the creature. She could feel it shooting down through her arms. It tingled in a slightly painful way, accelerating as amber light burst into the room, blindingly bright.

For a moment Rosemary couldn't see anything, and she wondered if she'd been knocked unconscious, but as the light faded she was still standing upright and perfectly fine.

The beast, however, had vanished. In its place was a very naked bookshop keeper.

"Liam! What the bloody hell was that?" Rosemary said as her childhood sweetheart opened his eyes and looked around the room blearily.

"Rosemary. What did you do?"

"What did *I* do? I just came in here to try and smooth things over with you. That is all I did! You, on the other hand, lunged at me in the form of a raging beast. What is it? A werewolf?"

"You got me," he said, raising his palms towards the ceiling. "It's not something I can help."

"So what, you just inhabit the shop sometimes in monster form and hope that nobody notices?"

Liam sighed heavily. "No. I'm usually shackled in a basement at this time of the month. The full moon caught me off guard. I was distracted thinking about...something else. I obviously didn't make it in time. I usually shut the shop, but I didn't even realise. What day of the week is it?"

"Thursday," Rosemary said.

"Thurs– Wait a minute," said Liam. He looked at her, puzzled. "How am I in human form?"

Rosemary shrugged. "Beats me."

"You did something," Liam said.

Rosemary glared at him. "You're accusing *me* of doing something after you attacked me?"

"No, it's not a bad thing. It's bloody brilliant!" said Liam. "What was it that you did?"

"It was just magic," said Rosemary. "I don't know."

"It's incredible. I've tried so many things over the years to stop the shift. But this...just happened. You did it without even trying."

"Fluke, I guess," said Rosemary, still shaking from adrenalin and not entirely ready to forgive Liam for the attack.

"I'm so sorry, Rosemary," he said, getting up.

Rosemary blushed and turned away.

"Oh, I better cover myself up," Liam said.

"I take it werewolves don't have the same convenient clothing magic as shifters, then," said Rosemary, recalling what Athena had told her about her school friend.

"I'm afraid not." Liam picked up a blanket that had been lying over a chair and wrapped it around his body to shield himself. "I'm still not quite in my right mind. But maybe...you've saved me somehow."

"That's great," said Rosemary. "Can we...can we just forget about this whole thing?"

"Yes, please do," said Liam. "Just don't tell anyone, okay?"

"Don't tell anyone that you turn into a raging beast at the full moon?"

"Exactly," said Liam with a gulp. "It's not exactly acceptable to be a werewolf in the magical community...to be infected. It's the disease, you see. There's a certain stigma. If people know they will stop coming to my store, or worse. I'd probably have to move."

A dark, brooding expression came over his face.

"I'm sorry," said Rosemary. "But you really expect me to not say anything after I was attacked?"

"I don't think it will happen again. Especially not if we can figure out how to harness your magic."

Rosemary felt as if a huge weight of expectation was suddenly being foisted upon her. She had no idea how she'd help Liam and she had far too much on her plate already.

"Even if I wanted to do that, we'd definitely need help," said Rosemary. "I barely know how to use it at all, and I'm not going to come over here and zap you once a month just so that you don't turn into the Big Bad Wolf."

"You're really not open to helping then?" Liam asked.

"I don't know," said Rosemary. "I just need to process, and I process by talking about things. And I talk to Athena even though she sometimes doesn't want to listen to me. But if I don't talk to anyone, then how can I figure out my position on all this?"

"You can talk to me," Liam said. "Look, take some time to process and come back later. Let's have a cup of tea."

"No," said Rosemary. "You just toddle on down to your dungeon or whatever and chain yourself up, because we don't know when this wolf mutation disease thing is going to come back on."

"You have a point," said Liam. "On Sunday, then? It'll be over by then."

"Right," said Rosemary sarcastically. "Because that's exactly how I want to spend my Sunday afternoon, being a magical counsellor to my ex-boyfriend with wolf issues."

“Okay,” said Liam. “Take your time, but just...”

“Very well,” said Rosemary. “I’ll have a cup of tea with you at some stage, and I'll try to keep quiet until then.”

“Thank you,” Liam said, with unnervingly adorable puppy dog eyes totally dissimilar to the terrifying eyes of the beast he’d been just moments before.

Rosemary left the shop feeling at least seventeen times more confused than when she first went in. Not only had life in Myrtlewood just got a whole lot more complicated, but she had a new secret to keep, and she hated secrets. She had no idea what to think of werewolves and didn’t understand why the townsfolk seemed so prejudiced about them, but her instinct told her that the mild-mannered bookshop keeper wasn’t in any way evil. But even if he meant no harm, that didn’t mean he wasn’t dangerous.

So much for Liam being a nice normal bloke.

Twenty-Two

Rosemary arrived at work on Friday feeling flustered, as she was late. Athena had been mucking around and didn't think it was her problem if Rosemary wasn't on time, since school didn't start until mid-morning.

"I tried my best," Marjie said, flinging her arms around Rosemary. "But alas, even my most powerful finding charm came to naught. I've no idea where your necklace is. Whoever took it must have been clever at covering their tracks."

"I don't get it," said Rosemary. "If magic can be used to disguise something like a necklace, why couldn't it be used to cover up the abduction of a child?"

"Excuse me, dear?" said Marjie. "I don't understand."

"Maybe Gretchen hasn't been taken to some other realm after all. Maybe someone kidnapped her and covered their tracks, just like whoever took my necklace. It could have even been the same person."

"Like who?"

Rosemary wrung her hands, wondering if she should let Marjie in on her suspicions. It wasn't that she didn't trust her dear family friend, it was possible that one of the customers innocently nibbling their cakes and scones was listening in. Besides, Rosemary was worried about coming across as paranoid. Even so, Marjie knew the town better than most people. It was worth the risk.

"Someone involved in the Bloodstone Society, probably," said Rosemary quietly. "I couldn't see who most of them were when they attacked the house. All those stupid dark cloaks got in the way. It could be anyone around town, maybe even the mayor. He's acting very suspiciously."

"Now don't go thinking like that," said Marjie. "You'll get your knickers in a twist with all that worry and it won't do you any good."

Rosemary sighed. Maybe she *was* just being paranoid, after all. She smiled apologetically at Marjie. "Thanks anyway for the finding charm. It was worth a try. I suppose I may never get the necklace back."

"Are you certain someone broke in and stole it?" Marjie asked. "Any ideas who it might be?"

Rosemary sipped the cup of tea that Marjie passed her. "A lot of people commented on it the other day," she said. "Mr June went a bit strange over it, remember?"

"Is that why you're worried about him?" said Marjie with a chuckle. "I do recall he made you feel uncomfortable. But I cannot imagine him like a common burglar, climbing in through a window or anything. He's much too pompous for that."

Rosemary smiled. "Good point." But she wasn't entirely convinced. Maybe Mr June had paid someone else to steal it, or used some pompous type of magic.

"Was anyone else at your house around the time?" Marjie asked.

"Only Sherry," said Rosemary. "And I can't imagine her doing anything nefarious."

"You're right," said Marjie. "Sherry is a sweet lass. I've never known her to be dishonest, though you could ask her if she saw anything suspicious."

"I could. I've been meaning to talk to her anyway," said Rosemary, picking at her fingernail. "I want to know what it was like when she was... you know..."

"Taken by the fae as a child?" Marjie prompted.

"Yes, and how it was that she got back."

"Tread carefully, there," Marjie warned. "You need to be aware that not everyone can talk about such things. In fact, it's a rare thing to hear more than a peep. Fae have powerful binding magic. I always wonder if it's to hide their dark secrets."

Rosemary shuddered. "That doesn't sound good. Who would have thought faeries would have dark secrets. I always thought of them as sparkly and fun."

"Well, they are strange folk," said Marjie. "I'm not meaning those with a bit of fae or nymph heritage, but the fully fledged high fae. They are bound to rules and etiquette."

"What does that mean?" Rosemary asked.

"Well, for one thing, they cannot lie, you see, and so they must bind themselves and others against revealing their secrets."

"*Why* do they need to be so secretive, though?" Rosemary asked.

"That's what I've always wondered. Probably just to protect themselves against vampires," said Marjie. "Speaking of vampires, look, it's your favourite lawyer."

"Where?" Rosemary asked, glancing around the shop.

"Just coming in from the underground entrance," said Marjie.

Rosemary turned back to the kitchen to see that Burk had indeed emerged from the trap door at the back and was brushing down his expensive-looking suit jacket.

He turned towards Rosemary and smiled, causing her to feel like a deer trapped in headlights.

"Rosemary," he said. "Marjie. Good day to you both."

"I suppose it is," said Rosemary.

"Listen, do you have time for a coffee?" he asked Rosemary.

"I'm a tea drinker," said Rosemary, "and I already have a cup of tea. Besides, I only just started work and I haven't done anything yet, other than stand behind the counter, chatting to Marjie."

"Nonsense!" said Marjie. "Off you go. Have a nice chat. It's a slow morning anyway and I've got no catering to do until tomorrow." She shepherded them both out from behind the counter with a cheeky wink and sat them down at a table.

"Will you be having the usual?" she asked Burk.

He nodded, returning Marjie's warm smile.

Marjie disappeared back to the kitchen and returned a moment later with black coffee in a floral tea cup.

Rosemary eyed it warily, wondering if it was blood-enchanted and what it might taste like.

"It's just coffee, Rosemary," Burk said.

"Oh, I didn't..."

"We can consume liquids fairly easily," said Burk. "But solid food makes us violently ill, as you've probably been told. Blood-enchanted food actually makes the food a lot like liquid, while maintaining its appearance of structure. It gives food some nutritional value we can actually absorb and a pleasant bloody taste."

Rosemary grimaced.

"My apologies," said Burk. "I forget that to most non-vampiric people, blood is hardly palatable."

"Don't get me wrong," said Rosemary. "I love a good black pudding. I just...umm...does it taste like human blood?"

"Mammalian blood tastes fairly similar, regardless of where it's from," said Burk. "Human blood is a lot like pigs' blood, which makes up the majority of what we eat."

Rosemary couldn't help but grimace again.

Burk gave her a quizzical look. "I'm just being upfront with you."

"Err, thank you, I guess," said Rosemary.

Burk shook his head dismissively. "Let's talk about something else."

"Okay," said Rosemary. "What do you have in mind? Surely you didn't just want to imbibe a hot beverage with me to tell me about your dietary habits, or is this a key part of educating a new worker at your local café?"

"No," said Burk, smiling. "I had something else in mind."

"Which is?"

"I intended to ask for your company for...an evening."

"What?" Rosemary was feeling dazed, her mind still miles away with thoughts of Gretchen and the necklace and the dodgy mayor.

"Would you do me the honour of your presence?"

"My presence where?"

"I suppose it could be anywhere."

"Wait a minute," said Rosemary. "Is this some obscure old-fashioned way of asking me out on a date?"

Burk seemed to pale a little. Then he cleared his throat. "You could put it like that."

"Oh!" said Rosemary, at first relieved that she'd worked out the mystery and then anxious about the entire situation. "Oh...well, you see, you're kind of my lawyer and also my grandmother's lawyer and that surely is multiple conflicts of interest right there, and also, I don't mean to be blunt but you are possibly about a million years old and the age gap is a little creepy. I mean, what am I supposed to tell Athena? I'm dating someone that could be my great, great, great, great, great, great grandfather? And also, I don't date."

Burk eyed her warily.

It took him a moment to reply. "I'm not that old," he said finally. "Well, I'm not a million. That's ridiculous."

Rosemary shrugged. "Close enough. It's not like you've told me anything specific about your age or what time in history you come from."

"It's a long story, and one I don't often share," Burk said. "I don't think you require my legal services anymore, which is why I've waited until now to ask."

"The answer would still be no," Rosemary said apologetically. "I really don't date."

"Why is that?" Burk asked. He was infuriatingly handsome at that moment, leaning back in his chair and stroking his chin with his index finger.

"Largely because I have literally the worst track record with men – notably one man – notably Athena's father."

"I see. So one bad apple has spoiled your appetite for the rest," said Burk.

"I suppose so. Also, my life is complicated enough with Athena, and discovering magic, and lurking looming dangers that seem to come at me every single week, and also, I'm setting up a business, so I have plenty of other stuff to think about and no time at all for romance."

"That's understandable," said Burk.

Rosemary felt a twinge of disappointment.

"Wait a minute," he said. "You're setting up a business? This is new."

"It is," said Rosemary.

"Anything you want to tell me about? Perhaps seek legal advice over?"

"You're not my lawyer anymore, apparently," said Rosemary. "And anyway, I don't feel ready to talk about it just yet. I want to let it bubble away and allow the energy to build up first."

"That sounds wise," Burk said.

"Thank you," said Rosemary. "People don't usually call me wise."

Burk smiled at her.

She was surprised that their previous date-related conversation hadn't seemingly made things awkward between them, unlike the situation with Liam. Perhaps having a few hundred years to overcome one's sense of personal rejection made all the difference.

"There you are!" said a hoarse voice from behind them. Rosemary turned to see Ferg in a fire-truck red three-piece suit. His arms were loaded up with baskets filled with little potted plants and eggs.

"Oh, hi Ferg," said Rosemary. "We were kind of in the middle of a conversation here."

Ferg looked from Rosemary to Burk.

"Don't mind me," said Burk. "I better get back to the office, anyway." He got up and walked towards the back of the tea shop, leaving Rosemary nursing her mild disappointment.

"What is it, Ferg?" she asked flatly.

"I've been meaning to check in with you about Ostara," said Ferg, panting.

"Ost...what? Oh that's right, the Easter thing that's actually the Spring Equinox with disappointingly non-chocolate eggs. Do you think you could make them chocolate, just this time?"

"No."

"For the children?" Rosemary asked.

"No. This is for you." He handed her a basket of little plants.

"Erm..."

"You've got a conservatory at your house," said Ferg. "I've seen it. Plus, you can use a bit of magic to speed up the growing process so that these tulips can flower. Old Galdie always helped us out a bit with that, leading up to the Spring Equinox."

"Ferg, I'd love to help, really, I would..."

"Excellent," said Ferg and turned to walk away.

"But!" said Rosemary. "There's just too much going on at the moment. I don't have any headspace to spare on gardening, or clearing out the old conservatory, which is in a right state. I'm too worried about that missing girl and trying to protect Athena. Besides, I don't even know how to use my magic to get things to grow, so I'm afraid you'll have to ask someone else."

Ferg gave her a stern look. "Rosemary, listen to me. If you really care about that little girl, you'll do what you can to help make this ritual work."

"Oh really?" Rosemary asked. "Why on earth...?"

"The equinoxes are when the veil between human and fae worlds is the thinnest," said Ferg. "If we have any chance of getting her back soon, it's through the ritual. Having a powerful witch like you involved will make all the difference."

"I told you I don't know how to."

"It doesn't matter if you don't have a full grasp of your powers yet," said

Ferg. "The power is there, with you and Athena both. Besides, it will give you a chance to practice your growing magic on the plants."

Rosemary sighed. "Really?"

"Yes, really," said Ferg.

"What is he doing?" Marjie muttered, coming over towards the table. "Ferg, are you bullying Rosemary into volunteering again?"

"I'm doing nothing of the sort!" said Ferg. "I'm simply informing her of how useful her magic will be for the equinox, which is also our greatest chance of getting little Gretel back."

"Gretchen," said Marjie and Rosemary simultaneously.

"Whatever," said Ferg.

"I suppose you do have a point there," said Marjie. "That was how we got wee Sherry back, after all, though it had been a whole year by that point."

"Sherry was gone for a year?!" Rosemary asked, in shock. "How awful for her family."

"It was a terrible time," said Marjie. "Little Liam could barely stop crying, at least at first. They were very close as similar-aged cousins, but after Sherry came back she was different. It has taken them years to form a solid friendship again."

"That's strange," said Rosemary. "I wonder if Sherry can give us any tips for how we could help Gretchen."

"She may not be able to speak of it," said Marjie. "But if you can summon an audience with your Granny's ghost, she might just be able to tell you how she helped Sherry cross back over."

"Granny did?" Rosemary asked.

"That's the story I heard," said Ferg. "And that's exactly why we need your help – we need the Thorn magic."

"I hate to say it, but he does have a point," said Marjie.

"I can try," said Rosemary. "But don't get your hopes up. Right now, my magic is utterly useless unless you're wanting an avalanche of blankets."

"Not right now, thank you," said Ferg with a deadly serious tone. "I will let you know if I get chilly though."

"Ahh, alright," said Rosemary.

"I'm certain that helping to grow these tulips will be a good opportunity for you to practice focusing your magic," said Ferg.

"I suppose, if I don't kill them all," Rosemary replied.

"Great. So it's settled then. You will help with the equinox."

“I suppose so,” said Rosemary grudgingly. “But I’m not crossing over into faery land. I’m staying firmly on this side of reality.”

“Excellent,” said Ferg. “I’ll bring around the trailer with the rest of the plants later on.”

He turned on his heels and strode out of the tea shop before Rosemary could say anything else. She sat down, her mouth gaping, staring after him.

“Trailer load…?” she said weakly.

“Ferg doesn’t do things by halves,” said Marjie.

“That’s for certain,” said Rosemary. “That man is…something else.”

Later, when Rosemary picked Athena up from school, the teen looked thoroughly embarrassed.

“What’s all that crap in the back of the car?” Athena asked, gesturing to the baskets on the back seat.

“I was actually hoping you could help me with that,” said Rosemary. “I’ve…uhh…volunteered to help Ferg with the equinox. Those are plants that I’m going to try to grow. I thought you be of some assistance.”

“What?!”

“It’s a long story. Basically, he convinced me that having the Thorn family magic involved would make the ritual more powerful and therefore make it more likely to get Gretchen back.”

“And you believed that weirdo?”

“We aren’t allowed to use the “w” word in a derogatory way anymore, remember what Granny said.”

“Who died and made her queen?” Athena asked.

“She did, I suppose,” said Rosemary. “Anyway, I don’t want to go around offending people’s religion or spiritual beliefs or anything, so I’m just trying to get out of the habit.”

“Honestly, I don’t care anymore,” Athena said. “From now on, I’m just focussing on my school work and my friends. You can deal with everything else.”

“I’m glad to hear it,” said Rosemary with a grin, though deep down she was sure life was just on the brink of getting far too complicated for both of them.

Twenty-Three

It was a cold, frosty morning. Rosemary's breath formed clouds around her in the air as she drove along the narrow twisting road leading up a hill to a large mansion.

She had spent all night going around in circles in her mind, thinking about both the disappearances of her necklace and the little girl. It seemed too much of a co-incidence.

If the finding spells didn't work for either, surely the same person could be responsible. The mayor seemed likely as a suspect. He was acting suspiciously and had a drive for immortality. Maybe he was using the excuse of the equinox to steal a child in order to use magic...somehow. Rosemary wasn't sure of the details, but she knew it would sound mad to most people, even Detective Neve.

There were so many ridiculous rumours floating around the village that Rosemary was sure no one would take her suspicions seriously. Instead of calling the authorities, she decided to take matters into her own hands in an attempt to get some solid evidence first.

She'd asked Marjie for directions to the Mayor's house. Her concerns had grown after everything she'd heard about the Mayor, Mr June, in recent days. Besides, he had taken such an interest in the emerald necklace when she saw him that she was sure he must be the culprit.

Rosemary even wondered whether he'd used the dinner party she'd thrown a few weeks before as an excuse to scope out the house for valuables or to plant some kind of magical assistance that might help him to rob her later on.

She approached the big black door and knocked on the shiny brass knocker, shaped like a goblin face.

An attractive man answered, tall with dark skin and piercing amber coloured eyes. He was wearing a purple satin dressing gown.

"Sorry to bother you," said Rosemary.

"Are you here for Don?" the man asked. "I'm his husband, Zade."

"Yes. Don, as in Don June. Mr June, the Mayor," Rosemary rambled.

"Come in," he said. "If you'll excuse me, I'll go and change."

"No, don't trouble yourself," said Rosemary.

"Don't worry," said Zade, with a warm smile, "I need to change anyway. I've been lounging around for too long already. Just make yourself at home. Don will be right down." He ushered Rosemary in and disappeared off upstairs.

Rosemary stood in the hallway wondering how such a nice man had hooked up with the greasy and pompous mayor. She glanced around at what she could see of the house. Everything looked expensive, if a little gauche for her tastes.

"Ah, Rosemary," said Mr June, coming down the stairs. "What can I do to help you? As you know, I'm always here to listen to the concerns of my citizens."

"Well," Rosemary began, but Mr June cut her off.

"Actually, it's very fortunate you came," he continued. "I have some business that I want to discuss with you regarding certain magical artifacts."

"Oh yes?" said Rosemary, surprised.

"Yes," said Mr June. "I do believe the late Madam Thorn had quite a few special treasures that I might want to purchase if you would deign to sell them to me."

Rosemary looked at the mayor suspiciously. Why would he want to bargain with her if he had just robbed her? She wasn't sure if he was genuine, or whether this was some kind of red herring to throw her off the scent.

"Look," she said.

"Oh, my," Mr June said, cutting her off again. "Where are my manners? Please come into the parlour, make yourself at home, and of course, I must offer you a beverage. What would you like? Tea? Coffee? An early morning pick me up?"

"Tea will be fine, thank you," said Rosemary, relieved when the rather overbearing man stalked off to the kitchen, leaving her in peace.

Rosemary paced the parlour, keeping an eye out for anything that looked suspicious. A polished wooden side table with a drawer caught her eye. She listened out for footsteps, but the house seemed silent enough. She knew she shouldn't, but her curiosity got the best of her. She crossed the room towards the drawer and pulled it open. The inside seemed to be largely filled with papers, but Rosemary rummaged through just in case there was anything incriminating.

"Excuse me," said a voice. Rosemary jumped.

Zade stood in the doorway.

"Sorry!" she said. "I was just admiring this table. What wood is this?"

"Mahogany," he replied dryly.

"Here you are!" said Mr June, re-entering the room brandishing a cup of tea. Rosemary took it and tried to hide her embarrassment.

"Ah, there you are, darling," Mr June said to Zade, who gave him a peck on the cheek and then walked past him towards wherever the kitchen must be, leaving Rosemary feeling relieved.

Mr June looked at Rosemary with a rather jolly smile. "Now, Ms Thorn! How can I help you?"

"I noticed you admired my necklace the other day," said Rosemary.

"Indeed, I did. I apologise for the misunderstanding. Are you willing to part with it?" he asked. "I do believe that item would be a wonderful addition to my collection."

"Yes, well, it's missing," said Rosemary.

"How unfortunate," said the mayor, though he didn't seem all that surprised.

"I'm not sure what happened," said Rosemary, watching Mr June carefully.

"Would you like me to try a locator spell for you?" Mr June asked.

"Marjie has already tried that," said Rosemary. "In fact, I must confess, that's the reason I've come here."

The mayor raised his eyebrows.

"Suspicions have been raised that maybe...you took it," she said quite frankly.

"My dear girl! How dare you come to my house and accuse me of petty theft!"

"That's the thing," said Rosemary. "It wouldn't be petty theft if it's a valuable magical item."

"That's even worse," said the mayor. "I will not stand for this! I'm outraged!"

"What's the matter, dear?" said Zade, standing in the doorway.

"This woman has the audacity to come to my house and accuse me of stealing!"

Both men looked at Rosemary. She felt distinctly uncomfortable. "Look, it's just...I heard some things. I thought maybe...maybe you knew something."

"That's not what you just said," said Mr June. "I think you should be going now."

"I caught her rummaging around in your drawer earlier," said Zade.

"Really? How outrageous! Why didn't you say anything?"

"She said she was admiring the woodwork, and I gave her the benefit of the doubt."

"I thought Madam Thorn would have taught you better than to invade somebody's personal property!" said Mr June.

"I'm sorry," said Rosemary. "You must understand that the necklace is very important to me."

"I understand enough," said the mayor.

"You'd better get out of here," said Zade.

Rosemary's heart began to race as she realised the trouble she'd gotten herself into, but it was for a higher purpose. She had to figure out what was going on.

"Just wait a minute," said Rosemary. "What about the missing girl?"

"Excuse me?" said Mr June.

"Gretchen. She disappeared around the same time as my necklace and finding charms don't work on either situation and...and..." Rosemary suddenly became aware how foolish she sounded. "If it wasn't you, then why aren't you out there looking for her? Surely, as the mayor you should be doing something about this!"

Mr June just stared at her, gobsmacked.

"Now you're accusing my husband of kidnapping?" Zade said, appalled. "Is this some kind of witch hunt? Are you prejudiced against us because—"

"No! Nothing like that," said Rosemary, even more alarmed. "I'm...okay, I'll admit it. I'm grasping at straws here. Are you sure there's nothing you can tell me? If it's not you, then who else would have an interest in my necklace?"

"A great many people, I dare say," said the mayor. "How awful that you've jumped to conclusions like this. I might not be the most popular person in town, but I'm a public figure and I deserve your respect."

"Okay. I'll just be going then," said Rosemary, anxiously backing out of the room.

"Not so fast," said the mayor.

"What? I thought you wanted me to leave."

"Not before I hand you over to the authorities," said Mr June. "I was just stalling. I've tripped the switch and the police will be here any minute."

"The police!?" said Rosemary, her panic quickly turning into dread. "But I didn't do anything."

"You came into my house under false pretences and proceeded to go through my personal things. That's breaking and entering."

"Oh, it was not," said Rosemary. "You let me in yourself."

"That was before I knew about your uncouth behaviour."

There was a knock at the door.

"Come in!" the mayor called out, and Constable Perkins entered the room followed by Detective Neve.

"Miss Thorn!" Constable Perkins bellowed, his cheeks red. "What kind of trouble are you getting into now?"

"This woman came into my house and accosted me – accused me of stealing, and kidnapping! She invaded my house and rummaged through my things. It's unacceptable, criminal behaviour."

"Rosemary?" Detective Neve's voice rose in pitch and Rosemary mourned for the potential friendship that was quickly slipping away due to her own reckless behaviour.

"Well, I suppose that's all true." Rosemary conceded. "But criminal? That's going a bit far."

Neve's expression was clearly unimpressed.

"Look, the only reason I came here is because I think he might have stolen my necklace."

"Why didn't you just tell us about your suspicions?" said Neve.

"I didn't have any evidence," Rosemary admitted. "And I didn't want to look foolish." She blushed, feeling much more foolish now.

"Of course there was no evidence," said the mayor. "Because I've done no such thing. Now arrest her, immediately."

Constable Perkins took a step forward, but Detective Neve held him back. "Arrest her for what exactly?"

"Yes, what exactly?" said Rosemary, crossing her arms and feeling relieved that Neve seemed to be taking her side.

"Invasion of private property!" said Mr June.

"Didn't you let her in?" Neve asked.

"That's beside the point," he replied.

"Look. I'm sorry," said Rosemary. "I just really need to get my necklace back. I feel all strange without it and maybe that's caused me to be a bit irrational and jump to conclusions." She looked at the mayor, deciding that now was not the time to repeat her suspicions. "You're right. I didn't have any evidence. It was just a hunch."

"She didn't really do anything wrong," said Zade.

"Aren't you on my side?" Mr June folded his arms.

"Of course I am. It's just...well, she was just having a nosy around. It's not like she damaged anything."

"Look," said Detective Neve. "I think this time the situation just calls for a warning. Rosemary, please don't break into anyone's house again."

"I didn't break in," Rosemary insisted. "We just went over this. He let me in."

"Still..." Neve shook her head and began to gently lead Rosemary to the door.

"I'm sorry," said Rosemary again as she walked out of the house with Neve. "I promise I'll go to the police next time something goes wrong or I have a suspicion about anything."

"Thank you," said Detective Neve, sounding like a harassed kindergarten teacher.

"It's just..." Rosemary stammered, as she made her way towards her car.

"I hate to say this because I think you're a great person. But can't you *do* anything?"

Neve's posture deflated.

"Sorry," Rosemary repeated.

"Thanks for triggering my impostor syndrome," said the Detective with a sad smile. "As one of the few non-magical people in this town, I went into law enforcement because I wanted the power to help. Only, it turns out I'm totally helpless at times like this."

"Oh," said Rosemary. "I didn't know."

"I'm doing everything I can – by the book. Plus a lot more. I'm leaning on my own personal connections to try to figure out how to get that little girl back, but it's a brick wall at every turn. Do you want us to look into your necklace as well?"

"No. You clearly have enough on your plate," said Rosemary. "Maybe we can work together. Only, I suppose I'd only cause you more trouble. The present situation is a prime example of that."

"Thanks for trying to help," said Neve. "Let me know what you find out, or if anything else goes wrong, and who knows, maybe we can work together at some point."

Twenty-Four

Athena walked across the road towards the town square feeling nervous. She'd never met up with friends outside of school before. In fact, she'd never really *properly* had friends, considering they moved around so much and she didn't fit in with most other kids her age.

That was, until recently. Elise and Sam had started to become pretty good friends at school, even if they did hang out with some ridiculous hooligans, like Felix in particular. Deron was okay and so was Ashwagandha, who sometimes joined in, sitting with their group at lunch time.

She recognised Elise's hair from across the square, easily spotting her standing next to Sam. They waved to Athena as she made her way over.

"Hi," Athena said, hoping she didn't sound stupid.

"You've made it!" said Elise.

"Yeah, Mum let me out of the house for a change," said Athena. "She reasoned that in the middle of the day with all the people around here I'd be safe enough."

"Your mother is a tad over-protective, isn't she?" said Sam.

"Tell me about it," said Athena. "I can barely do anything without her breathing down my neck these days."

"We're going to meet Felix and Deron later," said Elise. "Is that okay?"

"Sure." Athena shrugged. "I don't mind."

She hoped that her new friends weren't just interested in her for the novelty value or because they'd heard about her family's power. They seemed nice, and genuine enough. It would be awful if they got bored with her or were terribly disappointed when they figured out that she didn't really have any aptitude for magic.

"So what are we going to do?" Athena asked. "You said something about ice cream. Is it from the grocery store?"

"Oh no," said Elise. "We have to go to Mervyn's."

"Mervyn's?" Athena asked.

"Yes," said Sam. "Mervyn's ice cream parlour."

"I didn't realise we had an ice cream parlour in Myrtlewood," said Athena.

"Mervyn's is the best!" said Elise. "It closes up over winter, but at this time of year, it reopens again. And there are always a few extra surprises."

"That sounds amazing," said Athena. "Lead the way!" Then she wished she hadn't said that.

Athena tensed at her choice of words. They came out overly cheesy, as if she was on some sort of children's television show. She bit her tongue to try and stop herself from saying too much more. But fortunately, Elise and Sam didn't seem to notice, and Athena allowed herself to relax a little.

She followed them to a shop with pastel blue-and-pink-striped awnings out front. Inside it looked like an old fashioned ice cream shop through the window.

"This does look awesome," said Athena. "I love the little booths."

The booths were striped in various shades of pastel as well, like something out of a 1950s television show.

"Shall we go in?" said Sam.

"After you," said Elise.

Athena pushed the door open and a little bell tinkled above her. She cautiously approached the counter. A man stood behind it. He had long hair tied up in a bun and was wearing a pastel striped apron with a huge smile on his face.

"Welcome!" he said. "You're my first customers of the season. Ice creams are on the house to celebrate!"

"Oh wow!" said Sam. "Excellent. I won't have to use up all my pocket money.

"That's great," said Elise. "How sweet of you, Mervyn. How are you, anyway? Did you have a good time at sea?"

A faraway look came over Mervyn's face. "Yes, it's always marvellous."

"How long were you away?" Sam asked.

"Two or three months, I think," he said. "That's the only time I can get away and be with my people."

"Your family live at sea?" Athena asked.

Mervyn gave her a wink. "You're new around here, aren't you?"

"I'm afraid so," said Athena.

"I'm Mervyn Wade, your humble local town Merrow."

"Merrow?" Athena asked.

"That's the old Irish word," said Elise. "It means—"

"Mermaid Man...err Merman," said Mervyn. "You know, I'm trying to use the human terminology. It always confuses me. What's the difference anyway? Genders are much the same."

"You can say that again," said Sam with a giggle.

"You're a Mer er...person?" Athena said, stuttering over the words.

"Of course," said Mervyn. "Not many of us live on land, but the ones who do still need to spend a decent amount of time at sea. Otherwise, we get land sick."

"Land sick, like seasick?" Athena asked.

"You catch on quickly," said Mervyn with another wink. "Now what would you like?"

Athena surveyed the array of ice cream spread out before her. There were some regular flavours like chocolate and strawberry ripple, among other more unusual flavours like blackberry and thyme, boysenberry and sage, and frankincense and dark chocolate.

"Wow, so much to choose from," said Athena.

"I'll have the usual," said Elise.

"Blueberry coconut cream," said Mervyn. "With a half scoop of blackberry and thyme."

"That's the one," said Elise.

"That sounds good," said Athena, baffled by the choice. "I think maybe I'll just have the same."

Mervyn got to work scooping their two cones.

"It's so hard to choose, isn't it?" said Sam. "I think I'll just have regular old chocolate. Can't go past the classics."

Athena smiled at them, now wondering whether she should have chosen a simpler flavour.

They took the ice cream and sat down in one of the booths.

It was still fairly early in the day and so there weren't too many people around. Athena tasted her ice cream to find it was absolutely delicious and complex. The flavour was almost dizzyingly good.

"So how's it going?" Elise asked. "Are you settling into Myrtlewood okay?"

Athena was too absorbed in her ice cream to answer straight away. Eventually, she looked up and cleared her throat.

"I guess so," said Athena. "Mum is still a little bit frazzled. She's paranoid that I'll go missing like that little girl. Also, some special necklace of hers has disappeared, which hasn't helped things. She's super anxious. She probably just lost it behind the couch."

Sam and Elise both laughed, putting Athena at ease.

"Is your dad around?" Elise asked.

"No," said Athena. "At least it's better when he's not."

"Mine either," said Elise. "My father wasn't magical. He freaked when he figured out what Mum was. I don't really know him. Sometimes I wish I did, though, especially when Mum's being a pain. I wish there was somewhere else I could go to escape her new moon cleaning sprees."

Sam laughed. "Your mum is such a character, Elise."

"My dad has sort of been in and out of our lives," said Athena. "I think he's missing at the moment, but really that's nothing unusual."

She didn't want to say too much at first. After all, she hardly knew Elise and Sam. She often found herself bursting with rage at her father and hardly ever had anyone to talk to about it since Rosemary made excuses for him that just made her angrier. It was nice to have other people to talk to, and Athena couldn't help but express a few resentful sentiments about how Dain had never been helpful, how he'd taken their money and gambled it away.

"That sounds awful," said Elise. "Maybe I'm better off not knowing my dad after all, if he's anything like that."

"Don't you ever want to forgive him though?" asked Sam. "People say forgiveness is a good thing."

"No, he hasn't done anything to deserve my forgiveness or my trust."

"I wouldn't forgive him," said Elise. "Just because he donated his DNA to your cause, doesn't mean you owe him anything."

Athena laughed at Elise's way of putting it.

"I'm serious," said Elise.

"But he's family," said Sam.

"Just because somebody's family, it doesn't mean that they should be in your life," said Elise. "If someone is really toxic like that, it's better to cut them out altogether."

"True. Sometimes I wish I could cut off various limbs of my family," said Sam. "As accepting as the village is of my identity, my brothers are pests. No matter what I say or do they still won't respect that I'm non binary. They keep calling me by a very gendered version of my name. It just really upsets me. It's like they're taunting me with it deliberately. They're trying to show that they have the power in the situation and they're not going to respect me and my identity."

"That's awful!" said Athena.

Sam shrugged. "It sucks but I guess I'm used to it. I just hope they stop being such pests at some point."

"One can only hope," said Elise with a strange look on her face. "Speaking of pests, Felix just texted to say that he's not going to be in town after all. He's got some other family thing."

"Is there something going on between you and Felix?" Athena asked Elise before she could stop herself from blurting out the invasive question. There was a moment of silence in which Athena blushed and then added, "You're not together or anything?"

"Oh no," said Elise. "No, we've known each other for too long. In fact, I think he likes you."

Athena practically spat out her ice cream, but she didn't want to waste any of it as it was so good.

"That's an incredibly awkward thing to say," said Athena. "I mean, I know my question was awkward too. Sorry."

"*I'm* sorry," said Elise. "I shouldn't have mentioned it."

"Is there someone else you like, then?" Sam asked.

Athena blushed.

"There is!" said Elise. "Are you going to tell us?"

"I don't know," said Athena. "It's...it's a bit personal."

Elise shrugged.

"No pressure," said Sam.

Athena really wasn't used to sharing confidences with anyone. In fact, she was mostly used to trying to hide any personal details from her mother's prying eyes. But it was nice to be able to share with her new friends. And so, she offered a little bit of an explanation.

"There is this one guy," said Athena.

"Ooh!" said Elise. "Anyone we know?"

"I don't think so," said Athena, thinking of Finnigan's picture up in the school. "He's not really from around here."

It wasn't entirely true, but it was the closest Athena could get to the truth, without going into an explanation that she didn't understand how to clear up, seeing as the whole situation with Finnigan was shrouded in mystery.

"I hope it works out for you," said Elise.

Athena smiled. "What about you, is there anyone you like?" she asked.

"Not really," said Elise, with a blush.

"Me neither," said Sam. "Which is just as well because I don't think there'd be anyone who'd like me back."

"Don't be so defeatist," said Elise. "You're a wonderful and very cool person and you have lots of excellent qualities."

"Now I feel foolish," said Athena. "I told you about my crush and neither of you have one."

"There's nothing to feel foolish about at all," said Elise. "We won't tell anyone and I promise I'll tell you the next time I like someone." She smiled at Athena.

Suddenly, the embarrassment of the situation lifted and Athena didn't feel so awkward or self-conscious anymore. It was nice having friends.

Twenty-Five

Rosemary was relieved to find that Athena returned from her outing, not only safely, but in a good mood. They spent the rest of the day watching old movies and reading books. In the evening the house felt rather chilly, so they both decided to go upstairs and put on warmer clothing.

Athena paused on the upstairs landing and stood silently, looking ahead.

"What is it?" Rosemary asked.

"It's...the door!" said Athena. "The one you told me about."

Rosemary tilted her head to see around her daughter. It was indeed the door, the mahogany door gilded in roses, the magically-appearing-then-vanishing door that led to the tower.

"Do you...do you think *she* wants to talk to us?" Athena asked.

"Who? Granny?"

"Yes. Isn't that how you had that chat with her last time?"

"I suppose it could mean that," said Rosemary. "Or it could just be the house."

"Do you think we should go up?" Athena asked.

"I suppose so," said Rosemary.

They approached the door cautiously, unsure whether any sudden movements might make it disappear again.

Rosemary rummaged in her pocket for the key, but the door had other ideas. It sprang open without so much as a push, causing Rosemary and Athena to scramble back in surprise.

"Is it safe?" Athena asked.

"Of course it is," said Rosemary, though her tone was far from certain.

She took a tentative step towards the open doorway. Nothing seemed amiss, so she proceeded up the stairwell with Athena following close behind.

"This is amazing!" Athena said as she looked around the enormous tower room, which Rosemary could have sworn was even bigger than when she'd first discovered it.

"It is, isn't it?" said Rosemary. "I guess this was where Granny did most of her magical workings. At least that would explain all the equipment on the table."

"And the giant cauldron," said Athena.

"Yes, and that."

"Hello, dears!"

Rosemary and Athena both jumped and then turned in the direction of the mirror to see Granny standing there, clad in bright purple, her wild white hair tied back in a red scarf, hands firmly on her hips.

"Granny!" Rosemary cried, happy to see her favourite elderly relation, despite the circumstance.

"Who else would it be? The ghost of Christmas past?" Granny asked.

"Umm, hi," Athena said.

Granny grinned at her. "My, how you've grown," she cooed.

"It has only been a week or something since we last saw you," said Athena.

"I didn't mean grown in size," said Granny. "I mean in power."

"I wish!" said Athena. "Mum's the only one with real powers. I just hear inconvenient noises in my head."

Granny tutted as if she knew much better.

"Granny Thorn," said Athena. "Can you help me learn proper magic? Is there anything up here – maybe a book – that can help?

"You don't need a spell book to give you powers," said Granny. "You, my dear, are twice blessed."

"What does that mean?" Rosemary asked.

"It's like I told you before, if you ever bothered listening," Granny said. "She has other magic on her father's side. Of quite a different variety."

Rosemary's jaw dropped. "You did *not* tell me that. What are you saying about Dain?"

"Athena's father? Oh yes. He's definitely one of them."

"Them?" said Rosemary. "You don't mean–"

"The fae," said Granny.

"And you didn't think to tell me that?!" Rosemary asked.

"I thought you must have known, deep down, dear," said Granny. "Athena has always had that otherworldly nature about her."

"Fae magic?" Athena asked, not sounding surprised at all, just curious.

"You *knew*?!" Rosemary asked her daughter, before turning back to the mirror. "And you! You're telling me you knew that my daughter is a faery?" Rosemary asked.

"That's part of her heritage, of course. I really thought you would have worked it out by now."

Rosemary sighed. "What else have you been keeping from me, I wonder?"

"Plenty of things, no doubt," said Granny, winking. "I'm an open book for the most part though, so feel free to ask if you think of anything."

Rosemary sighed. "Sure, you're chatty as all Hermes when you don't have anything useful to say."

"Try me," said Granny, crossing her arms.

"Children are going missing," said Rosemary. "And that reminds me – I don't know how this keeps slipping my mind, but Athena's father is missing too, isn't he? That's what you told me last time."

"Away with the faeries," said Athena.

"What?" Rosemary asked.

"I've been reading about it in the school library. Fae have the power to make you forget," Athena said. "That's why you keep forgetting about Dad. In fact, I'm willing to bet that it's also why you keep forgetting things in general. You spent so much time with Dad – more than anyone should considering what a deadbeat he is – and it must have messed with your memory."

"You mean on top of what Granny's spell to hide our magic already did to me?" Rosemary asked, glaring at her grandmother.

Athena shrugged. "Maybe."

"Wait a minute. So that's why you hear voices? Fae can read minds?" Rosemary clasped her hand over her mouth in surprise. "Oh no! You're saying Dain could read my mind all these years? No wonder he always found my money stash no matter how hard I tried to hide it."

Athena sighed.

"And you!" said Rosemary. "How did you know about this?"

Athena shot her a slightly guilty look. "Finnigan told me a little."

"Finnigan!" Rosemary cried, feeling her blood beginning to metaphorically boil. "That boy! He's to blame for all this!"

"What on earth are you talking about?" Athena asked.

"Well, he's fae, isn't he? That explains it. And fae took that little girl – and he's always trying to get you to disappear off with him, like at the pub that first time."

"Mum, you're sounding quite mad."

"I don't care!" Rosemary shouted. "I don't want you seeing him."

"Calm your britches!" Granny's voice boomed, as if over loud speakers.

Rosemary visibly deflated, like a small child being scolded.

"What's this about a child disappearing?" Granny asked. "Give me details."

Rosemary explained about the situation with the little girl who'd gone missing, and the suspected abduction by faeries, or perhaps something more sinister.

Granny tutted again. "First Dain, now this. They really should have learnt by now not to meddle."

"What does this have to do with Dad?" Athena asked.

Granny scratched her chin. "The specifics evade me. Has anything else happened that seemed suspicious?"

"My necklace seems to be missing as well," Rosemary said. "I left it on the bathroom bench by the sink and Athena swears she didn't take it."

"Oh, I know about that," said Granny.

"You do?" Rosemary and Athena both asked.

"Yes, I have certain abilities to detect the goings on in my house," said Granny.

"So what happened?" Rosemary asked. "Who took it?"

"That remains a mystery," said Granny. "Whoever took it knows how to magically cover their tracks, so to speak."

Rosemary felt a creeping discomfort.

"You're saying someone came into the house and stole it?" said Athena. "I was sure Mum just lost it behind the couch or something."

"Quite probably," said Granny. "Or they found some other way to get it out of here, but that is less likely. The house is well-protected."

"So you think the missing necklace might be connected to the missing girl? Or Dad?" Athena asked.

Granny shrugged. "Beats me. But the fae folk are known for taking shiny things, and that boy of yours sure was a shiny one."

Rosemary glared at her grandmother. "He's not mine, and he's not a boy. Apparently he's not even human!"

Rosemary pulled out her phone and began dialling.

"What are you doing?" Athena asked.

"I need to file a missing person's report regarding Dain, before I forget again."

"You think the authorities are going to believe it when you say he was captured by faeries? Who are also his own kind?" Athena asked.

"Fortunately, we're in Myrtlewood," said Rosemary. "So yes. I'm calling Detective Neve."

Athena and Granny waited while Rosemary called the detective, saying she needed to report a missing person, and gave some brief details about Dain. Neve said she'd be right over.

"Come on," said Rosemary, feeling grumpy that her grandmother hadn't thought to tell her any of this before. "Let's go downstairs and wait for her."

"Suit yourselves," said Granny.

"But how do we get up here again, Granny Thorn?" Athena asked. "How can we get to this awesome tower room when the door keeps disappearing?"

"It's *my* room and I'll let you in when I feel like it," said Granny Thorn firmly.

"What happened to 'the dead shall have no claim over the living'?" Rosemary asked. Granny was beginning to fade out, and as grumpy as she was, she had a pang of regret that Granny would soon disappear again.

"I'm not claiming you living folk, just my special room. You have the whole rest of the house, which you can care for as you see fit. Besides, I don't see why you're sleeping in that tiny room when you can have my old bedroom and get rid of all the junk that's in there."

"I thought it was out of respect, actually," said Rosemary. "Really, Granny? You just want me to throw out all your stuff and move into your room and deck out the house as I see fit?"

"I left it to you, didn't I?" Granny said, her voice becoming quieter.

"All except the tower, apparently," said Athena. "What's the point in living in a big old house if I don't get to sleep in the tower?"

Granny grinned at her. "I like her. A girl after my own heart!"

"Wait," said Rosemary. "If the fae magic doesn't affect Athena because she's fae, why did she forget about Dain and about the car?"

It was too late for a response from Granny, who had disappeared, leaving the mirror looking perfectly ordinary.

Athena shrugged. "Maybe I just didn't care enough to remember, or I blocked it out because I can't stand Dad. Or maybe it was a different spell that time, on purpose. Oh, I know, the fae might have human witches working for them and they used a special kind of magic because they wanted me to forget..."

ATHENA CONTINUED to hypothesise as they made their way back downstairs to wait for the detective, but she stopped on the landing, in front of Rosemary. "What's that creaking?"

Rosemary groaned. "Not more surprises!"

The sound was coming from Granny's old room.

Rosemary tentatively peeked in through the open door to see Granny's possessions had vanished. The old rickety bed had been replaced by a larger four poster that looked to be carved out of cherry wood. Rosemary watched in delight as it made itself with a plum-coloured quilt, lavender sheets, and far more pillows than anyone could reasonably use.

"I guess this room is mine now," said Rosemary. "If Granny insists."

She checked the closet to find her clothes had already been magically transported there, and noted her other belongings were tidily arranged around the room.

"Finally!" said Athena. "I thought you'd never move out of that kid's room. I suspected it was some kind of childhood regression thing."

Rosemary shrugged. "Maybe it was. But don't we all need to regress once in a while? Curl up in the foetal position, that sort of thing."

"I guess you have gone through a lot of change lately."

"We both have, love," said Rosemary.

"Now you have a much cooler bed than me," Athena grumbled and looked out the windows to the darkening sky.

They continued on downstairs. "I suppose I should rustle up some dinner," Rosemary muttered. "Beans on toast?"

"Fine," said Athena, glancing at her mother. "What? What are you frowning about?"

Rosemary was indeed frowning. "Don't think I've forgotten that you knew all this stuff about fae and didn't tell me."

"Actually, I was hoping you *would* forget about that," Athena said.

"It's not a joke, Athena. This situation is dangerous. I can't have you holding things back from me like that."

"I'm still coming to terms with it, okay?" Athena said. "How would *you* feel if you found out your whole life had been a lie?"

"Kind of terrible, actually," said Rosemary. "Remember, it happened about a week ago."

"No one told *me* my father was some kind of mythical being."

"That's not my fault," said Rosemary. "No one told me, either."

"It's clearly *his* fault," said Athena. "And you never even get mad at him, which I assume is to do with his fae magic too. I've been mad at him for years and now I don't even know what to think."

"You still should have told me," said Rosemary sternly. "I'm your mother. I need to know things."

"And I need my privacy!" Athena shot back.

A knock at the door interrupted their argument. Detective Neve had arrived. She was dressed in somewhat more casual clothing than Rosemary had seen her in before, jeans and a knitted woollen navy jumper.

"Tell me what you know," Neve said. "When was the last time you saw Dain?"

"The thing is," said Rosemary, "I didn't exactly see him. I texted him and he appeared to have arrived with the boxes of our stuff from Burkenswood. Our old car was even here, but he had disappeared."

Neve nodded. "No sign of him since?"

"Nothing," said Rosemary. "The car seemed to disappear too. I'm not even sure when. I didn't remember. Actually, I keep forgetting everything about it."

"It does sound a lot like fae magic," said Neve.

"We think Dad is fae, too," Athena said. "At least, that explains all the noises in my head."

Neve gave her a quizzical look. "You're saying your father is high fae and was living in the human world?"

Athena nodded. "That's what we think. Not that he was any good at the human world stuff. He was totally useless, as a matter of fact."

"It's very rare," said Neve. "Those with both fae and human heritage can get on alright here, for the most part, but fae without any human DNA to ground them... Well, they tend to stick to their realm and only cause trouble here occasionally. For one to be living here for years is almost unheard of."

A tingle of fear ran down Rosemary's spine that she couldn't quite explain. "Do you think this has anything to do with the little girl who went missing?" she asked.

"It's hard to say," said Neve. "Children have gone missing before. Usually it happens around the equinox."

"Marjie mentioned that. It's just awful!" said Rosemary. "Why would anyone live here when such a thing happens?"

"Actually," said Neve, "some families with young children choose not to live here for that reason. You won't see many babies around, because fae have a long-standing habit of trying to swap them for their own kind."

"Changelings," said Athena.

"That's right. They cause havoc. But with older children, disappearances are rarer. Besides, they can happen anywhere. It's only a little more common in places like Myrtlewood where the magical energy is so strong. It thins the veil between the worlds even further."

"What happens to the kids that disappear?" Athena asked.

"They sometimes do come back," said Detective Neve. "Though people say they are different. They won't have aged as much as they should have because time works differently on other planes."

"It happened to Sherry, didn't it?" Rosemary asked.

"I can't talk about personal details unrelated to your reported case," said Neve with a tired smile. "You should ask her about it if you want to know more."

"I just keep thinking about that woman – Prue," said Rosemary. "The expression on her face..."

"I see a lot of things in my line of work," said Neve. "But when children are involved, it's always heart-wrenching. We are going to be busy down at the station, so don't be surprised if I have to delay our dinner invite for a while."

"I completely understand," said Rosemary. "Dinner is a low priority."

Her stomach chose that exact moment to protest such a statement with a loud growl, making them all laugh, though given the circumstances, it came out as half-hearted chuckles.

"The other thing," said Neve, "is that I'm going to have to go out of town again. I won't be on duty, but feel free to call me. Leave a message if I don't answer."

Athena and Rosemary shot each other worried glances.

"A work emergency?" Athena asked.

"I'm afraid not," said Neve. "This is a personal matter. It's my aunt, you see. She was totally fine until just recently, but now she's talking about missing children and babbling."

"Missing children, like Gretchen?" Athena asked.

"No," said Neve. "Someone else who never existed, I'm afraid. We think it might be dementia."

"I hope it all works out," said Rosemary, though in her mind she was wondering whether this could be another wild goose chase taking the only competent law enforcement out of town at a critical moment. Neve had been away during their last enormous crisis, leaving them to deal with Constable Perkins who caused more harm than good.

"Thanks," said Neve. "Take care, and I'll update you when I find out anything else about Dain and the circumstances of his disappearance."

"Thank you," Rosemary said, seeing Neve out.

As soon as the door was closed she rounded on Athena.

"I still cannot believe you didn't tell me about you being a faerie. Or about Dain!"

"Settle down, Mum. I told you, I'm still processing."

"You can process when we're out of danger."

"I'm not a baby. Why do you think we're in any kind of danger?"

"What if they come for you?" Rosemary asked.

"That's ridiculous," said Athena. "Why would they?"

"They came for Dain, didn't they? Isn't that what Granny implied?"

"He probably owed them money!"

Rosemary sighed. "You're not taking this seriously."

"I'm still grappling with the fact that we are in a situation warranting taking faeries seriously!"

"Athena!"

"What?"

Rosemary looked at her daughter's defiant expression and it only fuelled her rage. "You're grounded until further notice."

"Don't be ridiculous. I didn't do anything wrong."

"You didn't tell me something which was very important," said Rosemary. "And I am going to take this seriously even if you are determined not to. The danger is very real."

"You've never grounded me before. This is stupid!"

"I've never needed to," said Rosemary.

Athena crossed her arms and scowled. "Fine. I don't care. Take away all my human rights and imprison me for all I care."

"And you're forbidden from seeing that faerie boy – Finnigan – too," said Rosemary.

"What?"

"It's too dangerous!"

Athena gave her mother a disgusted look, then turned on her heels and stormed upstairs.

Twenty-Six

Athena paced her room. She didn't feel hungry. Well, she did, a little, but she didn't want to take her mother's peace offering of beans on toast, left outside the door, because that felt like admitting defeat or conceding on something important.

Rosemary was clearly out of line. Just because fae might be responsible for one disappearing human child and for claiming back one of their own kind, it didn't mean all fae were bad. Besides, there was no conclusive proof that the fae were behind any of this. For all they knew, it could just be spurious rumours or someone making it seem like the fae so that they could get away with it. Whatever *it* was.

Athena was sure that Rosemary was jumping to conclusions, and worse, she was being fae-phobic or species-ist or perhaps something else that hadn't been adequately named by humans because almost the entire population wasn't aware any of this existed.

It wasn't fair to discriminate against Finnigan, who had done nothing wrong, just because Rosemary was scared of the fae.

On top of that, Athena was furious that her mother was being insanely over-protective. I can look after myself! I might not have Mum's Buffy-strength or vampire-slaying powers, or anything that resembles useful magical defences, but I'm not a baby!

She badly wanted to call Finnigan and talk to him about all this, but she didn't dare. Though she knew she could talk to Elise at school and maybe even Sam or Ash, it wasn't quite the same as talking to Finnigan.

He understands me in a way that others don't, but he's so damn evasive.

Athena felt a pang of longing and wanted to call out to him, but she knew now that Granny would be watching. And, mad as she was with Rosemary's controlling behaviour, she also didn't want to make things worse for herself by revealing how simple it would be for her to call out to the fae boy, how easily she could slip away into the night and never have to deal with her mother's annoying over-protectiveness ever again.

Instead, she patted the little kitten on the end of her bed with a resigned sigh.

"At some point, Mum is going to have to let go of control," she muttered to the cat. "Or I'll have to take matters into my own hands."

Twenty-Seven

Rosemary opened her eyes, feeling awful. It was far too early to be awake and there was a banging sound that simply would not go away.

It took her a moment to realise the noise was somebody knocking at the door downstairs that continued into what seemed like endless drumming.

She groaned.

The sound continued, only punctuated occasionally by slight pauses, before it continued rat-a-tat-tat.

Who on earth would be knocking so persistently at this ungodly hour?

Rosemary moaned as she got up, covering herself in a dressing gown, and made her way downstairs.

Ferg was at the door.

"What are you doing here?" Rosemary asked.

"I'm here to deliver the plants, of course," said Ferg.

"Plants?" Rosemary asked as something familiar clicked in the back of her mind. "Oh, that's right. How did I sign up for this?"

"You wanted to help with the Spring Equinox," said Ferg. "And help you will!"

Rosemary groaned again. "Fine, I'll show you around to the greenhouse."

"Excellent," said Ferg. "The trailers are here and ready for unloading."

"Trailers, plural?" Rosemary peeked behind him to see two cars with large trailers laden with plant pots. "What have I done?"

"It's not what you've done. It's what you're doing for the goodness of the town. And we're very pleased. We appreciate it very much, Rosemary."

Rosemary gave a half-hearted wave to the eclectically dressed people standing by the trailers.

"Shall I introduce you?" Ferg asked.

"Don't bother," said Rosemary. "At this time of day I'm never going to remember anyone's name."

"Very well," said Ferg.

"The greenhouse is this way." Rosemary pulled a coat on top of her dressing gown. She stumbled outside, and around the side of the house.

The greenhouse, unlike the central part of the house, was in a dishevelled state just like the two wider wings of Thorn Manor.

"Oh no, this simply won't do," said Ferg. "Oh, no, no, no."

"What?" Rosemary asked, unimpressed.

"Tulips are beautiful divine blooms. They require a lovely environment. This is objectively un-lovely."

"Where are we going to put them?" Rosemary asked. "Outside?"

"At this time of year?" said Ferg, outraged. "No, they must go in the house."

"In the house? No way!" Rosemary protested.

"But they'll need your constant care and attention," said Ferg. "You'll need to work your magic on them."

"Constant?!" Rosemary asked.

"Well, not a lot of attention, perhaps not constant," said Ferg. "But regular."

Rosemary sighed. It was too early in the morning for her to properly process what was going on, let alone adequately fight Ferg, who seemed to have a will of steel.

"I guess I've got to pick my battles," Rosemary muttered. She stumbled back into the house. "You can just put them in there." She waved in the general direction of the living room. "I'm going back to bed."

"Very well," said Ferg with a cheerful smile. "I'll see you again soon, Rosemary. Thanks for all your help."

Rosemary waved weakly and wandered back upstairs feeling bamboozled. She had no idea how to magically grow plants, or even grow them the regular way. But it was far too much to think about at this time the day. She'd have to look at some possible options in Granny's books later. After all, she did still want to help get little Gretchen back. She didn't see any other way around it.

She fell back into bed with a thump, wondering how she'd ever gotten herself into such a mess.

Twenty-Eight

It should be easy, Rosemary told herself. She focused on the bucket of water sitting on the kitchen bench, willing it to rise.

Nothing happened.

She tried again, concentrating as hard as possible.

"What are you doing?" Athena asked.

"Concentrating," said Rosemary. The water slopped over the side of the bucket.

"Well, if you were trying to make a mess on the counter, congratulations I guess," Athena said.

"I'm *trying* to use my magic to make the freaking plants grow."

"Mum, have you lost your marbles?" said Athena. She wandered out of the room. "Ah! What happened to the lounge?"

"Ferg," said Rosemary, as if the single word was explanation enough.

Athena looked at her and then burst into hysterical laughter. "This is you helping with the ritual?" she asked, catching her breath before laughing some more.

Rosemary narrowed her eyes at her daughter. "I was trying to use my elemental magic, you know...master the element of water or something. Plants need water to grow."

"You might want to try moving a bit closer to the targets," said Athena.

"Fine." Rosemary picked up the bucket and placed it in the middle of the living room, which was now filled with hundreds of plant pots. "This is ridiculous. House – I hope you've got this covered." She tapped the wood of the wall nearest to her.

"Now who's ridiculous?" said Athena.

"I don't want everything getting soggy, okay?"

The house creaked. Rosemary chose to take that as a sign of agreement. "Here we go." She held her hands in front of her, focusing on the bucket, visualising the element of water, of emotions and connection, but all she connected with was her frustration and sense of overwhelm at being in far over her head.

"Nothing?" said Athena. "Maybe you're full of too much hot air to work with elemental water."

"Hey," said Rosemary. "That's a bit harsh."

"No," Athena said. "I mean, your elemental make up is more fire and air. You know, I've been learning about this in Cosmos and Astrology class. You're a Sagittarius with a Gemini rising, plus you've got a bunch of other fire and air in your chart."

"I thought star sign stuff was all nonsense," said Rosemary. "I've read my horoscopes in magazines. If I was a true Sagittarius I'd be out in nature, travelling and having big adventures, plus everyone would think I was wise."

"Yes, but because you have a Gemini ascendant people think you're shallow and ditzy, even if you've got a bit of depth underneath."

Rosemary frowned. "That's true, I suppose. And you're no typical Leo or you'd be off performing."

"Virgo ascendant," said Athena. "With a changeable Pisces moon. It's no wonder I burst into tears so easily as a child."

"What does all this have to do with growing these blasted plants?" said Rosemary.

"If you can't connect with water easily, maybe try it another way. Use your magic – use the air to carry the water."

"Oh," said Rosemary. "I see. That's not a bad idea. I'll give it a shot."

She closed her eyes again, imagining her magic shooting out into the water. The element of air came easily to her, like Athena said. It was light and quick, and clear. She pushed her hands out, as if directing a current of air towards the bucket. A gentle spray landed on her skin. She opened her eyes to find the water spraying out in delicate sprinkles, all over the plants, miraculously missing the living room furniture.

"Brilliant!" Rosemary exclaimed.

A slow clap sounded from Athena. "I'm impressed. You're finally learning how to use your magic intentionally when you aren't even in crisis."

Rosemary shrugged. "I figured this ridiculous plant situation is a good excuse to experiment."

"Aren't you supposed to be using magic to make them grow super-fast, not just to water them?"

"Yeah, don't remind me. I have no idea how to do that."

"There are plenty of books, Mum."

"You know I can't follow instructions. It's just like when I cook. I have to be intuitive."

"Alright, have it your way," said Athena. "I don't even know why you agreed to help with this anyway. What a sucker."

"Ferg convinced me that it's the best way to help get that little girl back."

"Well, you're going to have to try a little harder."

Rosemary looked around the room at the glistening plants. Her gaze drifted outside the window. "I have an idea," she said, closing her eyes.

The element of fire is new beginnings, she recalled. Passion, energy, instigation...

She connected with the fire within herself, with her strong will and drive, then she imagined the plants all growing, remembering a lush spring day in her childhood when she was visiting Granny, running across the lawn, picking daisies, helping to pot bulbs in the greenhouse.

"Wow! Mum!"

"Don't distract me."

"No seriously, look!"

Rosemary peeked to see bright green were springing up in every plant pot in the room.

"Amazing!" said Rosemary.

Athena beamed at her. "Very impressive. I bet you can get them to bloom in no time."

"That's a relief," said Rosemary. "Maybe I will be able to help get that girl back after all."

"Hey, you're not going to the fae realm, are you?"

"There's no way in Cerridwen's Cauldron," said Rosemary. "It's too dangerous. I don't even know if humans can go in there."

Athena shrugged and looked out the window.

"You want to go there, don't you?" Rosemary said. "We all want to find out what happened to Dain, but Athena, it's not safe."

"I told you I don't want anything to do with Dad."

"That's probably just as well," said Rosemary. "Because I absolutely forbid you to go to the fae realm."

"You know you can't protect me forever," said Athena. "I mean you can barely protect me as it is. I can look after myself. I don't belong to you."

Rosemary was bereft. Never, in all the years since she'd had Athena, had she felt so alone.

"Athena, you're all I have," she said.

An expression of guilt crossed Athena's face. "I can't be everything to you, Mum, I need to have my own life. And I'm not all you have. You've got a whole big house. You've got tons of money. You've got Marjie and your job. You've got your business to set up. You've got everything, and what do I have?"

"I thought you liked it here," Rosemary said.

"I do," Athena replied. "I just...I don't have cool powers like you and I'm still trying to figure everything out. Let me figure it out on my own. You can't do everything for me."

Rosemary sighed and raised her arms, walking towards her daughter to hug her. "I know you're good at looking after yourself. Just understand. I can't bear the thought of anything bad happening to you."

"I'm not a kid anymore." Athena gently pushed Rosemary away. "I just need some space." She stomped out of the room and upstairs.

Rosemary's feeling of triumph at using her magic to water the plants quickly evaporated.

"Time for some tea, I think," she said to herself.

Twenty-Nine

Athena was clearly in a foul mood when Rosemary picked her up after school on Monday.

"I shouldn't have to wait half an hour for you to finish work," she said as she got into the car. "I'm perfectly safe walking around in broad daylight."

"That little girl disappeared in the middle of the day," said Rosemary, steering Granny's lovely old Rolls Royce out into the street.

"I'm not a bloody five-year-old!"

"You sound hangry," said Rosemary.

"I'm just plain old angry."

"Not hungry at all?"

"No."

"Well, that's too bad, because I thought we could go to the pub for an early dinner."

"Fine," said Athena. "Do whatever you want, just like you usually do."

"I thought it would be a nice thing to do," said Rosemary. "Friday night at the pub, fish n' chips for dinner."

Athena sighed. "Whatever."

"Aren't you glad the week is over?"

"No," said Athena. "That just means I have more time imprisoned with *you*."

"Oh, don't be so dramatic," said Rosemary. "There's your Leo side showing."

They spent the rest of their drive in silence.

Athena's mood didn't lighten, even after they arrived into the warm, cosy atmosphere of the pub.

Rosemary looked around for Sherry, who didn't appear to be behind the bar. She had called the pub earlier to try to arrange a catch up after she'd heard about Sherry's involvement with the fae, but no one had answered. Rosemary reasoned that surely if Sherry had disappeared into the other world and come back, she might have some useful information that could help to bring Gretchen back, provide some clue about Dain's whereabouts, and protect other children in Myrtlewood.

There were no staff in sight, and as it was so early, only a few customers were present, clustered around some of the tables. Rosemary didn't recognise any of them in particular, though they seemed to give her a look that said they knew who she was.

It was a strange thing to be known and revered, purely for her family's reputation. Rosemary gave a polite nod and led Athena to what had already become their usual table.

She grabbed the menus that were propped up by the salt and pepper and handed one to Athena who gave her a glum look.

"Oh, come on!" said Rosemary. "This arrangement isn't forever, just until it's safe."

"And what if it's never safe?" Athena asked. "Are you going to try and keep me locked up until I'm thirty?"

"Of course not," said Rosemary. "But I'm currently legally responsible for you, and as you keep saying, you don't have any clear magical powers that can defend you yet."

"Actually, I do," said Athena, pulling a small arsenal of charms out of both of her pockets and dumping them on the table.

"Put those away before Constable Perkins shows up and tries to arrest us," said Rosemary. "I mean, it's good you've got all that but... Wait, when did you even have time to make them?"

"It's not like I have much else to do these days," said Athena. "I set up a little production stand in my room just so I have something to do at night. Maybe I can start a business of my own selling exploding charms and make enough money so I can afford to move far away from *you*!"

"Don't be ridiculous," said Rosemary. "I'm not that bad."

"You are," said Athena. "I don't even want to talk to you at the moment." She looked away from Rosemary and around the room instead.

"You're looking for *him*, aren't you?" Rosemary asked. "You're in a terrible grump with me because I told you that you're not to see Finnigan."

Athena chose not to respond and the silence was deafening.

"What will it be then?" a tired-sounding woman's voice said.

Rosemary looked up to see Sherry, looking very pale.

"Oh, it's you two," Sherry said with a wan smile. "Sorry I haven't returned your call from the other day, I've just been so exhausted lately."

"Is everything alright?" Rosemary asked. "You don't look very well."

"It's this time of year," said Sherry. "It always gets me. The thinning veil does strange things to my constitution, ever since...Anyway, what will you be having? Dinner is it?"

"Fish 'n chips, please," said Rosemary.

"Same, thank you," said Athena, giving Sherry a bright smile and then returning to glare at Rosemary.

"Lovely," said Sherry. "And I'll bring you some mulled mead, on the house!"

Sherry's voice sounded as if she was trying for enthusiasm, but it didn't carry through to her expression.

Rosemary tried to give Athena a meaningful look, but the teen was staring at the table. Clearly, there were no young fae men around to distract her from the fascinating wood grain. The food arrived a few moments later, as prompt as usual.

Rosemary eyed the crispy golden battered fish and fried potatoes with mouth-watering anticipation. She tasted it, only to be utterly disappointed.

It was bland and somehow bitter, even though none of the ingredients should have been bitter to begin with.

"Maybe the oil has gone bad," Rosemary said.

Athena didn't respond. She ate her food in silence, as if trying to punish her mother by withholding her verbal participation.

Rosemary took a sip of mulled mead. It, too, tasted bland, and for a moment she wondered whether there was something wrong with her sense of taste, and then she remembered Sherry's tired and pale demeanour.

"Stay here," said Rosemary.

She got up from the table and made her way towards the bar where Sherry was polishing glasses.

"It's terrible, isn't it," said Sherry as Rosemary approached.

"The food? It's...not quite as good as usual," Rosemary admitted.

"I'm sorry. My magic has gone all weak and our usual chef is on leave tonight."

"It's fine," said Rosemary. "I'm more worried about you, actually."

"I'll be right as rain in no time," said Sherry. "Once the equinox passes, that is."

"There's still a couple weeks to go," said Rosemary.

"Don't remind me."

"Is there anything I can do to help?"

"Nothing as far as I'm aware, unless you have some kind of antidote to the pull of the fae."

"Is that what's going on?" Rosemary asked. "What is the pull of the fae?"

"You probably know already that I was one of the children who was taken. The whole town has been talking about it, what with poor Gretchen going missing," said Sherry.

Rosemary nodded.

"Well, that place," Sherry continued. "It does things to you. It's almost as if a part of me was left behind there. I've never felt whole since."

"I was meaning to ask you about that," said Rosemary. "I wondered if there was anything you could tell me about how you got back. Anything that would help us get Gretchen back."

Sherry shook her head.

"It's awful," she said as tears visibly welled in her eyes.

"I'm sorry," said Rosemary. "I didn't realise. Was it traumatic – your experience over there?"

"No, quite the opposite," said Sherry. "But it's awful that I can't talk about it. All these thoughts spiral around in my head, but their magic is so powerful. I can't say anything. It kind of...drives me mad."

"Marjie said the fae have strong magic that stops people revealing too much information about them," Rosemary said. "It must be strange to have all that going on in your head and never be able to communicate about it."

"People said I came back changed," said Sherry. "But it was mostly just... so much in my head. A whole other world, that I can't even speak of at all. Though, even if I could, I don't know how I could even begin to explain."

"And it gets worse at this time of year?"

"Yes, I can almost forget about it at other times, but right now I feel like that little lost girl all over again. The memories come back. It's almost as if I can taste it. The other world is so close, and my spirit longs to cross back over."

Sherry clamped her hand over her mouth as if to stop herself from saying anymore. She looked surprised at what she'd revealed.

"It's okay," said Rosemary. "Let me know if there's anything I can do to make you feel better. We have a lot of books at the house and apparently a lot of magic even if we don't know how to use it properly yet."

Sherry shook her head. "It's no use. I'll just tough it out, as usual. Fae magic is far too strong."

Rosemary patted her friend on the shoulder reassuringly.

"It will be okay," she said, even though she was in a position to make no such promises.

Thirty

As Rosemary made her way back to the table she noticed some familiar faces sitting across the way. She double checked to make sure Athena was accounted for and then headed towards Agatha and Covvey, the two eccentric townsfolk who had invited themselves to her dinner party not so long ago.

"Good evening, Rosemary," said Agatha. "Pull up a pew and join us."

"I won't trouble you for long," Rosemary said. "I hope you're both having a lovely evening."

"As good as any," said Covvey gruffly.

"I'm trying to find out about something," said Rosemary. "And I just remembered that you're a famous historian."

"How did you know?" Agatha asked suspiciously.

"Marjie told me, and apparently one of Athena's teachers is related to you."

"That little minx," said Agatha.

Rosemary wasn't sure if she was referring to Marjie or the teacher, but it seemed irrelevant. "But it's true, isn't it?" She smiled at Agatha.

"I might know a thing or two about magical history," Agatha conceded.

"Well, if you wouldn't mind, I'd quite like to know a bit about the fae realm and how all of that stuff works. I imagine a local historian would have some information."

"You don't want to go messing about with that stuff," Covvey growled. "Keep well away. You don't know what you're getting into."

Agatha sighed. "Since that little girl went missing the other day, people keep asking me as if I know blimin' everything. And you will find bits of information scattered around in *The History of Myrtlewood* and various other publications of mine, but I'm afraid there's not a lot to say."

"What is it with this place?" Rosemary asked, exasperated. "People aren't allowed to talk about who's a vampire. No one will tell me anything about fae, never mind the awful crap they do, and shifters are bound to attack at any moment."

"Watch your mouth," said Covvey, sounding hostile.

"I didn't mean to hit a nerve," Rosemary replied. "I just can't get my head around all these different magical creatures."

"Who are you calling a creature?" Covvey said aggressively.

"No one in particular," said Rosemary.

"Now listen young lady," Covvey continued. "Your Granny knew a thing or two about how to behave in polite company, and it would serve you well not to go around talking smack about things you don't understand."

Rosemary raised her hands in innocence. "I didn't mean to say anything offensive."

"Don't mind him," said Agatha. "Something's got his goat tonight and he's always a little bit sensitive when people talk badly about shifters. You know he's a wolf shifter."

Rosemary's eyes widened.

"Why'd you have to go and tell her?" Covvey said. "She's obviously prejudiced."

"Don't be silly," said Agatha. "You're not sensitive like vampires. You don't care who knows as long as they're magical."

Covvey folded his arms and looked down at the table with a stony expression.

"A wolf shifter?" Rosemary said, remembering the incident with Liam and how he'd been so sensitive about his otherness. "Like a werewolf?"

A vein bulged in Covvey's temple. He looked up at her with fire in his eyes. "How dare you! I'm no bloody werewolf! I'm a natural-born shifter, not infected by some heinous virus."

Rosemary felt her cheeks redden in embarrassment. Liam wasn't exaggerating when he talked about the prejudice against his kind. "I'm sorry. It looks like I stepped on your toes too many times this evening already. I'll just excuse myself."

She quickly nipped back to the table where Athena sat, staring at her phone.

"Let's get out of here," said Rosemary. "I feel like I've offended half the town without even meaning to."

Athena blew out a puff of air. "Fine. It's not like you care when you only offend me."

As they left the pub, Rosemary noticed Burk sitting across the room. She raised her hand to wave to him, but then noticed he was seated at a table next to a rather attractive woman with slick, wavy brown hair and a glamorous outfit.

Rosemary felt a bitter taste in her mouth and pang of emotion that she didn't want to call jealousy.

"What is it?" Athena asked, following her gaze. "Oh, so now will you admit you like him?"

"Don't start," Rosemary said.

Rosemary and Athena didn't talk on the drive home, but as they pulled into the driveway a strange light began to filter through the trees.

Rosemary's heart began to accelerate as they drew closer and it became patently obvious that something was very wrong.

Alarming bright yellow and red lit up the way ahead of them.

The car drew close and Rosemary's jaw dropped.

"No," said Athena.

"What on earth?" Rosemary cried, slowing the car. "Thorn Manor! It's on fire!"

Athena was silent in shock as the full realisation hit both of them.

"Not just part of it," said Rosemary. "Not just a small fire. The entire thing is in flames!"

Even the tower was covered in a vibrant blaze.

"I can see that," said Athena, her voice croaky.

"Not good," said Rosemary.

"Is that all you can say?" Athena asked. "Not good!?"

"My words aren't working properly," Rosemary mumbled.

"Who do we call?" Athena asked. "Is there even a fire department out here?"

Rosemary had been in so much shock she hadn't even thought of that.

"Good question. Maybe the police will know?" Rosemary fumbled for her phone.

"It's probably too late. We've lost everything," Athena said, her face ashen. "Everything we own is in that house."

The loss began to sink in for Rosemary. It was more than mere possessions. It was the only place she'd felt at home and had huge sentimental value. Never mind that it had been in the family for generations. And what did this mean for Granny's ghost?

Rosemary could barely breathe. She finally found her phone and started looking up the Detective Neve's number.

"It's going to be too late," Athena said. "By the time the fire truck gets here, it'll all be gone."

Rosemary couldn't respond. Athena was surely right. The flames were huge, and yet, from where they were in the car Rosemary could feel no heat and see no smoke.

"Wait a minute." She got out of the car.

"Mum! What are you doing?" Athena asked.

"Just checking something."

Rosemary stared at the flaming house, noticing that the flames made no sound, either. Not a crackling. Not the sound of the wood beams bowing in the heat. In fact, the fire didn't seem to be doing much at all.

"What's going on?" Athena got out of her own side of the car to join her mother.

"I wish I knew," Rosemary said. "It's not...real."

Athena took a step closer.

"Wait," said Rosemary, holding back as Athena raised her hand. A ripple formed in the air, as if she'd touched upon some kind of membrane surrounding the house.

The fire flickered for a moment, like a dying light bulb, then they brightened.

"Wow!" said Athena as the flames burst into leaves and flowers in vibrant green and pink. "Are we tripping?" she asked Rosemary.

"I don't think the food at the pub was *that* bad."

Rosemary stepped forward, ready to try to channel her magic and protect them from whatever attack this surely must be.

The flowers and leaves grew to cover the entire house. Athena tapped against the membrane again and the foliage transformed into violet butterflies.

There was a moment of stillness followed by a gust of wind.

They all took flight, glowing in the air as they formed the words STAY AWAY, before vanishing completely.

"What – on – earth?" Rosemary stammered.

"It's the fae," Athena said in an eerily certain tone. "You've been asking too many questions and they know it."

"Hasn't everyone?" Rosemary asked. "The whole town is wondering about the missing girl."

"I think that was a warning for us, in particular," Athena said. "The fae don't want anyone to know about them."

"Well, if they don't want anyone to know about them, they shouldn't go around taking children. Should they?" said Rosemary. "We can't just leave poor Gretchen in their realm. What do you know about all this, anyway? Why are they so secretive?"

"Something to do with vampires, I think," said Athena. "Like, they've been at war for thousands of years. Fae taste delicious, apparently. The vampires hunted them to near extinction or something."

"I've heard mutterings about this," said Rosemary. "But how does it all connect?"

"I don't know. The fae have got a whole lot of binding magic so you can't talk about them, and it hurts the people who do know stuff if they say anything. I tried to find out and that's pretty much all I've got."

"Vampires," Rosemary said, feeling a cold discomfort in the pit of stomach as she thought of seeing Burk at dinner with another woman earlier.

"That's a good point," said Athena. "You should ask Burk. Didn't you say he's a million years old or something? He might have even been around when the war started."

Rosemary gave her daughter an exasperated look. "I don't think so."

"Mum," said Athena. "You want to get to the bottom of this, don't you?"

Rosemary nodded grimly.

"And I want you to stop being so freaking over-protective and leave me alone, which you did swear to do, once this whole fae thing is resolved."

"I'll think about it," Rosemary said. "Wait a minute. If this is really true, then aren't all the vampires after you?"

"The fae have powerful magic. Don't you think they would have thought about that and put protections in place?" Athena said in frustration. "No one can even see what I look like." She explained about the drawing situation with Sam.

"But that's ridiculous. How? And why would no one have noticed it before?" Rosemary asked.

"I think it must be in my genetics," said Athena. "There's something that obfuscates me somehow, so people don't see my face for too long. Sam had to because it was part of the class. I don't recall anyone ever trying to draw me before."

"I know what you look like," said Rosemary.

"I've been thinking about that," said Athena. "You stare at me far too much. Maybe the genetic link overrides the fae magic. And other fae folk can see me too, I think."

"Why didn't you tell me any of this before?" Rosemary asked.

"I would feel more comfortable telling you about my life if you weren't so invasive and over-protective," Athena said.

And with that, they both went into Thorn Manor, to find it all exactly as they'd left it. The fire illusion had changed nothing.

Thirty-One

Athena paced her room. It was now or never. She'd been holding off on leaving, but every day that went by made her more desperate to know the truth about herself, just as time passing made her miss Finnigan more.

It was an ache in her heart that felt more like a drug addiction than anything she could imagine.

He'd told her to call when she was ready to go to the fae realm.

She needed to understand her heritage, to understand her powers and where half of her DNA apparently came from.

The closer they came to the equinox the harder it was getting to leave unnoticed. Rosemary barely let Athena out of her sight. Unfairly grounded as she was, she wasn't allowed to go out alone. The only privacy Athena had was in her bedroom.

She smiled to herself. If only Mum knew that this is the most dangerous place.

She looked around her room with its magically created balcony, that Rosemary thankfully hadn't yet noticed. She knew it wouldn't take much effort to climb from the edge of the balcony, down the side of the house, and head towards the forest. Granny might be watching her every move, but once Athena was gone there would be nothing either her mother or Granny's ghost could do about it.

Athena had done some research into the fae, although the internet was probably not the most reliable source of information. She'd scoured all the books she could find on the subject too.

In light of everything she'd learned, she packed her bag with useful supplies: Jaffa Cakes, a bar of chocolate, and two small packets of crisps in case she needed sustenance. She'd read that eating in the fae realm could be dangerous.

She wasn't sure if the charms and potions she knew how to make would work in a different realm, but she'd prepared and packed a whole bunch just in case, along with some shiny trinkets from her jewellery box, crystals and glass pebbles, and a vial of salt. She'd read that the fae were partial to cream, and so included a couple of little bottles of it in case they proved useful.

Athena popped downstairs to make herself a thermos of tea after Rosemary had gone to bed. *Tea is important.* She might be going into another world, but it was important that she had her priorities straight.

Packing everything tightly into her backpack with a couple of small spell books, Athena tried to put on the bag but found it awkwardly heavy. She remembered a quick charm for lightening the load and quickly brewed up the relevant magical powder.

She dusted it over her bag and discovered, to her delight, that it was as light a feather, "at least in this world," she muttered to herself.

She put it on over her warm coat and patted the little black kitten one more time.

"Goodbye Serpentine, or Fuzzball, or whatever your name is. I'll see you again soon...I hope."

She was dressed for travel with her sensible leather boots and jeans. She paced the length of her room again, several times, building up the courage, and then, without thinking too much, she braced herself against her fear.

Athena slipped out to the balcony to find it quickly morphing to include a trailing staircase all the way down to the lawn below.

"Thank you, house," she said softly. "Look after my mother for me. Will you?"

She stepped quietly down to the lawn and then ran to the edge of the forest.

"Finnigan," she called out. "I'm ready."

This was where he'd told her to meet him when she'd talked to him through her mind earlier. In an instant he was there beside her, his pale skin glinting in the moonlight.

"Athena, you came," he said, his expression gleeful like a small child at Christmas.

A thrill rolled through Athena and she couldn't help but smile.

"Are you afraid?" he asked.

"I'm terrified," Athena replied. "Quickly, let's go before I lose my nerve."

He took both her hands in his. A pale green light emerged from between their palms and then shone out ahead of them, shifting into a dotted line through the forest.

"Now what?" Athena asked.

"We follow," he said.

He let go of her right hand, keeping hold of her left, and they walked through the trees following the lighted path.

"What should I be expecting?" Athena asked.

"You'll see," Finnigan replied.

As they reached the end of the sparks of illumination, the flecks of light gathered together again like a shimmer of fireflies, then dispersed and reformed, creating an archway in front of them.

"Fairy lights," Athena said. Finnigan gave her a curious look. "Never mind."

"We go through," he said. "Keep hold of my hand."

Athena took a deep breath, and, grateful for the warmth of Finnigan's hand, she stepped with him through the archway and into another world.

Thirty-Two

A sudden burst of light shocked Rosemary out of her slumber. She ran to the window to see a bright flare of blue and white in the forest.

"Oh no. No, no!" Rosemary cried. "Athena! They're back – the Bloodstones."

She ran towards Athena's room, only to find it empty.

"No, no, no, no...Athena!" Rosemary called out. She ran quickly to search the rest of the house, her heart hammering in her chest, breath catching in her throat. Her daughter was nowhere in sight.

The world seemed as if it was blurring. Time slowed. Rosemary struggled against the riptide in her mind that was trying to pull her under.

The door to Granny's secret room was nowhere to be seen. Rosemary hammered on the wall, just in case, but nothing happened.

Cold, cold anguish and panic took over, immobilising Rosemary.

She stood on the landing, unable to function, barely able to breathe.

Athena's gone...Athena's gone, she thought, over and over in her head. She had to do something, anything.

A thought flashed through her mind. She ran back to her bedroom to find her phone and called Detective Neve. There was no answer. Rosemary left a frantic message. Then she called Marjie. She didn't know what else to do and this, if anything, seemed like a good excuse to disturb somebody's peace.

Marjie answered on the second ring. "What time is it?" she asked groggily.

"Athena. She's gone. They've taken her," said Rosemary.

"Who's taken her, dear? Do you think she's run off with her friends or something?"

"No," said Rosemary. "I'm sure it's the fae."

"Take a few deep breaths in and out," said Marjie.

Rosemary tried to do as she was told. Her breath shuddered in her chest, disobedient.

"Now, where was she when you last saw her?" Marjie asked.

"She went to bed," said Rosemary. "At least, she was in her room."

"Is there anything unusual about how she left it?" Marjie asked. "Any sign of struggle?"

Rosemary checked. "The bed's still made. They must have gotten her before she even went to sleep. I can't believe I let this happen," said Rosemary as her eyes fell on a small blue envelope lying on Athena's pillow with the word 'Mum' written on it. "I think there's a note."

"What does it say?"

"What if it's not safe to touch?"

"Do you want me to come over there and check?"

"No, it's fine." Rosemary picked up the note and nothing happened. Her heart sank when she recognised Athena's handwriting. "Do you think they made her write it?"

"I don't know, dear," said Marjie. "Have you read it yet?"

Rosemary tried to hold her shaking hand still and concentrate as she read.

I'm sorry I have to leave so abruptly, but it's the only way. I need to find out for myself about my heritage. This is not about Dad and it's not about you. It's about me. I need to do this for myself. I know you'd never let me go, so I only hope you forgive me.

"I can't believe it," Rosemary said after she'd read the note to Marjie. "Athena wouldn't do this without someone leading her astray. It's that boy!"

"That might be so," said Marjie. "But right now you have to deal with the fact your daughter's gone to the fae realm."

"How do I get her back?" Rosemary asked. It was her single-minded focus and she was absolutely determined to do it.

"Now that might be a little more complicated."

Thirty-Three

"Granny!" she yelled, but no answer came. "Granny! I need you!"

Silence.

Rosemary walked slowly down the stairs. She could barely see through the dark feelings of anguish clouding her mind. At a normal time of crisis she would automatically put the kettle on in pursuit of the soothing power of tea, but this was not a normal time.

She could not think. She could barely breathe.

She walked without awareness of her body or of what she was doing. One foot automatically placed itself in front of the other, her mind scrambling to tell her this was an anomaly, a delusion, a dream, and that surely she would wake up any minute.

Rosemary found herself in the living room, surrounded by tulips. The tulips she had helped to grow with her magic. She'd managed to make them bloom, but that seemed like a lifetime ago. The flowers were out of place. They taunted her with their bright tones of red, yellow, and purple, when surely given the present situation the entire world must have lost all hope of joy or colour.

This can't be real.

Rosemary pinched herself, trying in vain to wake up.

It's not a dream.

Athena is gone. From this world, at least.

She opened her mouth and an unearthly wail escaped, along with it, a great rush of dark grey energy.

"Nooooo!" she bellowed.

The energy expanded out from her and then dispersed, leaving a trail of destruction in its wake.

As the cloud cleared, Rosemary looked around in shock to find that every last tulip had withered and died back into the soil.

A darkness inside her preened in satisfaction. If Athena is gone, then surely nothing bright and beautiful belongs here.

The dark energy that had escaped left Rosemary feeling limp and haggard. She collapsed there, on the living room floor, unable to bear any more of the present reality.

Rosemary opened her eyes and looked around. She was in bed, in her room. Her lovely new room with the carved wooden bed and plum décor. Everything should have been normal, but it wasn't. She felt as if she'd been run over by a truck and then backed over again several times.

She was burdened by the lead weight of emotion from what must have surely been a nightmare.

She breathed a sigh of relief and then was startled by a knock on her bedroom door.

"Athena?" Rosemary mumbled.

"Don't mind me," Marjie said, bustling in with a tea tray. "I'm just here to help."

"What?" Rosemary asked, confused.

"I came as quick as I could and found you collapsed on the floor surrounded by dead plants. I told that silly Ferg your magic wasn't ready to help with the plants."

"No, no, no," said Rosemary. "She's really gone."

Marjie gave her a sympathetic look.

"It wasn't a dream?" Rosemary asked.

"I'm afraid not," said Marjie.

Rosemary lay in bed, unmoving, a deep grief washing over her.

"Now, now," said Marjie. "Sit up. Here. Drink your tea."

Rosemary allowed Marjie to prop her up in bed with a stack of pillows because it seemed easier than trying to refuse. She took a sip of Marjie's special tea and immediately felt a warmth spreading through her, though it wasn't nearly enough to lift the burden of grief.

"Thank you," Rosemary said. "I feel a little better. I'm no use to anyone if I can't move."

"Oh love, now you must take it easy. What did you do to the plants, then?" Marjie teased gently.

"I actually...made them grow," Rosemary said. "Then, after I found out Athena was missing, something happened, and they all died at once. Anyway, we've got more important things to think about than plants."

"You might say that," said Marjie. "But remember we need the blooming spring bulbs for the equinox ritual – to pay tribute to the Goddess. If that doesn't go to plan, then who knows how we're going to get Athena or little Gretchen back."

"Do you think it will work for Athena too?" Rosemary asked hopefully.

"There's nothing sure about it," said Marjie. "None of us knows what Galdie did to retrieve Sherry from the fae realm, or whether it was pure luck. And I suppose it also depends on whether your girl is ready to return."

"What do you mean?" asked Rosemary, narrowing her eyes.

Marjie sighed. "You think she went with that boy?"

"Either that or she was taken by somebody else."

"The situation with Athena could be quite a different circumstance from the situation with Gretchen," said Marjie. "We know that young children have disappeared to the fae realm multiple times, but I've never seen a fully-fledged teenager wandering in there of her own accord. It should be impossible, but I suppose one with her heritage..."

"Don't tell me you knew about that as well!" Rosemary said.

"I'm sorry, dear. I forget you were living in the mundane world almost completely until just recently. You *so* belong here that it's hard to imagine you anywhere else."

"That's a nice thing to say," said Rosemary. "But how did you know about Dain?"

"Galdie told me the minute she met him that her granddaughter was involved with a fae boy. I thought she meant a dryad or a nymph, but she was quite sure he was the real deal."

"And you didn't think to tell me?"

"I thought you knew, dear. It was rather obvious to your grandmother. I've never met any of the true high fae myself, so I wouldn't know, but I trust

Galdie. They're said to be quite clever at disguising themselves, but I was sure Athena had that otherworldly look."

Rosemary grimaced. "High fae? Is that a rank thing or are they just smoking magic pixie weed?"

"I suspect it's more like a species."

"Well, I had no freaking idea that all those years I was involved with a mythical creature."

Marjie gave her polite smile. "Would you like some more of my special tonic?"

"Make it a triple," said Rosemary. "I don't know how I'm going to get through the day. I need all the help I can get."

"I'll give you the maximum dose," said Marjie. "Anymore and you'll feel all squishy."

"Thank you," said Rosemary. "And thanks for coming to look after me. I don't know what to do with myself."

"It's no trouble at all," said Marjie. "I'm here to help."

"What about the shop?"

"Herb will look after it for the day," said Marjie. "He made a fuss, but I told him where to shove his little trains."

Rosemary gave an involuntary laugh, despite the fact that she wasn't feeling like amusement should exist in the same world as her other emotions right now.

She couldn't stay in bed. She had to get Athena back.

"I have to go," Rosemary said.

"You might want to get changed first," said Marjie. "It took a lot of effort to magically bring you up to bed, but I didn't go to the trouble of trying to change your clothes. You look like you might need to shower as well, before you go into town."

"No, I mean I need to go to the fae realm. I need to follow Athena and bring her back now."

"That will be tricky," said Marjie. "Children may have been known to slip across when the veil is thin, or be taken, but adults are another matter entirely. Athena may have been able to go through easily because of her heritage. I suppose she would have the DNA to unlock the gate."

"There's a gate?" Rosemary asked. "Where is it?"

"From what I understand, it can be summoned, but it doesn't belong in a fixed location in this world, although there are places where the veil is thin

– all those stories of the fairy rings between mushrooms, and obviously Fin's Creek has been the location of many disappearances."

"There must be some kind of spell," said Rosemary. "Some kind of magic that can get me there."

"Fae magic is different from ours," said Marjie. "Not something witches can perform or even comprehend. They've protected themselves well, against the vampires of course."

"Will you help me?"

"Of course, dear," said Marjie. "Though our best bet is to prepare for the equinox."

"But that's not for two weeks!" said Rosemary. "I can't wait that long. Anything could happen to Athena in that amount of time."

"It's possible Athena will pop back by then," said Marjie. "I bet that girl is more powerful than even she realises."

"We can only hope." Rosemary took a big sip of tea, feeling Marjie's soothing uplifting magic at work. It did nothing to dispel her extreme dread, but it did calm her nerves a little.

Marjie excused herself and went downstairs to the kitchen. Rosemary was left alone for a moment before the little black kitten appeared, jumping onto her bed with a trill and prancing towards her.

"Hello, little Fuzzball," said Rosemary, raising her hand to pat the purring furry creature. "Or should I call you Serpentine? Athena would like that."

The kitten nuzzled at her palm.

"You miss her too, don't you," Rosemary continued. "Don't worry. We'll get her back."

The furry creature looked her in the eye with such knowing that Rosemary felt goosebumps prickle her arms.

This is no ordinary cat and the Thorns are no ordinary family.

She pulled together every ounce of strength she had, determined to retrieve her daughter, no matter what the cost.

Thirty-Four

Rosemary was vaguely aware that she looked dishevelled, but she didn't care. Her hair was a frizzy mess and her clothing was even more mismatched than on laundry day as she strode across the town square.

"Good morning, Rosemary," said Ferg. "How are those tulips growing?"

She was not in any state for small talk let alone having to explain what happened to the blasted flowers.

"Not now. I'm in a hurry," she said, brushing past him. At least that's what she intended to say. The words came out as more of a murmur.

She pushed her way through the doors of Burk's law office, feeling a twinge of embarrassment on top of everything else. She didn't really want to see the annoyingly attractive vampire after feeling jealous of seeing him at the pub with someone else. She smothered the emotion. She had more important things on her mind.

Rosemary had remembered, as she lay in bed trying to sleep the night before, that if vampires and fae had been at war for a long time, then surely vampires would know something. Athena had even suggested that before she went missing. But Rosemary had been too stubborn or too proud to listen.

Rosemary needed to find out what Burk knew, even if it was just what wouldn't work. Any information could save her time. The sleek silver-haired woman at the front desk eyed her suspiciously.

"I need to see Burk," Rosemary said.

"Mr Burk is not available right now." She flashed a false smile. "You can make an appointment."

"I need to see him now," said Rosemary, realising she sounded unhinged. "Look, I'll just call him."

"Don't trouble yourself," said Burk, emerging from the passageway. "Rosemary, come into my office." He held the door open for her.

Rosemary gave the receptionist a strange look. "She said you weren't here."

"Charlotte tries to protect me from interruptions," Burk explained dismissively as she followed him into his office. "Rosemary," he said, turning to her. "What's wrong? I've never seen you look so troubled."

"It's Athena," Rosemary said, not able to hold back the tears. It struck her that she hadn't cried. Not when she first discovered Athena was missing, not the next day, and not in the night when she was trying to sleep, but now being asked a simple, kindly worded question was all too much.

Burk disappeared from the room, jolting Rosemary, but he was back a moment later with a box of tissues. He held one up for her.

"Thank you," she said, taking a few more from the box. She dabbed at her eyes, trying to stem the stream of water that was now running down her face.

"Take your time," he said.

"Athena...she's gone missing."

"Where did she go?" Burk asked.

"It's the fae. They took her."

"That's impossible," said Burk. "She's too old to be abducted by those vile creatures."

Rosemary felt mildly offended on Athena's behalf, but she didn't let on. "I don't know the full story," she said, deliberately withholding Athena's fae heritage from the vampire who might very well not be able to control himself if he knew what she was. "I don't know how it happened. All I know is she's gone. I need to know how to get her back."

Burk crossed his arms and looked down to his desk. "If she had gone anywhere else I might have been able to help you."

"You must know something," said Rosemary desperately. "First that little girl went missing and now Athena." She burst into tears again.

Burk consoled her for a moment before another idea struck.

"Do you think this could have something to do with the Bloodstone Society?" Rosemary asked. "Are the fae involved with them?"

Burk shook his head. "The fae keep to themselves."

"Or maybe it's all a trick – the Bloodstones could be setting us up, making us believe it's the fae when really they are to blame."

"That's possible," said Burk. "But from what I understand the Bloodstones are still dispersed, just like their power. I suspect they'd have a hard time organising all this. Besides, it's not their style."

"Well, if you're sure. I need to know everything I can about them – *the fae* – anything at all that you can tell me."

"They are cold creatures."

"That's a bit rich coming from a vampire."

Burk frowned. "Is that what you think of me?"

"I'm sorry," said Rosemary.

"You should surely know that vampires tend to retain whatever values they had as mortals. Fae are...different. They have their own way of doing things, their own kind of code with very strict rules. They have never made any sense to me. During the war..."

"The war in which they were hunted by vampires?"

Burk gave her a pained look.

"What? Athena told me – your kind finds fae blood irresistible."

"That's true," said Burk. "But they weren't exactly helpless or blameless. There were attacks from both sides while the war lasted."

Rosemary looked at him sceptically. It sounded like Burk was making excuses for his kind, to make them not sound that bad. But this was hardly the time to argue with a vampire. "So the war ended. Then what happened?"

"A kind of cold war, I suppose," said Burk. "The fae keep building their protection. Over the last hundred years or so the borders have been closed. Young children can cross over sometimes, but adults can't, and I thought it would be impossible for a teenager."

"Well, it turns out they can take teenagers if they want to," said Rosemary, relieved she hadn't told him about Athena's heritage, especially after he'd just admitted that her blood was irresistible!

"Just tell me anything you think might be of help, so I can go to the fae realm and bring her back."

"I can't tell you how to get there," Burk said. "Although your best hope is probably the Spring Equinox."

"So everyone keeps telling me," said Rosemary. "But I can hardly wait that long. I've got to do something now."

"I think you're underestimating how hard it is to get to the fae realm," Burk said. "As far as I know, it has not been done by an adult human in over a hundred years, despite many seasoned witches trying."

Rosemary felt awash with hopelessness. "But Marjie said Granny helped get Sherry back... the Equinox?"

"Don't believe everything you hear," said Burk. "If the ritual is performed properly, the veil will lift for a moment, and you might have a chance. The only problem is you'd need to be in two places at once to actually get through."

"What do you mean?" Rosemary asked.

"The town square where the rituals are performed is a sacred space, designed to protect people from disappearing. The regular rituals honour the gods and goddesses so that they offer their protection. If the Goddess Eostre is satisfied at the Equinox she will bring good fortune to the town."

"For real?" Rosemary asked.

"You're saying you are willing to believe in vampires and fae but not goddesses?"

Rosemary hadn't thought about it a lot, but she did recall the appearance of cloud formations that could well have resembled the goddess Brigid around the time of Imbolc.

"Sure, fine, I'll go along with it," said Rosemary, furrowing her brow. "But at least I can *see* you in the flesh."

Burk gave her an odd look. "The point is, the ritual is performed in the town circle, but you won't be able to cross-over there."

"No, that can't be right," said Rosemary. "Ferg said they need me for the ritual to work. I have to be there."

"That makes sense," said Burk. "The more powerful the ritual, the more likely the veil is to lift enough to let someone through on either side."

"But you said I can't cross into the fae realm from there?"

"No. The centre of Myrtlewood is too well protected. There will be no entry point to the fae realm from the circle itself. If you're able to get from the town centre at the apex of the ritual to a weak point in the veil you might be able to cross over."

"Like Fin's Creek?" Rosemary asked. "That's where that child went missing."

"Yes, that's probably your best bet," said Burk.

"But how? I can't teleport. This isn't Space Trek or whatever."

"That is beyond me," said Burk. "I only wish I could move fast enough to carry you there in time."

"A noble sentiment," said Rosemary.

"The point is," said Burk, "I'm committed to helping however I can. I'll see what else I can find out. I have some sources who are very knowledgeable on magic."

"I appreciate it," said Rosemary.

As she got up to leave, Burk took her hand and gave it a little squeeze. She caught a look of vulnerability in his eyes. It was hard to believe that those same eyes belonged to someone capable of ruthless violence, of someone who found fae blood irresistible. She made a note to keep Athena well away from him when she came back, because Athena was going to return. Rosemary was absolutely determined about that.

"If you need anything – anything at all – don't hesitate to call me," said Burk.

Over the next few days, Rosemary kept herself busy, combing through Granny's books, looking for potential ways to enter the fae realm. She was surprised at how little information on the fae was contained in Granny's vast magical book collection.

She wondered multiple times if Dain, too, had been abducted by the fae and wished that he was still around so she could ask him to explain everything. *What could his own kind want with him? Maybe he owes them money! Do they even use money in the fae realm?*

She was almost totally clueless.

Much of the information she found online seemed like speculation and conspiracy theories, none of which was helpful.

Rosemary had managed to amass a sizeable collection of items said to be in some ways effective for warding off fae. In her desperation, she'd spent hours wandering through the forest around the house, hoping that whoever cast the illusion to make the house look as if it was in flames might return.

Based on something she'd read in a book, she set traps in the forest around Thorn Manor in an attempt to capture any faery creatures that might turn up, using saucers of cream as bait in the hopes of getting more information. So far she had caught one drunken dryad clad in nothing but leaves and a tiny blue pixie.

The only information she'd been able to divulge from threatening the dryad was that the politics in the fae realm was incredibly complicated. He rambled on about a missing prince and warring factions. Rosemary's eyes had glazed over. Surely none of this information was in any way useful to getting Athena back.

The pixie was even less useful and far more impolite, leading Rosemary to utter a string of expletives before setting it free.

She hadn't given up on Ostara as a last-ditch attempt to save Athena. With help from Ferg and Marjie she'd managed to re-plant hundreds of pots with tulip bulbs and use her magic to regrow them, so at least they were prepared for the ritual.

Every day brought the Spring Equinox closer.

Rosemary felt the tension in her gut increasing. If everyone around town was correct, this was the one chance she had in the foreseeable future of getting Athena back. The risks were immense. All she could do was prepare as much as possible, to research and practice following instructions so that she could actually get her magic to work properly, at will. This proved no easy feat, but every day she was getting a little better and making fewer mistakes around the house. Water and Earth elements were still a challenge, but Rosemary had gotten quite proficient at air and fire elemental magic, and could create fireballs at will. She could even combine the two to create a purple lightening ball which not only looked impressive, it did a decent amount of damage when she hurled it at an old tree stump in the garden.

Athena would be proud, thought Rosemary. *If only she were here to see it.*

Thirty-Five

Athena held tight to Finnigan's hand as she stepped through what felt like many layers of silk except...it was all just energy...floating.

As she entered the fae realm, it also entered right through her skin.

It passed through her entire being, every layer taking with it any doubt or fear she'd held about leaving her home behind, along with her exhaustion she'd been carrying for years.

In fact, it seemed to Athena that some knots had been released in her body, as if some old wounds, remnants of her former self, were being stripped away and lost forever. With that realisation came a sense of powerlessness. After all, she hadn't chosen to go through any particular internal change.

But even still, it didn't feel bad. In fact, Athena felt much better, more like her actual self. As they continued walking through many layers of subtly coloured mist, she began to see the outline of tall, oddly spindly lavender coloured trees, backlit against a deep violet sky.

Tiny lights dotted the air above them, which Athena quickly realised were many thousands of glowing butterflies.

"This way," Finnigan said, leading her towards a cobbled path that shone silver though there was no moon in the sky.

"Where are we going?" Athena asked.

"I'll take you to my home," he said. "But first, we need to get permission for you to be here."

"I don't know about that," said Athena, nervously pressing her fingernails into the palm of her hand.

"It's not my rule," said Finnigan. "If you're here without a proof of passage you're bound to be hunted."

Athena gulped.

"Fine," she said.

Being hunted by fae after the performance they put on at her house the other night did not sound like fun.

They passed enormous toadstools growing in purples and reds and greens. Athena longed to reach out for them, but Finnigan pulled her away.

"Don't touch anything unless I say it's okay," he said. "The fae realm might look like a beautiful fairy tale, but it's very dangerous here. There are plenty of risks that you won't recognise."

Athena nodded and continued on.

As they walked along the path, Athena noticed a large pond dotted with pastel coloured lily pads. She glanced towards the water to see an otherworldly creature there, which moved when she did. "It...it can't be," said Athena. "My reflection? Is it enchanted?"

"No," said Finnigan. "You look different here as well." That was when she noticed that Finnigan had also made some kind of transformation from entering the fae realm. His skin was glowing and his ears appeared more pointed. His hair had taken on a silver gleam, but she'd not noticed it before in the low light under which everything had looked vaguely more purple than usual.

His limbs appeared longer and more distinctly slender, though his clothes seemed to fit just the same.

"Am I taller?" Athena asked, examining her own long limbs.

"It's all a matter of perspective," he replied.

As they continued walking Athena had the distinct feeling of being watched. "Do you think someone's following us?" she asked Finnigan.

"Undoubtedly," he said. "All the gates are watched."

"Is that because you need to protect yourselves against the vampires?" Athena asked.

"Shush," said Finnigan. "Don't say that word around here. It will not go well."

"Okay, I get it. You don't like them," said Athena. "But they're not all bad."

Finnigan gave her a piercing look. "I don't think you should say that around beings who have been persecuted by them for thousands of years."

"Sorry," Athena said. "I guess I should have thought about that."

Finnigan ignored her and carried on. "When we go to the high office, just tell them that you have fae heritage and ask that they grant you refuge."

"Refuge?" Athena said. "I'm not in danger."

"Just say it," said Finnigan. "Otherwise, you might not be allowed to stay."

Athena's chest tingled in a silent alarm. "I just pretend that I'm in great danger? That I've been hunted by...err...things that I can't talk about."

"Exactly," said Finnigan.

"Is there anything else I should know before I make a complete fool of myself and become the target of half of the fae realm?"

"Just don't say anything," Finnigan said. "If you're not sure, I can help you. I can speak for you."

"Really?" Athena asked, raising her eyebrows.

"Come on," said Finnigan, pulling her faster along the forest path.

Athena was taken aback by Finnigan's gruffness, though she was too lost in wonderment at the stunning landscape around her to worry. The trees above glowed in all shades of purple. It was breathtakingly beautiful if only Athena had time to appreciate it as they hurried along.

"It does feel nice here," said Athena. "I thought it would feel strange and weird, but it feels..."

"Like home?" Finnigan asked with a smile.

"A little," said Athena. "Even my body feels more comfortable, like I'm not all weighed down."

"The atmosphere is different here," said Finnigan.

"Like a different gravity," said Athena. "Or whatever the magical equivalent of that is."

"Gravy tea?" said Finnigan.

"Never mind."

Athena realised how different they were, really. Finnigan may have visited the earth realm, but it seemed he'd never lived there. He hadn't been schooled there since he was very young, and that was in a whole different time in history, and yet, he was somehow more similar to her than almost anyone else she'd met.

The thought made her feel even more alone in all the worlds.

Up ahead she could see the spires of some kind of grand structure. "Is that where we're headed?" Athena asked.

"Sort of," said Finnigan.

"What do you mean, *sort of*?" Athena asked.

"You'll see soon enough." They approached the large structure, which Athena hesitated to assume was a building. It was shaped like an elaborate circus tent in varying shades of natural colours. It had towers that looked a lot like acorns. The entire structure seemed to be made entirely of leaves.

"It's so cute!" Athena said. "Please say that's where we're going."

"Over here," said Finnigan, leading Athena around the side. She felt disappointed, as she wanted to enter the odd building.

"Isn't this the office?" she asked.

"Technically yes," said Finnigan. "They don't really like to be indoors."

"Then why have buildings at all?"

He shrugged. "Maybe it's for keeping up appearances. Or maybe it's shelter. I don't know. They're always around the back, anyway."

They walked around the side of the building towards a clearing at the back. At the centre of the clearing was an enormous table made out of an old tree stump. Dotted around it were large mushroom stools, and perched on the stools sat an assortment of bizarre looking creatures.

Their skin seemed to glow in the violet light. It almost looked translucent. Their limbs were long and their ears were sharply pointed. Their eyes gleamed with a preternatural light and they were clad in skeleton leaves that appeared to be pasted together with sap and other natural fibres to form elaborate ball gowns and suits with matching hats.

"Who dares interrupt us at this hour?" said a haughty voice. It came from a figure to the left of the table dressed in a white skeleton leaf ballgown. She stood and strode over to them.

"Young Finnigan. Have you caught a prize?" She eyed Athena suspiciously.

"No, my lady," said Finnigan, bending into a low bow that seemed a little bit excessive to Athena, but she followed suit and gave a kind of half curtsey.

"Apologies for the interruption," Finnigan said. "In my scouting of the earth realm, I discovered one of our own. She seeks safe passage."

"Let her step forward," said a deeper voice, coming from the head of the table. Athena looked towards the figure, perched elegantly there, who wore a top hat made of green leaves and a dapper suit to match.

"Ismalia," Finnigan said with another bow. "Please meet my friend Athena Thorn. Athena, this is the high clerk of the Western Gate, Ismalia."

"A human?" Ismalia said, her eyes wide.

All eyes around the table watched Athena. She felt a sudden chill of danger.

"Tell them," Finnigan said, elbowing Athena.

"I think I need...to be a refugee...erm, safely. I need to run away. I'm in danger..." Athena rambled, feeling a lot like her mother.

Ismalia raised her eyebrows. "Come closer."

Athena stayed still until Finnigan pushed her forward.

"Let me have a look at you," said the fae, taking off her top hat. She raised her hand. The tip of her delicate long index finger glowed. She swirled it over Athena and her face lit up in a smile. "I think you do indeed have royal fae blood."

"Royal?" said Athena, before remembering to keep quiet.

Ismalia's green eyes lit up in a way that made Athena distinctly uncomfortable. "Very well," she said.

She let her finger glide down until it touched Athena's nose with a little ting.

Athena felt seasick.

"Don't worry, it'll pass," Ismalia said as the other fairies giggled.

Finnigan took Athena's hand and spoke to the unusual fae. "Many blessings upon you for your graciousness." He bowed. "We'll be going now."

"Do stay for some tea," said Ismalia.

"We're in a hurry," said Finnigan.

"Nonsense. You know you must stay, if we invite you to tea. Have you forgotten our Lore?"

Finnigan straightened his back, bowed, and sat down on one of the empty mushrooms. He pulled Athena towards the table on the other side.

"Tea?" Ismalia asked, brandishing a teapot that looked to be made out of a mushroom.

"I'm okay," said Athena. "I bought my own." She reached into her bag for her thermos.

"What are you doing?" Finnigan whispered.

"I read that I can't eat the food here."

"Don't worry about that," he said quietly. "You're fae."

"How adorable. She's overly cautious," said Ismalia. "It's alright, my dear. You can eat the food here."

"Err...Excuse me," said Athena. "How can I trust that what you say is true? I know nothing about this place."

Ismalia laughed. "Surely, as an earthly being you know that the fae cannot lie?"

Athena remained silent.

"You have safe passage here," Ismalia continued. "One such as yourself, with your heritage. Anyway..." She laughed again.

Athena shot Finnigan another sceptical look. He nodded reassuringly and she relaxed a little. After all, she was in dire need of a cup of tea.

"You know, as a child this would have been the highlight of my life," said Athena. "Having tea with fairies!" A silence fell around the table. "Oh no. I've done it again, haven't I? I've said something offensive."

"Never mind," said Ismalia, although there was a definite tension in her voice.

"We don't use that word," said Finnigan.

"Thanks for telling me," Athena hissed in a low whisper. "Can you please let me in on the other rules while you're at it?"

"For a start, don't ever say thank you to the fae," Finnigan whispered back. "It's considered incredibly rude."

"How odd," Athena muttered quietly. "I mean, I'm sure I read that online, but I didn't think it was true."

"We do have a rule about having to be polite," Finnigan continued, keeping his voice down.

"Really?" Athena rolled her eyes.

"Yes, really," said Finnigan. "Don't roll your eyes, whatever you do. It is not polite."

Athena sighed and raised her hands in surrender. "I apologise," she said, looking around the table. "I'm new to all of this."

"And you'll be forgiven. For a few more moments, at least," said Ismalia, grinning from ear-to-ear, clearly listening in on their conversation. "After that, we will not to be so generous."

Athena felt a cold chill. She knew that these creatures might seem delicate and harmless, but she could tell they were really very deadly, much more frightening than vampires, at least the nice vampires that she had met.

Ismalia poured an indigo liquid into a cup that looked to be made of a tulip-like flower.

"Tha— I mean, I accept your gracious hospitality," said Athena, reaching forward to take the cup, which was soft and supple in her fingers, just like real petals. The saucer that came with it was a large round lily pad leaf.

"At any rate, we cannot tell you *all* the rules," said Ismalia. "That is also part of the Lore."

"That's...just great," said Athena taking a sip of the tea. It tasted exactly like perfectly ripe blueberries. She couldn't help but smile as her whole body lit up at the delightful flavour.

"See, now that wasn't so hard, was it?" said Ismalia.

"It's delicious!" Athena said, and then she remembered what Finnigan had said before about not speaking as much as possible. She made a note to stay as quiet as she could for the rest of the engagement.

Thirty-Six

Rosemary stood at the kitchen table, practicing a spell. The house around her was chaotic, reflecting her inner state. She'd been experimenting with the elements and potions. She had no time for chocolate, and the various bunnies and eggs cropping up everywhere had only reminded her of what Athena was missing.

Getting her daughter back was consuming Rosemary's entire focus. She just needed a clue as to how. She'd gone to great lengths to read up on astrology, though reading the stars seemed far too complicated. She'd had a go at using Granny's tarot cards but kept getting scary looking outcomes, like The Tower, so she'd turned to tea leaves instead but could not make any sense of them.

In a fit of desperation, Rosemary had even gone to see Crystal Cassandra, the gossipy woman who called herself the town psychic, only to be told some nonsense about her aura being too foggy to read. Rosemary had been eager to leave. That woman gave her bad vibes.

Rosemary sprinkled the powder in front of her into the small copper bowl and muttered the incantation from the spell book. Nothing seemed to happen. She sighed.

She hadn't been to work in days. She was relieved that she didn't need the money anymore. At least in the short term, she was fine financially. She didn't want to be any more of a burden on Marjie than she already had been, but Marjie insisted she was fine at the shop and continued to drop around meal parcels at every opportunity, making sure that Rosemary and the kitten were both fed. She didn't even stop to chat, obviously because she had gotten sick of Rosemary refusing her delicious gifts.

There was a knock at the door.

Rosemary gave up on the spell, and assuming the knock came from Marjie, she went to the front door. Marjie's car was disappearing down the driveway.

Rosemary couldn't help but smile at her kind friend who felt more like family at this point.

She went to retrieve the package from the front door step. She could have sworn she had the feeling that something was watching her from the trees around the house.

She looked up, trying to make out any unexpected movement from the forest.

Just then there was a rush of air. A figure appeared. Rosemary shouted and raised her arms. A blast of energy shot out.

"Hey!" Burk said, shielding his eyes.

The handsome vampire stood on her doorstep, looking ruffled.

"Oh! You scared me," said Rosemary.

"I'm sorry," he said, standing back. "Rosemary, I just came to..."

"What?" She looked at him curiously.

"To give you this book," he said, reaching into his pocket and producing a tiny green fabric-bound volume.

"A book for miniature people?" Rosemary asked. "Sorry, I can't even make a joke anymore. I just say whatever thoughts come into my mind and most of them aren't that coherent."

"Understandable," said Burk.

"What is it?" Rosemary asked, reaching towards the book.

"It was over a hundred years ago that this book was made. It was commissioned by the High Councillor of vampires."

"You guys have a council?" asked Rosemary. "I had no idea being undead could be so bureaucratic."

"Painfully so," said Burk. "How else do you think we keep young vampires in line?"

"What did they commission a little book for?" Rosemary asked. A small glimmer of hope began shining inside her mind. *Could this be the missing piece of the puzzle?*

The small book barely filled her palm. There was no title on the cover or spine.

"It's about fae," said Burk. "This book was written by the wisest magical scholars around. This was a way we could gather enough information to combat them, and their tricks."

"I thought vampires hunted fae to near extinction," said Rosemary suspiciously. "Why would you need a book like this?"

Burk laughed. "If only it was that simple." He took a small step towards Rosemary. "Be aware, Rosemary. Be wary of the fae. They can be cruel. They have a totally different sense of morality from humans or vampires. The war was predominantly between our kinds, but believe me when I say that many magical humans were in support of us."

"That seems strange," said Rosemary. "Given you drink human blood – at least traditionally."

Burk looked mildly offended and slightly amused. "We are not the hideous demons we're often made out to be in all the stories." There was a bitterness in his voice. "Fae sought out and destroyed most of the volumes of this book. It contains some information that will be of use, just remember that it was written a long time ago, before all the protections were in place. It won't get you through the veil."

"Then what use is it?" Rosemary said, feeling the fluttery hopes that had awakened by the book wither and die in her chest.

"It has more information on the fae than you'll find elsewhere," said Burk. "And if you do make it into the fae realm, I believe there are some recipes here that will help to fortify you, both on your entry and to ensure your safe return."

"You sound so formal when you talk like that," Rosemary said.

"Modern language is, as they say, 'a stretch' for me," said Burk. "I've been around a long while and most of that time the language structure was more formal, at least in my circles." He rubbed his fingers through his perfectly styled hair.

"You know, you sound like a bit of a snob when you say that," said Rosemary.

Burk chuckled.

"But thank you for the book," she continued. "It's very kind of you."

"I only hope it helps," said Burk. "I'll keep researching to see what more I can find. Our Council keep a close eye on any activity happening at the edge of the veil, including any disappearances. It all happens too intermittently to predict."

Rosemary nodded. "Thanks again," she said, taking the little book and slipping it into her pocket.

"Rosemary, I..." Burk's words faltered. "I want you to know that I'll do whatever I can to help and that I...I care for you."

Rosemary felt a strange tug in her gut, but it did not seem like the right time to be having any feelings. It was kind of Burk to give her the book, but the last thing she needed was to get involved with a vampire lawyer who probably had boundary issues. Also, she hadn't forgotten that she'd seen him having dinner with an attractive woman only a few nights before. If he really cared for her then would he be dating other women? Not that that was any of her business.

"As I said before, let me know if there's anything I can do." He reached out and took Rosemary's hand, lowering his head and planting a kiss on her knuckle.

Rosemary gave him a quizzical look.

"I'm sorry," Burk said. "I'm just realising how strange the gesture must have seemed. I'm an old-fashioned chap."

Rosemary pulled her hand away. "Uhh... thanks, I guess. Have a good night."

She turned away to pick up the package of food that Marjie had dropped off and heard the rushing sound behind her telling her that Burk had left. She had no time to think about the vampire and his strange antiquated manners and his handsome features and his gorgeous eyes. She had far more important things to do.

She went inside and placed the pie and salad that Marjie had left her onto a plate. It was blessedly still warm. She took it to the table with the little book and began to study its pages, careful not to spill any food since it was no doubt irreplaceable.

As Burk had said, there were indeed useful-sounding recipes for things such as miniature cakes and biscuits that, prepared correctly, would fortify human strength and protect against the dangers between the realms, and also for adjusting on the return to the human world.

None of the recipes seemed particularly useful for vampires, although the book did say that vampires, regardless of their strength or enchantments, could not easily pass into the fae realm and could not survive there long even if they did.

Perhaps they had been training human spies to go in there and sabotage the fae. Rosemary wondered whether she could trust Burk. He always seemed quite genuine, if a little arrogant. He had been kind to her and Athena. But there was no way she could risk him finding out what Athena was.

Rosemary sat at the table, reading the book, until she could barely keep her eyes open.

She couldn't help but feel that Burk was being deceptive, at least to make it sound as if his side – the vampires – weren't really that bad.

Rosemary must have nodded off because she woke with her head on the table and a crick in her neck, lines from the book creasing her face.

It was a noise that had woken her, the sound of frantic knocking.

Sherry was at the door.

"Goodness," Rosemary said, feeling groggy. "What time is it?"

"Time?" said Sherry, her voice rough and high-pitched. "Who has a care in the world for time?"

It was then that Rosemary noticed Sherry was not at all pale or tired looking like she had been the last time they'd seen each other. Her eyes seemed to be almost glowing and a maniacal smile curled her lips.

"Sherry, are you okay?" asked Rosemary.

"I am magnificent!" said Sherry. Then she lowered her eyes. "Except, I heard about Athena and I am very sorry to hear of your loss."

"Is there anything I can do to help you?" Rosemary asked, in a tone of genuine concern.

"Help me? Oh, no, I'm on top of the world or...at least I will be very soon." She shot Rosemary another cunning smile.

"I thought the equinox made you feel drained."

"Usually it does, but I found something that makes me feel much better. In fact, I think I can help you."

Rosemary's heart thudded in her chest as her mind raced with the realisation that Sherry might be on some kind of magical drug. Even still, she could not ignore the possibility that she might be able help get Athena back.

"How could you help?" Rosemary asked.

"Just make sure you bring the following ingredients to the equinox." She brandished a crumpled shopping list with a bunch of herbs and crystals scrawled on it. "We need to create a doorway to get into the fae realm."

"You want to go back there?" Rosemary asked, surprised.

"I have some unfinished business with the fae." A troubled look crossed

Sherry's face. "They took something precious from me and now I can finally get her back."

"What are you talking about?" Rosemary asked, but it was too late. Sherry had turned towards the forest. Rosemary caught a familiar flash of gold around the woman's neck as she ran away into the trees. Rosemary wondered for a moment whether she should go looking for her, but decided against it, as the forest had been giving her the creeps for weeks. Instead, she called Detective Neve and left a message.

LATER THAT NIGHT, as Rosemary was lying in bed, her mind ran through the encounter with Sherry. The glimpse of gold around her neck was from a chain, Rosemary realised, and it was so familiar because it was part of the missing necklace.

Rosemary had only caught a brief glimpse but she was sure of it.

Sherry must have taken it when she was visiting the house.

Rosemary got out of bed. She needed to talk to Granny, but there was no secret door visible on the upstairs landing. She went to the part of the wall where the door had once been and knocked. There was no response.

Rosemary knocked again and then began hammering at the door.

She took a deep breath as sobs wracked her chest. She wiped away her tears with the back of her hand.

"Granny! I need to talk to you. Right now! I don't care if this isn't a good time for you. You're a freaking ghost. I'm sure you have all the time in the world."

There was no response, so Rosemary raised her palms to the door, calling for her magic. Light radiated behind her hands. Nothing happened for a moment and then slowly golden edging appeared, tracing the outline of the door.

"Thank you," Rosemary said to the house. She opened up the newly-formed door and climbed the stairwell at pace.

"Listen here, old woman," Rosemary said, storming into the tower room.

"Can't you tell I'm busy?" said Granny, materialising in the mirror.

"I don't care if you're busy," Rosemary shouted. "Your great grand-daughter has gone missing!"

"I'm quite aware of that," said Granny. "That's what I'm busy with."

Rosemary stepped back in surprise. "I didn't realise you keep such close tabs on us."

"Of course I do," said Granny. "The two of you are so dense sometimes. Somebody's got to watch out for you. But rest assured, Athena is fine."

"She is not fine!" Rosemary stormed. "She's been kidnapped!"

"Rubbish," said Granny. "It's just a romp, that's all."

"A romp!" Rosemary was appalled. "We might never get her back. You should know how hard it is to get through the veil."

"Well, the equinox..."

"I know!" said Rosemary, still fuming at her grandmother's flippant attitude. "That's what everyone keeps telling me. But how? Marjie seemed to think you'd know."

"I just follow my intuition as far as magic is concerned," said Granny, with a little wave of her hand. "There are no instructions for any of this, not since they closed the borders when I was a little lass. But don't worry, the girl will surely be having the time of her life."

Rosemary was livid. It took her a while to calm down enough to speak again. Clearly Granny was too disconnected from the earth to understand the gravity of the situation. There was no use in getting into a pointless argument when Granny might be able to help, whether she realised it or not. Instead of fighting over whether Athena was in danger or simply romping about, Rosemary gritted her teeth and changed the subject.

"That's not the only thing I need to tell you about," said Rosemary eventually. "I just realised that Sherry was the one who took the necklace."

"That girl." Granny shook her head. "I wonder why she would have done that."

"I suppose she was the obvious culprit," said Rosemary. "After all, she had visited the house around the time it went missing. I just didn't believe she could have done it." She was silent in contemplation for a moment, then asked. "Do you think the necklace would have a strange effect on her?"

"There is no doubt in my mind," said Granny. "It's a powerful relic. The Thorn family have held onto it for generations, partly because our magic makes us strong enough to wear it. I doubt there's anyone else in the town who could pull that off."

"Thanks for warning me," Rosemary said. "What if I'd lent it to a friend?"

"How dare you lend out priceless family heirlooms!" said Granny. "I thought even *you* had more sense than that."

"I wouldn't have," said Rosemary. "I didn't even let Athena wear it. Sherry was in a very odd state. I thought she was high."

"She probably is. That magic is powerful."

"But she's had the necklace for at least a week," said Rosemary, "and the last time I saw her she was nothing like that."

"Maybe she only just tried it on?" Granny suggested.

"She said something about helping me get Athena back."

"I wouldn't trust her as far as you could throw her, love," said Granny. "Not when she's under the influence."

"She seemed really serious about it though," said Rosemary. "Loads of people have offered to help me, but when Sherry did my intuition told me she was genuine, despite her state. She said something else too. She wants to get something back from the fae realm – something she lost there."

"Now," said Granny. "That sparks a memory. Did she say something or someone?"

"Why do you ask?"

Granny waved her arm and a large drawer rolled open from the big wooden desk at the side of the room. It was filled with old fashioned files. "Let's see, where is it?"

Papers shuffled around and then a manilla folder flicked up and landed on the desk. "Here," said Granny.

"What is it?" Rosemary asked, crossing the room towards the desk.

The file opened and papers flittered around, leaving one on top. It was an old newspaper clipping with pictures of two girls on the front. One was clearly a young Sherry. The other had darker hair and a serious expression.

"Mei Lee," Rosemary said, reading the name under the picture. "She went missing at the same time. Why didn't anyone say anything?"

"It's one of the problems with living where the veil is thin," said Granny. "Fae magic affects everyone's memory, especially where *they* are concerned. When Sherry came back, no one knew who she was."

"How awful," said Rosemary. "Not even her parents?"

"They recognised her eventually, but I understand it was quite traumatic for her at first, coming back and finding herself treated as a stranger in her own home."

"I bet," said Rosemary. "No one is going to make me forget Athena. Just please try to help get her back."

"Fine, fine," said Granny. "But you're the key here. Your magic, now that you are using it properly, should protect you somewhat from memory loss, but the fae are strong. That's why I keep a record of the goings on. You can never be too careful."

"I think there was a recipe to help with this actually," Rosemary said. "Burk gave me a little book with useful information on fae. There's a lemon tart that protects against their charm."

"That does indeed sound useful," said Granny, giving her a knowing look. "That handsome vampire really is going out of his way for you, isn't he? Oh, to be young again!"

"It's not like that," said Rosemary.

"Whatever you say," Granny said, grinning.

Rosemary ignored her and looked back at the newspaper cutting.

"Do you think everyone forgot about the other girl?" she asked.

"Possibly everyone, except for Sherry," Granny replied.

Thirty-Seven

As Athena finished her tea cup she realised the sky above them was lightening.

"How long have we been here?" she asked Finnigan. She was feeling slightly odd, and she didn't know whether it was due to the beverage she'd just consumed or just to being in a different world. It felt as if she'd only been gone twenty minutes, and yet she knew time didn't follow the same patterns as in the earth realm.

The creatures around her laughed at her question.

"Not long," said Finnigan. She noted the anxious look in his eyes. "But we'd better be on our way. We appreciate your splendid generosity," he said, standing and bowing towards the fae.

Athena followed suit.

"Leaving so soon?" said Ismalia.

"I'm afraid so," said Finnigan.

"Do keep us informed of your activities," said the fae clerk, tipping her leafy top hat. Athena was sure there was a hint of threat in her voice.

A light snoring sound interrupted them. Athena glanced over to see that one of the elaborately dressed fae had fallen asleep at the other side of the table.

Ismalia gave the sleeping fae a sharp kick and then clapped her hands together. "The night shift has ended! Time for the day to take over."

Her voice travelled across the lawn of wildflowers as if magnified by a microphone, towards the leafy building. A trumpet sounded.

Finnigan pulled Athena away and they headed off towards a path in the forest. She couldn't help but turn around to see the commotion, as half a dozen smartly dressed fae in red coats left the house and made their way out towards the table, clearly in order to replace the night shift.

"I'm not even going to pretend to know what that was about," said Athena.

"What? You expect them to work all night and day?" Finnigan asked. "Even fae need rest."

"No, not that," said Athena. "The night and day shift makes perfect sense. It's all that stuff about manners that I don't understand, and the strange tea. I'm sure it made me feel funny. Look, you told me you'd bring me here to explain things and you have explained almost nothing of any use to me. I've got far more questions than answers."

Finnigan ran his hand through his hair. "What is it you want to know?" he asked as he continued to lead her along the cobblestone path that glowed pearlescent under the soft lilac early morning light.

"I want to know what is going on in my brain when I hear the voices inside people's heads. Wait a minute. I haven't heard them. I haven't heard any voices or any fuzz since I got here."

"I think you'll find that particular ability works with humans, not fae, unless they are very closely connected to each other," he said.

"But it works with you," said Athena, wondering how she could feel so close to someone from the instant they'd met.

"It does," said Finnigan. "I assume it's only because I have both human and fae heritage, like you, remember?"

"You're just assuming this?" Athena asked. "Shouldn't you *know*? Have you ever seen any humans in the fae world or fae in the human world?"

"That's not as common as you might think," said Finnigan, giving her a slightly strange look.

"And why couldn't you just tell me all this before?"

"I told you I could say very little," said Finnigan.

"So what's new?" Athena said, feeling frustrated.

"What else do you want to know?"

"You told me you'd help me to hone the power, but I can't even use it here."

"Being here will help you," he reassured her. "Don't you feel it? This place is the natural home for you, for your body."

Athena closed her eyes for a moment, standing still on the path. She did feel peaceful, much more than she ever had before. It helped that her mind was still. Not having to deal with voices was a nice change, but even before the telepathy power had come in, she'd never felt this deep sense of calm.

"See, you know yourself better here," said Finnigan. "Besides, there's someone else who can help you."

"Who is it?"

"The Countess of West Eloria."

"West Eloria?" Athena asked. "Where is that?"

"All around you," said Finnigan. "This part of the fae realm is West Eloria. It's ruled by the countess."

"Are the other parts much different?" Athena asked.

"I can't tell you that," said Finnigan. "I've never been into any of the other regions. I'm...I work here."

"Oh, okay," said Athena, catching a slightly strained tone in Finnigan's voice. "What's she like, the countess?"

"She's strong and beautiful," said Finnigan.

Athena felt a pang of jealousy and wondered how old this countess was.

They walked on in silence for a while, until something caught Athena's eye.

Up ahead, through the trees, some interesting characters were approaching. They looked to be wearing bright red tutus.

"Stay close," said Finnigan suddenly, grabbing Athena by the hand, sending delicate shivers through her limbs and torso. She wasn't sure if it was just the chemicals of infatuation or something more magical, but she was distracted from wondering about that by the seriousness in his tone.

"What is it?" she asked quietly.

"Tribute seekers," he said. "Do you have anything in your bag that might make a good tribute?"

"What kind of thing?"

"Something shiny," said Finnigan.

Athena mentally took stock at the contents of her backpack, feeling uneasy when she considered all the charms and potions she'd mixed up to use as protection or self defence against the fae. She recalled some of the other things she'd packed, too.

"Do you think they'd like gemstones?" she asked, remembering how she'd raided Granny Thorn's rather extensive collection of crystals before she left.

"As long as it's not lodestone or hematite," said Finnigan.

"Don't you think I know better than to take iron into the fae realm," she replied. "I might be mostly clueless, but I do know a thing or two about folklore."

"Fine, just find something quickly, can you?" said Finnigan, not looking particularly impressed by Athena's knowledge of fae-repellent minerals.

"Probably." Athena shrugged, then took off her backpack and rifled through one of the side pockets as the red-dressed creatures approached them. Unlike the other fae creatures they'd met, these ones were squat and almost bell-shaped. She wanted to ask if they were a different species, but it seemed highly probable that such a question would be rude considering the fae obsession with politeness. She pulled out a small piece of rose quartz. It clinked against a tiny bottle of cream as she took it out of the bag.

"Tribute! Tribute please! Tributes for our fair queen!" the strange creatures called out, holding up a large yellow pail which they jingled around.

"You can explain this later," Athena said to Finnigan.

"Will you choose to pay tribute to our fair queen?"

Athena looked down at the small piece of rose quartz, and all of a sudden it didn't seem to be quite enough. She put it back into the pocket of her bag and rummaged around, hoping to find something flashier.

The taller tribute seeker made a large exaggerated sniffing noise. "What is that?" it asked. "Could it be...? Could it be contraband?"

Finnigan shot Athena a warning glance. She produced a large chunk of agate and held it up to the creature to see its dazzling green eyes sparkling at the sight.

"Such generosity," said the smaller tribute seeker, reaching out for the crystal. It held the agate up and sniffed again. "Could it be?" The creature's eyes seemed to grow bigger and bigger. "Cream!"

The other creature joined in a high pitched squeak.

"Stay very still," said Finnigan.

"Turn out your pockets!" said the taller creature.

"This is not good," said Finnigan. *Tell me you didn't...* His voice sounded in her head.

So it turns out the telepathy does work here, Athena thought.

Athena! Finnigan's voice rang in her mind.

Athena thought of the charms and spells in her bag, wishing she knew whether their power would work in the fae realm. She hoped that the creatures didn't have the ability to read her mind too, but she had a feeling she was going to find out soon enough.

So what if I bought cream? she replied to Finnigan. *What's the danger?*

Cream is like heroin to the fae, he said. *It's expressly forbidden. Our best hope now is that they take the cream and run off with it to use themselves.*

And what's our worst hope? Athena asked.

If you're discovered with cream here, things are not going to look good for you. We'll be locked up in a dungeon and tried for high treason.

Thank you for warning me about this earlier!

I'll see if I can distract them, he said and turned back to the fae. "That's an awfully nice frock you're wearing."

That's your attempt at distraction? Athena said in her mind, grateful that the other creatures hadn't seemed to pick up on the telepathy.

What, they're prone to flattery. It's a major weakness.

Athena glared at him.

"How sweet of you to say," the bell-shaped demon said. "However, there are other more pressing matters at hand. Turn out your pockets and surrender to me whatever it is that smells like cream." A dozen spidery limbs emerged, protruding from both creatures' backs like wings as they reached towards Athena threateningly.

Fortunately, I've got a better distraction, Athena thought. She reached into the main pocket of her bag. *Get ready to run!*

Wait, Athena, what are you doing? Finnigan asked.

Athena removed a small bundle that looked remarkably like a bath bomb. She held it up in the air and the creatures' eyes followed her.

The creature stepped towards the bundle and Athena threw it hard at the ground, taking Finnigan's hand and running with him as a huge explosion rent the air.

It was as if a whole carton of fireworks had been set on fire, complete with colourful sparkles.

Finnigan and Athena were blown back several metres in the air, and Athena was grateful that the thickness of the fae realm atmosphere cushioned their fall.

"Thank the gods that charm worked," Athena said as they dashed away through the forest.

"What was *that*?" Finnigan asked.

"I don't know," said Athena. "I mean, it was a defence charm I made, but I didn't even know which one I grabbed or if it was going to work. I didn't know if earth magic worked here."

"Normal human magic might not work here," said Finnigan. "Or at least that's the rumour."

"Maybe it just doesn't work as expected," said Athena.

"And you brought an arsenal?!"

"It's something that I used when we were being attacked a few weeks ago by the Bloodstone society. But the charms didn't have anywhere near that effect in the earth realm."

"I suppose your magic must work differently here," said Finnigan,

"It's not really my magic," said Athena. "I just followed the instructions."

"Don't be silly," said Finnigan. "Following instructions doesn't automatically lead to magic."

They decided to pause for a rest in a glade by a stream, having judged the tribute seekers were now far away enough that there wasn't any present danger.

"My mother has magic. She doesn't need any potions or charms or even spells to utilise it. She just hasn't bothered learning how to use it yet. Typical."

"I think you might find you have even more power than her," said Finnigan. "Not only from your human side but from your fae side as well. It's no wonder she tried to keep you locked up in the earth realm rather than letting you come home."

"That's not what she was doing. You are way off base, though if I do have power it'd be nice if I could actually use it properly." Athena sighed. "I suppose there are no shortcuts. I'll have to figure out how to practice, how to harness it on my own, just like I do with this stupid telepathy thing."

"You're doing quite well, really," said Finnigan.

"What do you mean?"

"Well, just before you were channelling your thoughts straight to me. If you hadn't been protecting them against the tribute seekers, they would have heard everything we'd said to each other."

"Really?" Athena asked.

"It took me a long time to learn how to protect my own thoughts from the fae," said Finnigan darkly. "It's the downside of being human. They can pick up a lot of what you think. It took me years to figure out how to conceal my thoughts and avoid being punished for being impolite or resisting orders in my mind."

"You're saying I'm using it properly?" said Athena. "But how?"

"You focussed your thoughts," said Finnigan. "You didn't want them to overhear you. And you didn't put too much energy into worrying about it either. If you'd done that it would have just made it worse. Magic is always about will."

"Do you think I can use magic like Mum can? I mean, will my magic to just appear without a spell or anything?"

"Why not give it a try and we can see." He raised his hand as though to reach for her, but held it poised in mid-air. Athena reached her fingers out towards his until they were almost touching, then she concentrated on her very fingertips. Nothing happened at first, and then light began to glow from her index finger. It was joined quickly by her other fingers.

"Making light," she said, smiling.

"Is that what you're trying to do?" Finnigan asked. "I thought you'd do something more impressive."

"Hey!" She laughed and swatted him with her hand, forcing the light to die out. "Baby steps. I don't want to blow your brains out by accident."

"That's just as well." He laughed and pushed back at her and they found their fingertips interlaced. Smiles spread across both their faces.

"Athena, I..."

"Shush," she said. "I just want to enjoy this."

"Enjoy what?" he asked.

"I told you to shut up," said Athena teasingly. "Enjoy the moment. You silly boy."

"It just feels so lovely."

Athena grinned. "Something like that." She took a deep breath and closed her eyes, wishing that life could always be so sweet and so simple as it was in this very moment.

But the moment was short lived. As questions and worries surfaced from what felt like a former life.

"What happens to the children who disappear from the earth realm?" Athena asked.

"I'm here, aren't I?" Finnigan asked. "I survived."

"You're fae as well as human," said Athena. "What happens to the others?"

"I was collected, very deliberately, despite my father's attempts to ward them off." There was a bitterness in Finnigan's tone. He clearly resented having been kidnapped by the fae and Athena could understand why.

"A little girl went missing the other day, do you know about her?"

"It's not really my area of expertise."

"But you know something. You must," said Athena. "What would the fae even want with human children?"

"That's not something I'm privy too," he replied. "I suspect it's something to do with building a stronger species."

"What now?"

"The high fae are all terribly inbred, you see, like fancy dog breeds or royalty in the human world. I don't understand exactly how, but I suspect the young humans are being studied."

"How ghastly," said Athena. "Do you mean in a lab?"

"Not like that," he replied. "Just...observed, I suppose."

"Still, that seems wrong," said Athena.

"They seem perfectly healthy, though," said Finnigan. "I stumble across them from time to time. They're all so young and beady eyed."

"They don't grow up?"

"No, not here. They look happy enough, though."

"I guess that's some comfort," said Athena. "But it's still terrible."

"There's a different kind of morality down here."

"So I gather," said Athena. "I thought I was about to be executed for not showing proper manners earlier."

Finnigan shrugged. "That wouldn't have been out of the question."

"Really?! Well, you'll have to give me a lesson in how to behave properly before we get much further," said Athena, propping herself more upright.

"Never give your full name to the fae," said Finnigan. "And try not to accept any gifts because it might get you trapped into servitude."

"I know all that." said Athena with a wave of her hand. "Or at least, I read about it in books, so I wasn't going to fall into any of those ridiculous traps. I'm not a fool."

Finnigan looked offended at Athena's comment, though she couldn't quite fathom why.

After some refreshments, consisting of tea and Jaffa Cakes from Athena's bag, they left the glade and continued on.

“Where are you taking me next?” Athena asked.

“Hopefully to somebody who can answer more of your questions,” said Finnigan.

“Still so cryptic.”

As they walked along the forest path, occasionally creatures flitted through the trees. Most of them were small and waiflike.

“What are they?” Athena asked.

“Various types of fae creatures,” said Finnigan. “You have many of them in your realm too. They're not usually visible, but you might find you can see them now you’ve been here. It was good you brought food with you. Human food will help to keep you grounded. It seems to have made you less pale at any rate.”

Athena blushed, feeling decidedly less pale. “I've never heard of Jaffa Cakes being considered so healthy,” she said.

Finnigan laughed.

“I do feel more grounded,” she reflected. “And my arms and legs look a bit more normal. Hey, do you think, whoever it is you're taking me to will know what happened to the missing children?”

“More than me,” said Finnigan.

“I wonder how long it's been since I left home,” Athena said, stretching her arms in the air. “I wonder if Mum's discovered I’m missing yet.”

“It’s hard to tell. Perhaps a week or two,” said Finnigan.

“What?!” Athena cried. “You're joking.”

“I might be wrong,” he said, though she couldn’t shake the feeling he was trying to placate her obvious distress.

“I'm going to be in so much trouble!” said Athena. “Maybe if I can find those kids, Mum will forgive me. Where do you think they keep them?”

“Probably near the castle,” said Finnigan. “So it’s a good job that’s where we’re headed.”

“I don't get it,” said Athena. “If they need humans so badly that they’re willing to steal children, why did they look down on me for being human?”

Finnigan laughed. “Have you met the fae? Have you seen how arrogant they are?”

Athena sighed. “I'm afraid so.”

“The thing is, human and fae relationships... well they’re not considered appropriate now,” said Finnigan. “But I heard that a long time ago, the fae would cross over into the human realm as often as they liked and steal potential mates, kidnapping them, bringing them back here.”

"That's awful," said Athena. "Are you saying they forced—"

"Not exactly. You know, they're so polite and can be quite charming. But I don't think the human world appreciated it so much. It's probably why they teamed up with the vamps, to stop the fae."

"Is *that* what happened?" Athena asked. "From what you said before, I thought the vampires were in the wrong."

"Well, you didn't hear it from me," said Finnigan. "Around here those bloodsuckers are always in the wrong, but, from spending time in the human world, I'd say both species are at fault in some way. Vamps are natural predators for us, but the fae have no real grounds to be sanctimonious. Don't tell anyone I said that."

"You're upset that they took you," she said.

Finnigan paled. "I never saw my father again. By the time my mother got bored with me and sent me back, he was gone. Decades had passed. There was nothing left of my old home."

"How awful," said Athena. "I'm sorry." She reached out and took his hand.

"It's not all bad," he said. "At least I got to live in this time and meet you."

Thirty-Eight

Rosemary stood at the kitchen bench, midway through a spell. Against her nature, she was trying her hardest to follow the instructions. She did her best to ignore the state of the house around her. In her single-minded determination, she'd turned much of the available space into a kind of lab – experimenting with potions and elements. She'd dragged equipment into the living area from Granny's tower room and other things she'd found in the dusty wings of the old house.

As she worked the spell, light began to shoot out from her fingertips like tiny lasers, entwining in front of her into a loose weave over the items she'd laid out – amethyst, sage, salt, and black pepper. This was one of the recipes from the book that Burk had given her, though Rosemary was unsure whether it had ever worked particularly well, let alone whether it would work now, given how outdated the information was.

She was interrupted by a knock at the door. The light disappeared from her hands. She sighed, thinking it was probably just Marjie, delivering her some lunch. She held up her hands to try again. But then she heard another knock. Not Marjie then. Not unless there was something she actually wanted to talk to Rosemary about in particular.

Marjie had been very good at respecting Rosemary's wishes to be left alone. She'd had few interruptions, though she continued to be well fed. She did wonder whether she was racking up such a huge tab of gratitude to her family friend and employer that she would never be able to repay her in a thousand years.

A more urgent knock sounded at the door.

"Fine," said Rosemary. "I'm coming."

She opened the door to see four young faces looking at her. Not smiling exactly, though there was something like excitement in their eyes. Was it fear?

"I'm Elise," said the girl with blue hair. "And this is Sam, Felix, and Deron."

Rosemary nodded. "Athena's school friends."

"Yes," the girl continued. "We're sorry to hear about Athena."

"How did you find out?" Rosemary asked in a guarded voice.

"News travels fast around here," said the boy with red hair and a cocky expression on his face who'd been introduced as Felix.

"So it does," said Rosemary. "How can I help you?"

"We're worried about Athena too," said Elise. "We want to know if there's any way we can help you."

"Thank you for the offer," said Rosemary. "But, as the most experienced magical beings in this town can't seem to help me, I'm not sure there's much use. I'm sorry."

"We want to go with you," said Sam, who matched the description Athena had given of her non-binary school friend.

"Go with me where?" Rosemary asked.

"You're going after her. Aren't you?" said Felix.

"It's hard enough for me to figure out how to get into the fae realm," said Rosemary sternly. "And I wouldn't want to take the risk of bringing other people's children there. It's too dangerous, so please stay as far away as possible."

"Elise has pixie heritage," said the other boy with dark hair.

"Shut up, Deron," said Elise. "I am not a pixie. You know that my mother is a naiad."

"I'm afraid I don't know what that is," said Rosemary. "I assume you're some sort of otherworldly creature."

"Something like that. I've never been to the fae realm," said Elise. "But my grandmother grew up there."

Rosemary leant forward in a conspiratorial manner and said, "Look, I mean it. I don't want to bring any of you into this. But if your people know anything that might help me, please let me know."

"The fae are good at keeping secrets, aren't they?" said Elise with an awkward smile. "Your best bet is the equinox, but I'm sure you already know that."

"That's what everyone keeps telling me," said Rosemary, pulling back and resuming her normal volume of speech. "The only problem is the ritual needs to be performed at the town square and I need to be there. Apparently, my powers are important to make it effective, to have a chance of bringing Gretchen back, or Athena..." Her voice trailed off as her breath caught in her throat, overwhelmed with grief.

"I might be able to help you there," said a high pitched voice coming from the side of the driveway. They all turned to see a girl with her hair held tightly in a bun.

"What are you doing here, Beryl?" Elise asked.

"I heard you talking in town. I knew that this was where you were going, and I followed you."

"Why? asked Felix.

"I don't have any particular affections for any of you, but as you know, I'm an accomplished witch, and my family...Well, my family knows a thing or two about magic, you might say."

Rosemary was getting distinct impressions that reminded her of her own nasty, snobbish cousin, Elamina. There was something quite snobby and snarky in Beryl's manner.

"So what are you doing here, then?" Rosemary asked. She eyed the girl warily.

"It's not good for the town that people go missing," Beryl said. Every word was laboured. "It creates a nuisance, and the fae need to be put in their place. My family – the Flarguans –helped to push them back a hundred years ago."

"So where are your parents? Do you think they could help?" Rosemary asked.

"They're out of town on business as usual, and no, I'm not sure whether they *would* help. They tend to be quite occupied with their own interests." Beryl's tone was icy, as if she was concealing pain.

Rosemary's voice softened. "Did you come here to help?" she asked Beryl.

The girl nodded curtly, as if she'd prefer not to be there at all. "There's a spell. It can help you move time and space, so that you can bring two points together. I've been thinking about this all week. It's no use to try to move the equinox ritual from where it's been performed for hundreds of years. That will only weaken its power. And the weakest point in the veil, as you probably know, is at Fin's Creek, where that little girl disappeared. It's a complicated spell, far more advanced than any of you could pull off, more advanced than anything I've ever done," she admitted glumly. "But it's worth a try."

"Where is it? Can you give it to me?" Rosemary asked.

"I can deliver you the instructions," said Beryl. "But it requires some unorthodox ingredients." She looked at Rosemary, clearly uncomfortable. "We have some of them around the house. But the key magical supplies are not accessible for me or my sisters. In fact, I don't even know if or where my parents keep things like that. If you happen to have contacts in high places with a lot of money, then this would be the time to call on them."

Contacts in high places with a lot of money...Rosemary's shoulders sagged even further as her cousins came to mind. "I could ask Elamina and Derse."

"Oh, you know the Bracewell family?" Beryl asked, raising an eyebrow.

"I have the misfortune of being related to them," said Rosemary.

Beryl gave her a curious look as if she'd misjudged her somehow. "Well, now would be a good time to call in any favours."

Rosemary laughed. "I don't think they would consider that they owe me any favours at all, despite the fact that I restored the family magic, but they did seem to take a liking to Athena. Maybe they will help," she said, although in the back of her mind, she wondered, *at what price*?

She pushed that worry away, knowing that any price would be worth it if it brought her daughter back safely.

"Alright," said Beryl. "I'll bring you the spell and a few of the ingredients. I'm not going to help you cast it."

"And I don't want you to, either," said Rosemary. "Children should stay away from this, Beryl." All the other teens on her doorstep looked offended. "Look, I don't mean this as an insult. It's just too dangerous."

"Oh yeah?" said Felix. "And what exactly do you plan on doing to find Athena once you get to the fae realm?"

"Excuse me?" said Rosemary.

"What's your plan?" he asked, leaning against the doorframe. "You're just going to wander there and start calling out for her?"

"I've been doing what I can to prepare," Rosemary said.

"Well, you keep doing that," said Felix. "But bear in mind that you might just need us."

Thirty-Nine

As soon as Beryl had arrived the next day with the instructions for the spatial relocating spell, Rosemary quickly fired off an email to her cousin Elamina asking for help. She'd found the email address among Granny's contacts and hoped that it was still a current one. She also hoped that her irritating cousins would actually turn out to be useful for a change.

With no time to waste, Rosemary set to work, gathering the spell ingredients that she knew were the simple ones to find. To her surprise, later that day a silver Rolls Royce pulled up the driveway.

Rosemary went out to meet it to see that there were no passengers, just a driver. Rosemary recognised him from her cousins' previous visit.

"The mistress wanted me to deliver this parcel to you," he said in a slightly disapproving tone. He held out a square-shaped package wrapped in inconspicuous brown paper and tied with twine.

"Not Elamina's usual style at all," said Rosemary.

"There's a note," he said as Rosemary took the package.

He handed over a rather elaborate gold and purple envelope.

"That's more like it," she muttered, wondering whether the brown paper of the package was supposed to be a clever disguise to make it look less conspicuous.

"Thank you," Rosemary said to the driver. He nodded and drove away.

Rosemary went back into the house. She closed the door behind her and leant against it, feeling her heart beating in her chest. She was one step closer, hopefully, to finding her daughter.

"What's all the fuss about, then?" said Granny, appearing in the mirror on the wall across from where Rosemary stood.

"Your other granddaughter is helping me get Athena back," said Rosemary.

"You must have been desperate to call in a favour from her," said Granny.

"Of course I'm desperate," said Rosemary. "Didn't you say you were trying to help us?"

"I was at first, but then I thought about it."

Rosemary stared daggers at her grandmother's ghost. "You thought what exactly?"

"That as she went willingly, it wasn't really my place."

"How can you say that?" Rosemary asked. "She's been gone for a week!"

"You don't think she'll just wander back in at any moment?" Granny asked. "Like I said, she's just gone for a romp with a boy."

"Stop calling it a romp! She's far too young to be doing that!" said Rosemary.

"I wasn't implying any explicit details," said Granny. "But surely, if she can get to the fae realm because of her heritage, she should be able to get out again."

"We don't know that Athena can get back by herself," said Rosemary. "Tell me, how did you help to get Sherry back all those years ago?"

"Is that what you've heard?" Granny said. "The funny thing is, all I did was perform the ritual properly at the equinox. Sherry showed up at Fin's Creek. She must have done something herself at the same time in order to get out, only she'd never tell me what. I don't think she could."

Rosemary was appalled. She'd been hoping Granny could shed more light on what had worked in the past. "You're infuriatingly unhelpful!" she said.

"I still think you're overreacting," said Granny. "When I was her age I ran off with a rather handsome wolf shifter and didn't come back for a month!"

"Spare me the details!"

"All I'm saying is things have a way of working themselves out."

"I admire your optimism," said Rosemary, "but I'm not taking any chances." She opened the envelope from Elamina.

My dear tragic cousin, read the refined loopy handwriting. *I have gone to quite some trouble to source the ingredients that you seek. Unfortunately there was one item that is exceedingly rare and highly illegal in the magical world due to its danger, but you should find everything else in this box. Best of luck in figuring out what to do with all these items. I take it the spell is rather complex, and well beyond your abilities. I'm afraid it won't work at all unless you can source the remaining item. However, since I have gone to great trouble, you surely must agree that you're now indebted to us, and please believe me when I tell you that we intend very much to recall the favour.*

Rosemary gulped. "What a fancy way of saying, you owe me one," she said to herself.

"Well, I'm just glad that you're finally practicing your magic," said Granny. "I forgot to mention, I was quite impressed with that plant growing trick."

"And you were no help at all," said Rosemary.

"Well, what do you expect? I'm dead!" said Granny, raising her arms. "And have far better things to do, but I'm glad you have everything under control here." And with a little pop, she was gone.

Rosemary sighed. Being dead sure seemed to have the effect of making Granny less concerned with the perils of the mortal world.

She took the package to the dining room table and opened it up, finding that it did indeed contain the ingredients she'd asked her cousin for. They were packaged elegantly in glass vials and little wooden boxes. She checked them against the list. All the items were accounted for except for werewolf blood.

"And it just so happens that I know where to get some of that," she said to herself.

Rosemary hadn't seen Liam since she'd barged into his shop and been attacked, nor had she returned the two phone calls he'd made to her, as she'd had other things on her mind. This seemed like as good a time as any to pay him a visit. The full moon had passed, so she felt comfortable that he would be in human form.

She pulled up in the car outside his shop. The lights were on, and there didn't seem to be any customers milling about.

Perfect.

She got out and made her way inside.

The doorbell tinkled and Liam came out from the back room to stand behind the counter. "Rosemary!" he said. "What a surprise. I...thank you for coming. Have you had a chance to consider my offer?"

"Your offer for me to help you with your...situation?" Rosemary asked. "It just so happens I have a proposition for you."

"Okay, good!" Liam interlaced his fingers nervously. "What is it?"

"I need your blood," she said.

"My...my blood?" Liam asked. "Rosemary, it's not a good idea to try to turn yourself, or anyone else for that matter, into a werewolf."

"No. That is not what I mean," said Rosemary. "You might have heard Athena has gone missing."

"I heard a rumour," said Liam. "I didn't realise it was true."

"She's gone to the fae realm and the only way that I can figure out to get across there to fetch her back involves very specific timing and a very specific spell with very, very specific ingredients."

"You have a spell that requires *my* blood?" Liam asked.

"Werewolf blood," said Rosemary. "It's not specific to a particular werewolf, or to you. The spell is old, and it requires a whole lot of weird ingredients like ground narwal horn and roasted newt, hair from a dryad...odd things from a bunch of magical creatures."

"You're calling me a creature now?"

"Well, I don't know what to call you. But apparently everything we say is wrong and offensive, so maybe I'll just carry on talking all day and upset everyone else in the town while I'm at it," said Rosemary.

"I'm afraid it's impossible," said Liam.

"Oh no, I really could ramble on all day, just watch," said Rosemary.

"Not that. Getting my blood is impossible," Liam explained. "And not only is it expressly prohibited in the magical world, it's extremely dangerous. I've had to use a number of protections on myself so that I don't accidentally infect anyone if I get a paper cut."

"So it's your blood that causes the magical disease to spread?"

Liam shrugged. "It's a virus that can be spread through a number of different means. The most common is a bite."

Rosemary gave him a peculiar look. "Do you protect your teeth as well, then?"

"Of course," Liam said. "I've employed every magical protection that I could work up on my own. I haven't told anyone else. Not even Sherry, though she does look at me curiously, when I'm sick so often."

"There are obviously a lot of prejudices out there in the community," said Rosemary. "I want you to know that I don't have any of those myself, being quite frankly too naive to this entire world to know the difference between a werewolf, or shifter, or dryad, or anything else."

"That's actually somewhat reassuring, believe it or not," said Liam.

"Let me continue," said Rosemary. "I need to do whatever I can to get to the fae realm on the off-chance that I can get my daughter back. There are lots of risks and I might fail completely, but I have to try. I have to exhaust every possible option."

"Look, I get it," said Liam.

They stood for a moment in silence. Rosemary looked down at her feet, wondering what she could do or say to convince him.

Finally, Liam spoke. "I can...I can help you."

"Thank you so much," said Rosemary.

"On one condition."

"Name it."

"I need you to help me figure out how to get this...condition...under control."

Rosemary started to protest. She didn't have the time for this.

"Not right now," he said. "I mean, your focus is on your daughter. I get it, but please, at some point, fairly soon, I would really like for you to figure out if you can use your powers to stop this nightmare or at least keep it under control."

"Liam, I'll do what I can."

"You didn't sound like you would the other day."

"I was in shock," said Rosemary defensively. "What do you expect? You'd just attacked me as a great big wolfy beast."

"Okay. I get it," said Liam. "But I have your word?"

"Fine, anything," said Rosemary. "If I survive this, I'll help you."

Liam eyed her cautiously.

"Okay," he said. He closed his eyes as if mentally preparing himself, then he waved the palm of his right hand over his left. Rosemary watched as a pattern of shadows flowed out over the area. He took a letter opener that looked like a miniature sword from the drawer in front of him and raised it.

"Wait a minute," said Rosemary. "You're going to bleed all over the place if you stab yourself like that. Let me get something."

She reached into her handbag where she'd had the foresight to bring some of Granny's glass vials and corks to fit them.

"Here." She passed him a wide-lipped vessel.

"Thank you," Liam said, placing it down on the desk in front of him. He leaned over and pierced the skin on his palm. Oddly thick dark red blood oozed into the glass.

"Be very careful with this," he said, finishing up and handing the vial to Rosemary.

"I will," she reassured him.

She turned to go. Then, remembering her manners, she glanced back. "Liam. Thank you," she said.

"And thank *you*," Liam replied. "Not just for what you've promised and bargained for, but for keeping my secret."

"It's not mine to tell," she said.

She made her way back to the car with a lightness in her chest for the first time since Athena had disappeared. She hadn't solved the entire puzzle yet, but she had all the ingredients to help her get into the world her daughter had been taken to. There was nothing in her way. At least nothing that wouldn't move with a good hard metaphorical kick.

Forty

It was finally that time of year. The air seemed to thicken in anticipation, though the weather was fine. The morning of the equinox dawned crystal clear skies.

Rosemary arrived at the Ostara ritual an hour early to find that Ferg had already set up the hundreds of tulips she'd helped to grow. He'd collected them from her house with a group of his eccentric volunteers earlier that day before Rosemary had gone to Fin's Creek to place especially enchanted crystals in a circle there for the spell.

She'd dressed for travel, with her sturdy leather boots and warm fleece-lined coat. She was even wearing the bundle around her neck that Athena had insisted she make a few weeks earlier to protect her from Dain's influence. It was a long shot, but she was hoping the protection might extend not just to her ex's fae magic, but also to fae, more generally. She also carried a number of other hopefully-useful-items.

She had everything she needed in her large handbag, or at least everything she could think of. A backpack would have been more practical, but a handbag seemed less conspicuous. The ingredients for Beryl's spell, once prepared, amounted to only a small volume and didn't take up much space. She also had a few other items that she'd prepared to help her get in and out of the fae realm from the recipes in the book that Burk had given her.

"You're dressed awfully casually for a ritual," said Ferg. He was wearing a pale blue-and-pink-striped cloak with midnight blue robes underneath.

"And you're looking very formal," said Rosemary, trying to make polite small talk while her mind was clearly in another place entirely.

"I am," said Ferg proudly.

"I've been doing some research." Rosemary tried to sound casual. "In Granny's library, I found some useful additions for the equinox ritual." It was true that she'd scoured Granny's books, but she'd only found a few useful tips for dealing with fae.

"Oh yes," said Ferg, sounding interested.

"Well, you said you wanted me to lend my family's magic for the equinox ritual, and I did my research, so I'm just going to place these crystals over here in a little circle right in the middle. And these small bundles go on the outside."

"This is very unorthodox," said Ferg. "Your grandmother never did any of this."

"Well, you know, I don't want to take my chances."

"And how exactly do you think it will help convey our blessings to the Goddess and the guardians of all the other worlds, and especially to the fae realm, in the hopes that they grant us their good favour?"

It sounded a bit flaky to Rosemary. "I'm sure it will," she said.

She continued preparing in accordance with Beryl's family's spell on the off-chance that Ferg's grand notions of the Goddess conveying her favour wasn't enough to get her daughter back.

By the time she'd finished setting up, a bunch of people, many of them dressed in robes, had started to arrive. They milled around the circle.

Rosemary recognised a number of familiar faces, including the teenagers who'd visited her house. *Don't get any ideas*, she thought, giving them a suspicious look.

The beginning of the equinox ritual seemed quite similar to the last one that Rosemary had witnessed, though she hardly paid attention. The quarters were called and the circle was cast. A woman with long wavy blonde hair stood in the centre, and said some beautifully crafted words about the Goddess Eostre. Rosemary registered that it was lovely and poetic, but her main concentration remained focused on what she needed to do next.

As part of the ritual, a group of young children walked around with baskets of dyed eggs, handing them out to the circle participants. Rosemary smiled as she took the pink and blue painted item, finding that it was heavier than she expected. It was indeed a hardboiled egg rather than a hollow shell. She tucked it into her pocket because she knew she'd need her hands free.

For the next part of the ritual Ferg nodded to her. It was her turn.

"Now, if everyone will close their eyes," Rosemary said, "and chant with me: *the earth, the air, the fire, the water.*"

The circle around her did as they were told, except the young children among them who looked on with curiosity as Rosemary stepped into the centre between her carefully laid crystals. She held out her hands and focused her energy, muttering the memorised chant, from the spell, which was drowned out by the chanting around her.

This had been part of her plan to distract everyone from the sneaky magic she had to do. But at the same time, she could feel the energy from the chanting contributing to her own power, emanating out into the centre of the circle and weaving around the light that began to shine from her fingertips. It lit up an intricate network between the crystals on the ground. Rosemary stepped into the centre and raised her arms.

She said the final words of the spell, commanding the magic to life.

Silence fell around her, though she could tell the circle of people were still chanting.

Rosemary waited with bated breath as the light between the crystals shone brighter.

A ring of dark blue swept up around in the air in front of her. It formed a portal with gaseous flame-like patterns around its outside. Ripples swam across its inky black surface.

She could see the willow trees surrounding the portal, transparent, just as she could see the circle behind of the townsfolk who were still chanting.

"This is it," she said to herself.

She'd done it. She'd created the spatial warp needed, connecting Fin's Creek and the centre of the town. Both were now temporarily in the same place.

She took a deep breath and stepped through, glancing back, only to see that others were following her.

"No!" Rosemary cried out.

It was too late. Sherry tumbled through, giving Rosemary a push, followed by Athena's school friends.

"No..." Rosemary tried to push them back into the earth realm.

It was too late.

The portal closed, but they weren't in Fin's Creek or the town centre. They all looked around, finding themselves surrounded by an eerie violet light.

"So this is the fae realm," said Felix, looking around.

"Why did you follow me?" Rosemary asked. "I told you to stay away. It's too dangerous."

"We needed to help Athena," said Elise.

"And we're not convinced that you know what you're doing," Felix added.

"Thanks very much for the vote of confidence." Rosemary turned away from the teens in exasperation. One teenager was more than enough, and now she had four on her hands, though right now there were bigger problems.

"Sherry," Rosemary said, taking hold of the woman's shoulders.

Sherry still had the otherworldly gleam in her eye.

"Sherry, did you take my necklace?"

"It was the only way," she said. "I'm sorry, Rosemary, I needed to come through. I'm not a powerful witch like you or a young one like these teens. I wouldn't have been able to follow without it."

"But why?" Rosemary asked. "I thought you hated this place."

"I needed to come back for her. I promised."

"Your friend?" Rosemary said.

"You know about Mei?" said Sherry in shock. "Everyone forgot her. Even her family. It was like how no one remembered me when I came back. Like I didn't exist. But I remembered everything. I could never forget my friend."

"My granny found a newspaper clipping just recently," said Rosemary. "The little girl, she disappeared when you did."

"I promised her I'd come back," said Sherry. "And now that I have, I'm not going to leave without her."

Forty-One

Everything was different – the sounds, the scents, the creatures. As they continued their journey through the fae realm, Athena marvelled at the physical terrain that unfolded around them. The shimmering plants and fungus seemed larger than life and came in all different colours. Enchanting mists swirled around them in spiralling patterns.

"Can you feel it?" Finnigan said.

"Feel what?" Athena asked.

"You belong here."

Athena winced, feeling the truth in his words but also recalling her mother and everyone she cared about back in the earth realm. Her old life seemed like a distant memory.

"How long have we been away?" she asked again.

Finnigan shrugged. "Not long."

"I think I should get back," said Athena. "It feels like it's all slipping away from me. Everything human, everything that I knew."

"If you need some grounding just eat some more of the human food you brought with you."

Athena reached into her bag for her Jaffa Cakes, only to find them crumble into dust in her hand. "What happened?" she asked. "I can't imagine them being so stale. Surely I only opened the pack a few hours ago. It shouldn't have changed that much."

"Things work differently here," said Finnigan. "Maybe it reacted to the air."

Athena opened a bag of crisps to find them in the usual condition. She ate the entire bag just in case, offering some to Finnigan, though he declined.

"You don't need to eat human food?"

"I spend most of my time here," Finnigan said. "I don't belong in the human world. Not anymore." A sad look crossed his face and Athena felt sorry for him, but he didn't seem to want to talk about it, so they continued walking on in silence.

"Okay. I really think I should turn back," she said again as mist grew thicker around them. "I need to go home."

"There's something you need to see first," said Finnigan, his voice sounding a little anxious.

"Alright," said Athena. "Then we'll go home. You promise?"

He nodded. "I intend to return to the earth realm as quickly as possible. I just need to show you something first."

Athena had an uneasy feeling, but she chose to follow him, not knowing how to navigate alone through the thick mist. A structure came into view ahead of them that looked like it was composed of dozens of enormous mushrooms.

"What is this?" Athena asked.

"The castle of West Eloria," said Finnigan.

"Is that what you wanted to show me?"

"Yes, I just have to introduce you to someone. It'll make everything clearer."

Athena hesitated.

"You'll love this. And besides," Finnigan coaxed, "the missing girl is probably here."

Athena's intuition was flaring. Something wasn't right, but what choice did she have? She didn't know how to navigate the fae realm alone, and besides, finding Gretchen and returning her to Myrtlewood would do a lot to appease her mother, who was going to be dreadfully mad.

Athena followed Finnigan uneasily towards the strange building.

The large doorway ahead looked to be made of silvery tree bark.

"You wanted to see what it was like inside a fae building," Finnigan said mischievously.

"I did, didn't I?" said Athena, marvelling at the odd organic architecture. "I didn't realise that we'd go to an actual castle."

"Here." He took her hand and pressed his other hand to the door. It opened, leading to grand hall. Athena walked in, holding Finnigan's hand.

The door closed behind them, jolting Athena.

At the other end of the building stood an enormous, glimmering throne set high up. It was surrounded by numerous other chairs and elaborate ornaments of fae creatures. As they neared, Athena could make out a figure on the throne with tumbling silver hair and a crown of flowers and leaves. Her dress too looked as if it were made entirely of rosebuds and spring blossoms.

"She's beautiful," Athena whispered as they walked closer.

When they got to be a few metres away, Finnigan bowed and Athena followed suit.

"Finnigan," said the woman who, Athena guessed, was none other than the Countess of West Eloria Finnigan had mentioned earlier.

"*What* have you brought me?"

"A halfling," said Finnigan.

Halfling? Athena shivered, feeling uncomfortable at the way he'd referred to her, noting that many of the other chairs on both sides of the throne were filled with powerful looking fae and flanked by guards.

"A halfling, yes," said the countess with scorn in her voice. Athena immediately disliked her.

"Not just any halfling," said Finnigan. "I do believe that her father is none other than the Queen's son, Prince Dain."

Prince! Dain! Athena was stunned. My deadbeat dad is not only fae, but he's also a prince?!

A tiny gasp escaped the countess's mouth and she clapped in excitement, causing a flurry of butterflies to fly up from her hands. Her eyes flared with a preternatural glow as she looked at Athena.

"You're telling me," said the countess, "that the prince got up to mischief on his little earth realm escapade? Oh my! You have done well, Finnigan. She's a pretty creature, even if she is only half fae."

Athena grimaced. Finnigan had told her it was rude to refer to people as half fae, but that obviously didn't apply to the countess. The way they were talking made her progressively more anxious. All she knew about fae politics was that it was complex, and the fact that her father was missing did not bode well with the news he was some kind of royalty.

"Finnigan, what is all this about?" Athena asked.

"Athena is special," said Finnigan. "She's not just half fae. Her mother is from a powerful witching family."

"Oh, indeed, this is a worthy prize!" The countess shrieked and stood up from her throne.

Athena turned to the boy she thought she knew.

There was a roaring in her head that eclipsed everything else as the realisation sunk in.

"You!" She looked at Finnigan. "You set me up. All along you *were* just a filthy spy. You captured me and played me for a fool. I'm some kind of prize to you? So you'll be rewarded by the fae? Is that it?"

Finnigan raised his arms as if to protest. "Athena..."

"How could you do this?!" Athena yelled.

Finnigan's face was clouded with unreadable emotion. "I had to. I was bound by the countess. Indentured...to carry out her will."

Athena sensed all previous feelings she'd had for the boy wither into bitterness and disgust. "And I suppose you had no free will of your own? Wait a minute, you planned this the whole time, didn't you? All of it. You cast that illusion on our house. So that Mum would know it was fae who were after me. This is all part of a bigger plot."

A smile crept across his face. "I was rather clever, wasn't I?"

Athena gasped. "It was you!" she glared at Finnigan. "You kidnapped my father!"

"I think of it more as 'guiding him back home'," said Finnigan. "He had been missing for a long time..."

"Don't tell me you also stole our old car?"

Finnigan shrugged. "I might have."

"You deceived us. But fae can't lie!"

The countess threw her head back and crowed with laughter. "Oh, that's such a good one," she said. "I absolutely love how humans still believe that rubbish. Of course we can lie!"

The dread was setting in, along with a cloudy feeling. Athena rubbed her eyes as if trying to wake up from a bad dream. "I don't understand," she said. "I need the truth. Tell me what's really going on here. Tell me what it is you're trying to do."

"Now, why would he go and do a silly thing like that?" said the countess. "You already know far too much. You cannot ever return to the human realm. We will keep you right here."

"No!" Athena cried as guards crashed forward, surrounding her. "You will not take me. You will *not* capture me!"

The fae guards were bulky and dressed in the red uniforms Athena recognised from the day shift at the clerk's office. They were armed with spears and bows. She closed her eyes, determined that everything she had would go into this fight.

She could feel them drawing nearer, her hope of escape diminishing, but her determination burning strong. Her sense of betrayal, anxiety, fear, and rage was bottling up inside. There was a roaring in her ears as the pressure became too much.

Just as a hand reached out for her, she released the tension she'd been holding.

A surprising spurt of bright light shot from Athena's fingertips, bursting out to fill the room.

All the creatures froze still, like statues, except Finnigan and the countess herself.

"No! Grab her!" the countess cried.

"No freaking way," said Athena, and she ran towards the nearest door, at the side of the throne room.

She busted through to find long winding passages. Wishing she'd had the foresight to run back outside instead, now she found herself trapped in the countess's castle, and it was only a matter of time before more guards or soldiers, or worse, came to attack her.

Footsteps sounded after Athena as she ran down the passageway. She had no idea of what she'd done before to freeze the guards. It had been some kind of automatic self-defence, but at least it was magic. *Real magic.*

Still, her energy seem to be flagging. She worried she'd have nothing left to fight off another attack.

She opened the door to what looked like a storeroom filled with boxes. Her heart thudded in her chest as she closed the door behind her quietly, then snuck in and hid behind a large stack. It would only be a matter of time before they found her.

She closed her eyes, wondering whether there was anyone who could help her now. She recalled what Finnigan had said about how she could communicate telepathically in a controlled way, getting herself to only be heard by people she wanted to communicate with.

It was a stab in the dark, but she'd run out of other options. There was nothing else she could think of. She had to try, even though she had no idea whether there were any friendly forces in the entire realm, or whether it was possible to talk to anyone back in the human world...her *own* world.

My real home.

Athena focused her mind outwards, calling out to anyone who genuinely had her best interests at heart, an ally, anyone who she could consider friendly.

To her astonishment, a voice called back.

I'LL HELP YOU, if you can help me.

Who are you? Athena asked, wondering whether it was possible her communication had been intercepted by some fae servant of the countess, trying to draw her out.

I'm locked in the northern tower.

How do I know I can trust you? Athena asked.

Athena, it's Dad.

Dad? Athena responded in surprise. What are you doing here?

The cogs started to turn in her mind. Of course he was here. Finnigan had captured him and brought him here. The countess had imprisoned her father in much the same way she intended to imprison Athena.

I've been stuck here for weeks, possibly months, Dain replied. *The countess has held me hostage.*

You probably deserve it, said Athena drily. Her father always brought trouble.

I might do. I don't know the difference anymore. I just...I want to help you, even if it means risking my life. I owe you this.

You're right. You owe me this, said Athena. *Mum might forget how terrible you are and forgive you, but I don't.*

Fair enough, said her father. *Come and find me. I'll send a signal.*

Athena felt a low pulse like sonar through her chest, pulling her in a particular direction.

Her father was the last person she wanted to seek help from. In this situation, he might also be the only person who could help. Sure, she had been let down by him for years, but it was nothing compared to the fresh sting of very deliberate and wilful betrayal from the boy she'd thought she could trust.

Mum was right, Athena thought to herself. *We do have bad taste in men in this family.*

Hey, I heard that, said her father in her mind.

Athena's lips curled into a smile. There was something totally absurd about the situation, though it shouldn't be at all funny.

She followed the pulse, carefully darting along passageways, avoiding the scurrying fae who would no doubt be searching for her. They probably thought she was trying to escape, not running to one of the tallest towers, so at least she had that to her advantage.

After a while of scurrying around the castle, Athena found the door to the mushroom tower only to see that it was bolted with a heavy padlock.

Athena knocked softly on the door. "Dad, I'm here. It's locked."

"You can get through the lock, Athena. You're powerful. Use your fae magic," said Dain.

"I don't know how," Athena said.

"Just close your eyes and imagine the lock turning and...uhhh...twiddle your fingers around."

"Do I have to do that part?" Athena asked.

"No, but it'll help you to concentrate."

Athena did as instructed, and to her surprise, she heard a subtle click. The door sprung open, and for the first time in many months Athena laid eyes on her father.

He looked far paler and skinnier than usual. And she wasn't sure if that was just because he'd been in the fae realm for some time or whether his captors had also been starving him.

"Why are you locked up like this?" Athena asked, observing the shackles around Dain's wrists and ankles. "What did you do?"

"I didn't do anything," he replied defensively. "They kidnapped me. Look, Athena I know I haven't been a good father. You probably realise this by now...but I'm fae."

"You don't say," said Athena, observing her father in his fully fae form for the first time in her life. "I never would have guessed, despite your slender limbs and pointy ears."

"I know I haven't done anything to deserve your trust. But there's nothing more that I want right now than to help you."

"And what about Mum?"

"Is she here too?" he asked, surprised.

"No, forget it," said Athena. "We can talk about Mum later. Can you help me get out of here?"

"I can," said Dain. "At least, I can help a little. I don't know how to get back through to the earth realm alone."

"Seriously?!"

"There are a lot of protections put up against the fae," said Dain.

"Against the fae?" Athena asked. "I thought the protections were put up by the fae against the vampires."

"It's more complicated than that," said Dain. "The only way that I was able to escape this realm, many years ago, was because I followed a little girl back through on the equinox."

"But Finnigan could get through easily."

Dain scowled. "Yes, but Finnigan is part human like you. The little girl I followed was human. I helped her to tear a hole in the fae side of the veil, and it worked...with the help of her human magic. We needed both to get through. She helped me escape, though she never saw me. I'm thinking that, with your human side, we might be able to do the same."

"How do I get you out of the shackles?" Athena asked.

"It's complicated magic," said Dain. "I don't know. Do your best, or your worst."

She held up her hands, willing the shackles to open. Sparks flew in front of her and they clicked open immediately.

Dain looked astonished. "How did you do that?"

"I don't know!"

"That's your grandmother's magic!" said Dain. "That's the Thorn family magic. I thought it was hidden and bound."

"How do you know about all that?" Athena asked suspiciously. "Oh, never mind. Let's just get out of here."

She managed to break her father out of the rest of his shackles without too much magical effort.

"Thanks," said Dain. "Look, I'm not very strong right now. I haven't been fed properly."

"Can you eat human food?" Athena asked.

"Not right now. It would make me ill. I have to get used to it slowly."

"I can't really help you, then," said Athena.

"It's all right," said Dain. "I've got enough energy to do this and I can forage some berries on the way."

"Do what?" Athena asked.

"It's like teleportation."

"You can teleport!"

"Only in this realm. Quick. There's no more time for chit-chat. Take hold of my hands."

Footstep sounded in the corridor outside.

"Now!" he commanded.

Athena reached for her father's hands.

"Close your eyes," he said.

She did. It felt as if a wind whipped around them in that room, and when she opened her eyes again they were in the forest, surrounded by trees that glowed in the violet light.

Forty-Two

"Are you okay?" Rosemary asked Sherry. She was looking peakish.

"I'll be fine," Sherry replied. "Let's just go. We need to find them."

"Can you give my necklace back first?" The brittleness in Rosemary's voice made Sherry stiffen.

"I would," said Sherry, "but I don't think I'll survive here for long without it giving me the magical boost."

"What about these children?" Rosemary asked. "Will they survive?"

"Everyone should eat one of these," said Sam, holding up some small pink cupcakes.

"What is it?" Felix asked.

"Maam made these cakes. She said they helped people go into the—"

"Wait a minute," said Rosemary, rummaging in her handbag and producing a small bag of baked goods. "Those look a lot like these ones that I made. How did your Mum get her hands on the books that the vampires had made about the fae?"

Sam laughed. "Where do you think the vampires got the information from? People always underestimate folk magic. Sometimes it's the simple things that work the best."

Rosemary opened her own bag, feeling slightly woozy herself. She took some cake and offered the rest around.

"No offense, lady," said Felix, "but I think Sam's ones look better. They're not all burnt."

Rosemary glared at him.

"We don't have time for bickering over baking," said Sherry. "How are we going to find them?"

"I have a locator spell," Rosemary replied. "It's supposed to track down humans, and I hope it works on Athena."

"Why wouldn't it?" Sherry asked.

"Never mind," said Elise, and Rosemary got the impression she knew more about Athena's heritage than Rosemary did. "We'll have to hope it works at all in the fae realm," Elise continued.

Rosemary brushed away her annoyance about being left in the dark. She tried to cast the spell by muttering the incantation and wiggling her fingers. There was a tiny poof but nothing else happened.

"Oh blast!"

She attempted it several more times to no avail.

"Let me try?" Elise suggested. Rosemary grudgingly handed over the crumpled piece of paper with the instructions on it. Elise and Sam looked it over, muttering to each other. Felix tried to weigh in, but his suggestions of adding more 'zazz' were declined.

Rosemary felt a little bit as she did with new technology, which young people seemed to always be so adept at.

"Okay, here goes," said Elise. She held out her hand and waved her fingers about in a complex pattern unlike Rosemary's attempts, saying the chant for the spell in a lower tone. A little glowing blue light appeared in front of her, shaped like a small diamond.

"I think it will help if we all concentrate on it, give it more energy."

They stood in silence, focusing.

The diamond began to glow brighter. It bopped in mid-air and then began to move through the trees.

"I think we're supposed to follow it," Sam said, taking off at a run.

Felix, quick as lightening, transformed into a fox and bolted ahead. *That's right,* Rosemary recalled. *Athena said he was a shifter.*

She and the others followed through the forest.

The light was moving rather quickly.

As they continued, the terrain became more rugged. Huge mossy rocks dotted their path that seemed to glow in various shades of pastel.

“This one smells like lemon sherbet,” said Sam. “I almost want to lick it.”

“Don’t!” Elise cried.

“I’m not that stupid.”

A yelp sounded from Felix. Clearly, in his fox form, he hadn’t been able to resist the appetising scent. They gathered around him as he writhed on the ground, peach coloured bumps popping up all over his furry body.

“Get him to water!” Sam said decisively.

“Why?” Rosemary asked.

“Just folk knowledge,” said Sam. “Maam always said, with otherworldly magic, water helps things flow through. I don’t know if it will work...”

“It’s worth a shot. I have water in my bag, here,” said Rosemary, holding out her drink bottle.

“No, it has to be running water,” said Sam.

“I don’t know if such a thing exists around here,” said Sherry, sounding rather dazed. “Or even exists at all. What exists? What does that word really mean?”

Rosemary ignored Sherry’s deranged rambles. This was serious. They needed to act fast.

“If only he could talk,” said Elise. “He’d have his fox hearing, but even if he can understand us I don’t think he’s in any state to move.” She turned to Deron and gave him a meaningful look. “What do you think?”

“Worth a try,” Deron replied.

“What is—?” Rosemary asked, but before she could continue what had built up to be a rampaging monologue of questions in her mind she gasped.

Deron was sprouting fur, all over his body.

“Not you too!” Rosemary said, turning to Elise. “Which thing did he lick?”

“Just wait,” said Elise, placing a calming hand on Rosemary’s forearm.

Rosemary watched in astonishment as Deron, who was already reasonably tall, puffed out and grew two feet.

“Oh, I see, another shifter,” Rosemary muttered.

Standing in front of them was a black bear. He growled, making the hairs on Rosemary’s arms stand up on end. Then, she watched as he picked up the writhing spotty fox in his arms and began to run.

“What about the diamond?” Sherry called out as they all followed. “Shiny, shiny diamond!”

“One thing at a time,” said Rosemary.

Running in the fae realm felt a lot like moving through water, but at a faster pace. The effect gave her motion sickness.

Sure enough, up ahead a stream appeared. Deron was already there by the time they arrived, lowering Felix into the running water.

They watched with baited breath, not daring to express the possibility that fae realm water, with its otherworldly violet glow, might not have the desired effect, but might in fact do something even worse.

After a moment, Felix stopped writhing and became unnaturally still.

"Is the poor little dilly-dally going to be okay?" Sherry asked.

"Shush," said Rosemary, unsure if she was seeking silence or trying to soothe Sherry and indeed herself.

The spots were fading from Felix's body, and he'd transformed back into human form, but other than that, he remained still, carefully held by the friendly bear.

"Felix," Elise said gently. "Can you hear me?"

Rosemary's mind was racing with anxiety. What on earth was she going to tell the parents of these children whose lives she'd inadvertently endangered?

"Felix!" said Sam in a booming voice. "Time to wake up now!"

Felix coughed and spluttered and then grinned. "That was an adventure!" he said.

Elise looked daggers at him.

"Do not lick anything!" she said as they prepared to continue on. "Do not even touch anything unless I say so."

"Yes, ma'am," he said cheekily.

"It's not funny," said Sam. "We were worried, you could have—"

"Alright, I get it. I'm sorry for licking the peachy moss. I'll be more careful."

"Do you think he'll be able to return?" Rosemary asked. "I read that if you eat here you can't leave the realm."

"Who knows," said Sam. "Let's hope that only applies to food offered by the fae, not random moss. Or that it's just nonsense."

Rosemary crossed her fingers and muttered her own private spell, with the intention they'd all get out of the realm safely.

Fortunately, the shining diamond they'd summoned earlier had followed them. It hovered in the air patiently, waiting to lead them on.

Rosemary felt famished all of a sudden, only she didn't feel like the special shortbread that Sam was passing around to the others, or any of the baking she'd prepared either. She needed something more substantial. She reached into her pocket and found the egg from the ritual. *How convenient,* she thought, and ate it, glad for the protein boost.

They continued through the forest, careful to avoid any creatures coming their way, and definitely not licking anything.

After what felt like hours they stumbled across an enormous mushroom speckled with violet and lime green dots. It was as wide as a house, and seemed to be fitted with windows and doors.

The diamond hovered in the air above the arched front door.

They approached cautiously.

"It's locked," said Sam.

"How do we get in?" Rosemary asked.

"I think Felix will know how to handle this," said Elise, looking towards the mischievous boy who seemed to have recovered from his earlier mishap. "He always seems to know how to break into places he's not supposed to be."

"Stand back, ladies," said Felix.

"Fine, as long as you stop calling us that," said Rosemary. Sam gave her a grateful look, as did Deron.

Felix held out his hands. The lock cracked open, sending sparks flying.

Rosemary flinched as sparks hit her.

"I told you to stand back," said Felix.

The door swung open and inside, in the low light emitted from the crystal chandeliers above them, shone the faces of half a dozen young children.

Forty-Three

The sky above them had darkened to deep purple, but the trees seemed to glow in a silvery light. Athena would have appreciated the effervescent beauty if it wasn't for the impending doom. "How do we get through the veil?" she asked her father.

"You'd know better than I do," said Dain.

"What do you mean? You said you could help me. Plus, you're a powerful fae."

"Sure," said Dain. "But like I said, the only way I could get through was to follow a human girl when she found her way back on the equinox, remember?"

"How did she do it?" Athena asked. "I'm still trying to get my head around the idea that the protections on the veil are cast from the other side."

"Of course they are," said Dain. "Humans have a lot of fear of the fae."

"And all this time, I thought they were protecting themselves from vampires," said Athena.

"Vampires are worthless bottom-feeders," said Dain. "I can't stand the bloodsuckers. But they're no big threat, especially now that they can't detect us anymore."

There was a whooshing sound, and bright light beamed through the trees.

"They've come after us," said Dain. "Quick. We've got to find some way to hide. If we're out in the open like this, they'll find us in no time."

"I know!" said Athena, remembering the leafy building she'd seen not long after first entering the fae realm. "Why don't we break into the clerk's office?"

"You're definitely my daughter," said Dain with a grin as he plucked a few berries from a nearby bush.

She pierced him with a glare. "Don't say that again."

"Sorry," he said as they ran quickly towards the familiar cobbled path which would lead them directly to the clerk's office.

"Can you go any faster?" asked Athena. "Or can you just teleport us or something?"

"Oh yeah," said Dain. "I've been out of the fae realm so long that I forget I can do that. Come on. Take hold of my hand."

Athena grabbed her father's hand and quickly found herself inside a strange room. The walls were made of leaves.

"That was an easy way of breaking and entering," said Athena. "Remind me to take you along next time I have to commit some petty theft."

"It really is unfortunate that it only works in the fae realm," said Dain. "But what did I just tell you?" Dain winked at her.

"Don't say it," said Athena. "You know, I'm not going to forgive you for the way you treated us."

The swagger and sparkle disappeared from Dain's demeanour. "I'm sorry. Really, I don't deserve your forgiveness. I was terrible at playing human, just like I was terrible at being a fae prince."

"I still can't believe you, of all people, are a prince, whatever that means here," said Athena.

"Please understand that I didn't know what I was doing."

There was a booming sound outside. "Err, that's great, Dad, but we kind of have bigger problems right now."

"No, please let me finish. Wait, you're calling me Dad again?"

"We don't have time for this," said Athena.

"But I owe you an explanation."

"Fine," said Athena, crossing her arms. "Tell me, why were you so terrible then? What's your excuse?"

Dain sighed and his shoulders slumped forward. "You need to understand how it all happened. When I was here I never cared for the pomp and ceremony. I especially couldn't stand the politics. It was awful."

"Uh huh," said Athena, tapping her foot.

"I found the earth realm relatively refreshing, in comparison," Dain continued. "Although I was so young when I went through the veil and I knew nothing of human customs. I guess that's why I was a target for the authorities. They picked me up and I ended up hopping from foster home to foster home."

"Oh?" Athena asked. She'd never heard anything much about her father's childhood before.

"Needless to say, I didn't exactly have the ideal upbringing. Some of the families I was placed in were kind, but I couldn't help it. I'd always get in trouble, run away or do something mischievous. And then I'd be moved. A lot of the time there was...violence. I won't go into the details. I just wanted you to know."

"Why did you never tell us this?" Athena asked.

"I was always the fun guy," Dain replied with a sad smile. "I didn't think anyone wanted to know my sob story."

"Well, all we saw was an irresponsible deadbeat messing with our lives, not to mention Mum's memory!"

Dain looked abashed. "I'm sorry about that. I never meant to do her any harm, either of you. The effects of fae magic are hard to predict on humans. Anyway, I'm not here to cry about my past. I was a terrible father. It didn't help that I had an addiction to cream, which led to a gambling problem among other things."

"We didn't know about any of that either. What is with the cream?"

Dain shrugged. "Haven't you always been partial to cream?"

"Sure," said Athena. "In a fairly ordinary way."

"Your human side must protect you," he said.

"What exactly is the effect that cream has on the fae?" Athena asked.

"Why? Do you have some?" Dain asked, looking back at her with a preternatural gleam in his eyes.

"Just explain it to me, Dad," Athena said, realising the renewed silence outside was even more worrying than the previous booming sound.

"It gives us quite a rush," said Dain. "Makes us lose all sense of rationality. That's the reason why I got kicked out of a lot of foster homes. I mean, it puts you in a wonderful mood at first. I would generously give away all of the money I had, even the shirt off my back. And then it would wear off and I'd feel awful."

"Interesting," said Athena. She felt her mind clicking away, calculating something.

"What do you have in that bag of yours?" Dain asked.

"Mostly explosives," said Athena. "Don't get any ideas."

Dain laughed, just as a loud bang rent the air.

"They're coming for us," said Dain, peeping out of the windows. "Quick. Let's find some way we can get a better view."

"They know we're here?" Athena asked, running through the leafy rooms. The building was quite a marvel. If only she'd had the time to admire the architecture.

"It looks like it," said Dain, peeping out of another window. "They're headed right this way.

Suddenly, the air began to swirl around them. An explosion of light cascaded through the building, reducing it to a great pile of leaves, sending them tumbling to the ground amid a writhing pile of foliage and the clerk's office staff.

"There you are," said the countess. "So careless of you to run from me. You know, there is no place you can hide in this corner of the realm."

Athena reached into her bag.

"Don't get any ideas," said the countess.

"What do I have to lose?" Athena asked.

"A riddle?" The countess looked puzzled and then she grinned. "Oh, I do love riddles."

The soldiers continued to advance towards them. Athena grabbed hold of a round shaped charm she'd prepared earlier and threw it out in front of her, towards them.

The explosion sent several of the fae guard flying back, but it wasn't enough.

Another guard lunged at Athena. Her survival instincts kicked in, along with her magical ones, and she reached out, grabbing the hefty guard with both hands, and flung him far and wide.

"I have the Buffy powers, too!" Athena exclaimed.

"What?" Dain asked.

"Never mind," she said as she punched and kicked and swept more fae guards away.

They kept coming.

Athena threw charm after charm, and hurled guard after guard, but eventually succumbed to the mass of uniformed fae, who pushed both her and her father's hands behind their backs.

"Athena!" a familiar voice called out.

"Mum?!" Athena turned, astonished to see not only her mother, but also her school friends, and Sherry from the pub, with a small group of young children in tow.

They were approaching the enormous pile of leaves which used to be the structure of the clerk's office.

"Leave my daughter alone," said Rosemary, light glowing from her hands.

"I would advise you not to try anything stupid," said the countess. "Otherwise, your daughter won't last much longer."

"She's bluffing," said Dain.

"Dain!" Rosemary said in shock, clearly only just realising he was present. "What are you doing? How did you get here?"

"It's a long story," said Dain.

A fox circled the clearing, growling, and Athena recognised him as Felix. Seeing him gave her a warm mischievous feeling. Felix was always up to trouble, and he was full of ideas that would create the perfect disruption. Seeing him prowling around sparked something in Athena's mind, connecting the dots in the pieces of knowledge she had of the fae, weaving them into the perfect plot. It was a mad idea, but it just might work to get them out of there.

"Any last words?" asked the fae countess.

"Actually, yes," said Athena. "I would like to invite you to tea."

"Tea?" the countess asked. A hushed silence fell around them.

Rosemary looked at her daughter, gobsmacked.

"Yes, tea. I would like to invite you to tea right now," said Athena.

"Oh," said the countess, shocked. She seemed to be struggling, inwardly, with the request.

Athena smiled, knowing that the fae were tightly bound by the rules of etiquette.

It was more than just custom. It was the law, or perhaps the Lore. It was deep within them, compelling them to obey.

"This hardly seems to be the time," the countess said.

"Oh, but it's the perfect time," Athena said. "I've even brought the tea with me, all the way from the earth realm, in a show of gracious hospitality."

The countess paled. "But of course. How kind of you to offer. And... where is this tea party?" She struggled against her own words.

"Right here, of course," said Athena, waving her arms and gesturing towards the log table with the mushroom seating where the clerk had entertained her on her arrival.

The countess smiled, though it looked more to be a grimace. "How kind," she said coldly. "Though I wouldn't want to trouble you on such short notice."

"It is no trouble at all," said Athena. "But if you'd be so kind as to tell your guards to stand down—"

"Of course," said the countess. "Guards. Stand down. You may retreat to the outside of the clearing."

Athena smiled. This would at least buy them some time, and she had something else in mind. She knew there was still enough tea in her thermos for at least a few small cups. As soon as they'd sat down on the mushroom stools, she picked up an empty vessel from the table that looked like a magnolia flower and poured out some rather tepid tea for the countess. Athena took care to hide what she was doing as she added a good dollop of cream from the little bottle in her bag.

"Tell me," the countess said suddenly, making Athena flinch. "What is that delightful smell?"

Athena glanced back to see a genuine smile spreading across the countess's face along with a gleam in her eye.

Dain looked at his daughter incredulously, knowing exactly what she was doing. He grimaced and grasped the table in front of him, as if visibly restraining himself from diving towards the cream.

"Here you go, your...err...highness," Athena said, handing her the cup. She then poured out the remainder of what was left in her thermos out into more cups, despite there only being a tiny amount to go around. She didn't add any cream to these, but handed them around the table to her mother, school friends, Sherry, and her father, who had all sat down for tea with the countess.

"What gracious hospitality," said the countess, half glaring maniacally and half smiling, equally maniacally. "It is actually quite delightful to find so many humans here. Surprisingly so. I see you discovered the children we took."

"Oh, umm..." said Rosemary, smiling at the children who stood nearby, all in a row, watching with curiosity.

Athena looked across at them. There was a red-haired boy who was taller than the others, a dark-haired girl who reminded Athena of someone she knew, two blonde girls who looked to be around four or five, and strawberry blonde twins who were young enough to be toddlers.

"Why did they stay so young?" Rosemary asked.

"That's something we're working on," said the countess. "We'd like for them to be a little older, so that they could breed."

"Breed?!" said Rosemary, clearly mortified.

"You, however." The countess pointed a finger around the table. "All of you might be of breeding age."

"We are most certainly not," said Rosemary. "Especially not the teenagers!"

"A pity. Our genetic variety is very low, you see," said the countess. "But don't tell anyone else I said that. In fact, remind me to put an enchantment on you so you'll all forget. We can't have anyone else knowing we'd even consider the possibility of cross-breeding with mere humans." She took another sip of tea, becoming sillier by the minute. "I do say, this is the most delightful beverage I ever drunk...drunken...drunkie dunk."

Athena noticed that the countess's cheeks had become rosy and her eyes glowed brighter and brighter.

"What delightful company you all are," the countess said, waving her hand. Sparks flew out from her fingertips and lit up the air like fireflies. "Oh, what an enchanted evening!" With another wave of her hand the sparks began darting about. The children laughed in glee and began chasing them around the clearing. The countess was clearly high on dairy fat and wouldn't be much of a threat, but the guards were unaffected, and there surely wasn't enough cream to go around them all. Athena considered how she might spray it everywhere with magic and create chaos in which they might escape, but then the countess spoke.

"This has been quite delightful." The countess drained her cup. "I feel so wonderful. How will I ever return your gracious hospitality?"

"Err, if you'd be so kind..." said Athena. She'd had an idea.

It was a longshot, but it was worth attempting, especially since the countess seemed to be in such a good mood. If Dad lost all sense of reason and became so generous he gave all our money away when he'd had cream, then surely there's a chance...

"To return our hospitality," Athena continued, "you could simply take down the fae side of the enchantments on the veil, so that we can get back to the human world."

The fae countess threw back her head and cackled hysterically.

Athena felt herself tense in preparation for battle, but then the countess pulled herself up straight, still smiling brightly. "But of course! It would be rude not to," she said and giggled gleefully. Then, with a wave of her hand, she sliced a crescent moon shape in the air above the table. It peeled back to form a door.

"What now?" Rosemary whispered.

"We have to get through the human magic on the other side," said Athena. "Okay, we're all going to have to work together on this one." She stood, taking her mother by the hand.

"What?" Rosemary asked.

"You've been practicing your magic, haven't you?" Athena said. "I could tell by the way your hands were glowing before."

Rosemary nodded. "Yes, but I don't know how to get through."

"The Thorn family magic is incredibly powerful," said Sherry. "This wall in front of us is powerful too, but mostly against fae magic."

"She's right, Mum," said Athena. "We can do this. It's nothing compared to what we're capable of. We just have to imagine the protections dissolving."

Rosemary and Athena both held out their hands towards the door, visualising the defences on the other side peeling right back like the fae side had moments before.

"It's working!" said Sherry.

Athena looked to see green trees visible through the hole in the veil.

"Oh, what clever little creatures you are," said the countess. "You want to get back? Here, off you go!" She raised both arms dramatically.

Ribbons of magic flew out, sweeping up all of the earth beings.

Athena instinctively reached out and grabbed Dain's wrist as they were all pushed through the portal.

Bright light shone out, and then faded.

Rosemary, Athena, Sherry, Dain, the other teenagers, and the children who had been lost, all found themselves standing in the middle of the town square.

The whole area was now deserted, except for Ferg who was sweeping up some petals nearby.

"Oh, it's you lot," he said flatly. "Don't make a mess. I've been cleaning up from the Equinox for at least half an hour."

Rosemary and Athena looked at each other and then both collapsed in exhaustion onto the soft earth realm grass, laughing and relieved beyond belief.

Forty-Four

"I'm so sorry," said Detective Neve as they all sat around the police station. Rosemary had one of the six children on her lap, the little boy with bright red hair, who said his name was Harry.

"I have a feeling bad things happen when you get called out of town," Rosemary said to Neve. "Was it another trick to get you out of the way?"

"It really was a family emergency, like I told you," said Neve. "Just a coincidence this time."

"Is everything okay with your aunt?" Rosemary asked.

"Something's happened to her memory, as we feared. She seemed fine until a few weeks ago, but now I'm afraid she's got sudden-onset dementia. She keeps ranting about her little girl who went missing. It's unfortunate my auntie is so far away. My family moved out of Myrtlewood years ago."

"Oh, how awful to lose a child," said Rosemary. "Think of what the parents of these children must have gone through."

"That's the thing," said the detective. "My aunt didn't have a child. Seems a strange thing to make up."

Rosemary shrugged. "Stranger things have happened around here."

"You bet," said Neve, looking around at the children. "So these are all the ones who disappeared over to the fae realm."

"All the ones we could find," said Rosemary. "They were all kind of clustered together in a giant mushroom."

"The mind boggles," said the detective.

"It doesn't make much sense to me either," said Rosemary. "Even though I was there to witness it."

Just then, Prue burst through the doors of the police station. "Gretchen!" she cried. The little blonde child ran into her arms.

"It's just as well the mother remembered," said Sherry. "It wouldn't have been long before she would have forgotten all about her, just like I was forgotten about." She cradled a little dark-haired girl on her lap who looked to be about seven years old. "Mei and I went missing at the same time."

A strange shiver ran down Rosemary's spine. She turned back to Detective Neve, recognising some familiar features.

"Your aunt used to live in Myrtlewood, did she?" Rosemary asked Neve.

"Well, she did a long time ago when I was growing up," said the detective.

"Sherry, what's Mei's last name?"

"Lee," said Sherry.

"That's funny," said Neve. "That's my mother's maiden name."

Rosemary waited for the penny to drop.

The detective looked at her, startled. "That's my aunt's last name..." She clamped her hand over her mouth and looked at the little girl. "But how?"

"Sherry can explain in more detail," said Rosemary. "When she came back from the fae realm all those years ago her family had totally forgotten about her. It took a long time for them to remember her again, even after she'd returned."

"It...can't be!" said Neve. "I'm going to call my auntie straight away." She hurried from the room.

"What was that about?" Athena asked.

"It seems this little girl might well be related to our favourite police detective."

"No way!" Athena said, smiling at her mother. "Mei is supposed to be the same age as Sherry, isn't she?"

"Yes, we were good friends, growing up," said Sherry.

"And you never forgot her all those years after she disappeared," said Athena.

"I promised to bring her back," said Sherry. "I've been trying this whole time."

"It's almost enough to make me cry," said Rosemary. "So sweet...Even though you stole my necklace."

"Here you go," said Sherry, reaching around her neck to unlatch the clasp.

"Umm... Thank you," said Rosemary, taking the precious pendant in her hands. "This is turning out to be quite a good day after all."

Athena beamed at her.

"But don't think I haven't forgotten how you ran away with that boy," said Rosemary.

"Don't remind me about *him*," said Athena.

"You haven't escaped being grilled by me yet," said Rosemary. "Just wait 'til we get home. Also, you're grounded indefinitely."

"I probably deserve that," said Athena, crossing her arms. "And I'm kind of going to lie low for a while anyway. But please let me see my friends." She draped her arm around Elise, who smiled.

"I suppose I owe them that," said Rosemary. "They shouldn't have run through the gap in the veil either, but I suppose they did help, and it shows how loyal they are. Even that Beryl girl."

"Beryl? What did she do?" Athena asked, shocked.

Rosemary filled Athena in on the help provided by Beryl.

"She probably only wanted to do that so she could prove how much better she is than me. She just wanted to have something to rub in my face."

"That's a little bit harsh," said Rosemary.

"Well, that's Beryl for you," said Elise. "But she really did help."

"I suppose I'll have to thank her," Athena muttered bitterly.

Dain stepped out of an interview room, followed by Constable Perkins.

Rosemary clutched the anti-Dain protection bundle around her neck.

"Hey," Dain said. His smile was still disarming, regardless.

Rosemary had barely said two words to him before Constable Perkins ushered her into the interview room for her turn. She grudgingly followed the grumpy old officer and was grateful when the interview didn't last too long. As expected, it was just a series of baseless accusations and ridiculous questions from Perkins, but after a while the constable gave up and let her go.

By the time Rosemary returned back to the lobby all of the teenagers had been picked up by their respective families. Though there was still the remaining matter of the foundling children.

Gretchen had gone home with Prue, and Mei was talking excitedly with Neve. Rosemary looked at the four other young children.

Harry, with the bright red mane, said he was six, and little Elowen had white-blonde hair and seemed about four or five. They were currently in the corner of the reception, playing with a small basket of toys that Detective Neve had found.

The twins, with their strawberry blonde curls, were probably less than two years old and didn't speak. Athena had taken the liberty of naming them Thea and Clio, and was sitting with them both propped on her lap.

It was adorable, however the fact remained that they had nowhere to go, and Neve didn't have a bed ready for Mei, her newly discovered cousin.

"What are we going to do?" Rosemary muttered.

"I suppose we could call Child Protective Services," said Neve, approaching Rosemary. "Until we can track down the remaining families."

"But who knows how long they were in there? They don't age in the fae realm, remember?" said Rosemary.

"It would be better if they avoided foster care," said Dain, who had clearly been eavesdropping. "Believe me. You never know what kind of luck you'll get. Besides, they might well be highly magical, especially after so much time spent in that realm."

"They can come back to our house," said Athena. "We've got room."

"Wait a minute." Rosemary felt a rising panic at the thought of suddenly being responsible for all the foundlings from the fae realm. "Hold your horses. I've got enough work looking after one delinquent child, let alone a whole barrel of kids."

"I'll help you," Athena insisted. "Maybe that can be my punishment. It will teach me how to be responsible, or something."

She smiled down at the twins who were falling asleep on her lap.

"Well, I suppose it wouldn't hurt to have them around for a few days," said Rosemary.

"That's the spirit," said Marjie. She'd arrived soon after Rosemary had called her to let her know they were all back safely and had been hanging back, minding the little ones. "I'll help out. Herb can spare me for a few days."

"And what about you?" Rosemary asked Dain. "Where will you go?"

He shrugged.

"Oh dear," said Athena.

Rosemary gave her daughter a warning look, hoping she wasn't going to verbally abuse her father too much, especially not around so many young children.

"Why don't you come back to our house, too," said Athena.

Rosemary was so shocked she almost fell out of her chair.

"Just for a few days," Athena continued. "We might even be able to see if there's some kind of magic we can rustle up to protect you from your little cream problem."

Rosemary almost choked. "You've got to be kidding me!" she said to her daughter. "I thought you were angry at your father for everything he did. And what's all the fuss about cream?"

"I'll explain about the cream later, but we all make mistakes and bad choices, don't we?" said Athena, giving her mother a meaningful look. "I haven't forgiven him, not completely. But I think I've started to understand him a little bit better. He hasn't had the most normal life, or the most stable childhood. So can he come, or not?" She folded her arms.

Rosemary grinned. "Of course he can come to our place, as long as he stays firmly away from our wallets and doesn't steal anything."

Dain raised his hands in innocence. "I promise. A few weeks shackled in a tower in the fae realm has really given me a new appreciation for the freedoms of life, and I don't want to abuse that."

"It's settled then," said Athena. "Let's all go home to Thorn Manor now. Are you coming, Neve?"

"Me?" Detective Neve said.

"You can bring little Mei," said Athena. "And all the other kids too. They need somewhere to sleep and we have plenty of room."

Rosemary bit her lower lip, worried about the mess she'd left the place in. Surely, nobody would mind a bit of chaos, given the circumstance.

"Oh," said Neve. "I hadn't thought about that. Maybe I could come over. I'd just have to call my girlfriend."

"Nesta's welcome too. I'm sure we can accommodate all of you," said Rosemary. It was true that Thorn Manor was huge enough to fit all of them, and plenty more besides. Although Rosemary was mentally trying to figure out how to fit them in comfortably, as both east and west wings were notoriously dusty and shabby the last time she'd gone in there, let alone the huge experimental jumble she'd created when cooking up possible ways to get into the fae realm in her many failed attempts.

"We can always make some makeshift beds in the living room now that all of those plants have been cleared out of the house," Rosemary said. "I'll just have to move a few tables of potion equipment."

Neve didn't look too convinced.

FORTUNATELY, the house seemed to have heard the call, and by the time Rosemary and Athena and the others arrived back at the manor, all Rosemary's magical paraphernalia been tided away, and the door to the west wing was open for a change.

Rosemary peeked in to see it was no longer a dusty mess, but was sparkling and gleaming as if it had just been cleaned by a maid service and was perfectly well maintained. Even more conveniently, a large nursery had appeared that Rosemary was certain hadn't been there before, complete with five little beds. A few adjoining rooms held queen sized beds.

"How does it *know*?" asked Athena.

"I don't know. But I think it's best we treat it with kindness," Rosemary replied, tapping the wood of the door.

The little black kitten scrambled out from under one of the small beds where she'd clearly been investigating. Athena scooped her up.

"I've missed you," she said, nuzzling against the cat's head.

"Sweet little Serpentine," Rosemary cooed, reaching out for a pat.

"You've named her properly!" said Athena, beaming. "And you chose my preferred name."

"That's right," said Rosemary. "May I formally introduce Miss Serpentine Fuzzball Thorn, her Royal Cuteness."

Athena giggled.

"This is very organised of you," said Nesta when she arrived, after following Neve into the nursery. "How did you know?"

"It wasn't us," said Athena. "The house has its ways."

"Now I know why they say the Thorn family magic is so strong," said Neve, clearly impressed.

Marjie arrived with baskets of Ostara buns and chocolate eggs for supper, which Athena was almost as excited about as the young children seemed to be, sleepy though they all were.

While their guests adjusted to Thorn Manor, Rosemary and Athena retreated back to the kitchen. Athena put the kettle on for tea – both the electric one and the old fashioned one – to make enough for all the additional visitors. Meanwhile, Rosemary made a saucepan of warm milk with cinnamon and honey for the children.

As the smell of sweet spice drifted through the kitchen, Rosemary smiled at Athena. "I'm so glad to have you back."

"That was quite...an adventure," said Athena.

Rosemary looked at her daughter. "Don't go running back to the fae realm, now," she said sternly.

"No. I'm relieved to be back. You know, I quite like our strange little magical life here."

Rosemary's smile widened even further. "You know what? You're right. Aside from all the risks and danger and creepy things, which I decidedly do not like, everything else in Myrtlewood is just fabulous!"

Combustible Magic

MYRTLEWOOD MYSTERIES BOOK THREE

Prologue

As Rosemary and Athena slept peacefully in their beds, a woman stood on a hill under the light of the waning moon, overlooking the village of Myrtlewood.

Her eyes gleamed in joy at the news – such good news. Her contacts had come through, finally. A girl had entered the fae realm, and not just any girl, the one she'd been looking for all these years.

"Right here under my nose," she said to herself and cackled in glee.

There was finally a path in sight, a way to cut through to the realm, and this held the key to unlocking many years' worth of plotting.

"The power will be ours," she said to her companion, who hung back, overshadowed by trees.

The woman raised her arms, her dark hood sliding back slightly to reveal pale hair that gleamed pearlescent in the moonlight as she began chanting the ancient words, not heard for centuries.

She signalled for her companion to open the crate as the spell reached its apex. A burst of red and orange flew out. Circled in the air and then sped away.

The woman held her breath, unsure whether the spell had worked. It had been too fast, too much of a blurr to catch the details of what had been unleashed. She surveyed the countryside, looking for some kind of clue.

Down in the fields of Myrtlewood, all was quiet.

Then, as if from nowhere, a gust of wind swept through the back of the old Twigg farm.

The barn that had stood there for a hundred years suddenly burst into flames.

Agatha Twigg looked out her back window in horror as the bright orange fire engulfed the structure before turning an unearthly pink.

"Oh dear me, Marla!" Agatha called out to her niece. "Ring the authorities. Something big is coming!"

One

It was a charming late spring day. Athena lay on the grass next to Elise on the lawn at the back of Thorn Manor. They both looked up at the sky.

The foundling children ran around on the other side of the lawn. Athena could see Harry's red hair as he ducked behind a magnolia tree, chasing dark haired Mei, light haired Elowen, and the tiny strawberry blonde twins who Athena had named Clio and Thea. It was peaceful to watch them play from a distance, although staring at the tufts of white clouds drifting through the clear blue sky was even more tranquil.

"You're lucky to live somewhere like this," said Elise. "It's beautiful here."

"It would be more beautiful if I was allowed to go out and do stuff on my own," said Athena. "Outside of school, I'm pretty much stuck here. Unless Mum feels like taking me out for a walk like a little dog."

"I hate to say it, but there might be good reason for that," Elise said. "Your mum was in quite a state when we saw her after you disappeared. We were worried about you, too."

"I know," said Athena. "I'm sorry. It was stupid. I never should have trusted him."

"You don't have to keep apologising," Elise said. "I mean, as long as you've learned your lesson." She twirled a daisy between her fingertips and then flipped it at Athena.

"Hey!" Athena jokingly slapped at her friend. They giggled for a few moments. "Thanks for coming over. It's gonna be a long time before Mum lets me actually go out and visit other people's houses."

"She'll loosen up soon enough," said Elise. "I mean, you're sixteen. It's not like you're a baby. You're almost an official adult."

"That's what I keep telling her," said Athena. "But does she listen? No. She's so stubborn."

"Just like someone else I know," said Elise, reaching for a little wad of grass. Which she ripped up and threw at her friend.

Athena blasted the grass away with a burst of air.

"You seem different ever since you went through," said Elise.

"I am different. For a start I couldn't really use my magic before. Not properly. There was something about that place that kind of sparked it all...kicked it off."

"It's not just that though," said Elise. "You felt it, didn't you? That feeling...when I went through. It was like...*going home.*"

Athena turned towards her friend, giving her a knowing look. "It was the best thing I've ever felt," she admitted. "But I can't possibly tell my mother that. My father might understand, although I can never be sure with him. Plus, I can't really talk to him about that stuff. It's too personal."

"Fair enough," said Elise. "But he probably does understand, in his way. It's his home, his only true home. He's fae. For us, at least, we're part human. We should belong here just as much as we do there."

"Then why doesn't it feel like this?" Athena asked. "Why does this place feel so..."

"So heavy and lifeless?" Elise suggested.

"Exactly," said Athena. "I mean, I know that there's life all around me, but it all feels so dull compared to the other realm. It's like, it's like I was living in black and white, colour blind, and all of a sudden, everything's in Technicolor. You know, like in that old Wizard of Oz movie."

"That's exactly what it's like," said Elise. "My mum's never been through. But my grandmother grew up there and she knows. The doorways used to always be open. And people could just wander through. Sometimes they'd pop in for dinner and exit at the end of the evening."

"I wish it was still that way," said Athena. "But that was, I don't know, a hundred years ago or something."

"Yeah, my grandma's really old," Elise replied. "Naiads live for a long time."

"That's good to know," said Athena, smiling at her friend. "Hopefully you'll live for a long time, too. Sometimes it feels like you're the only one who understands me. I can't talk to Mum about any of this."

Athena held out her hand towards Elise.

Their fingers met, sending sparkles all around them. It reminded her a little bit about the moment she'd shared with Finnigan.

Despite the usual heaviness to her heart when she thought of him, the sparkles that shone out lightened everything again.

Athena didn't need to waste her energy on him. She wasn't going to make a stupid mistake like that ever again.

Two

The envelope sat on the kitchen table. It had been delivered with the morning post, but Rosemary hadn't opened it yet. She knew exactly who it was from. No one else would send such elaborate gold and purple brocade stationery.

"What do you think it says?" Athena asked.

They both stood over the table as Serpentine prowled around them as if she owned the house. Thorn Manor was unusually silent. Nesta and Dain had taken the foundling children to the park. The lack of background noise only made the envelope seem more ominous.

"I don't want to think about it," said Rosemary. "I know it's from our cousins."

"I'll open it," said Athena, picking up the envelope.

Rosemary's heart thudded in her chest. She was worried Athena would see something she shouldn't. "No. Give it here." She took the envelope and sat down at the table with her cup of tea. She'd asked for the favour from Elamina because she'd been desperate, and it wasn't the teen's fault. She didn't want Athena to feel like she was some kind of object to be bargained over. "Okay, here goes."

She opened the stiff expensive card of the envelope and pulled out an equally expensive looking piece of paper, complete with the Bracewell-Thorn's gold monograph in the corner.

"What does it say?" Athena asked.

"It's an invitation to dinner. Not exactly what I was expecting."

"You thought they were going to ask for your firstborn child?" Athena joked.

Rosemary gave her a serious look. "I'm indebted to them for the help they gave me to get into the fae realm. I told you..."

"So what? That was just a little favour. They gave you some spell ingredients. What's the big deal?"

"I'm afraid they're going to make it into a very big deal. And don't joke about firstborn children. You know, Elamina seems to quite like you. I wouldn't be surprised if she tried to steal you."

"I'm not a thing to be stolen, Mum."

Rosemary eyed her daughter warily. Elamina could be deceptive and charming when she wanted something. She hoped Athena wasn't naïve to that fact.

"Exactly, but my cousins might see you as some kind of pet," said Rosemary. "You know, they assume most other people are beneath them. Especially me."

"So we're not going to go and see them," said Athena.

"I guess we have to," Rosemary replied.

"Maybe going to dinner will be returning the favour," Athena suggested somewhat optimistically.

"I very much doubt that. But I do need to find out what it is they really want. And this is the best way to do that. I can ask them directly."

"When's the dinner?" Athena asked. "And do we have to dress up really fancy?"

"Tonight. And wear whatever you like," said Rosemary. "A brown paper bag would be fine. Least it would give them something else to be mocking and scornful about rather than just my very existence."

"What if we turn up butt naked?" said Athena.

"Sounds a little bit gross."

"Yeah. I don't know. Just making conversation. Doesn't it seem impolite that they summoned us for dinner at such short notice?" Athena looked at the invitation, which Rosemary had finally let go of. "What if we had plans tonight?"

"Exactly," said Rosemary. "They don't think much of us. Any plans we have are inconsequential to them."

"Some kind of weird flex," said Athena. "It's kind of rude, though, isn't it?"

Rosemary sighed. "They just wouldn't really think of us as real people."

"Though it is a little bit strange, isn't it?" said Athena. "Aren't they supposed to deeply value decorum?"

Rosemary shrugged. "Maybe they think they're honouring us with the invitation."

"All right. We'll go see them. I've always wanted to check out their house. You said it was a massive mansion."

"I've never been invited before," said Rosemary. "But that's how Granny always described it. Actually, I wonder what the old bat would have to say about this." She went upstairs, followed by Athena, half expecting not to see the little door to the tower. She was a little surprised that the door was visible from the upstairs landing, and even more shocked when she got there to see that there was a note pinned to it.

"More mail," said Athena. "We're popular today."

"I didn't know ghosts could write," said Rosemary. "It's definitely Granny's handwriting." She opened it up to read aloud.

My dearest descendants. I'm so relieved that Athena is back and that you are both well. I take this as my cue to leave you.

"Aw," said Athena. "She was growing on me."

"Like a delightful fungus," said Rosemary, although she did feel a pain in her heart at the thought of Granny not being around anymore. She continued reading.

This is not a final goodbye. It's merely a fare-thee-well-for-now. There are matters in the spirit realm that are calling me, requiring my utmost focus and urgent attention.

I apologise for not saying goodbye in person. I did not want to wake you or to disturb you.

Besides, I get the feeling having a batty old ghost hanging over your shoulders is starting to cramp your style.

Take care, my loves. I'm afraid you won't be able to summon me from where I'm going, but I will be back one day.

Until then, farewell and blessed be.

Rosemary felt sadness well up. "It's like I'm having to say goodbye to her all over again."

Without any warning, Athena put her arm around her mother's shoulder and gave her a little pat. "It's okay, Mum. She'll come back. And when she does, you can give her a right telling off."

Rosemary smiled.

"I suppose we'd better figure out what to wear tonight," said Athena.

"That's right." Rosemary sighed, remembering the dinner that she'd temporarily been able to forget. "Family," she said. "Even when they don't live with you, they have the amazing ability to drive you up the wall!"

They stood outside an enormous, looming black stone mansion belonging to the Bracewell-Thorns.

"Foreboding is the word to describe it," said Athena.

Rosemary rang the doorbell and some kind of fancy butler answered. He was tall with a black and silver waistcoat and a stony expression. They were shown in to an elaborately adorned cloak room, and the butler took their coats and then lead them through to an even more elaborate waiting area.

"Looks like we're inside a palace," said Athena. "And to think, these family members knew we were in poverty and never once offered to help."

"It's a bit gauche for my tastes," said Rosemary bitterly.

The butler disappeared into another room and then returned a moment later. "The Bracewell-Thorns are ready for you now." He bowed slightly and gestured for them to enter into a long stone hallway, lit with flaming lanterns.

"You've got to admit this part is cool, though," said Athena.

The hallway opened up into a large room with a high ceiling. Rosemary eyed the lengthy dining table with seating for over a dozen, complete with lit candles in crystal stands that glimmered, casting reflections back and forth between the chandeliers that loomed large on the ceiling. The whole room smelled like lily of the valley, Elamina's favourite perfume, but fortunately it wasn't too overpowering.

Rosemary's two cousins stood at the far side of the room. Elamina stepped forward. Her long white-blonde hair was done up as if she was prepared for a ball and she wore a grey and mauve evening gown, tailored perfectly to outline her petite figure.

Derse was dressed in a suit as usual, and glanced across at them, just as aloof as ever.

"Rosemary...Athena, how wonderful of you to join us."

Rosemary shot Athena a confused look. In all the years that she'd known her cousin, Elamina had never once before been so gracious or willing to acknowledge Rosemary's presence. She almost seemed warm in her demeanour.

It certainly must be an act, Rosemary thought, wishing that Athena would read her mind so they could have a conversation. Ever since she'd come back from the fae realm, Athena, having learned how to control the voices in her head, had very deliberately turned them all off, saying she didn't need the extra headache.

This was occasionally frustrating, but also a welcome relief. Overall, Rosemary preferred not to have to worry about her own mind being pried into by a nosy teen. It meant that Rosemary had slightly less to be teased about, at any rate.

Elamina, with a genuine smile on her face, or at least a genuine gleam in her eyes, came forward, taking both Rosemary's and then Athena's hands in a kind of half handshake. She then air-kissed them on both cheeks in turn.

"How wonderful of you to join us," said Derse, though his voice sounded wooden, almost robotic. Rosemary was surprised to hear him speak more than a word at a time. Whatever this charade was, he'd clearly been let in on it but couldn't act to save himself.

Elamina turned to him with a slightly wild look in her eyes, her smile faltering a little. She turned back to Rosemary, eyeing her rather casual outfit. "You look...well. It's so refreshing when middle-aged women give up the need to dress to impress."

That's more like it. Her cousin's passive-aggressive tendencies were strangely more comforting than the horrendously fake smile plastered to her face. Athena just looked surprised and vaguely amused. Rosemary didn't even bother trying to return the backhanded compliment.

"Please take a seat." Elamina gestured to the table.

Rosemary noticed little place cards with their names on them. Athena's place was right next to the head of the table, where Elamina sat down.

Preferring to ignore the assigned roles, Rosemary took Athena's seat and swapped the place cards over.

Athena gave her a mischievous look.

All was silent for a moment and then Elamina shook her head with a little giggle that was so out of character it shocked Rosemary.

"Thank you so much for joining us on such short notice." Elamina looked at her delicate silver watch. "And only half-an-hour late. I'm very pleased to hear that Athena returned happy and well." Her voice was almost musical.

"Erm," Rosemary started, unsure of what to say. Her cousin seemed to be locked in an internal battle between being her normal caustic self and taking on the faux-happy persona of a children's television presenter.

"Oh, now look," said Elamina crossly as two young servants approached with trays. "The entrees are arriving before I've even offered you a drink." She waved them away.

Rosemary felt her stomach rumble. She hadn't eaten before the rather long drive to the fancy neighbourhood. Her terrible sense of direction had sent them off on a round-about journey before Athena insisted on using her phone to navigate.

"Now, what would you have to drink?" Elamina asked. "Sherry? Wine? What do people like *you* drink?"

Athena stifled a giggle. Rosemary pressed her mouth into a thin line to avoid laughing. It was comical how much her snobby cousins were trying desperately to accommodate them, while also clearly having no idea how to be normal people.

"Red wine is fine," said Rosemary.

"Do you have any lemonade?" Athena asked.

"Certainly." Elamina smiled at Athena then clapped her hands. Servants stepped forward and she relayed the drink instructions. Moments later they returned with the beverages.

"Excuse me for asking," said Rosemary, feeling like she should at least attempt to be polite, given the comical situation. "But was there a particular reason for the invitation?"

"Oh, you don't beat around the bush do you?" Elamina batted her eyelids, as if trying to be charming. "I just wanted to see you – my poor dear cousins – after all you've been through. And we wanted to celebrate that Athena is back, safe and well. Isn't that a lot to celebrate, Derse?"

Derse just nodded.

"Thank you," said Athena. "It is nice to be back." She took a sip of her lemonade and squinted as if it was far too sour.

Rosemary followed suit and took a gulp of her own wine, which she admitted to herself was delicious and probably incredibly expensive.

"Now we can have the entrees." Elamina clapped her hands and the servants returned with silver domed trays.

"So, just a celebration?" said Rosemary. "Great. That's...That's lovely."

"Yes. And how was it?" said Elamina. As if asking about a holiday.

Rosemary gave her a deadpan look. "How was what?" she asked flatly.

"The fae realm, of course," said Elamina with a little laugh.

"It was..." Athena's voice trailed off and she stared blankly at the candles.

"I see, it's complicated," said Elamina. "I'm so sorry for asking. I've heard such wonderous things. I just...I don't mean to pry. But if you ever do feel like talking about it, let me know. I hear it can really cut to the heart of you...A place like that."

Rosemary raised her eyebrows as her cousin nattered on.

"I knew someone of fae heritage once," said Elamina. "Who'd been brought up in the fae realm but had somehow slipped through."

"Oh..." Athena started, but Rosemary shot her a warning look. This was not the time to talk about Dain's genetics. In fact, it was a time to withhold as much information as possible.

"That's interesting," said Athena. "I wonder how they got through. It's quite a hard thing to do, apparently."

"Indeed. I'm dying to know how you did it," said Elamina, looking between the two of them.

"It was a stroke of luck really." Rosemary tried to keep her expression neutral, though it was all she could do to stop herself glaring suspiciously at her cousin. *What is she up to?*

"Luck," Elamina repeated, sounding unimpressed.

"Yes, luck and a dash of cream," said Athena.

Rosemary shot her another warning glance. *Too much information*, she tried to think loudly, hoping that Athena had dropped her psychic barriers temporarily in honour of the occasion.

"Well, I don't know how we did it," said Athena. "Maybe...barriers like that tend to ebb and flow, don't they?"

"Indeed," said Elamina. "I hear it used to be quite an open thing. Quite easy to slip back and forth. If you were magically inclined anyway. Such a shame that the old ways have been forgotten. Things have changed and not always for the better. I hear there is much potent magic there."

Oh, so that's what it is, Rosemary thought loudly. *That's what this is all about. She's hoping you have some fae magical secrets that she can get her hands on.*

"I must admit I did manage to slip through the barrier when I was a wild young child, on an equinox or two," said Elamina. "It's a pity I had no idea of the true potential of the magic it held."

"I can't see why you'd want to do that," said Rosemary. "It's really not all that hospitable over there, despite their obsession with manners."

"Oh?" said Elamina. "Do tell me more."

Rosemary bit her tongue to stop from rambling. She'd already shared far too much information.

"Is that what this is all about?" Athena asked, rather more forward than Rosemary was comfortable with. "Are you trying to get back there? Are you trying to get through the veil?"

Elamina gave a little laugh. "Oh, darling girl. I'm afraid that was merely a passing fancy...a childhood phase. I've moved on to much, much bigger things with my ambitions. That's all I'm going to tell you about that."

So that's what it is, Athena's voice projected into Rosemary's head. *She's trying to get to the fae realm and she's trying to get information out of us.*

I knew it was something like that, Rosemary replied. *And we are not going to help her. It's far too dangerous.*

Rosemary thought the appetisers were overly complex in terms of flavour profile, and not terribly enjoyable, while the main was bland.

Athena seem to be enjoying it well enough. They ate mostly in silence aside from the odd question about the fae realm or the family magic posed by Elamina. Derse, in his typical style, hardly said a word.

"Now, Athena, you're growing very powerful, aren't you?" said Elamina. She gave a flourish of her hand as she gestured for the staff to clear away the meals. "Now tell me about your magic, my dear cousin. How does it work for you?"

"I'm just figuring it out, really," Athena demurred.

Rosemary wanted to ask why Elamina was so curious about Athena, rather than about her. She didn't want to bring up the subject of her daughter's father's heritage in case it was revealing her hand too much in a game she didn't know how to play.

"Wouldn't you love to train with some *real* magical experts?" she asked Athena.

"Oh," Athena started. "I don't know." She paused for a moment.

"Actually, Athena has come a long way recently," said Rosemary. "We're both quickly learning to master our magic without any help from *you*."

She didn't mean it to come out sounding so bitter.

Elamina's smile never faltered. "I know!" she said, with a little clap. "How about you come and stay with us regularly, my darling little cousin."

The term of endearment made Athena wince. Clearly Elamina was not used to spending time with the teen folk.

"Uhh...That's okay," said Athena.

"As I said, we're perfectly fine with our magical training," said Rosemary.

"Come now, I have no children of my own," said Elamina.

Probably because you didn't want to risk losing your figure, Rosemary thought inside her head, wondering if Athena was still listening, and sure enough, the teen reached for her mouth as if to stifle a giggle.

She wants to keep you as a pet, Rosemary continued as a fluffy pink dessert course was placed in front of them.

"I can understand your hesitation," said Elamina. "After all, we've never been a very close family now, have we? I must admit, I was always jealous that you and Granny got on so well." She gave Rosemary a meaningful look.

Rosemary was startled by that revelation. It wasn't like Elamina to let her guard down.

"I know, I'm not the most friendly and well-liked person around," said Elamina.

You can say that again, said Athena's voice in Rosemary's head.

"I can't help the way I am," said Elamina. "But I'd like to make amends."

"I thought you brought us here because I owed you something," said Rosemary. "After you helped with that spell."

"Oh, nonsense," said Elamina. "What's a favour among family? Besides, it helped you get your daughter back...my dear cousin."

"I don't know what you're trying to bargain for here," said Rosemary. "Athena's not some kind of pawn. She's a human being, not a play thing. You helped me when I needed it and as you made clear in your letter, I do owe you one, but I don't owe you her." She gestured to Athena.

Elamina's smile dropped away from her face. "Very well," she said coolly, putting down her tiny dessert fork. "You've made your hostility perfectly clear, Rosemary." There was an edge to her voice that made Rosemary feel tense.

"I won't bother you," said Elamina. "Just know that I'm acting with goodwill. I'm trying to make amends for not being the best cousin or the best...person. And I may well have a lot more work to do on that score. But I'm trying and that's all I can do."

Rosemary nodded, feeling slightly ashamed of herself. “Okay. Thank you. I guess.” She took the last bite of her overly sweet dessert.

“It’s getting late. I think we’d better leave,” said Athena. “It’s a school night.”

Elamina sniffed a little. “I'll have Charles fetch your coats.” She clicked her fingers, summoning another servant.

On the way back to the car Athena gave Rosemary a very concerned look. “What was all that about?” she asked.

“Beats me,” said Rosemary. “Perhaps our dearest darling cousin is finally losing the plot.”

Three

Athena sat in class, feeling unfocused as she often had recently. She'd been unable to sleep the night before and was sure she'd heard strange sounds coming from the forest, though it could have just been her mind playing tricks on her in a half-dreaming state.

Mr Spruce waffled on about automancy, which was apparently the art of magically getting something to work for itself.

Instead of focusing on the topic at hand, Athena was miles away. Her eyes closed, just slightly, and she could almost picture it.

The fae realm...

Those purple trees and pearlescent cobblestone paths.

...that feeling like a fish being dropped back into water, at home again.

She'd wanted to come back home to escape the countess. And, of course, because after Finnigan's betrayal everyone she knew and cared about was in the Earth realm. But coming back seemed to take a toll on her body.

Everything felt so heavy.

"At least attempt to pay attention," Elise whispered, next to her.

Athena opened her eyes again and looked around the classroom. Mr Spruce hadn't noticed that she'd been daydreaming and almost napping in class, but Beryl certainly had and shot Athena a smug smile.

Beryl had been bragging about how it was only because of her that Athena had come back from the fae realm. The nasty girl had been lapping it up...How disengaged Athena had been...How poorly she'd performed at school recently. But it was hard to focus around things that seemed so grey and lifeless compared to the other world she'd briefly inhabited.

For most of the others in her small circle of new friends who'd gone over to rescue her, the fae realm had the opposite effect. It had felt unnerving and confusing and unpleasant. They were relieved to get back to the solid reality they were used to.

But Elise understood.

Athena reasoned it was because she was naiad on her mother's side, and they were beings from the fae realm. Elise felt the connection and the glorious joy of being there, that sense of finally fitting in and being comfortable.

Mr Spruce cleared his throat. "Now for something practical!"

He rummaged in the pile of odd implements behind his desk and brought out a box containing some old brass instruments. He handed them around to the class.

"Are they some sort of magical contraptions?" Felix asked.

Beryl laughed. "These are obviously just torches of a regular kind."

"Torches?" asked Deron. "This don't look like no torch to me. We've got a lot of plastic torches at home."

Beryl shot him a disgusted look.

"These are indeed dynamo torches," said Mr Spruce. "And we've been using them to teach this class for many decades. So while they might be dated I can assure you they work perfectly well. The point is that for automancy you must use your mind, not to influence the kinetic energy around the device in order to move it, but to connect with the device itself. The idea is to get the device to turn on, in its natural essence, and therefore move itself. Let me demonstrate."

He sat down at his desk, placing one of the brass windup torches in front of him. Then he put his hands on his temples and kind of zoned out, going cross-eyed as he looked at the device.

Felix laughed at the face Mr Spruce was making, and Elise elbowed him. It was clearly still her job to keep everyone in line. Athena gave her a supportive smile.

Mr Spruce hummed a little, and the handle of the dynamo began to turn, just slightly at first, and then a little faster. And faster still, until a light began to shine out of the front of the torch.

"There you have it!" said Mr Spruce proudly, lowering his hands as the handle stopped moving. "Now, you will practice. And don't even think about using kinetic energy to move the handles. They've been especially charmed so they'll only work with automancy."

The class began practicing. Athena didn't feel interested enough to engage in the task. She looked around to see Beryl, focusing in frustration as she stared cross-eyed at the device. Athena would have laughed, only none of the torches in the classroom were moving at all.

Felix looked like he'd given up and was shooting magic shaped like tiny paper planes back and forth with Deron who had abandoned his dynamo too.

"Ugh, it's no use," said Beryl, screwing up her face. "Why bother with automancy when kinetic energy is perfectly sufficient?"

Mr Spruce bellowed a laugh. "Miss Flarguan, surely you know that automancy is far more than just getting a torch to light up. It's a whole magical speciality. We are starting small because it's challenging to master."

Athena tried to stop herself from smirking at the obvious discomfort of her nemesis, but Beryl was right, there was hardly any point in trying. She folded her arms and leaned back in her chair. If none of the other students could get the thing to work she had a fat chance of succeeding.

"Not even going to try?" Mr Spruce asked.

"Err," said Athena. "I'm having trouble concentrating today."

"Go ahead," said Mr Spruce. "I have it on good authority that the Thorn family are experts in automancy."

"That might have been the case a long time ago," said Athena, thinking of the way their magical manor house liked to do things automatically as if it was a sentient being. "Unfortunately, my mother and I don't quite yet know what we're doing with magic."

"Now, now, this speciality is complex. It takes most people many years of studying, even just to get the basics. You hear that class?" Mr Spruce said, scratching his long, white, frizzy beard as he addressed the room. "You're not expected to move mountains today. I'd be delighted if any one of you got even an inch of movement from the contraption in front of you. I expect it will take you some weeks to get it to turn on at all."

Beryl had an expression of ardent determination on her face as she continued to stare at the dynamo, clearly hoping to prove herself.

Athena sighed and stared at the torch in front of her, but it wasn't long before her eyelids began to droop again, revealing some sort of imprint of the purple light shining through the fae realm at night and that feeling of connectedness.

Every time she thought back to that place, it came with the sting of betrayal.

Finnigan.

She'd trusted him. And yet, all he did was hand her over to his mistress, the Countess of West Eloria. The memory made her surge in anger, followed by sadness. But the worst part was that she still had feelings for him.

She couldn't escape from her own emotions. There was something that felt good about being with Finnigan, and about the fae realm in its entirety, which is why she'd stuck close to Elise when she was at school. Elise understood.

It was the same with the young foundling children who were temporarily housed at Thorn Manor. Being around them reminded her a little of that unearthly place. They, having lived there for so long, glowed with some of its essence. This was also perhaps why she didn't mind all the time she was spending with her fae father, despite not completely forgiving him for how he'd behaved when she was a child.

Dain was fae and she was fae. And as much as part of her wanted to cut herself off from all of that, along with the pain of betrayal, another part of her delighted in it so much that she simply couldn't. In the fae realm things worked for her. Her magic came easily. Her mind was clear. Even being there a short amount of time had helped her hone her powers in a lasting way, far more than months of practice in the Earth realm had before. It was like she was made for that place. She fitted there. It worked.

She glanced back down at the brass object in front of her, still half in a restless daydream. It was like she could see through the layers of metal. It had been created for a purpose. It belonged...Just like Athena felt she fitted when she was at home in the fae realm.

There was something about the dynamo contraption that oddly reminded Athena of the house that she lived in. Thorn Manor had this intense sense of purposefulness about it, like a being alive in its own right.

All of a sudden she could see it – sense it – as if it were an innate truth. Everything had such a spark within it. And when activated, it could do so much more than expected.

She focused closely on the device in front of her. In her mind she could see down, through the layers of brass, through the cogs and screws, into the heart of the object: its essence. Athena felt the inner spark light up like a fire igniting to life.

The handle of the dynamo twitched.

Yes!

There was a humming sound. All eyes turned towards Athena's desk, to the contraption that was now moving of its own accord. It began to turn, quicker and quicker, out of control, so much so that the torch spun around on the table, shining a light throughout the whole room.

Mr Spruce stood up, bursting into loud applause. "Oh brava! Brava!" he cried out. "I've never seen such a thing! That was simply stupendous for a first attempt!"

Athena felt a swell of pride. She noticed Beryl glaring at her from across the classroom, but she couldn't help smiling. Despite the fact that she hadn't even been trying very hard, at least she'd managed to do one thing right this term.

Four

Rosemary watched from the kitchen window as Athena and Dain ran around on the lawn outside, entertaining the children. Little Clio and Thea had finally started talking, though they didn't remember anything about their past, not even the names they'd had before Athena had given them new ones. They giggled as they ran around, guided by the vivacious Harry and shy Elowen. Mei was there too, only she, unlike the other foundling children, had a known family. The others remained mysteries.

"They're such placid children, aren't they?" said Detective Neve, who sat at the nearby table, sipping a cup of freshly brewed tea.

"Maybe that's part of the magic of the fae realm," said Rosemary. "It's true. They hardly ever cry or bicker. They're nothing like the challenge Athena was as a little one."

"You're probably right," said Neve. "They're ethereal, like that place rubbed off on them. At least that makes them easy to look after."

Rosemary readily agreed. The children had been no trouble at all. All she needed to do was make sure they were fed and bathed, and Dain was doing a great job of entertaining them. Two weeks had passed since their return from the fae realm, but this wasn't a permanent home for them, and the uncertainty was starting to bother Rosemary.

"How's Athena going?" Neve asked.

Rosemary beamed. "Brilliantly, at least today. She came home raving about autofancy or something. Apparently school went well today!"

They watched as Athena swung Harry around in a circle, while the other children squealed with glee. The children were so sweet and full of wonder.

"What do you think will happen to them?" Rosemary asked.

"We've been trying to track down the families, as you know," said Neve. "But the magical authorities are busy with emergencies."

Rosemary raised her eyebrows questioningly.

"I probably shouldn't tell you," said Neve. "Police business, but as for finding the families these children belonged to, our best leads are old historic cases." She took out a manilla folder from her bag and opened it on the table. "I'm not technically supposed to show you this, as it's a police investigation. But in the circumstances..."

Rosemary excitedly skipped over to the table to look at the documents.

"We've got the groceries!" Marjie said, bustling into the kitchen in a multi-coloured floral dress. Nesta followed close behind wearing her usual bright-red cape over plain black clothing. Her dark hair was pulled up in its customary high bun.

Rosemary smiled. Nesta had become a good friend over the past few weeks as she and Neve had assisted with the foundling children. Rosemary was used to hearing her soft musical voice with its slight Welsh lilt.

The house had recently been full of friends, something Rosemary had been sure she would tire of quickly, but it was actually quite nice.

"Don't worry," said Nesta, approaching the table and seeming to read Rosemary's mind in the way she often intuitively did. "We won't stick around forever. We just want to help with the children until...oh, is this the file, love?"

Neve shot her girlfriend a smile. "Yes, just don't tell Perkins I showed it to you or he'll blow through the roof. You know what his temper is like."

"It's really no trouble having you all around," said Rosemary. "In this big old house I can still have my own space if I want to, I just have to wander into one of the many empty rooms. Besides, how else would we cope with all the kids?"

"They don't have to be your responsibility," said Neve.

"As I said before," Rosemary responded, "I don't want to risk them going into foster care in case they have a horrible time. Besides, it's giving Athena a good chance to learn to take more responsibility."

Rosemary watched through the window as her daughter threw tiny blonde Elowen high up into the air.

"Or at least that's the idea," said Rosemary with a sigh. She crossed to the back door and yelled out to Athena. "Be careful not to injure them!"

"Is that little Elowen?" Marjie asked, squinting. "She just loves to be thrown around. She thinks it's hilarious when Herb holds her upside down!"

"She's a sweet kid," said Rosemary. "Barely knew her own name. I think she's about four years old."

"From the old newspaper records, we think she's little Elowen Dawson who went missing forty years ago," said Neve.

"A lot can happen in forty years," said Nesta. "Where are her family now?"

"The last report we have says they left town. Moved to Burkenswood, probably to keep the other children safe."

"I don't blame them," said Rosemary. "Who would want to stick around somewhere that constantly reminds you of your missing baby?"

"Have you spoken to the family?" Marjie asked.

"Not yet. I tracked down a sister. The parents have passed away."

"It's strange, isn't it?" said Rosemary. "Tracking down family members and trying to find out whether they want to adopt their missing siblings or cousins who disappeared decades ago but are still little kids."

"It's certainly not normal police business," said Neve. "And we can't involve the mundane child welfare office because..."

"How do you explain something like this?" said Rosemary.

"Exactly," said Neve. "We've never needed a magical child services department before. Occasionally children have gone missing or returned, but it's quite rare, especially coming back from the fae realm. The problem is, so much time has elapsed over here, but the kids are still so young. And to make matters worse, the families don't tend to remember anything."

"Oh. That's right," said Rosemary. "So why did they move away?"

"The specific magical amnesia seems to take a while to kick in," said Neve.

"We'll have to watch that we don't all forget what happened to us as well," Rosemary muttered, feeling bitter about her memory and how it had been tampered with. "I wonder if there's some kind of spell that might stop the memory magic from happening." She looked out the window towards Dain, who was running around with Harry and the twins. She didn't want any more fae meddling with her mind.

"I can try to help you with that," said Marjie. "My Aunt Morwenna was an expert when it came to memory. She had some spiritual books..."

"Don't remind me," said Rosemary. "Dain wasn't the only one that messed with my memory, remember? My own grandmother cast a spell to bind the family magic, making me totally forget it ever existed."

"Now, now," said Marjie. "You know she had her reasons."

Nesta astutely assumed that this was a good time to change the subject. "So you're going to call on them?" she asked Neve, gesturing to the files. "Elowen's family, I mean. It looks like you've tracked them down. Surely you have to let them know."

"I was planning on going there tomorrow," said Neve. "To visit the sister." She turned to Rosemary. "Maybe you could come with me and help to explain about the fae realm and the memory loss, since you understand it better than most."

"Don't you think that would be crossing a line?" Rosemary asked. "I'm not a cop or anything. It might be weird."

"I could bring you in as a sort of external consultant," said Neve. "We'd pay you an hourly rate, just like other contractors."

"You know, I never expected I'd become a professional consultant in magical memory loss and faeries," said Rosemary. "But Perkins will hate it, so count me in."

Neve smiled at her. Just then, a little dark haired girl ran to the kitchen and wrapped her arms around Neve and then around Nesta.

"Mummies!" she said.

"Mei, we've had this conversation before," said Neve. "I'm your cousin, remember."

The little girl giggled. "I know, Connie," she said, using what was clearly a childhood nickname, shortening Neve's first name, which happened to be Constantine. "But it's like you're big enough to be a mum. How did you get so big, anyway?"

"A lot of time passed, remember," said Nesta. "You were in the fae realm, and time was different there."

"But where is Mummy? My real mummy?"

The two women shot each other an uncomfortable look. "Your mummy's a lot older now," said Neve gently. "She didn't go to the fae realm like you. You stayed very small, and the rest of us got bigger and older."

"She must be huge!" said Mei.

"Not so much, actually," said Neve.

"When can I see her?" Mei's smile faded.

"I've actually arranged for her to fly in this weekend," said Neve. "She's going to stay at our house. Remember, the one we visited yesterday?"

"Why not here?" Mei asked. "Can she stay here with me and my friends?"

"Mei, we thought you might want to come and stay with us, too," said Nesta.

Mei pouted. "But I want to stay with my friends."

"We don't want to trouble Rosemary for too long," said Neve.

Mei looked at Rosemary expectantly.

"All things change, darling," she said. "It's up to Neve and Nesta when they're ready to move on. You're no trouble, really." Rosemary looked at Neve. "Don't rush. We've got plenty of room. And I'm sure even if we run out, the house will whip us up some more." She patted the wood of the house affectionately. "Nice house."

"Well," said Neve, looking slightly troubled. She kneeled down and took Mei's hands. "We'll see where your Mum wants to stay. You must remember that a lot of things have changed since you disappeared."

"I know!" said Mei excitedly. "Athena showed me amazing things."

"Amazing things?" Rosemary asked.

"Yes! She has this little box like a rectangle, and it glows. And you can do *everything* on it. You can even talk to people who aren't there, but not like a telephone, but like...their faces. And it's got all the information in the world! It's magic."

"I see," said Rosemary, smiling.

"Athena calls it her phone," said Mei. "But phones have cords and they are much bigger. I told her!"

Nesta and Rosemary grinned at each other.

"This is going to be an interesting adjustment period," said Neve with slight concern in her voice.

Five

Athena stared at the wood panels on the ceiling. She was having trouble sleeping again. As she lay in bed, all she could think about was the fae realm and how good it had felt to be there.

She looked around her room. Everything about this place felt too heavy and hard and dense. It was home in many ways, except the way that sang to her heart.

The wind rattled the windows and whispered through the trees outside as she lay there.

Sure, everyone she knew and loved was in the Earth realm, but being here just felt wrong. At her lowest points, she almost wished she could talk to Finnigan, despite his betrayal. At least he might understand. What she really missed was the Finnigan she'd thought she'd known, not the one who had turned her over to the fae countess, but that boy didn't exist.

She wasn't ready to talk about her emotions or anything personal with her mother. The last thing Athena needed was Rosemary getting overprotective and possessive again. Even still, she couldn't keep going around in circles. She needed to do something.

There was nothing for it.

Athena climbed out of bed and got into her slippers and warm dressing gown. She opened the door out to her balcony.

For a moment, she thought she heard whispering voices, but when the wind stilled all was silent. Athena felt so alone.

Of course, she couldn't call to Finnigan, and she wouldn't have wanted to see him even if he did come looking for her. Worse, she suspected he wouldn't bother, now that he'd got what he wanted out of her, using her as a bargaining chip with the countess.

She might still have lingering feelings for him, but she wasn't completely stupid. And most of those feelings right now were different forms of anger, anyway. She pushed him out of her mind.

There were more important things than boys, after all.

The wind picked up again as Athena stepped silently down to the lawn, grateful that the house hadn't decided to remove her own personal exit, despite Rosemary's yelling and complaining about it when she'd realised the balcony and staircase had appeared. Though her mother's histrionics *were* probably more to do with Athena running away to the fae realm than the magical renovations in particular.

She crossed towards the forest where Finnigan had led her. She couldn't help but look around for him in the trees, though she had half a mind to blast him with her magic if she did catch sight of him.

If only there was a way that she could figure out how to get back to the fae realm without him, even just temporarily. It was almost as if that place was calling out to her, beckoning her home, but she knew she had to stay.

Maybe I can try to cut through the veil, just a little bit. That would be enough to keep me sane and contented for a little while.

She attempted to remember what Finnigan had done, vaguely recalling there had been lights in the air. They formed a kind of archway. But she didn't know how to make that happen. It was all a bit hopeless.

A gust of wind whipped through the trees; it almost sounded like whispered chanting, but Athena knew better than to let her imagination run away on her.

I'm a powerful witch...and powerful fae. I can do this. I don't need him and his theatrics. I have all the power I need.

She raised her index finger with the intention of trying to cut a door through the veil from this realm into the next.

If Finnigan can use his fae and human magic to get through both sides of the veil, then surely so can I.

Athena focused on the fae realm, that beautiful sensation, the feeling she'd had of being free and relaxed, contented and truly alive. It was the feeling of being at home in her heart. Images of the purple light filtering through the trees swam through her mind.

A tiny light burst from the tip of her finger. She moved it up and over, sensing a thickness behind the usual night air. It was almost like moving her hand through jelly as she cut into the veil.

A blast of energy shot through, bowling her over onto the grass.

Athena picked herself up and tried to see what she'd created. The air shimmered in front of her. She held out her hands and felt a warm liquid sensation floating through her.

Gorgeous patterns of light wove through the air as bursts of red, blue, and purple flew through from the fae realm.

Athena sighed and basked in the energy.

It was that same beautiful feeling, though it was only fleeting.

This is it, she realised. *This is the feeling of home. If only I could bottle it and take it with me wherever I go.*

After a few moments, the feeling was gone and the veil had stitched itself back together. Despite the temptation, Athena didn't dare try to make another opening in order to get through, in case she couldn't return again.

She slipped back up the stairs and got into bed, hoping that the contented feeling would last for at least a little bit longer.

Six

Rosemary and Neve stepped out of the car in a modest neighbourhood of Burkenswood. The morning air was still thick with a stubborn fog. Rosemary felt a slight thrill of nervousness at the prospect of helping Neve with policework, which put her at risk of rambling.

"I forget how early children wake me up these days," said Rosemary. "I didn't even realise it was still morning."

Neve smiled at her. "Are you ready?" she asked. "This could get interesting."

Rosemary nodded. She had put her hair up into a band, a bit like the style of ponytail the detective wore. She had dressed in some quite conservative clothing, a plain navy shirt and black pants, so that she didn't give off her usual vibe, which Athena referred to as Grandma-toddler-yoga-attire.

Neve knocked on the door. After a moment, a woman answered, pale with greying hair and a tired expression on her face. She held a piece of toast in one hand.

"Tamsyn Dawson?" said Neve.

"What's this about?" the woman asked. "I'm running late for work."

"Sorry to bother you. Shall we come back at a better time?" Rosemary said.

"No. Just tell me." Tamsyn sounded impatient. "Are you selling something, because if so you can shove—"

Detective Neve held out her badge and introduced herself.

Tamsyn's expression became even more serious. "What happened?"

"It's a long story," said the detective.

"I guess you'd better come in," said Tamsyn. They followed her into the open-plan kitchen and living area of the house. It had a musty smell. Rosemary noticed the linoleum yellowing and the veneer on the kitchen cabinets was cracking from age.

"You may not remember this," said Neve as she sat down at the kitchen table. "But forty years ago, a little girl went missing, who was related to you."

The woman shook her head in disbelief. "Is this some kind of cold murder case?" she asked with a look of horror.

"Not exactly," said Rosemary. "She's still alive."

"You're telling me I have a long lost relative who was kidnapped?"

"Sort of," Rosemary said.

Neve shot her a glance and Rosemary decided to let the detective do most of the talking.

"Look," said Neve. "To be perfectly frank with you, there was magic involved."

Tamsyn shook her head in shock. "No, no. We moved away...to get away from all that."

"Why did you move away from Myrtlewood? Do you recall?" Detective Neve asked.

"Something happened," Tamsyn said with a cloudy look. "I don't know what it was. Maybe my parents didn't tell me. But something bad happened and we had to move away. We weren't allowed to talk about magic anymore. Oh gods, I missed it. I missed it so much."

"Would you like to know about the thing that happened?" Rosemary asked tentatively, unable to stop herself from talking completely.

"It's been a long time," Tamsyn said. "My parents are gone now. I suppose...I don't have to follow their instructions anymore." She shook herself. "Okay, sure. Hit me. What happened?"

"The little girl who went missing was your sister," said Detective Neve.

The woman's jaw dropped. She shook her head slightly in disbelief.

"She was abducted by the fae into their realm," the detective continued. "This is why you don't remember. They have a powerful magic that makes people forget things that might compromise them."

Rosemary nodded, relieved that the detective had a way of communicating that was so clear.

"It's not possible," said Tamsyn, crossing her arms. "I didn't have a sister. I would remember something like that."

"We understand this is a shock," said Neve.

The woman's posture stiffened. "Look, I don't know who you are and what kind of game you're playing. But I would've remembered something like *that*."

"Please," said Rosemary.

"No. Get out of here!"

"Do you want to know more about her?" Detective Neve asked.

"This is *not* happening," Tamsyn said. "It can't possibly be true. Leave now before I report you to the *real* authorities."

Rosemary and Neve shared a troubled look. The detective shrugged and gestured for them to get up from the table. Rosemary went along with it. The woman was clearly stressed and arguing with her wasn't going to help. They left the house and made their way back to the detective's car.

"Well, that was awful," said Rosemary.

"It could have gone a lot worse. Believe me," said Neve. "At least we got through the door. At least she knew about the magic, even if she is about to dob us in to the 'real' authorities."

"It's a lot," said Rosemary. "Isn't it? It's horrible having your memory mangled. Like your whole sense of reality is being challenged. I know what that's like."

Neve sighed. "We should have started with that. You could have talked about your experience and gently led her into it. I was too abrupt."

"No," Rosemary reassured her. "You were great. So clear and calm. I suspect there's not a perfect way to deal with a situation like this. And even if she does eventually believe us, what then? We can't just dump a little girl on the doorstep of a woman who doesn't remember her."

"This job is a lot harder than I thought it was going to be," said Neve. "You know, usually when the police return abducted children, everyone is overjoyed and relieved about it. It's a huge win, but this..."

"I wonder if there is something I can do to help," said Rosemary. "Some kind of spell."

"Thank you. That's the other reason I wanted to bring you along. I thought it might motivate you to see what you can do."

"Fair enough," said Rosemary. "I'm a total novice with magic, you realise. And as for police business? Well, I probably shouldn't have said anything at all, but I can’t help it. My mouth just operates of its own accord.”

Neve laughed. “You actually weren’t that bad back there. And magically, you're more powerful than you think. You've already done the impossible. Twice. You've taken down the Bloodstone Society, which I thought would never happen. And you've made it to the fae realm. I think you can crack something as simple as memory magic.”

“I fear there’s nothing simple about it,” said Rosemary. “And you make me sound much more impressive than I am. But sure. I'll see what I can do.”

Seven

Rosemary's limbs felt heavy and tired as she and Neve arrived back at Thorn Manor. They found Athena, Nesta, Dain, and the foundling children all sitting around the dining room table. Clearly, it was morning tea time.

Athena poured tea out for the adults and milk for the children. Thea and Clio immediately began slurping their drinks happily while Harry blew bubbles in his before being told off and beaming.

Athena offered Nesta milk.

"I'm afraid we're only allowed a low fat milk in the house, still," said Athena, looking at Dain. "It's not safe for him to be around cream."

Nesta smiled. "I know, love. Don't worry. I don't mind what kind of milk it is."

Athena served Nesta and then turned to Rosemary. "Find out anything interesting?"

"I'm afraid I'm not at liberty to discuss my serious police business," said Rosemary, slumping down in a chair under the weight of disappointment. "As a trusted and professional consultant..."

"Give me a break," said Athena.

"Well, we can say that it wasn't a particularly successful endeavour," said Neve grimly.

"Surprising," said Athena ironically. "If somebody showed up on my doorstep trying to pawn off a child that nobody remembered and who hadn't been seen in decades, I would be over the moon!"

The children laughed and clapped, not understanding the sarcasm in Athena's voice. Rosemary shot her a warning.

"Look. They're delightful," said Athena. "But it's an odd situation, you've got to admit."

"Shouldn't you get to school already?" Rosemary asked.

"Teacher only day. Anyway, I'm sure I'm learning a lot more about the responsibility of life just by having to look after all these kids."

"I'm sure," said Dain. "You're doing plenty by playing and having tea parties all day."

"Speak for yourself." Athena crossed her arms. "Somebody around here has to be responsible."

Dain sipped his black tea, raising his eyebrows at his daughter and smiling. "You turned out pretty well considering, I have to say."

"Considering what?" said Rosemary sternly. "It's not like you helped very much."

Dain made a face and Athena laughed.

"Considering that I have both of you for parents," said Athena.

Rosemary sighed. "Being a mother is the most thankless job!"

There was a knock at the door.

"Come in!" Rosemary called. But Marjie had already let herself into the house. "I'm back, and I brought cakes!"

The children cheered. Marjie carried two boxes into the dining room and set them on the table. Athena opened the one closest to her to reveal half a dozen assorted little cakes topped with cream.

Cream!

"Ahh, Marjie," she said, a note of worry in her voice.

Rosemary stared at the cakes, the hairs rising on her forearms in warning.

"Yes, dear," said Marjie.

"There's...on the cakes...Crea—" Athena stuttered.

"Oh!"

All adult eyes in the room turned towards Dain.

His eyes, locked on the cakes, seemed to glow as if covered in gold dust.

"This is not good," said Athena, quickly covering the cakes. "Mum. You have to hold him back."

Rosemary quickly moved to Dain's side of the table and gripped him by his arms. He began to struggle away from her, towards the cakes.

"Dain. No! You have a problem. But you've got to calm down."

For a moment, Dain held preternaturally still.

"I'm so sorry," said Marjie. "I should have remembered to check. I told the new girl at the shop, Lamorna, not to give me any of the cream ones for you, but she's obviously forgotten."

"Get them out of here!" Rosemary cried.

Athena picked up the box and made a dash towards the kitchen.

Rosemary heard the door to the back garden slam, just as Dain wrestled free of her grip. He flung open the other cake box to find there was no cream in sight, then he took a great leap over the dining chairs towards the door.

"Stop at once!" Rosemary cried. She watched Dain disappear in hot pursuit of the cream cakes, suppressing her urge to use magic. She didn't want to risk debris flying towards the children.

"Oh blast it all!" Marjie cried.

Rosemary ran after him. "Dain, I'm warning you," she said.

His hand was on the doorknob that Athena must have magically locked as she'd fled.

Rosemary could see her daughter heading quickly towards the trees, still carrying the box, but Dain could be much quicker. With his fully unleashed fae speed that he sometimes used while chasing the children she knew it would only take a moment for Dain to catch up.

Dain's hand was still on the locked door, scrambling to get it opened.

"Remember what happened last time?" Rosemary said, but the logical part of his mind had obviously vacated the building. "One more chance." She held her hands in front of her, and a light shimmered behind her palms. "I'm serious."

A growl issued from Dain's mouth. It sounded more like purr. He snapped the handle off the door as if it were no stronger than a candy cane and flung it wide open.

"That's it," said Rosemary.

She called forth her magic.

A golden ball of light issued from her hands and flew across the room, hitting Dain in the back. He sprawled forward, clearly concussed.

"It took you long enough," Athena said as she crossed back towards the house.

"I had to give him a warning," said Rosemary.

"Why? You know he doesn't think properly when he's in sight of a fix."

"We've got to do something about this," said Rosemary.

"Yeah, that's what you said last time," said Athena as they strolled back through the house. "And what have you done about it?"

"I've done some research," said Rosemary defensively. "I tried that spell from the old book Burk gave me, but it just made Dain sick, remember?"

"Oh well, at least we get to have whipped cream for morning tea, now that Dad's unconscious." Athena's voice was tense when she called Dain "Dad." It was a new development for her to casually refer to him in this way and Rosemary hoped it was a good thing.

The children, who were now in earshot, cheered and clapped at the news. They were big fans of Marjie's cream cakes, despite the fact that they were hardly ever allowed them, except on rare excursions to town. On those occasions, Dain had to stay locked in the car for his own protection and everyone else's.

Rosemary understood that cream had an effect on the fae worse than most mind altering substances known to humans. They would lose all sense of integrity or propriety and become exceedingly generous. Fortunately, this didn't seem to apply to Athena, who must have skipped those parts of the genetic lottery and merely had an enthusiastic fondness for dairy.

Aside from its dangers, cream had proved to be exceedingly useful. Under its influence, the fae countess had sent them back to the human realm without so much as a second thought, even though she'd been pursuing them with violence moments earlier. Athena had cleverly laced her tea with cream that she'd smuggled into the fae realm.

Understanding the power of cream had helped to clear things up for Rosemary regarding Dain's history of irrational behavior, his gambling, and the way that her wallet had a habit of disappearing when he was around, back in the days when they were together.

The explanation hadn't meant she'd forgiven him. It was hard to come back from something like that. Despite often forgetting her anger towards Dain in the past, due to the amnesiac properties of fae magic, being betrayed over and over again by your first love took its toll.

It had almost made matters worse that she hadn't gone through the appropriate anger with him, or processed it.

Athena, who was immune to the fae memory magic, had been dreadfully angry and resentful of her father, but recently, she'd seemed to warm to him slightly more than Rosemary was comfortable with.

While she hadn't been happy about Athena being previously so mad at Dain, Rosemary now had to contend with them both ganging up on her from time to time, even if it was just in a playful way.

Back inside the house, Rosemary helped herself to a chocolate tart and took a sip of tea, which Marjie had especially spiked with a generous helping of her special formula.

"Have you gotten any further with a cure for him, love?" Marjie asked.

"I keep asking her that," Athena said.

"I think I'm going to have to make up another spell entirely," said Rosemary. "I'll get to work on it after I visit Liam. Not that I know what I'm doing."

"Why are you visiting Liam all of a sudden?" Athena asked. "Don't tell me you two have a thing going on."

"Oh, really?" said Nesta. "Liam from the bookshop? He's quite handsome."

Rosemary felt her cheeks flush. "Nothing like that. I just promised I'd help him with something."

"But she won't say what," said Athena.

"It's not something I'm at liberty to share."

Marjie gave her a curious look.

"Oh, well," Athena continued. "At least if you're seeing Liam, you're less likely to get back with dad again. And we know that never was a good idea to begin with."

"I'm not getting involved with anybody, thank you very much!" said Rosemary. "We all know that only leads to disaster."

"Oh, it would be nice to see you with a nice man...or woman," said Marjie. She smiled at Nesta. "We don't discriminate."

Nesta gave her an awkward smile. "I know. You don't have to spell it out."

"Why don't you give us those spells that you tried last time on Dain?" said Marjie. "Athena and I can get started on some variations while you're out."

"Really, you don't have to go to any trouble," said Rosemary. "You've done so much already."

"Nonsense," said Marjie.

"What's the matter?" said Athena. "Are you worried that I'll figure the spell out before you do and show you that I'm better at magic?"

"That's the least of my worries," said Rosemary. "I wouldn't be surprised if anyone was better at magic than I am."

Athena sighed. "There's your imposter syndrome again, making everything worse." She gave her mother a sympathetic smile. "Don't worry, leave it to us. We'll have the spell cracked in no time. But at some point you're going to have to tell us what's going on with Liam."

Eight

Rosemary drove down the quiet country lane towards the address Liam had given her. He'd asked to meet her at his home rather than at the bookshop, for the sake of his privacy.

Liam's cottage was a small white one with pale blue trim, a sweet little house to look at from a distance. But as Rosemary drew closer, the peeling paint and cracked whitewash became more evident. *It definitely could use a bit of care, and a fresh coat of paint.*

She stepped out of the car and headed for the front door, but just as she neared it, she heard the snap of a breaking twig from behind her.

She turned back to see a tall hooded figure wearing black robes and a grey mask, and carrying a giant metal spear.

"Not this again!" said Rosemary. The figure didn't say a word, but ran towards her at an alarming pace, raising the spear, poised to strike.

Rosemary was caught off-guard. She lunged out of the way, narrowly missing the attack.

It must be that cursed Bloodstone Society!

The figure turned back to face her.

Don't show fear, Rosemary instructed herself. *You're a powerful witch. Show them who's boss.* "Reveal yourself, you coward!" she said with mock bravado.

The attacker laughed a deep throaty chuckle. "Rosemary Thorn," a raspy voice said. "Prepare to meet your fate!"

"What a cliché. You really can't come up with anything more original than that?"

The figure laughed again. "You are a weak mortal. You will not stand in our way. We will return, victorious!"

"Yeah, yeah." Rosemary's patience was wearing thin and that helped her channel some of her pent up rage into a fireball the size of a small melon. She held it in both hands, staring down her foe.

The hooded figure hesitated. "You...I was told you knew nothing of your power. That taking you out would be easy."

"Then you were misled or someone got their wires crossed," said Rosemary with a frustrated sigh. "But either way, I've never been a fan of drawn-out fights, not even in movies, and definitely not in real life. Get out of here before I blast you to another dimension."

Rosemary had no idea how to do that, but she bit her tongue to save from rambling. This was hardly the time.

"Consider this a warning!" The figure raised the spear as if to throw it, but Rosemary was quicker. She shoved the fireball towards the weapon, blasting it out of the attacker's hand.

The figure shrieked and rushed towards her, but Rosemary was more prepared this time. She made use of the strength and flexibility that seemed to only work as a magically-induced survival mechanism and gave them a quick stiff kick to the head, hoping to reveal their identity.

The hood remained in place, however, as the attacker reared back, clutching their face.

Rosemary caught a glimpse of an emblem under the cloak. It was the familiar shield bearing the Bloodstone Society crest. She sighed. "Look, I'm sick of your crowd. Leave me alone. I've got places to be."

"There are hundreds of us and we are gathering power!" the figure shrieked. "We will return!"

A crackling sound burst from behind Rosemary.

She felt dread rising as she turned, preparing for more attackers. Instead, her eyes were met with a solid wall of fire.

"What the...?" Rosemary turned back to see that the mysterious attacker had disappeared.

The red and orange flames rose swiftly, in a mesmerising pattern.

Rosemary wanted to watch, but her instincts made her step back and check for other risks.

Her abdominal muscles clenched as the fire spread dangerously close to the side of Liam's house.

"This is not what I expected for my morning," Rosemary muttered to herself.

"Rosemary!" Liam called, coming out from his house. "What's going on? What did you do?"

"Nothing!" Rosemary replied. "I was just attacked...And now, well, I guess the attacker lit a fire somehow."

Liam looked at her, unimpressed.

"It wasn't me!" said Rosemary defensively.

"Fine. But can't you do something?"

"Not without a lot of water," Rosemary replied. "I don't know how to put out fires magically."

"There's water in the pond," said Liam. "Can't you..."

"Actually, I think I can help with that, now that you mentioned it."

Rosemary focused her attention on the water from the pond, not far from the back of the house. Surely, it wasn't all that different from watering the plants she'd tended in her lounge only a few weeks before.

She closed her eyes and visualised the water spouting out, using the power of air to pick it up and pour it over the fire.

"It's working!" said Liam.

Rosemary looked to see that indeed, the water was spouting from the pond, sprinkling all over the flames, which had died back.

"Thank goodness for that," said Rosemary. "Sorry, Liam. Your house almost got singed."

"I thought you said it wasn't your fault."

"It wasn't. I'm just sorry it had to happen. And while I didn't make the fire, that attacker knows exactly who I am and knew where to find me. So you might want to reconsider whether you want to meet here."

"Who was it?" Liam asked.

"I'm not sure exactly." Rosemary described the mysterious figure. "I'm willing to bet it has something to do with that stupid secret society that seems to have it in for us. I'm sure I saw their emblem."

"The Bloodstones?" Liam asked.

Rosemary nodded. "I thought they'd given up, but apparently not."

Liam's lips pressed into a thin line. "Sherry told me she'd heard rumours of them making a comeback, or attempting to."

"Just what we need. Oh well, I suppose if we've vanquished them once it can happen again."

"The problem is, with their leader gone, there will be some kind of power struggle. They might get desperate." He rubbed his chin in contemplation. "Now that I think of it, some suspicious customers came into the book shop the other day. They weren't from around here, but they were seeking out texts on ancient vampire lore. One of them asked an oddly specific question on parallel dimensions."

Rosemary frowned. "Do you think they're trying to bring Geneviève back? I don't understand why they'd need the little brat."

Liam shrugged. "Their leader might have looked like an innocent child, but her reputation was infamous. She is believed to have caused chaos and destruction wherever she went for centuries, including instigating several wars and two near-apocalypses, and that was *before* she went undercover as the leader of a magical sect."

"Well, that's ruined my mood. I suppose I shouldn't visit your house if I'm only bringing you danger."

"Rosemary, if they knew to come to my house, then I'm no safer with you anywhere else, am I?"

Rosemary shrugged. "Fair enough."

"Come in."

She followed Liam inside. The cottage was simple with pale cream walls and plenty of bookshelves. Rosemary noticed many of Liam's books were old and leather bound, though she spotted a large collection of fantasy novels. She was surprised by the rather dainty watercolour paintings of flowers that adorned the walls. The furnishings were comfortable, not flashy. Old sofas and armchairs were draped with crochet blankets and there was a large fluffy rug on the floor. The lounge was cosy, especially when Liam lit the fire to take the chill out of the air.

Rosemary sighed and warmed her hands near the hearth. "I much prefer your fire to that one outside. It gave me the creeps."

"It was unusual. I wonder if it's anything to do with the fire at the Twigg farm a couple of weeks ago."

"I didn't hear about that," said Rosemary. "Which is strange in such a small town."

"Strange indeed. It was so warm this morning. And now all of a sudden it's freezing."

"Stranger things have happened," said Rosemary. "What is it you think I can help with?"

"We've talked about this," Liam said slightly defensively.

"Yeah...I know, in general, what you want me to do. I just don't know how to do it."

"Look, Rosemary, last time when I was in wolf form, you shocked me with your magic and it made the wolf go away, and it freed me temporarily. The next full moon is coming up in just over a week."

"Are you saying you want me to wait until you turn into a wolf, then shock you with magic every month?" Rosemary asked, unimpressed.

"If it comes down to it, then maybe," said Liam. "But I'm hoping there's a way you can bottle that sunshine stuff you produce out of your hands."

"Sunshine?" Rosemary wondered if what Liam had noticed might actually be some kind of combination of elemental fire and air – the two elements that came most naturally to her.

"That's what it felt like," said Liam. "I know it sounds strange, but maybe the sun kind of counteracts the moon."

"But you're still a werewolf during the day when it's full moon," Rosemary reminded him.

"Yeah, sure. It sounds silly and...I don't know. It's just my guess. The Moon is full when the Sun is opposite it, you know. The Sun and Moon have a kind of polarity."

"That sounds lovely and poetic," said Rosemary, though she wished Liam would get to the point.

"Look, I'm not sure about the actual scientific or magical truth. I'm grasping at straws," Liam admitted. "Do you have any other theories?"

"I'm afraid not," Rosemary said. "We can go with yours for now. Surely there must be lots of books on werewolves? You work in a magical bookshop. Don't you know these things?"

"There are lots of books on how awful we are," said Liam. "The most useful things I've found are protection spells—the kind of thing I use a lot, to make sure I don't infect anyone else. But until the other day I'd never heard of anything like what you did. As far as I know, it's never happened before."

"Well, that's just ridiculous." Rosemary put her hands on her hips. "I don't know what I did. It was a fluke. We're totally in the dark."

"Could you try bottling it? Liam asked. "You know, like pouring your energy into some kind of vessel, and then when I need it I can just open it up."

"Why not smash it on the ground for dramatic effect?" said Rosemary. "Or, I know, in the bath. Maybe you want a magical bath bomb?"

"You're not taking this seriously."

"Forgive me if I'm a little wound up. I've just been attacked and had to deal with magical arson and now you tell me we have no clues as to how to deliberately work the magic you have such high expectations on me for."

"So you don't want to help me?"

"I certainly can try," said Rosemary. "Though, if I do manage to bottle some energy, we won't know if it works until it's already too late."

"That's true," said Liam.

"You'll have to chain yourself up in the basement, just in case."

"If I'm chained up, how am I going to have a magical bath?" Liam asked, amused.

"Liam, I'm afraid there are some things that I'm not going to be able to help you with." Rosemary laughed. "I draw the line at bathing you."

"I suppose I'll have to manage," said Liam with a wry smile, then his expression became more serious, his eyes stormy. "Thank you for trying to help. This *condition* has been plaguing me for years and I finally have hope that I'll be able to live a normal life without constant fears of hurting people or being ostracised by the magical community. I even wonder if there'll be some kind of cure."

"You mean if I can zap you with enough magic to stop you from ever changing again?" said Rosemary.

"I'm not sure if it's about enough magic," said Liam. "Or if it's about finding the precise kind, woven in the right way."

"Yeah, I get it," said Rosemary. "I wish I could ask other people for help because I have no idea what I'm doing and I don't want to hurt you. I only blasted you at the shop because I was being attacked by an enormous wolf creature. I don't really want to do that when you're standing here as a human, let alone as a friend."

"I've missed our friendship," said Liam in a soft voice, his eyes downcast.

"Me too," said Rosemary. "You were starting to act weird."

"I'm sorry. I just...I got a bit jealous after you shot me down. You've been hanging out with that vampire a lot. It gives me the creeps."

"Wow," said Rosemary. "Discrimination, much?"

"They're not natural, Rosemary."

"Any more than a werewolf is?"

"That's very different," said Liam.

"Is it, though? I mean you've both been infected with some kind of magical equivalent of a virus or something."

"That's one way to put it," said Liam. "But vampires are cunning, and they've been around for a long time. They're very strategic."

Rosemary thought of the very handsome vampire she'd taken a shine to. Burk had gone out of his way to help her when Athena went missing. He seemed trustworthy, but was that all a part of his vampire charm, luring her in?

"They amass a lot of resources," Liam continued. "And they have a different sense of morality. I mean, they feed on blood."

"And blood-enchanted food." Rosemary grimaced. "And apparently a lot of pig's blood."

"Still," said Liam, "I get the feeling they enjoy being what they are. Whereas, it's not like I can use my wolf to my advantage. It's only a curse, there's nothing good about it. I'd do anything to be properly human again."

Rosemary gave him a sad smile. "So you think this is something we can practice when you're not in your wolf form?" she asked. "You want me to shoot magic energy at you? I suppose you could give me feedback on whether it's had any effect on the wolfiness. If you're attuned to it enough to be able to tell."

"I think so," said Liam. "When infected with the virus, it's like a kind of wolf lives inside you. That's part of the reason I was so jealous. The wolf can make me aggressive sometimes, even when it's not the full moon. I do my best to quell it, but it's hard to control."

"So you can feel it there all the time?" Rosemary asked.

"Yes."

"Then I'll practice shooting you with magic and we can see how we go."

Liam gulped.

"Not too scared?" Rosemary asked him, her voice slightly teasing.

"Scared of what? Only the most powerful witch in town, shooting me with magic lasers?" Liam asked. "Why would I be scared of that?"

"They're not lasers," said Rosemary. "I'm a great ball of sunshine, remember?"

Liam laughed. "That you are, Rosemary. That you are."

Nine

Despite the pleasant hour she'd spent with Liam, Rosemary felt heavy and drained by the time she returned home. It didn't help her mood that the kitchen looked like a bomb site.

"What on earth is going on?" she asked.

Athena popped her head up from behind the counter, looking frazzled. "We've been trying to make a potion, but it keeps exploding. This magic stuff is way unstable."

"Tell me about it," said Rosemary. "Where's Marjie?"

"She's gone to the bathroom to clean herself up while I had a wee sit down on the floor."

"Oh dear," Rosemary said, approaching her daughter and giving her a fortifying hug. "This situation with Dain is not going to improve anytime soon, is it?"

Athena shook her head as Rosemary led her over to the window seats to rest properly.

"Magic is complicated where fae are concerned," Athena muttered.

"I was hoping we could get his little problem dealt with," said Rosemary. "I suppose he's just going to have to work on his self-control, which is tricky when fae don't seem to have any around a particular high-fat dairy product. Come to think of it, isn't it odd that butter doesn't have the same effect?"

Athena shrugged. "Butter has the fat, but it has some of the other stuff taken out of it. Maybe it's the processing or maybe it's just that it needs all the components of cream to create that effect."

"How did you get to be so smart?" Rosemary asked. "Wait a minute, where are the kids?"

"Don't worry, my dear," said Marjie. "Nesta took them out back. She's so good with children. She's always wanted some of her own, Neve told me."

"She's welcome to take some of ours," said Rosemary flippantly. "We've got plenty here, and I'm a little bit worried that the next seasonal festival is all about fertility. Seeing as magic is real and all, we hardly need any more children at this time!"

She looked at Athena.

"Gross, Mum. Don't look at me. I'm not having any children, and you won't have to worry about accidents considering I'm never having relationships, ever!"

Marjie shook her head and tutted. "Why don't you go and get yourself cleaned up?" she said to Athena, who grumbled as she shook herself and stalked off towards the bathroom.

"What's all that about?" Rosemary asked.

"The sting of betrayal," said Marjie. "It takes a long time to get over your first crush."

"Athena won't tell me the details of what went on," said Rosemary. "Just that Finnigan sold her out to some fae countess. I assume they wanted her and Dain to use as political bargaining chips. He was locked up in the same castle."

"And you can't see why she's bitter about relationships?" Marjie asked.

"Of course I can," said Rosemary. "It's just...she's cutting herself off from a whole world of human experience. It's bugging me how much she reminds me of myself right now."

Marjie gave Rosemary a knowing look. "And how will this insight affect you?"

"Oh Marjie, you know I have rotten luck when it comes to men."

"When it came to one man with a very specific dairy product addiction who isn't even human."

"That's a bit harsh."

"I don't mean offence by it. It's just the truth. Maybe if you were involved with anyone other than Dain it wouldn't be such a disaster."

Rosemary sighed. "I let Athena down so badly with my choices. I'm not going to do that again."

"And yet, here we are," said Marjie. "Listen, think about it this way. If you were giving advice to a good friend in your current situation, what would you say to her?" And with that, the older woman stood up, brushed off her apron, and started cleaning up the kitchen, leaving Rosemary boggling at the astute question.

She got up to help Marjie as Athena returned and joined in the cleaning too. "Okay, so talk me through what you've tried so far, and I'll see if I can figure out what's going wrong," said Rosemary.

"Well," Athena said, "the first phase of the spell involves a fresh egg, quartz crystals, and plenty of sage, as well as salt."

"Sea salt to be precise," Marjie added.

"Yes, I know that," said Rosemary. "I tried it myself, remember. This one made Dain awfully sick. It didn't explode the kitchen, though."

"We've been trying to swap out ingredients," said Marjie. "Seems like any variation of the spell just creates total chaos...makes it unstable."

Rosemary read through the spell again, holding the piece of paper she'd copied it onto by hand to save the book from getting messy. "It's such an old spell and it was originally supposed to deter fae from cream, but that was before the fae magic changed to protect them from vampires, and before the veil barriers were put up. If only I could understand how it's supposed to work. Then maybe I could make it better."

"I'm afraid I'm not really the expert here," said Marjie.

"I could try asking one of the teachers from school," Athena suggested.

"That's not a bad idea," said Rosemary. "They're bound to have a lot more experience in this sort of magic, even if they haven't focused on fae."

"It's almost like a healing spell," said Marjie, looking at the text again. "Actually, come to think of it..."

"What? said Rosemary.

"I feel daft for not mentioning it earlier," said Marjie. "It never crossed my mind that we should have been consulting Ashwyn at the local apothecary."

"What's that?" Athena asked.

"Oh, you know, the apothecary across the square from the bookshop," said Marjie. "They make all sorts of remedies. Well, perhaps not all sorts, otherwise we would have just got a pre-made one for our little fae spell. But they do specialise in treatments for all kinds of magical ailments and some mundane ones as well."

"This is more than just a regular magical ailment," said Rosemary. "Do you really think they can help?"

"It's worth a shot," said Marjie. "After all, they're experts at what they do. They're not going to be able to cure vampirism or stop someone from being a horrible werewolf, but for something like this, where the primary focus is actually an addiction, they might be able to do something or at least explain to you how this spell is supposed to work."

Rosemary grimaced at Marjie's werewolf comment. It seemed like blatant discrimination and it made her fear for Liam, if his secret ever got out. *If the loveliest woman in town is awful about werewolves, I hate to think how anyone else would react...*

"Do you think it's safe to tell your friend at the apothecary what Dad is?" Athena asked Marjie. "I don't even know if fae are supposed to be here in this world. Mum wants me to keep what I am a secret from vampires."

"Good point," said Rosemary. "We've got to play it safe. But the police know what Dain is. I'm pretty sure we could mention it to the local magical equivalent of doctors."

"They see all sorts of things around here," said Marjie. "And I'll vouch for Ashwyn and her lovely sister. They are good sorts."

"Alright, let's go then," said Athena.

"I can introduce you," said Marjie.

"We'll just have to check to make sure that Nesta is okay with minding the kids a little bit longer," said Rosemary.

"I'm sure she'll be fine," said Marjie. "I just checked a little while ago and she's got them down for their afternoon nap. Well, most of them. Mei was reading quietly in the corner of the nursery."

Rosemary smiled. "It still surprises me how the house knew to make us a nursery, even before we got home."

"All right, Mum," said Athena. "Let's go. Before Dad wakes up."

Ten

Rosemary and Athena followed Marjie into the apothecary and were surprised to see a familiar face.

The woman behind the counter had long, blonde, wavy hair. It took a moment for Rosemary to recall that she was the one officiating at the Ostara ritual a few weeks before.

Rosemary looked around the shop to find dozens of shelves neatly stacked with assortments of bottles, all with neat white and green labels.

Athena had already become distracted by the different items on sale and had veered off to examine them. A large flower arrangement sat in the middle of the small shop, made up of freshly picked wild flowers and herbs.

The way everything was set out gave the shop a spaciousness and lightness. The whole feeling of the space was one of peace, which no doubt was partly attributed to the tranquil presence of the woman who ran it.

"How can I help you today?" said the woman, smiling.

"Ashwyn! How nice to see you," said Marjie, introducing Rosemary and Athena. "We were just wondering if we could trouble you to help us out with a little problem we've been having, which is rather...complex."

"Of course, Marjie," said Ashwyn. "You know how much I adore little complex problems."

"Not so little, I'm afraid," said Rosemary. "Nothing is quite so simple when it comes to the fae."

"Let's see how we can help." Ashwyn regarded them with a knowing smile. "Please take a seat."

She waved her arms and four little stools appeared, surrounding the table.

"I see...Would you like some tea?"

"We just had tea," said Rosemary.

"Since when has that ever stopped you?" Athena asked.

"I just mean, don't go to any trouble," said Rosemary.

"It's no trouble at all," said Ashwyn. "I just happen to have herbal formula brewing. It's my new calming blend."

"That sounds wonderful," said Rosemary.

Ashwyn disappeared into a back room and Marjie smiled. "She always has some kind of tea brewing to offer people who enter the shop at any time. One of the nice things about coming here."

"If I'd known about that, I would have popped in more often," said Rosemary. "You know, my nerves can always do with some calming,"

"That's right, Mum. You should definitely be a regular client."

Ashwyn returned with tea. She was followed by another woman of similar height with long brown wavy hair. "This is my sister, Una," Ashwyn said.

There was something luminous about Una's skin. Rosemary thought she looked a little like Athena. The teen approached and sat down at the table. She smiled at the brown-haired woman and the woman smiled back, a glint of recognition in her eyes.

"What seems to be the problem?" she asked.

"It's my father," said Athena. "He's always had a problem. He can't help himself."

"Dairy addiction?" Una asked.

Athena gasped in surprise.

"How did you know?" said Rosemary, gobsmacked. She looked from one sister to the other, feeling her paranoia rising. Who were these women, really? They seemed so nice and genuine, but could that be a ruse?

"I might have some experience in that realm," Una replied. "I'm both human and fae, just like you." She looked at Athena, who put her hand to her mouth in surprise.

"You are? I thought there was something familiar about you," Athena said.

"Yes," said Ashwyn. "Our mother was a gifted healer, but we have different fathers."

"I didn't know my father," Una added. "But Mother would talk about him sometimes. She said it was a summer fling. But anyway, back to your problem. What's happening?"

"Dain has always been erratic," said Rosemary. "Flipping out and gambling and giving away everything we own."

"That happens when he has cream?" Una asked.

"Wait a minute," said Rosemary. "If you didn't really know your father, how do you know about this?"

"I might have suffered from something quite similar," said Una. "As I said before, Mother was a gifted healer and she was able to help me."

"But if you're like me," Athena said, "then why don't I have that problem?"

Una shrugged. "It could be genetics."

Ashwyn's brow furrowed. "I wouldn't be surprised if the power of your legendary magical genes had something to do with it, given that you come from the Thorn family."

"How do you know that?" Rosemary asked, raising her eyebrows.

Ashwyn laughed. "Marjie just introduced you. Besides, it's a small town. Everyone knew Galdie. I'd be surprised if there was a local here that doesn't recognise you already."

Una looked at Rosemary and Athena curiously.

"But your mother managed to help you," said Rosemary excitedly. "So, you have a remedy for us?"

"Not exactly," said Una. "The one that our mother managed to concoct for me was a potion and a spell. But it fortified my human side. If your father is a fully fledged fae, then that's not going to work."

Rosemary deflated in disappointment, her shoulders hunching.

"That's not to say we can't help," said Ashwyn. "We might be able to give you some pointers."

"Please, if you can help in any way," said Rosemary. "I had previously just thought that Dain was a totally irresponsible human being and I'm now having to adjust to the realisation that he's actually a fae prince with an unfortunate predilection for flipping out over cream cakes. It would really help things if he didn't become a total fruit loop and lose his mind every time he saw a cream bun—"

Athena cleared her throat and Rosemary stopped rambling. "We've been working on something," Athena explained. "It's from an old book about the fae."

Rosemary pulled out the tiny green fabric bound volume that Burk had given her.

"Where did you get this book?" Una asked as she flipped through the pages. "I've never seen anything like it."

"I can't say," said Rosemary. "But it's quite rare. I'm not sure if there are any other copies. It's rather outdated, I suppose."

"It is," said Una. "But there are some things in here that I might find quite useful, if you lend it to me."

"I don't know..." said Rosemary.

"Oh, maybe you can just pop around and read it from time to time?" said Marjie. "I'm sure Rosemary wouldn't mind that."

"No, that would be fine," said Rosemary, smiling. "I'm already borrowing it from a friend and I don't think I can lend out somebody else's book."

"I totally understand," said Una with a warm smile. "I just got a bit excited there. It's so rare to find any proper information on the fae that isn't just idle speculation or fantasy."

"Like that rubbish about them not being able to lie," said Athena bitterly.

"Tell me about it," said Rosemary. She filled Una in on some of the details and talked about their recent experiences.

A look of the greatest surprise crossed both sister's faces as they heard the brief story of Rosemary's venture into the fae realm.

"I would have thought it impossible," said Una.

"I remember you being at that ritual," Ashwyn added. "I remember the crystals on the ground, and chanting. And then it all gets a bit foggy."

"Funny how the fae manage to do that, isn't it?" said Rosemary. "Come to think of it, that's another thing I'd like your help with. Do you have any miracle cures or remedies to both protect against the memory altering magic, and also to repel it?"

"We'll have a think about that," said Una. "But in the meantime, this is the spell, is it?" She'd flipped to the bookmarked page.

Rosemary nodded.

"I see. So it's trying to work on the fae side," Una continued. "It's just possible that if we combine what we know from this spell with the one in my mother's Grimoire we might be able to come up with something that works."

"That sounds promising," said Athena.

"Unfortunately it all hinges on something that's totally out of our control," said Una.

"What's that?" Rosemary asked.

"Love," Una replied.

Athena scrunched up her face, looking mildly disgusted.

"What do you mean by that?" asked Rosemary.

"There needs to be love on both sides," Ashwyn explained. "It's in our mother's spell, anyway. There needs to be something that he loves more. To have power over the addiction. And it needs to be cast by people who love him."

"Sounds tricky," said Rosemary. "They can't be many people who Dain's formed any kind of deep emotional attachment to."

"He did with you, Mum," said Athena.

"That was a long time ago," Rosemary replied. "And while he's very charming. I am not in a position to be able to...do that. You're his daughter, you're probably better placed."

"Maybe," said Athena. "He's starting to grown on me...Although I wouldn't go that far."

"We can worry about the specifics of it later, dear," said Marjie. "It's just important that we get the ball rolling on this. I better pop back to the shop, but I'll check on you later at your place."

"I guess we'd better leave too," Rosemary said. "Thanks for your help."

"We haven't done anything yet," said Una.

"Even just a little bit more information is something," Rosemary replied. "We've been totally in the dark apart from the spell in this book. If you'd like, you're welcome to pop around in the next day or two. I'll be home most of the time, keeping an eye on those foundling children and making sure Athena stays out of trouble."

Athena glared at her mother, and then turned back to Una with a smile. "You could come over for a cup of tea."

"That sounds lovely," said Una.

Eleven

Athena left the apothecary with a lingering feeling of warmth. She'd arranged to meet Elise at Marjie's shop for cake a bit later, so instead of going back to Thorn Manor she said goodbye to her mother and wandered across the circular park in the centre of Mytlewood. This park, sometimes called the town circle, was where the village rituals were held. It was surrounded by roads forming a square, lined with shops and other businesses that faced inwards, giving Athena a sense of safety. No one would attack her here, not in broad daylight. Still, as she crossed beneath the hawthorn trees in full bloom, she had the sensation of being watched by someone with malicious intentions.

She looked around, but everything seemed to be in order.

Don't run wild, she scolded her imagination. *I'm totally safe.*

She deliberately drew her attention back to the warm feeling she'd had at the apothecary, the sense of recognition when she'd met Una and the tingling sensation that spread right to her fingertips.

She'd rarely met anyone with such similar heritage to her and wondered if it was something to do with her genetics that inspired the reaction.

Finnigan was the only other person she knew with high fae and human parents, and he was the last person she wanted to see.

This particular reaction to Una was different. It was almost as though they were bonded somehow – connected, like family despite never meeting each other before.

Athena certainly hadn't felt anything like that when she'd met any of the creatures in the fae realm. She tried to push thoughts of that realm out of her mind, along with the guilt that came from her late night activities.

She knew she needed to make friends with Una and spend more time with her. Being in her presence had not only dissipated the uncomfortable, heavy feelings from the physical plane but had also made Athena feel light and safe and contented.

It was a little bit like the feelings she had at night when she cut her way through to the fae realm itself.

Stop it, she scolded. *Focus on the present. There's no point in pining for another world.*

As she neared the tea shop, she recognised Elise's blue hair.

Athena smiled as she opened the door. "You're early."

Elise beamed back at her. "So are you! It must be fate."

"Maybe it's a sign we need to have extra cake."

"That sounds right," said Elise with a nod.

They hugged and made their way up to the counter.

Marjie's new helper, Lamorna, greeted them with a broad smile. Marjie said she had just moved to Myrtlewood from St Austell and came from a magical family. Today, she wore an oversized knitted jumper. Her blonde hair was pinned up into little bundles which Athena thought looked cool in an old '90s sort of way – though she knew Rosemary would have balked at the '90s being considered old-fashioned.

"I'm so sorry about the mix-up earlier," Lamorna said. "I totally forgot about the cream situation."

"That's okay," said Athena, hoping not to sound too uncool. "No big deal."

Lamorna nodded, then gestured to the cabinet. "What will it be?"

"Oooh," said Elise. "I really want chocolate, but I don't tolerate animal products well. I'm pretty sure that one's not dairy free. I wonder if I can handle a bit of cream..."

Athena shook her head. "Not if it's going to make you sick."

"You know what," said Lamorna, with a wink. "We have a fresh triple chocolate cake cooling out the back and I made it with coconut oil instead of butter. You know, I can't tolerate it either. How about I bring some out with cashew cream?"

"Perfect!" said Elise.

Athena grinned and ordered the shortcake and a large pot of her favourite strawberries and cream tea.

They sat down at a table by the window to await their feast.

"She's so cool!" said Elise.

Athena nodded. "There's something unusual about her though. I wonder if she's part fae."

Elise rubbed her chin in thought. "Maybe. Lots of people can't have dairy, though."

"Speaking of part fae," said Athena. "Have you ever met Una at the apothecary? She's awesome."

"I vaguely know her," said Elise with a frown. "She's one of Mum's friends."

"You don't like her?"

"Oh no, it's not that. She seems lovely."

"What is it then?" Athena asked.

"Nothing," said Elise. "I guess I'm just hungry and need an extraordinary amount of cake, right now!"

It wasn't long before their cake and tea arrived. Athena ate and drank, quietly pondering the connection she felt with Una. There was only one person who might have any clue about it who was accessible.

She made a mental note to talk to her father when he'd woken up from his little magically-induced nap.

Twelve

That evening, Rosemary opened the door to find a familiar woman standing there, her greying strawberry blonde hair looking as if it needed to be brushed. She was holding a large casserole dish.

"Sherry?"

"Hello," said Sherry. "I just dropped around to bring you some of my famous beef and Guinness stew. I'm so sorry about everything."

"I understand," said Rosemary, still feeling slightly awkward about the situation. "You lost someone. I would do the same thing if I had to...to get Athena back."

It was true. Rosemary did understand. But she didn't entirely trust Sherry even though she wanted to. It had been invasive. The woman who was supposed to be a friend had stolen a priceless and magical heirloom from Rosemary's bathroom, all so she could have enough power to go to the fae realm to try to rescue her childhood friend, Mei.

"Can I see her?" Sherry asked.

"Sherry!" a voice called out, and little Mei ran towards the front door and wrapped Sherry in her arms. "How did you get to be so big?" she asked.

"I told you this before, Mei," said Sherry. "You were gone for a long time."

"It wasn't really very long," Mei insisted.

"It may not have seemed long where you were," said Athena, following along behind Mei. "But time passes differently here."

Mei giggled, beaming at Athena, clearly star-struck by the teen.

"Won't you join us for dinner, Sherry?" Rosemary asked.

"I don't want to trouble you," said Sherry. "I just thought I'd bring you something to eat since you're so busy looking after all the children."

"Nonsense," said Rosemary. "Come on, stay a little while. It'll give you a chance to catch up with Mei. I'm sure there's a lot for you to talk about after all these years."

Sherry smiled and joined them at the dinner table where they had not only the stew but also roasted vegetables and chicken drumsticks that Athena had already made.

Rosemary smiled at her daughter. "Your cooking is improving. This is really good."

"I suppose I'm getting a lot of practice at the moment," said Athena as she shot little Harry a warning glance across the table. He'd been trying to steal a chicken drumstick from Elowen's plate while she was occupied trying to sneak a piece of stewed beef to little Serpentine under the table.

"It's a lot of work to feed so many mouths," Athena continued. "Speaking of culinary tastes, have you made any progress on your chocolate shop? Other than looking at derelict old shops, I mean."

"What's this about a chocolate shop?" Sherry asked.

"Oh, nothing," said Rosemary. "It's just a kind of pipe dream I had. Now I've got the money for it, it's not impossible anymore. I've always wanted to work with food, and being a chocolatier would be amazing. I'd love to have a little shop. But I've been rather distracted lately. Nothing's really happened aside from looking at signing up for a bunch of courses and getting deeply confused."

"Well, the two cakes you made while you were still working in my shop were lovely," said Marjie. "I really do hope you make it happen."

"Yes! You must," said Sherry. "That's exactly what we need in town. Everyone loves chocolate. And it's such a mood booster."

"Now that I'm getting better at using my magic," said Rosemary, "I might even be able to do something magical with the chocolate. Like little harmless charms to boost concentration or improve people's emotional state, that sort of thing."

"What a wonderful idea," said Neve from across the table. She and Nesta had all but moved into Thorn Manor recently, though they still went home sometimes in the evenings, usually taking Mei with them.

They'd turned Nesta's office into a bedroom and Nesta was considering renovating the small cottage in their back yard so she could work from there instead.

"Mum doesn't really know what she's doing yet," said Athena. "But she's already considering renting a shop in town."

"Is that the one next to Liam?" Sherry asked. "Perfect! You should ask Covvey about it. I'm sure he'll give you a good deal."

"Why Covvey?" said Rosemary.

"He's the landlord," said Sherry.

"That's right," said Marjie. "Didn't I mention it?"

Rosemary grimaced. "I don't think I'm in his good books at the moment. I might have accidentally called him a werewolf."

"Why on earth would you do something so ghastly?" said Sherry. "I mean, I'm sorry, but there's hardly a worse thing you could have called a shifter."

"Well, I don't know about any of this stuff," said Rosemary. "I didn't grow up in this world."

"I'm sure he'll forgive you," said Marjie.

Sherry gave her a questioning look.

"Well, maybe he'll need a little time," Marjie added. "He is very stubborn."

"Oh bother," Rosemary said. "Maybe I can find another shop to rent, just in case he holds a grudge."

"There's not much around, I'm afraid," said Sherry. "But don't worry. We can help you talk Covvey around. He hasn't leased it for a long while despite people asking."

"Why not?" Rosemary asked. "Surely it's just costing him money without being leased out."

"You'd think that," said Sherry. "He's got some emotional attachments to the bar that he used to have, despite the fact it was a bit of a seedy dive."

"The mayor shut him down," said Marjie. "Wouldn't renew his license to operate. Said it brought down the whole tone of the town."

"Judgmental," said Rosemary.

"Well, he wasn't wrong," said Neve. "We had to break up so many fights in there."

Marjie tutted. "That's right. The place seemed to draw in all sorts of riffraff, even werewolves."

"Why does everyone hate werewolves so much?" Rosemary asked.

Silence fell around the dinner table and everyone stared at Rosemary, except Athena who looked just as surprised at the reaction as her mother felt.

"If you'd ever met one," said Marjie, "you wouldn't be asking that."

Rosemary shrugged awkwardly. "It's some kind of magical virus isn't it?" she asked with what she hoped was a light and casual tone of curiosity. "Why are people so mean about something that others can't control?"

"It might be a virus. But it seems to have the unfortunate effect of turning people quite rough," said Neve. "They might seem normal for a while, but as time passes they become more and more ragged and rude, quite violent at times."

"Not to mention the fact that on the full moon, they go around attacking and biting people, murdering...and spreading that foul curse," said Marjie.

"Wait, is it a curse or a virus?" Rosemary asked, wondering whether Liam was becoming more aggressive.

"A bit of both, I think," said Sherry. "Sort of like a cursed virus."

"Have you ever wondered whether the reason people might become so hard to deal with is because everyone's horrible to them?" Athena suggested.

Rosemary was pleased that her daughter had asked the question that she hadn't dared to ask. She was worried about accidentally outing Liam by saying too much.

"You would understand people's reactions," said Marjie, "if you'd ever come across one of those horrible beasts, let alone had a loved one killed by them." Her eyes clouded over.

"I'm sorry, Marjie," said Athena. "Did something awful like that happened to you?"

"My little brother Jowan was murdered by a werewolf." Tears welled in Marjie's eyes. "I will not abide them!"

"Something similar happened to my cousin," said Sherry.

"Liam?" Rosemary asked, surprised.

"Course not! Liam's still alive." Sherry looked taken aback. "No. He and his brother, Treave, were out walking in the forest one day. Of course it must have been the full moon...and a werewolf attacked them. Liam was lucky to escape with his life."

"How awful." Rosemary's mind rang with the realisation that the event Sherry just described probably led to Liam's present condition, though no one else in the town seemed to be aware of it.

Athena gave her a puzzled look and Rosemary shot her glance, warning her daughter to stay out of her mind.

There was a sound of footsteps in the hallway and Dain entered the dining room looking sheepish and bleary eyed.

"I'm sorry," he said. "It happened again, didn't it?"

"I'm afraid so," said Athena. "Sit down, Dad. Have some dinner."

Dain did as he was told, helping himself to a good portion of food. "I don't think we've ever properly been introduced," he said to Sherry. "I'm..."

"I know who you are," Sherry said with a little shy smile. "I'm Sherry."

"Of course." Dain leaned back in his chair and cradled his arms behind his head.

"We met during that rescue escapade," Sherry said.

Dain's lip twitched. "I was actually going to say, I'm the fae who followed you back out of the realm when you were a child."

The whole table sat in stunned silence.

Sherry gasped. "What? Really?"

"Sure," said Dain. "You probably didn't see me, but I remember you. I figured you were my only hope of escaping Leithrein."

"Leaf rain?" Athena asked.

"Leithrein, the Countess of West Eloria. I hid in the bushes, near the thin part of the veil, and I worked my fairy magic to bring down the protections on the inside to let you through. I hoped you had enough magic that you could get past the human protections. And when you did, I ducked out after you."

"You kind of stalked me," said Sherry, sounding slightly uncomfortable.

"Not exactly," said Dain. "I needed to get out of there. I knew the countess was after me. After I played a trick on her and her guards."

"Some fae don't take kindly to trickery." Sherry's brow furrowed. "I had some uncomfortable experiences."

"The countess also had a vested interest," Dain added. "She wanted to use me as some kind of bargaining pawn against my mother."

"So that was why she captured you," said Detective Neve. "You didn't tell me that during the police interview."

"I try to keep out of fae politics." Dain shrugged. "It's easier that way. And safer."

Sherry's eyes were moonlike. "You helped me escape. You helped me get out of there and back home."

Dain flashed her charming smile. "And I do it again in a heartbeat."

"To suit your own interests," said Rosemary, worrying a little at how Sherry was gazing across the table at her ex. He did have a way of charming the ladies, and Rosemary was sure there was some kind of magic at play.

"What do you take me for?" Dain raised his hands defensively. "I'm not just out for myself. At least not when I'm sober."

"Thank you," said Sherry. "I had no idea how I was able to escape it the first time. I just knew I had to get back in there to get Mei out again." She smiled at the little girl across the table who giggled. "I had to do anything that I could to help my friend."

"Well, if you ever need any fae magic again, you know who to ask," said Dain, winking.

Rosemary's gut tightened at the obvious flirting. She frowned and Athena gave her a cheeky grin.

"Have you noticed anything strange around here lately?" Detective Neve asked as they cleared up from dinner.

"Stranger than usual?" said Rosemary. "Are you wondering about anything in particular?"

Detective Neve lowered her voice. "I was wondering if you'd noticed any fires?"

With a jolt of recognition, Rosemary replied. "Yes, actually the other day when I went to visit Liam, a fire just burst out of nowhere."

"You told me it was a person who attacked you," said Neve.

"It was, at least at first. I assumed the fire was related to the attacker."

"You didn't think to tell me about the *fire*?"

Rosemary gave the detective an apologetic look. "You know what my memory's like, after everything Granny and Dain did to muddle it. Whether they realised it or not, it seems to have had a long-term effect. The fire slipped my mind. I haven't even told Athena yet. I only mentioned the attack to you earlier because it popped into my head."

"I would have thought you'd have called me straight away." Neve frowned. "Especially after you'd been attacked by somebody in a dark hood. You think it's *them*?"

"I do, actually," said Rosemary. "I'm ninety-nine percent sure it was the Bloodstones. Anyway, straight after I was attacked this fire appeared. So obviously the same person, or people, caused it."

"Perhaps," said Detective Neve. "At least that's a potential lead."

"Why do you ask about fires?" said Rosemary.

"Mysterious fires have been popping up around the place. Nobody seems to know why. They're not huge, but they might be getting bigger."

"That *is* concerning," said Rosemary, as she rinsed dinner dishes.

"But there doesn't seem to be anything causing them to appear," Neve added. "I've had two reports in the last twenty four hours. At first, I thought it was kids playing pranks. But now it seems like too much of a pattern."

Rosemary nodded. "And besides, kids aren't usually careful enough not to get caught. It could be the Bloodstones starting fires all over the place, though that seems odd."

"It might be tactical," said Neve. "Perhaps they don't have big enough numbers here to go on the offensive. They're just strategically trying to scare people. Throw them off the scent of what they're actually doing."

"Maybe," said Rosemary. "Either way, it makes me uncomfortable."

"What are you talking about?" Athena asked, carrying some more of the dishes to the kitchen.

"Oh, you know, just the usual." Rosemary smiled. "Mysterious fires and a high chance of a secret magical society attacking me."

Athena groaned and Rosemary filled her in on the details.

Athena squinted at her mother. "You know, it's funny. I'm sure I saw someone peeking through the windows of Thorn Manor when you were out at Liam's house. Maybe it was one of *them* – spying on us!"

"Why didn't you say anything?!" Rosemary asked.

Athena shrugged. "Why didn't you tell me about being attacked?"

"My thoughts exactly," said Neve, putting her hands on her hips.

"Like I said, it's been a busy week," Rosemary said. "And a long day. I'm more than ready for a cup of tea and a good night's sleep."

Thirteen

Athena wiped down the bench and kitchen table, cleaning up after breakfast. She still had an hour before school started.

She hadn't had a chance to talk to her father, yet.

She'd been meaning to ask, the night before, about the unusual reaction she'd had to meeting another person with fae heritage. But Dain had gone to bed shortly after dinner, claiming that he was far too tired for someone who'd slept off a magical concussion all day.

Athena didn't blame him, he seemed exhausted. But she kept it in mind for the next morning, after Harry, Elowen and the twins had excitedly woken her up to make them breakfast.

Now, her burning curiosity was enough to overcome any hesitancy she had about trying to have a meaningful discussion.

Dain seemed happy that morning, grabbing a piece of jam toast from the table, he'd immediately begun to chase the restless young children around, making them squeal with delight as they ran out to the lawn.

She waited until he was tired from running around the garden, and had collapsed under the shade of a large magnolia tree. Athena admired it, in full bloom, as she walked over. It's enormous purple flowers reminded Athena, of the fae realm and she felt a pang of longing for that illusive place.

"I wanted to ask you about something," she said, approaching Dain.

"Ask away."

"Yesterday we went to the apothecary and met this amazing woman who was definitely of fae and human descent."

Dain nodded. "There's a few around, although they're not very common."

"Anyway," said Athena. "It gave me a strange reaction... when I met her, a sort of warm feeling. I don't know quite how to explain it, but it's different from when I've met other fae."

"I know you're about as uninterested in fae politics as I am," said Dain. "So I won't bore you with the details. But the different regions within the realm are governed and populated by various fae factions. Each has a unique blend of magic of their own. Most of the fae you would have encountered are likely to be linked to West Eloria, though."

"Because that's the region bordering here?" Athena asked.

"Yes."

"I thought the gates to the fae realm moved around," said Athena. "The one that Finnegan opened in the forest led almost exactly to the same part of the realm as the one that Mum opened from Fin's Creek."

"You're right," said Dain. "It's difficult to explain. You can think of the two worlds, as if they joined together by a kind of string that connects to each realm in multiple places in each region. The fae realm has its own separate pieces of string that connect to different parts of the earthly realm."

"So, you're saying you could go through any of the gates created around here and end up in the same place over there?"

"Yes," said Dain. "There's a complex matrix of probability around each one. But there's also a lot of synchronicity at play."

Athena nodded, not quite understanding.

"Actually," said Dain. "I'm not sure what any of that means. It was just more or less what I was told as a child."

"Good," said Athena. "Because I was just pretending to know what on earth you're talking about. But what does this have to do with Una?"

"Who, now?"

"The woman from the apothecary; that's her name."

"Ah, so more to the point, the different regions and their fae populations have diverging specialities."

"So you think my reaction is to do with Una's particular speciality? I wonder where her father was from.

Dain shrugged. "I couldn't tell you. Maybe if I met her I'd know more."

"That's fair," said Athena. "Why do you have to be so calm and reasonable all of a sudden? I'm so used to you being a rash and irresponsible. I don't know how to adjust to this new version of my father."

"You want to go back to being angry with me?" Dain said, grinning.

"I'm still angry with you," said Athena. "You don't get off scot-free for years of bad behaviour, just because you had a little problem with cream."

Dain shrugged. "That's fair, too."

"Anyway, speaking of little problems," Athena continued. "The women at the apothecary thought they might be able to figure out some kind of magical solution. If they did, would you be interested?"

Dain shook his head and scrunched up his face. "I tried those remedies that your mum gave me. They just made me sick."

"Those ones didn't work," said Athena. "But does that mean you're just going to give up like you gave up on us?"

"Oh, harsh," said Dain. "I guess I deserve that."

"And a lot more, besides," said Athena.

"Of course I'll try," he said. "I'm trying to redeem myself, remember. There's nothing like spending weeks locked up in a mushroom castle, being stabbed and tortured, to make you rethink your life choices."

Athena grimaced. "Was it that bad?"

Dain shrugged. "In a way, it was all worth it."

"What do you mean?"

Dain stared down at the earth around him. He paused for a moment and then said, "Well, if I hadn't gone through all that and had a chance to help you get back here, I might never have been able to spend any more time with you again with no chance to try to redeem myself."

Athena felt her heart soften.

Dain looked up at her. "It's been good, getting to know you as an almost adult."

She smiled. "Tell that to mum."

"Your mother is a tad overprotective," said Dain. "Though I guess I don't have any parental rights to say so."

"No, I don't think you telling her that is going to make any difference at this point. But I do appreciate you trying to stick up for me."

Dain shrugged. "I can understand why she does it. She cares a lot for you."

"Obviously, she does," said Athena. "It's mostly just been the two of us. And Mum never really had to be protective of me before because I never really did very much. I didn't get along with other kids and so we just stayed home and watched a lot of movies and ate popcorn. Now that I have more of a life she doesn't know what to do with herself."

"She's gonna have to figure it out eventually," said Dain.

"That's what I keep telling her," said Athena. "Anyway, I've got to go and get ready for school. Thanks for the chat."

Dain smiled and his eyes held a flicker of hope. "I mean what I said," he called out as she walked away. "I'll do what I can. If there's any way that I can possibly win back your trust..."

"We'll see," Athena called back across the yard.

Fourteen

Athena had just left for school, Dain was playing hide-and seek with the children in the back garden, and Rosemary was putting on the kettle for morning tea when a knock sounded at the front door of Thorn Manor. She went to answer it and was delighted to see the two sisters from the apothecary.

Una came in holding a large old book.

"Good timing," said Rosemary. "I'm just making tea."

"That's sounds lovely," said Una. "How about we do a swap over tea? You can read our book and I'll have a look through yours?"

"Excellent," said Rosemary. She showed them through to the living room and returned a few moments later with a tea tray.

"Before we get started," said Ashwyn, "I had an idea regarding your other request."

"Which one?" Rosemary asked, trying to think back to the conversation they'd had only the day before.

"Your memory," said Una.

"Oh, yes. My memory is atrocious," Rosemary admitted. "Though it's not entirely my fault. Both fae magic and my granny's binding spell are probably to blame for that."

"Yes, exactly," said Ashwyn. "I was thinking about all that. At least the parts that you told me. And while I could give you a general memory tonic, I don't think that would work."

"That's a shame," said Rosemary.

"It seems like whatever components your grandmother put into the binding spell, she mimicked fairy magic in order to make it stick," Ashwyn continued. "Normally, memory spells don't last for very long."

"You're saying my grandmother was using fae magic?" Rosemary asked.

"I suspect so," said Una. "If only there was a way we could ask her to make sure."

"Well, the next time I see her…" said Rosemary.

Una gave her a questioning look.

"Metaphorically, I mean," Rosemary said. "Or it was a joke? Maybe it was a joke. Yeah…"

The fact that Granny's ghost still inhabited and haunted the manor was a secret Granny did not want them to share with anyone else lest she had more than just her own descendants bothering her for spells, or trying to exorcise or banish her, for that matter. Rosemary gathered that ghostly housemates as stubborn and vibrant as Granny Thorn were rare, and that hauntings were usually much more subtle. She also didn't know if anyone else could see Granny's ghost, or just those wielding the Thorn family magic, and Granny didn't seem keen to test this out, as she was tremendously busy in the spirit world.

Rosemary brought in a tray with tea and biscuits. Ashwyn pulled out a large old book. "Swap you?"

Rosemary handed the small green volume on the fae to Una and grasped the heavy leather-bound grimoire that Ashwyn had passed her. It had the resemblance of a book kept in the family for generations. She found the spell used to stop Una's cream addiction had been bookmarked.

"Oh, and there's this," said Rosemary, handing over a piece of paper. "Athena found it in an old book, all marked up. She thinks Granny might have used it to bind my memory."

"It's just like I thought," said Una. "Fae magic. Look – for the memory issues, there may be an antidote."

"Really?" Rosemary asked.

"I have a tonic that might work," said Una, looking at her sister. "It's a surprisingly simple recipe. Just take some fennel and sage, spring water. In fact, it's coincidentally the exact tonic I use for migraines."

"Seriously?" Rosemary frowned. This seemed like far too much of a coincidence.

"Yes," said Ashwyn. "Actually, it's one we carry with us as part of our herbal first aid kit. Did you remember to bring it, Una?"

"I think so." Una opened an old fashioned doctor's bag and pulled out an emerald green glass bottle. "Migraines work along the same neural pathways as this magic seems to, so it makes sense that unblocking them will solve both kinds of problems. Take a teaspoon of this and see how you feel."

"It's worth a try," said Rosemary. She took the little bottle from Una and retrieved a teaspoon from the kitchen. Returning to the lounge, she sat down on a couch across from the two sisters and poured out a little of the pale green liquid to fill the spoon and then swallowed it.

The taste was aromatic and slightly bitter, leaving an astringent residue on her tongue. "Well, I feel quite normal," said Rosemary, realising quickly that she'd spoken too soon. Stars formed a border around her vision before obliterating everything inside.

Rosemary opened her eyes, feeling woozy, with the dreaded sensation that she might have been tricked. She blinked, looking up at the ceiling. It took her a moment to get her bearings. "What happened?" she asked.

"I've never seen a reaction like that before," said Una.

Rosemary pulled herself up from the couch, reassured that everything seemed to be in order. She was glad that she'd had a soft landing when she'd evidently passed out. "Oh my goddess!"

"What is it?" Ashwyn asked, sounding concerned.

"My head feels so clear!" said Rosemary. "I feel like I can look right back into the past and see everything, even things relating to Dain."

"Everything?" Una asked.

"Okay, maybe not everything, but before it was all blurry. I couldn't remember specifics at all and now...Wow. Thank you!" A thought struck her. "Do you think this will work on other people?"

Una and Ashwyn gave her a quizzical look.

"I mean, others that have had their memory meddled with by the fae?"

"I don't see why not," said Una. "It worked on you."

Rosemary sighed. "The problem is, how do we get people to ingest something when we don't know them and they're unlikely to trust us? Do you think the formula would bake into muffins that we could leave on someone's doorstep?"

Ashwyn gave her a sceptical look for a start. "Would *you* eat muffins that were left on your doorstep?"

I suppose not," said Rosemary. "Unless I was absolutely sure they were from Marjie. I see your point."

"I don't think that would work anyway," said Una. "It'll have to be in liquid form, otherwise the tannins in the sage will bind to whatever else you combine it with."

"I see," said Rosemary. "What about a fine mist?"

"That could work," said Una. "If somebody could inhale or ingest enough of it."

"Only one way to find out," said Rosemary. "How much of this do you have?"

"I've got a whole supply of it back at the shop," said Una. "You can pick some up tomorrow if you like."

"I think I might just do that," said Rosemary. "Maybe now, with my enhanced memory, I'll be able to figure out this spell and help Dain." She blinked, feeling a whole new mix of emotions where previously she'd just felt only confusion.

Five minutes before, Rosemary would have vaguely recalled that Dain had screwed her over so many times, especially with Athena's many reminders over the years, but none of the specific memories had been able to shine through. Now, after taking the tonic, they stabbed painfully in her chest when she thought of him. Even more overwhelming were the whole wave of happy memories that flooded in. Memories of when they were together and very much in love, memories of them both playing with young Athena.

Now, everything about the cream addiction made a lot more sense. If only she'd known back then what she knew now. She could have asked Granny for help to figure out a solution. Of course she could still ask Granny now, though the old woman in her ghost form had been quite evasive, and that was before she'd up and left them with nothing more than a goodbye note. Perhaps ghosts weren't supposed to meddle in the affairs of the living.

"I think I might have an idea for how this might work," said Una, poring over the small book Burk had acquired on the fae. "If you'll let me copy a few things out of your books, I can examine the basic mechanisms and see if I can come up with some sort of template for a spell to help Dain."

"That would be fantastic," said Rosemary. "Copy away!"

Just then, the children ran in from the back garden, bright eyed, rosy cheeked, and panting, followed by an exhausted looking Dain.

Rosemary wasn't quite ready to confront all the memories and baggage that had re-emerged from Una's tonic, so she tucked that into a side-cupboard in her mind for later, smiled politely, and introduced them all. The children were quite taken with Una and Ashwyn, and convinced them to join in several rounds of ring-a-ring-a-rosy.

Dain pulled Rosemary aside during the second round.

"She's fae, isn't she?" he said, gesturing discreetly to Una.

Rosemary nodded. "On her father's side, I think. But don't get any ideas. I know she's gorgeous, but she's a new friend and I don't want you making things awkward."

Dain's jaw dropped in offence. "What do you take me for?"

"You don't have the best track record," Rosemary pointed out.

"Maybe not, but that's not my angle here."

"Then what?" Rosemary crossed her arms and gave him a pointed look.

"She's just familiar, is all," said Dain. "And I can't recall, but maybe I've met her before?"

"It seems unlikely, unless it was around here. Una never met her father and was raised here in Myrtlewood by her witch mother." She was going to add something about the patterns of fae fathers but was interrupted as Ashwyn and Una approached.

"We'd better get back to the shop," said Una. "If you're sure you're okay after the memory thing..."

"Memory thing?" Dain said.

"I'll tell you later." Rosemary turned back to the sisters. "I'm feeling fine. In fact, I'm feeling a lot better than I have in quite a long time. Everything feels so crystal clear in my head. I've even thought of a few things that I'd forgotten I needed to do."

"That sounds promising," said Ashwyn as Una packed up her things.

"I've copied down the information I need," said Una. "So if you swing by the shop tomorrow I'll have some things ready for you to pick up."

"Wonderful," said Rosemary. "Let me know how much I owe you."

"Oh no," said Una. "This is definitely on the house."

"But you hardly know me," said Rosemary.

"Still, given the involvement of the fae, it's personal," said Una. "I'd feel uncomfortable taking money, especially when it's so rare to come across someone who's like me. Is Athena around? I'd like to see her again."

"She's gone to school." Rosemary was unsure if she should be suspicious of the woman's interest in her daughter. Una and Ashwyn seemed lovely, but she hardly knew them. Then again, Athena had seemed to light up around other fae people, including Una. "But I'm sure she'd love to chat to you sometime about what it's like. You don't have that telepathy thing, do you?"

Una shook her head. "I'm not sure what you're talking about, so probably not."

"Athena hasn't mentioned it recently, but it was bugging her a while ago," said Rosemary. "She said it was kind of like having a radio in her head. She picked up on people's stray thoughts."

"I must have missed out on that ability in the genetic lottery. I haven't experienced anything like that. But I'm sure we have other things in common and I might be able to help with some of them."

Rosemary smiled and showed the two women out. Then, she immediately texted officer Neve, to tell her about the new discovery of the memory tonic, just in case she forgot. She didn't know how long the tonic would hold, and neither did the sisters. Una had explained that people had to take the tonic for every migraine because the neural pathway patterns tended to re-emerge, but with the fae magic, perhaps it would stay gone. Either way, Rosemary was determined to make the most of her new-found clarity. She texted Athena, as well.

We need to fight.

Mum, I'm at school, came her response a few minutes later. *What's this about? What have I done now?*

No, Rosemary wrote back. *I mean, we need to train, we need to practice fighting.*

It was a thought that had occurred to Rosemary after the recent attack by that hooded figure and she'd only just remembered it along with everything else. She and Athena might be getting used to using magic, but they needed combat skills, especially if the Bloodstone Society was coming back.

Sounds great, Athena texted back. *Any excuse to throw you around.*

Rosemary smiled. Despite the sass, it was good to have Athena back.

She went to the kitchen to make herself some toast for lunch and returned her attention to the other topic that had suddenly begun weighing on her mind.

When she'd sipped that sage tonic, other things had become clear in her memory, and one of them in particular was bothering her.

A few weeks earlier, she'd seen Burk at the pub having dinner with an attractive brunette woman, and now that she remembered the details, she was sure it had been Una.

At the time, Rosemary had to suppress a pang of jealousy. She and Burk were just friends, sure. And yes, she had politely turned him down when he'd asked her out to dinner. But that didn't mean she didn't harbour some small and conflicting feelings for him, despite her better judgement.

Burk was incredibly good looking, suave, and genuinely helpful, if a bit arrogant. He'd gone above and beyond to help Rosemary in the short time she'd known him. He might be a vampire and incredibly old, despite still looking like he was in his thirties or early forties, but that didn't mean he wasn't an eligible bachelor, or that he didn't deserve to date other women. Knowing this, Rosemary had done her best not to get in the way, but now that she realised who it was he was dating...What she was...

Una, being of fae descent like Athena, should be kept away from vampires. Rosemary understood that. She wasn't about to leave Athena alone with Burk either. Not that the fae were innocent, but vampires were clearly a threat to them. Despite the fae politics and how freaky they were, and their unsavoury habit of kidnapping young children, they needed protection from vamps who had hunted them for centuries.

Does Una know about all this? Rosemary wondered as she spread butter and raspberry jam on her freshly made toast. She didn't know her father—maybe she was in the dark about how vampires find fae irresistible.

The situation had been so dangerous for the fae that they'd fused protections into their DNA, so that vampires couldn't smell them, or recognise them. Athena said that people couldn't see her face properly, they just saw some kind of projection, something that Rosemary found troubling, as she was sure she could pick her daughter out of any line-up, though perhaps it didn't work on mothers.

If Una was at risk, then Rosemary had to warn her. Burk might seem harmless, but he possessed the preternatural strength and speed of a vampire. Rosemary had only been able to fight them off because of her own magic. She didn't know what kind of magical abilities Una had, aside from clearly being a gifted healer.

If neither of them knew the true nature of the situation they were in, it could be a recipe for disaster. He might not mean her any harm, but if he were to discover Una's true nature, say, if she spilled a drop of her irresistible blood, he might well lose all sense of control.

Rosemary battled with these conflicting emotions as she scoffed down her toast, the understanding deepening in her mind that she had no choice, she had to warn her new friend about the very handsome and often quite considerate vampire.

Fifteen

Rosemary gritted her teeth as Detective Neve drove around a tight corner. They were on their way to the house of Elowen's sister again, having picked up supplies from the apothecary just moments before. Una had been busy with other customers, so Rosemary didn't have a chance to talk to her about Burk.

Surely she must know. Being a magical person in a magical town, everyone here probably knows who the vampires are. But then again, even if Una knows, maybe she isn't aware of the issues between vampires and the fae. Una was raised by witches and hardly anyone knows much about the fae. Maybe Una doesn't realise what danger she's in if Burk finds out about her true identity.

Rosemary opened the brown paper bag that Una had left on the counter for her. Inside, as promised, was a spray bottle containing the sage tonic, which she could use to create a kind of mist effect that would hopefully help to jog the woman's memory about her missing sister.

There were a few other items in the bag too and some written instructions. Rosemary tried to make sense of them, but her mind was in too many places at once.

"This must be something to do with the spell to help Dain," she muttered.

"That sounds promising," said Neve. "Una and Ashwyn are talented. It was good you talked to them. I hadn't even thought of that myself."

"They seem to know a lot," said Rosemary.

"I wish they could help me with my other case," said Neve. "Right now, I wish anyone could. We're out of leads."

"The fires?" Rosemary asked.

"Yes, there have been two more since yesterday. The first one we know about was on the old Twigg farm, and so far they seem to be fairly random and out in the rural areas, like the one that sparked up near you. They seem to be getting bigger."

Rosemary gulped. "Any idea if they are connected to the Bloodstones?"

"There's been no link so far," said Neve. "In fact, I wouldn't have even thought of it if you hadn't mentioned you'd been attacked by somebody wearing a dark hood."

"It seems like too much of a coincidence not to be related though, doesn't it?"

"Anyone can wear a dark hood," Neve pointed out.

"That's true," said Rosemary. "Although the only people that have attacked me wearing them have been involved with that stupid society. Besides, I'm sure I saw the Bloodstone crest on the robes."

"Unless that's a ruse," Neve suggested.

Rosemary pondered the possibility for a while, looking out the window. "You know, my cousins have some fiery magic, on their father's side. They once set a law office on fire."

Neve raised her eyebrows. "It's worth checking out."

Rosemary laughed. "Although, now that I think of it, Elamina is far too fancy and snobby to be hanging out on the old Twigg farm. I'm sure the modest countryside is beneath her and she wouldn't want to get her expensive shoes dirty."

"Well, let me know if you have any other ideas," said Neve. "But witches with a known predilection for fire are definitely on our list to investigate."

They pulled into the driveway of the slightly dilapidated house where Tamsyn, little Elowen's now much older sister, lived.

"What's the plan?" Rosemary asked.

"You tell me."

"It's going to look weird if I squirt her in the face with this stuff," said Rosemary. "Maybe when you knock I can try creating enough mist to have an effect when she opens the door."

They stepped out of the car into a strong wind.

"Or maybe not," said Rosemary.

"It's worth a try," said Neve. "But if that doesn't work, you might have to go on the offensive."

"Is that legal?"

"No, but it would be a hard thing to press assault charges for, or even make a formal complaint – a light mist in the face."

Rosemary shrugged. "It's not like she likes me anyway."

They made their way to the door.

"Ready?" Neve said.

Rosemary held up the spray bottle, ready to push the trigger as Neve reached out to knock on the door.

Just as Rosemary sprayed, the door flew open, and Tamsyn was misted right in the face.

"What's the name of..." she cried out.

"Sorry," Rosemary called. "That wasn't my intention."

Tamsyn's eyes glazed over and she teetered on the spot.

Rosemary reached out to steady her, but she managed to stay upright. "What...has happened?" Tamsyn asked. "Everything went white."

"Hopefully we've restored your memory," said Rosemary.

"My...my *memory*? Everything feels so clear. Oh goodness. You weren't lying to me before." A look of utter bewilderment crossed her face. "I had a sister. Elowen. She went missing. It was a long time ago. So clear now in my mind that it almost seems unreal. Is this a trick?"

"I'm afraid not," said Rosemary. "The trick was whatever memory magic stopped you from remembering your own family member for so long."

Tamsyn shook her head. "She was only four years old."

Rosemary nodded. "You'll find she still seems to be about that age."

"No! Really? How's that possible?"

"Your sister was taken to the fae realm," Detective Neve explained.

"That's right. I think you'd better come in again," Tamsyn said, opening the door wide.

Over the next half an hour she apologised profusely for how she'd treated them the first time they'd come calling. After a while, a look of deep exhaustion crossed her face. When Rosemary and Neve had finally finished explaining everything to her, Tamsyn rested her head in her hands on the table.

"This is all just so surreal," she said. "Please forgive me."

"You didn't do anything wrong," said Rosemary. "I'm sure I would have reacted much worse in your situation. I probably would have blown whoever was on my doorstep to smithereens thinking they were the Bloodstone Society—"

"The what?" Tamsyn asked.

"Never mind that," said Detective Neve, shooting Rosemary a warning glance.

"Yeah, don't worry about that," said Rosemary. "I have a rambling problem. It would be best to only listen to twenty five percent of everything I say. Anyway. The long and short of it is that you now have a sibling who's still a young child."

"Obviously in a situation where children go missing," said Neve, "the normal response is to return them to their families. We understand your parents passed away quite some time ago."

Tamsyn nodded. She sighed deeply. "Do you know it's funny? I always felt like something was missing. Something I couldn't name. Now it's like the missing part of my life is being handed to me. I probably should be overjoyed but...I...the shock..."

"It'll take you a while to get used to it, I imagine," said Rosemary. "These kinds of situations must be incredibly rare and you probably need to have a good night's sleep and think."

Tamsyn nodded. "You're probably right, though I don't know if I can sleep, knowing what I know now." She looked around at her kitchen and sighed. "My husband left after the kids grew up. They all live abroad now, and I hardly see them. I felt like I was stuck in a rut here, but I couldn't quite leave. Maybe this is why. I'm sorry. I'm the one rambling now."

"That's perfectly understandable." Rosemary patted the woman on the shoulder. "Change is hard, and this situation is exceptional."

"We can leave you to have some time to think. Give me a call anytime," said Neve, handing the woman her card.

Tamsyn shook her head. "No. I need to go. I need to see her now. Can I come with you?"

"Are you sure you're feeling up to it?" Rosemary asked.

Tamsyn nodded, resolute.

"Of course," said Detective Neve. "We can leave straight away."

Sixteen

Tamsyn sat in silence in the back of the car as they drove towards Myrtlewood. Neve and Rosemary kept the conversation to a minimum as well, wanting to give the woman as much peace as possible, considering what she was still processing.

A phone call came through as they drove. Neve pulled over to answer it.

"Okay, I'll be right there," she said after a long pause.

She turned to Rosemary. "I just need to make a quick detour. It's urgent. You can stay in the car with Tamsyn; make sure she's okay."

Rosemary nodded. "Has there been another one?"

Neve raised her eyebrows in a silent 'yes'.

Rosemary could see smoke up ahead as Detective Neve pulled down a familiar road which began to wind up a hill.

"No," said Neve, looking at the clouds of black wafting through the sky. "This looks a lot worse than I thought. I should have dropped you home before I came."

Rosemary gritted her teeth. "No time. Who's going to put out this fire? Surely the regular fire service can't be expected to deal with magical infernos!"

"Hopefully the Myrtlewood fire brigade will be there by now," said Neve.

"We have a fire brigade?" Rosemary asked. "Why does no one tell me these things?"

"Never mind. Just stay in the car and stay out of trouble." Neve shot Rosemary a warning glance.

"I'm not a child." Rosemary folded her arms indignantly. "I know how to behave myself."

Neve grinned at her. "Sure you do."

They pulled into a very grand entrance to a driveway that wound up the hill.

Rosemary gasped. "Oh no, it's not..."

"I'm afraid so," said Neve.

Rosemary recognised the driveway from the last trip she'd made to Mr June, the mayor's house. "He's not going to like that I'm here."

Neve shrugged. "Like I said, stay in the car."

Rosemary stared at the mayor's house. It was alight in flames that covered the whole left side of the building.

"What a shame," said Tamsyn from the back of the car. She'd clearly snapped out of her trance.

Rosemary turned back towards her. "Sorry to drag you into this. Neve didn't realise it was a full-on house fire."

"I hope nobody's in there," said Tamsyn.

"I'm sure his lordship will have gotten out quickly, along with his prized possessions," said Rosemary.

"That sounds a bit harsh," said Tamsyn as a siren blared behind them.

"You're probably right," said Rosemary. "I had a bad run in with the mayor last time I was here. He tried to get me arrested. And let's just say his personality leaves a lot to be desired."

Neve pulled over to allow a bright red old-fashioned fire engine to tear up the driveway, with lights and siren blazing. They followed the truck up towards the house and parked nearby.

Rosemary watched as a muscular black woman emerged from the driver side door of the fire engine, strapping on a fireproof jacket.

"Another one!" she called out to Neve, who nodded. "All right then. Let's hope this one behaves just like the last ones." She pulled out her firehose.

Rosemary watched in awe as the clearly magically-enhanced device spirited water all over the building in a way that no normal hose could manage. The jets of liquid twinkled in a supernatural way as they seemed to seek out each point of flame and extinguish it quickly.

"That's something else," said Tamsyn from the back of the car. "I've never seen anything like it."

"I'm glad we have a fire department here," said Rosemary. "Though I wish someone told me these things!"

"Why wouldn't you?" asked Tamsyn. "Oh that's right, I forgot how magical this place was. Maybe I need more of that magical spritzer."

"Feel free to take a whole spoonful," said Rosemary. "I'll give you a bottle. I'm not sure if it wears off, or if it's something you only need the once."

"I better get my own supply, just in case," said Tamsyn. "I still can't believe all that happened to my memory. It breaks my heart that my parents died not remembering little Elowen."

"It's very sad," said Rosemary.

She was distracted by tapping at the car window.

"Returned to the scene of the crime, I take it," said Constable Perkins, tugging at his suspenders. His nose was as red as usual, and his stance just as arrogant as the first time Rosemary had met him. "I'm glad that you're already safely in the detective's car, Rosemary Thorn," said Perkins. "I didn't realise Constantine had so much sense and worked so quickly."

"Oh, you didn't, did you?" said Neve, standing behind him, raising her eyebrows.

"Oh, Detective Neve. Sorry I didn't see you there," Constable Perkins bumbled.

"Don't you worry," said Neve. "Rosemary is here to help with official police business. And no, she did not have anything to do with setting the fire."

Constable Perkins spluttered and waved his fingers as though he was about to protest.

"Shouldn't you be comforting the mayor and taking his statements?" Neve said, waving him away.

Rosemary smiled apologetically at Neve as the police officer slinked off.

"He's really got it in for you, hasn't he?" said the detective.

"He sure does," said Rosemary. "I don't know what it is about me that rubs him the wrong way."

"He and Galdie never got on either," said Neve. "She always bested him in his investigations. That's partly why they brought me on board in the first place. They needed somebody who wasn't always putting their foot in their mouth and getting in the way."

"How is all of this magical law enforcement organised?" Rosemary asked as they watched the fire crew work their magic.

"Orders come from Glastonbury," said Neve.

"I would have thought it was London." Rosemary frowned. "Isn't that where all the bigwigs are supposed to sit?"

"Not the magical bigwigs," said Neve. "In our community, they all live near the base of the Glastonbury Tor. They say it's where the magic is strongest in Britain, anyway. Though the global authorities are in Bermuda, of course."

Rosemary nodded. "I guess that makes sense. I'm not sure if the bigwigs have a good handle on it given the state of Perkins' performance."

"You're probably right," said Neve. "But, just like in any job, once somebody is firmly established it's quite hard to get rid of them."

"That firefighter woman's amazing," said Tamsyn from the back of the car.

Neve nodded and smiled. "Who, Sid? Yes, she is rather..." There was a tightness to her voice. "She's also my ex, so we keep things as professional as possible."

Rosemary nodded, wondering why Neve was being so candid despite being at work.

Neve obviously wondered the same thing. Shaking herself, she said, "Sorry, I better get back to business."

"Before you go," Rosemary said, looking across at the blaze that was very clearly engulfing half the mayor's house in red, orange, and bright pink flames. "What's going on with these fires? Any ideas?"

"Your guess is as good as mine," Neve said, then walked away, leaving Rosemary to ponder in silence. She zoned out a bit as she sat in the car waiting for Detective Neve to return from whatever police duties were occupying her at the mayor's house after the fire.

She heard Tamsyn cough behind her. "What's going on out there?" Tamsyn asked.

Rosemary shrugged. "I don't know, just some sort of professional emergency response stuff."

"It doesn't look all that professional to me," said Tamsyn. "They look a little bit...*cosy* over there."

Rosemary squinted in the direction of the house to see Neve standing next to Sid, rather too closely. In fact, the firefighter's arms were stretched out and she was stroking her hands down the detective's upper arms.

"I thought she said that woman was her ex," said Tamsyn.

"She did. Plus, she's very happily and monogamously engaged to someone else now. Or at least we're hoping they'll get engaged soon."

"And it looks like they're not the only ones getting cosy either," said Tamsyn.

Another firefighter had her hands all over a tall, handsome man that Rosemary recognised as the mayor's husband, Zade.

"Excuse me a minute," Rosemary said.

She got out of the car and sprinted over towards the house, knowing full well that she'd been told to stay put. But she figured that in exceptional circumstances, she had to break the rules.

"Neve!" she called out, approaching the two women. Neve's eyes flicked over to Rosemary. She had a drunken smile plastered over her face.

"Oh, Rosemary," she said, and giggled. "Have you come to join in the action?"

Sid turned towards the interruption. "Aren't you going to introduce me to your pretty friend?" she asked Neve and reached out towards Rosemary.

"I'm not sure what's going on here," said Rosemary, "but this is not normal."

That was when she felt it.

A warm wave emanated from the house, drifting over from the smouldering embers on the left side of the building that had now caught alight in a bright pink flame, though none of the firefighters seemed particularly interested in it anymore.

"Oh," said Rosemary. "It's quite warm, isn't it."

"You're clearly overdressed," said Sid, reaching out to tug at Rosemary's cardigan. Rosemary did indeed feel overdressed. In fact, it seemed like the most natural thing in the world for them to all take off their clothing and frolic naked, indulging in all the hedonistic pleasures of the body.

She shook herself. Something wasn't right. But another wave pulsed out from what remained of the fire, loosening her inhibitions and melting her logic like ice in hot water.

Sid pushed Neve up against the fire engine and wrapped her in a passionate embrace.

Alarm bells rang in the back of Rosemary's mind and a little voice screamed out: *Something's not right!*

Rosemary remembered the ancestor with silver hair that she'd met in some kind of void world, and the process she'd gone through to unleash the old Thorn family magic that had been bound. That voice seemed to be communicating with her now.

Stop it at once!

A wave of gold light pulsed out from Rosemary, seeming to freeze the people where they stood.

Clarity returned as the dazed feeling fell away.

It's the fire! It's meddling with people's minds. Put it out!

Rosemary grabbed the hose that was dangling from one of the firefighter's hands, the woman having clearly forgotten her duty to put out the fire in the heat of the moment, too wrapped up in whatever magic had them all spellbound.

Rosemary twisted the nozzle, turning the hose up and holding on for dear life. The water sprayed out, touching not only the fire, but also the people standing around it. As if dousing the invisible flames of lust they'd been entrapped in, one by one they seemed to come out of the daze.

Rosemary continued directing the hose across the fire until nothing remained but smoking embers.

"What on earth is going on? Explain yourself, Rosemary Thorn," said Constable Perkins.

He was standing arm in arm with the mayor. Upon realising this, he blushed and stepped away.

Everyone else seemed to have a similar reaction, clearly coming to their senses.

"Don't blame me," said Rosemary. "I was the one who saved you."

"Trespassing again!" cried Mr June.

"Excuse me," said Rosemary. "Unless you wanted to have a magically-induced orgy, you should be thanking me right now! I was perfectly happy to stay in the car. But alarm bells started ringing, and I thought I'd better come over here and stop you from making terrible mistakes."

She gave Neve a meaningful look. The detective appeared to be shell shocked.

"Thank you, Rosemary," she said, her voice wavering a little, her posture stiff and awkward. "I think we'd better be going."

As the two women walked back to the car, Neve asked, "Do you have any idea what happened there?"

Rosemary couldn't help but feel she was being accused of something. "Like I said, I was in the car. Tamsyn pointed out there was something strange going on with you and your ex and I came over to see what in Hades was going on. As far as I can tell it was something to do with those flames. Did you notice the fire had sparked up again from the embers and turned pink?"

"I don't recall," Neve admitted.

"Whatever it was, it made everyone lose their panties for a minute."

Neve glared at her.

"Metaphorically, I hope," said Rosemary. "Although, you weren't far off."

"Please don't tell Nesta," said Neve. "She's already jealous of Sid."

Rosemary shook her head. "Look, I'm not going to get involved in your relationship politics. But as far as I can see, *you* are the one who should tell Nesta about this, and you should do it soon, because if she finds out some other way, it's going to cause a lot more damage."

Neve sighed. "You're right. I just need a few minutes and a good stiff drink to do some processing."

Rosemary nodded. "That, I can arrange. Let's get home and I'll bring out the good scotch."

Seventeen

By the time Rosemary finally got home with Neve and Tamsyn, she was heavy with exhaustion. She opened the front door to find the house empty.

"This is a nice big place," said Tamsyn. "We used to live in a big old house, not quite this big, back when we were in Myrtlewood. We had to downsize when we moved and I always missed living in a place like this—"

"Tamsyn?" Rosemary asked.

"Yes?"

Rosemary smiled kindly. "It's alright. I recognise nervous rambling when I see it. I've had plenty of experience. Take a deep breath and calm down. The kids are probably out back."

"Okay," Tamsyn said, inhaling deeply.

Neve nodded. "You've got nothing to worry about."

"She might hate me," said Tamsyn quietly, as if admitting a secret. "I wasn't the nicest older sister in the world. I'd get jealous when she got attention, and I hated it when she stole my toys."

"Tamsyn..." Rosemary tried to sound reassuring.

"Or worse, what if she doesn't remember me at all? It has been such a long time and I look so different."

Rosemary stopped with her hand clasped on the back door. "Do you need a hug?" she asked.

Tamsyn nodded.

Rosemary held out her arms and gave the woman a big reassuring cuddle. "It's all going to be fine."

"I'm sorry," said Tamsyn. "You hardly know me, and here I am acting like a big baby."

"Totally understandable," said Rosemary.

"Ready now?" Neve asked from behind them as Rosemary pulled away from Tamsyn.

"As I'll ever be."

"Think of it this way, it's not every day you get to meet your abducted baby sister, finding her still alive four decades later. This is a fairly unique experience."

"Not helping," said Tamsyn.

Rosemary zipped her mouth and opened the door.

The children were running and skipping across the backyard, circling a red-and-white-checked picnic blanket where Nesta was sitting cross-legged. Tamsyn looked overwhelmed as she tried to make out their faces.

"Tamsyn!" cried a little blonde girl, skipping over to where they stood. "It is you, isn't it? But how did you get so big?"

"How does she recognise me so easily?" Tamsyn asked Rosemary.

"I have no idea, they seem to pick things up again fairly well after so much time in the fae realm. I'm surprised their memory isn't addled too. Maybe they absorb some of the excess memory that's syphoned away from the people in the earth realm."

"That's not such a bad hypothesis," said Neve. She shot Rosemary a smile as Tamsyn knelt down to wrap her baby sister in a hug.

"Really? It's more of a throwaway comment than a hypothesis," Rosemary said.

"No, really," said Neve. "Magic doesn't work in a vacuum, it's often about altering the polarity of something to shift the result."

"Huh. I really should be going to magic school like Athena."

"Hearing you all talk about this stuff like it's normal is so refreshing," said Tamsyn.

"That's not what you said when you kicked us out of your house," Rosemary joked, and Neve shot her a glance as if warning her to be more professional.

"No, I'm sorry about that. It's just, after Elowen disappeared everything changed. We weren't supposed to talk about magic anymore. It's a shame really. My parents were really talented Rúnsealls."

"Come again?" said Rosemary.

"Rúnseall is a magical specialisation," Neve explained. "They are experts at finding hidden things. Any old witch can perform a seeking spell, but a true master Rúnseall can often find something even if magic has been used to mask it. They can also detect traces of magical intent and figure out which witch cast a particular spell, but that's quite a complex technical process, as I understand it."

"I could have used some of that when my necklace was stolen," said Rosemary. "Or in countless other situations."

"It's a shame, then," said Tamsyn. "Supposedly it's in my blood, and I showed great promise, but true masters work in pairs like my parents. It almost killed them when Elowen disappeared...knowing *where* she'd gone, but they still couldn't get her back. They walked away from everything. It's so sad. I miss all this." She waved her arm around vaguely. "I miss casual conversations where magic is real."

"You can always move back to Myrtlewood," said Rosemary. "We can help you get set up. It will probably be good for Elowen to be in a familiar place close to the other kids she knows. They are all quite close."

"Are you saying I can just...*keep* her?" Tamsyn asked, confused, as Elowen ran off to play with the other children.

"She's your family," said Neve.

"Aren't you even going to do a background check?" said Tamsyn.

"Already done," said Neve. "We completed that before we knocked on your door. We just need to make sure you'll be able to provide her with a safe home where she'll be loved and looked after. That's what children need."

Tamsyn nodded. "I couldn't just up and move, could I?" Her eyes were wide.

"It's up to you," said Rosemary. "Do what feels right."

"I just..." Tamsyn looked around in awe. "I suppose it's something people do. Make snap decisions. Uproot their lives. I just never thought that was me."

Neve smiled patiently. "Take some time and think it over."

Tamsyn shook her head. "No. I don't need time. I know that this is right." She beamed at them.

Rosemary could almost see her transform before their eyes. The downtrodden and worried woman they had met a few days ago in Burkenswood had vanished. Tamsyn stood there, strong and vibrant.

"I might have to take you up on your offer to help me move back here.

There's nothing much for me back home, not after my two kids moved to France and Portugal. Just a depressing office job and an underutilised gym membership."

"We'll be happy to," said Rosemary. "Just tell us what you need, and I know someone who will be thrilled to help you find a cottage here. Don't worry, she's not an estate agent, just a wonderful friend."

Tamsyn gave her a confused look, and then returned to smiling.

Eighteen

Athena sat next to Elise in History of Folklore and Mythology class, studiously avoiding Beryl's glare. It had been an awkward morning. Just as Athena had predicted, her snobby classmate was livid after the dynamo incident. Beryl hated to be bested in anything.

It had come as a shock to Athena to hear that the girl she sometimes thought of as her arch nemesis had been instrumental in aiding her return from the fae realm. Beryl had given Rosemary the spell she'd needed in order to get through to help. Although, as Athena kept insisting, she was the one who figured out how to get back on her own, without needing her mother or anyone else.

Still, Beryl had gone out of her way to give Rosemary the spell and Athena felt some mixed gratitude about it. She hadn't even had the chance to properly thank Beryl because every interaction she'd had with her had continued to be so unpleasant.

Athena gazed out the window, longing for the delightful lightness of the fae realm.

"You're zoning out again," Elise whispered. "Listen."

Athena tried to refocus on Ms Twigg, just as she said, "Has anyone heard this passage before? 'When the wheel begins to turn, let the Beltane fires burn.'"

Beryl raised her hand quickly and enthusiastically. Nobody else did.

"Yes, Beryl?"

"It's a quote from the prominent witch, Doreen Valiante."

"Very good," said Ms Twigg. "Beltane is the next seasonal festival approaching in our calendar year. It was customary in the days of the ancients to celebrate fertility in the early summer, so as to bring about a good harvest."

"Eww, gross!" said Felix.

"Yes. Thank you, Mr Lancaster," said Ms Twigg. "As gross as fertility might sound to a group of teenagers, it's also an important part of life."

"And here I was thinking I could escape sex-ed class by going to a magical school," Athena whispered to Elise, who couldn't help but giggle.

"No such luck," she replied.

"Part of the ritual involves lighting magical fires, enchanted with fertility blessings," Ms Twigg continued, ignoring the rowdy class, or at least so it seemed until she slammed a book down on Felix's desk. He tensed.

"Mr Lancaster, would you care to read aloud to the class from the following passage?" She pointed to an open page.

Felix gulped anxiously and then started reading. "It is believed that fire sprites were traditionally involved in Beltane festivities in the rituals of old, bringing with them the potent fertility magic present in the element of fire. Their presence has not been detected for some time since most fire sprites were believed to be chased out of the earth realm by the witching authorities due to their habit of causing havoc."

"Very good, Mr Lancaster. Now, in Myrtlewood, this time of year has always had an interesting significance," she said. "The Beltane fires have granted many fertility blessings. Much more so than in other places."

"Are you saying all this to warn us off getting pregnant?" Elise asked.

"No, Miss Fern," said Ms Twigg. "It occurred to me, recently that something odd is at play. We've had a number of unexplained fires around, including one on my family farm – a rather otherworldly fire, it was."

Athena sparked up and paid attention. Her mother and Neve had talked about the fires.

Ms Twigg continued. "I suspect there might be something magical afoot, and I thought it would pay to prepare you for what might come."

"By getting us to study musty old books?" said Felix, then he stiffened as Ms Twigg's slender forked tongue darted out of her mouth like a frog's and she fixed him with her reptilian eyes.

"Indeed," she said. "We must pay close attention to the lessons of the past so that we do not repeat them. In *A History of Myrtlewood*, written by none other than my aunt Agatha, there is a strong mention of Beltane fires, including the Cavalia."

"What are you talking about?" Sam asked, clearly confused by this unusual diversion from a normally dry class.

Beryl raised her hand. "If I could explain? The Cavalia is believed to be linked to astrological alignments that only occur every two or three hundred years. Last time it happened, in 1763, over one hundred people were killed."

"Doesn't sound very cheerful," said Felix.

"Beryl is correct. It was an enormous fire in Glastonbury and mythical beasts were seen to be involved," said Ms Twigg. "It was rumoured to be brought on by the fire sprites. But as I said before, they were chased off a long time ago, and they can't easily sneak through from the fae realm anymore." She gave Athena a meaningful look before continuing. "And those of us with slightly longer memories or an interest in history have been concerned about the recent fires."

"Why are you telling teenagers about this as if we can do anything to help?" Athena asked, feeling slightly nervous about the way the teacher looked at her. Surely she couldn't know what Athena had been pre-occupied with recently. "Shouldn't you be talking to the police?"

"Rest assured, we've informed the authorities," said Ms Twigg. "Not that that matters a wink."

"Why aren't they taking it seriously?" Elise asked.

"This may surprise you," said Ms Twigg dryly, "but no one takes history seriously enough. That's why it appears we are doomed to repeat the mistakes of the past. People never learn. It's a treacherous flaw. But I fear that our students might be in danger. Young people are especially prone to the magic of fire sprites." Ms Twigg glared around at them all. "It behoves me to warn you and to make this an assignment."

"Aww really?" said Felix.

"Yes, really," said Ms Twigg. "I think it would be in all of your best interests to pay attention. I expect you to write and submit a five page essay on Beltane by next Thursday."

Athena grimaced. Essays were not her favourite thing. She'd had very little assigned work since starting at Myrtlewood Academy and didn't have much experience in the conventions of writing essays about magical things. But something in Ms Twigg's warning was even more disconcerting.

She needed to talk to her mother and Neve about all this, and she needed to do it fast. The class wrapped up, and as the students filed out, Athena recalled another thing she meant to ask her teacher about.

"Erm, Ms Twigg?"

"Yes, Miss Thorn?"

"Do you know anything about fae magic? It's just that—"

"What have you heard? It's all malicious rumours!" Ms Twigg's whole body stiffened, and tiny as she was, Athena took a step back in fear.

"S—sorry," she stuttered.

Athena wasn't sure why Ms Twigg was acting so very strangely, and maybe she never would completely untangle the mystery of the small reptilian-like teacher-librarian, but for the first time she could understand why Felix had such a fear of her.

"I think it's time for you to leave, Miss Thorn," she said sternly.

Athena nodded and scrambled out of the room as quickly as possible.

Nineteen

The morning was thick with fog as Rosemary made her way to Liam's cottage. Though the damp air eased some of her concerns about the likelihood of fires, it did nothing to quell her anxiety about potential Bloodstone Society attackers.

She kept her wits about her as she made her way to Liam's front door. She was relieved not to be interrupted by any scary hooded figures.

"You made it!" Liam said, stalking out from behind the house. "Come this way. I've set us up for some practice."

He led her around to the back garden.

"Are you sure this is the best idea?" Rosemary looked around at the surrounding farmland. "We're so out in the open. People might see us."

"I warded off the area," said Liam. "We should be safe."

"Why do we need to be outside?"

"I want to avoid any collateral damage," said Liam. "Remember how we talked about the fact that I can feel the wolf inside me at all times?"

Rosemary nodded and gulped. "You're not suggesting that we have a practice session where you try to bring it out?"

She wasn't prepared to be faced by an enormous hairy werewolf any more than she was excited about the prospect of a Bloodstone Society attack.

"Not exactly," said Liam. "I just thought you could try shooting me with your magic again and I could see if it has any effect. Only, I don't want to be blown into my bookshelf or break anything else around the house while you're firing off blasts at me."

"I'm not sure this is a good idea," said Rosemary "Last time, I was just protecting myself automatically. I didn't have any particular spell I was doing. I don't think I could replicate it."

"I think it's worth a try," said Liam.

Rosemary agreed, with some trepidation.

"You stand over there," he said. "And I'll stand a few paces away. Just try and blast me with your magic."

"My magic doesn't always comes out the same," said Rosemary. "And I'm still not sure exactly how to control it. I can pull off some relatively complex spells if I try, and I have been practicing, but I think it's going to take years to master."

"Just give it a try," said Liam.

Rosemary held her hands out in front of her and visualised golden magical light. She was trying to recreate what she'd done in the bookshop weeks before. As she connected with her magic, a blast surged from behind her fingers and pulsed out towards Liam, hitting him in the chest and knocking him onto the ground.

He pushed himself up to a sitting position, looking startled.

"Anything?" Rosemary asked.

Liam shook his head. "Aside from the shock, the wolf's still the same. How about if you close your eyes and imagine the scene in the bookshop. Imagine that I'm attacking you in my wolf form."

Rosemary closed her eyes and thought back to the bookshop where the huge beast was making its way towards her and growling.

She sent out another blast of magic.

"Oh no," said Liam. Rosemary opened her eyes to see that his muscles were bulging right out of his shirt. He was growing taller by the second. And hairier too. His teeth grew long and pointed until standing in front of her, baring its teeth, was a huge wolf.

"I...think I accidentally magicked you *into* a wolf," Rosemary murmured in a low voice. "Uhh, sorry, Liam...Wolfie."

She took a few steps back, but the creature growled and prowled towards her. Rosemary wanted to run, but she knew she could never be fast enough.

Her mind raced through possibilities in panic, but there was nothing for it.

She couldn't out-run an enormous beast like this.

She held out her hands, reaching instinctively for her own survival magic.

Come on...come on...

She blasted the creature with a wave of golden light.

By the time it dimmed, Liam was lying in a heap on the ground with his clothing in tatters, or what was left of it anyway.

Rosemary grimaced, hoping the poor man wasn't badly hurt.

"Sorry, Liam," Rosemary said. "I think that backfired."

Liam blinked and looked around before picking himself up.

Rosemary checked to see he was fine and then stood there awkwardly for a moment. "If you're alright, I think that's enough for the day. I might get going."

"No, wait," said Liam, his eyes widening. "That actually worked! I can feel the wolf inside me, still, but it's diminished."

"Liam, if you didn't notice, that was a total disaster," said Rosemary. "I made you turn into a werewolf *outside* of your normal cycle, and then blasted you to the ground."

"You did," he agreed. "But you also made me change back!"

"It seems like I can turn you back just out of my will to survive," said Rosemary. "But I don't know how to replicate it."

"It's progress," said Liam. "I'm tired now, but maybe we can try again in a few days."

"I'm not sure."

"I didn't mean to attack you," said Liam apologetically.

"I'm aware of that. It's just, it's quite dangerous, and not just for me. I don't know if it's also hurting you as well. You look a wreck."

"You promised to help me," Liam said.

Rosemary felt a stab of guilt, and perhaps something else akin to duty or loyalty. In werewolf form, Liam terrified her, but as much as she wanted to run away, she also cared about him.

"I will help, if I reasonably can." Rosemary clenched her hands together. "But for now I think I need some time and space to process all this. I'm not convinced that turning you into a werewolf and then blasting you back into human form is a good way forward. And I hope you're not expecting me to make a house call every full moon."

"That would be something," said Liam.

Rosemary narrowed her eyes at him.

“Okay, fine,” said Liam. “We've got another week and a half until full moon. You can take a few days to process, but maybe then we can regroup and come up with a plan.”

Rosemary nodded, still feeling shaken and unsure.

Twenty

Rosemary opened the door and entered Marjie's teashop. It had become a regular occurrence that Marjie would drop off morning tea for the children, and anyone else who was around at Thorn Manor. Today, she'd asked Rosemary to stop in and pick it up instead, as she was too busy to make the delivery herself. It was the least Rosemary could do, considering how helpful Marjie had been.

The teashop was bustling with activity. There were plenty of customers, and Rosemary felt a little pang of emotion in her chest when she saw Lamorna, the new employee, behind the counter. If Rosemary was completely honest, she'd been avoiding the shop recently. It didn't quite make sense, rationally. Since the foundling children had moved in and Rosemary was signing up for courses towards her chocolate business, she hardly had time to help Marjie out anymore, but she still felt a twinge of emotion seeing her young replacement with the lush blonde hair.

Rosemary had quite enjoyed working at the teashop when she was first settling into Myrtlewood. It had given her not only a sense of independence, but also a sense of purpose and helped her to feel like part of the community. Seeing the new girl in her place sometimes had the effect of making Rosemary feel a bit dislocated, somehow.

Lamorna seemed lovely, and reasonably competent apart from a few mix-ups, but Rosemary couldn't help but dislike her for some reason.

"There you are, love. Take a seat," said Marjie. She strode out from behind the counter wearing a floral apron in her usual style.

"I don't need to stay long. I don't want to trouble you," said Rosemary.

"Nonsense. Sit down. I'm going to bring you something."

Rosemary sighed and did as she was told. Marjie returned with a tea tray.

"Really, don't bother about me. Go and help your customers," said Rosemary.

"My customers are perfectly fine. Mind your own business," said Marjie with a grin.

"You know I didn't mean it that way. I just don't want to be any trouble."

"And that is part of your problem," said the older woman.

"What do you mean?"

"You've been doing everything to help out everybody else. And nothing for your own self. Here, sip this tea — yes, it does have some of my special remedy in it — and think about what you want to do for yourself and for your *own* future. You've been spending so much time looking after the children, helping Neve, looking out for Dain, and supporting Liam with whatever it is you're doing for him. Your whole life is helping everybody else."

"You're one to talk. You're always helping other people."

"That's because I figured out what makes me tick a long time ago. It took me a few false starts, mind. But after the fiasco with the recyclable toilet paper business I realised what I really like doing is nurturing people, feeding them, making them smile. You, on the other hand...Well, you're not a natural nurturer, dear. No offense or anything."

"None taken," said Rosemary. "You're right. I'm surprised I've kept Athena alive all these years. I'm more interested in making food – and eating it – than giving it to people."

Marjie smiled. "You still have your whole life to live. You need to be the main character, not just a supporting role. You've told me about the chocolate shop dream that you've had. And I've taken a few liberties..."

"You've *what*?" Rosemary's eyes widened.

"I just made some inquiries on your behalf. That's all."

"Oh no...really?" Rosemary said. "I've already got so much to think about with trying to get the children re-homed and Dain's addiction, not to mention trying to keep Athena out of trouble and everything else. I don't think I could start a business right now."

"Take it from somebody who's learned this the hard way," said Marjie sagely. "Helping other people is a lot easier than helping yourself."

"Says the woman who spends most of her time helping people."

"Not at my own expense," said Marjie. "And what can I say, it's a calling. But for the longest time I resisted it. I wanted to save the world with my inventions, despite the fact they often backfired on me. It's an ironic truth of life that doing what you really need to do can be the hardest thing. Meeting your own needs and dealing with your own issues is much, much harder than trying to save other people, but it's also far more important. If you don't do what you need to do for your own dreams, then you'll wither inside. And then you'll be no real help to anyone else."

"Oh, Marjie," Rosemary said, giving her friend a frustrated look.

"Now, don't protest, you know that I'm right."

"You *do* sound right," Rosemary admitted grudgingly.

"Alright then. It's settled."

"Settled?" Rosemary asked.

Just then, the bell tinkled above teashop door, and a tall, gruff, older man walked in, complete with scars on his face and a grumpy demeanour.

"What's all this about?" Covvey barked. "You tell me to come down here, old woman, and here I am."

"Speak for yourself," said Marjie. "I'm a spring chicken! You're the grumpy old bag of bones around here."

Covvey grunted.

"I have someone here who wants to do business with you," said Marjie.

"What kind of business? What are you talking about?" said Covvey.

Rosemary balked as Marjie gestured to her table. "Take a seat."

"What's *she* doing here?" Covvey asked suspiciously, clearly reminded of the last run-in he'd had with Rosemary when she'd inadvertently accused him of being a werewolf, which, to Rosemary's mind was only offensive because everyone was so prejudiced about the poor cursed beings.

"Yes, Rosemary's interested in leasing your vacant shop,"

Covvey sat down and folded his arms. "It's not on the market."

His words were spoken with a decisive finality that made Rosemary's heart sink, but Marjie was having none of it. "Don't be silly. It's not like you planned to do anything with it. And I'd say you have a good sweet tooth on you."

Covvey's brow furrowed. "What is it you want to do with it?"

Rosemary let out the breath she'd been holding. "Look," she said. "I'm not quite ready yet, but I would love to have a chocolate shop one day."

"A chocolate shop," said Covvey. "Well, I'm sorry, the premises is pretty much condemned. That mayor won't let anyone near it with a ten foot pole."

"That's not what I heard," said a familiar, silky voice.

"Mind your own business, ye blighter," said Covvey.

Rosemary glanced around to see Burk approaching. "The premises are sound," he said to Covvey. "The reason that the mayor won't let you operate is because he didn't like your previous establishment."

Covvey growled and Burk raised his hands. "I'm not one to judge, *believe* me, but as it stands, you're just wasting money, having to pay rates while the shop sits empty. You might as well lease it to someone else, at least that way you'll get rent."

"What makes you think I'd take advice from one of your kind?" Covvey barked.

"Do you mean a lawyer?" said Burk, with a slight raise of his eyebrows.

Rosemary suppressed a giggle.

Burk continued. "Look, I'm happy to throw in the legal work you'd need on both sides for free."

"Why would you do something like that?" Covvey's voice was tense and suspicious.

"It's a shame to see that shop sitting vacant. And I'd quite like to see what kind of chocolates Rosemary can make." He flashed her a stunning smile that Rosemary pretended not to react to.

"I do like chocolate," said Covvey slowly, raising his hand to his chin and pondering. "And old Galdie would have liked it...Your idea. She was a fierce one. And we didn't always get along. But she was loyal, a good strong woman. We had history, we did."

Rosemary nodded. "I'm sorry if I caused you offence the other day."

Covvey raised his arms dismissively. "No. It's all forgotten. All in the past." He began to stand up to leave. "I'll think about it. But I'm not making any promises."

He stomped out of the shop and Marjie beamed. "See, I told you I'd made some inquiries. There'll be nothing to it."

"It didn't sound too positive," said Rosemary.

Burk flashed her a soul-melting smile.

Rosemary turned away and looked at her phone, hoping to avoid a conversation. She reminded herself that Burk was dangerous, especially to the fae. She needed to keep Athena away from him, along with anyone else with similar heritage.

She'd been planning to call in to see Una after the tea shop. She needed to warn the fae woman about associations with a vampire.

"Rosemary," said Burk, his voice slightly strained. "Is something the matter?"

"I've got to go."

"I insist," said Burk.

"Please don't," Rosemary said, aware that her tone was cold. "I need to make sure we keep out interactions at a professional level." With that, she got up from the table and left Marjie's teashop, forgetting about the treats she'd gone in there to collect.

Rosemary crossed the town circle towards the apothecary only to find it shut up. There was a note stuck to the door saying that the shop was closed for personal reasons and that it would reopen next week.

A tingle of warning ran through Rosemary's nervous system.

"For personal reasons," she muttered to herself. "That doesn't sound good."

She went back to her car to find Marjie waiting there with a box of freshly baked ginger biscuits and a puzzled expression.

"What?" Rosemary asked.

"What happened back there?" Marjie asked. "With Perseus?"

"I forget his name is Perseus," said Rosemary. "I always think of him as Burk."

Marjie shrugged. "Don't change the subject. You're acting rather off."

"Marjie, I'm worried about Una."

"What's the matter with Una?" Marjie asked. "She seemed alright when I saw her earlier."

"You saw her today?"

"O'course I did. Her cousin Matilda's just had a baby. She and Ashwyn have gone out of town for a few days. They stopped to pick up some cakes for the family."

"Oh," said Rosemary. "I wondered what the personal reasons for the shop being closed were."

"Is that all you're worried about?" Marjie asked her, a little suspiciously.

"No," Rosemary admitted. She looked around to make sure nobody was watching. "Marjie, the other day, when I had the tonic from Una, a whole lot of memories came back to me."

"That's excellent news!" Marjie said. "Finally cleared out all those fake cobwebs in your head."

"Exactly. Only, it took me a little while to realise that Una was having dinner with Burk at the pub a couple of weeks ago."

"And?" Marjie raised her eyebrows.

"Well, okay, to be honest, Burk and I...well, there may have been a little spark between us at one point."

"So you might be jealous," said Marjie. "But that doesn't explain why you'd be worried."

Rosemary folded her arms. "I might have been a little bit jealous. But then it occurred to me that Una being fae...Don't you think she should be staying well away from vampires?"

"Oh, I see," said Marjie. "This is really about Athena."

"It is *not*," said Rosemary.

Marjie shook her head and smiled. "You're projecting your fears for your daughter onto Una, because you know they have similar parentage."

"I never thought of it that way." Rosemary crossed her arms. "Isn't it dangerous though?" she asked, lowering her voice. "I thought fae blood was irresistible to vampires."

Marjie shrugged. "Burk isn't one to lose control, though, is he? I'm not saying you shouldn't warn Una. She may well be unaware of all that. All I'm saying is Perseus Burk is a perfect gentleman. I've never once seen him lose his composure, or fly off the handle, or attack anyone who didn't deserve it."

"But you have seen him attack people?" Rosemary said.

"I've seen you attack people, too, including Dain," Marjie pointed out. "And you don't do it with quite so much composure or rationality."

Rosemary frowned. "Okay, fine. Maybe it is a little bit to do with Athena. I don't know. Everything's so complicated at the moment."

"That's because you've been trying to help too many people, like I said. Why don't you go home and have a nap and daydream about the chocolate shop. You could even have a go at making some chocolate. Do something for yourself, you know?"

Rosemary tried to protest, but the more she thought about it, the more she realised Marjie was right. She'd been putting off looking after herself. Worrying about other people was far easier than dealing with her own problems. "Alright, you win," said Rosemary. "I'll see you later."

Twenty-One

"Mum!" Athena called. "Mum!"

"What is it?" Rosemary's heart raced at the urgency in her daughter's voice. She grabbed hold of the porcelain sides of the large bathtub, trying to push herself out but underestimating the slipperiness of the sides. Water slopped over the floor. "I'm in the bath," she called out.

"Oh, don't worry then," said Athena. "This can wait until you're out."

Rosemary sighed, slipping back into the warmth of the bathtub, but she couldn't relax until she knew whatever it was that Athena was clearly concerned about.

"Can't you just tell me through the door?"

"Not really," said Athena. "It's too awkward. Besides, you might need a cup of tea for this."

"Okay, give me a minute. I'll meet you downstairs."

Rosemary got out and dried herself off, putting on the first clean clothing she could find. She'd been trying to take Marjie's advice and do something nice for herself, but clearly fate had other ideas.

"What's going on?" she said, making her way out to the kitchen where Athena was making tea.

"What on earth are you wearing?" Athena asked, her eyes boggling.

Rosemary looked down to see she had on a sunshine yellow top over forest green pants with a hot pink cardigan. She frowned. "I *thought* you had something important to say. You sounded worried."

"I did, but your outfit is also disturbing."

"Leave my outfit out of this," said Rosemary. "It's my new look. I'm calling it clashing Titans."

Athena giggled. "Okay, let's sit down."

"Now I'm really worried," said Rosemary.

"It's not bad news...exactly," said Athena as she carried the tea tray over to the window seats. "It's just that I learned something at school and I think it might be a clue as to what is going on."

Rosemary gulped. "Don't tell me you've been studying werewolves?"

"No," said Athena, looking confused. "Why would you guess that?"

"Erm...nothing," said Rosemary, feeling foolish for the slip-up. "It's just, I'm scared of werewolves after what Shelly and Marjie said."

Athena gave her a strange look as if she wasn't quite convinced. "Anyway," she said. "Today in Folklore and History, Ms Twigg – that's Agatha's daughter."

"Yes, I remember that," said Rosemary. "It's so nice to have my memory back."

"Pay attention, Mum," said Athena.

"I'm sorry. What did Ms Twigg say?"

"Wait." Athena crossed the floor and pulled out her notebook from the schoolbag she'd carelessly flung on the floor earlier. "Here it is," she said, making her way back to the window seats.

Just then, Detective Neve burst into the room. Her clothing was singed and the scent of smoke drifted across the house towards Rosemary.

"What happened" Rosemary asked.

"Another one," said Neve. "And they're getting worse." She slumped down next to them on the window seat."

"Another *heated* scene?" Rosemary asked.

"Fortunately we got this one early," said Neve. "But that reminds me. Is Nesta out back?"

Rosemary nodded.

"I still haven't told her about...that other thing." Neve groaned.

"I'm sure you'll have plenty of chances," said Rosemary, trying not to begin rambling, as Neve clearly didn't want to air her dirty laundry in front of the teen. Instead, Rosemary changed the subject. "Athena was just in the middle of telling me something."

"Was it another fire?" Athena asked. "Where was it?"

"It was out by old Briar castle," said Neve. "They seem to happen either in relatively powerful places, or around groupings of two or more highly magical people. That's the only pattern I can detect."

"None have happened here," said Rosemary.

"You're lucky this place has been warded up to the nines by old Galdie," said Neve. She turned to Athena. "What were you about to say?"

"I was just about to tell my mum something that they said at school. Only, I'm not sure if you'll take it seriously," said Athena.

"Try me," said Neve.

"Well, Miss Twigg told us all about the Beltane fires and the fire sprites and how in previous times they were involved in worshipping the god Balanus."

Neve nodded.

"Anyway," Athena continued. "Miss Twigg seems to think all that has something to do with these fires happening at the moment. She set us all assignments on it and I've been doing some research. One source I read said that every few hundred years the planets align in a special way with Uranus and Jupiter in Aries, and Mars joining them. It sets the scene for something called the Cavalia. It hasn't happened in a long time, but that might be because there aren't enough fire sprites to instigate it. I read that fire sprites used to be involved in the old rituals of the Cult of Belamus. But you don't see many of them around these days. My guess it they all got sealed in the fae realm when the veil borders closed."

Neve shook her head. "Why's she telling schoolkids about all this and not the police?"

"Well, she said that lessons in history are important." said Athena. "And apparently she did tell the police, though I'm not sure if anyone listened."

Neve sighed. "I'm gonna have to have words with Perkins about this. Not telling me things that notable people in the community have said is definitely along the lines of obstruction of an investigation."

"He probably didn't take her seriously," said Rosemary. "He doesn't seem to take much seriously apart from himself."

"Harsh but true," said Neve. "If you'll excuse me, I have to go and make a very grumpy phone call."

Rosemary looked at her daughter. "It was good you told us. Nice work, kid."

"I'm surprised either of you took me seriously," said Athena. "People don't usually listen to teens."

"You're not just any teenager," said Rosemary. "You're my daughter. I know you're incredibly clever. And you don't suffer fools. I'm sure if you thought the teacher was having you on you wouldn't have spared them a second thought."

The two Thorns sipped their tea in silence until Neve returned a moment later. "Perkins wasn't happy about that," she said.

"What was his response?" Rosemary asked her.

"He complained that if he had to relay every half-brained thing the ridiculous townspeople told him he'd never get on with any of his other more important work."

"It sounds like something he'd say," said Rosemary. "Anyway, I'm glad we have you on the case. At least you've got plenty of brains."

"Thanks. I might pay your teacher a visit later," she said to Athena, and then turned back to Rosemary. "But now, I'd better go and talk to Nesta. Wish me luck."

"What's going on with them?" Athena asked as Neve left the room.

"Hopefully nothing," said Rosemary.

"Oh, fine," said Athena. "But tell me, what was it you said about fighting you?"

Twenty-Two

"You'll pay for that!" Athena drew energy into her hands. It sizzled, a white blob of light flecked with green. She raised it above her head and lobbed it at her mother. "This is really helping me to work out some anger issues."

Rosemary ducked, spun, and hurled a golden ball of light back. Athena only just got out of the way. The ball landed on a nearby tree, burning a charred mark into the bark.

Dain and Marjie were out shopping and Nesta had taken the foundling children inside so that the Thorns could use the back lawn for training purposes. Though the excitement had meant there was now a row of very interested little faces peeping through the back windows of the house.

Rosemary and Athena stood five metres away from each other, crab-walking slowly around in a circle as they practiced both attacking and defending with magic.

"I'm glad you found an outlet for your anger," said Rosemary, shooting a fireball.

"Hey!" Athena dropped to the ground to avoid it. "At least give me a chance to retaliate."

"Our enemies won't do that."

"Fair point. That was a heavy one," she said as she got to her feet again.

"I'm glad you noticed," said Rosemary. "I constructed it out of my rage at all the injustices in the world."

Athena smiled. "You know, we also need to practice close range combat." She lunged towards her mother and kicked out.

Rosemary raised her hands, and a blast of white light shot out, blowing Athena back across the lawn.

"How did you do that?" asked Athena. Her magic had come in much more strongly since she'd left the fae realm. It was even stronger on the mornings after her night time escapades that had continued, recently, where she tried to cut a door through to the other world.

She knew she shouldn't, but she couldn't help it, just to get that sensation of feeling warm and connected and at home in her own body.

Of course, Rosemary didn't know anything about it and Athena wasn't about to tell her mother. Rosemary was only just starting to relax a little after the fae realm debacle. Athena was doing all she could to play the sympathy card of Finnigan's betrayal, even though it made her feel sick to her stomach to do it.

"We can't just fight with magic," said Athena. "Our attackers might have weapons."

"Let's try hand to hand combat before we add in dangerous weapons, shall we?" Rosemary jumped forward and threw a punch towards her daughter.

"That was terrible," said Athena, leaning back. "Even if I'd stayed perfectly still it would have hardly hurt at all."

"Well, forgive me for not wanting to hurt my own child," said Rosemary.

"If you're not going to properly attack me this is not really going to work."

"You're right," said Rosemary. "We need a proper trainer. Only, I don't know anyone who fits the bill."

"Maybe Marjie will know someone," said Athena. "Or you could always ask your vampire friend."

Athena watched as her mother visibly stiffened.

"Stop that."

"I will, if you stop denying it. You definitely got jealous when you saw him at the pub with another woman."

Rosemary looked uncomfortable. "Feelings don't always make sense, as you well know," she said.

"Sure thing, Mum. It seems like you've moved on with Liam now, anyway."

"That's *not* what's going on, and you know it," said Rosemary.

"It's a shame though," said Athena. "It would probably make you less wound-up."

Rosemary shot a huge ball of a sizzling electric purple light towards her daughter.

Athena blasted it out of the way with her own magic. "I guess I deserved that." She caught a glimpse of her reflection in the windows of the house. Her hair stood up on end from the near miss. "How did you do that? I want to play with electricity."

"I think it's a mixture of elements, but I have no idea," said Rosemary. "That's part of the problem. And if you must know, I'm trying to help Liam with a medical issue, one that I'm not privy to discuss."

"Oh...*Oh*!" said Athena. "I see. Is it gross?"

Rosemary narrowed her eyes.

"You're right," Athena continued. "I don't want to know if it's gross."

Rosemary laughed and Athena made the most of her mother's distraction by lobbing another ball of pale green light. It hit Rosemary in the chest, making her fall straight back.

"You got me," she said, staring up at the sky.

"It's not fair that I can only do balls of light and you can do fire and all sorts of weird stuff," said Athena.

"I'm just playing with my emotions," said Rosemary. "Maybe if you weren't so closed off about yours you'd be able to make cool stuff too."

"Touché." Athena lunged towards her mother, kicking and punching before being blasted back again by a ball of energy that was big and fluffy and baby-pink. It wrapped her up, lifted her into the air, and held her, hovering above the ground.

"Not fair!" Athena shouted from the giant pink bubble. "Put me down!"

"You're protected by my love," said Rosemary, laughing.

Athena closed her eyes and imagined a dart of magic, shooting out. The bubble popped with a bang, and she collapsed to the ground in a disgruntled pile.

"Had enough for the day?" Rosemary asked.

Athena lay there on the ground, grumbling unintelligible noises, not bothering to pull herself up.

"Marjie dropped over some homemade lemonade," Rosemary coaxed.

"Sure," said Athena, her voice a whimper.

Rosemary helped her up. "We can try again tomorrow. But I do really think we need a trainer, otherwise we're not going to get very far. We need to be on our game if these creepy things keep showing up and attacking us."

As if in answer to her words, a deep crackle like the sound of thunder shocked the air around them. They turned to see three figures appear at the side of the house. They were all shrouded in dark hooded cloaks.

"Oh no. No you don't!" Rosemary crouched down, already on the offensive. She threw her arm to the side and a silver disc of light shot out, taking out one of the enemies at the rear.

"Uh...Mum...What's going on here?" Athena felt a flutter in her chest as she realised the danger their unexpected guests posed.

"My guess is it's the Bloodstones," muttered Rosemary, as the figure at the front raised her hands in the air. Lightning sizzled between her palms and the hood fell back revealing long silvery blonde locks. Her face remained concealed behind a butterfly mask that gleamed, iridescent. All Athena could see of her face were her eyes, which flashed blue in the sunlight.

"Who's that?" Athena asked. "She looks familiar."

"Whoever she is, I don't think she's entirely human," said Rosemary.

Athena looked at the woman. Her limbs were slender like the fae, but there was something different about her.

"Join the club," Athena replied. "I've got this." Her hands trembled a little as she held out her arms, creating an enormous ball of magical light energy, and then gave it a huge shove, pushing it towards the woman, who dived out of the way.

One of the woman's cronies ran at Rosemary. Athena watched as her mother's super strength magical instincts kicked in. She threw the attacker to the ground, but another crony emerged from the bushes and was close behind. Athena was prepared to attack, but Rosemary was faster, blasting magic instinctually. It burst out as light and air in a wave of energy, stripping the hood back from the attacker. For a moment they saw that he was a dark-haired man with pasty skin, before he burst into dust.

"Didn't your mother ever tell you to wear sunscreen?" said Rosemary.

Athena cringed at her mother's cheesy line and laughed at the same time. "Seriously, who brings a vampire to a daylight fight?"

"I see you're not unprepared," said the masked woman in a gravelly voice. "No matter. I'm merely here to relay a message."

"What's the message?" Rosemary asked.

"We're here, all around you. We are coming for you. There is no way you can run or hide. We're bringing our leader back."

In a flash of lightning, the hooded attackers were gone.

"Holy Hades," said Rosemary. "That was bloody unexpected."

"You're sure it's the Bloodstones?" Athena asked, her blood running cold.

"It must be," said Rosemary. "Especially with their penchant for wearing black robes."

There was a crashing sound and Rosemary made a dash towards the house, Athena following close behind. They got inside to find the place ransacked. Chairs were strewn around and shattered porcelain littered the floor. The children were hiding underneath the couch, Nesta huddled close by, trembling.

Athena gasped. "What happened?"

How did the Bloodstones get through the wards? Athena wondered. *They must be packing some pretty powerful magic.*

"It was a distraction," said Rosemary, her tone certain.

Athena bit her lip in concentration, trying to make sense of the situation. "I'm surprised they're so organised. Didn't you kill their annoying little vampiric leader?"

"I thought so," said Rosemary.

"Unless..." Athena's mind raced. *The Bloodstones were looking for something, otherwise why bother to create a diversion? They're trying to make a comeback.* She tried to think of magical items they might be after, but her mind kept returning to the box that the Thorn family magic had been bound inside.

"Unless what?" Nesta asked.

Athena looked at her mother. "You don't think they're looking for the box?"

Rosemary frowned. "Why would they do that? It's empty, remember? Geneviève picked it up – the power was already released."

Athena crossed her arms. "Mum, didn't you say Liam had suspicious customers asking about magical dimensions?"

"Something like that."

"And when Geneviève was vanquished – or at least that's what we thought – it wasn't a normal dusting, was it?"

Rosemary's eyes bulged. "You don't think...?"

Athena nodded. "They wanted to keep us busy. So they could get *some-*

thing from inside the house. There's a chance she might have been flung into the magical dimension created inside that box – or at least, the remaining Bloodstones might think so."

She and Athena looked at each other and then took off towards the library.

The door had been flung open. Books lay strewn around the room, and the wooden little box that had once held the Thorn family magic had vanished.

Twenty-Three

Rosemary tried to slow her breathing. She and Athena stood in shocked silence, looking at the spot on the desk where the box had once been.

Athena frowned. "You really believe she could still be in there?"

"At least, that's what her followers think," said Rosemary.

They turned towards the sound as the front door of the house swung open.

Dain and Marjie had returned from their shopping expedition. Rosemary noticed that Dain was already dressed in some new jeans and a crisp white shirt. He beamed at her, and then he took in the carnage around him and his expression pressed into concern.

"What happened?" he asked.

"Did you try that spell again and mess up the house?" Marjie asked.

Athena shook her head. "No, we were attacked by the Bloodstone Society."

Dain ran forward, sweeping both Rosemary and Athena into a ferocious hug.

"My girls," he said, his voice cracking, in a gesture that was both caring and protective. "Are you alright?"

"We're fine." Rosemary's body stiffened in awkwardness as her ex continued to hug her. "It was just a distraction. They attacked us outside when we were training, but what they really wanted was in here."

"What was it, dear?" Marjie asked as she stepped around the group hug, surveying the damage.

"The box," said Athena. Rosemary was surprised her daughter was continuing to allow her father to hug her. "You know the one that used to house our family magic."

"But the magic's not in there anymore," said Marjie. "Surely they know that."

"We suspect they think Geneviève is still in there, somehow," said Rosemary, wondering what the best way to pry herself out of this awkward hugging situation. It had clearly gone on for far too long, but there was only sweetness and concern in Dain's demeanour. She thought back to what Una said about the spell for the cream addiction.

It requires love.

It was quickly becoming clear to Rosemary that despite Athena's long-held resentment towards her father, there was definitely a more positive attachment there too. And now that Rosemary's memories had cleared up, she could remember the good times and the bad. It gave her a new perspective, coupled with the knowledge about Dain's addiction.

She finally managed to extricate herself from the hug with the knowledge that there was definitely a feeling of warmth between them. She wasn't sure if it was romantic, but it did feel a lot like love.

Rosemary turned towards Athena, who had a slightly overwhelmed expression on her face. "It's time to try the spell."

Twenty-Four

"These notes are quite complicated," said Athena. "Are you sure we're up to doing this?"

They were standing in the lounge an hour later, after cleaning up from the attack, in which the house helped a great deal. They'd had lunch and begun preparations for the spell.

"It's nothing compared to the spell I had to do to create a temporary warp in space in order to try and rescue your silly arse from another dimension," Rosemary replied.

"How long are you going to keep reminding me about that for?"

"Probably until you're retired," said Rosemary. "That'll give me a good few decades of ammunition."

Athena sighed.

Rosemary rubbed her hands together. "Alright. Let's start."

"Don't you think we should wait until Una comes back from her family thing? She might be able to help."

"We could do," said Rosemary. "Although, I don't think we need her here to do the spell. Her notes say it should be cast by the people closest to the fae in question."

"No, that's not what it says," said Athena. "It says we have to love him. I don't think that we qualify."

"I wouldn't have said so either," Rosemary said. "But I think something has changed. Or maybe a whole lot of things have changed over time. You can still be angry at someone that you love. You can even hate them sometimes. In fact, sometimes the reason that feelings are so strong is because of the love."

"Sounds like a self-help book," said Athena. "I don't mind Dad. In fact, he's kind of growing on me a little bit. But that doesn't make up for the facts."

"It doesn't make up for it," said Rosemary. "You're right. And it's not about making up for it. We just have to deal with the situation...wherever we are. And this is where we are right now."

Athena narrowed her eyes. "Why are you so focused on this? Don't you have a million other things to worry about? Like Liam's little health disorder and all these fires and the children still running wild around the house, not to mention getting your own life together, and setting up your business?"

"One thing at a time," said Rosemary. "I've just got to tick this off my list. The less I have to worry about Dain, the easier it will be sort out those other things. It makes me nervous having him around when we never know if he's going to lose the plot. It seems even more dangerous to kick him out."

Athena shrugged. "Okay. Let's set up, then."

They gathered together the ingredients for the spell: amethyst crystals to be placed at the four direction points; a bundle of sage and another of rosemary; three sprigs of thyme and one of vervain; and nine cardamom pods. They applied the anointing serum to their temples, made with essential oils of black pepper and juniper. It smelled wonderful.

They pushed the couches out of the way in the lounge and lay the herbs and the crystals in a circle and said the basic blessing to create a sacred space. Then they called Dain in. He'd been waiting in the kitchen blindfolded, as the instructions said he had to enter the ritual space that way. He stumbled a little bit, tripping on the arm of a chair that had been pushed a little too close to the doorframe.

"Can we help?" Athena whispered.

Rosemary nodded. They stepped forward and led Dain to the circle.

"Sit down," said Rosemary.

Dain did as he was told, sitting cross legged on the floor. Athena and Rosemary stood above him, joined hands, and began to chant.

By the power of our love for you, we bind you.
We shackle you to free you.
We bind you so that which would tear you from us now only sickens you.

We bind you, Dain, in our love.
We bind you to free you.

A burst of light emanated from the centre of the circle, above Dain's head.

It radiated out in between where Rosemary and Athena stood. It shone out in an intricate paisley-like pattern and then contracted around the three of them.

Rosemary felt something shifting.

It was as if a new lens had come over her way of seeing.

The world stilled for a moment, then her vision went blank.

There was a heavy darkness and Rosemary realised she must have passed out. She tried to open her eyes, only to find everything different. She was still standing, holding onto Athena's hands, but she was also somewhere else entirely, in her mind.

A reel of memories ran through her head, but they weren't Rosemary's.

It was Dain's perspective as a young fae, peeking through the veil, leaving behind everything he knew, entering into the human realm.

Rosemary felt the extreme heaviness of emotion, and the disconnection he'd experienced. He'd been running from something big and terrifying and found himself in another world, a much harder, heavier world where nothing made sense.

She watched as he was picked up by the authorities, not understanding anything about the way the world operated. She watched his memories stream past as he was passed from foster home to foster home, often to be beaten and yelled at and threatened.

She watched through his eyes as he saw her for the first time.

Rosemary, beautiful and young, her red hair blowing in the breeze on a crisp spring morning as she stopped to pick a bluebell on her way to high school.

He could see the magic all around and inside of her, even though she couldn't see it herself. It was the magic that drew him in. It was her personality that kept him anchored to her.

Rosemary felt the deepest love swim through her. Only it wasn't her emotion. It was Dain's. It was a beautiful sensation that gripped her heart, only to be interrupted by shame and failure.

No matter what he tried, Dain could never do things right. Rosemary saw her own weariness through his eyes, as things got harder and harder to manage. She felt the heaviness he experienced, just being in the earth realm. His disappointment in himself was enough to break her heart.

She saw herself yelling at him for refusing to do the grocery shopping when she was up all night with a sick child. He'd gone to such great lengths to control himself, to avoid his addiction, it was backfiring on him. He left their small flat and walked the streets. He knew he couldn't trust himself at the grocery store where Rosemary worked. Getting too close to his weakness could cost him everything. Instead he went to a bar and sat in the darkness. There was no point in trying anymore. No matter what he did, he wasn't good enough.

Rosemary watched through Dain's eyes as he ordered an Irish cream liqueur. He downed it in one gulp and suddenly he felt good again. There was lightness. But there was also a lack of control. That was when it all fell apart. He'd hang out in bars and gamble with his new friends. He lost all semblance of control, but managed to keep hiding what he was from his family.

He kept going back to the cream bottle over and over again because it made him feel good when nothing else was right. He couldn't stop himself from being reckless. Wasting every chance he got.

The memories faded and she heard Athena sob. Rosemary pulled her closer, but Dain was in the way. They tripped and fell into a pile of family on the floor.

The ridiculousness of the situation made them laugh, even though Athena and Rosemary were both in tears.

"What...what happened?" Dain asked.

"It was so sad," said Athena, not bothering to get up from the floor. "I mean, you told me you had a rough life. You told me bits and pieces, but it was like..."

"It was like we were there," said Rosemary, beginning to move in an attempt to extricate herself from the puddle. "Like we went through everything you did, although, obviously the Reader's Digest version."

"Well, I didn't come here to get embarrassed," said Dain, pushing himself up. "I'll just show myself out."

"No, it was important," said Athena. "We needed to see all that. It means something."

"It does," said Rosemary. "Our lives might have been tough, and you are probably the cause of most of that to be quite frank."

"Thanks," said Dain in a caustic tone. "That makes me feel so much better."

Rosemary gripped his arm. "But we didn't know what you'd been through."

"I've been angry at you for so long," said Athena, shaking herself. "You didn't know any different."

"That's right." Rosemary nodded. "In some ways, I understood that, intellectually. But to experience it is a whole other thing."

"Great," said Dain, still sounding unimpressed. "Did it actually work?"

"We'll find out," said Athena.

Twenty-Five

"Is this really necessary?" Dain asked.

Athena laughed at the absurdity of the situation. "Yes, Dad," she said, wrapping the rope around him one more time before fastening it to the chair he sat in. "You might not remember it very well, but you totally lose your head when the cream comes out. We need to make sure you're restrained and are no danger to yourself or others."

Rosemary nodded. "It's really a surprise you've lived this long."

"What can I say? Fae are resilient creatures."

"That does not give me much hope for us when the Countess figures out how to get her revenge," said Athena.

She had been thinking about this possibility a lot lately. Every time she cut another door through to the fae realm there was a risk that fae could push their way through. It seemed like they hadn't figured out how to do it yet. Something came through when she sliced into the veil, but it wasn't solid.

She hoped that the Countess had no idea what she was doing, and considering Finnigan could go back and forth between the worlds as if he had dual-passports, the Countess could probably mount her own attack without Athena accidentally enabling it, though that thought wasn't exactly reassuring.

Worse still, it was a far greater risk that she'd encounter her infuriating ex crush, and she did not want to think about him.

“Stay very still,” said Rosemary, strapping Dain’s hands down onto the arm rests with duct tape.

“This is all a bit much for a little cream,” Dain protested.

“Quiet, you,” said Athena. “Marjie will be here any minute with cream buns or something. It will all be over soon enough and we’ll see if the spell worked.”

The door opened and Marjie came in, brandishing a bottle of cream. “Are you sure this is a good idea?” she called out, hesitating in the doorway.

“Don't worry, we've got him restrained,” said Rosemary.

“And the kids are all out at the park with Nesta, just to be safe,” Athena added.

Rosemary watched as Marjie took a deep breath.

“Right then,” she said, entering the room.

It had been a few days since they’d cast the spell. Dain had been exhausted afterwards and had spent most of the elapsed time sleeping.

Una’s instructions said to let him rest and wait two to five days before they tested it by carefully allowing him near high fat dairy products.

“Are you ready,” Rosemary asked Dain.

“As I'll ever be,” he replied. “But if it doesn't work, please knock me out gently and forgive me for anything stupid I do.”

Athena smiled. “Happy to. We know it's not your fault. At least you're trying Dad.”

Dain’s eyes lit up with hope.

Rosemary smiled. “It warms my heart to see my daughter getting along with the father who had always been such a thorn in her side.”

Athena glared at her.

“What? Animosity wasn't doing either of you any good. And though we won’t forget the past, it’s about time we stop living in its shadow.”

“All right, here goes,” said Marjie. She cracked open the bottle of cream and peeled back the foil seal.

They all watched Dain, nervously.

Instead of lighting up gold, as they usually did in reaction to cream, his eyes had a greenish tinge. In fact, his whole face looked rather pale. All of a sudden he coughed and then wretched.

The chair rocked backwards as his whole body convulsed.

Athena turned away as Dain was violently ill, all over himself and the floor. Rosemary tipped the chair to the side so that he didn't choke on his own sick.

"I wasn't prepared for that," she said.

"Disgusting," said Athena. "I wish I didn't have to see it.

"Well, the spell did something," said Rosemary as Dain continued to vomit on the floor.

"Not exactly what we bargained for," said Athena.

"He was sick the last time he tried the remedy from that old book," Rosemary pointed out. "This time, maybe it will actually work, if cream makes him sick in the long term."

"But the point is, Dad should be able to get over his problems, and function in society, regardless of what dairy products are being served. We can't have him curling over and making a mess every time he seems a cream cake."

Rosemary sighed. "At least he's not going to take all my money and gamble or give it away."

"Wait a minute," said Marjie. "I'm going to get Una on the phone."

"Isn't she away?" Rosemary asked.

"Haven't you heard of cell phones?" said Marjie.

Rosemary blushed. "It's not like I know her all that well."

"Look, here you go. It's ringing," Marjie said, holding up the phone.

Rosemary raised her hands in protest not quite sure what to say.

"Oh fine," said Marjie. She spoke into the receiver. "Hello dear. Yes, I'm perfectly fine. Look, we've got a situation here. The Thorn girls tried the spell and they thought it worked but Dain was violently ill. Oh, I see."

Marjie raised her eyebrows and Rosemary gave her a questioning look.

"Here," said Marjie. She handed the phone to Rosemary.

Twenty-Six

"Uh, hi," said Rosemary, grabbing the phone reluctantly.

"Oh, Rosemary. I'm sorry," said Una's voice. "I should have warned you that this might happen. It wasn't so severe with me, but I can see how things could have been a lot worse."

"What do you mean?" Rosemary asked.

"Cream made me nauseous," Una explained.

"Are you saying he's going to continue to be sick like this every time he smells cream?" Rosemary asked.

Athena frowned.

"I don't think so," said Una. "The nausea wore off after a few weeks, so don't worry. Hopefully the same will happen with Dain. Then you'll be able to take him out in public without fear of cream buns."

"Thank you," said Rosemary. She sighed with relief, feeling the exhaustion of the past few weeks catching up on her. "So you're saying the spell worked?"

"It sounds like it worked rather well," said Una. "He wouldn't have had such a reaction to cream if the magic wasn't potent. You must really..." Her voice trailed away and Rosemary interrupted her.

"Oh, there was something I wanted to tell you." Rosemary was thinking about the situation with Burk, but then she hesitated. This probably wasn't the appropriate time and place with Athena, Marjie, and Dain all listening in.

"Yes?" Una asked.

"Never mind," said Rosemary. "It can wait until you get back. When are you back, by the way?"

Tomorrow morning," said Una. "Maybe we can catch up for a cup of tea in the next few days."

"That sounds perfect," said Rosemary. "Thanks again, for everything." She hung up the phone. "Good news," she announced. "The spell worked and Dain's not going to be sick forever, though he won't be wanting to be around dairy any time soon."

"Fabulous!" said Athena. "We can probably untie him now."

"I was gonna ask when you were going to remember that," said Dain. "I'm quite uncomfortable here, tied up in a pool of my own vomit."

"Well, it's not the best situation for the rest of us either," said Athena as Rosemary got started on the rope.

"Una thinks the extreme effects should wear off after a few weeks," said Rosemary. "And then you'll probably just be left with a mild dislike for dairy products. You can tell people you're lactose intolerant."

"True enough," said Dain. "It might not be the lactose, but I don't tolerate nausea well." He was out of the chair and looking rather dishevelled. "If you'll excuse me, I'm going to go and have a shower. Don't worry, I'll clean up when I get back."

"How considerate," said Athena as Dain wandered towards the bathroom. "He's not too bad to have around, after all."

Later that day, Rosemary, Athena, and Marjie sat in the window seats, watching as the children played with Nesta outside. Marjie had insisted on staying to clean up the mess.

"Thank you for everything," said Rosemary.

"It's no trouble, my dear." Marjie patted her arm. "I know Dain had offered to do it when he woke up, but that seemed both unfair on him, being sick and all, and unfair on you for having to deal with it until he got himself in order."

"I was hoping the house would do it for us while I got changed." Rosemary said.

"Actually, you're right. Most of the mess was gone by the time I got to it."

Rosemary smiled. "As long as Dain doesn't get too used to Thorn Manor picking up after him."

"Don't worry, Mum," said Athena. "There will be plenty of opportunities for him to help around the house in the future. Hopefully none of them will be quite so gross."

Rosemary rested her chin in her hands in thought.

In future sounded like some kind of commitment. Sure, Dain had been hanging around for weeks after being rescued from the fae realm, and sure, they had plenty of room at Thorn Manor. It *was* nice that Athena was building a healthier relationship with her father. Dain had helped out a lot with the foundling children and Rosemary didn't mind his company, now that she seemed impervious to the fae magic that previously kept her swooning over the guy, though she wasn't sure whether that was to do with the memory tonic, her magic being unbound, or the complex set of charms and wards that Athena had insisted on setting up.

This arrangement can't be permanent.

Rosemary had assumed Dain would just drift off eventually, like he usually did. But perhaps this time it would be different. He hadn't asked her for money, nothing had noticeably gone missing from the house, and given the spell they'd just performed, perhaps he would settle down. Rosemary just wasn't sure she was ready to think about a situation where her very troubled ex was settling down *in her house!*

"You need to relax, dear," said Marjie, clearly troubled by Rosemary's expression. "After all that...I have a present for you."

"Oh no. No you don't," Rosemary said. "You've done quite enough."

"When are you going to come to your senses and stop resisting my way of showing I care?" Marjie asked, and there was a cutting edge to her tone that shocked Rosemary out of her resistance. "You and Athena are family to me now, and I'll spoil you as much as I possibly can. That's the truth, whether you want to accept it or not."

Rosemary sighed and smiled sheepishly, not wanting to disrespect her very generous friend, who was indeed starting to feel more like family.

"Rosemary, I'm serious. Stop trying to take on the world by yourself. You're used to being alone, but you're not anymore. You've got us now. And goodness knows we have to take care of our family, wherever we find them."

"Thank you," said Rosemary, as Marjie's words warmed her heart.

"Not yet. I haven't even given it to you."

"What is it?" Athena asked.

Marjie fished in her handbag and pulled out a cream coloured envelope. "This is for you, both. Take it and relax. You need it. And stop apologising for being yourself. You're a strong determined woman and you've been looking after everyone else for too long. Now that you've sorted out Dain's cream addiction, take a little breather."

Rosemary opened the envelope to find a voucher for a local spa. "Oh Marjie, how thoughtful! I've never been to anything like this before."

She gave the older woman a big hug.

Rosemary might have resolved Dain's problems, at least for now, so he didn't need babysitting so closely, but Liam was still wanting her help, and there was still the looming issue of the mystery magical fires, and the attacks from hooded figures, but overall, it seemed like a relatively good time to take a little break from it all.

"You can enjoy a whole day of pampering. Take Athena, the voucher will cover it."

Athena's eyes lit up in excitement. "We'll be just like film stars with cucumbers on our eyes, Mum."

Rosemary laughed. "That actually sounds perfect."

Twenty-Seven

The plants outside seemed greener than usual, lush from the heavy rain the night before. Rosemary left Thorn Manor relatively early for a Saturday morning and drove towards the spa. She followed the directions from her phone. Nesta was going to drop Athena off later, as the teenager didn't feel comfortable with Rosemary's first planned activity of getting a nice long relaxing massage. It seemed like heaven to Rosemary, but Athena was squeamish about the idea of strangers touching her.

The spa was a little off to the west side of the village, further up the coast from Thorn Manor. Rosemary drove along the seaside road. It was soothing to see the ocean waves rolling in.

Despite living relatively close to the sea, they'd barely spent any time at the beach. It was often too windy, but now that the weather was warming up perhaps that would change. She needed a day of relaxing, especially since she was now training with Athena every day, with Dain sometimes helping. They were quickly improving, but the magical fight practice took its toll.

As Rosemary drove, she glanced up towards the hill on her right to see the mayor's house peeking through the trees from a distance as she passed by. It looked slightly different, though she couldn't see the details from this far away. Perhaps it was scaffolding for the repairs, following that fire.

Thinking about Mr June left a bitter taste in Rosemary's mouth. He had not been happy to see her and she was more than happy to avoid him for the foreseeable future. She only hoped that their little run-in a while back where he'd accused her of breaking and entering into his house hadn't dampened her chances of getting a license for the chocolate shop.

She was more determined than ever to go ahead with the business, especially now that Covvey had agreed verbally to lease her the building, but she felt a frightened flutter in her heart every time she thought of it. She didn't know the first thing about running a business.

She'd found numerous online small business courses alongside the chocolatier qualifications that she was still trying to decide between.

Marjie was right. It was much harder to think about herself and get on with the things that she wanted to do in life than it was focusing on other people's problems and trying to sort out their issues.

But today, she didn't have to worry about any of that. Not the children, not Dain. Not Liam, not even the police investigation into the fires, or the Bloodstone Society, touch wood. She reached out to knock on the polished wood panel in the dashboard of Granny's Rolls Royce.

Today was about relaxing. First of all, just by herself as a person in her own right, and then later Athena would be joining her for facials and footbaths and manicures and pedicures and all sorts of other cures.

It sounded almost too good to be true, despite the fact that Rosemary had never done any of this stuff and had a sneaking anxiety that it might actually be rather awkward and uncomfortable.

She pushed away her fears as she drove into the carpark of an exquisitely landscaped area with little rock gardens dotted around the outside. The building itself had enormous gates made of wood up front. It looked like a luxury resort and Rosemary wondered who in the modest magical village of Myrtlewood was keeping a place like this going.

An engraved silver placard on the door read that the Myrtlewood Spa was a treat for magical people from across the world.

"That would explain it then," Rosemary muttered to herself as she continued to read.

Enjoy the exquisite luxury of the spa, complete with magical treatments such as you've never seen before. We have everything required to put your mind, body, and spirit at ease.

"That sounds lovely."

She rang the bell, and a smaller door opened from within the gate. It seemed to move all on its own. Rosemary wasn't sure if it was through magic or some kind of electric-powered mechanism.

Through the door, a smooth cobbled path wove along more elaborate gardens with ornamental rocks and tropical plants.

As Rosemary began to wander along she heard the sound of trickling water from a small stream which flowed to her right. She took a moment to admire the water feature bubbling out of some rocks forming a tiny waterfall. Being there was already relaxing.

She made her way up to reception and entered to see a familiar face behind the counter.

"Ferg?"

He was wearing a brown pinstriped suit, suitable for a Saturday by his standards. He looked up from the book he was reading. "Ah, Ms. Thorn," he said. "I see you're right on time for your massage."

"You...work here as well?" Rosemary asked. She was used to Ferg as an event organiser, taxi service, and sometimes gardener. She wasn't expecting him here as well.

"It's my weekend job," said Ferg, sounding proud. "Got to keep busy! Please take a seat and we'll be with you shortly."

"When do you sleep?" Rosemary asked.

"I've never found sleep to be particularly interesting," said Ferg.

"Oh, sorry," said Rosemary. "I didn't mean to ask personal questions."

"Personal how?" Ferg asked.

"Never mind," said Rosemary. She took a seat in one of the plush purple velvet chairs in the waiting area and picked up a magazine. She'd expected it to be a regular women's magazine, or even one of those nice, healthy lifestyle ones with the thicker paper. She was surprised to find it was titled *Magical You*. On the front there was a picture of a pixie-esque woman with a bluish tinge to her skin and pointed ears.

"Can't escape unrealistic body standards even in the magical world," Rosemary mumbled.

"What was that?" said Ferg.

"Nothing." Rosemary smiled warmly at him.

Ferg gave her a stern look and walked away.

Rosemary looked back at the image of the blue woman on the magazine. She was surrounded by various fonts of text that read: sixteen ways to charm him with spices, the secret magic of cinnamon, harmless garden hexes to keep the pests at bay, and fire up your love life – advice from a rare fire sprite.

Rosemary giggled and began flicking through the pages. "Where do I subscribe to this? It's hilarious."

Ferg approached again, carrying a tray laden with objects.

"Ms Thorn, I'd appreciate it if you kept your voice down, please."

"But we're the only ones here," said Rosemary.

"The spa is a peaceful place."

"Ferg, what are you, a librarian?"

Ferg gave her a serious look. "I thought we discussed this. I work here in the weekends. And please call me Mr Burgess while I'm here. It's more formal."

"Okay," said Rosemary shrugging. "I didn't realise this was a formal place. I thought it was supposed to be relaxing."

"Formalised relaxing," said Ferg, straightening up the paisley-lined collar on his blazer. "Now, I've brought you some artesian spring water from a sacred well in the north of Ireland. Its properties help to ease your worries and strengthen your essence."

"Uh, sounds lovely," said Rosemary, looking at the tray that Ferg was holding.

"And also an assortment of fruit," said Ferg.

"Does that have any special properties?" Rosemary asked.

"No, should it have?"

"Just ordinary fruit then?" said Rosemary.

"I can go and check if you like." Ferg looked concerned and slightly bothered.

"It's okay," said Rosemary, but Ferg had already stomped off after placing the tray down in front of her.

Rosemary sighed, hoping that Ferg wasn't going to be doing the treatments too. If he was, this could be quite a long day.

After a few moments and a good slug of the artesian spring water, which made Rosemary feel all sparkly and happy inside, she managed to eat a few strawberries and a piece of kiwifruit before a petite woman with blue hair came to collect her for the massage.

"You look familiar," said Rosemary.

"I think our daughters know each other," said the woman. "I'm Fleur. Elise's mum."

"That's a clever play on words, like the song," said Rosemary.

Fleur gave her a quizzical look. "I'm sorry, I don't understand."

"Never mind," said Rosemary with an awkward smile. She followed Fleur down an ambient passageway and into a candlelit room with ocean sounds.

"Where's that noise coming from?" Rosemary asked, not seeing any kind of speaker or stereo system in the room.

"From the ocean," said Fleur.

"Oh, I see," said Rosemary. "Why didn't we hear it out in the lobby?"

"The sound in here is magically enhanced," said Fleur.

"That's pretty clever," said Rosemary. "I wonder if I can do that with my magic."

Fleur smiled at her. "You're very unusual." She said it in a friendly way that Rosemary chose not to take offense to.

"I'm just going to slip out of the room," said Fleur. "Just get yourself ready and get on the massage table."

"Oh...okay," said Rosemary. "How?"

Fleur gave her a quizzical look.

"I've never had enough money to get a proper massage before," Rosemary explained.

"Just remove your clothing and get under the sheet," said Fleur.

"That's not usually what I do for my daughter's friend's parents," said Rosemary, blushing as she realised she'd put her foot in her mouth again and made the situation unnecessarily awkward.

"Well, it's a fairly ordinary situation for me to be in," said Fleur, taking it in her stride. "I can assure you it's not as racy or exciting as one might be led to believe from the way you just phrased it."

"Given how racy and exciting my life's been lately, I'm rather pleased about that," said Rosemary. "Excitement is not all its cut out to be."

"Thank you for helping my daughter get back to the earth realm," said Fleur. "I just needed to say that. I would have thanked you before, but I didn't really know how to approach you."

"That's okay," said Rosemary.

"I warned her not to go. But you know what teenagers are like."

"Do I ever."

"She hasn't been quite the same since." Fleur sighed. "I'm sure you know what I mean."

"What *do* you mean?" Rosemary asked.

"Oh, you know. The fae realm does things to people."

Rosemary gave Fleur a quizzical look. "What kinds of things?"

"It might not be the same for you, as you're not of fae heritage, are you? And you weren't there long. But, you know, if Athena has been quiet and withdrawn lately, it'll just be that she's missing home."

"Home?" Rosemary asked, feeling her shoulders tense. "She's *at* home. I went and got her and brought her home. That was the whole point."

"Of course she's at her earth realm home," said Fleur. "That's the way my mother explains it. The fae realm is different for us who are biologically natives of that place. It calls to us. It sings in our bones, like we're part of it."

"Athena hasn't mentioned anything," said Rosemary. "Maybe it didn't affect her that way."

"Maybe," said Fleur, though she didn't sound convinced. "I've never been, so I wouldn't know exactly what it's like. Elise has been a little quieter lately. Anyway, I'll leave you to it."

Fleur left the room, and Rosemary stood for a moment, pondering the conversation. Had Athena been quieter and more withdrawn than usual? She didn't think so. It was hard to tell with a surly teenager. She slipped out of her clothes, leaving them in a pile on the chair, and got under the silky sheet on the massage table. Lying there in the warm candlelit room, listening to ocean sounds was relaxing enough in itself, but when Fleur returned and began to knead at Rosemary's back, using magically enhanced oils that smelled like frankincense, it seemed to lull Rosemary into a kind of healing trance. All of the worries slipped away from her mind, at least temporarily.

She was finally doing something that was just for herself and it actually felt ridiculously good.

After the massage, Rosemary hardly knew herself, in a very good way.

She couldn't remember ever feeling this relaxed before and was tempted to schedule in regular massages, at least every month for the foreseeable future.

She put on the fluffy white and purple bathrobe which was heavenly soft, along with matching slippers and went out to the lobby to wait for Athena.

She was surprised to find that a lot more people were milling about.

Must be rush hour.

Athena wasn't there yet, so Rosemary sat down in the waiting room, reading the pamphlets and leafing through other magazines, while also discreetly ogling the various guests who walked through.

She read in one of the brochures that people came and stayed in the various bungalows around the main building, to restore and replenish their energy. It was a destination for magical people from all around the world.

A woman with flaming red hair and a bright red dress, who looked like she was almost on fire herself, sauntered through the lobby. Rosemary wondered what kind of creature she was.

A large man wobbled in looking as if he was almost made of jelly. He became increasingly less human though kept on his bowler hat as he approached the reception area. Ferg ushered him into a room at the side.

There are all kinds of creatures out there that I hardly know anything about.

It was hard to believe that a few months ago she'd thought magic was something entirely confined to fairy tales and fiction, and now she found herself heavily immersed in a fantastical world.

A group of people in lime green business suits walked through. It looked as if they were all part of the same club or on a business trip. Rosemary caught a glimpse of someone walking away, down the passageway behind them, in pastels with a familiar black bob cut.

Rosemary stood up and began to walk after her, heart hammering in her chest, and the palms of her hands beginning to itch.

Despina!

She hadn't seen the woman since the Bloodstone Society's thwarted attempt to steal the Thorn family magic, months before. Rosemary had put a stop to it, including destroying the leader, a young looking but ancient vampire who had been masquerading as Despina's niece. The very same niece who may well somehow still be alive and trapped in the little wooden carved box that had been stolen from Thorn Manor recently.

Rosemary hadn't seen Despina since. The woman disappeared down the hallway and Rosemary ran after her but was stopped by an arm catching her shoulder.

"Mum! What are you doing?"

Rosemary turned to find her daughter there.

"Despina was just here. We've got to stop her."

Athena gave her a strange look. "Are you sure?"

"Of course I'm sure," said Rosemary. "My hands were itching and everything."

"Mum, we've discussed this. Your allergy to realtors is completely psychosomatic; it's not a real thing."

"A little while ago you thought magic wasn't a real thing," Rosemary reminded her daughter. "How is an allergy to realtors any less bizarre? Anyway, we don't have time. We have to go after her."

Athena shrugged and followed her mother down the corridor, but the woman had disappeared. Rosemary tried to go into a few of the rooms, but after getting yelled at by a few unusual creatures she decided she'd better not create any more disturbances.

"Did you even see her face?" Athena asked.

"Not exactly," said Rosemary. "But she was in pastels."

"Mum!"

"We should go home. It's not safe," said Rosemary.

"On a hunch? You must be joking. I thought you were supposed to be here to relax."

"I was totally relaxed until a moment ago. And now, I don't think I can afford to be."

"No," said Athena. "No way."

"What is it?" Rosemary asked.

"There is no way that you're ruining this. Not for you and not for me. Even if you glimpsed the back of someone who really was the estate agent vampire involved in attacking us, we've got no reason to believe that she knows we're here. And even if she does, we are way more powerful than we were before. The Bloodstones have been keeping relatively quiet, aside from a few weird little attacks. But if they came after us now, this would be the worst place to do it."

"Why is that?" Rosemary asked.

"Look around," said Athena. "We're surrounded by powerful magical beings and I'm pretty sure most of them aren't in league with a particular almost disbanded magical secret society."

Rosemary shrugged. "Okay, fair enough. You have a point."

"This way," Ferg called, motioning them towards the front desk. "Your lunch is being served by the pool. And then your facials will follow."

Twenty-Eight

Athena sighed she let her feet sink into the foot spa and relaxed back into the unnaturally comfortable reclining chair. "I told you. This is just what we needed."

"Lovely, isn't it?" said Rosemary. "How sweet of Marjie to look after us like this."

"Aren't you glad you didn't go running off after an estate agent vampire look-alike?"

"I suppose so. But I'm still worried."

"Look," said Athena. "You've got to leave things like this to the authorities. I know you think you're some kind of detective now. But really this isn't something you should be sticking your nose into. You've already called Neve and told her your wildly paranoid theories. Now let her deal with it."

"You're probably right," said Rosemary. "It's just that the authorities haven't exactly had a great track record. Don't get me wrong. Neve's smart and I'm sure she's good at her job. But she has the habit of disappearing when things get gnarly. And I haven't exactly seen proof of her effectiveness yet. I know she's smart and I don't mean to speak ill of a good friend..."

"But Mum, you haven't exactly let her show off her effectiveness because you keep meddling in everything and getting in the way."

"Who knows what would have happened if I just let things take their course?" said Rosemary. "We would probably have been killed by the Bloodstones, and even if we'd managed to survive their attack you'd be stuck in the fae realm."

"It's also possible your meddling made things worse before you made them better."

Rosemary sighed. "Maybe. Marjie keeps telling me off for getting involved in everyone else's problems instead of solving my own."

"Well, Marjie is absolutely right." Athena glared at her mother.

"Time for your facial," said the spritely attendant whose name Athena had already forgotten, though with a shock of orange hair and baby green eyes, her appearance was certainly memorable. "Here's your facialist, now."

"Thank you," said Rosemary. The door opened and a familiar face peered in, shrouded in long wavy light blonde hair.

"Ashwyn!" said Rosemary. "What are you doing here?"

"I come here in the weekends, and sometimes do special treatments during the week," said Ashwyn. "It helps to keep our business in the black, to have a few additional income streams on the side."

"But aren't you supposed to be out of town?" Athena asked. "Mum said something about your cousin's baby."

"We just got back this morning." Ashwyn took out her phone and showed them a few photos of a very chubby newborn with a squished up face.

"Why do newborn babies always look like aliens?" Athena asked.

Rosemary nudged her gently with her elbow. They were seated far enough apart that she couldn't reach to have any jarring impact and Athena was grateful for that.

"What? It's true," she continued.

"You're right," said Ashwyn with a musical laugh. "Newborn babies do look rather odd, don't they? Anyway, I had to come back this morning in time for work. Now, tell me, is there any special kind of effect you want from the facial?"

"What do you mean?" Athena asked.

"Well, sometimes people want more luminous and glowing skin and other people want to look a bit younger. We get all sorts here. But they mostly fit into two camps. The ones going for health and the ones going for more 'special effects' shall we call them?"

"Is it a little bit like magical plastic surgery?" Athena asked, feeling awkward.

"Something like that," said Ashwyn. "Though it only lasts for about a month before the glamour starts to wear off."

"Well, I don't think it matters too much for me," said Athena. "Apparently, no one can see my true features anyway, unless they're fae."

"That's a good point," said Ashwyn. "My sister has the same thing. People can tell she's gorgeous. But it's like they don't really *see* her. They can't recall the specifics."

"So strange...the fae magic," said Rosemary.

"Tell me about it," said Athena.

"I don't want to go overboard," said Rosemary. "I mean, I still want to look like myself. Just, you know...make me look like I've had a few good nights of sleep and a lot of adequate hydration. That should do the trick."

Ashwyn laughed. "I'll give you our classic skin healing and hydration treatment then." She went about mixing together various items from tubes and bottles into a little bowl before she started applying it to their faces.

"Are you going to do the thing with the cucumber?" Athena asked. "I've always wanted to have that."

"Then of course," said Ashwyn. "Everyone always wants that. I think because it's so popular in the movies."

"I certainly feel like a celebrity," said Athena.

A few minutes passed, and Ashwyn finished applying the healing face masks and the cucumber slices over their eyes, then she left them to relax.

Athena took a deep breath, feeling more tranquil than she had since she'd entered the fae realm. "My skin's all tingling. It feels nice."

"While you're a captive audience," said Rosemary.

"Oh no, Mum. This is not the time to start heckling me about anything. It's bad enough that I can barely leave the house these days."

"I wanted to talk to you about something that happened earlier."

"We've already talked about that," said Athena.

"No, not that," said Rosemary. "I mean, before, when I first arrived. The woman who gave me the massage was the mother of your friend Elise."

"Oh," said Athena. "It's funny. I've never met her. And now you have. It seems a bit weird, doesn't it? I know, maybe it's because *you never let me go to my friend's houses*!"

"Something like that," said Rosemary. "But Elise and her mum do seem lovely. I might be comfortable waving that rule for a special situation, especially seeing as it seems you've learned your lesson for now."

"Really?" said Athena, with a spark of excitement. "You'd let me go and visit Elise's place?"

"As long as you don't go doing anything stupid. Anyway..."

"Oh, I see," said Athena. "Now, having dangled the carrot, you're going to give me the stick."

"I just wanted to ask you about something," said Rosemary. "Fleur was telling me her daughter seemed quite tired and withdrawn lately. She said it was something to do with going to the fae realm."

"Mum," Athena started. She didn't want her mother to pry into her personal experiences, but she knew it was inevitable.

"Fleur seemed to think that anyone of fae type heritage, who went into that realm, felt like they were much more at home there. She said it felt so good there they just wanted to return, and that was what was making Elise feel so low."

Athena was silent for a minute, mulling it over. What could she tell her mother that wouldn't just stir her worries and make things even more challenging at home? She didn't want to lie about this, mostly because she didn't think she could get away with it.

"I have felt a bit like that," Athena admitted.

"Why didn't you tell me?" Rosemary asked.

"Why do you think, Mum? This is a situation that you've constructed. You're so paranoid, and I can't do anything. You're so worried about me that it doesn't exactly make me want to reveal the whole truth to you, does it?"

"I thought we were over this," said Rosemary. "I thought we were done with secrets."

"You just make it so hard," said Athena. "I can't tell you everything because I'm scared you're going to overreact and make my life even worse."

"I thought you were *glad* to be back."

"I was," said Athena. "I am. It's just...I can't help the way I feel. When I went there, it was like...well, sure it was weird and strange. You were there. You understand. But the thing is, I kind of lit up like I belonged there. I'd never felt anything like that. It's like that place stripped away a whole lot of my worries. In comparison to being there, this world feels so heavy. I'm still getting used to it."

Her mother was silent for a moment and Athena wondered whether she was getting herself into even more trouble.

"Okay," Rosemary said eventually. "Thanks for telling me."

"You're not going to confine me to my room?"

"Of course not. That's hardly going to help the situation is it?" Rosemary sighed. "I guess I'm just realising that I need to build back your trust, just like you need to build mine."

Athena felt a stab of guilt. She hadn't told her mum the whole truth. She certainly wasn't about to start talking about how she'd snuck out at night several times over the last week to cut a hole to the fae realm in her nightie just to get a hit of that good feeling again. She wasn't going to risk losing what small freedom she currently had, even if it was something she had to steal in the middle of the night.

"It helps, hanging out with people like Elise," said Athena, hoping her mother would give her a little more freedom. "And even Una. It gives me a little bit of that feeling again without having to go anywhere."

Athena wasn't lying, even if she was angling for a particular outcome.

"That's good to know," said Rosemary. "We can work with this. Maybe...maybe you can see more of your friends. And I'll let you go to Elise's house if that's what you want to do. Just promise me—"

"We'll be careful. I promise," said Athena. Her guilt was only intensifying.

Twenty-Nine

Rosemary and Athena left the spa feeling calm and relaxed after all the pampering.

"I haven't felt this good in a long time." Rosemary checked her glowing reflection in a window as they headed to the car. "Thanks for making me stay."

"Anytime you need somebody to boss you around, you know who to call," said Athena.

Rosemary smiled. It was wonderful to see her daughter in such a good mood. She thought back to the conversation they'd had earlier over the comments that Fleur had made, and realised that Athena had seemed reserved lately. In comparison to how she was now, at least, with her eyes sparkling.

Rosemary started up the engine and they began to drive. "You know, I haven't seen you light up like this in quite a while. How was your morning anyway? What did you get up to before you came to the spa?"

"It was nice," said Athena cheerfully. "I just played with the kids and the kitten, and did some work on my essay for folklore and mythology. Granny's got some really good old books. I have to be careful with the pages."

"Find anything interesting?" Rosemary asked.

"Actually, I think I did. Beltane is supposed to be named in honour of one of the very old gods, and there's not much information about him around. There's plenty on Brigid and Cerridwen and Cernunnos and all of those younger ones. They've only been around for a few thousand years."

"Spring chickens then," said Rosemary, wondering exactly how old Burk was.

"Exactly," said Athena. "But the old gods...well, it's really hard to know what they were all about. Beltane is named after the ancient god Belamus, who was also called Belli."

"That's kind of cute," said Rosemary. "It reminds me of a dog. You know, when they roll over and they want belly rubs."

"I'm pretty sure that's offensive Mum." Athena rolled her eyes. "And I don't think he was cute, exactly."

"That's a shame," said Rosemary. "A cute god sounds much more palatable than most other forms of god I can think of."

"Yeah, well, we might have a problem," said Athena. "The books hint that if the Cavalia happens again, we might have a very, very old God on our hands."

"What do we know about him?" Rosemary asked.

"Well, it was a cult that worshiped him all the way across ancient Italy," said Athena.

"Not so cute sounding." Rosemary looked out on the countryside as they drove, checking for fires. "What did they do?

Athena shrugged. "That's kind of the problem. Nobody seems to know. In fact, the only thing that I could find out about him was that he's thought to be the grandfather of many of the gods from around here. And he's something to do with light."

"Light?"

"Yes, god of light," said Athena.

"Love and light," said Rosemary weakly. "It sounds kind of hippy dippy, and I'm not a fan of toxic positivity, but surely light is better than carnage or something?"

Athena made an uncertain sound. "Granny's books have some details about how he would ride across the sky on a great golden chariot."

"Subtle guy," said Rosemary.

"Oh yes, quite flashy, and I think he's got horns on his head or antlers or something." Athena continued on babbling away enthusiastically about the tidbits she had pieced together from the old books.

Rosemary smiled warmly. It was so nice to see her daughter really happy and enthusiastic about something.

She felt proud, not only that Athena was getting into her schoolwork for a change, but that she was coming into her own. She could certainly hold up against Rosemary's magic the other day, which gave her hope regarding future attacks.

Athena would be able to look out for herself.

Rosemary wasn't sure about this Belamus character and she hoped he wasn't about to show up on a flaming chariot and turn the town into soup or cinders, but she didn't want to worry too much in this moment. She just wanted to enjoy listening to her daughter.

After everything they'd been through over the past few months, all the ups and downs, and all the arguments they'd had, they seemed to have found a new even keel.

Rosemary felt like she just might be ready let go of the reins a bit more, to let Athena demonstrate her sense of responsibility, and have a little more freedom along with it.

The sunlight was beginning to fade as Rosemary pulled up in Myrtlewood town. It was part of their gift from Marjie to have afternoon tea at her shop after the spa, though the pampering had taken so long that it was almost closer to dinner time. Fortunately the tea shop stayed open later on Saturdays in case people wanted to stop in for Marjie's signature pies and pasties.

"You both look so radiant, you're practically glowing!" said Marjie as Athena and Rosemary walked into the shop. "And just in time for tea!"

"Oh Marjie," said Rosemary, giving the older woman a big hug. "Thank you so much. We had a wonderful time."

"Yes, thanks!" said Athena.

"I hope you haven't gone to too much trouble over afternoon tea," said Rosemary as she surveyed the table Marjie gestured them over to, heavily laden with tea and delicious looking treats.

"Oh," Marjie blushed. "I might have prepared with special versions of your favourite cakes," she said.

"These are the two cakes we had the first time we came to the tea shop," said Athena. "You remembered! I had chocolate and Mum had lemon sponge."

"How sweet of you," said Rosemary. "And there are the strawberry tarts I can't get enough of."

"You're so wonderful," said Athena, giving Marjie a kiss on the cheek.

"Oh, it's nothing," said Marjie. "You know I enjoy fussing over the two of you. You're the family I never managed to have. And giving you a special day of pampering is exactly the kind of thing that brings me joy, followed by a late afternoon tea – my treat."

"Marjie, you're exactly the kind of person I want to be when I finally grow up," said Rosemary with a laugh.

Athena shot her a wry look.

"Don't grow up too soon, mind," said Marjie. "You've still got your whole life to live. You might as well look and feel radiant while you do it!"

"I do feel like I'm glowing," Rosemary said. "Or at least I'm rather relaxed. I don't even need any of your special remedy this time."

"No," said Marjie. "I'm afraid if you had some of it now you might drift away and float right out of the tea shop."

They ate their cakes and sipped tea in silence, enjoying the good feelings soaking in post-spa. As they sat there, the bell above the door tinkled and Una walked in, her shiny brown hair falling in perfect ringlets.

"Good to see you," Athena said as Una approached.

"I've so been looking forward to catching up!"

"Come and join us," said Rosemary, remembering what Athena had said about feeling even better around other fae. She swept a cream cake to the other side of the table and gestured for her new friend to sit down.

Una smiled. "I can only stay for a minute. I need to go and sort of few things out at the shop before we reopen again tomorrow. I'll have my usual," she said to Marjie who returned moments later with another pot of tea and some bliss balls.

"I take it you don't go in for chocolate cake?" said Athena.

"I'm afraid to say it doesn't agree with me," said Una. "Which is a shame because it looks delicious." She glanced longingly at Athena's plate. "I can't really have dairy."

"Oh, of course," said Athena. "I'm sorry."

"No, no, it's fine," Una replied. "I'm used to it, and wheat gives me a rash as well. It's not really ideal either way. But Marjie does a lovely job of accommodating me and makes me these very delicious, healthy bliss balls. They're not quite the same as cake. Now, there was something you wanted to talk to me about?" she asked Rosemary.

Rosemary looked at Athena, wondering whether this was an acceptable topic to broach in front of her teenager, then decided she might as well. It might be good for Athena to hear the conversation anyway, considering what she *was*. Rosemary just hoped she didn't get teased too mercilessly about it afterwards.

"Well, it was a few weeks ago," said Rosemary, "and I didn't realise it at the time—and in fact, I didn't remember until after I'd had your special memory tonic—but I saw you sitting at the pub with Perseus Burk."

Athena coughed and Rosemary could tell she was trying not to giggle.

"Oh, yes. He and I are friends," said Una.

"Okay then," said Rosemary. "That's...that's nice." She shot Athena a warning glance. It looked as though the teen was teetering on the edge of bursting out with something inappropriate.

"The thing is," said Rosemary. "I just wanted to talk to about it because..."

"'cause Mum likes him!" said Athena. "And she's obviously jealous."

"No, it's not that at all," said Rosemary, blushing. "We've covered this a billion times before."

Una was blushing too.

"No, the reason I wanted to bring it up," Rosemary continued, "is because you know what he is...uh...You know what he is, don't you?"

Una raised her eyebrow. "Uh...a Capricorn?"

Rosemary stuttered, knowing that it was considered very rude to *out* vampires without their consent. "Not exactly."

Una laughed. "I'm joking. I know what he is."

"Oh, good," said Rosemary. "But do you know that...'Capricorns'..."

"You can say it, Mum," said Athena. "It's not like we're in the fae realm, and no one else is around."

"Okay." Rosemary felt a ramble coming on. "Vampires. They...they have a sort of long and sordid history where they hunted your kind to the brink of extinction in the human realm and I just wondered if you knew about that and whether it was safe for you to be hanging out with them because I'm just trying to look out for you."

"Oh," said Una. "I see what you mean."

"Sorry, if it's patronising," said Rosemary. "It's just that...I thought since you weren't raised around your own kind, and you don't necessarily know very much about it, I worried that you might not be aware and it might be dangerous. And I wanted to warn you."

"I get it," said Una.

"Mum, you can stop talking now," said Athena, stifling another laugh.

Rosemary cleared her throat and took another sip of tea to try and quell her own instincts which inevitably led to her babbling uncontrollably in any possible awkward situation.

"Yeah. I know a little bit about that," said Una. "But there's nothing to worry about. The thing is with, with Perseus he's...he's not like that. You know as vampires age they often get more refined and controlled."

"But his brother," said Rosemary.

"His brother was a bit of a deadbeat," said Una sadly. "But anyway, Perseus is a perfect gentleman. He's lovely."

"And do you think he knows?" Athena asked.

"Knows what?" Una asked.

"Knows what you...we...are?"

"I think so. I mean, it's not something we explicitly talk about."

"I thought you said you were friends." Athena pushed her plate away and crossed her arms.

"We are friends," said Una, looking slightly embarrassed.

Rosemary had a creeping sense of jealousy again.

"And I'm sorry, I didn't realise you had feelings for—" Una started.

"It's not like that," said Rosemary.

"I can assure you it's not like that with us either," said Una. "We just catch up from time to time and have dinner. Believe me, you are in safe hands with Perseus, he wouldn't hurt a fly. Well, okay, he would hurt flies and probably other vampires and demons..."

"Demons?!" said Rosemary, her eyes widening. "Demons are real too?"

"Of course they are," said Una.

"I was kind of hoping they weren't," Rosemary admitted.

"What kind of world do you think we live in?" Una asked.

"I'm wondering that more and more every day," said Rosemary.

"Anyway," Una continued. "I'm sure Perseus wouldn't hurt any of us. He's really a lovely person. Athena's in safe hands around him. In fact, I bet he'd protect you both, no matter what, even if it was putting himself at risk."

Rosemary felt her shoulders soften as she visibly relaxed, surprised at how relieved she felt that Athena would be safe around Burk.

"See Mum? I told you there was nothing to worry about," said Athena. "I'm safe. We're fine. We can carry on with our lives now."

Una smiled. "You know, it's so lovely being in your presence," she said to Athena. "It's refreshing."

"Umm, thank you?" said Athena.

"You're welcome to come and visit us again sometime," Rosemary said.

"I'd like that," Una replied. "How about tomorrow afternoon?"

"It's a date," said Rosemary.

Thirty

Rosemary glanced out the tea shop window at the darkening sky. A bright red flash her eye.

She gasped. "No!"

"What?" asked Athena, turning around.

They watched as bright flames flared from the town square, growing higher.

"Gross," said Athena. "This isn't one of those magical fires that makes people get all icky, is it?"

"I'm afraid so." Rosemary watched as the red and orange fire became tinged with pink. "Stay in here."

"Mum!"

Rosemary shot her daughter a concerned look. "Seriously. You do not want to go near this."

"Fair enough," said Athena. "This is one dangerous situation I really don't want to get involved in. But do you ha—"

"I'm glad you see it my way." Rosemary ran towards the door before Athena could stop her.

"Don't lose your head or your panties!" Marjie called out, waving from the kitchen as Rosemary stormed past the counter. "There's a fire hydrant outside if you need it."

"Thanks." She pushed open the door and stalked out.

"Run away!" she yelled towards the people gathered in the town square who'd stopped to look at the sudden appearance of fire. They didn't seem to respond. "It's not safe!"

"There'll be an explosion if that builds up," said Ferg, popping up out of a hedge to Rosemary's left.

"No, there certainly will not," said Rosemary. "Listen, just get as far away as you can, and take people with you."

"Roger that!" said Ferg, taking off at a gallop. He began moving the dazed bystanders along, seemingly unaffected by the blaze. Rosemary recalled what Sherry had said about Ferg not being a romantic or sensual sort. In this situation it seemed ideal!

Rosemary needed water. Unfortunately she didn't have the first idea of how to open a fire hydrant. She could see the sign and the little square tile on the ground in yellow. But obviously she didn't have her own fire hose and she was...feeling rather warm as she stood there in the fires glow. Warm and melty.

She pushed through the carnal flush from the flames and was grateful that nobody else was around to see it as she reached down and tried in vain to open fire hydrant to turn it on. Nothing happened.

"Desperate times call for desperate measures," she muttered to herself, feeling her legs press together in a rather pleasurable way. She focused on the hydrant, trying to push the seductive feel of the magic away.

"Stop it, Rosemary," she scolded herself. She needed to concentrate. Just then, she remembered something that Athena had told her about automancy, the kind of automatic magic that the Thorn family apparently specialised in. That was exactly what she needed.

"Come on then," Rosemary said to the fire hydrant. "Come on. I know you're in there."

She focused down on it.

"There's something in you that just wants to spill water everywhere," Rosemary said encouragingly. "Wake up. You know you want to!"

"What are you doing?" said Ferg.

Rosemary jumped.

"Magic," she grumbled. "Go away."

"It's not like any magic I've seen before. It seems like you're just talking to an inanimate object. Haven't you noticed the fire's getting bigger?"

"Ferg," said Rosemary with a warning in her voice. "Unless you're also a part time firefighter who knows how to—"

"Okay, okay," said Ferg. "I know when I'm not wanted. I'll just go and check on those folk who were in the square. They're all acting a bit weird."

Rosemary ignored him and focused back on the fire hydrant, willing it to life.

A moment passed and she had the strange sensation that she was staring right into the heart of the object.

Something clicked in her mind and it sparked to life.

There was a clunking sound and then a gurgle. Water burst forth, showering Rosemary, but not going anywhere near the fire.

"Good," she said to the hydrant. "That was the first step, now..."

"Rosemary! Get out of there!"

Rosemary turned towards the familiar voice to find Burk careening right into her.

"*You* get out of here!" she yelled, gripping the arms of his suit, which were quickly soaking with water.

Burk was the absolute last person she wanted to see when she was feeling like this.

"Rosemary?"

She grimaced. "It's bad enough having to sort out my own dramas involving you, let alone you actually being here in person."

"What are you talking about?"

"Listen. I've got the situation under control. You can leave," said Rosemary, though Burk did seem awfully tantalising standing there in his crisp white shirt and expensive-looking drenched suit.

Rosemary knew she had other more pressing matters to attend to. But surely they could wait just a few moments...

She reached towards his starched collar.

"Rosemary, what do you think you're doing?" he said.

"Less talk, more action," she said, and pulled him into a kiss.

Something in the back of Rosemary's mind screamed at her. This wasn't the time or the place.

She pulled away.

Burk stared at her in stunned shock and Rosemary came to her senses.

"Oh no...Oh no, no, no! What have I done?"

A growl sounded behind them and Rosemary tuned to see Liam standing at the front of his bookshop staring daggers.

Burk cleared his throat. "This is..."

"You're obviously not affected by this magic," Rosemary muttered, pushing Burk away. She was battling desire, confusion, embarrassment, and social awkwardness all at the same time.

Morbid embarrassment perhaps was a better word as she realised Athena, Marjie, and countless others were watching the whole fiasco from a safe distance.

Liam lunged towards Burk.

Rosemary sensed a blast of her magic automatically coming out of her hands in some kind of defence mechanism.

Liam fell backwards.

Another growl sounded, this time not from Liam but from the fire itself.

"*What...*was that?" Rosemary asked.

She turned to see a beautiful, delicate creature looking at her through the flames.

"You growl?" she asked the creature, before noticing that behind it was a great horned beast.

"Oh no you don't," said Rosemary. She flung her hands towards the fire hydrant, willing the water to spray in the direction of the fire. The effect was a bit like putting a thumb over the top of a running hose.

The water spurted out sideways, not only blasting the fire, but also hitting Rosemary, Burk, and Liam, covering them all with water.

Rosemary ducked out of the way of the strong spurt and then pivoted around to aim it more directly towards the fire.

The flames grew brighter and it began to sizzle, then a great cloud of steam rose up and the entire blaze disappeared, creatures and all, leaving nothing but a scorch mark on the grass.

Rosemary shook herself. "That was a close call." She wasn't sure if she was talking about the situation with Burk and Liam, or the fire itself.

"Oh my *goddess*," said Athena as she emerged from the tea shop.

"I don't suppose there was a chance that you happened to miss seeing all that?" said Rosemary.

"Not a chance in Hades," said Athena. "In fact, I think the entire town saw."

Rosemary looked around to see that indeed, many of the townspeople were standing around, ogling her.

"I'm just gonna go home and hide in my bed for the next forty odd years," said Rosemary. "If you'll excuse me."

"That's some love triangle you've got going on, Mum," said Athena as Rosemary drove them back to Thorn Manor. "I mean, I knew it was bad, but I didn't realise it was *that* bad."

"It's not a love triangle," Rosemary argued, gritting her teeth as she drove. "It was merely...a misunderstanding."

Athena laughed hysterically for several minutes. "I love how you kissed that very old, but also very-attractive-for-an-old-guy vampire in the middle of town, in front of your ex-boyfriend who you happen to be spending a lot of time with lately for 'medical reasons.' And you call it 'merely a misunderstanding'."

"It was the magic of the fire," said Rosemary. "I told you the spell or whatever it is makes people go wigity."

"Wigity?" Athena asked.

"Okay then, frisky," said Rosemary.

"Gross!"

"Well, how would you explain it in ways that won't be uncomfortable for you?"

"Look," said Athena. "I'm just saying it's obvious that there's something going on there. And then if you add Dad into the mix—"

Rosemary laughed. "You're dreaming."

"Come on! There's something there."

"Stop with your obsession with my romantic life," said Rosemary. "It's time for you to think outside the box."

"Yuck!"

"That's not what I mean," Rosemary grumbled. "All I'm saying is you're treating this like some kind of romance novel. We're not in Jane Austen, or one of those godforsaken paranormal romances I sometimes catch you reading."

"They're good books!" Athena insisted.

"Be that as it may, it's not reality is it?" said Rosemary. "I have a lot of feelings..."

"Eww!" said Athena. "Please keep them away from me. I do not want to hear about your feelings."

"You're a walking paradox sometimes," said Rosemary. "The point is, none of my feelings make very much sense at all. And it doesn't help that you're teasing me all the time."

"What else am I supposed to do for fun?" said Athena. "It's not like you're letting me out on the town much these days."

Rosemary sighed. "I haven't told you the worst part yet."

"There's a worse part than my mother making an absolute fool of herself in front of the entire township?"

"I'm afraid so," said Rosemary grimly.

"Out with it," said Athena.

"So, I'm pretty sure nobody else was close enough to see them," said Rosemary. "But there were creatures..."

"Creatures? What do you mean? Did creatures cast the fire? It wasn't the Bloodstones?"

"Who knows?" said Rosemary. "They might well have been responsible, but the creatures I saw were actually in the fire."

"Oh no! Do you think they're okay?"

"They seemed more than okay. In fact, I think they were part of the fire. It was more some sort of pixie-ish thing and a big beastie with horns."

Athena inhaled sharply. "This is not good. Do you think it could be *him*?"

"Who?"

"You know, Belamus, the Old God."

Rosemary shrugged. "Honestly, I have no idea. It could've been a Satyr for all I know or some other mythical beast. But maybe it is the old god dude."

"Okay then," said Athena. "My guess is it's one point for Ms Twigg and zero to Constable what's-his-face."

"Perkins," said Rosemary. "And yeah, I suppose if you don't actually have any theory about what's going on you're not going to get any points at all. We have to tell Neve!"

Fortunately, Detective Neve was at Thorn Manor when they arrived. Nesta had made a giant pot of chicken soup with her grandmother's recipe. The children were all sitting around the dining room table. Tamsyn was there too, sitting next to little Elowen.

Tamsyn had been visiting the house a lot over the past week, and Elowen had been spending time at the small cottage in Myrtlewood that Marjie had helped Tamsyn to find. Marjie had all the connections. Clearly she was a good person to know. Rosemary wouldn't hesitate to call her the backbone of the community.

Elowen was happy alternating between the two homes but was transitioning towards living in the cottage.

Over a bowl of hearty and satisfying soup Rosemary and Athena filled Neve and Nesta in on the details of what had transpired that day. Athena took pains to describe the scene of Rosemary's morbid embarrassment, making the children giggle about kisses.

"But other than that you had a good day?" Nesta asked.

Rosemary smiled. "I guess so. It's hard to remember now. But yes, the spa was lovely."

"It was," said Athena. "In fact, it was probably a perfect day. And then it was made even more interesting. Mum is never going to live this down, although I'm slightly mortified of what my friends are going to say at school."

"It could have been a lot worse," said Neve.

Nesta gave her an uncomfortable look.

They'd obviously had the talk about what had happened at the mayor's house with Neve and her ex-girlfriend.

"That magic is incredibly powerful," said Rosemary. "Despite all my supposed magic, I really struggled to resist it. Although Burk seemed impervious."

"That makes it so much worse," said Athena.

"It does make it more embarrassing," Rosemary conceded. "It was kind of a one-sided thing."

"But he let you kiss him?" said Nesta.

The children giggled again.

"I think he was just shocked, actually," said Rosemary. "He didn't seem particularly enthusiastic. He asked me what on earth I was doing."

"Still, vampires move incredibly fast, don't they?" said Athena. "He could have pulled away at any time. And in fact, he could have stopped you from even getting close to him."

"What are you implying?" Rosemary narrowed her eyes. "Never mind, I know exactly what you're implying. This is not one of your paranormal romance novels, for the millionth time!"

"You're right," said Athena. "In a romance novel there would be far more kisses!"

Rosemary had the feeling that Athena had said that just to make the children giggle again, which of course they did.

"Alright, enough about me," said Rosemary. "How are you settling in?" she asked Tamsyn.

"Well, thank you," said Tamsyn. "I mean, things have been a little bit strange, but overall, it's great. It was wonderful of Marjie to connect us up with a cottage to rent. Elowen seems to be adjusting well to living with me. Though she still thinks it's funny that I got so old."

Elowen giggled.

"There is far too much giggling here tonight," said Nesta with a grin, which of course made the giggling even worse.

"I'm glad you're settling in well," Rosemary continued.

"Everyone's so lovely here," said Tamsyn. "I can't believe my family ever left this place. It already feels like home."

"Tell me about it," said Rosemary, though she noticed Athena had a sad look in her eyes at those words.

Rosemary reached out to pat Athena's shoulder. "Why don't you invite Elise over next weekend? Or...I suppose you could go to her house. If that's okay with Fleur."

Athena smiled. "Thanks, Mum, I'll message Elise."

With her daughter's sadness averted, Rosemary focused her full attention on finishing the delicious hearty soup, pushing all worries of fiery beasties out of her mind.

Thirty-One

Rosemary was just finishing up her soup when she noticed that Dain had a serious expression on his face. He'd been sitting at the table but had not joined in on the conversation. She hadn't been paying much attention, but as the giggling died down, Athena also seemed to notice something wasn't right with her father and abruptly changed the subject.

"Anyway, Mum. What's the next step for your chocolate shop?"

"I suspect it's mountains of paperwork," said Rosemary. "Plus, I need to learn how to run a business and how to professionally make chocolate. It seems a bit ridiculous doesn't it? What on earth am I getting myself into? I don't know the first thing about being a chocolatier."

"I'm sure you know the first thing and the second," said Nesta. "Probably the third and fourth too. You might not know everything, but you've got a lot of life experience."

"It does seem like a frivolous thing to be focused on," said Rosemary, "when there's so much else going on here. That fire today, Neve, it was something else. Athena was excited to tell you about how I made a fool of myself. But there's more. Before I put the flames out, I saw creatures staring out at me from inside the blaze."

"What creatures?" Neve asked.

"It was some sort of fae or pixie-like thing."

"Inside the fire?" Neve said incredulously.

"It sounds a bit ridiculous, I know," Rosemary admitted.

"It sounds like what Athena was talking about the other day, actually," said Neve. "We need to look into this. I'm going to ask your teacher to come into the station and give a proper statement."

"I'm really glad that none of your records get transferred to the regular police stations," said Athena. "Can you imagine what that statement would look like?"

"Even the magical authorities are going to have a hard time with this," said Neve. "They might know magic, but this is something else, something ancient."

"That's what I was thinking," said Athena. "I've been working on my essay for folklore and mythology and I can hardly find anything about Belamus even though everyone's heard of Beltane."

"I hope you don't mind sharing the research you're doing with me," said Neve.

Athena smiled proudly. "I don't mind at all. It might not be all that helpful, though."

"There must be someone casting the spells or doing something to summon the fires," said Nesta. "These things don't just happen willy-nilly. Something different is going on here."

"We can try and find out," said Neve. "Of course we are already following our usual processes, but nothing's coming up. If only we had a real Rúnseall. It would make a huge difference if we could track down whoever is causing this."

"It's sad that my parents aren't around anymore, they were expert Rúnsealls," said Tamsyn. "But I could give it a whirl."

"Doesn't there need to be two of you?" said Rosemary, recalling a conversation they'd had earlier.

"There are two of us," said Tamsyn, reaching out to take Elowen's hand on the table.

The two sisters smiled at one another.

"I didn't realise a four year old was up to advanced magic," said Neve.

"Of course she isn't," said Tamsyn. "But I've been looking through my parents' old spell books. I found some of them in boxes in their attic after they passed away. And having the two people there isn't so much about them both needing to be advanced. It's more creating a kind of channel. Elowen has our same genetics, so hopefully she's inherited gifts, too. I know I can do some of the magic, but I haven't gotten into too much of it. Mum and Dad were always trying to get me to stay away from it after we moved. I think it was too painful for them."

"But it's worth a try," said Neve, looking tired. "You might not come up with anything, but I don't have any leads at the moment. Every single one that's cropped up so far has been a dead end."

"Okay," said Tamsyn. "It's the least I can do after everything you've all done for me...for us. I'll need a few days to practice and memorise some parts of the spell."

"Great, how about we reconvene on Tuesday?" Rosemary suggested. "And see what happens."

"Sounds good." Tamsyn was practically beaming. "I'm actually quite excited. I've been so looking forward to doing magic again."

Rosemary noticed a strange look passing across her daughter's face and Dain still seemed oddly serious, but she pushed her concerns away. She'd had enough to think about for one evening.

Rosemary was looking forward to curling up in bed, perhaps after a hot chocolate or two. She was on her way to the kitchen when there was a knock at the door.

She answered it, curious about who the night-time caller might be.

Liam was standing there, looking slightly dishevelled.

"Rosemary, I'm sorry to come so late. I just wanted to apologise for...*before*. I didn't mean what happened. It was sort of instinctual."

Rosemary gave a him a strange look. "It's instinctual for you to try and attack people?"

Liam nodded. "Unfortunately, the moon is waxing," he said quietly.

"Full Moon is not for another week." Rosemary was unimpressed. "I've been keeping an eye on it in the witchy calendar Marjie gave me."

"I know that," said Liam, lowering his voice and looking around to make sure no one was listening. "My wolf grows stronger in this part of the month, as the moon waxes."

"I have a right mind to wax you!" Rosemary said.

Liam gulped, but looked slightly excited by the possibility.

Rosemary blushed. "Oh, you know what I mean! You can't just go around attacking people. It's not socially responsible."

"I thought I had him under control."

"Him? Your wolf?" Rosemary asked in a hoarse whisper. "Do you have a name for him?"

"Fluffy," Liam admitted.

Rosemary was torn between laughing out loud and slamming the door in Liam's face. A rogue werewolf named Fluffy was the last thing she needed.

"Anyway," said Liam. "What you did the other day worked, or it seemed to for a few days...but clearly it hasn't stuck. When I saw you—"

"That's just great," said Rosemary. "Well, it's time for you to go home and tend to Fluffy yourself. Sorry I couldn't be of more help."

"Don't tell me you've given up," said Liam. "Rosemary, I need this. You can't just—"

"Hey. I'm not the bad guy, here," said Rosemary, feeling frustrated. "If there's something in you that goes around attacking people in town for no good reason, even in your human form, you can't make that all my problem."

"It's not like that," said Liam. "The only reason I attacked the vampire was because he had his hands..."

"On me?"

"Yes. I felt..."

"Possessive? Jealous?"

"I couldn't contain myself," said Liam.

"That makes it slightly more awkward," said Rosemary.

Liam looked downcast. "I can't help the way I—"

"Look," said Rosemary, feeling bad for him, but also desperately not wanting him to talk any more about feelings, especially when Athena could appear at any moment and listen in. "You're right. It's not your fault you have this...virus."

"It's not your fault either," said Liam. "I'm sorry for making it seem like you had to take responsibility for me and my problem. I don't expect anything of you, I just hope...This is the closest I've come to a cure. If there's anything you can do to help in the next few days...I'll do anything to return the favour."

"I'll see what I can do," Rosemary said. "But don't expect too much."

Liam's gaze moved from Rosemary's face to a point just behind her. She turned back to see Dain, standing with his arms crossed.

"Oh, I'm sorry," said Liam awkwardly. "I didn't realise you had company."

"No, no," said Rosemary. "He just lives here. Liam, this is Dain, Athena's father. Dain, this is my friend, Liam."

She expected them to reach out and shake hands, but instead they both stood there, staring at each other like a couple of staunch tomcats.

"Really?" said Rosemary. "What is with this?"

"What?" Dain asked.

"This territorial behavior," she said, looking back and forth between the two men. "This is ridiculous!"

When neither of them budged or said a word, Rosemary turned back towards Liam. "Thank you for visiting," she said. "You should go now."

"Yes, it's time to go now, Liam," said Dain, waving to him with a smile.

Rosemary fixed Dain with a glare. Liam was also glaring at him when she turned back.

"Rosey, I'm sorry for bothering you." Liam had clearly decided to ignore Dain and focus on her instead. "And I'm sorry for my behavior before. You've done a lot to help me. I mean it, if there's anything I can do to help you, anything at all, just let me know."

"Thanks, Liam. Have a good night," said Rosemary, closing the door.

"Yeah, have a good night, Liam," Dain called, smiling even more broadly as he waved again and the door clicked shut.

Rosemary elbowed him. "That wasn't necessary."

"I'm just having a little fun," said Dain. "You seem to have a lot of suitors lately, *Rosey*."

"Rosey was a childhood nickname, and I don't have any suitors, thank you very much." She folded her arms. "Why doesn't anyone believe me?"

"Maybe because a beautiful woman such as yourself shouldn't be single. It's a crime."

"I'm sure that's sexist," said Rosemary. "I don't need a man to complete me – or a woman, or any kind of romance. Also that sounds like a pickup artist line."

Dain raised his arms in innocence. "I can't do anything right, can I?" he said. "I'm just the guy who lives here and has no life."

Rosemary smiled sympathetically. "You've actually done a lot of good things lately."

Dain looked at her questioningly.

"It's been nice to see you getting on so well with Athena and you've been great with the foundling kids. So, as weird as it is to have my ex living here, it's been good to have you around."

A big grin spread across Dain's face. "I'm glad you think so. I can think of a way you can properly thank me." He winked, and Rosemary felt the slight draw of Dain's fae magic, or perhaps it was just his natural charm. Either way, she was far too strong for it to get the better of her.

"Nice try," she said. "But I'm not falling for it."

"Pity," said Dain. "But you're right. It's been so good us being back together again."

"*We're* not back together," Rosemary insisted. "You know that. 'Us' was never going to work."

"Wasn't it?" Dain asked. "Or was it just that my problems were always ruining everything?"

"Your problems had a huge role to play," Rosemary admitted. "But we can't go back in time. It's too late for us. I'm not the young, innocent girl you met all those years ago."

"I don't want you to be innocent," Dain said, his lip curling.

"Dain, so much has changed since then. I need you to know that we're not together, okay? We're not going to be together. Athena needs you in her life—if you're going to be a good influence, anyway. She's been having trouble."

"What kind of trouble?" Dain said. It looked as if a storm cloud crossed over his face. "Is it that guy again?"

"No," said Rosemary, smiling at his reaction. "I think she misses the fae realm."

Rosemary explained the conversation she'd had earlier with Fleur.

"It makes sense," said Dain. "This world is a lot heavier. It's one of the things that I struggled with so much in coming here, why I was so prone to weakness when I couldn't give up my addictions."

"And now?" Rosemary asked.

"I'm stronger now," he said. "I was tortured for weeks, Rosemary. When you've been right to the brink of your own experience, you've been so far that you didn't know if you'd ever survive, and you've come back from that, you know what you're capable of. And you know what matters to you. You and Athena are what matter to me. I've been through hell, but I'd do it all again in a heartbeat."

Rosemary felt warmth spreading through her chest. "I appreciate the sentiment." She was going to continue with some kind of statement like 'but it doesn't matter' or 'but it's too late' or 'but that doesn't change anything', but nothing came out. So she left her previous words hanging. She didn't need to ruin the moment.

"How about some dairy free hot chocolate?" she offered and continued on to the kitchen.

Thirty-Two

As was tradition in Myrtlewood, the school was closed in the week leading up to the seasonal festivals. Beltane was to be the following weekend. Yet that didn't mean all the work had to stop. Athena still had her essay due on Wednesday, but it did mean no classes, which also meant that Rosemary allowed Athena to visit Elise's house, even though it wasn't a weekend.

A sleepover; it was actually something Athena had never done before. She'd missed out on slumber parties with friends when she was younger because she never really had any close friends, only a few acquaintances who she spent time with at school. Besides, Rosemary and Athena had never really lived anywhere nice enough before to bring company, so if she had been invited over, she wouldn't have been comfortable returning the favour.

Now, however, things were different. Rosemary was dropping Athena off on the condition that she got to meet the parents, despite the fact that she'd already met Fleur.

"As long as you don't embarrass me," Athena said as they drove into the dense forests northwest of Myrtlewood.

"I'm surprised anyone lives out here at all," said Rosemary.

"Why not? It's lovely," said Athena. "All these green trees."

"What's wrong with our trees?"

"There's nothing wrong with trees," said Athena. "That's kind of the point. Besides, it's not a competition. It's not like they've asked me to move in or anything. I'm just saying. It's nice."

"It's nice where we live, too." Rosemary had been oddly defensive since the conversation at the spa where Athena had admitted to missing the fae realm, making Athena's other secret even harder to share with her mother.

The road became narrower and more gravelly as they continued on.

"I hope there's some way to turn round at the end," said Rosemary.

"She would have mentioned if there wasn't," said Athena. "I doubt you're the first person to drive down here. It is a road, after all."

"I suppose you're right," said Rosemary. "I'm just feeling nervous. I've never had to deal with anything like this before."

"Just relax, Mum. Why don't you go home and book in for another massage?"

"Ohh, maybe she offers them from home," said Rosemary.

"No, Mum. Absolutely not. You're not crashing my sleepover."

"That was a joke," said Rosemary. "Sort of."

"I'm serious," said Athena. "Don't you dare ask for a massage while I'm visiting my friend."

"Fine," said Rosemary. "Look. Here we are."

The little wooden house was almost camouflaged in the trees in front of them, painted green and brown and hoisted above the ground on stilts. Athena noticed little bridges made out of rope and wood running between the trees.

"It's adorable," said Athena.

"It's kind of like in that Star Wars movie with the bear creatures," said Rosemary.

"Mum," Athena said with a warning in her voice.

"What?"

"You're being weird – weirder than usual. Perhaps it would be better if you try to keep your mouth closed as much as possible. And don't stay long."

"All right, all right," said Rosemary. "I just want to meet them."

They got out of the car and made their way up a rickety wooden staircase towards a bell-shaped front door.

"It's like a fairy house," said Rosemary.

"Shush. Don't say things like that. It might be offensive. Remember, they are fae folk."

"Well then, it shouldn't be offensive," said Rosemary.

Athena shot her another warning glance and made a motion for her mother to keep her mouth shut.

The door opened before they could knock. A pretty blue-haired woman stood in front of them.

"You must be Athena," she said. "I'm Fleur."

"Hi," Athena said.

"Mum!" Elise called out, coming to the door. "It's okay, I've got it."

"Nice to see you again," Rosemary said, smiling at Fleur as Elise grabbed Athena's arm and pulled her into the house.

"Bye, then," Rosemary called out.

"Remember what I just told you," said Athena, hoping her mother wouldn't embarrass her.

Rosemary waved dismissively.

Athena pushed concerns about Rosemary's behaviour out of her mind as she followed her friend. "Your house is awesome."

"It's not enormous and fancy like yours," said Elise as they passed through a small cosy living room complete with quilts and crocheted pastel rainbow coloured doilies. "But it's quite nice here. This is my grandma, Ambrosia."

"Hello," said a woman who didn't look a day over fifty, smiling at them from a rocking chair where she sat knitting.

Athena barely had time to reply before Elise whisked her out of the room again.

"I thought your grandmother was supposed to be over a hundred years old," said Athena.

"She is," Elise replied.

"She doesn't look anywhere near that old. You've got good genetics."

Elise smiled. "Come up here. This is my room." She climbed up a wooden ladder. It was painted bright blue, almost matching Elise's usual hair colour.

Athena followed her to a kind of loft space. The ceiling fell in a triangle. There wasn't much room, just a reasonable sized bed, low to the ground, and little bookshelves lining the walls.

"It's lovely," said Athena. "What a nice space."

"It's not much," said Elise. "But it's home."

"You don't sound very enthusiastic when you say that."

"Oh, you know. When I say that word now it just reminds me of—"

"The fae realm," Athena said. "I totally understand."

"It's nice to have *you* around, though," said Elise. "When you're not here, I feel kind of drained and tired."

"I know the feeling," Athena admitted. She wanted to share the secret she hadn't told anyone else about, but now wasn't the time. "Things have been weird, recently. I didn't want Mum to know about it. Turns out she knows now though. It didn't help that your mother talked about it when she was giving Mum a massage."

"I'm sorry," said Elise. "Parents are so weird."

"That's the understatement of the century," said Athena. "Never mind. It's okay now. It's probably for the best. At least Mum will let me out of the house to see you more often because she knows that it makes me feel better about being here in this world."

"That is a fortuitous turn of events," said Elise, folding her arms. "Now, would you like some tea?"

The rest of the afternoon passed in an enjoyable blend of tea and cake and conversations, followed by a supper of roasted fern roots and chestnuts which Athena found surprisingly delicious.

Later that evening, as they lay in Elise's bed, Athena felt inspired to let her friend in on the secret that she hadn't shared with anyone yet.

"I want to show you something," she said. "Just promise you won't tell anyone."

Elise gave her a look that was both excited and suspicious. "What is it?"

"Can we get outside from here? Without anyone noticing?"

"Of course we can," said Elise. "This way." She opened the window and showed Athena how to climb down the sturdy vines that grew up the side of the house. They scrambled down until they reached one of the rope bridges and made their way across to a little platform between three big old trees.

"This place is so awesome," said Athena. "I can tell why you like living here."

Elise smiled. "What is it that you want to show me?"

"Something you're going to like," Athena replied. She held out her index finger and took a deep breath before she began cutting a door in the air, just like she had the other nights recently.

"What are you doing?" Elise asked in a slightly panicked whisper.

"You'll see," said Athena.

A light glowed in the air, making a trail behind her finger. Elise gasped as whisps of fae realm magic flowed through. "Oh my goddess!" she said.

"It's feels good, doesn't it?"

"Yes," said Elise. "It feels amazing. It's wonderful!"

Athena beamed at her.

"Have you been doing this often?" Elise asked.

"Most nights," Athena admitted. "I probably shouldn't. It's dangerous, I know, but I can't help myself. It just feels like...like I'm meant to be there. Even though everything important in my life is here."

Elise nodded and took Athena's hand.

Just then, a large reddish coloured whisp in an almost human shape flew through the veil with such speed and force it pushed the two friends apart.

"What was that?" Elise asked.

"I don't know," said Athena. "That happens sometimes. I wonder if I'm letting things through that shouldn't be in this realm, but no high fae have tried to come through yet, so that's something."

"It's concerning, though," said Elise.

"I know."

"No...I mean like really concerning."

"Why?" Athena asked.

"Because I think sometimes when things pass between the realms, they do it in an incorporeal kind of way. That's what my Grandma said used to happen, back when the realms were more open. It was like she'd dissolve a bit when she came through and re-form on the other side."

"So you're saying—"

"You could be letting anything in!"

"Even fae?" Athena practically choked the words out.

"I don't know," said Elise. "I'm just a bit worried."

"Why, though?" said Athena. "I mean, aside from that nasty countess and her henchmen, it's probably fine. There's plenty of faery type creatures in the earth realm. What's wrong with a few more? Your grandmother seems harmless."

"You should see her in a temper. But anyway, plenty of us *are* harmless. The real reason I'm worried is that I got a sense...from whatever it was that just drifted through that it could potentially be something dangerous."

She reached for Athena's hand again and the light faded.

"You're really that worried?" Athena asked.

"I am." Elise gave Athena a knowing look. "I have a feeling that could have been a fire sprite."

"Oh...Oh, no," said Athena. "Are you sure?"

Elise shook her head. "I'm not a hundred percent sure. I just got that kind of vibe from it."

"Have you met one before?" Athena asked.

"In passing," said Elise. "But obviously not in this kind of situation. I've heard that the fire sprites who've been here for generations are quite different from the wild creatures in the fae realm."

"Do you think it's possible that I'm the one responsible for all the fires?" Athena asked, her voice rising in panic.

"I don't know," Elise said. "And part of me doesn't want to find out."

Thirty-Three

Rosemary joined roughly two hundred other residents of Mytlewood as they crowded the town hall. Some faces were familiar, some were rather odd.

Marjie had phoned her early on Monday morning to tell her about the special meeting that night, called by Mr June, the mayor. Rosemary hadn't wanted to show her face after the recent interactions with his highness, lord of pompousness, as she liked to call him inside her head, but Marjie had insisted that it was important.

The town hall was an old Edwardian building with high ceilings. Rosemary had never been inside before and was relieved by the strong turn-out. She hoped it meant the mayor and his charming husband wouldn't notice her.

Ferg stood up first and did a sort of blessing, thanking the elements of the four quarters and the town's patron goddess, Brigid. Next, it was Mr June's turn to speak. He approached the podium with his black hair gelled back, wearing a long black and purple cape, edged in gold and draped over a three piece suit in matching colours, which Rosemary thought was a rather dramatic choice of outfit.

"My dear townsfolk," said the Mayor. "I'm sure you understand the gravity of the situation we face, at least in part."

There was a murmur of concern from the crowd.

Mr June had a gleam in his eye as he continued. "There have been no less than sixteen fires around town over the past week or so."

Movement caught Rosemary's eye. She turned her head to see Detective Neve, clearly a late arrival, excusing herself as she slipped down the row to take an empty seat next to Rosemary.

Mr June cleared his throat and glared in their direction.

So much for not being noticed, Rosemary thought.

"What's happened?" Neve asked in a whisper.

"Nothing yet."

"If. I. May. *Continue*," said Mr June, emphasising every word in a way that was laboured and unnecessary. "I'm sure you are all concerned for your safety and the safety of your families. We understand that the fires are both real and also magical. That is, they can burn like an ordinary fire, but they also have some...unexpected effects."

"That's an understatement," said Neve under her breath.

"I will allow our Chief Firefighter to come up here in a moment to give you more details on what to watch out for, but first, I must make an announcement. It is with a heavy heart that I must officially cancel the Beltane festivities."

A murmur of surprise and disappointment rolled around the room.

"But...that's outrageous!" said Ferg, standing up, clearly unable to hold himself back.

"Please sit down, Mr Burgess," said the Mayor. "You can ask questions later."

Ferg sat down, but Rosemary could still see the look of outrage on his face.

"I'm aware that this is almost unprecedented," Mr June continued. "We haven't had to cancel a ceremony in my entire time as mayor, though we did postpone the winter solstice once due to a stray banshee."

The audience laughed, though Rosemary didn't get the joke.

"In fact, no ceremony has been cancelled in this town since the fae troubles a hundred or more years ago. But, in the interests of your own safety and the wellbeing of the town, we cannot risk a large gathering at this time. Not until we are clear of the dangers posed by the fires. Therefore Beltane will be cancelled, with a possibility of rescheduling it, if, and only if, this fire business is cleared up forthwith, though I'm afraid our local law enforcement are clueless as to the culprit."

He glared at Neve and then panned the room, his eyes narrowing in suspicion.

"If you have any information at all on these fires, please come forward to the authorities."

The audience broke into conversation as the mayor finished up and passed the microphone over to Sid, the firefighter who also happened to be Neve's ex.

Neve had a slightly uncomfortable expression as they watched her speak about the risks posed by the fire, something they already knew rather a lot about, from personal experience.

"What is it?" Rosemary asked.

Neve sighed. "We're going to be overrun with hearsay and rumours for days after what he just said. I'd bet on it. Besides, it's not going to help."

"The rumours?" Rosemary asked.

"No. Cancelling Beltane. It won't reduce risks. In fact, I think it will only make things a whole lot worse."

"And that," said Rosemary, "is exceptionally suspicious!"

Thirty-Four

Athena paced her room, late into the evening hours. She'd been so stressed since she came back from Elise's house earlier that day.

She'd tried to hide it from her mother but had failed miserably. Thankfully, Rosemary had bought the excuse that her anxiety was over the essay on Beltane being due on the next day.

It was true that Athena had spent hours researching it, though she still wasn't very happy with the lack of information and how she'd tenuously tried to thread it together. Athena had never cared so much about school work before, and had never wanted to do well, but she loved Myrtlewood Academy, and besides, she wanted to beat Beryl just to wipe the smirk off her face.

It was slightly stressful, and the Beltane-related school work was only the tip of the iceberg. She hadn't been able to sleep the night before, not after realising that all of the problems happening around town with the fires might well be her fault. Rosemary already seemed overwhelmed with all the magical danger posed by their new life. Athena hadn't voiced it, but she was scared that one more disaster might push her mother over the edge and make her move them both out of town, and back to the mundane world where nothing made sense anymore.

The last thing Athena needed was for her already over-protective mother to find out that she might be the one responsible for the fires.

There might be no way to hide it if Tamsyn was able to do the finding spell...Unless Athena could come up with some kind of magic powerful enough to contradict it.

She had poured over Granny's most potent books but hadn't been able to find anything of use, until she came across a spell in one of the old Thorn spell books in the tower room.

The spell did look promising. Athena was hoping it would do the trick and that her now-functioning Thorn family magic would be able to get it to work well enough to mask her presence.

She couldn't risk Rosemary finding out and lose her freedom again.

She felt guilty to hide something as big as this, but she needed to stay hidden long enough that she could figure out how to fix what she might have done. That was a whole other mystery that she hadn't figured out how to solve yet.

Perhaps some kind of summoning spell would work. She could call all of the fire spirits or sprites or whatever they were and led them back through the veil.

Rosemary wasn't exactly going to get on board with anything like that. Especially not if it involved Athena going into a different world again. So even though she did feel terribly guilty, she pushed it down, suppressing it.

"I have to figure out how to solve this on my own," Athena muttered to herself. "If I've created the mess, I'm going to clean it up."

She crossed her room, back to the old spell book that she'd brought down from the tower, and read over the spell again.

It looked complex at first glance and Athena had had to use a special book on old British runes to decipher some of the symbols. Though the more she looked at it, the more the magic intuitively made sense to her, apart from one perplexing piece – how could the tiny quantity of ingredients fill an entire cauldron?

Once she was sure Rosemary was fast asleep, she took the spell book back up to the tower room, grateful that it had been accessible to them ever since Granny had apparently vacated the building.

Athena needed to use the large cauldron and some of the ingredients up there that she'd previously catalogued in case they were of use.

It was a strange spell and Athena couldn't quite figure out how it all came together. There didn't seem to be enough liquid involved to fill the cauldron by any stretch. She sprinkled in the dry belladonna leaves and said the ignition charm to light the cauldron.

The leaves started to smoulder and she added in river stones, acacia bark, and four crushed dried hornets from Granny's supply cupboard, along with a spoonful of honey. The next step was to prepare a glass of enchanted spring water. Rosemary never bothered with expensive over-priced bottled water, but fortunately Thorn Manor prevailed. The fridge must have heeded Athena's mind's call. She found it stocked with dozens of bottles of water, complete with labels saying it was from a local spring. This was simple enough for Athena to enchant with an easy spell, though she did hope the remaining water disappeared before her mother saw it.

As the spell instructed, she began to slowly pour the glass of enchanted water into the cauldron at a trickle, while stirring with her other hand.

To Athena's astonishment, one small cup of water managed to fill the entire enormous cauldron.

Athena chanted the words that she didn't entirely understand, with the intention of hiding herself.

A scent a lot like lavender filled the room, along with billowing clouds of steam.

Satisfied, Athena took three drops of the potion on her tongue. It tasted like raspberries and had the unnerving effect of emptying the entire vessel so the cauldron became completely dry and clean as if she'd never put anything into it in the first place.

She felt an odd sizzling sensation inside her, and then a thudding like the beat of her heart, only heavier.

She checked herself in the mirror, but she looked quite ordinary. She stood for a moment longer, observing her reflection. She almost jumped as four large tendrils of light, like the legs of an octopus, sprang out from her back and wrapped around her, tucking her in like a new born baby into a blanket.

It would have been terrifying if the sensation wasn't so comforting.

As she stood there, the light faded away to nothing.

"Well," Athena muttered to herself. "Hopefully that worked and I'll be protected for a few days. If not, I suppose I'd better have a backup plan."

She offered a small prayer to the goddess Brigid and then slipped back down the stairs and into bed.

The next day, Athena woke feeling rested after a good night's sleep. The spell seemed to have the side effect of making her feel far more relaxed than she'd previously been.

She went downstairs for breakfast to find that Rosemary had already made pancakes.

Dain and Nesta were sitting around the dining table with the foundling children. Thea and Clio were staring determinedly at a fork as it levitated between them and Harry was cheering them on.

Definitely not normal children.

"I'm afraid we're not going to be here for too much longer," said Nesta to the children.

"Aww." They sighed. "Why not?"

"Well, Mei's mummy is well enough to travel. She's arriving soon," Nesta explained. "Mei and Neve are going to spend more time in our house with her. She's a little bit older and she needs some extra care."

"It'll be a shame not to have you around much," said Rosemary.

Athena nodded, although she did wonder whether it would be easier to keep a secret without having a detective in the house all the time.

The past few days, Neve had occasionally given her funny looks and Athena was worried that she might be found out.

"So that's the plan for today, then?" said Athena, trying to put a jolly tone in her voice.

"Yes," said Nesta. "Neve is picking her aunt up from the airport soon and is going to bring her here. We'll hang around for a bit while we get to know each other, which will give Tamsyn plenty of time to try the finding spell."

"Isn't it a bit much to do all in one day?" Athena asked, hoping to delay the inevitable.

Rosemary shrugged. "There's plenty of us around. If Neve has to go off for a little while to investigate anything, I'm sure we can hold the fort."

"But wouldn't we want her to be here for support?"

"Maybe," said Rosemary. "If that's the case, then we can do a bit of digging and report back."

Athena gulped. She hadn't even started eating her pancake yet. She squeezed some lemon juice over it and sprinkled on sugar, though she barely paid attention to what she was doing.

She tried to think it over in her mind. She barely noticed the tangy, sweet flavour of her breakfast as she ate it.

"Oh look, here they are now," Nesta cried, getting up and going over to the doorway. Moments later, Neve and Nesta led in an old woman wearing a big grey coat, her black hair streaked with grey.

"Where is this you've brought me?" she said.

"Aunty, these are my friends, Rosemary and Athena," said Neve. She introduced them all.

"What is this house, Constantine?"

"This is Rosemary's house," said Nesta.

"No...this house. I recall...this is the house of Galderall Thorn."

"Yes, it was," said Rosemary. "I'm her granddaughter."

"Connie, where is my little girl?"

"Mummy!" Mei cried, running over and wrapping her arms around the legs of the old woman. "You got so old!"

The older woman laughed. "Yes. Yes, I did...I did get old. And you stayed so young."

It would have been enough to bring tears to Athena's eyes. And indeed, she noticed a few in the eyes of those around. She couldn't properly enjoy the moment as she was feeling too anxious about what was to come.

"You there!" Meng called out, pointing at Athena. "You. You are evil! You don't belong here."

Athena's eyes widened and her pulse quickened.

"Auntie, now, now," said Neve. "We've been over this. I'm sorry, Athena, she's still suffering from dementia, I'm afraid."

"Come on, come outside," said Nesta. "It's a lovely day." They led the old woman away.

Athena stood still, mortified.

"Sorry, love." Rosemary put her arm around her daughter's shoulder. Athena didn't even shrug it off. Her heart pounded in her chest and she didn't know what to do. "Don't worry," said Rosemary. "You know she doesn't know what she's saying."

Athena tried to smile and nod and shrug casually, all at the same time. The problem was the old woman knew exactly what she was saying. She knew far more than anyone else seemed to about the real nature of the situation.

"I think I might just go to my room," said Athena.

"Wait," said Rosemary, turning back towards the front door. "Tamsyn's here."

Tamsyn came in with little Elowen. They were both dressed in red T-shirts with blue jeans.

"Elowen is excited about matching outfits," Tamsyn said with a smile.

Rosemary beamed. "Adorable!" She turned to Athena. "Put some tea on, will you love?"

"Okay," Athena replied weakly.

She went to the kitchen and started making tea as if on autopilot, trying not to think because thinking wasn't doing any good. She could hear the conversation nearby between her mother, Neve, and Tamsyn, which only made her feel worse.

"How does the spell work?" Rosemary asked.

"It's based on what we know about the fire sprites being involved," said Tamsym. "Whoever is behind that should be revealed to us."

Athena's hands trembled and she put in too many tea leaves. She poured them all out and then she realised, on her second attempt, that she was putting tea leaves into the kettle instead of the tea pot. She had to wash the whole thing out and start again.

On the third attempt, she finally made tea and carried it into the living room, only to find that her hands were shaking so much when she was pouring it that she slopped it all over the tea tray.

"Go and get a cloth," Rosemary said, not seeming to realise the state that Athena was in. Rosemary could usually tell things like that and Athena wondered whether the binding spell was indeed protecting her, not only from spells, but also from her mother's perfectly ordinary intuition about what was going on with her.

She went to the bathroom and washed her face, then to the kitchen where she found a cloth to wipe up the mess. By the time she got back to the living room after giving herself a pep talk in the mirror, the spell was already underway.

Athena was trying to think of an excuse to make herself scarce when her mother said, "Come in and close the door."

Athena's heart shuddered in her chest. *Does she know?*

But Rosemary's expression seemed perfectly normal.

Athena wondered whether she could get away with closing it, but it was too late. She tried to press herself up against the wall, making herself as invisible as possible despite the fact that everyone could see her perfectly clearly.

If only I had found an invisibility spell, if such a thing exists. Then they wouldn't be able to find or *see me.*

Tamsyn moved her hands in a particular and unusual pattern, saying an enchantment that sounded Latin, or maybe French. She took hold of little Elowen's hands while they walked around in a circle over a map of Myrtlewood that had been placed on the ground.

"Here it goes!" said Tamsyn as a tiny spark of light shot up from between them and hovered in the air then plunged down towards the map, spinning around in circles over the township.

The spark vanished into the air in front of them.

"Did it work?" Rosemary asked.

Athena realised she was holding her breath.

Tamsyn shook her head. "It seemed like it was going to," she said. "But I can't see anything on the map that wasn't there before."

Athena let out the breath she'd been holding, grateful that nobody was paying any attention to her in all the confusion and excitement of the spell.

"I'm sorry," said Tamsyn. "I was sure we'd got it sorted. We've been practicing on my cat all morning."

"You've been doing spells on your cat?" Rosemary asked.

Elowen laughed. "Dixie! His name's Dixie!"

"Kind of," said Tamsyn.

"We had to find Dixie on the map," said Elowen, smiling.

"That's very clever," said Rosemary. "It sounds like a useful spell for when we can't find Serpentine, or someone else I know." She looked over at Athena, who tried to smile and shrugged.

"Hey, you pretty much always know where I am anyway, and I'm not a cat."

"You do have some cat-like tendencies," said Rosemary. "But we won't go into that now. It's a shame we don't have any leads on whoever is summoning these fires, if that's what's happening."

"Never mind," said Athena. "I'm sure we'll figure something out."

"I can try again, or maybe use another spell," said Tamsyn. "I'm not sure what happened, but it really should have worked."

"The other finding spells didn't work," said Athena.

"Most finding spells aren't that powerful," said Tamsyn, sounding confused. "But the ones in my family that fit with our magic...they should be able to find almost anything. I just...maybe it's my fault. I'm not as good as my parents."

Athena felt guilty, but she couldn't very well reveal that the spell would probably have worked perfectly well, had she not put in adequate protections against them.

"Never mind. You did your best," said Rosemary. "That's all any of us can really do."

Athena nodded and smiled and felt terrible.

Thirty-Five

Rosemary stirred the bubbling pot of porridge on the stove as she cooked breakfast for the remaining three children, herself, and Dain. The house was quiet, though she occasionally heard squeals and laughter from the back yard. Neve had promised that good foster parents were being lined up, though Dain still wasn't sure that was the best idea, given his bad experiences, and the paperwork was taking so long to process that Rosemary wondered whether the children would be teenagers by the time things were all organised.

Athena had left early for the day, despite Rosemary's protests. Since Beltane was officially cancelled, so was Athena's school break. The teachers had taken an extra day to organise themselves and then expected everyone back at school as if the seasonal festival had already happened.

Mr June obviously thought this was the best way to return to 'normal', but Rosemary disagreed. She didn't really want her daughter trudging off into the fiery wilderness when Neve thought it was only going to get *more* dangerous.

More fires had been reported across Cornwall since the mayor's announcement, two with serious injuries requiring hospitalisation.

Rosemary had tried to get Athena to stay home, even promising that she'd be able to help with the investigation by rifling through Granny's books, but Athena had other ideas. She clearly didn't want to stay cooped up at home and Rosemary could hardly find a good enough reason for

Athena to miss more of her education. She had already skipped a few weeks while stuck in the fae realm. Besides, it was refreshing to see Athena so interested in school work for a change.

There was a knock at the door and Neve let herself in. Rosemary had insisted on keeping the revolving door policy for her select closest friends, mostly because it saved her from having to open it so often.

Tamsyn followed close behind Neve with little Elowen in tow.

"Welcome," said Rosemary as Elowen caught site of the other children outside and ran out to join them. "Tell them breakfast is almost ready," Rosemary called out after her. Then she turned back to Neve and Tamsyn. "Would anyone like some tea?"

"Yes please," said Tamsyn.

"I could do with something stronger," said Neve. "My aunt has been quite a handful. But as it's still morning, and I'm technically on duty, I'd better stick with tea."

"I have some of Marjie's special tea tonic," said Rosemary.

Neve waved the offer away. "I'll be fine. I just need a moment of peace."

"How is Mei adjusting to the change?" Tamsyn asked.

"Mei is fine," said Neve. "In fact, sometimes I worry about how fine she is. Time in the fae realm sure seems to make children docile and easy going."

"I only wish it had that effect on teens," said Rosemary. "Or even on me! I'd love to feel relaxed and easy going."

Neve and Tamsyn laughed.

"She does miss the other kids. That's the only thing that seems to upset her," Neve continued. "It's the worry I have about fostering out the other three kids. What do they really know of this world apart from us and each other?"

"Hopefully we can keep them close enough to visit," said Rosemary.

"That's the problem," Neve said. "All the available foster homes are in Burkenswood or further afield."

Rosemary sighed. "As adorable as they are, I really don't think I'm cut out to foster three more children. I can barely cope with Athena sometimes."

Neve smiled. "We never expected them to stay here in the long term. Don't worry. We'll figure something out. You've already done more than enough to help, and it pains me to ask you for anything else, but—"

"I take it this isn't just a social visit, then?" Rosemary asked, her voice tightening in concern.

Tamsyn gave her a pointed look. "I called Neve because I think I've figured out how to cast the finding spell differently so that it doesn't rely on a map. For some reason, that didn't work last time."

Neve nodded. "From what Tamsyn told me on the way over, we should be able to just follow the spell and find out who is letting all those fire sprites into this realm."

"Where's Athena?" Tamsyn asked. "Does she want to help with the spell?"

"She went off to school early today," said Rosemary. "Now that the holidays for Beltane have been cancelled, she can't wait to get away from me."

"Teenagers are so surprising sometimes," said Neve. "It's like she doesn't want to have a holiday at all."

"I suspect she just wants to see her friends," said Rosemary, smiling.

They drank their tea quietly while Rosemary multi-tasked, finishing off the children's breakfast. They'd graciously slept in that morning, leaving the adults to get a bit of extra well-needed rest.

"Alright then. Shall we get started?" said Tamsyn.

Rosemary turned the pot of porridge off. "I'll just check with Dain to see if he's okay to feed the kids breakfast and look after them while we do the spell."

She went out the back and called out to Dain. He looked exhausted from running around with the kids, and was perhaps a little emotionally distant, but happily agreed to mind them for an hour or two.

"What would I do without you?" Rosemary said.

"Find a new man slave," said Dain with a grin.

Rosemary couldn't help but smile at his teasing, though it also made her want to throw something at him. There was no time for theatrics. She went back inside to find Tamsyn and Neve setting up in the lounge.

"All right," said Tamsyn. "Technically, this is a simpler spell. But I'm hoping that the way I've worked it will make it more powerful than the last one. I'll just go and get Elowen and then we can begin."

Neve looked at Rosemary. "Thank you for helping so much with this. I have to say I'm in over my head with all of these magical investigations lately. Not being terribly magical myself, I feel kind of at a loss."

"You're a heck of a lot more competent than Perkins," said Rosemary.

"Low bar," said Neve. "There's something about this whole situation that doesn't make sense. But hopefully we'll figure it out soon enough."

Tamsyn returned with Elowen in tow. "I think it'll help if you join us this time," Tamsyn said to Rosemary. "I'll be able to draw on your magic as well. You can join in too, Neve."

"Oh no. I'll probably just dilute things," said Neve. "My mother always said my magic was like tepid dishwater."

"That's a bit harsh," said Rosemary.

"I used to think I made up for it with my cleverness. Being a good detective was a way that I could help out even though there wasn't much else I could do when things went wrong. Anyway, enough about me."

"I think it will help," said Tamsyn firmly. "Come and join us."

"If you insist," said Neve.

It only took a few minutes to set up for the spell, using rosemary and onyx for protection, with ginger and tiger's eye crystal to reveal the truth.

The four of them held hands. Rosemary crouched down one side to reach Elowen's tiny hands; the soft little fingers reminded her of when Athena was small. She missed those days in some respects, but in other ways she was relieved to be free from many of the struggles of raising a small child, other than all the foundling children she seemed to now be surrounded by.

"Alright, Elowen," said Tamsyn. "Remember the poem we practiced?"

They began chanting.

Essence of will. Let us be still.
Reveal to us the source. As a matter of course.
What is hidden, let us see. So mote it be.

All was silent. Rosemary wondered if the magic was working at all, and then she felt a little tug. It was as if her magic was being pulled downwards.

She could see it coalescing like gold dust in the air in front of them, forming a small cloud of light.

"Alright," said Tamsyn. "Now just focus on the light with our intent to find the source of whoever is creating the fires."

They all focused in on the gold dust floating in the air. It began glowing and sparkling, forming the shape of an arrow. Rosemary thought it looked like a slightly translucent hood ornament.

"Now we just have to follow it," said Tamsyn.

"Okay," Rosemary said. "Wait, it's moving fast!"

The arrow flew right through the wall, leaving trails of gold sparkles in its wake.

"We've got to go," said Rosemary. "Come on, quick!"

"Elowen, you stay with the other kids," said Tamsyn.

"Okay." Elowen skipped off as the three women dashed out to the front of the house.

Rosemary could see the arrow headed down the driveway.

"It should stick to the roads, at least," said Tamsyn. "I didn't think about walls!"

"We should have cast it outside," said Rosemary.

"With the car running," Neve added. "Never mind, we can still make it. Get in!" She gestured towards her police vehicle.

They all jumped in and took off, following the arrow as it zoomed towards the village and then sped around the streets of Myrtlewood, only slightly above the speed limit. Neve popped the sirens on so they could legitimately drive faster.

"It seems to be heading past the town centre," said Rosemary.

"Maybe it's going to someone's house," said Tamsyn as it continued on into a suburb.

"Wait a minute," said Rosemary as they turned down familiar street. "This is close to Athena's school. I hope there's nothing terrible going on here that could affect all those kids."

"I think it's worse than that," said Neve as the arrow stopped right outside Myrtlewood Academy, hovering in the air next to the old stone buildings.

"I think we have a problem," said Tamsyn.

"At least now it's being patient," said Neve.

The arrow seemed to be waiting for them, so they parked and got out of the car. They followed it as it moved, much more slowly now, right into the school grounds.

"This is bad," said Rosemary. "I wonder if it's one of the teachers...or one of the students."

"Shush," said Neve. "We don't want to give ourselves away. Stay quiet and walk as if you're just going about an ordinary task."

Rosemary sighed. "I think I've forgotten what it's like to have ordinary tasks."

She followed Neve through the courtyard between several buildings, trying not to look too suspicious. The arrow moved in an organic kind of way, almost like a little dog. It seemed to be looking around for something.

Rosemary's phone buzzed. She glanced quickly at the screen to see that Liam was calling.

That's right. I was supposed to meet him today to help with his little problem, Rosemary recalled. *That will have to wait.*

They followed the arrow through an entrance way and along a corridor until it stopped outside the closed door of a classroom.

"Ohh, this is going to be awkward," Rosemary muttered. "If Athena catches me here, she will be so mad!"

She hoped like anything it wasn't Athena's classroom they were standing outside.

Neve knocked on the door and poked her head in. "Excuse me," she said.

Rosemary craned her neck, but she couldn't see much through the slither of open door.

"Yes?" said a voice of someone who must be the teacher. "Oh...Detective. Can I help you?"

"I just need to come in and ask someone a few questions," said Neve. "Nothing serious."

"Who do you need to talk to?" said the teacher.

"We'll see in a moment." Neve opened the door wide so that the now-very-patient arrow could move in.

It hovered around the room, above the heads of the students.

Rosemary, standing in the doorway, saw Athena sitting there with a look of absolute horror on her face.

Oh no, Rosemary thought. *She's going to kill me!*

She continued to panic until the arrow came to rest right above Athena's head.

"Miss Thorn," said the teacher. "I believe the detective here wants to have a word."

"Come with me, please," said Neve.

Athena stood up.

"There must be some mistake," Rosemary mumbled as she looked at her daughter. "Maybe it was looking for the person missing from our house. Yes...that must be it." She chuckled awkwardly.

Just then there was a sound of gasps and screams coming from the other students in the classroom. Rosemary turned back and looked across the room. Out the window, enormous orange and red flames burned.

"Oh, no. Oh, no, no, no! This is the last place we need *that* to happen!"

Rosemary ran outside. "Get back!" she cried. "Get all the kids as far away from the fire as soon as possible."

"Obviously!" said a teacher with pink plaits and orange robe. "Line up, class. Get away from the flames this instant." The teens didn't seem to listen though.

"The school has things well under control," the teacher said. A blast of air emanated out from her hand, knocking the students back, away from the flame. A further blast, scooping them up and escorting them all to a designated area.

"It's just protocol," said the teacher.

"Yeah," said Rosemary. "Well, this is no ordinary fire, and you'd better stay away too because I don't think you're my type."

Neve followed close behind as Rosemary dashed towards the flames.

She knew that she could at least handle a little bit of their beguiling magic. The fire seemed to start in the front entrance to the school, but it had quickly spread all along the corridor.

"This is bad," she muttered to herself.

"I'm going to go and find a source of water," said Neve, leaving Rosemary alone, facing the flames.

Rosemary caught sight of a very tiny teacher and a very large bearded teacher canoodling nearby.

"Get away!" Rosemary called. They didn't pay any attention to her. She blasted them with her light magic, and they flew back. She could only hope that the rest of the school had been evacuated as far away from the flames as possible.

She felt a warm, relaxing sensation coming over her, but this time she wasn't going to be fooled. She knew how to fight it. She used her protective light energy to coat her entire body so she was impervious to the seductive lure of the flames.

I need water.

She attempted to summon the feeling of water to see if that worked, but nothing came out of her hands.

It was a relatively clear spring day, but even so, she tried to reach for the small tufts of clouds floating in the sky, pulling them down towards the fire with her magic.

They did nothing but sizzle in the extreme heat. The fire grew bigger.

A flaming beast emerged, seven feet tall and horned with gleaming red eyes.

"This is what I was worried about." Rosemary glared at the beast, adopting her best mum voice. "Get back in there, you freaky flaming thing!"

"You could use some help with your swearing," growled the beast.

"Oh really? Are you some kind of god, then?"

"Ha, ha, ha," laughed the beast. "I'm merely a minotaur. My master will be here shortly."

He stalked towards her through the flames.

"Oh no you don't," said Rosemary. She hurled a ball of lightning towards the creature, blowing him back several metres.

The lightning appeared to do no damage whatsoever.

He laughed again and then lunged at her. There wasn't any time for punches and kicks. She could feel the heat coming off his body from metres away. One touch could melt her or burn her to cinders. So she fortified her magical protections and concentrated with all her might, pouring her magic forward, like a steady stream of water.

She felt it, flowing through her hands, emanating the very elemental feel of a river. This was the element Rosemary struggled with the most. She was mostly fire and air, as Athena had pointed out with her Sagittarius sun and Gemini rising. She wanted action and quick thinking, but water was slower. To connect with elemental water, she needed to relax and let go.

She closed her eyes. All she could hear was her own heartbeat, pumping blood around her body. Her body made mostly of water.

It shouldn't be this hard!

Rosemary struggled against her own instinct for control.

Relax, came the intuitive voice of the ancestor. *Let it come to you.*

Against her own instinct, Rosemary let her shoulders slump. Her breathing slowed.

Water came gushing through her as if channelled from another place entirely. It spurted against the beast, causing a cloud of steam to rise up.

"Impressive," he growled. "But you are no match for me."

He continued to march towards her. Rosemary bolstered herself and blasted him back with more ferocity this time. The minotaur fell back into the flames just as a great burst of water came forth from behind Rosemary.

She turned to see Neve's ex-girlfriend, Sid, standing there.

Reinforcements had arrived, just in time.

Rosemary sighed with relief and stood back as the firefighters took over, blasting the flaming school buildings with their magical hoses. It gave her a moment to take stock of the damage, which was far more extensive than she'd realised, but at least the students and staff had all been evacuated to the far lawn and there had been no casualties. Rosemary overheard Sid talking about this with her colleagues.

As she watched, the fire slowly died down at the hands of the six magical firefighters, possibly all of the crew they had in town, and certainly more than had arrived at the mayor's house.

"Amazing," said Sid as she turned off her hose and walked towards Rosemary. "I've heard legends of fire-dwelling creatures connected with the old gods, but I didn't believe it until now."

"Alarming, wasn't it?" said Rosemary.

Sid nodded. "This fire was a big one. Much worse than the others. It's just as well you were here to hold it off. The school is going to be out of commission for some time."

"Oh," said Rosemary. "Can't it just be magically repaired?"

She shook her head. "No. The properties of this fire seem to withstand that kind of magic. The magic is old and complex. It seems to withstand our contemporary repairing spells. The mayor's house is being rebuilt the old-fashioned way and he keeps complaining that it's taking such a long time."

"That's a shame," said Rosemary. "Where will the kids go?"

"That's a worry for another day," said Neve. "Come on, we better go and find Athena."

Rosemary followed Neve to the lawn where all the school students and teachers had assembled. Athena was standing off to the side looking mortified.

"That spell worked, didn't it?" said Rosemary.

"I'm so sorry," she said. "I didn't mean to..."

"Let's find somewhere to sit down," said Neve. "It seems Athena has some explaining to do."

"She certainly does," said Rosemary.

Athena broke into tears before she'd even sat down. They were in a little alcove on a bench outside the staff room, an undamaged part of the school. Rosebushes in full bloom surrounded the bench, perfuming the air, but Athena barely noticed them.

"I'm sorry," she said. "It's all my fault."

"It's okay," Neve said in a calm voice. "Just tell us. Tell us what you think happened."

"I didn't realise," said Athena. "I...at first, I was just experimenting. At night I'd go down to the forest. I thought of it as a kind of practice."

"What were you practicing?" Neve asked, nudging Rosemary, clearly to keep her quiet.

"Just practicing cutting a door through to the fae realm," said Athena.

Rosemary gasped.

"It felt so good," Athena explained. "I…I really miss being there."

"Where did you get the idea?" Neve asked.

Athena shrugged. "I don't know. I saw Finnigan do it to let us through. When I came back everything felt so grey. Actually, I might have thought of it after the dinner we had with our cousins. Elamina wanted to talk about the fae realm, at least. Mum never did. It got me thinking that I might be able to cut through. Just a little bit. Being there was *amazing*. It felt like home and maybe…it's kind of addictive. I don't know. I couldn't stop thinking about it and I felt really good. But I was so tired and drained when there wasn't enough fae realm energy around and…I had no idea I was letting anything through until…"

"Until what?" Rosemary said.

"Until I showed Elise when I was at her house. I didn't cut all the way through, ever, just a tiny bit. Just enough for some of the energy to come back to me. Elise understood why I'd do it. She missed the fae realm too. But she saw something fly out. And she said it was some kind of fae and a spiritual form. Maybe a fire sprite."

Rosemary and Neve looked at each other.

"I'm so sorry," said Athena. "I didn't mean to cause any trouble at all. I wasn't trying to create a fire or anything. You believe me, don't you?"

"It's actually really hard to believe you right now," said Rosemary, her voice heavy with disappointment.

Neve sat down in the seat next to Athena with a great sigh.

"I'm sorry, Neve," said Athena. "I really didn't mean to."

"It's not that," said Neve. "In fact, I think the problem is even bigger."

"What do you mean?" Rosemary asked. "Athena just explained it to us."

"Well, we found the source…of the person who let the fire sprites in to the earth realm," said Neve. "That's who the spell led us to."

"But?" said Rosemary. "There definitely sounds like there's a but here."

"If Athena was only letting them in by accident, then there's somebody else we're looking for."

"What do you mean?" Athena asked.

"Based on the research I've done, fire sprites are relatively friendly. In fact, I've interviewed a couple just to get more information. They were hard to track down as there aren't many around, and the ones that live here, well they are much more stable and well-adjusted than their wild counterparts, but even they wouldn't just go around lighting magical fires and summoning the Cavalia."

"See, you are good at your job," said Rosemary. "You have way more of an idea of what's going on than I do."

Neve sighed. "From everything I've learned, I'm absolutely certain there is something deliberate going on here. These fires are serious. It couldn't possibly have all happened by accident."

"I swear it wasn't on purpose," said Athena. "As soon as I found out what I was doing I stopped."

"I'm not accusing you," said Neve. "Besides, I don't see what your motive could possibly be. Someone else must be behind this. I'm not sure if they knew what you were doing. They're definitely using it to their advantage."

"That's giving me the creeps," said Rosemary. "Do you think it could be somebody close to us?"

Neve looked around suspiciously, confirming Rosemary's fears.

"Why are you so sure it's deliberate?" Rosemary asked.

"Those kinds of fires wouldn't happen by accident," said Neve. "Like I said, fire sprites tend to be quite peaceful unless they're specifically summoned and charged with doing something else. We may have found the source who's letting them in." She looked at Athena. "But we haven't found the source of the biggest problem."

"It couldn't have just been a coincidence?" Rosemary asked as Athena dried her eyes.

"What we're dealing with is really old magic," said Neve. "Someone has been weaving it together expertly, in a way that allows the fire sprites to connect with the divine plane."

"The what?" Athena asked.

"The divine plane, where the gods are."

"There's another plane, all together?" Rosemary asked. "I'm going to need a multi-dimensional map for this."

"Anyway," said Neve. "The only reason I'm more concerned now, is that it seems like you've played some kind of role in someone else's plan without even knowing it."

"I didn't mean to," said Athena.

Rosemary let out a long, slow breath. "It's okay."

"You're not angry?" Athena asked.

"I am angry," said Rosemary. "But I'm starting to realise something."

"What?" Athena asked.

"You didn't want to tell me any of the stuff about missing the fae realm because you were worried about me being over protective, right?"

"Right," said Athena.

"And if you hadn't been worried about that, you would have talked to me more about this stuff."

"Exactly," said Athena. "So it's really your fault."

Rosemary narrowed her eyes. "I wouldn't go that far."

"Also, if I'd been able to hang out with Elise more often she probably would have told me what I was doing wrong, much earlier."

"Don't rub salt in wound," said Rosemary. "You're still in trouble."

"I'll be grounded forever, right?"

"No," said Rosemary. "I'm starting to see that grounding you is part of the problem. We're going to both have to work on being more open and trusting, okay?"

Athena sighed. "Okay, Mum. I'll be more open with you if you stop being so freaking controlling."

Rosemary made an exasperated noise. "Fine. Now we just have to figure out who the creepy spies are who've been manipulating us and taking advantage of the fact that you missed the fae realm so much."

On the way back to Thorn Manor, Athena and Rosemary sat next to each other in the back of Neve's car while Tamsyn sat in the passenger seat. Athena's school had sent all the students home due to the fire, and she'd been far too embarrassed and overwhelmed to stay anyway.

On the drive, they collectively mulled over the suspects.

"Do you think it could be Dad?" Athena asked.

"He's certainly got the fae realm experience," said Rosemary, feeling her blood run cold. "But why would he want to do something like that?"

"He's quite mischievous, you know," said Athena.

"True." Rosemary groaned. "I never should have trusted him again. Or gone to all that effort to help him."

"Mum, it was just a possibility. I doubt it's him."

"Well, if it is, he's got another think coming."

"There are actually lots of possible suspects," said Neve as she turned into the driveway of Thorn Manor. "A lot of people have been around the house lately."

"Obviously Marjie and Nesta," said Athena. "But I doubt either of them would have any motive to summon deranged fire beasts."

"Then there's Sherry," Rosemary added. "She has a record of being deceptive in the past."

"That's true," said Neve. "But I wouldn't have thought she'd want anything chaotic to happen after what she's been through."

"We've had quite a few visitors," said Athena. "And it could even be somebody who hasn't been to the house at all. Someone with other ways of spying on us who knows what I've been up to."

"They could even have been subtly influencing you with magic," Rosemary said.

Athena shook her head. "No. That gives me the creeps. I don't like it. Maybe it really is just a coincidence. Someone was doing this magic and happened to make use of all the extra fire energy around."

"It's a pretty big coincidence," said Neve. "This is complex magic. They're not fooling around. I suspect they needed the fire sprites in order for it to work, a bit like Marla and Agatha Twigg. Not many people have the power to open up doors between the realms the way you do, because of your fae and witch heritage, and most people don't know that about you, either."

"That's true," said Athena. "But I'm not the only witchy fae person around."

"Not Finnigan!" said Rosemary. "You haven't heard or seen him again since you left the fae realm?"

"No, of course not," said Athena crossly.

"What if he's behind it?" Rosemary continued. "He might have been letting through a lot more fire sprites than you."

"That's certainly a possibility,' said Neve. "There are a few people with fae heritage around."

"Like Una," said Rosemary. "But I have no idea what kind of motive she would have."

"That's the problem," said Neve.

"The Bloodstone Society could have spies everywhere. Athena thought that blonde woman looked familiar – the one in the mask who attacked us – but who is she?"

"That's true," said Athena, looking her mother in the eye. "How many blonde women do we know?"

"There's Ashwyn," said Rosemary. "And Elamina, of course, but I'm sure I'd recognise my own cousin, even masked, and I'd be able to smell her sickly perfume a mile away. Besides, she wouldn't be caught dead in an outfit like that."

"What about the new girl at Marjie's shop? Lamorna?" Neve suggested. "We don't know anything about her."

"It's silly, really," said Athena. "We're grasping at straws. The woman was probably wearing a wig."

Neve sighed. "You're right. Oh, by the way, I checked the records at the spa the day you were there. Apparently there was a woman checked in who looked a lot like Despina, registered under the name Merriweather Wurster."

"I knew it!" said Rosemary. "I bet it was her."

Neve frowned. "The problem is we just don't know enough. If we'd been able to find the person responsible today then we would hopefully have had a little time before Beltane tomorrow night."

"I would offer to try again," said Tamsyn, "but it'll take a few days for my magic to recharge after such a big exertion."

"Never mind that," said Neve. "Whoever is doing this found some very clever ways to hide their tracks. Another seeing spell might just lead us to Athena again or someone else who's unwittingly helping them, and there's not enough time. All these other fires are just dress-rehearsals. If my deductions are correct, then whoever is doing this is going to want to celebrate Beltane, whether the rest of the town is there or not."

"So we'll be able to find them," said Rosemary.

"Exactly," said Neve. "Tomorrow night is our best bet."

Thirty-Six

"You saw it, didn't you?" Rosemary asked Neve as they sat around in the living room later on that day, after returning to Thorn Manor.

"Yes. That beast was terrifying," said Neve. "What did he say he was? A minotaur?"

"That's right. Sid said she's heard rumours of fire beasts like that." Rosemary leaned back in her armchair, grateful that she wasn't the only one to see it. She was also pleased to be freshly showered and feeling much better. However, the atmosphere was tarnished with anxiety.

"What was it like?" Athena asked. "I couldn't see anything from where we were standing."

Rosemary tried to explain the terrifying flaming minotaur.

"Your mum was incredible," said Neve. "She somehow summoned water out of thin air...or made it. I've never seen anything like that."

Rosemary shrugged. "I didn't know what I was doing. I really wish that I did."

"But you killed it, did you?" Athena asked.

"Not exactly," said Rosemary. "I just pushed it back through. The fire was sort of like a portal."

"That makes sense," said Athena. "The fire sprites' energy must be being used to open up a portal to the Divine Realm to let Belamus through. Beasts will come through, along with the ancient god of light. That's what the

Cavalia is supposed to be. According to Granny's books anyway. It's all becoming clearer."

"God of light. That sounds kind of nice," said Nesta.

"I don't think there's anything nice about it, unfortunately," said Athena. "The Old Gods aren't like Brigid or any of the other ones that we normally hear about. They come from a different time and aren't likely to value human life all that much, or so I've read. Although I admit, there's not all that much written about them."

"Do you think the gods are trying to come in and take over?"

"Or maybe somebody else is trying to bring them through so that *they* can take over," said Rosemary.

"Quite possibly, something along those lines," said Neve.

"Compared to how epic the Cavalia sounds, the flaming huge beast I fought today was probably nothing," said Rosemary.

"I bet it's Sid," said Nesta bitterly. "She's suspicious. Plus, aren't firefighters all secret pyromaniacs?"

Rosemary looked between Neve and Nesta. "This is one conversation I'm not going to get involved in, but I'm pretty sure the blonde woman who attacked Thorn Manor wasn't Sid – not even in a wig."

Nesta sighed. "It's probably a good thing that Beltane was cancelled."

"Neve didn't seem to think so at the town meeting," said Rosemary.

"Why not?" Athena asked.

"Without the Beltane celebration, I'm worried it will only get worse," said Neve. "Whoever is doing this is bound to hold a ritual anyway, to draw on the energy of the season, and no one will be there to stop them."

"You're probably right about that," Dain chimed in. He'd been sitting quietly, as if lost in thought, for some time. "They're increasing in intensity and frequency. It's got to build up to something. But we could use that to our advantage. Beltane could be a chance to confront whoever's doing this and put a stop to it, maybe even to push some of the sprites back through the portal."

"So you're saying we should have the ritual anyway?" Athena asked.

"If we don't take control of it, someone else will," said Neve. "That will be the benefit of leading the ritual ourselves. At the moment, whoever is behind all this has scared everyone off, successfully."

Rosemary felt a prickle of suspicion as Neve continued to talk. The mayor had cancelled Beltane. Maybe he wanted them out of the town centre for a reason. "So you're saying if we don't go down there and take charge, then they'll have the whole run of the place?"

Neve nodded. "They'll be in total control, which is what they're wanting. And we can't risk that. But then again, it's not fair for me to put you at risk either."

"We want to help," said Rosemary.

Neve looked around the room. "I've tried to call in more enforcement from the magical authorities, but I'm afraid they're not taking this very seriously. They think the real Beltane ceremony is in Edinburgh. I'm afraid they're stationing most of their enforcements up there, even though many of the fires have been around Myrtlewood."

"But not all of them?" Rosemary asked.

"No. In fact, there have been some in Burkenswood, and a few dotted all over the country. The authorities are trying to keep them quiet in case whoever is doing this is just wanting attention. My superiors were hoping they'd just stop on their own."

Rosemary and Neve shared an unimpressed look.

"I had no idea there've been so many," said Athena. "I'm so sorry for whatever role I've played."

"We'll let you make it up to us later," said Neve with a smile.

"You're on dishes duty for a very long time," Rosemary added.

"I suppose I deserve that," said Athena. "Luckily, we have a very cooperative house that likes helping out."

Rosemary squinted at her daughter. "Don't try and get out of this, someone needs to teach you that there are consequences for your actions and your deceptions and not telling your mother about them."

"Yeah, tell me about it," said Athena. "I'm never gonna live this one down, am I? Is there any way I can help?"

"I'd prefer to keep you well out of it," said Neve. "But I'm afraid we're going to need all the help we can get to hold the ritual and hopefully stop whatever is trying to come through."

"Do you think it will be in the town circle?" Rosemary asked.

"I assume so," said Neve. "That's where all the rituals are, it's a kind of nexus of power for the town, right in the middle of those ley lines. That's an obvious choice."

"Maybe it's too obvious," said Athena. "Maybe they'll try and hold it somewhere else. Like in the forest somewhere."

"That's quite possible," said Neve. "Though that could be to our advantage as well. The town circle holds so much energy that we could use it to channel a lot of the Beltane energy and divert any other attempts that somebody tried elsewhere to summon the Cavalia."

"Sounds dangerous," said Rosemary. "Maybe we're playing right into their hands. I hope you've got a plan."

Neve gave a stiff nod.

"Tell me where to sign up," said Dain.

Rosemary looked at him, feeling slightly suspicious. They'd allowed him to sit in on the conversation since the children were all occupied eating pudding. Rosemary had wanted to see his reaction to all this. He'd taken it very calmly, so far, perhaps a little too calmly. Though, what he'd have to gain from all this chaos, Rosemary had no idea.

"You want to be part of this?" Rosemary asked.

"Of course I do," Dain said. "I'm not just a glorified babysitter, you know."

There was an edge of anger to his tone. He got up and stomped out of the room.

Rosemary followed him. "Dain, what's going on? Tell me the truth," she asked.

"I don't think you want to know," said Dain.

Rosemary felt a lead weight in her gut. "Do you have something to do with all this? The fires? If you do then tell me right now."

Dain laughed. "Don't be ridiculous, I'm not a fan of fire sprites at the best of times, let alone the old gods."

"What do you know about them?" Rosemary asked.

"Enough to know that I don't want anything to do with them, that's all," said Dain. "They're dangerous and archaic, hard to understand, not something you want to mess around with."

"So why are you in this mood, then?" Rosemary asked.

"Because you keep side-lining me," Dain said. "No matter what I do, I can't seem to make up for the past and I know it'll take time but...give me a chance."

"I've given you a lot of chances," said Rosemary.

Dain sighed, pressing his hands over his face. "Look, it's hard for me, seeing you with all these suitors, hearing about you kissing some vampire in the middle of town."

"Nonsense. I don't have any suitors, for the last time! And the only reason that town incident happened was because of the stupid fire."

"No, it isn't," said Dain. "I know you, Rosemary. I know you wouldn't be caught dead kissing anyone that you weren't already attracted to, magical pull or not. You're powerful, more than even you know. And it's not just your magic."

Rosemary recalled seeing herself through Dain's eyes...the warmth of the love he had for her.

"Why won't you open up to me?" he asked.

"This is not about you," said Rosemary. "We've been through way too much, Athena and I..."

"And part of that was my fault," said Dain. "I accept that. I just wish you'd give me another chance, now that I'm free of my addiction. I wish I could show you how much I care."

Memories of his past tenderness swam through Rosemary's mind. She closed her eyes. Dain stepped towards her and grasped her shoulders. Rosemary opened her eyes and looked into his.

She shook her head.

"We're meant to be together," he said. "And it hurts to think of you with anyone else."

She stepped away from him. "No, we're not, Dain. There's nothing destined about us. We were just two kids that found each other in the wrong place at the wrong time, had a terrible turbulent relationship, and managed to get a wonderful daughter out of it. That's all."

"It can't be all," said Dain. "You're everything to me. You and Athena."

"And that's part of the problem," said Rosemary. "It's not healthy, I can't be everything to anyone. You need to have your own life."

"I know I do," said Dain. "I've been thinking about that. I want to start a business. And I probably need to move out of here."

Rosemary sighed, wondering what she'd do with all the children without Dain's help.

"See, exactly," said Dain. "You're worried about how you'll cope with the kids. You treat me like a babysitter. You just want me here to help out around the house. You don't want *me* here."

"Thank you for all your help," Rosemary said. "I know the fae don't like to be thanked, but seriously, thanks for all the things you've been doing to help with the kids. I'm not sure what we would've done without you, probably shunted them off into substandard foster homes by now. It's taking a lot longer than I thought to find them homes."

"It hurts that you only need me because of them," Dain said.

"And because of Athena," said Rosemary.

"She doesn't need me." He looked down at the ground, his voice cracking as he said it.

"She does. She needs her father around. As long as you're going to be a good influence." Rosemary nudged him with her elbow. He took hold of her hand, gently, and looked her in the eyes.

"Just tell me, Rosemary. Honestly, I need to know the truth. Tell me you don't have feelings for me."

Rosemary looked into Dain's eyes, feeling a wave of vulnerability. She couldn't say it, because it wasn't true.

A cheeky grin spread over his face. "I knew it! You do! You do have feelings for me."

She elbowed him again, hard this time.

"I can't help the way I feel about anyone," she said. "We have a past. And I admit, we have chemistry. But..."

"Yeah, I know you're not having any relationships. That's fine," said Dain, maintaining his grin. "I just need to know that there's still hope. Take all the time you need, Rosemary. You're not getting rid of me anytime soon. Not unless you really seriously want me out of your life. And if that ever happens, you're going to have to tell me. Be straight with me. I've never loved anyone like I love you. I don't know if I could."

With that, he walked away, leaving Rosemary feeling dizzy, confused, and heartbroken all at the same time.

Yes, she had feelings for Dain. She always had, despite the fact that she'd tried to suppress them a lot of the time. And if she was completely honest with herself, she also had feelings for Burk, and possibly for Liam as well.

"Feelings," Rosemary muttered. "Who needs them? Way too complicated."

"Are you talking to yourself again, Mum?" Athena asked, coming out of the living room. "What was up with Dad? Why did he storm out?"

"I think he's just sick of being treated as the babysitter, like you thought," Rosemary replied. Clearly she wasn't going to tell her teen anything about the conversation she'd just had. Rosemary had enough to be teased about already.

"Oh yeah?" said Athena. "So if he quits his job as a babysitter, what are we going to do with the kids?"

"I have no idea. Hopefully, the authorities can find them some good foster homes as quickly as possible."

"They need to be magical foster homes," said Athena. "The kids aren't really practicing magic yet, but they sure are otherworldly, and strange things will happen around them from time to time, things that mundane people will struggle to understand."

"That's why it's taking so long to find them homes, I think," said Rosemary. "But you're right. We need to come up with some other kind of solution, because even the most placid children in the world are a handful."

"Thank you for what you said before," said Athena. "I know you were just trying to control yourself. Because there were all those other people listening in. I know that you're still mad at me."

"It was the truth," said Rosemary. "I've never had to worry about protecting you so much before because you never went to parties or got into trouble like other teenagers. And now that things have changed since we've been in Myrtlewood, I've gone totally overboard, treating you like a toddler when you're almost an adult, as you keep saying. If I treated you that way from the beginning, then you wouldn't have gone to the fae realm without telling me. Well, you might have, but things could have been different. And you would have told me how you were feeling about that place. We could have figured it out together instead of you sneaking out at night and cutting holes in the veil."

Athena nodded. "I guess if you didn't pry into my life so much, then I wouldn't feel like I needed so much privacy or to protect myself from you."

"I guess it's time for me to let go a little bit," said Rosemary. "You're so strong. You can protect yourself. You know your own mind. I'm incredibly proud of you. I'm still angry, but also incredibly proud."

"Thanks Mum," said Athena, giving Rosemary a playful push.

"What was that for?"

"Just trying to break the tension. I'm a teenager, I can't handle these serious earnest conversations, remember?" She giggled. "So since you're going to trust me to live my own life, you're going to let me come to this Beltane ritual, right?"

"My initial reaction is not on your life," said Rosemary, looking her daughter in the eye. "It's bound to be dangerous, possibly more dangerous than anything we've faced yet, including the Bloodstone Society, although I wouldn't be surprised if they are the ones behind this. I have a feeling that if I try to hold you back and keep you at home with the kids, not only will we be in more trouble, because we won't have you there with your powerful magic, but you'll also find some way to sneak out anyway. And then we won't be well-orchestrated. And we'll be in even more danger. So, this is me, living up to what I've said. Walking the talk or whatever."

"No one says that anymore, Mum."

"I'm not trying to be cool," said Rosemary. "It's just a figure of speech."

"I'm glad you're not trying to be cool because I don't think it would ever work," said Athena. "But also. Thank you."

"I'm trusting you to make up your own mind," said Rosemary. "I still don't think you should come. But if you are going to, then let's work as a team."

"I think you already know that I'm definitely coming," said Athena. "And I'm bringing my friends too."

Thirty-Seven

"I know you're up to something," said Marjie, the next morning. She'd arrived at Thorn Manor a few moments before, carrying a big box of Sally Lunn buns, including some dairy free ones for Dain. "Don't even think about not including me."

They sat around the table, drinking tea and eating the fresh baked goods.

"It's going to be dangerous," said Rosemary. She filled Marjie in on the details. "Actually, it'd be great if you could stay here with the kids."

"I'm not just some babysitter, Rosemary Thorn," said Marjie. "Not when there's danger that I could help to fight. I'd ask Herb to help with the kids, but you know he's not the best, with his bad leg. He won't be able to run after them. How about Una and Ashwyn?"

Rosemary glanced at Neve across the table, wondering if the sisters could be trusted.

"What was that look about?" Marjie asked. "Don't tell me you're suspicious of those two. They're both absolutely lovely and highly trustworthy."

"How can you be sure?" Rosemary asked, a whir of different suspicious thoughts flicking through her mind. "Una's father was fae, and maybe she could have some kind of motive to do with their realm."

"That does sound like a stretch when you say it like that, Mum," said Athena. "Una is so nice."

"Nice people can do terrible things, remember that sweet little girl who turned out to be an ancient vampire and came after us?"

"She was *not* nice," said Athena. "Geneviève was pure evil. I could tell from the very beginning."

"Don't be silly," said Rosemary. "You were just jealous."

Athena pierced her with an evil look.

"I know!" said Neve, clearly trying to break the tension. "How about we invite them over and ask them some questions. We can ask if they'll babysit. And that will also give us a chance to make sure that they're comfortable with the kids before we leave them with the children."

"I don't know about that," said Rosemary. "Can't you just stay?" she asked Nesta.

"I'm afraid not," Nesta said. "When Neve's working I'm only able to go out for short intervals at the moment, when my neighbour pops over to look after Neve's aunt. I can't very well leave her and Mei alone for hours at a time in the evening."

"They could all come here," said Rosemary.

"My aunt's refusing to leave the house at the moment," said Neve. "She says there's too much evil afoot."

"That's probably true," said Athena. "She was right about me after all."

"What you did wasn't evil, love," said Rosemary. "Just misguided."

"Thanks for the vote of confidence," said Athena. "That's what it will read on my tombstone. 'Not evil, just misguided.'"

"You're not going to have a tombstone." Rosemary frowned. "At least not while I'm around."

"That is not exactly inspiring confidence," said Athena.

"Are you sure you don't want to stay, Dain?" Rosemary asked hopefully.

"Absolutely not," said Dain. "There's no way I'm going to miss out on the chance to see you fighting." He laughed.

Rosemary glared at him.

"But more seriously," Dain continued, "I need to be there to help protect you two."

Rosemary sighed. "Fine. We'll call Una and Ashwyn and see if they're able to come over and look after the children. But – I want Neve to interview them before we allow them anywhere near the kids. Use your detective interview powers Neve."

Neve gave her a questioning look. "You want me to interrogate them? Have you got a swinging lightbulb in a bleak concrete room?"

Athena laughed. "We can just ask them some questions. If they're acting weird, we'll tell them not to worry about it, and then we'll follow them around until they do something evil. And otherwise, we'll have a babysitter."

"It still doesn't seem like the wisest idea," said Rosemary.

"It might not, but we're running out of options." Athena held up an old leather-bound book. "We need to get organised. This book makes it sound like we'll have to appease the gods in some way."

"That doesn't sound good," said Rosemary. "In fact it sounds rather 'adult', especially when you think about the effect that the fire seems to have on people. I'd really prefer if you didn't come," she said to Athena. "Can't you babysit?"

"No, Mum. We've been over this. You need my magic."

"How do you appease the gods, then?" Rosemary asked.

An idea popped into her head relating to magical protection. She could use a shield spell and adapt it to cover the Myrtlewood residents to protect them from the fire. It would be complicated, but it might just pay off.

"We can try milk and honey," said Athena. "That's the kind of thing that Brigid likes."

"Okay, add that to the shopping list," said Rosemary. "What else do we need?"

"Yellow topaz, carnelian red agate, ruby, garnet," said Athena. "Basically all the red, yellow, and orange stones."

"We should make some more battle charms," said Marjie. "That's how I'm going to help."

"Sounds great," said Rosemary.

"Plus, I'll make sure you're all fed. I've got a batch of beef pies, baking in the shop. In fact, I better go and get them. I'll meet you in town later on."

Most of the day was spent in preparation for the ritual. Rosemary was relieved that there were no more fires and nobody had tried to attack her for a change, but there was lots of work to do in the meantime to prepare for the evening.

"We'll arrive in town, just after nightfall," said Neve, who was in charge of strategy. "That way we'll have less chance of the mayor finding out and kicking us out of the town circle before we can set up."

"Alright," said Rosemary.

She checked her phone to find another missed call from Liam. Her heart sank. She had promised she would help him soon. But she had other more pressing issues. Surely, he could just do whatever he normally did if it was too close to the full moon. He'd been caught out a couple of months before, but he'd assured her that wasn't normally the case and he had some kind of cage setup that he usually used when he went all wolfie. She pushed thoughts of Liam out of her mind. She had plenty of other things to think about.

There was a knock at the door.

Rosemary opened it to find Burk standing there, his skin looking pasty. He was holding an umbrella.

"I didn't know you could go outside in daylight," said Rosemary. It was only slightly awkward seeing him for the first time since their little incident in the middle of town.

"It's a cloudy day," said Burk. "Plus, I'm wearing incredibly high SPF sunscreen and the umbrella's for shade."

"I figured," said Rosemary. "What do you want?"

"Can I come in? It's a bit risky being out here."

"Sure." She stepped aside and let him in through the front door. "How can I help you?" There was slight rigidity in her voice considering everything else that was going on. She hardly needed the disruption.

"I know you're doing something for Beltane to try to stop the fires," said Burk.

"Did Marjie tell you?" Rosemary asked. "There's no such thing as a secret in this town, is there?"

"I might have just figured it out myself," said Burk. "I heard about the fire at the school. The mayor thinks that cancelling Beltane is going to help settle things down. But he's wrong, isn't he?"

"That's what I think," said Neve, stepping towards them. "Look, you're not going to be able to stop us. We know it's risky, but we've got to do something."

"I'm not trying to stop you," said Burk. "I'm trying to help."

"Oh, good," said Rosemary. "Now...you can help by staying out of the way and stepping in if necessary."

"Is that all?" Burk asked, sounding a little disappointed.

"Do you actually want to help?" Rosemary asked. "Or are you just getting your action kicks?"

Burk gave her a slightly offended look.

"I know you're a vampire. You've been around a long time, life gets boring. Maybe you're here for a little entertainment."

"I'm just offering to help," Burk said defensively. "Is something wrong? Did I do something to offend you?"

Rosemary shook herself. “No, sorry. I'm just a bit stressed. Sure you can help. I just I don't have the bandwidth to figure out how at the moment.”

“Never mind, leave that to me,” said Neve. “Come this way. Mr. Vam...I mean Capricorn man.”

Rosemary laughed at Neve’s deliberate use of the code word for vampires that she and Athena had come up with.

Burk raised his eyebrows questioningly, but didn’t ask any questions.

As Burk followed Neve through the house, Dain came out of the living room, raising himself up to his full height and squaring his shoulders in some kind of display of alpha-maleness.

Rosemary giggled.

“What's *he* doing here?” Dain said.

“Helping,” said Rosemary cheerfully. “Which is what you're supposed to be doing, remember? And it would be in your best interests to listen to Neve, instead of bothering me. I've got enough to think about with the spell.”

“What's the spell? I might be able to help,” said Dain.

“Since when do *you* do spells?” Rosemary narrowed her eyes.

“I have fae magic,” said Dain defensively.

“Yes, but fae magic is not the same as witch magic,” said Rosemary.

“Just run along and see what Neve’s strategy is, and we'll ask you to pitch in with the magic if necessary.”

“Okay, fine,” Dain huffed and walked away.

“All right, then,” said Rosemary, walking into the kitchen where her daughter was dutifully doing her chores. “As soon as you're finished that, I need you to help me with a few things.”

“Okay, Mum, but I meant what I said. I asked around, and my friends are going to help us.”

“Do their parents know?” Rosemary asked. “Actually, it's probably better if you don't tell me. We need the numbers. This might be dangerous, but it's going to be a heck of a lot worse if we don't pull it off.”

“I'm glad you think so,” Athena said, crossing her arms in satisfaction.

There was another knock at the door. Rosemary sighed dramatically. “Not more disruptions!”

Athena opened the door to find Una and Ashwyn. “Thanks for coming,” she said.

Rosemary felt more guarded than Athena seemed to be, judging by her cheerful smile.

"Come through here." Athena showed them into the dining room, as the living room was currently occupied by the strategy department, meaning Neve, accompanied by Burk and Dain.

Rosemary had plenty of prep work to do and she would have much rather been watching the rooster-like behavior of the two men and laughing at them than having to have this awkward conversation.

"Maybe I'll go and get Neve," she said.

Athena shot her mother a warning glance.

What? Rosemary asked in her mind.

"I'm going to go and make tea," said Athena, slightly too loudly. "Why don't you sit down and be polite, Mum?"

Rosemary reluctantly sat down at the table.

"You look stressed," said Una. "What's going on?"

"It's complicated," said Rosemary.

Neve came in a moment later. "Oh, you're here!"

"What's this about?" Una asked. "I thought it was supposed to be babysitting."

"Yes, err..." Rosemary wanted to leave the room, but Athena had made it too awkward. "We just have a few screening questions first," she said.

Neve gave her an odd look.

"Why can't I do anything right at the moment?" Rosemary asked.

"Look," said Neve. "Something strange is going on around town and we want to make sure that you're not part of it, so we do want to ask you a few questions. If that's all right."

"Of course," said Ashwyn, smiling in a friendly way.

"Is this to do with the fires?" Una asked, concerned. They both sounded so genuine and earnest. With each question they were asked Rosemary ceded a little bit more mental ground to the realisation that they must be innocent in all this.

Athena brought in the tea and Rosemary followed her out.

"What was all that about?" Rosemary asked.

"You were trying to avoid an awkward situation," Athena said with an accusatory tone.

"So what?" asked Rosemary.

"Mum, you're the suspicious one here. If you're really worried about those two, you needed to be there to hear them out. Otherwise you weren't going to stop being suspicious of them, and it would defeat the whole purpose."

"Oh fine," said Rosemary. "You have a point."

"And?" said Athena, bracing her hands questioningly.

"And they seemed perfectly innocent to me," Rosemary conceded. "I'll trust them to look after the kids."

"That's perfect," said Athena. "Now come and help me with this spell."

"I thought I was in charge of the magic," Rosemary said, crossing her arms.

"Mum, don't pout. It's ridiculous." Athena laughed. "You're just getting wound up. Why don't you go have a bath and relax? You're no good to any of us if you're frazzled. You need to recharge your batteries."

"There's no time for baths," said Rosemary.

"Yes, there is. We've still got several hours and everything is in hand. I'll make you a cup of Marjie's special tea and your job is to relax."

"Why is relaxing the hardest thing to do sometimes?" Rosemary complained. But after a lot more magical preparation, she took Athena's advice and stalked upstairs to have a bath. After all, baths were important.

The relaxation actually did help her to clear her mind somewhat. She remembered several things that would be helpful for the ritual. She also remembered to put on the heirloom emerald necklace to help her focus. She had avoided wearing it recently because she wanted to hone her powers without the crutch of the magical talisman, but tonight, she wasn't going to take any chances.

Thirty-Eight

Rosemary emerged in her fluffy bathrobe after what had turned out to be a rather long and relaxing soak in the tub. A glorious sunset lit up the sky outside her bedroom window.

"Athena!" she called out. "Look."

Athena came through from her own room and they watched the fiery sky.

"I should be getting dressed," said Rosemary. "But just look at that."

"Red sky at night, shepherd's delight, isn't it?"

"I hope it's not a warning," said Rosemary. "Although we hardly need a warning for danger when we know we're going straight into the thick of it."

"We'll be alright, though," said Athena. "We always are. We've gone through lots of dangerous situations before, at least since we moved here."

"I told you this town was trouble," said Rosemary.

"It might be that," said Athena. "But is there anywhere you'd rather live?"

"No, of course not," said Rosemary. "Plus, I figure now we've got access to the Thorn family magic, danger is going to follow us wherever we go."

"That's right," said Athena. "And this town needs us. It's good to be needed."

Rosemary thought back to what Dain had said earlier about how they didn't need him. They'd done all right in his absence. That was true, but she could see that there was pain behind his words. He needed to be needed.

Everyone needs to belong and be part of something that isn't just themselves. And this little quirky and oddly dangerous town is where we belong.

"You're right. We'll get through this," she said to Athena. "But either way, you're not going to get out of doing the dishes."

"I wouldn't dream of it," said Athena with a smile. "Now, get dressed, or we're going to be late."

Thirty-Nine

As soon as darkness fell, they left Thorn Manor, driving in procession to the town centre.

Athena felt a nervous flutter in her chest as they drove through the quiet streets. "There would normally be a lot more people around on the night of a seasonal festival," she muttered from the back of the car as Rosemary drove with Dain in the passenger seat.

He'd insisted on coming with them. Burk had taken his own car and so had Neve.

"It does seem awfully quiet for a Saturday night, in general," said Rosemary. "But I guess the shops do close early around here."

Athena felt even more nervous as she realised how eerie the deserted town seemed.

They pulled up next to Marjie's tea shop. She was waiting outside, holding a rolling pin.

"What's that for?" Rosemary asked.

"It's a weapon," said Marjie. "I've got a broom too."

"Maybe try a sword or something," Athena suggested.

"Where are your weapons, then?" Marjie asked.

Rosemary held up her hands and twiddled her fingers around. "This is all I need."

"Dear, dear," said Marjie. "Look, the pies are ready."

She nipped inside the shop and returned with a tray containing paper bags of delicious smelling beef pies.

"Feel free to pop in if you need anything to drink," said Marjie. "I'll leave the door unlocked while we're here."

Athena took a pie and bit into it. Despite the fact that her brain was occupied with a million different worries, she couldn't help sighing at the delicious, rich gravy and crumbly pastry.

"Marjie, you're a legend," she said with her mouth half full.

"Close your mouth when you're talking," said Rosemary. "I mean, don't speak with your mouth...eat with your mouth full, don't speak with your mouth open up. Oh! You know what I mean!"

"Athena!" a voice called out.

She turned to see Elise approaching with Felix in his fox form just behind her, followed by a rather large bear. Sam brought up the rear.

"You came!" said Athena.

"Of course," said Elise.

Athena smiled and gave Elise and Sam hugs. "Thanks for coming," she said. "We're in way over our heads. We have no idea what we're doing."

"We wouldn't miss it," said Sam.

"I'm a little surprised, actually," Athena admitted. "I wondered if...after yesterday at school, nobody would ever want to talk to me again."

"I figured what must have happened," said Elise. "I hope you don't mind, I explained it to the others."

"That's fine," said Athena.

"But we were sure you hadn't done anything on purpose," said Sam. "And then when you texted today...Well, of course we had to help."

"You're our friend and that's what's important," said Elise. "Regardless of what you accidentally let into the earth realm."

"Thank you," said Athena. She was still getting used to having real friends.

"Umm..." She ogled the slightly terrifying bear who she knew was probably Deron. "What are we going to do with a couple of stray animals?"

"They're much stronger in their shifter forms," said Elise. "You'll see."

"Ahh," said Marjie. "There you all are!"

"You knew we were coming?" Elise asked.

Athena looked around awkwardly, hoping Marjie wasn't about to send her friends packing.

"Of course you'd come. I prepared some special charms just for you. If any creatures appear, throw them and duck." Marjie held out a brown paper bag to both the humanoid children.

Felix looked up expectantly.

"You're only allowed one if you're in human form," said Marjie sternly. "Foxes can't throw."

Felix looked down at the ground, making a whining noise, and skulked off.

Athena laughed nervously. She knew the evening ahead was going to be dangerous and hoped she didn't regret inviting her friends. Even with the additional people they were still going to be a bit light in terms of holding a proper town ritual, let alone fighting off potential hordes of flaming beasts.

Mum's protection spells better work!

"Right. So what's the plan?" Elise asked.

Neve frowned and turned towards Rosemary. "Are you sure it's a good idea to allow children to be here?"

"We're almost adults," said Elise. "And Mum's even here."

"She is?" Rosemary asked.

They turned to see Fleur locking up her car, holding a big tray of something sparkly.

"I told her all about it," said Elise. "She insisted on coming to help."

"And so have I!" said a familiar voice. Ferg appeared from a side street. He was wearing a brown cloak.

"What are you doing here?" Rosemary asked.

"I've come to officiate, of course," said Ferg.

"I thought you'd be following the rules," said Marjie.

Ferg looked stern. "Unfortunately, this was a difficult situation for me. I'm usually a stickler for the rules as you know, but I can't abide a town festival being cancelled, especially not on such short notice. It was outrageous."

"Great," said Rosemary. "The more the merrier!"

They began setting up the ritual, placing the red crystals at strategic points in the town circle.

Athena noticed that her father and Burk seemed to be studiously avoiding each other. She found it hilarious, the pickle her mother was getting herself into with these various men who were obviously interested in her and Rosemary's flat-out refusal to be involved with any one of them. Though she did feel a little bit sorry for both men. For Burk, who had done nothing but be the perfect gentleman, and who Rosemary was treating with slight coldness, and also for her father, who might have been totally useless at times. He wasn't so bad, and it wasn't just because he'd had a hard life that Athena was close to forgiving him. There was also everything he'd done to try and make up for it lately.

Everyone deserves a chance to redeem themselves, she thought. *If people can forgive me for letting the fire sprites into the earth realm, then maybe I can work on forgiving dad.*

They began laying out crystals and herbs to prepare for the ritual. Marjie set up the Beltane fire. Meanwhile, Ferg walked to the centre of the circle and set a little brown drawstring pouch gently on the ground.

"What's that?" Rosemary asked, her hands poised with a bundle of protective herbs she was laying around the perimeter.

Ferg didn't reply. He took three paces back and muttered a charm under his breath.

The brown pouch twitched slightly and then out popped a candy-striped pole, ten feet high and strung with ribbons.

"The maypole, of course," Ferg said.

Athena clapped and her friends cheered.

Rosemary narrowed her eyes at Ferg. "You could have warned me. I was getting worried."

Ferg turned towards Rosemary. "Nothing to worry about." He saluted and then walked off towards Marjie and her fire, leaving Rosemary shaking her head.

Forty

Rosemary glanced around for one final check to ensure the herbs and crystals were all in place for the protective spells she'd prepped for.

Everything was laid out in preparation for the ritual and they'd arranged themselves in a loose circle on the grass, leaving enough space in the middle for something dangerous to enter.

I hope this works!

Ferg stepped slightly further into the centre and began to officiate the Beltane ritual. He was so comfortable, as if this were a normal festival and not a last minute attempt to stop arsonist cults.

"At this time of year, we give thanks to the start of summer," he said. "And the many blessings of richness and fertility it bestows upon us."

Rosemary had a prickling at the back of her neck as if she was being watched.

She looked around to see more people from the town had appeared, including Nesta who must have found someone else to look after the child and old woman at their house. Sherry was there, and so was the mayor's husband, Zade, along with Agatha Twigg and Covvey. Ashwyn appeared too. Either she'd come to help once the children were settled in for the night, or perhaps something more sinister was afoot.

It seemed that a lot of people had kind of summoned themselves to the ritual, and Rosemary was slightly suspicious of all of them.

She eyed them one-by-one, wondering if any or all the uninvited guests were involved in the fires.

Mum, stop glaring at people. It's awkward. Athena's voice sounded in Rosemary's head.

But how did they know to come here? Are they all Bloodstones?!

Athena gave her a meaningful look from where she stood across the circle. *Didn't you stop to think that this ceremony has been practiced here for centuries? People weren't going to stop just because some mayor called it off.*

Rosemary made a point to smile instead of anything that could be misconstrued as glaring. *Maybe you have a point, but they shouldn't be here. They probably have no idea they're putting themselves in grave danger.*

Athena didn't respond. Maybe she had stopped listening in to Rosemary's thoughts.

As Ferg continued to talk, Rosemary wanted to warn them all off. It wasn't safe. But she knew it was too late. Even if the townsfolk tried to leave now there was no guarantee they'd escape what was to come, and besides, there was a certain strength in numbers.

Instead, she connected mentally with the earth beneath her. She could sense the crystals and flowers she'd placed strategically around the circle. She linked her magic through them now – both the old Thorn family magic that coursed through her veins, and her own unique brand of magic.

She felt the crystals respond to her as her magic pulsed through them, beginning to weave the spell around them all, protecting the circle from harm, wrapping delicate white protective light around them.

Ferg raised his hands and announced that the circle be cast.

Marjie walked around the perimeter, waving a little wooden wand with a crystal stuck to the end of it, adding her own magic to that which Rosemary had already woven, strengthening their protections further.

A third source of magic joined in the mix. Rosemary glanced at Athena, who nodded. She smiled back. Her daughter's magic was powerful on both sides. The fae magic from Dain's side had a distinctly aromatic quality that Rosemary hadn't noticed before. It reminded her of elderflower cordial.

"The circle is cast. We are between the worlds. Beyond the bounds of time," Marjie said. "Where light and dark meet as one. Together we are safe. Together we are strong."

She resumed her place in the circle.

It was time for the directions and elements to be called.

Athena turned to the east, and everyone followed suit. She summoned element of air, with intellect and clarity.

Then turned to the south and Rosemary summoned the element of fire, passion and drive.

Marjie summoned the element of water, emotion and empathy, and then finally, Neve summoned the element of earth, matter, prosperity, and the physical world, grounding and determination. Rosemary smiled as she felt the energy click into place. Neve had been hesitant to take part as she wasn't particularly magical, but that kind of grounded practicality was just what they needed for the earth element.

After the quarters and the elements were summoned, Athena called out to the maiden goddess, Brigid.

Oh great maiden, Brigid, we honour you tonight.

Then Rosemary did the same for the crone goddess, Cerridwen.

Cerridwen, we call you forth to our circle, oh grandmother, guardian of the old ways and of inspiration, goddess of transformation and rebirth. We honour you.

They had figured if an older god was trying to break through, it wouldn't hurt to have some of the more modern, and hopefully more spry, god relatives present, or at least in their favour.

They lit the small fires they'd prepared inside the circle, then began to circle around it, as was the traditional practice at Beltane.

It seemed a rather solemn affair compared to what Rosemary would have expected from a usual festival. After all, they were supposed to be celebrating fertility and the beginnings of summer.

As the ceremony continued, the atmosphere lightened to one of merriment. Ferg began patting a drum to a jaunty beat. Fleur pulled out panpipes and played a little tune.

The participants came forward, taking handfuls of flower petals from the baskets that Marjie had brought, to scatter around the circle. Some took ribbons from the maypole and skipped around it, weaving the colourful strands over and under each other as they went.

Sherry, Zade, Agatha, and Ashwyn began dancing around the circle and were joined by others, as they made their way towards the small Beltane fire.

Traditionally, those who wanted children or to bring something to fruition in their life, would jump over the fire, thinking of what they wanted. And Rosemary figured, since nothing else in a dramatic nature had occurred, she might as well jump over it thinking of her dream chocolate shop. Though she was pleased to see that Athena didn't jump over it at all.

Rosemary certainly wasn't ready to be a grandmother yet.

She carried on around the circle, turning back to watch as Nesta jumped over the tiny fire, tripping a little as she did so, landing with a laugh as Neve caught her. Rosemary smiled at her friends. They really did make a lovely couple.

The joy and laughter of the celebration was interrupted by a shriek and then a banging sound.

Rosemary turned to see the dreaded and familiar hooded figures approaching.

"I knew it!" she cried out to Athena. "It's the Bloodstone Society. They are the ones behind all this."

The woman in the middle peeled back the hood of her cloak. Her pale blonde hair gleamed in the low light of the lanterns around the town centre.

Rosemary breathed a sigh of relief that her paranoid suspicions about her various blonde friends were unwarranted. She glared at the woman. "Still masked, I see. What's the matter? Not brave enough to show your face?"

The woman threw back her head with a gravelly laugh. She removed her gleaming butterfly mask to reveal a beautiful pale and familiar face.

"Lamorna!" Marjie shrieked. "I cannot believe this! I trusted you to work in my shop and all the while you were plotting against us."

"And spying, no doubt," said Athena.

Lamorna smiled in glee. "It was so easy to put on a simpering act and win your trust," she said, pouting.

"Shut it, blondie," said Rosemary. "It's time for you and your Bloodstone cronies to get out of my town!"

"I don't think so," said Lamorna. "In fact, we quite like it here."

"Move out of the way," Rosemary cried, motioning to people to run around to the other side of the circle. She sent a blast of bright purple energy out towards the newcomers.

It seemed to hit an invisible barrier on the inside of the magical dome that encased the ritual. Rosemary hadn't realised that when they'd cast the circle they'd created an actual energy membrane or forcefield, an unfortunate own-goal.

The energy ball made its way through with some encouragement but it was too slow. The Bloodstone members just stepped to the side.

Lamorna laughed. "You told me she was silly, but I didn't realise she was this silly."

"That's just my Gemini ascendant," Rosemary muttered.

Athena gave her a sympathetic look.

"Anyway, who are you talking to? Who told you I'm silly?"

Lamorna turned to the figure next to her whose cloak slipped back enough for Rosemary to recognise Despina with her perfect shiny bob of hair and her pastel pink collar.

"Not now!" said Rosemary. "The last thing I need is to get a rash."

"She's not an estate agent anymore," said Athena from the east of the circle. "I told you your so-called allergy was psychosomatic."

"Once an estate agent always an estate agent."

"What are you talking about?" Lamorna asked. She was clearly the leader.

Rosemary grimaced. "Well, at least it looks like we're protected in here. Plus, we've got way more power than the three of you. Why don't you just go on home?"

Lamorna threw back her head with another gravelly laugh. "We have reinforcements coming."

"Of course you do," said Rosemary. "Why wouldn't you have planned ahead when you've orchestrated all this?"

Lamorna looked at her in shock. "What do you mean? We thought you and your silly witch friends were behind the fires."

"Why on earth would we do that?" Rosemary glared at Lamorna. "It's not like we're in a dodgy power-mad secret society or anything!"

"Don't act all innocent," Despina said. "Why else would you be here when the ritual was supposedly cancelled?"

"Wait a minute," said Athena. "If you're not here for the Cavalia, what are you doing here, then?"

"We're here to stop you," said Lamorna. "Messing with the old gods is a step too far. The Bloodstone Society is coming back, and believe me when I say that *we* are going to be the major magical power in these parts. No old gods are getting in our way."

Rosemary looked around the group in confusion. "So you're here to stamp out the competition?"

"That's right," said Despina. "Whatever cult of Belamus you're trying to start here – it's not going to happen!"

"I'm not bloody starting any cults!" Rosemary cried.

Despina rolled her eyes. "Then who?"

There was a sudden crackle from the tiny fire in the circle, and the little cauldron burst into life as an enormous fire lit the centre of where they stood.

Rosemary reached for her magical light barrier, sending more energy through it, around the circle, in the hopes that people wouldn't be affected by the magical fire.

"It's too late," said Despina. "He's here."

"Let's go!" Lamorna cried.

There was a great crackling sound followed by booming laughter.

A series of beasts burst through the flames.

Rosemary looked back at the Bloodstone members to see their eyes bulging.

"I think we'll just leave you to it," Despina said and they backed away into the shadows.

Rosemary thought about going after the Bloodstones, but she had bigger fish to fry. Her problems had just grown astronomically larger. She eyed the flaming beasts in horror. Some were at least eight feet tall. Others had wings. "This is going to get messy."

"Let us out of the protection," said Marjie, hammering against the invisible barrier that Rosemary had put up, which seemed to have grown and warped to encase all the ritual participants individually. "We need to fight. We're prepared." She held up a bright yellow bundle from her patchwork carry bag.

Covvey growled and flexed his muscles. "Let us fight, lass."

Rosemary tensed. "It's not safe."

"We came prepared to fight," said Fleur.

Rosemary looked around to see Ferg holding a staff and Ashwyn with bottles of potions. Everyone had some kind of weapon or magical tool. Even those who Rosemary had assumed had just wandered into town for the ritual.

"But how did everyone know to bring weapons?" Rosemary asked.

"After Elise told me what was going on I called up some allies around the town," said Fleur. "We couldn't let you face this alone."

It was all kind of moving, but Rosemary didn't have time to be sentimental.

"Alright, then," she said. "I'll drop the barrier, but if things get out of control I want everyone to run away."

"We're not stupid," said Sam. "We're here to fight, not to be annihilated."

Rosemary allowed her magic to shrink back, so that it was no longer a barrier, but she kept a small coating in place, covering the participants, to protect them against any inappropriate effects of the fire.

A huge minotaur lumbered forward. He raised a gleaming golden bow, aiming a flaming arrow towards Rosemary, and let fly.

She raised her arm and blocked it with a magic shield, just as Marjie hurled a yellow parcel at the beast. It exploded into dozens of enchanted butterflies that swarmed around its head and chased, tripping it to the ground.

"That was unexpected," said Athena.

Covvey shifted into an enormous wolf and growled just as Felix in fox form lunged at one of the fiery nymphs.

Rosemary shrieked. "Don't get burnt!"

"Don't worry," said Elise. "His fox form is impervious to fire."

"Including magical fire?" Rosemary asked.

"We'll soon find out," said Athena.

Rosemary strengthened the protective magical barrier over herself and extended the same favour out to the townsfolk around her, hoping that it would keep them from danger of either the violent or seductive kind. She could sense Athena's magic working with hers, fortifying their protections.

Rosemary looked towards her daughter, just as Athena cried, "Mum!"

She turned to see a fiery centaur running towards her.

"Don't worry, I've got this," Athena said and blasted it out of the way with a big sizzling ball of lightning.

"That was impressive." Rosemary beamed. "You've been practicing!"

The fight continued. The giant wolf that was Covvey barrelled down multiple beasts at a time before taking a break and shifting back to human form to help Agatha as she wielded an enormous double-headed staff that shot blasts of water in multiple directions.

"What's that?" Rosemary called out.

"One of my little inventions," said Agatha. "I call it the Aquifyer."

"Handy!" said Rosemary. She noticed Fleur and Elise nearby as they sparred with some fire nymphs not far away, moving with a kind of fluidity that Rosemary wouldn't have thought possible. It almost looked like a dance as they ducked and kicked and punched the nymphs that darted around out of their reach and then circled back, baring their teeth and claws as they hissed at their opponents.

Elise and her mother joined hands. Bright rainbows burst from between them, circling the fire sprites, delicate flaming creatures that they were, and wrapping around them, binding them and sending them sprawling into the ground.

Zade wielded an impressive-looking glowing sword. He stood back-to-back with Ferg who got to work using his staff like a spear. He battled a large hairy fire creature bearing a flaming pitchfork. Ferg was nimbler than Rosemary had expected. The creature lunged for him with the sword and Ferg ducked, rolled on the ground, and then sent his staff straight towards the chin of the creature.

Burk stood off to the side with an intense expression on his face. No doubt he was holding back because of the damage the fire would do to his vampire form. Dain, on the other hand, was right amongst it, punching nymphs, sprites, and beasties alike. He was a ball of chaos, grabbing them and spinning them around, flinging them into each other.

Rosemary raised her hands, pressing her fingers together. She wove a much stronger fire-protection spell in mid-air and sent it floating towards Burk. His expression transformed into one of glee as it coated him like liquid. He nodded in her direction and then barrelled into the fire, no longer afraid of the flames.

Ashwyn threw a potion towards the centre, nearly striking the largest beast who had been standing there, roaring for a while. The beast stepped out of the way and continued roaring. The potion hit the ground, crackled and hissed, sending bright silver sparks into the air in a cloud of steam. The earth beneath it melted.

She sure knows how to brew up something nasty. Remind me to never get on her bad side.

The battle was in full swing. The smell of smoke and charred earth hung thick in the air, but above that was a sweeter scent note, it was heady, almost soapy, but Rosemary didn't have time to think about it. Between sending out blasts of magic and hurling flaming beasts to the ground as they attacked, Rosemary watched the chaos unfold all around. The bear and fox and various magical people all attacked or were attacked by the fiery creatures.

Sid and her firefighting team had been called in by Neve. They lined up around the outside of the town square. They had hoses and all the hydrants on full blast, dousing the flames that tried to escape the outskirts of the circle, but they hadn't gained much ground.

Rosemary tried to connect with the element of water, but it evaded her. It turned out that in the heat of battle, she needed to fight fire with fire.

The Myrtlewood townsfolk had managed to hold back the swarm of flaming beasties well, but the tide seemed to be turning, as more and more creatures emerged from the flames. Some flew through with fiery wings. Others formed a stampede.

Rosemary threw up the barrier spell she'd practiced, but it was all she could do hold them back.

Suddenly, there was an air wrenching crack and an enormous chariot burst through, hovering in mid-air. It glistened and gleamed in gold. Atop it sat an enormous man, who gleamed golden himself with huge horns stretching up into the sky.

"The Cavalia begins!" he cried. "I have been summoned."

"Belamus!" The fire creatures all began to chant and bow before him.

"Heed my power and delight!"

"Delight?" Rosemary called back. "What kind of delight is this?"

"It is a celebration of all that is bright in the world!" the old god bellowed. The sheer size of him made Rosemary feel tiny.

The old god's voice rumbled through them; Rosemary felt it shaking her bones. "Thank you for summoning me, human creatures, frail as you are. I heeded your call."

"It wasn't us," said Athena, but Belamus took no notice.

"Now I'm ready to receive my sacrifice."

"Sacrifice?" Rosemary asked. She looked around at the other townsfolk who were all looking as equally terrified as she felt. "We didn't hear anything about a sacrifice."

Belamus roared. "You must sacrifice a beast to me. A beast of the earth to appease and delight me." He looked around. "But here, you have only young little beasties." He gestured towards Deron and Felix. "Is this meant to be a befitting sacrifice?"

"No!" Athena shouted. "They're not sacrifices!"

Just then, a howl sounded off in the distance.

Rosemary looked around, but she couldn't see anything.

"Are you saying you summoned me here without a sacrifice?" Belamus growled.

"The thing is," said Rosemary, her heart racing almost as fast as her mind as she struggled to come up with a solution to their catastrophic predicament, "we didn't exactly want you here at all. It's all a big misunderstanding and I hope you don't mind just turning around and going home. Sorry for the inconvenience."

The god glowered at her. "You frail and worthless humans! How dare you insult my power like this!"

There was another howl and Rosemary turned to see a huge wolf-like creature stalking towards the circle.

Oh no! It's Liam!

She hadn't returned his calls and now it was too late. Somehow, he'd not managed to keep himself shackled up and had come to join the party.

Marjie and some of the others were glaring at the huge wolf-man as if he were part of the evil, and for all Rosemary knew, maybe he was. He certainly wasn't up to any good.

"Aha!" said Belamus. "A great beast! A great beast befitting to be sacrificed for me! That will do. Kill him!"

"No!" Rosemary shouted as Liam, or at least the werewolf that Rosemary assumed was Liam, lunged towards the circle.

Rosemary raised her arms to try to stop him, but hesitated. If she blasted him with her magic, his secret might well be revealed in front of half the town. Before she had time to weigh up the risks, Burk flew across and attacked, blocking the werewolf's path, and so did Dain.

"A great battle in my honour!" Belamus bellowed again and laughed.

"Werewolf, vampire, and fae," Rosemary muttered. "It seems remiss not to make a bad joke about a bar." She wasn't bothering to censor herself as she wondered how much water she could draw from the four hydrants around the town.

"Not now!" said Athena. "We've got plenty of time for your awful sense of humour later on. We've got to stop them!"

"I'm sure they'll be fine," said Rosemary.

"No, not them." Athena gestured back towards the flaming beasts, who were slowly advancing towards Rosemary's would-be suitors.

"What about your essay?" Rosemary asked.

"This is no time to be asking about schoolwork, Mum!"

"No. Just think. Is there anyone we could call on...anything that could stop Belamus?"

"Depending on which source you believe, once the beast is sacrificed," said Athena, "the door will be flung wide open, and thousands of fiery creatures will come through and ravage the human realm, bringing a renewed era of Belamus!"

"You didn't think to tell me there was a sacrifice?!" Rosemary asked. "Oh, never mind. That part's not very helpful. Anything else? If only there was somebody who could stand up to him."

"Now that gives me an idea," said Athena, ducking out of the way of a flaming arrow. "Remember how we called on the gods as part of our ritual. What if I actually tried to summon Brigid?"

"Brigid? Why Brigid? Do you think she's any match for this dude?"

"I don't know," said Athena, blasting a nymph with her magic. "But she is the patron goddess of this town. Maybe she'll be listening. Granny's books say that reciting Brigid's ancestry will bring protection."

"Worth a try," said Rosemary as she hurled a flaming beast aside. "Only...Do we know what it is?"

Athena pulled out her phone. "Hold them off for a second."

Rosemary blasted white light out towards all the fiery creatures nearby, knocking them back. " I won't be able to hold this up for very long."

"Here goes!" said Athena, and she began to recite.

This is the genealogy of the holy maiden, Brigid.
Radiant flame of gold,
Daughter of Dugall the Brown,
Son of Aodh, son of Art, son of Conn,
Son of Crearer, Son of Cis, son of Carmac, son of Carruin,
Every day and every night
That I say the genealogy of Brigid,
I shall not be killed, I shall not be harried,
I shall not be put in a cell, I shall not be wounded,
Neither shall Spirit leave me in forgetfulness.
No fire, no sun, no moon shall burn me,
No lake, no water, nor sea shall drown me,
No arrow of fairy nor dart of fay shall wound me
And I under the protection of the great goddess
And my gentle foster-mother is my beloved Brigid.

Athena raised her arms in the air and said, "Fair Brigid, patron goddess of Myrtlewood, our people need you. Please come forth. I summon you, I beseech you!"

"That was a bit dramatic," said Rosemary. "Remind me to sign you up for drama lessons."

"Shush!" said Athena. "I'm trying to focus."

The air around them seemed to still and then a big gust of wind blew through, bringing a flurry of flower petals with it. The maypole ribbons began to spin as it swept around the circle. With it came the warm floral scents of spring.

An enormous white light burst into the town square.

Rosemary shielded her eyes and peered through the glare. An enormous being stood there, towering over them, six stories high.

"Goddess Brigid," said Athena.

The goddess looked down at them curiously and then turned her attention across the circle, fixing her gaze on the old god.

"Ah..." said Athena. "As you might notice..."

Belamus stood there with a somewhat sheepish grin now plastered across his face.

"Grandad!" said Brigid. "What are you doing here? This is *my* town."

"I'm...I'm here for the Cavalia," said Belamus. "These people summoned me. They...need my help. They want to bring things back to the old way."

His words stirred something inside Rosemary's memory. She couldn't quite put her finger on what.

"No, you absolutely will not do that," said Brigid. "The old ways are over, granddad. You're coming with me." She snapped her fingers, and the entire fiery scene in front of them vanished, along with the beasts, leaving no trace behind, not even scorch marks.

"Fair people of Myrtlewood," said Brigid. "My apologies for the disruptions. I'm afraid I must go now, to attend to some family matters."

"Thank you!" Rosemary and Athena both called out after her as she vanished slowly, leaving a floating trail of spring blossoms hovering magically in the air in her wake.

"Well, that was unexpected," said Rosemary. "I'm glad your Brigid thing worked."

"Yeah. Thank goodness I'm becoming a bit of a swot. Getting geeky about my assignments."

They surveyed the carnage, including a large scorch mark in the middle of the town square, much bigger than the one from the previous fire from a few days before. At least a few people seemed to be limping or mildly injured. Everyone was accounted for.

"Everything's going to be alright," said Rosemary, somewhat surprising herself with this realisation. "We did it."

"I did it, you mean," said Athena. "You just stumbled and floundered, then I led us to victory."

"You're still on dishes duty," said Rosemary. "For a very long time."

Athena sighed. "Oh, well. It'll be good practice for my automancy magic, I suppose."

Rosemary elbowed her playfully. "Seriously though. Thank you," she said. "I'm pretty sure we wouldn't have gotten out of this mess without you, at least without any serious injuries."

"No problem," said Athena. "When I make a mess, I like to be the one to summon a goddess to clean it up."

"That's how I raised you," said Rosemary proudly.

People milled around asking each other how they were for a few minutes, and then began cleaning up.

"You're all welcome back at my place," Rosemary announced.

"I'll bring the cake," said Marjie.

"I'll bring the wine," Sherry added.

"All right, it's settled," said Athena. "I'll take these bags to the car."

The scent of lily of the valley wafted over the town square and Rosemary turned to see someone standing in the entrance to one of the side streets.

"I'll meet you there," she said. "I've just got to take care of something."

She bolted after the shrouded figure, chasing them down the street next to Burk's law office.

"Stop where you are," Rosemary called. "Or this is not going to be pretty."

The person stopped and then turned back and lowered the scarf from around her head.

"I knew it!" said Rosemary. "Well, I didn't at first, but I did suspect you were up to something when you invited us to dinner, and then I got caught up with thinking it was the Bloodstone Society..."

"Must you ramble?" Elamina asked.

Rosemary noticed that despite her haughty tone, her cousin looked somewhat dishevelled. Her white blonde hair, normally perfectly in place, looked mussed, as if she'd been through some quite frantic endeavours, herself.

"Did the Bloodstones have no idea what was going on?" Rosemary asked. "Or was a that lie? Are they secretly working for you?"

Elamina threw back with a haughty cackle. "Those plebs? I wouldn't dream of working with anyone of their station."

"So even when you've been apprehended, you still insist on being an arrogant nutball?"

Elamina glared at her. "What gave me away? You all seemed perfectly occupied. You didn't even notice that I was watching from a distance."

"For a start, there's the stench of that god awful flower," said Rosemary. "That's a dead giveaway. Plus, when you invited us over for dinner at your house, you did talk about wanting things to go back to the old ways, which was kind of what that big horned guy said. I didn't remember until just before."

"You speak about the gods with such disrespect," said Elamina.

"Who's being disrespectful now?" Rosemary asked. "It's pretty rich accusing me, considering you set the town on fire and almost blew up the whole place. I've heard about blue-blooded conservatives romanticising the past, but this is ridiculous. And probably a whole lot more carnage would have happened if we hadn't stopped that guy."

"*That guy*," said Elamina, "is an ancient and respected being. He's incredibly powerful!"

"I don't really see the appeal," said Rosemary. "He's a little bit large and hairy for my liking."

Elamina scoffed. "If you only knew."

"Look," said Rosemary. "I don't mean to kink-shame you, but what on earth did you think you were playing at?"

"I'll have you know that I've managed to do what my father had been aiming to for decades."

Rosemary raised her eyebrows. "I don't want to know about your daddy issues! How did you even do it?"

Elamina glared at her. "There were various manoeuvres necessary, if you must know. For a start, I managed to get hold of some wild fire sprites through some of my contacts. They were the missing link, you see. With the power of my magic, and drawing close to Beltane, I managed to light the first fire."

"The one at the old Twigg farm," said Rosemary. "But that wasn't enough for you?"

Elamina laughed bitterly. "Not by a long shot. To have a chance of instigating the Cavalia I needed more sprites, but the only way I could think of was through the fae realm. It was fate really, that my own little cousin held the key."

"That's why you wanted to spend time with Athena wasn't it? You knew she had the power to cut through the veil. You know *what* she is...But you don't know *who* she is. She's not a play thing. You manipulated Athena. How?!"

"I might have planted some seeds," said Elamina. "I might have tried to hint to her, very subtly so that you wouldn't pick it up, that she had the power to get back to the place she missed so much. The place that you would be trying to keep her away from."

"I don't buy it," said Rosemary. "You're not *that* compelling. And Athena isn't gullible."

"If you really must know it was a simple suggestion, over dinner, followed by some carefully crafted chants to lure her outside and make her think it was a good idea to open the veil. Then my own ancient magic had the power to summon them through. After that first time I simply attached an invisible charm to her and she did the rest. It was brilliant, if I do say so myself."

Rage rose like bile in Rosemary's torso and she hurled a ball of red lightning at her cousin. Elamina deflected, but it sent her reeling into the side of the wall.

"How dare you enchant my daughter!"

Rosemary expected retaliation, but Elamina merely shrugged. There was something odd about her; she seemed almost deflated.

"I didn't hurt her," Elamina said quietly.

"That entire thing was totally inappropriate and dangerous. Not to mention all the fires that we've had recently which sent people into all sorts of strange behaviours."

"Inconvenient, but necessary," said Elamina. "The magic on the other side of my family goes back many thousands of years. It comes from the cult of Belamus. To truly harness it and master it, we needed his return. All my life I was told tales of the great power of Belamus. My father mourned the loss of the old gods to history. I was merely fulfilling my legacy."

"And did you get what you wanted?" Rosemary asked, unimpressed.

"The old ways..." Elamina began, but her voice trailed away.

"Well, that's just lovely," said Rosemary. "But this was all about power. What were you *really* seeking here, cousin? Did you want some kind of apocalypse?"

“The power is rightfully ours. The Bracewell family...”

Rosemary laughed. “How foolish to think you could harness the powers of an old god.”

Elamina looked bitter, and Rosemary could tell she had regrets.

“I guess it’s a bit late for a be-careful-what-you-wish-for moment,” said Rosemary.

Elamina glared at her. “If you hadn’t meddled—”

“What? You’d have fire and brimstone raining down on us? Is that honestly what you wanted?”

Elamina crossed her arms. “Mama and Papa may have been mistaken as to the risks. It is difficult to understand ancient history as not much was recorded and many things that were are not entirely accurate.”

“I suppose that’s as close as I’m going to get to you lot admitting you were wrong,” said Rosemary. “At least you admit to all of it. That’s very convenient because I have a detective friend who’s right over there...I wonder what the magical authorities will think.”

“I don't think so,” said Elamina. “You owe me one.”

“I only owe you some potion ingredients,” said Rosemary. “It’s not a get out of magical jail free card.”

“Now, that's where you're wrong,” said Elamina. “You owe a lot more than that. Imagine my surprise when my sweet, innocent, yet somewhat idiotic cousin came to me asking for spell ingredients, only to ask for something totally banned and illegal. Of course I helped out with what I could, but werewolf blood? That’s something else entirely. If I was to possess such a thing, the authorities would come knocking on my door. Indeed, the witching authorities do not show mercy to people possessing and using dangerous illicit substances like that. Let alone the fact that it now appears that you *know* a certain werewolf...one who turned up here tonight, no doubt. I don’t suppose you’d like to end up imprisoned in Bermuda for the next decade or two?”

Rosemary was speechless. Though Elamina had not specifically issued a threat, she'd certainly laid it all out. If Rosemary went to the authorities now, Elamina would be sure to tell them about the werewolf blood, which would not only put Liam in danger when they tracked him down, it would also land her with a whole lot of charges for harbouring a werewolf and using illicit magical substances or some such things.

“How can you—”

Elamina smirked. “Now, I know you're going to tell me how much you care about your daughter. And I know you do. I also know you're not about to risk everything you care about and set yourself up to be locked up in a prison cell, where you can't care for her."

"You absolute garbage face," said Rosemary. "How dare you?"

"How dare I what?" said Elamina. "I have not threatened, dear cousin. I'll let you do that yourself. I have more important things to do with my time."

"So that's it then?" said Rosemary. "You create total chaos, unleashing an old god and a whole lot of fiery beasties, and then you toddle off to your castle."

Elamina looked bitter. "I didn't really get what I wanted to out of the whole thing."

"Oh great," said Rosemary. "So you're bitter that Belamus was sent back?"

"It is a shame he disappeared so fast, before Derse and I had a chance to harness his energy for our own gain. But there's no point in wasting anymore time, cousin. I'm afraid I can't stay much longer. Things to do, people to see. You know the drill."

Rosemary sighed. She hated being caught in a checkmate situation like this. She couldn't put Liam at risk and she couldn't go to jail. She needed to be there to protect Athena.

"I won't go to the authorities," Rosemary conceded. "You win on that front, there's too much at stake."

Elamina smiled – not the fake smile she'd put on over dinner, but her genuine smile which was a lot colder and more frightening.

"See now, cousin. You are a bit slow but you do catch up, eventually."

"Maybe I won't go to the authorities," said Rosemary. "But I can still kick your arse and you're not going to tell anyone about it."

Rosemary held up her hands, summoning a giant purple ball of energy, crackling with lightning and fire.

Elamina screamed and dashed out of the way before disappearing into the night.

Rosemary laughed at herself, trying ease the bitterness she felt at being trumped like that. "At least it solves the mystery," she muttered. "Though I don't know if I can actually explain any of that to anyone else."

"You don't have to, Mum," said Athena, stepping from around the corner. "I heard all of that." She looked around to check that nobody else was listening. "It's Liam, isn't it? He was the werewolf."

"Athena, I..."

"I know. I won't tell anyone," said Athena. "It seems that werewolves are rather stigmatised in magical society. It seems a bit prejudiced if you ask me."

"I thought so," said Rosemary. "Anyway, what did you think about our dear cousin?"

"She's a nasty piece of work, isn't she?" Athena linked arms with her mother as they walked to the car.

"I'm glad you realise that," said Rosemary. "I'm sure Elamina thought I'd hide it from you so that I didn't share Liam's secret. She's still going to try and use you for something. I can tell by the way she talks about you as if you're some kind of treasured prize."

"That's one thing you don't have to worry about," said Athena. "Hell's going freeze over before I let that happen."

"Don't say that," said Rosemary. "I'm sure this town has a seasonal festival for exactly such a thing."

Athena laughed. "Okay, then." She put her arm around her mother. "Let's go home. We can talk about all of this and what it means another time."

"That sounds like a good idea," said Rosemary. "I'm in the mood for hot chocolate and a bit of good conversation, followed by a lot of very quiet time."

Forty-One

Rosemary stirred the enormous bubbling pot of hot chocolate on the stove, inhaling the heavenly scent.

Most of those who had been at the impromptu ritual had decided to come over to decompress after the dramatic events of the evening.

Marjie lined up mugs, ready for hot chocolate for Rosemary, while Athena showed her friends around the house, since only Elise had seen the inside of it before. Ashwyn admired Granny's crystals and chatted to Sherry while Fleur and others followed Dain into the living room. Of course, Liam was nowhere in sight, and Rosemary hoped he was okay. Dain had informed her that Burk had escorted him away from the town square and was keeping him somewhere safe. Rosemary wondered if this would mean letting the vampire in on his secret, but that wasn't her issue to worry about.

Rosemary added an extra pinch of cinnamon and a dash of vanilla into the brew of hot chocolate.

"Mmm, smells delicious," said Ferg. He sat at the kitchen table as if he were someone incredibly important, staff still clasped in hand, while the foundling children stood around him, looking awestruck.

Rosemary had returned to find them all tucked up asleep in their beds, and Una sitting in an armchair with a book looking slightly tired herself, but satisfied. The children's slumber had not withstood the sounds created by so many people arriving. They had gotten up, confused and excited, and proceeded to run around the house. They were all going to be tired in the morning, but Rosemary didn't mind. Hopefully that would mean a proper sleep in.

With over a dozen visitors, Rosemary was pleased to see that the living room had grown to be bigger than usual. She and Marjie carried in trays of mugs filled with steaming hot chocolate.

Rosemary and Marjie entered the living room to find that the mayor had arrived at Thorn Manor.

"That's funny," Rosemary whispered to Marjie. "I thought he'd be too embarrassed to show his face after cancelling the ritual and everything."

"Oh, Don never misses a party. He must have snuck in," said Marjie. "I didn't notice him arrive."

Mr June insisted on doing a round of speeches, in which he thanked the townsfolk for all their hard work and somehow made it seem as if all of the good ideas were his own.

"How does he manage to take credit for everything when he wasn't even there?" Athena asked. "While he's supposed to be thanking us all?"

"Must be a gift," said Rosemary quietly, smiling at her daughter.

"Never mind," said Ashwyn, who was sitting next to Rosemary. "This hot chocolate is so divine that it makes up for any pompousness."

"Believe it or not, it's his way of apologising," said Marjie. "I know it sounds silly, but he's got a bit of a complex, and he's trying to include himself in things to show how much he approves."

Rosemary shrugged. "Oh well, it shows I have a lot to learn when it comes to our most esteemed town official."

Una giggled. "I'm so relieved it worked out. Ashwyn did some scrying after you left and saw what kind of danger everyone was going to be in. It really could have gone either way. So she decided to join in."

"It was probably good that she did come down," said Rosemary. "It was kind of touch and go there for a while. A lot of chaotic influences, including our local neighbourhood secret society and a couple of enormous gods."

"Sounds like quite the adventure," said Una.

"What about you?" Rosemary asked. "How did everything go?"

"It was lovely," said Una. "The kids are wonderful, so charming. I always wanted to have a big family. I love children, I just can't have any of my own."

"Well, they're free to a good home," said Rosemary.

"Seriously though," said Una. "What is going to happen to them? Surely they can't stay here indefinitely."

Rosemary pressed her lips into a thin line. "That is a problem. Now that

Neve and Nesta are back at their house all the time, and Dain wants to have a life of his own...I don't know how we're going to manage. Neve's tried to find them foster homes, but they are clearly magical and need special supervision."

"They certainly are," said Una. "That's partly why I find them so delightful. They remind me of something. Maybe it's to do with my fae lineage, I'm not sure, but I find being around them so soothing."

"They are particularly placid aren't they, for young children," said Rosemary. "Still, they need to run around a lot and they need to eat and so on."

"I managed to get them to make their own sandwiches for supper," said Una.

"That's an impressive start," said Rosemary. "You'll have them doing chores in no time."

Una watched the three children across the room. They were now all sitting dotingly around the mayor who continued to speak. He'd moved on to telling grand stories about the town and its relationship with gods and Beltane over the centuries, some of which would have been helpful to know before the evening's fiasco.

Rosemary watched Una's face light up at the sight of the children, before turning back.

"You wouldn't..." Una started. "I mean, I'm hardly qualified, but Ashwyn and I could look after them, at least for a while. I've always wondered about being a foster parent."

"Really?" Rosemary asked. "It's a big job. They're quite placid for children, but still, any kind of parenting is a lot of work."

"We have a big old house, not quite this big," said Una. "And if we can figure out some kind of childcare arrangements for during the day while we're in the shop..."

"Marjie has been talking about enrolling them in the local kindergarten," said Rosemary. "We just didn't know how long they were going to stick around Myrtlewood for, or whether they'd have to go further afield to find suitable foster homes."

"They really have nowhere else to go?" Ashwyn asked.

Rosemary shook her head. "Neve's tracked down some of the historical records she thinks relate to their families, but the problem is they're all from so far in the past that we have no idea whether their very distant, great, great nephews and so on, would want anything at all to do with them. We certainly can't force them off into people's lives like that. We really need to find foster carers who are ready, willing, and able...really prepared to have children around."

"They shouldn't leave Myrtlewood," said Ashwyn. "Surely not after all the change they've already gone through."

"That's probably right," said Rosemary. "Are you really serious, you'd consider adopting them, or fostering them temporarily at least?"

"Of course," said Una. "I was talking to Ashwyn about it, wasn't I? After we met them at your house a little while ago, I knew they needed a more permanent home, but I didn't want to be too pushy or anything. It's quite a big deal to come into somebody's house and say I want to foster the children you found in the fae realm."

"I'm almost certain nobody's ever done that before, actually," said Rosemary. "It's quite a unique predicament. But I'm thrilled that you're even considering it. Right now we've got so few options."

"Really?" said Una. "That's wonderful, isn't it, Ashwyn? We might be able to foster the children!"

Ashwyn grinned at her sister. "What are we getting ourselves into?"

Rosemary smiled and rubbed her hands together with glee.

Everything seemed to be falling into place. However, there was that small matter of Athena's school...the school that had almost completely burnt down in a magical fire.

Perhaps she'd be home-schooling Athena for a while, which didn't sound like the sort of endeavour either of them were prepared to embark on, especially when Rosemary was supposed to be trying to set up her own business.

After the hot chocolates, the townsfolk went home, leaving Athena, Rosemary, and a blissfully quiet house, after Una had offered to put the children to bed and sleep in the adjoining room.

Rosemary was glad she and Ashwyn hadn't got cold feet about the potential foster situation. Dain had called it a night, yawning and excusing himself, saying he'd had quite enough excitement for one millennia.

Athena was dutifully doing the dishes, although Rosemary did notice she was staring quite intently at the sink, perhaps trying to use her automancy magic to get the job done a lot faster.

"I wish I could show you," said Athena. "You should have seen that dynamo go...and the look on Beryl's face. It was priceless!"

"Speaking of school," said Rosemary. "It's such a shame about the fire.

You know it's funny, with all those children gone the house is going to feel quite empty. Think we'd have room for a few dozen more kids?"

"What are you talking about?"

"Just my very random thoughts. I've seen your school. There's only a handful of pupils in each class. Surely there's not more than fifty on the entire campus, despite how big and sprawling those old buildings are."

"Probably something like that." Athena's voice had a sharp edge to it. "Why are you talking about this now?"

"Maybe Thorn Manor can temporarily be Rosemary Thorn's Educational Establishment for Challenging Magical Students."

"Is that the official title?" Athena asked with a laugh. Rosemary laughed too. It was clearly a joke.

"That would be terribly embarrassing," said Athena. "I've got to keep you as far away from my classmates as possible. Although, imagine the look on Beryl's face if she found out she had to go to school at my house!"

A cracking and rumbling shook the house.

"What was that?" Rosemary clenched her fists as the rumbling continued. Then they noticed a shimmer of gold running around the room.

"Oh no," said Rosemary and Athena simultaneously.

"It's the house!" said Rosemary as they followed the sound to the west wing of the house. She pulled open the door to find the cobwebs being cleared from before their eyes, as the dusty abandoned looking wing was swept clean, and the wood began to gleam. New rooms formed around the corridor.

"Oh no!" said Athena. "I think the house was paying a little bit too much attention to your joke, Mum."

"Maybe it wasn't a joke." Rosemary crossed her arms.

"It's making classrooms!" Athena cried. "It's kind of amazing, but also, there's no way I'm going to school at home."

"It would just be a temporary arrangement," said Rosemary. "After all, your education is very important."

Epilogue

Lightning crashed through the sky, followed closely by rolling thunder.

The cloaked figures assembled in the old ruin of a castle, high up in the tower, overlooking the stormy ocean. Wind whipped through the busted stone walls.

A bald man with a pointed nose spoke first. "Why did you call us here, Despina? The weather is atrocious!"

Despina said nothing, as if she wouldn't dignify his protestations with a response. She merely pulled her pastel pink cloak tighter around her shoulders to protect her from the cold.

All eyes turned as a woman entered via the old spiral staircase. She wore a deep blue cloak and her white blonde hair tumbled out from the hood making her easily recognisable among her fellow society members. "We have more important things to think about than weather, Geoffrey," said Lamorna, her pale skin glistening in the moonlight.

Her mouth twitched at the corners as they all stared at her. They could tell she wasn't quite human, but none of them knew her secret. Not yet.

A loud wave crashed outside and Lamorna smiled.

"Hem, hem," said Despina. "Now that all the cell leaders of the Bloodstone Society are present and accounted for...and quiet." She eyed Geoffrey as she spoke. "We have some news."

There was a pause so full of anticipation, Despina wanted to prick it with a pin, but she drew it out, waiting for Lamorna.

"Those Myrtlewood pests with their fire sprites have given us a brilliant idea," Lamorna said. "Of course, you'll be aware of the rather fortuitous celestial alignments coming up this Solstice. Neptune will be in harmonious aspect to the full moon eclipse in Capricorn."

"Will you stop babbling about the stars already?" Geoffrey grumbled. "It's freezing!"

"Very well," said Despina. "You might be more interested in this!"

She pulled a black cloth from the small table in front of her.

Gasps echoed through the room as they all took in the sight of the small carved wooden box.

Geoffrey scoffed. "You really mean us to believe *she's* in there? After all this time..."

Despina frowned and glared at him. "Three months is hardly a long time where other dimensions are concerned. You're just trying to make a play for leadership. But guess what? It's not going to work, werewolf. You're too weak!"

The man growled and looked up at the half-moon, visible through the gaping holes in the ceiling. He bared his teeth and lunged for the box.

"Stop!" Despina cried, but Lamorna opened her mouth and a strange sound escaped.

Geoffrey froze, spellbound. They all watched, transfixed, as Lamorna opened a tiny silver vial, humming as she did so.

Glimmering liquid rose up from the small vessel as if coaxed by her voice. It sped towards Geoffrey, covering his face.

He screamed as the metallic liquid hissed, burning through his skin and clothing. He stumbled around the room and leapt from the open side, screaming as he fell.

The remaining attendees looked out to see that he was dead.

"Now then," said Despina, dusting her hands together. "Are there any others who feel like challenging us?"

Order Myrtlewood Mysteries book four!

(and read on for a special bonus scene - Burk's perspective of first meeting Rosemary!)

A NOTE FROM THE AUTHOR

Thank you so much for reading this box set! I had a lot of fun writing it. I love Myrtlewood with all its quirky characters and cosy magical atmosphere.

I wanted to write this series, in particular, because I've hardly ever come across solo parent main characters in fantasy, urban fantasy, and paranormal mystery books.

The inspiration came, one day, in an Urban Fantasy books group, when someone posted a request for books a bit like Gilmore Girls, but with magic. She particularly wanted a magical village with lots of interesting characters, like in Stars Hollow. I followed the recs with interest. There weren't many options and so I decided to write this series!

I was raised by a solo mother, and have also been one, myself. I've noticed that there aren't many books, movies, and shows that focus on this kind of experience, so I wanted to bring this project to life.

I've also always been interested in magical things, consider myself a bit of a kitchen witch and also belong to a Druid grove. Writing magical books allows me to draw on my own witchy experience and boost it with fantastical elements. For instance, you may notice that this book is based around a traditional magical festival, as are the following episodes in the series. They are a lot of fun!

If you have a moment, please leave a review or even just a star rating. This helps new readers to know what kind of book they're getting themselves into, and hopefully builds some trust that it's worth reading!

If you're keen to read more, you can *order Myrtlewood Mysteries book four!*

You can also join my reader list or follow me on social media. Links are at the end of this book.

P.S. You can also subscribe to my Patreon account for new chapters and other writing before it's published as well as real magical content like meditations and spells, and access to my Myrtlewood Discord community. Subscribing supports my writing and other creative work!

For more information, see: www.patreon.com/IrisBeaglehole

Read on for the bonus scene - Burk's first meeting of Rosemary told from his perspective!

Bonus scene

PERSEUS BURK'S FIRST MEETING OF ROSEMARY THORN

It should have been an ordinary day, only it felt different. The early spring blossoms stirred in the trees as Perseus Burk glanced out the window of his office, across the town square of Myrtlewood.

He had been around long enough to know it. Some new kind of magic was in the air.

He sat down at his desk, flipping through a thick stack of papers, before returning them to the file marked: Thorn - SECRET.

He slipped that file into a mahogany cabinet and locked it, then returned to his desk to go over the smaller, simpler Thorn file, which he re-read as he waited for his client to arrive.

He didn't usually work on Saturdays, largely because no one seemed to want to spend weekends with their solicitors, but this case was important enough to make an exception.

He stood up and glanced back out the window to see a woman with wild red hair running frantically across the town towards him. Perseus frowned. This does not bode well.

The Thorns were a powerful and ancient line of witches: a beacon that would lure the worst sort of enemy. The death of the matriarch, Galderall, was a significant vulnerability, especially given what she'd told him of her children.

This granddaughter of hers might be a fully grown adult, but Galderall had confided in Perseus that Rosemary knew nothing of magic. On top of all that she was running late. His frown deepened. He could not fathom how little respect many mortals had for time, given they had so little of it.

When they'd spoken on the phone the day before, Rosemary had seemed argumentative, bubbly and somewhat odd. Despite all this, the sound of her voice had stirred a lightness inside him that he did not recognise.

He heard the sound of the front doors opening and made his way out. As he expected, it was the woman with wild red hair and piercing green eyes. She was out of breath and clearly flustered, looking towards the counter. She hadn't seen him. He cleared his throat.

"Uhm, hello," she said. "I'm looking for Percy Burk."

Percy?

"I'm Perseus Burk."

"Oh, yes...Perseus, right. Like the ancient warrior or something?", the woman mumbled. "You sounded older on the phone, and more...well, kind of old-fashioned, but you must be younger than me..." She continued talking, somewhat unnecessarily.

"I take it you're Rosemary Thorn," Perseus said, decisively.

"That's me."

"You're late." He chuckled internally, "And I assure you, I'm certainly not younger than you."

Despite getting his name wrong, Perseus couldn't help being drawn in by the woman's natural fiery energy and unapologetic nature. She was beautiful in her own peculiar way, as was the fresh spicy scent that she carried, like cherries, cinnamon and chocolate. Delicious.

"Right this way, Miss Thorn," he said, trying to reign in his unexpected craving for her blood. It had been many decades since he'd had such an urge – centuries, even.

Rosemary gave him an unimpressed look. "Okay, but please don't call me 'Miss'."

Perseus raised his eyebrows. Living for as long as he had, he felt he should be used to the way the world continued to change, but modern informalities often threw him. "Ms then?"

"Just Rosemary, please."

"Very well. Please take a seat." He ushered her into his office where she sat down, awkwardly.

He couldn't help but study her closely, taking in every detail of her appearance. Her cheeks were rosy against her milky complexion that only added to the intensity of her eyes. He clothing was somewhat shabby, but she looked good in it none-the-less. She was unlike any other client he'd ever had.

Rosemary looked at him questioningly. "So, what's this all about, then? The letter said that Granny's will instructed you to meet with me alone."

"Indeed, it did." Perseus found himself flustered – an uncommon experience for him – and he didn't know where to begin with the serious discussion ahead.

"And...?" Rosemary prompted.

"Miss–" he started before correcting himself. "Rosemary."

She smiled as if privately amused.

He cleared his throat. "You may be aware that the circumstances around your grandmother's death were... unusual."

"Unusual how?"

Perseus hesitated. He wanted to tell her everything, but he couldn't reveal too much without driving her from his office in a panic. There wasn't much at all he could say about Galderall Thorn without mentioning magic. "I'm not permitted to discuss any details that may still be under investigation by the authorities," he said, hoping she would accept his explanation.

"But there is an investigation?" Rosemary persisted. "Someone hurt Granny."

Perseus could see the panic in her eyes and he felt a pang of sympathy. He could almost feel her inner turmoil as if it was his own. He wasn't used to connecting this way with people, let alone with mortals.

She began to cry while mumbling to herself and all he could think to do was pass her a box of tissues.

"Thank you," Rosemary said, dabbing her eyes. "It was a risk to have me come here without my chaperone. She usually stops the worst of it."

"Your chaperone?" Perseus asked, slightly mortified.

"My daughter, Athena. She knows when to shut me up."

Perseus couldn't help but chuckle, finally realising that Rosemary was joking. "I see," he said, trying to hide his amusement.

This woman was surprising in everything she said and did. It made him feel as if the solid ground he was standing on was crumbling beneath his feet.

"But why was it you wanted me to come all the way here today?" Rosemary asked, her voice serious once again.

Perseus frowned, knowing that he couldn't avoid the question any longer. "My apologies, Rosemary," he said, pulling out a stack of old papers. "Your grandmother's will states that you, and your daughter, are the sole heirs to her entire estate, which she intends for you to look after with great care and pass on to your descendants."

"Excuse me?" Rosemary said, clearly stunned by the news. "I didn't quite catch that last part. It sounded like you said Granny left everything to me. But that can't be right. I hadn't even seen her in years!"

"It is, in fact, right," Perseus said, trying to maintain his composure. "It seems the late Madame Thorn had a very old will."

"Oh - well, I guess that makes sense," Rosemary said and then began rambling again. Perseus could understand the need for her to have a chaperone, though her nervous habit was endearing.

“If you'll allow me to finish,” Perseus said, not unkindly. “Her will was very old, however she changed it just two months ago...”

“Oh,” Rosemary said. “So I don't inherit–”

Perseus cleared his throat again, trying to regain control of the situation.

“Sorry,” Rosemary said. “I'll shut up now.”

“That might be wise if you want to hear the rest,” he said, his voice curt, though internally he was feeling rather bemused by the whole situation. This was not normally how estate settlements went. He eventually managed to inform her about her inheritance.

“Fortune?” Rosemary's eyes widened. She took the will and pored over it in rare silence.

He couldn't help but observe her shock. She clearly had no idea that her grandmother's estate was worth so much. It was a welcome change from the usual reactions he received when delivering such news – many people were either greedy or entitled. But Rosemary seemed genuinely surprised and unsure of how to handle the situation.

“Now, it isn't for me to judge,” Perseus said, carefully. “And please understand that from our legal perspective, Madame Thorn was of sound mind at the time she composed this will. However, just between you and me, the police may find it suspicious.”

“Suspicious?”

“Suspicious that she changed her will significantly only weeks before her death – which they also consider suspicious.”

“Oh, I suppose it is,” Rosemary said, folding her arms and frowning.

Perseus felt momentary concerned for her welfare as if she were a close friend and not an odd woman he'd just met. He wanted to help. “If you know of any reason that she may have done so, I'd be happy to discuss the legal ramifications with you, free of charge – off the record, of course.”

"Reasons?! Are you implying tha–"

"I'm not implying anything." Perseus wanted to calm her down but words clearly weren't helping. Instead he adopted a more relaxed posture, interlacing his fingers and leaning back in his chair. "I'm merely offering you support – just as I intend to offer you support to sell the house."

He was testing her intentions. Would Rosemary Thorn respect her grandmother's wishes? Or would she settle up and leave town a wealthy woman. He, himself, has some interest in Thorn Manor and its many magical artefacts, as did the Vampire Council. If it were to come on the market he would definitely consider purchasing the old place.

Rosemary gaped at him. "I don't think that will be necessary. I can't very well honour Granny's memory if I'm selling her house the moment I inherit it."

"Take you time; think it over. In fact – here are the keys."

Perseus Burk watched as Rosemary took the keyring from his hand, her touch sending a shiver down his spine.

She shivered. "Are you alright?" she said.

"Why do you ask?"

"Your hand – it's freezing."

Perseus gulped. Rosemary was used to the mundane world. The less she knew about him, the better. "It's just a condition I have. It affects my... blood-pressure. I'm prone to cold extremities."

"If you say so," Rosemary said, sceptically. "Uhm. Thank you, I guess."

"It has been a pleasure, Miss Thorn," he said, realising too late that he's used the formal address for her by mistake. She didn't correct him that time.

Rosemary left and the room seemed strangely empty. Perseus found himself feeling a strange mix of wariness and attraction towards her. It was a craving he hadn't experienced in a very long time. He needed to see her again, despite his better judgement, and he suspected that their paths would surely cross again in the near future.

Her delicious scent still hung in the air, reminding Perseus that he'd have to be careful around Rosemary Thorn. But he couldn't shake the feeling of significance that arose from their meeting. He needed to know more about her.

He watched from the window as Rosemary left the office, heading in the direction of the tea shop.

Perseus Burk had a sense of unease. He wasn't used to people, let alone clients, challenging him the way she had. He began to regret giving her the keys to the house. All of a sudden, he didn't like the idea of her staying in the old Thorn Manor, given the circumstances surrounding Madame Thorn's death. He glanced towards his locked mahogany cabinet and made a mental note to keep a close eye on the situation. After all, it was his duty as a lawyer to protect his client's interests, and his duty as a vampire to report anything of note to the Council. He couldn't shake the feeling that something nefarious was afoot.

If you've enjoyed reading the first three books you can order Myrtlewood Mysteries book four!

A NOTE FROM THE AUTHOR

Thank you so much for reading this box set! It was so much fun writing it. I love Myrtlewood with all its quirky characters and cozy magical atmosphere.

If you have a moment, please leave a review or even just a star rating. This helps new readers to know what kind of book they're getting themselves into, and hopefully builds some trust that it's worth reading!

You can also join my reader list to keep up with my releases.

P.S. You can also subscribe to my Patreon account for new chapters and other writing before it's published as well as real magical content like meditations and spells, and access to my Myrtlewood Discord community. Subscribing supports my writing and other creative work!

For more information, see: www.patreon.com/IrisBeaglehole

About the Author

Iris Beaglehole

Iris Beaglehole is many peculiar things, a writer, researcher, analyst, druid, witch, parent, and would-be astrologer. She loves tea, cats, herbs, and writing quirky characters.

facebook.com/IrisBeaglehole
twitter.com/IrisBeaglehole
instagram.com/irisbeaglehole

Printed in Great Britain
by Amazon

49678460R00442